MY TREASURED OBSESSION

"Wherever you go, I will always follow, doll."

MARZY OPAL

My Treasured Obsession

Copyright © 2025 by Marzy Opal

All rights reserved.

This is a work of fiction. All characters, names, places, events, organizations, businesses used in this book are a product of the author's imagination or if real, used fictiously. Any resemblance to a person living or dead is purely coincidental.

Paperback ISBN: 978-1-7383050-6-3

Published by Marzy Opal
www.marzyopal.com

Editor: Emily A. Lawrence (Lawrence Editing)
Cover: Manuela Soriani (Art) and Gabriele Zibordi (Colour)
Interior Illustrations: Manuela Soriani (Art) and Gabriele Zibordi (Colour)
Cover Typography & Interior Formatting: Qamber Designs

WARNING

This book contains strong language, sexual content, graphic scenes,
and dark themes that may be triggering to some. The heroine is a mob
princess, so this story has mafia elements and a mystery plot. There is a
final showdown with a kidnapping scene and brief animal injury (but no
death as the animal recovers). Reader discretion is advised.

For a full list of triggers, check out my website:
www.marzyopal.com

Please note: Montardor is a fictional city based in Central Canada.

For all the queens who crave a sweet, gentlemanly,
dirty-talking hero that would do anything for you...

AUTHOR'S NOTE

Dear Reader,

Thank you for picking up *My Treasured Obsession*. This story idea came to me in June 2024, when I was wrapping up *Trapped With You (Remastered)* for publishing. I couldn't stop thinking about Hunter and Gabriela's love story, so much so that I knew it would be my next release. This is the first book I wrote after recovering from burnout and finding my spark again. I'm so happy that I finally get to share it with you <3

    This book is a new adult romance featuring university football, mafia elements, found family, a loyal girl gang, and romantic suspense. Timeline wise, it takes place after *Trapped With You (Remastered)* and the main characters are 20 years old. Gabriela is a mob princess and Hunter is the star quarterback that's utterly obsessed with her. These two were so much fun to write, from their playful dynamic, flirty banter, and soft adoration for one another. I hope you love them just like I do!

    This book, like everything I write, is dedicated to my readership. Thank you for still being here and supporting me through it all.

    Happy reading, queens!

Love,

Marzy

Spotify Playlist

PLAYLIST

Ariana Grande – Dandelion
Ariana Grande – Knew Better/Forever Boy
Ariana Grande ft. Lil Wayne – Let Me Love You
Ariana Grande – Needy
Ariana Grande – R.E.M
Beyoncé – Blow
Beyoncé – Cuff It
Beyoncé – Move
Beyoncé – Naughty Girl
Calvin Harris and Rihanna – This Is What You Came For
Camilla Cabello – Never Be The Same
Edward Maya – Stereo Love
Flo Rida ft. David Guetta – Club Can't Handle Me
Isabel LaRosa – Pretty Boy
Jisoo and Zayn – Eyes Closed
Justin Bieber – Hold Tight
Justine Skye ft. Tyga – Collide
Katseye – Gabriela
Little Mix – Touch
Miley Cyrus – Adore You
Normani – All Yours
One Direction – Little Black Dress
One Direction – Stole My Heart
Rihanna – Where Have You Been
Sabrina Carpenter – Espresso
Sabrina Carpenter – House Tour
Sabrina Claudio – Everlasting Love
Sabrina Claudio – Frozen
Selena Gomez – Body Heat
Selena Gomez – Hands To Myself
Shawn Mendes – Treat You Better
Tate McRae – It's Ok I'm Ok
Tate McRae – Just Keep Watching
Tate McRae – Miss Possessive
Tate McRae – Sportscar
The Weeknd ft. Daft Punk – I Feel It Coming
Zayn – TiO

HUNTER SAINT WARREN

Twenty years old

GABRIELA REGINA BELLAFIORE

Twenty years old

LUNA BELLAFIORE

Eight years old

PROLOGUE

HUNTER

I finally knew what obsession felt, looked, and smelled like.

It felt like a constant thrum pulsing in my ribcage, growing in rhythm and noise when *she* entered my vicinity until the only sound rushing through my ears was that of my pounding heart.

It looked like blue eyes, sultry lips, red-wine-coloured hair, and a hot little body donned in a revealing dress that made her pale skin gleam like moonlight against the sensual black satin.

And it smelled divine—like warm vanilla and red roses. A mouth-watering scent that did nothing but fuel my desire to taste her flavour on my tongue.

My obsession was named Gabriela Regina Bellafiore, and she was currently ruining my goddamn peace of mind, dancing in the middle of the crowded university party with a drink in her hand, a lack of inhibitions, and the gazes of every red-blooded male within a ten-foot radius devouring her.

Tucked in the shadowed corner of the room, I took a pull of my drink, my eyes drawn to her gyrating frame like a moth to a flame. Everything about her—the roll of her hips, the fingers running through her hair, the come-hither smiles flashing on her lips—was sin personified. Like a fallen angel exiled from the heavens, now roaming the Earth and tormenting every man and woman with her seductive aura.

Every delineation on her person had been crafted to sheer magnificence, as though she were amongst the crème de la crème. Those upturned eyes set in a doll-like face, with round cheeks and plush, pillowy lips that you could lick, suck, and bite to your heart's content. That long, luscious hair that could be wrapped around your fist twice cascading down her back. And that petite but sculpted body, with hourglass curves meant to bring one to their knees.

Gabriela was so effortlessly beautiful. It was unreal.

Growing up, I'd harboured an extensive fascination with Greek myths and their various characters—gods, muses, titans—consuming the lore as my preferred choice of literature, alongside the classics. And as a kid, I'd had the tendency to associate some of the people in my life with these mythological personalities.

Watching Gabriela move on the dance floor, surrounded by a slew of jock fanboys and appearing like a beacon of light amongst them, the lights wreathing above her head like a halo, I finally came to my conclusion.

She reminded me of Nike. The goddess of victory.

Revered and worshipped by athletes like myself.

If given the chance, I'd worship at her temple and be a lifelong devotee.

I knew I should peel my gaze away from Gabriela. But I couldn't.

Looking at her hurt. Looking away from her hurt more.

"What are you staring at?"

My jaw clenched and I removed my eyes from Gabriela's form when Shaun, one of my good friends, unexpectedly sidled up beside me, a red Solo cup cradled in his hand. I met him over a year ago—before our freshman year—and we quickly struck up a friendship. Now he was the captain of Vesta University's hockey team, while I was the quarterback of the football team.

"Nothing."

He cracked a smirk. "You checking out Gabby?"

Kind of hard not to when she was the most stunning thing I'd ever seen. "No."

"You're lying."

"And you're annoying," I retorted, though my lips twitched in amusement.

Shaun was one of those rare individuals who were selfless. If he was friends with you, he'd always have your back no matter what. An overall stellar guy, really, when he wasn't ribbing me about Gabriela.

"You should finally make a move on her," he encouraged. "Or you'll regret letting her slip through your fingers."

I wondered if he was spewing wisdom from personal experience.

The truth was I first saw Gabriela four hundred and seventeen days ago at my best friend Josh's birthday party in the summer. She'd sauntered into the place, confidence and charm abutting her frame. And when our gazes connected amongst the crowd for mere seconds…time slowed. Every breath, every heartbeat, every sense felt sharpened and magnified.

I remembered thinking to myself if the word perfection had a face, body, and demeanour, she was it.

Gabriela then proceeded to break eye contact and chat with my other friends without sparing me another glance. Like I was inconsequential. A fleeting moment in time she'd never remember again.

She'd moved on like she hadn't set my world on fire with one look.

Meanwhile, I fell under her spell—hook, line, sinker—like a pirate lured by a siren's call.

I was so desperate that I cornered a nearly drunk Josh at his own party and demanded he tell me her name, alongside whatever else he possibly knew about the mysterious girl who caught my eye.

Once I found out, my obsession began taking root deep in my core.

The little minx bought real estate in my mind and parked herself front and center until she clutched my undivided attention in the palms of her hands. Every second, every minute, every hour in the day and night.

Since we had mutual friends, we ran in the same circles and I saw her often in many social settings. Like tonight. Gabriela was always a ball of energy and the life of the party. An extrovert through and through.

Whereas I was quieter by nature, struggling to find the confidence to approach her, afraid of rejection.

She had a tendency to go through men like tissues, and I wanted to be treated like more than her conquests. I wanted to matter *more* than those fuckers. And I wanted her to crave my presence the same way I craved to be in hers.

"Maybe I will," I finally answered Shaun when a small ruckus that erupted on our right pulled me out of my reverie.

"Tonight. Do it." He took a swig of his drink and clapped my back. "I'll see you in a bit, all right?"

Before I could say anything else, he moved into the thick crowd, his attention fixated on a girl with dark hair and green eyes.

My eyes automatically went back to Gabriela.

She stopped dancing and stared at a couple making out aggressively, a frown marring her pretty face.

I wondered what was on her mind.

She squared her shoulders and sashayed off the dance floor, heading towards what appeared to be the open bar on the other side of the room, further away from my needy gaze.

The urge to follow Gabriela beat at my chest like a gong. It was insane. Two decades on this Earth and I'd never felt this level of attraction for another human being until her.

Now a girl who barely acknowledged my existence ruled me.

The further Gabriela drew from my line of sight, the more my chest burned with the need to pursue her. I felt like a hunter, helplessly riveted by its prey. She was magnetic and I was enamoured.

My fingers flexed at my side before clenching into a fist when her tiny figure blended into the crowd and I could no longer see her.

Shaun was right. I had to make a move.

How long would I keep watching her from afar without doing anything?

How long would I allow my insecurity-fueled thoughts to win?

How long would I wait...before she slinked off to another target and I lost the chance to make her mine?

Taking another sip of my drink for liquid courage, I finally gave in, stalking after her.

CHAPTER 1

Moonlit Meeting

GABRIELA

To say I was bored out of my mind was an understatement.

Normally, parties were my scene. Especially those Shaun Jacobsen—the captain of the school's hockey team—hosted in his luxurious downtown Montardor penthouse located near the campus.

After a strenuous week of classes and work, some good music and a few drinks always helped me unwind.

Tonight, the music was great, the drinks were strong, and the closed-invitation party's crowd was packed with the familiar faces of my fellow peers, buzzing with heedless energy…and yet I wasn't feeling it.

Maybe because my mamma texted me earlier this evening, asking me to come home to meet her new beau—the sixteenth one in four years—and it put a huge damper on my mood. Mamma was a hopeless romantic and a serial dater. There was a void inside her chest that she longed to fill since divorcing my papà.

The last text she sent me three hours ago said:

I want to be loved, Gabby. I want us to be a big, happy family again.

Mamma's boyfriend, who was probably closer to my age than hers, wouldn't be the one to complete our family. She didn't realize that, despite her divorce from Papà, we were still a unit.

But Lucia Bellafiore was stubborn and forever wearing rose-tinted glasses. She was convinced that life had only the best to offer her and was continuously on a hot pursuit for domestic bliss. It was admirable but exhausting.

I didn't have the heart to tell her that Lady Luck wasn't always on her side.

If she were, Mamma wouldn't have fallen in love with a mob man, wouldn't have gotten pregnant with me, and wouldn't have ended up in her current predicament: lonely and missing her ex-husband.

At least Papà deposited a good chunk of money in our bank accounts every month to ensure we had enough food on the table, to house the nice roof over our heads, to afford my expensive schooling, and to sustain Mamma's and my shopping habits. But otherwise, he kept a respectable distance, dropping in periodically to check on us.

And unfortunately, I could see this new disaster—Mamma and her boytoy—waiting to crash like a train wreck. Just like all the other men. She'd introduce us, we'd all get along momentarily, and then he'd discard her like trash.

Once she was patched up, we'd ride this merry-go-round all over again. I was so tired of the same mistakes, of picking up her broken pieces, and of the fact that I couldn't break her out of this pattern and push her in the direction of the one she really wanted. My papà. Her first and only real love.

Sighing, I brought my drink to my lips to down the remainder of my spiked fruit punch before my gaze unceremoniously connected with a familiar pair of dark eyes.

My gut tightened.

The other reason why I wasn't feeling it tonight?

Taylor Prescott was here.

He was a second-year English major at Vesta University and one of the football players on the team. Up until recently, we had a short-lived, no-strings-attached, friends-with-benefits arrangement. But he ended it two days ago. In hindsight, I wasn't heartbroken or devastated. Taylor was a shitty lay and only knew how to fuck in one position: with me doing all the work on top. Not to mention, I was a commitment-phobe. My motto was *love 'em and leave 'em.*

I was always the first one to end it.

So the fact that Taylor beat me to it kind of bruised my ego.

To add insult to injury, he left me for none other than Morgan Huxley—one of my peers from the Women in Business Student Association—after sending me a simple text message that said, Hey, I'm done with you and I've found better.

Now Taylor and Morgan were eating each other's faces just metres away from me on the dance floor like it was their last supper. It was gross and disturbing.

Taylor even had the audacity to wink at me mid lip-lock while Morgan shot me a smug expression like winning his attention was an accomplishment. Ew. To both.

From the minute I joined the Women in Business Student Association, Morgan's had some sort of one-sided rivalry with me. I was uncertain why my presence vexed her when all I'd ever done was occasionally give her a smile during our weekly team meetings when I caught her staring at me or CC her in one of my work-related emails. Though maybe she disliked me because I got the position she was vying for—finance coordinator—and now she was annoyed. Regardless of the reason, Morgan was continuously rude during our team meetings. Cutting me off. Giving me the stink eye. Sighing exasperatedly when it was my turn to speak.

Dry humping my sloppy seconds at parties was also getting added to the roster.

As for Taylor? I regretted giving the jackass the time of day.

If Papà were here right now, he'd hand me his loaded gun and demand I finish off Taylor like the last slice of my nonna's tiramisu. Though tempting, I wouldn't want his blood on my conscience.

Therefore, I settled on the best course of action: removing these two idiots from my vision.

My drink was done anyway and I could use a refill, alongside some fresh air.

Cutting through the horde of bodies crowding the makeshift dance floor, I earned a couple of curious glances as I sauntered to the open bar setup in the corner of the room, their attention straying down my body in an appreciative once-over.

My dark red hair fell down my back in waves. My lashes were layered with thick coats of mascara. And my black dress had enough cutouts to bare my ribs, waist, back, and cleavage. I wasn't shy or modest. I knew I looked good tonight.

I returned a few flirtatious smiles to the boys on the hockey team before grabbing myself another spiked fruit punch and wandering onto the empty terrace.

The September night was warm, with a starless sky, a luminous moon the only light. A soft breeze cooled my skin as I walked towards the balustrade and placed my cup on the limestone surface. My phone buzzed at that exact moment and I pulled it out of my heart-shaped clutch encrusted with rhinestones. A flurry of messages populated the group chat with my two best friends, Anna and Layla.

The first message was a selfie of Layla and her boyfriend, Josh, having dinner at a popular Mexican restaurant with another couple slash friends of ours, Ella and Cade.

Hope you're all having a good night 🤍 Miss you both! —Layla

The second was a picture of a light pink bustier top on a mannequin, stitched with gold threading, freshwater pearls, and ornamental chains. It was so beautiful that I was speechless as I soaked in the artistry.

What do we think? It's still a WIP. —Anna

Anna was a creative genius and a fashion designer in the making. Her style was opulent with a hint of scandal. All of her creations contained lush fabrics and were embroidered with intricate patterns that made you feel like a million dollars. One day, she was going to be a Canadian powerhouse. We just knew it.

Omg! Anna, this is gorgeous. I want one. —Layla

I started typing up my replies.

Hi 🤍 I miss you all! The party's no fun without my girls. — Gabby

Anna, that is stunning. For yourself or a commission? — Gabby

Also, I want one too!! —Gabby

Thank you, beauties 🤍 It's for myself. Next time we hang out, I'll take both of your measurements and see what I can do. — Anna

And I miss you both too. Are we still good for brunch tomorrow? xo —Anna

We always did brunch on the weekends. It was our thing. I'd known these girls since our childhood days because our moms were friends. And although we were busier than ever with sophomore year of undergrad and various priorities, we still made time for each other. I firmly believed that showing up for the people you loved and cared for constantly was what kept relationships running like a well-oiled machine.

Once we confirmed our plans, I pocketed my phone and my posture deflated like a sagging helium balloon as a bout of loneliness slotted into my system.

There was a time when Anna used to join me for nights out like these, but that was before she got hurt in one of the worst ways possible. Now she was a bit more introverted like Layla. She would rather get lost in one of her sewing projects and Layla would rather get lost in her art or one of her culinary adventures.

Then there was me.

I never liked being alone.

Not when I was a kid and certainly not as an adult.

Perhaps I was more like my mamma than I thought. There was a void in my chest that needed filling too. And I filled it. With pointless parties, pointless men, pointless interactions.

I tried to stay a busy bee with school, work, and social commitments. Otherwise, my head got too loud and I didn't always like my own thoughts. Clearly, I had mommy and daddy issues—amongst many others like a seasoned magazine—but no will to truly work on them.

Sometimes I wished I were more like Anna and Layla. They were extremely comfortable in their own presence and silence. Me? I was needy. I *had* to be surrounded by people.

"This sucks," I muttered to myself. Being here without my friends, seeing my ex-fling with my current peer, and doing my utmost best not to let all these irritating thoughts cripple me mentally.

Maybe I should consider offing Taylor for having the audacity to humiliate me with Morgan. It would be one less thing to mull over...

Seconds later, a man's deep voice intoned from behind me, "What sucks?"

"Oh my God!" I flinched, nearly knocking my drink off the balustrade.

Hearing a chuckle in response, I whirled around, trying to find the source of the sound. A tall figure cloaked in darkness stood in the corner of the terrace, not close enough for me to properly see his characteristics.

"Give a girl a warning, would you?" I narrowed my eyes. "It's not nice to spy on people."

"I was here before you," he drawled. "If anything, I'd say you were spying on me."

"That's not possible." I flicked my chin in a haughty manner. "I didn't even see you. Ergo, I couldn't have been spying on you."

"So if you're not spying on me, what exactly is it that you're doing here?"

"Contemplating my chances of committing murder and getting away with it."

"That's very unladylike of you."

"Who said I'm a lady?"

"You look the part." He tilted his head, studying me from his position where he languidly leaned against the wall with a drink in his hand. "At least from here."

"Won't you come closer and introduce yourself like a *gentleman*?" I asked coyly. "I promise, I don't bite."

It was a white lie. I was a biter. But only if you asked for it.

He swaggered forward with unhurried, measured steps, his gait eating the distance between us. "Who said I'm a gentleman?"

Finally, he revealed himself.

And I sucked in a quick breath.

Light blue eyes fanned by impossibly long lashes. Straight nose with a small, faded scar at the bridge. A five o'clock shadow peppering his jaw. Black hair with a hint of a wave sitting just shy of shoulder-length. Pressed black pants and a navy blue dress shirt were poured over his muscular physique, the top three buttons undone, showcasing a silver chain looped around his corded neck, and the cuffs of his sleeves rolled up just beneath his elbows, revealing an expensive watch strapped over his thick wrist. He had an air to him, a *je ne sais quoi* that I categorized as upper class. But the tattoo on his left forearm that I couldn't properly decipher in the darkness of the night hinted at a rebellious streak.

To put it plainly, he was stunning, resembling a cross between a perennial hero from my favourite paranormal romance books and a timeless knight in shining armour from age-old fairy tales, minus the proverbial sword and protective covering.

Awed, I craned my neck back to stare up at his larger-than-life figure looming above me and suddenly...my eyes flared in recognition.

I knew this man. I'd seen him many times before.

Quickly composing myself, I cleared my throat and parroted, "You look the part. At least from here, *Hunter*."

His chest bowed with an inhale. "Appearances can be deceiving."

"Is that so?" I mused.

Hunter was a business student at Vesta University—like myself—and majoring in management with a focus on law. He was also the quarterback of the football team and best friends with Josh, who I remembered introducing us at his nineteenth birthday party last summer.

Given that our best friends were dating, Hunter and I saw each other a handful of times throughout the semesters. Though we didn't converse much beyond the occasional casual greeting.

Plus, I noticed Hunter was a bit of an introvert. He preferred to stick to every room's perimeter where he couldn't be seen, while the rest of his teammates partied and basked in the attention thrown their way.

"Mhm." He gazed at me as the late summer wind sailed against him, tousling the strands of his hair. "Whose murder are you planning?"

I hedged a saucy expression his way, letting loose a mock scandalized gasp. "Why? Are you offering to play my partner in crime?"

"Would you like me to?" He smirked before taking a swig of his drink.

I jokingly side-eyed him, still smiling. "I mean, I don't really know you like that…"

"Try me."

"Can you dig a grave?"

"I've got excellent shovelling skills, courtesy of many Canadian winters." He arched a bemused brow. "Does that count, Gabriela?"

Oh, I liked the way he uttered my name. Softly and with intention. "It'll do. Now how much can you lift? We're going to have to transport the dead body from location A to Z."

"I can lift two hundred. Give or take," he volleyed back. "Good enough for you?"

That was quite impressive. "Yeah, sounds decent enough."

He continued our banter. "What weapon are we using to commit this crime?"

I shrugged and grabbed my drink. "A gun obviously."

"Why is that your choice?" he asked, genuinely curious.

"Because I know how to wield one." I sipped my spiked fruit punch. "And it's efficient. One bullet through the brain and—*bang*—you're dead. No screaming. No struggle. No hassle."

"And where does a girl like you learn how to use a gun?"

"My dad. He's a…ranger." Well, he was a high-ranking member of the Irish mob, but semantics, right? "He taught me how to shoot when I was young."

"Interesting." Hunter's gaze ran over me, from the tips of my crimson heels to my black cutout dress, to my red lips, to the long rhinestone earrings dangling down my neck, and to my long, middle-parted hair. "You don't strike me as the kind of girl who plays with guns."

I gave him a shark grin. "Appearances can be deceiving."

He puffed out a small chuckle. "Now are we doing this or what?"

I cocked my head, staring into his soulful blue eyes that reminded me of a serene body of water surrounding a tropical island. "Not convinced yet that you're the right candidate for the job."

He popped an elbow on the balustrade, getting comfortable like he was here to stay until he convinced me otherwise. "What else would you like to know?"

"Your full legal name, for starters, would be great so I can draft a contract."

"Ah, planning ahead. Smart girl," he crooned. "My full legal name is Hunter Saint Warren. Yours?"

I was a simple woman. Praise me—especially for my brain—and I melted like a burning candle. "Gabriela Regina Bellafiore," I said. "Also—Saint? You're not beating the gentleman allegation, I'm afraid."

"I'm not?" he replied amusedly, leaning closer.

I liked how he smelled, his cologne a black ice and fresh leather mix. "Well, your middle name and the fact that you were quick to offer your execution services to a damsel in distress like myself says otherwise."

His eyes raked over me in a scorching manner. "You're far from a damsel in distress, sweetheart."

Butterflies fluttered in my stomach, causing the blood in my veins to rush faster and the beat of my heart to pound quicker than ever. Warmth suffused my face and I was grateful for the dark night. Otherwise, he'd see the blush smattering my cheeks.

How was it that I'd met this man numerous times, but tonight was the first time we were having an actual conversation?

Hunter and I followed each other on social media, and I'd already stalked his account in the past, so I knew the basics about him: he was single, kept a low profile, and was hot as hell. Now I was tacking on sweet and playful to his description as well.

"You're right." I smirked. "I'm not really a damsel in distress. I could probably execute the kill on my own and bury the body in the woods without blinking twice."

Hunter laughed good-naturedly. My smirk transformed to a grin at the sound of it.

Unbeknownst to Hunter, I wasn't kidding. That was the funny part. I really was my papà's daughter.

Once his laughter faded into the distance, silence trickled in. We stared at each other, a light tension and understanding—the start of a camaraderie—passing between us. It felt tangible, like it could be gripped in my hand.

Hunter peered down at me, eyes softening. "All jokes aside, what's bothering you?"

I blinked. "What do you mean?"

"You looked upset before I came along."

I swallowed thickly, surprised he was tentative enough to pick up on something like that. "It's not really a big deal."

"If you feel comfortable telling me, I'd like to know." He shrugged. "No pressure, of course."

Chewing my bottom lip, I stared into the moonlit sky, gathering my thoughts. Should I tell him?

I usually kept my business to myself unless I was relaying it to my best friends. But maybe it was the needy side of me that wanted to confide in another because I found myself blurting, "I saw my ex kissing the girl he left me for and I…felt a certain way."

Hunter's body jerked back, his eyes widening. "Who?"

Not sure why my words incited such a reaction from him. "Um, Taylor. He plays on the football team too."

After Taylor, I swore to never date or sleep with jocks ever again. I didn't have the best track record with them and I didn't see that changing anytime soon.

A muscle in Hunter's cheek ticked with how hard he clenched his jaw. "Taylor Prescott? You were dating that slimy motherfucker?"

Embarrassed about my poor taste in men, I tucked a strand of my hair behind my ear. "Well, I wouldn't call it dating. We had a casual arrangement. It ended two days ago. He texted me that he found better and next thing I know, he's cozying up with my peer."

"He's an asshole." Hunter cursed. "I'm sorry, Gabriela. You didn't deserve that."

"It is what it is." Though I appreciated his words. "And you can call me Gabby. That's what all my friends do."

An unnamed emotion passed over his face and when he spoke, his voice was a hint gravelly. "Gabby it is."

Our gazes intertwined, the moment charged with an electrifying energy that lit up all my nerve endings. There was barely any distance between us.

Now I was all too aware of the heat emanating from his robust body, the height of him towering over me, the masculine fingers slightly callused from years of playing football sitting close to my own on the balustrade, and the blue in his eyes darkening as it swept over my features as though committing me to memory.

A gust of wind lifted the ends of my hair, causing them to fan against his bare forearm in an intimate caress. I glanced away, unable to maintain eye contact any longer. "I guess I should probably head back inside. I'll see you around, Hunter?"

I really hoped I did. I enjoyed his company. Next time we went out with our group of friends, I'd make an effort to seek him out.

Hunter didn't reply.

Instead, he stared at me with furrowed brows, like he was pondering something.

When his lips parted and no sound emerged, I took that as my cue to leave. "Bye—"

"Gabby." His hand shot out swiftly to wrap around my wrist, halting me. "Do you want to get back at him?"

"What?"

"Taylor." He tightened his hold. "Do you want to get back at him?"

I chuckled. "I don't actually have murderous tendencies, Hunter. I was joking."

"I know." A small smile flashed over his lips. "But that's not what I had in mind."

"Oh." I frowned. "What do you propose?"

Never in a million years would I have expected him to utter the next words.

"Kiss me," he rasped. "Use me to make him jealous. Show him what he was stupid enough to let go of."

CHAPTER 2

Kiss Me

HUNTER

Once I said the words, there was no taking them back.

Hell, I wouldn't even if I could.

Tonight was about finally making a move on my dream girl and that's what I intended to do. Despite my methods being a bit unorthodox, I hoped she didn't shoot me down.

Gabriela was frozen, a deer caught in headlights look on her face. Until she finally sucked in a hissing breath through her teeth, breaking out of her motionless state. "Pardon me?"

"You heard me. Let's put on a show for him."

She shook her head. "This is ridiculous." And chuckled nervously with an airy tone. "Taylor won't care if I'm making out with another guy when *he* ended it with me."

"Trust me, he will." Taylor was the kind of dude who didn't like it when someone touched his possessions. Even the old ones he discarded.

Fuck, I was still wrapping my mind around the fact that she'd had a 'casual arrangement' with him—a purely physical one.

The burn of jealousy sizzled under my skin and coursed through my veins like lava as I imagined them together. His hands running over her skin. Her hands diving into his hair. Their bodies colliding. Over and over and over again.

Generally speaking, I got along with everyone on the football team and I took my responsibility as quarterback seriously—making plays and trying to be a good leader. However, Taylor was the exception. I hated the degrading way he viewed women. He had the obnoxious habit of discussing his girlfriends in the most classless manner. I usually tuned out his voice during locker room talk because it grated on my nerves.

Now I also hated the motherfucker because he'd had a piece of Gabriela when he wasn't even worthy of breathing the same air as her.

She deserved so much better than him.

God as my witness, if she gave me the chance, I'd show her what *better* entailed.

Gabriela placed a hand on her hip, eyeing me up and down like I had a hidden agenda.

I almost smirked. She had no idea about the extent of my desperation. Could you blame me, though? After more than a year of wanting her, desperate times called for desperate measures.

"What's in it for you?" she asked.

I get to feel the taste of your lips on mine after eons of longing.

"I can't stand Taylor. I have a personal bone to pick with him." *Now that I know he's hurt you.* "And I figured if we kiss in front of him, it'll be like killing two birds with one stone. You get your revenge and I get to piss him off."

Thankfully, Gabriela didn't ask what 'bone' I had to pick with him. Instead, she appeared to simmer over my words while I held my breath.

It took a lot of bravado for me to follow her out, to step out of my shell, to converse with her, and to ask for a kiss. If she said no, I didn't know what I'd do with myself.

Something in my expression convinced Gabriela as she suddenly nodded. "Okay. Let's do this. I want to get back at the asshole."

I ignored the excitement—because she said yes—and the slight twinge—because she only wanted to kiss me for his sake—travelling through my chest. A year of yearning turned me into a pathetic beggar who ached for crumbs of Gabriela.

Stepping ahead of me, Gabriela offered her hand. "Ready?"

My heart started racing embarrassingly fast as I zeroed in on her open palm. Fairer than mine and with gentle lines that made me wish I knew the art of palmistry so I could see what the future held for us. And if there was any possibility that I could weave myself like a stitch forevermore in the tapestry of her destiny.

Sliding my fingers against hers, I grasped her hand.

Electricity crackled at the touch.

We both jerked but didn't let go of each other.

"Ready," I said, my voice inexplicably hoarse.

"If you grip my hand any harder, I may lose blood circulation," she teased.

I winced and loosened my hold a wee bit. "Sorry."

She started walking, guiding me away from the terrace and back into the party.

I followed Gabriela Regina Bellafiore blindly like a wretched devotee living to please her every whim. The smile she gave me made her resemble a wicked witch getting her way with her lowly disciple. And like a fool, I would let her lead me anywhere she desired, including oblivion.

"Are you hanging in there?"

My gaze bounced around our surroundings. "Yeah."

"You don't like big crowds, huh?" She cut through a sea of bodies and ushered us onto the dance floor. Tendrils of drugs and alcohol ribboned the atmosphere like luring lovers enticing you to partake in salacious pursuits reserved for darker hours.

"How do you know that?" I asked when we reached the middle of the dance floor.

The music was louder than ever and the thumping bass mirrored my heart's drumming beat. I had to lean down to hear Gabriela speak and she had to rise on her tippytoes to be heard. "Whenever I see you," she enunciated loudly, "you're always standing in the corner of a room. You never party with any of your friends. I'm guessing you're more introverted?"

I blinked, stunned. The only thing I registered was that she noticed me. Multiple times. It made me think that maybe *this*—me and her—wasn't so far-fetched. Maybe there was hope for *more*.

When I didn't reply to her in a timely manner, she prompted, "Hunter?"

I cleared my throat. "You're right. I don't really like crowded spaces. Sometimes I get anxious. I'm more of a homebody, if I'm being honest."

Which was ironic since I was crushing on a girl who was basically a social butterfly and the complete opposite of me.

Gabriela's face gentled. "Do you want to abort this mission?"

"*No*," I said a little too hastily, causing Gabriela to jolt, before I softened my tone and added, "I mean, I'm fine. Let's do this."

She was here and I wasn't alone. Therefore, my nerves were more at ease.

Gabriela smiled. "You'll tell me if this gets too much for you?"

I liked that she cared about me, even if it was in this small capacity. "As long as you do the same."

"Deal." Gabriela tilted her head back as she slowly dragged her hands over my torso, over my shoulders, and over my neck until they braided at my nape. I shivered, starved for her touch. "Now dance with me, Hunter."

There weren't enough words to encompass the feelings running haywire through me. Wonderment. Shock. Exhilaration. Everything in between. My insides sparked like the First of July.

Gabriela soaked in my silence, taking it for something else. "Getting cold feet, pretty boy?"

The compliment had my heart nearly bursting out of its cage like a bird in a cuckoo clock. "You think I'm pretty?"

"Please, you know you're good-looking." She rolled her eyes playfully. "How does it feel to be one of God's favourites?"

The fact that my dream girl was calling me good-looking? I was a goner. "Great, actually. Thanks for asking."

She threw her head back on a girlish chuckle. I beamed at the sweet sound. Gabriela was like a ray of sunshine. Bright and vibrant. Like a shot of espresso. Warm and awakening. And like the most beautiful flower in the Garden of Eden. Magnificent and timeless.

"You're cheeky," she said. "And kind of adorable."

I couldn't remember the last time I smiled this much. "Right back at you."

She started swaying her hips to the music and my hands found her waist as we rocked to the provocative beat. Her fingers delved into my hair slowly, tipping my face down, and I nearly groaned at the sensation of her nails grazing my scalp in a way that could only be described as divine. I pulled her closer into me until barely an inch separated our bodies.

"What have you been drinking tonight?" she asked.

The world around us blurred. All I could see and feel was her. "Why?"

"I don't kiss boys who drink beer. Don't like the taste of it."

"One whiskey and Coke. That's all I drank." My palms skidded up her sides and my thumbs rubbed against the skin of her ribs, visible from the little cutouts in her dress. It was Gabriela's turn to shiver and I loved that I elicited that reaction from her. "Though I'll never touch a drop of beer again if it ups my chances of getting kissed by you, sweetheart."

A look of half disbelief, half pleasure flashed over her face, like my boldness charmed her. I meant every word. I'd do anything to have her mouth against mine.

"Hm." She licked her bottom lip. "Didn't realize you were so eager to kiss me."

Baby, you have no idea. "Can't help it. You're beautiful."

She grinned. "Damn, aren't you a charmer?"

The tiny gem gleaming on her top left canine took me aback. I found it incredibly sexy. "I aim to please."

Gabriela ran her thumb over my lips suggestively. I nearly moaned from the featherlight touch. "I can see that, pretty boy."

We simply watched each other without exchanging any more words, dancing to the song and letting our eyes do the talking.

Her fragrance vined around my frame, intoxicating me with its addictive scent. Her blue eyes held me hostage, rendering me speechless.

And her scarlet red lips hiked up in a kittenish smile, making me wonder what they would feel like against my mouth.

Gabriela enchanted me, just like the first time I'd laid eyes on her.

"Don't look now," she whispered, mouth hovering near mine. "But he's watching."

Slight disappointment caused my shoulders to droop. Of course this moment wasn't about us. I'd temporarily forgotten that I gave her free rein to use me. But glee quickly squashed my disappointment when I remembered that I was about to kiss Gabriela.

After waiting a few seconds, I slid a glance to my right. Lo and behold, Taylor lurked next to us. Despite dancing with another girl, his eyes were on Gabriela. He was frowning, probably miffed that she'd moved on to another man within days of him dumping her.

I hid my smirk against her jaw, gliding my lips along her skin. "He doesn't look too happy."

"No." Her exhale was my inhale. "But he can go fuck himself."

"You ready to put on a show for him?"

Her reply came in the form of a devious expression as she trailed her hands down my shirt, feeling my pectoral muscles before whirling around and surprising me by backing her perky ass against my lap.

I bit back a groan when she ground over my growing bulge while running my fingers through the strands of her hair sensually.

Gabriela knew she was hot and she wasn't afraid to flaunt it.

The undulating hips and the wink she threw me over her shoulder spoke volumes.

Winding my arm around her waist possessively, I rocked in unison with her in the dirtiest kind of dancing. We were garnering the attention of everyone around us. Some of the men eyed Gabriela like they wanted a turn with her.

But if I had it my way, she was never escaping my clutches. At least not tonight.

I brought my mouth to her ear. "Do you like it?" I murmured. "The way they're all watching you like you're the most beautiful girl in the room?"

She rested her head against my chest and raised her arms, wrapping them around my neck while she continued moving her hips in a rhythm meant to destroy me. "I like it," she murmured back as though it was a forbidden secret. "I like the attention. I'm...needy."

I loved that she was divulging this piece of herself. Fuck, all I really wanted was to give her the attention she desired. Cater to every one of her needs like it was my life's purpose.

"And what do you need right now?" I collared my hand around her neck. Her pulse thundered against my fingers, mirroring my own erratic one.

When I ground back against the split of her ass, Gabriela released this low sound that manacled around my cock and squeezed. Goddamn, I wanted to hear that noise again. Preferably when she was on top of me. Riding my cock like a hot little minx. And if I didn't hear it again in this lifetime, I might lose my fucking mind.

"Gabby?" I gripped her throat more firmly, more deliberately. "What. Do. You. Need?"

"I—" Her eyes briefly closed before opening and meeting my own desire-filled ones with anticipation. "I need you to kiss me, Hunter."

I need you to kiss me, Hunter.

Those seven words ignited a fire in my core. I didn't even care about the people staring at us.

The only thing I cared about was that Gabriela *needed* my kiss.

Driven by impatience, she fisted the hair at my nape and tugged me down to her mouth, but I paused when millimetres separated our lips. From this proximity, I could count every individual lash and speck of grey in her blue eyes. We breathed each other in and it was perhaps the most intimate moment I experienced, even if we were standing in the middle of a crowded dance floor with loud music pumping through the veins of the room.

"Say *please* like a good girl," I rasped. "And I will."

Then I gave in to the urge and sank my teeth into her plump bottom lip.

Gabriela whimpered at the sting. "*Hunter.*"

Hearing my name in that spoiled tone? I was done for and we'd barely kissed. "Say the words, Gabriela."

I relished the way her breath hitched and how she watched me, as if seeing me in a whole new light. Gabriela seemed like a girl who enjoyed having control but also relinquishing it.

"Please, Hunter. Kiss me."

Unable to deny her any longer, I slammed my mouth to hers in a kiss that was hard, titillating, dominating, and laced with the truth that I would never be the same ever again after this night.

She gasped into our kiss and I drank the sound with my own guttural groan, my tongue running against the seam of her mouth after I sipped from her top and bottom lip rapaciously. I needed more. So much more. And she gave it to me by parting her lips and brushing her tongue with mine. Gently at first. Demanding the next.

Our mouths devoured each other like the only thing that could quench our thirst was this kiss. The taste of her sweet drink and the smell of her floral scent pushed my pulse into overdrive. I tightened my hold around her petite body, including the hand wrapped around her throat. She moaned and fisted the strands of my hair, ensuring I didn't pull away from her. As if I had plans of going anywhere else when I had my arms wrapped around my fantasy and my palate full of her intoxicating flavour.

When we withdrew for oxygen, I spun her around to face me, keeping my hand around her neck, and stamped my mouth to hers again. The scene around us obscured to nothingness and time was measured by our heartbeats, our wet kisses, and our hands exploring each other curiously and greedily.

Her fingers were all over my jaw, stroking my stubble, and in my hair, clutching my roots. She strived for control. I didn't allow her any as I kissed her like a starved man. My fingers ran all over the curve of her thick ass and my tongue teased the rhinestone on her canine.

The music changed, the crowd thickened, and the world could have stopped right this instant, but I wouldn't have noticed. Not when Gabriela and her sensual kisses ruled my entire being.

A jarring push caused us to break apart from our heady lip-lock and stumble back a few steps on the dance floor. Some drunk girls bumped into us, shooting slurred apologies and bashful chuckles.

My arms remained securely wrapped around Gabriela as we paid them no mind and stared at one another almost trance-like. Our harsh breathing mellowed and Gabriela blinked, the glazed look in her eyes slowly evaporating. Her lips were kiss-swollen and I'd smeared her red gloss during our make-out session. Male pride filled me at seeing her slightly dishevelled from my ministrations but still beautiful as ever.

"Gabriela?" I tucked a strand of her hair behind her ear. "You okay?"

As if me saying her name snapped her out of a daze, she cleared her throat and took a step back. I instantly felt cold without her.

"I, uh." Her head swivelled around to evaluate our surroundings, taking note that Taylor and the girl he was with were no longer there. "That was…"

A fantastic, amazing, brain-chemistry-altering kind of kiss.

I'd never recover from it.

"I think we did a good job." She forced a smile that made my stomach sink. "Taylor and Morgan are gone. I'm guessing he got a good view of our show."

Right. Our show. Because it was all about getting revenge on Taylor.

Though I was elated that I finally got to talk to her, to touch her, to kiss her…I was also gutted that she appeared so unaffected. After all, her only goal was to get back at Taylor. Unlike mine.

"Yeah." I smoothed my hair back. "He did."

Gabriela shifted on her feet, awkward and a complete one-eighty from the girl I bantered and flirted with on the terrace. "I should probably, um, get going."

My brows slammed into a frown and an acerbic taste filled my mouth. I didn't anticipate that our night would end on such an uncomfortable note. It was palpable in the air, tightening like a noose around my throat. Had I done something wrong? Was I too eager in my desire for her?

Insecurity-laced thoughts ping-ponged in my brain. My skin crawled, but I fought against the feeling, wanting to keep her here with me for as long as I could. "Gabby—"

But she was already walking backwards, a frazzled smile pasted on her lips. "I'll see you around, Hunter. Thank you for tonight. I appreciate it."

She disappeared into the crowd and left me standing on the dance floor.

Alone, aching, and even more obsessed with her than when the night had begun.

CHAPTER 3

Plot Twist

GABRIELA

Brunch with Anna and Layla was something I looked forward to every week. It was like a reset button for me, spending time with my found family while gorging on French toasts, fruits, and lattes.

Who needed therapy when you could have girls' time with your best friends?

After eating, we hung out in Anna's impressive walk-in closet with the strains of an old Beyoncé song playing in the background as she took our measurements. The crystal chandelier above our heads illuminated the space, the walls decked out with velvet displays containing priceless jewelry, shelves with heels and thigh-high boots—Anna's guilty pleasure— pink silk hangers with rows of lingerie, and endless designer and thrifted clothes, including Anna's own creations, which, in my opinion, were far superior to anything you could buy on the market. She was incredibly talented and would one day have her own haute-couture label.

"I should have these bustiers done by the end of the month," Anna said, the statement earrings in her lobes swaying as she bent forward to wrap the measuring tape around Layla's waist. "What colour do you want for yours, Lay?"

I'd already requested mine be black.

Layla gazed at her reflection in the ornate mirror with a tilted head. "Normally, I'd ask for white, but Josh does love me in yellow. Maybe something in between...like a cream colour?"

Anna's hazel eyes found me where I leaned next to the glass showcase housing all her beauty queen pageant trophies, and we shared a knowing smile. Layla in love was a good look. For years, she'd been shy and closed-off, never allowing herself to feel too much. Then Josh entered her life and bulldozed through all her walls with his golden retriever energy. She'd never stood a chance against the determined mob prince.

Catching our expressions in the mirror, Layla narrowed her green eyes. "Stop that."

"What?" I shrugged, trying to tame the teasing nature of my features. "We haven't said anything."

Layla released a long exhale, rolling her eyes, despite her own smile twitching her lips. "I know, but you're all thinking it. I'm whipped."

"Hey—you said it," Anna piped up while writing Layla's measurements on her pink notepad. "Not us."

Layla combed her fingers through her dark hair and sighed. "Sometimes I have these moments where I wonder if all of this—*him*—is too good to be true. I feel like one day I'll wake up and it will just have been a dream. One big fantasy I concocted in my mind."

Layla rarely opened up to others. Josh was the first man she allowed herself to be emotionally available with and this was the most vulnerable she'd ever been. "You're a sure thing, Lay. You have nothing to worry about."

A wistful expression flashed on her countenance as she turned around to face us, adjusting the cap sleeves of her white satin maxi. "You're right. I do have the ring to prove it."

Josh bought her a sparkly diamond a few months ago—he was single-handedly raising all her standards—as a promise. They were saving themselves for one another.

The romantic in me swooned, but the cynic in me scoffed. Sometimes my track record with men made it hard for me to believe that maybe there were good ones out there who'd do anything for their significant others. But Josh was definitely one of them.

"Let's also not forget the tattoo on his chest that says Layla," Anna launched over her shoulder as she walked towards the mannequin in the corner of her closet, her pink thigh-high boots click-clacking. They were brand-new and she was trying to break them in. "If that doesn't prove that man is insane for you, I don't know what will."

Layla blushed.

"See?" I said. "You have nothing to worry about—"

Layla's phone ringing cut off the rest of my sentence. "Oh, it's him."

Speak of the devil. "Don't mind us. Answer it."

"Are you sure?" she asked.

"Yes," Anna assured and then chin-nodded at me as she placed the measuring tape around the mannequin's neck. "Gabby, come over here. I want to show you something."

With a grateful glance in our direction, Layla brought her phone to her ear, saying, "Hi, Jay."

"Josh and Layla, sitting in a tree," I sing-songed loudly and teasingly, skipping after Anna. "K-I-S-S-I-N-G."

Layla palmed her face with an embarrassed groan. Anna laughed and I was certain I heard the distinct sound of Josh singing along on the other side like a little shit. They continued their conversation in hushed voices, probably confirming their dinner plans for tonight, while Anna and I headed into her bedroom, a glamorous affair composed of pink, gold, and white accents.

She perched against her regal vanity laden with makeup and ornamental bottles of perfume, and I walked towards her queen-sized bed to take a seat. My eyes wandered over to the shelves beside Anna, holding all her crowns, sashes, and sceptres from past competitions.

"What did you want to show me?" I asked, sitting on my hands and wiggling my feet that barely touched the floor. Out of all my friends, I was the shortest. Anna was five-foot-nine, Layla five-foot-six, and myself? A whopping five-foot-two. Though I made up for my lack of height with my personality.

"Nothing." Anna picked a red nail polish from her stash and shot it my way. I caught it. "I just wanted to give Layla and Josh some privacy."

I shook the bottle of varnish and unscrewed the cap before meticulously painting my bare toenails. Red and black were my favourite colours and they were well-incorporated into my wardrobe. Over the last few years, Anna helped me curate my outfits based on my style, ranging from classy, business chic, dark academia, gothic-inspired to everything in between.

"Where are your mom and brother today?" I inquired after applying my first coat.

Pensive, Anna gazed down at her own sparkly pink nails. "Michael is hanging out with his friend, and Mom's at work. Too busy for us as usual."

I hated the sadness surrounding her. "Anna…"

Grief was the hardest emotion to process in my opinion. After all, it was love that had no place to go, locked inside the chest of your soul with the key floating somewhere in the river of your tears.

Anna's dad died almost a year ago and the wound was still very much raw and bleeding, barely bandaged and with no signs of healing soon. Michael was too young to fully grasp that his dad was gone forever, Anna's mom avoided their reality by throwing herself into work so she never had to stop and think about the loss of her soulmate, and our best friend? She was all too aware of his death and trying her best to cope without his presence. Some days were good, like today. And some days were really bad, where pulling herself out of bed and going through the motions of her daily routine felt too much. She was wracked with guilt and pain that never seemed to lessen.

Layla and I did our best to be there for her and offer all the comfort we possibly could. But I understood that with these kinds of tragedies, only time would heal the wound. I truly hoped Anna could one day live freely without all these demons haunting her.

Anna shook her head as if ridding herself of certain thoughts. "Anyways, how was the party last night? Did you have a good time?"

During brunch, I avoided the topic of the party, steering the conversation towards our busy school and work week instead. Naturally, Anna picked up on it.

"It was good. I had fun."

And I made out with the hottest man alive.

Done with her phone call, Layla chose that exact moment to breeze out of the walk-in closet, the train of her dress trailing behind her like an angelic cloud. "By the way, Josh mentioned you ran into Hunter at the party."

"Oh." My throat went dry. "W-what exactly did Hunter tell him?"

Anna and Layla sported matching frowns at my tone.

"Just that he ran into you." Suspicious, Layla crossed her arms over her chest and went to stand beside Anna. "Was Hunter supposed to tell Josh something *beyond* that?"

Huh. So he didn't tell Josh that we kissed. Not that I expected him to. Hunter didn't appear like the kind of person to kiss and tell. And regardless of what men claimed, they loved to gossip. Just like women. If not more.

My silence caused their frowns to melt and their eyes to sharpen into inquisitive stares filled with plenty of unanswered questions.

"Gabriela," Anna hedged calmly, the use of my full name not lost on me. "Is there something you want to tell us?"

I shrank under their undivided attention. Papà always said that if I ever got kidnapped and interrogated, I'd crack like an egg and spill every secret they demanded. I wasn't one of God's strongest warriors and I was okay with that. "Like what?"

"Did something happen between you and"—Anna and Layla exchanged a quick glance before fixating on me again—"Hunter?"

"Why would you say that?" I avoided eye contact and continued applying my second coat of nail polish. What a pretty shade of blood red. I loved it.

"Based on the way you're acting and squirming," Layla chimed in.

Fuck it.

Taking a deep breath, I blurted out, "I might have kissed Hunter last night."

It got so quiet that you could probably hear a pin drop.

Followed by a loud eruption of girlish shrieks. I pretended to block out their noise by cupping my hands over my ears, even though I grinned widely at their reactions. "Quiet down, you banshees!"

Layla shot a pink pillow my way. "Spill. Every. Single. Detail."

"I can't believe that wasn't the first thing you told us this morning," Anna accused with a mirthful edge. "Why so secretive?"

Layla mock gasped. "She didn't say anything because it meant something to her. She *liked* it. Otherwise, she tells us about every meaningless hookup."

"You're right. This one meant something." Anna's eyes flared. "You like him, don't you, Gabby?"

I groaned, capping the nail polish and setting it aside, satisfied with my pretty toes. "I have no idea what you're both talking about."

"Bullshit!" Layla said. "Now put us out of our misery and tell us what happened."

It was foolish of me to assume I could actually keep this tidbit a secret from my best friends, who were basically like my sisters. Though I was still trying to make sense of what happened last night...they weren't completely wrong.

Hunter's kiss deeply affected me.

My whole world tilted on its axis.

I'd kissed a lot of guys in my life, but no one had ever kissed me like him.

Passionately, with his hand wrapped around my throat possessively. Eagerly, like one kiss wasn't enough and he needed so much more. And hungrily, as though devouring my lips was the only thing that could satiate him.

Just remembering that hot revenge make-out session and the way Hunter called me *good girl* and *sweetheart* heated my blood. No doubt, I had heart eyes and drool at the corner of my mouth too.

Knowing Anna and Layla wouldn't rest until I told them everything, I relayed my story, beginning with seeing Taylor and Morgan on the dance floor. By the time I finished explaining how Hunter and I wound up putting on a show for Taylor, their jaws were slack, mouths hanging open.

Seconds later, I was subjected to more surprised squeals.

"I can't believe he said 'Kiss me.'" Layla chuckled. "Clearly, he saw his shot and took it!"

"One hundred percent," Anna agreed, grinning.

Confused, I said, "What are you talking about?"

Anna twirled a lock of her waist-length blond hair around her finger. "I mean, I've noticed he stares at you whenever we're in the same room. It's like he can't help himself."

"I've noticed that, too," Layla added.

Excuse me, what? Why am I only learning this now?

"And none of you thought to, I don't know, maybe tell me that?" I deadpanned.

"Honestly, at first I thought he had a staring problem." Layla winced. "Then I figured he found you so pretty that he simply couldn't look away. But after hearing what you just told us, I'm convinced he's been harbouring a crush on you the entire time."

"I concur," Anna said. "Why else would he jump at the first opportunity to kiss you, Gabby?"

I stayed mum, digesting this new piece of information and seeing our exchange from last night in a different light. Maybe Anna and Layla were right. Or maybe they were delusional, including myself, for even entertaining this possibility. Nonetheless, it didn't matter.

It was just one kiss, one night, one encounter.

Nothing would come of it.

I was a fling or one-night stand kind of girl. Hunter wasn't about to be another notch in my belt. Not only because it may ruin the dynamics of our friend group when things inevitably ended, but I had an inkling he was a long-term kind of guy.

The complete opposite of me.

Even though at one point, I'd been exactly like that. A long-term kind of girl. Someone who hoped to find her perfect match and settle down, with the whole white picket fence and two point five babies dream.

But perfection was a myth and most men frankly sucked.

"I don't think he has a crush on me," I concluded, shaking my head. "He barely knows me. And hypothetically speaking, if he does, why wait until now to approach me? The way I see it, yesterday was a one-off. We were just two people in the right place at the right time."

"Some people are shier by nature." Anna smoothed her hands down her baby pink, high-waisted miniskirt. "Maybe Hunter just didn't know how to talk to you before, and last night was the first time he found the courage to actually do so?"

When I pondered over our moment from the terrace, Hunter didn't appear shy. Only playful. But he did mention that he was a homebody. Perhaps he was more introverted than I suspected and that halted him from previously approaching me.

Still, I was choosing to treat the kiss between us as a successful business transaction. Nothing more, nothing less. But the next time I saw Hunter at a party, I'd go out of my way to hang out with him for the sole reason that I didn't like knowing he hid in the corner. Big crowds made him anxious and that, for some inexplicable reason, tugged at my heartstrings.

"Plus, you're a catch, Gabby." The thin gold bracelets adorning Layla's wrists jingled as she gestured towards me. "Can't blame Hunter for having a thing for you."

"Oh, God." I stood up, groaning. "Let's stop this conversation right here. For all we know, your earlier theory of him having a staring problem could be accurate and we're just being silly by thinking he has a crush on me." I put *crush* in air quotations. My ego wasn't so grand to assume that everyone with a dick in my vicinity had the hots for me. "And though he's cute and I'll admit that *maybe* I'm attracted to him, it doesn't matter because I'll *never* act on that attraction."

They both seemed genuinely puzzled.

"Why not?" Anna asked. "He seems like a nice guy. Not like…"

She trailed off, but we all knew about the elephant in the room.

Not like Franco, my ex-boyfriend.

The stupid fucker who birthed all my trust issues. I regretted giving him three years of my life. If I could turn back time, I'd undo all our memories and make sure to kick him where the sun didn't shine.

"Yeah, Hunter does seem nice." Reminders of my ex brought out a bitter note to my voice. "Alas, still a no."

My best friends didn't push the topic anymore.

Layla tried to ease the mood by wiggling her eyebrows and jokingly saying, "Do you want me to text Josh and ask if he thinks Hunter has a staring problem?"

Anna chuckled and a scoff escaped me.

"Please, don't do that," I pleaded, adjusting the strap of my structured black minidress so it rested better on my shoulder. "If this gets back to Hunter, I'll die of embarrassment."

We spent the next few moments exchanging goodbyes and making plans to meet up for a study session midweek. Since I didn't have my license yet, Layla drove me to my apartment, which was located in a complex owned by the Remingtons—Josh's family—and not too far away from Vesta University's campus.

The best decision I made was moving out of my childhood home for the sake of my mental health. I loved my parents, but distance really made the heart grow fonder. Moreover, I liked living alone, sans roommate. It helped strengthen my independence.

Maverick, the security guard who doubled up as a doorman, welcomed me as I neared the entrance of the building. "Hello, Miss Bellafiore."

I forced a smile. "Hey, Rick. Good day?"

"Better now that you're here." He gave me a suggestive once-over that made me want to gag. I resisted the urge to hurry up to my apartment so I didn't come off as a total bitch. "How's your day going?"

He put a pudgy hand on my waist under the guise of guiding me inside the building and I shuddered, quickly ducking out of his hold. "Great. Thanks for asking."

Maverick was in his early forties and a little too flirty and handsy with the female patrons living in the apartments. A few months ago, when I came back home after a night out, he propositioned me, asking me to dinner and well, everything that comes afterwards. I politely declined and he took it like a champ, never asking me out again. But he did make me uncomfortable with his creepy grins and leery-eyed looks.

I bet if he knew about the gun sitting in the drawer of my console table, he'd never look my way again. Nevertheless, I gauged Maverick to be relatively harmless and never bothered reporting his weird behaviour to management.

"I hope you have a great rest of your day," Maverick drawled with a wink.

But something about the way he said *great* and *day* had my gut tightening with instinct. I couldn't quite place my finger on the trigger, but I felt edgy. I tried squandering the feeling screaming inside of me that something was off as I headed for my apartment.

Visibly, everything was status quo. The usual potted plants sitting in the foyer. The speckled flooring from the '90s. The light smell of lemon-scented cleaning products. The gentle whirring of the air conditioning unit. The cockatoo from the ground floor apartment squawking faintly in the background.

But eeriness pulsed through the air as I climbed up the steps in the empty stairwell, the echo sounding like nails being pounded into a coffin. My skin itched like a hundred little ants crawling down my spine by the time I reached the third floor.

The hallway was exceptionally quiet. With every footstep, my senses whetted as I neared my apartment…and automatically halted.

My door was unlocked and ajar.

I pushed it open and stepped inside before thinking twice.

Once I did, my eyes widened in shock as I soaked in my wrecked place.

My favourite crystal vase, which used to rest on my console table in the entryway, was broken, shattered into tiny little pieces on the floor.

And the white living room wall before me bore an angry sentence, scrawled in crimson red paint.

Hell is empty and all the devils are here . . . including you, bitch.

Something jumped at me from my left and I flinched, letting out a bloodcurdling scream.

CHAPTER 4
New Neighbour

Hunter

Despite the soreness in my muscles from an entire afternoon of moving, a sense of satisfaction roamed through me when I glanced at my new place from the entryway. After a year of studying at Vesta University, the long commute finally got the best of me and I decided it was time to move out of my parents' home and find a place closer to campus.

Josh, my best friend and teammate on the football team, helped me set up over the last few hours, hauling boxes and building furniture until we were both exhausted.

"Hunt, come over here!" Josh called out from the kitchen.

I padded over to find him putting his phone back in his pocket and pouring Irish whiskey in two crystal tumblers.

"The whiskey is from me," he said. "And the glasses are from Layla. A little housewarming gift for you."

"Thanks." I slapped him on the back. "I appreciate it."

He inched a glass my way and we clinked our drinks together. "Cheers."

The whiskey was smooth, with gentle hints of oak and caramel.

"So what do you think of this place?" Josh asked after his sip.

Though most of my furniture was here, the place would feel more like a home once I started living in it. "It's great. I can't thank you enough, man."

Josh's family owned the building. If anyone asked, the Remingtons were strait-laced businessmen hailing from South Side, Montardor. However, those who actually conducted business with them were well aware that Vance Remington—Josh's dad—was a notorious kingpin and the leader of their criminal empire. They were the ones who got me the hookup for this apartment.

In fact, Josh insisted I move into this particular complex, on this floor, and in this unit.

"No problem. That's what friends are for." His brown eyes sparked with mischief and he grinned wickedly. "Now that you're settled in, want to tell me what really happened last night between you and Gabby?"

The mahogany cabinets in my kitchen suddenly intrigued me. I pretended to evaluate them as if I hadn't already done so before signing the lease. All to avoid Josh's gaze. "What do you mean?" I feigned ignorance. "I told you I bumped into her at the party. That's it."

Josh chuckled and ran his fingers through his dark brown hair. "Yeah, right. You're full of shit. Shaun texted the group chat a minute ago that he actually caught you making out with Gabby last night."

Guess it was bound to get out eventually. Especially when we kissed in such a public setting. I palmed the nape of my neck and relented, saying, "Fine, that did happen."

"Hallelujah!" Josh praised. "You finally made a move. I feel like a proud dad!"

I smirked and shook my head. "Don't get too excited. We only kissed because she was trying to get back at her ex. She was quick to leave once she got her revenge."

Part of me was still irked about that—that she couldn't be bothered to stick around long enough for us to share another drink, another conversation, or fuck, even another kiss. My mind was completely hazy after the feel of her lips against mine. My obsession fed, all I wanted was more, more, and *more*. I was completely smitten with Gabriela and the way she ran away almost cheapened our moment on the dance floor.

Worry coalesced into a lump in my throat. What if she didn't like the way I kissed?

Or worse, what if she regretted it?

"Who's her ex?" Josh's brows furrowed. "Don't think I recall Layla telling me Gabby was seeing anyone recently."

Before I could tell him about Taylor, a feminine shrill had us flinching and cursing in our spots.

"What the hell was that?" Josh spat, our shocked expressions mirroring each other.

"I think it came from the hallway outside." We deposited our glasses on the counter and headed towards my door. I peered into the peephole. "There's no one out there."

I unlocked my door and cracked it open a fraction. Josh hovered over my shoulder, trying to get a better look. An empty hallway and utter silence welcomed us.

However, the door to the apartment directly in front of mine was agape.

"Oh, fuck," Josh mumbled strangely. "We should check that out."

Perplexed by his tone but silently agreeing, I opened my door wider and Josh charged ahead before I could even blink. He knocked loudly on my neighbour's door. "Gabby? It's Josh. I'm coming in."

Every muscle in my body froze, including the breath travelling through my lungs.

Did I hear him right?

Did he actually say Gabby—as in *my* Gabriela?

When Josh pushed open her door and revealed the scene before us, it felt like a stake was driven through my chest, puncturing my skin and causing my breath to whoosh out of me in one fell swoop.

Distraught, Gabriela sat amongst a flurry of broken glass, with a dark grey cat clutching her. Both of them trembled pitifully.

Josh and I let ourselves inside, and he shut the door with a decisive thud, awarding us privacy from any potential onlookers.

I lowered myself to my haunches in front of her, glass crunching beneath my shoes. I didn't touch her, afraid to spook her further, but coaxed her with my gentle tone, "Gabby?"

Blue eyes with specks of grey that reminded me of a stormy sea rose to mine, glistening with unshed tears and so much despair. "Hunter?" Her voice was weak and her face surprised as if she just noticed our presence.

"You okay?" I whispered.

I think I actually felt my heart breaking for her when she returned a thick and watery, "No."

It took everything within me to stop myself from gathering her into my arms.

"What happened over here?" Josh asked the million-dollar question, lowering himself beside us. "We heard you scream."

The cat in Gabriela's arms hissed and pawed at Josh as if to scratch him for getting too close to its beloved owner.

"*Shh.*" Gabriela tried to calm it down before turning to us. "I...I don't know. I just got back home less than a minute ago. My door was open, and I found my vase broken and my wall vandalized. Then my cat jumped at me and I got scared." She sniffled. "I'm so sorry for screaming. I didn't mean to disturb anyone."

She had nothing to apologize for when she'd just experienced something traumatic.

Gabriela's mention of her vandalized wall had me giving a quick glance towards the culprit.

Hell is empty and all the devils are here... including you, bitch.

I sucked in a sharp breath, my face screwing with anger. Josh noticed the quote at the same time, dropping a low, "*Fuck,*" under his breath.

Who would break into her place and write something like that?

"Do you know who did this?" I urged.

She teared up some more, utterly miserable. "No."

I furiously searched my pockets for my phone. "I'm calling the cops so we can file a report. Maybe we can also talk to the building's security to help identify the intruder."

Because this wasn't just a regular break-in. Those horrendous words were personal. Someone clearly had a vendetta against Gabriela.

Right as I was about to dial 911, Josh and Gabriela protested. "No, don't!"

"Why not?" I demanded, their vehement reactions catching me off guard.

They exchanged grim expressions. Josh rubbed his forehead as he stood up. "With families like ours, we handle our business discreetly. We don't involve the authorities unless necessary."

Though I knew my best friend's family conducted their dealings in the underworld, Gabriela's family also participating was news to me. But I didn't argue, choosing to ask instead, "What do you propose?"

Josh crossed his arms over his chest, surveying the state of her apartment. "I'm going to have a crew come over within the hour. They'll try to find fingerprints and then clean up. I'll also take a look at the security tapes to see who entered and left the building in the timeframe that you were gone, Gabby." Josh pulled out his phone, took a picture of the quote painted on the wall, and typed a text on his phone. Afterwards, he glanced at Gabriela. "Do you have a gun or knife I can use?"

His question didn't faze her. "Knives are in the kitchen. My gun is in the console table's top drawer."

Gabriela wasn't kidding when she said her daddy was a ranger—which was a half truth if he was in the same circle as the Remingtons—or that she knew how to wield a gun. I supposed it was a given for a mob princess.

"I'm going to give your place a quick search, though I suspect whoever is responsible for this mess is already gone. But I just want to verify that there are no other surprises left for you." Josh opened the drawer and yanked out the gun, checking the chamber for bullets. "We'll figure out who did this. Don't worry, Gabby."

"Thank you," she said in a small, resigned voice, a far cry from the sassy, confident girl I conversed with last night.

"Why don't you come with me while Josh does his thing?" I offered, getting up and extending a hand towards her. "I'm right across from you."

Gabriela's throat worked with a swallow. "Really?"

"Yeah, I just moved in today."

My best friend conveniently managed to disappear down the hallway as soon as I said that. Josh knew I had a crush on her, knew she lived here, and knew this was the opening I needed. I wasn't even annoyed that he orchestrated this entire thing and kept me in the dark so I'd be taken by surprise.

"Oh." She attempted a weak smile as her slender fingers slid over mine and grasped firmly. Her soft skin against my slightly callused one felt perfect. "This isn't how I usually welcome my neighbours."

I lifted her off the ground. "How do you usually welcome your neighbours?"

"With my charming personality, a baked good, or a house plant."

"I'd say you've nailed the charming part," I teased. "Though I wouldn't be opposed to a baked good or a house plant."

I wouldn't be opposed to anything from you, baby.

Gabriela stared at me like I was an enigma. My face grew warm. Was that the wrong thing to say?

Her cat meowed between us and I was grateful for the distraction. "What's its name?"

"Her name is Luna."

Luna eyed me curiously, her head nestled against Gabriela's shoulder. I softly dragged my fingers down her back in a slow caress. "Hi, Luna."

She purred, closing her eyes and enjoying my touch. I basked in the satisfaction of Luna not hissing at me the way she did Josh. It was a small win in my book.

"C'mon." I tipped my head towards her door. "Let's go."

Still holding her cat, Gabriela followed me out. We had just a few minutes before Josh showed back up to mine and I wanted to milk every second alone with her.

Once we crossed my threshold, her eyes roved over my apartment, registering the cream walls, dark wood flooring, massive navy blue sofa in the living room, the glass-topped dining table, the brass-accented chandelier with low-hanging light bulbs that my older sister insisted I get to help bring my home's 'aesthetic' together.

"You have a beautiful place, Hunter."

"Thank you." It pleased me that she liked it. I led her to the kitchen. "Do you want some water?"

"I do."

I pulled out one of the stools for her, waiting until she was seated by the kitchen island before going over to the sink and filling up a glass of water. If I had food in the fridge, I'd make her something to eat. Wanting to make conversation and distract her from what occurred back at hers, I said, "I still need to add some finishing touches to my place. Maybe a painting for my dining room wall or a bookshelf in my living room. What do you think?"

When she remained quiet, I got worried and peeked over my shoulder. Her expression was forlorn as she gazed at the granite counter. "Gabby?"

She snapped out of her daze, sitting up straighter. "S-sorry, did you say something?"

Luna rubbed her head against Gabriela's neck, sensing her need for emotional comfort.

I handed her the glass and while she drained the water within seconds, I repeated in a vain effort, "I said I'm thinking of adding a painting to my dining room wall or a bookshelf in my living room. Thoughts?"

"Yes to both." She deposited the glass on the counter. "An abstract or landscape painting and a dark-coloured bookshelf will definitely tie up the apartment nicely."

"Noted." I tipped my chin towards her empty glass. "Do you want more?"

"No." She gulped. "But can I have some of that whiskey?"

"Of course. Help yourself." I pushed the bottle closer to her. "Is there anything I can do for you? Anyone I can call?"

She poured herself two fingers. "I'll text my parents and friends soon. You and Josh have already done enough for me. Thank you."

"You don't have to thank us. Not for something like this."

A faint smile curved her mouth. As she daintily sipped her whiskey, I walked around the island to take a seat next to her. At this proximity, I could smell her perfume and it brought forth memories of last night.

After I came back home from the party, I spent a long time in the shower, using my fist to fuck myself in her honour. Whenever I closed my eyes, all I saw was her sensual body on the dance floor, all I heard was her little noises, and all I felt was her fingers diving into my hair, her lips staining mine red with sinful kisses, her greedy tongue twining with mine, and her quick pulse fluttering under my hand on her throat.

"Hunter?"

It was my turn to snap out of my daze. I cleared my throat and angled my body towards hers, mildly ashamed for being unable to let go of that kiss. "Yes?"

I realized even sitting down side by side, I towered over her. She had to tip her head back to gaze at me.

God, she was so beautiful, with her blue eyes, rosy lips, little black dress, and a white bow holding half of her hair up, the rest of it trailing down her back.

"About last night—"

"Coast is clear!" Josh hollered, cutting off Gabriela as he entered my apartment. "Luckily, there's no other damage. My crew should be here shortly. But, Gabby, you can't stay here anymore. It's not safe."

Gabriela sighed, as though finally registering the magnitude of her situation. Someone was taunting her—someone who most likely meant her harm—and now she couldn't stay here. "Yeah, I know. I'll stay with my mom for a bit."

"You should tell your dad ASAP." Josh perched his hip against the counter where we sat and returned her gun. "And when you do, tell him to get in contact with me."

Gabriela nodded. "I will."

"Good. In the meantime, I'll keep you posted if we find anything else on our end."

"Thanks, Josh." She downed the rest of her whiskey, wincing slightly at the burn. "I should get going now."

Josh fished out his keys from his pocket. "I'll drive you."

Knowing this was my chance to spend more time with Gabriela, I cast Josh a meaningful glance. "Actually, I know you have to meet up with Layla soon for date night, so…" I turned my focus to Gabriela. "I can drive you instead."

Gabriela hesitated. "Are you sure?"

"Positive." I stood up. "Josh, I owe you one for today."

I owe you for a lot more than helping me move.

Josh smirked, understanding the double meaning. "Anytime, man."

CHAPTER 5

Nothing More Than Platonic

GABRIELA

The sun was setting, melting into the horizon, and shading the blue sky in gorgeous tones of yellows and oranges as evening fell upon the city. Normally, I'd have pulled out my phone and taken a picture to add to my gallery of sunset images. However, today was far from normal circumstances and my hands were otherwise occupied, fidgeting anxiously over Luna's carrier in my lap.

The only thing that seemed to calm me down was the scent floating in the sports car—a mixture of Hunter's cologne and the pine-scented air freshener suffusing the inside of his luxurious car.

"Gabby?" Oh, and Hunter's voice, calling out to me in his deep, husky tone.

It was a soothing sound in the chaos buzzing through my mind.

I dragged my gaze away from the blurring scenery in the passenger window and shifted in the beige leather seat to face him. "Yes?"

The hands holding the steering wheel tightened and I couldn't help but stare at the veins exposed due to his sleeves being rolled up. I'd always had a weakness for strong arms, and Hunter's physique was clearly honed from years of training and playing football.

The *pièce de resistance* was the realistic snake tattoo wrapped around his left forearm. The one I hadn't been able to properly see last night in the dark. Shaded in blacks and greys, it disappeared under the cuff of his shirt, no doubt stretching all the way up to his shoulder.

My goodness. Athletic, tall, muscular, and tatted?

Hunter was easily the handsomest man I'd ever seen.

His blue eyes met mine when he caught me staring. "You okay?"

Was I okay? Far from it. But would I be once we figured out who broke into my apartment and dealt with them accordingly? Yes.

"I'm fine," I croaked. "Thank you for driving me."

"You don't have to keep thanking me, Gabby," he insisted. "This is the least I can do for you."

I was correct in my assumption last night that Hunter was a well-bred gentleman. Offered me his services to conduct homicide and now he was driving me home like a personal chauffeur. All because he saw someone in need and was willing to extend his help.

The last twenty-four hours came crashing back to me and I sagged in my seat, completely spent. Finding my sanctuary broken in and knowing I may not be safe anymore was a harsh pill to swallow. And now, on top of all that, I couldn't believe I shared the hottest kiss of my life with a beautiful man who was my new neighbour.

I wasn't one to believe in cosmic interventions, but this felt pretty damn close. Like fate was playing with Hunter's and my strings, forcing us to collide with no choice but to obey.

The car suddenly rolled to a stop.

Lost in thought, I hadn't realized Hunter veered off the GPS-guided route and brought us to a café.

Before I could say anything, he directed a sheepish smile my way. "I'm really hungry after an entire day of moving and I could use a bite. I'll just grab something quick to-go. Can I get you anything?"

I recognized this place. Le Petit Moulin was one of the cafés in the city I liked going to during the week to get some work done. Pink, flowery, and with romantic girlish décor, they had a great selection of pastries and I had a voracious sweet tooth.

"Actually, can we sit inside for a bit?"

I was exhausted and not exactly eager to face Mamma and Papà. Though I loved them dearly with all my heart, they were loud, passionate, overbearing, dysfunctional, and I feared being in their presence would only speed up the headache that was already looming close. Before leaving Hunter's apartment, I'd texted my parents in our group chat, saying that we needed to have a family emergency meeting in an hour. I didn't build up on what was wrong, just that it was urgent. But anticipating their reactions made my stomach flip. Mamma would cry and Papà would go berserk.

"Yeah. I'd like that." He threw a glance at my cat. "Will Luna be okay inside?"

"Yup. She'll be okay. Plus, this café is cat friendly."

Chivalry obviously wasn't dead because Hunter turned off the ignition, unfolded out of his car, and quickly rounded the front to come open my door. Wordlessly, he grabbed Luna's carrier from my lap.

My throat tightened at his kind gesture and the way his gaze moved over my body in a lazy perusal that had my toes curling in my red platform heels.

Now that the adrenaline from the horrible situation was wearing off, I finally registered the polished loafers, the black slacks moulding to his muscular thighs, the grey Henley wrapped over his roped torso, and the same silver chain and watch from last night.

Hunter was a pretty rich boy if I'd ever seen one.

When he wasn't in football gear, it was clear he enjoyed the finer things in life.

From the outside, he appeared suave and put together, but the unshaven jaw boasting a five o'clock shadow and the black wavy hair carelessly tousled gave him a hint of ruggedness.

Dare I say, with the sun setting behind him in a picturesque sight, he even reminded me of the heroes from my favourite paranormal romance books. A night creature from centuries-old lore. He could pass as a charming vampire, a dominant werewolf, a filthy demon, and…my musings were a clear indication that my state of mind was currently far from okay.

"I like your bow," Hunter remarked with a low rasp that did nothing to tame the skyrocketing tension between us.

I enjoyed accessories and getting dolled up for any occasion. Whether it was for a night out with my girls or to run a quick errand. I never missed an opportunity to don my best. Smiling at Hunter's compliment, I returned, "And I like your chain."

Hunter smiled back and offered me his hand, helping me step out of his car. I ignored the way my skin buzzed at our fingers touching and smoothed a hand over the skirt of my black dress while he closed the door behind me.

Hunter walked ahead, his long-legged strides eating the distance from his car to the front door of the café. I almost wobbled in my heels, trying to keep up with him.

When we entered Le Petit Moulin, the aroma of coffee and viennoiseries wafted in the air. My stomach grumbled. I could go for a warm mochaccino and some donuts. The café wasn't packed as per usual since we arrived at a peculiar time—too late for lunch and too early for dinner.

Adjusting the heart pendant choker around my neck, I inspected their selection of sweet treats while Hunter sauntered to the counter, Luna in tow. He started chatting with the server, a pretty woman who seemed just a bit older than us.

"Gabby," Hunter called out after a few seconds. "What would you like?"

"I'll have a small mocha and half a dozen of the mini donuts."

"Assorted?"

"Yes, please."

I walked over to them, but Hunter already whipped out his black card from his leather wallet and paid for both of us.

"What are you doing?" I asked, baffled. "I was going to get my own."

Hunter crossed his arms over his barrel chest, pinning me with a serious look. "Don't take it personally, sweetheart. I never let a woman pay when she's out with me."

Hearing *sweetheart* again brought a flood of memories from last night. Once more, I could feel the phantom of his masculine hand collaring my throat. Could feel the outline of his ridge against my stomach. Could feel his lips on mine. Sinful, greedy, and impatient for more.

"Thank—"

"For the love of God," he teased. "Stop throwing around the T-word. I get it. You're welcome."

A small chuckle burst out of me. "Okay, fine, I won't. Just know that I'm thinking it."

I'd find a way to repay him. With a house plant, baked goods, and something else. Though I had a feeling nothing would be enough for the generosity he bestowed upon me today.

Quietly, we watched the woman prepare our order. She was wearing a minidress, strappy heels, a pink frilly apron, and her ensemble was complete with diamond jewelry and beautiful pin-up style waves that fell down her back. I'd seen her here often and was beginning to wonder if she was the owner.

Her name tag read Elsie.

She turned around with a radiant grin and a pink tray containing our food. Hunter took it from her, leaving her a generous tip in the jar. As we walked away, I couldn't help but tell her how great she looked. "You're gorgeous. I love your heels."

She blushed and chuckled lightly. "Likewise."

We found a secluded corner in the empty café. Hunter pulled out my chair for me, then sank into his. I plucked Luna out of the carrier and into my lap but kept her leash wrapped around my wrist so she wouldn't wander off. Noticing my sweet, furry companion, Elsie came over with a little bowl of cat treats and petted Luna, who relished the attention. Once she wandered off, Hunter and I dug into our food.

He'd ordered himself a salad with chicken breast and sparkling water. I watched as he placed a napkin over his lap, took hold of the pink cutlery—which his big hands dwarfed—and used his fork and knife to slice into the meat before bringing a forkful into his mouth and chewing thoughtfully. He was so posh, sitting across from me with a regal posture, eating like we were at a five-course restaurant and not a casual, cute café with cramped seating.

He ate his salad and I devoured half of my donuts, companionable silence floating between us. I relaxed further into my seat. With other people, I sometimes felt the need to fill the quietness with chatter. But not with Hunter.

His presence was steady and solid, demanding no words and offering solace in return.

I liked that.

A little too much.

"You have a sweet tooth, don't you?" Hunter asked after finishing his meal.

"What gave it away?" I joked. "The six donuts or the sugary drink?"

He chuckled, unscrewing his bottle of water. "By the way, you have frosting on your lips."

Oops. I licked at my bottom lip and glanced up. "Is it gone?"

Hunter paused, the bottle halfway to his mouth, his eyes fixated on *my* mouth.

Oh, God.

Too close.

That look was way *too close* to the one from last night before he hungrily stamped his lips to mine. And unfortunately, I meant it when I told my girls I wasn't planning on acting on this attraction. I wouldn't let Hunter's and my newfound friendship—if we could even call it that—develop into anything beyond platonic.

Although my tongue slipped back in his apartment and I almost asked him about last night, I realized it was best not to broach the subject. As far as I was concerned, we were both on the same page. It was a great kiss, but it was just that—a kiss shared between two consenting adults who found each other attractive.

Plus, our revenge plan worked. Taylor unfollowed me on social media this morning. Either because he realized he'd forgotten to do so before or because of my public display of affection with Hunter. Regardless of the reason, to a certain extent, Taylor's ego was bruised. In our one-month friends with benefits arrangement, I learned that he was a bit cocky and didn't like to be outdone by anyone else. And he may have claimed to have 'found better' with Morgan, but I was the one who hit the jackpot. Ditching the mediocre football player for the team's star quarterback?

Hah. I hoped Taylor had the worst week ever.

"Hunter?" I prompted when he kept staring at me, feeling self-conscious.

Hunter inhaled a sharp breath, forcing a smile onto his lips. "Y-yeah, all gone." He guzzled his water like he was parched, his Adam's apple rising up and down in his neck before inquiring cheekily, "Did you save a donut for me?"

I snatched a sprinkle donut, giving him a mock stink eye. "I guess you can have the last one."

He grabbed the remaining mini jelly donut and plopped it into his mouth with a wolfish smirk. "Which one was your favourite?"

"I'm a chocolate lover, so the chocolate-dipped one for sure." I pressed my cheek into my palm. "Do you have a sweet tooth?"

"I do." He dabbed the corners of his mouth with a napkin. So princely. "But I have to maintain a stricter diet during football season. Therefore, I rarely indulge."

Interesting. Wanting to learn about his hobbies and interests, I couldn't help but needle him for more information. "How did football become a thing?"

"My dad got me into it." He reclined back in his chair. "I started playing it when I was a kid and continued throughout my schooling. He always dreamed of me going pro."

"And is that what you want?"

"Nah. I want to be a lawyer like him and follow in his footsteps."

My face softened. "That's so sweet."

A sad smile curved his lips. "My dad was my best friend. I looked up to him my whole life. He was the greatest person ever." After a moment of hesitancy, he added, "Unfortunately, he passed away from cancer when I was nine."

"I'm so sorry to hear that." Hunter spoke about his dad with such unabashed hero worship, it made my heart clench for him. I couldn't imagine the pain he must have gone through with losing a parent so young. "I'm sure he'd be very proud of how far you've come. With your academic career and football."

The sad smile turned into one filled with fondness. "Yeah, he would be." He leaned forward on his elbows. "What about you? What incited you to pursue finance and the Women in Business Student Association?"

Despite us not conversing prior to the last twenty-four hours, it was abundantly clear to me that we'd both kept tabs on each other. Me through social media and Hunter through his conversations with Josh, perhaps.

"I've always been good with numbers. I debated going into mathematics briefly but decided to do my undergrad in commerce with a finance major instead and I'm quite happy with my decision. I enjoy the classes and my workload isn't too overbearing." I sipped my mocha. "As for the Women in Business Student Association, I attended some of their events last year and their message really resonated with me. I wanted to be a part of a group of individuals who helped educate and empower the university's student body by providing them the tools and resources needed to become successful future business leaders. The association has been great at creating events that give opportunities for students to learn about different industries and network with professionals to open doors for internships and jobs post grad. So far, it's been a very rewarding experience working with this team. I applied to be the finance coordinator this past spring and officially got the position just shy of summer."

Hunter appeared fully engrossed, like my passion for my work resonated with him. "That's amazing, Gabby. What exactly does your position entail?"

"I'm responsible for our overall budgeting. I get to decide how much of our capital gets allocated to certain events and activities. I work closely with the event coordinators, the sponsors, and our team president, Hera. We have a mixer event coming up in two weeks and we've rented out the entirety of the MacGregor Bar. Tickets are currently being sold." I bit my lip before biting the bullet and saying, "You should come."

Hunter's eyes widened a fraction, pleased.

"We host this every year early on in the fall semester. It gives the student body a chance to meet our team and familiarize themselves with what we do and our upcoming events. It would be a nice way to meet your fellow peers at the university." Hunter appeared to be considering it and I rushed out to add, "I know you don't like crowded spaces, but if you come, I'll hang with you. We don't even have to talk to anyone else. I promise."

"Okay," he said with a charming smile. "Since you promised to be with me, I'll look into buying a ticket."

It felt like an accomplishment that I could convince this homebody into leaving his comfort zone and come to an event that my team was hosting. "Great. Can't wait." My phone buzzed with a text. It was my dad. He'd just arrived home. "I hate to cut this short but…"

"I know." Was it my imagination or did Hunter sound a tad bit disappointed? He grabbed his keys. "Let's get you home, sweetheart."

Fuck, I was in trouble. I liked hearing him refer to me in all sorts of endearments in his voice. It was smooth, yet a hint rough. Like warm honey and whiskey.

After one kiss, I was already finding him irresistible and now I worried that *not crossing* another line with Hunter would be harder than I thought. I was also woman enough to admit that if it weren't for my own set of rules, I'd want to go all the way with him.

When I followed him out of the café with Luna back in her carrier, evening welcomed us, the sky faded in wondrous shades of blue, pink, and purple.

He opened the passenger door for me and we both jolted when a dragonfly flew between us, letting loose surprised chuckles.

I once heard that dragonflies signified courage, change, and new beginnings.

I dwelled over the good omen for the rest of the ride back home. It wasn't a long drive, but it felt like an eternity when I was all too aware of Hunter. The scent of his cologne. The soft inhales and exhales making his muscular chest bow rhythmically. The wind whipping through his window, causing his inky black hair to float just above his shoulders. The smooth way he handled his powerful car. All these things had my heart fluttering.

And dammit, I'd just invited him to my association's mixer, giving fate another opportunity to recreate last night's moment.

Maybe I was just as hopeless as my mamma when it came to love and infatuation.

We arrived at my childhood home shortly and Hunter parked in the driveway.

Papà was already waiting for me by the porch steps in his three-piece suit, black windswept hair silvering at the temples, infamous deadpan, and his leather-gloved hands in his pockets in a resting stance meant to portray his casualness but was actually a farce to hide his offensive nature.

When he saw that I arrived with Hunter, his face instantly morphed from passive to thunderous.

Hunter, sensing the shift, cajoled, "Is your dad going to polish his shotgun and threaten me if I step out to open your car door?"

I undid my seatbelt. "He...might."

"I'll take my chances." Hunter got out of the car and came to my side to open my door yet again. He grabbed Luna and I slid out, already anticipating Papà's reaction to a boy bringing me home. Any other day, I'd have freaked out. Right now, I was too depleted from the day's events to care.

"Will you text me your schedule when you have a moment?" he asked tentatively, low enough that Papà wouldn't hear. "We can grab a coffee together if we have a mutual break."

Coffee was friendly. Platonic. Very doable.

"Of course. I'd like that." I smiled. "Here, give me your number."

We swapped phones and added each other's contact information.

"Although you told me not to say the T-word, I feel the need to repeat it once more," I murmured. "Thank you for your kindness today. Talking with you helped take my mind off...the situation. I really appreciate it."

He grinned and it was so soft and swoon-worthy, my chest clenched at the sight. "Anytime, Gabby."

Then Hunter walked beside me as I headed towards Papà.

"Hi," I said to him. "This is Hunter. He's friends with Josh and lives in the apartment across from mine."

Hunter stuck out his hand first. "Nice to meet you, sir."

Papà sized him up with a scowl, wanting him to break a sweat. Hunter's hand stayed outstretched, not balking under his intimidation tactic.

Eventually, Papà returned his handshake, but I saw how firmly he squeezed Hunter's hand, sending a message across. "Thank you for bringing my daughter home." He pinned his unrelenting stare on me. "Gabriela, *entriamo*."

Papà addressed me in Italian in front of Hunter to alienate him. He was biding his time before he could pepper me with questions about my new neighbour. Papà wasn't fond of outsiders and after the last asshole who broke my heart, he was even more vigilant when it came to the men surrounding me.

Hunter read between the lines. He handed me Luna's carrier. "I'll see you around, Gabby. Take care."

I gave him an apologetic smile. "Take care, Hunter."

We waited until Hunter's car peeled out of the driveway before going inside the house.

I whispered a prayer under my breath, knowing that the next hour was going to be absolute chaos.

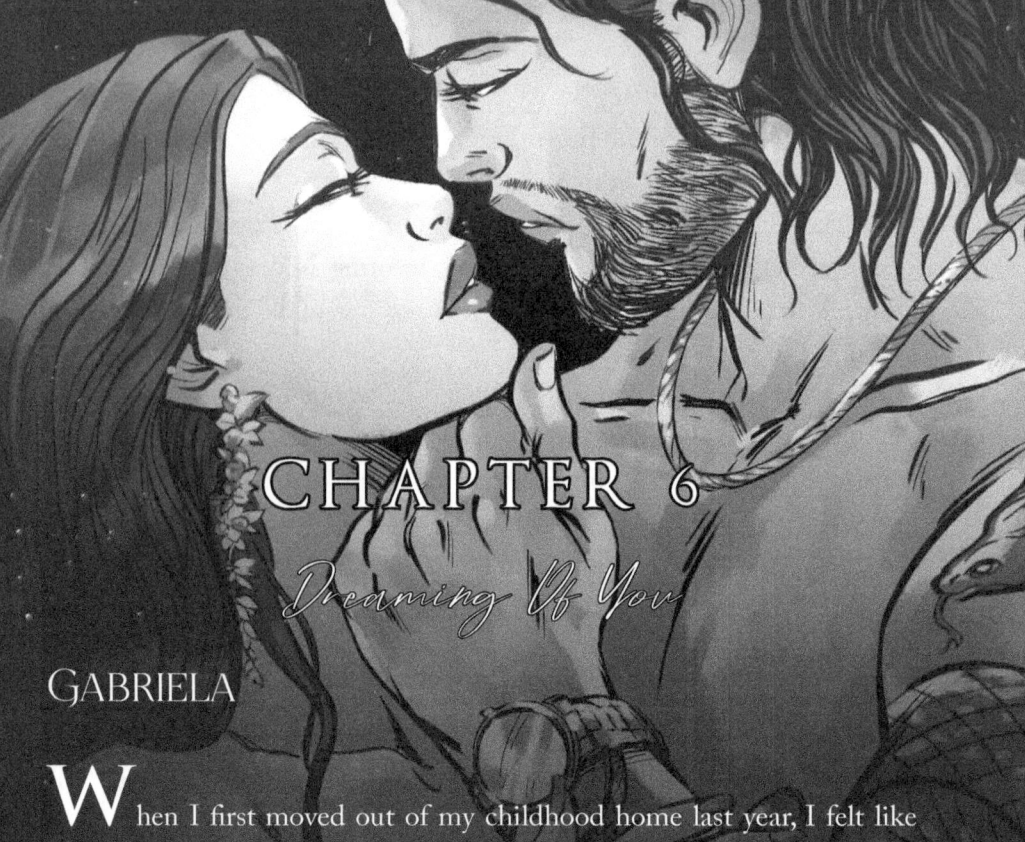

CHAPTER 6

Dreaming Of You

GABRIELA

When I first moved out of my childhood home last year, I felt like I could breathe properly for the first time. A huge weight was lifted off my shoulders and all the ailments plaguing me from living under the Bellafiore roof evaporated into thin air. The root cause of my occasional anxiousness—my parents' dynamics—was no longer breathing down my neck like a fictitious dragon. Serenity was a state of mind I quickly became acquainted with and it was one I realized that I took for granted.

Because the minute I crossed over the threshold of said childhood home, the pressure returned tenfold and rested on my sternum like a block of cement. My fight or flight response kicked in like a bird in a cage. Flapping its wings frantically to fight. But held hostage by the reality of its situation.

Seeing my parents sitting together on a love seat in the living room, mere millimetres separating their bodies, amplified the anxiety. Their postures were defensive and their armours coated with the ashes of their once flaming love. But if you paid close attention, their stubbornness was an undertone of their longing. When you spent years yearning for something without avail, it made you vexed at the world and all its inhabitants.

Being the child of divorced parents was hard, and it was harder when the divorcees were still obsessed with one another...yet too prideful to actually work on their issues.

In general, I tended to be forgiving because I understood that they were still human and it was their first time on this earth as well.

"Gabriela," Papà bit out through gritted teeth with barely concealed impatience. "Are you going to tell us why you called an emergency family meeting or do I need to keep sitting on the same sofa your mamma uses for her string of lovers?"

I pinched the bridge of my nose. *Here we go again.*

Mamma's back shot ramrod straight and she threw daggers at him with her gaze.

He smirked but didn't look at her, blue eyes like mine fixed on the coffee in his hand.

Running her fingers through her red hair—the exact shade I inherited—she harrumphed, "You don't see me complaining about the nauseating perfume radiating off of you from *your* string of lovers, *stronzo.*"

Her insult hit bullseyes. Papà placed the cup down on the coffee table with a prominent clatter. "How many times do I have to tell you—"

"I'm going to stop you both right there!" I waved my hands in front of them, forcing them to redirect their attention to me. I was sitting across from them on a singular fauteuil. "This meeting is about me. Not your failed marriage. So could you please halt your arguing and listen to what I have to say?" I gulped. "Something bad happened today and I'm scared."

To their credit, in the face of my distress, they both paled, instantly quieting.

With a deep inhale, I told them everything that occurred. From me coming home and finding my apartment door unlocked, my vase shattered, my wall vandalized with a nasty quote, my frightened Luna, and then Josh and Hunter coming to my aid after hearing me scream from across the hallway.

When I finished recounting the details, I was correct in my earlier assumption.

Mamma gasped and wept.

And Papà went berserk, kicking the corner of the coffee table as he stood up and paced in the living room like a lion locked in a den. "I told you it was a bad idea to let her move out," he spat, pointing an accusing finger at Mamma. "We should have never allowed it, Lucia. If she'd been home when the break-in occurred, who knows what could have happened to her. We're lucky she's alive!"

I shrank under his tirade. It definitely wasn't a good time to tell him that I didn't need permission to move out last year when I'd legally been an adult.

His anger stemmed from worry and it was valid.

Mamma glared at Papà. "You think I don't know that, Enzo? We both agreed that Gabriela could live closer to school for her own benefit!" She turned towards me, wailing, "You can't live there anymore. We forbid it. It's not safe. You must stay here."

My worst nightmare was unfolding before me. I appreciated the concern, but living under the same roof as Mamma, with Papà visiting, would do me in. Including the long commute from our West Side neighbourhood to downtown every day. "I know I can't live there anymore." Which pained me, considering how much I loved my apartment. "But I can live elsewhere. Still closer to school, though."

"Absolutely not," Papà barked and rounded the sofa to take a seat beside his ex-wife again. "Starting now, you're living here. I'll have one of my trusted guards stationed at the house at all times, and another one will follow you around. To school. To work. To wherever the hell you go. You're not to be left alone until I figure out which asshole had the balls to toy with my daughter and kill him."

My head spun. "Papà, *ti scongiuro*. I don't want your guards shadowing my every move. I'll go crazy. Furthermore, I can't have them sitting outside my classes or my meetings. That will draw unwanted attention towards me. Please don't do this. We'll figure out another solution."

"For once, I agree with Enzo," Mamma said disdainfully. She reached for the box of tissues on the coffee table and tore one out to wipe her tears and ruined makeup. "You're all we have. We won't risk you, Gabriela. Your safety is not something to be gambled with."

I started relenting under their beseeching.

Mamma and Papà conceived me when they were young and as a result, I felt like I grew up with them in a way where they were more like my older siblings than parents. But now, with their downturned lips, fear in their eyes, and ashen faces, they looked weary beyond their respective forty-one and forty-three years of age.

They were doing their best to stay strong, but this had shaken them to their core. They wouldn't budge from their decision and there wasn't much I could do to go against their wishes. Especially when I knew Papà would flex his muscles and have an army of his men barricading me if I refused.

I also wouldn't be the one to put them through any form of stress if I could prevent it. I loved them too much. Therefore, closing my eyes, I whispered the word that sealed my fate, "Fine."

Whereas Mamma's and Papà's postures deflated with relief, mine stiffened with vexation.

Needing to establish a game plan, I asked, "What comes next?"

"Starting tomorrow, I'll drive you to school," Mamma said. "And you'll remain in public spaces with other students—never alone—until I finish work and can pick you up."

"That's not convenient." And while I adored my parents, I could only handle them in smaller, healthy increments. Not such large doses. "My schedule isn't compatible with your hours at the salon. It won't work."

"Then I'll drive you, and on the days that I can't, one of the guards will," Papà stated, smoothing invisible lint from the sleeves of his suit jacket. "Nonetheless, you're not travelling solo. And I'll have a guard following you at all times even if it's from a distance, Gabriela. That's non-negotiable."

It was my turn to stand up and pace, my teeth nervously chewing my thumbnail. I should have gotten my license months ago. "What if I carpool with Anna and Layla?" That way, I could keep some of my sanity. "And on the days when that's not possible, a guard can drive me. Is that fair?"

"Fair." Papà pulled out his phone to check the time. "I have a meeting tonight with the Remingtons and the De la Croixes. Once that's adjourned, I'll ask Josh to show me the security footage from the building. One way or another, we're going to figure out who did this and make them pay. Understood?"

I was the apple of my parents' eyes. Regardless of our differences and flaws, they'd do anything for me. "Understood, Papà."

"Now that that's settled…" Mamma rose from the sofa and came over to me, framed my face and planted a tear-stained kiss on my forehead. "I'm so happy you're okay, *cara mia*." Throwing a dirty look over her shoulder at Papà, she added, "Enzo, I'm going to start preparing dinner. Feel free to leave before I serve it."

He scoffed, still scrolling on his phone. "Nice try. I didn't drive all the way here to leave unfed, *principessa*."

"Don't call me your princess, Enzo."

"What are you going to do about it, huh?" he goaded, going from a menacing mob man to a besotted fool for her. "Ask me for another divorce?"

"*Dio mio*, you grate on my nerves," Mamma grumbled as she sashayed in front of him on her way to the kitchen.

"Do I grate on your nerves when I send you a hefty deposit so you can afford your designer shoes, purses, and clothes?" He threw her a shit-eating grin when she flipped him the bird before disappearing down the hallway. "Yeah, didn't think so."

Mamma did well for herself as a hairdresser and nail technician. Though they were more hobbies than jobs at this point. She didn't really need to work. Not when her ex-husband kept her bank account well-padded and supported all her materialistic wishes. Mamma and I were similar in that sense. We both liked to spend Papà's money. And he doted on us, never once complaining.

When she was no longer within earshot, Papà tapped the seat next to him. I went over and he put his arm around my shoulders, hugging me to his side. "It's going to be okay, Gabriela. No one will ever hurt you on my watch."

I had no doubt. Even when I was a little girl, I knew Papà was a ruthless mob man working with the Remingtons—one of Montardor's dominating crime families—yet I'd never been afraid of him. I'd only been subjected to his loving and caring side. Come hell or high water, I knew he'd defend me with his dying breath.

"I know." I rested my head against his shoulder, inhaling his familiar scent. It hadn't changed since I was a kid and it always brought me a sense of comfort. "Thank you for always protecting me."

His reply came in the form of a kiss against my temple. "*Ti voglio bene*, Gabriela."

"*Ti voglio bene anch'io*, Papà."

After a few seconds of silence, he gathered enough courage to ask, "How's your mamma doing these days? Is she still dating those losers?"

"Please." I leaned back to pin him with a chiding stare. "Don't act like you haven't kept tabs on your precious Lucia. You already know who your ex-wife is and isn't dating. And if you want her to stop dating 'those losers', then maybe *you* should ask her out."

He rubbed his forehead like he was the one tired of dealing with these dramatics. Hah. Try being in my shoes for a day. "You're just like your mamma. Feisty and witty."

"I also happen to have your temper."

"And my good looks." He cast a yearning glance in the direction of the kitchen, where we could hear the clanging of pots and pans as Mamma prepared us a meal. "Hers too. Don't tell her I said that, though."

"You're hopeless." I laughed. "C'mon. I'm hungry. Let's go eat."

We walked down the hallway. I skipped ahead, the aroma of spices, tomatoes, and basil calling out to me. The landline started ringing. Papà ignored it and beelined for the kitchen, the urge to annoy Mamma too strong. But I paused at the half-moon table near our staircase, housing an antique rotary phone.

Before picking up the handset, I already knew it was my grandmother. She was the only one who called here and usually around the time Papà visited to make sure nobody had killed each other.

"*Ciao, Nonna!*" I announced in a TV show host voice, twirling the cord of the phone around my index finger. "It's your favourite granddaughter!"

"*Ciao, piccola.*" She chuckled at my silliness in her smoker, gravelly tone. I liked making her smile and laugh. "You're my only granddaughter."

"Still your fav."

"That you are." She coughed a bit. "Is everyone still alive?"

"For now," I whispered conspiratorially. I heard Mamma barking at Papà, probably for tasting the sauce.

"Good," she said. "Also, I packed some tiramisu for you. Enzo should have brought it when he came over."

I loved her tiramisu. "Thank you, Nonna. I adore you."

"Me too, Gabriela. Now tell me, how's everything with you?"

I didn't want to tell my grandmother about the break-in. She'd throw a fit if she found out. And if I thought my parents were overbearing, she could be worse. Nonna would strap herself to a chair in my apartment with a grenade and rifle, ready to kill whoever was messing with me. "Everything is going well. Just, you know, busy with—"

My sentence was cut off by the loud ruckus stemming from the kitchen.

"*Merda!*" Nonna cursed. "What's all the noise, huh? If I didn't know any better, I'd say you were living in a zoo."

"Close enough," I muttered. A loud *vaffanculo* rang in the background, followed by the swift crack of a spatula hitting flesh. Papà screamed. Mamma screamed louder. "They're having another passionate fight."

"Gabriela, some idiots are doomed to be together. Namely your parents. They just need to get their heads out of their asses and realize it. Your mamma was wrong and impulsive to ask for a divorce, and your papà was even more foolish for giving it to her. Now they're both miserable because they still miss and want each other. Their kind of love never really dies."

I wholeheartedly agreed with her. "I know, but who's going to make them realize it?"

"They'll come to that realization themselves. Whether it's tomorrow, next month, next year, or decades from now. But they will."

"Enough about them, Nonna. How is your book club going? What's this month's pick?"

"That blasted Arlene influenced Jenna to pick another alien romance this month." She sighed. "Can you believe it? I just finished reading about an immortal tentacle demon railing a sweet librarian. When I was young, literature like this would have never existed. It's all so…blasphemous!"

I guffawed. Arlene was a seventy-year-old tree hugger who dressed like a neon highlighter, cursed like a sailor, and drank too much coffee. She was my favourite lady from Nonna's gang. "But you enjoyed it, didn't you?" I jested. "Next thing you know, you'll have an entire shelf filled with alien romances—"

"Gabriela, dinner is ready!" Mamma hollered from the kitchen, exasperated.

"Yeah, okay, fine. I did enjoy it," Nonna begrudgingly admitted. "Anyways, go eat, Gabriela. I'll call you again later this week, *va bene?*"

"*Va bene,* Nonna. Speak soon. I love you." I felt the need to relay those three words to her, today having frightened me more than I'd like to admit.

What if I had been home when the intruder came in? What if they had hurt me? What if I never got the chance to tell my loved ones how much they meant to me because I was gone?

Those thoughts were a slippery slope and I needed to put a stop to them right now. The best I could do was count my blessings that I was safe and healthy and pray that it stayed that way.

After my call with Nonna, I went to the kitchen, finding my parents with flushed faces and throwing half-assed glares at each other from across the dining table as they waited for me to join them.

We said grace and I dove into the pesto pasta, garlic bread, and caprese salad with gusto. My family could be a little chaotic at times, but they were mine and I loved them with all my heart.

Once dinner was over, Papà hightailed it out of there before he was late for his meeting. Though not before two of his men arrived. They were currently patrolling the perimeter of our home, their guns hidden underneath their suits to avoid scaring off our neighbours.

Papà said to call him if we experienced any sort of distress or disturbance. He was also planning on coming back tonight to sleep under the same roof as us, a fact that pissed off Mamma.

I offered to do the dishes and clean the kitchen since she'd cooked. Once I finished my duties, I ascended the stairs to the second floor and paused when I reached the landing, spotting Mamma speeding down the hallway towards her bedroom. A cloud of perfume trailed around her. She was in her fancy silk pyjamas saved for *special occasions* and a bit of subtle makeup that made her glow.

"You look good." An amused grin pulled at my lips. "Did you get all dressed up for your ex-husband?"

She narrowed her eyes. The blush on her cheeks was answer enough. "Gabriela."

"What?" I shrugged innocently, almost comically. "It's an honest question."

"You should already know that I don't do anything for Enzo," she replied testily.

"Okay, if you say so."

She huffed, shaking her head. "Go to your room, you little hellion. You're grounded."

"You can't ground me anymore. I'm an adult."

"Of course. How can I forget?" Her tone was dry, but her expression was tender. "You've had a long day, *cara mia*. Don't stay up too late."

"I won't." I rose up on my tippytoes to plant a kiss on her cheek.

"Also, I want you to meet Neal soon. You'd like him."

Well, shit, how could I forget about her latest beau? I scrunched my nose. "Is that really wise?"

"What do you mean?"

Sometimes I really hated having to be the parent in the conversation. "Everyone knows you have unfinished business with Papà."

For a split second, I regretted saying it, before reminding myself that this was necessary. She needed to hear it. She needed to stop dating around aimlessly just to annoy him. And she needed to stop trying to fill the void in her chest that only he could fill.

"I'm not having this conversation with you." She swallowed. "I'm going to bed. Enzo has a key. Therefore, he can let himself inside."

"Where will he sleep?"

"On the couch," she snapped. "Or in the dog house."

We didn't have a dog house and Papà wouldn't be sleeping on the couch. In fact, we all knew that when he'd return home, he'd slither into her room—their old room—and sleep on the floor right next to his *principessa*.

I felt saddened for both of them. "Mamma…"

She paused at the threshold of her bedroom, mustering a weak smile. "Good night. I'll see you tomorrow. We'll have a girls' day, just you and me. I'll give your ends a trim and do your nails, all right?"

"Sounds good." I nipped the conversation in the bud for now as I walked backwards towards my own room. "Good night. Love you."

"Love you too."

Entering my own bedroom, its familiarity instantly comforted me. I may not visit often, but this place had always been my safe haven. My baroque-inspired furniture was black and gold, contrasting beautifully with the red accented pillows and blanket decorating my bed. My walls were lined with posters from my favourite bands and dark shelves, which contained my paranormal romance books, their spines weathered from years of reading. And my windowsills were laden with old, flowery candles, some melted and some unused.

My room was an amalgam of all the things I loved from teenagehood to now, and stepping back inside of it was like visiting a time capsule.

I didn't take much when I moved out a year ago, except for my wardrobe. Papà's guards would have to shuffle all my clothes from my apartment back here for the duration of my stay.

The second I plopped on my bed, spread-eagle, Luna jumped on my stomach with a graceful leap. I caressed between her ears and she purred. I got her when I was twelve years old and she was a tiny, three-week-old kitten. Papà found her by a dumpster. She'd die if left on her own, so he brought home the Nebelung kitty to me. I took care of her like she was my baby and loved her with all my heart. She'd been there for me through thick and thin. Luna was my protector and I was hers. If we were ever separated from one another, we'd always find our way back to each other.

"Hi, girl," I cooed. "We've had one helluva day, huh?" She meowed in response. "I know, I know. Today scared you." I couldn't imagine the fear she must have felt when a stranger broke into our place and violated it. Luna was hiding under the console table, trembling with fear when I entered the apartment. "I'm sorry I wasn't there. I'll make it up to you. I promise."

I was busy showering my Luna with kisses when my phone pinged with a notification. She pawed at me, unhappy that I stopped giving her attention, a little too similar to her mommy in that regard.

Flipping to my stomach, I belly-crawled on my bed to grab my discarded purse resting near the decorative pillows. Once I pulled out my phone, I realized it was a text from Hunter.

I'm still waiting... —Hunter

Smiling, I typed back a reply, my feet swinging back and forth in the air. Luna sidled next to me, pressing her head on my wrist, blinking at the screen with her yellow feline eyes.

For what? —Gabriela

For you to tell me if everything's okay on your end and to send me your schedule. —Hunter

Oh, I completely forgot.

I'm feeling much better than this afternoon. Thank you for checking in! My dad's looking into the situation now. Obviously this means I can't go back to my apartment yet. I'll have to stay here for the foreseeable future 😟 —Gabby

I attached a screenshot of my schedule.

Send me yours as well! —Gabby

Hunter read my message but didn't respond right away. I put my phone down and decided to take a shower to wash away the day. When I emerged back into my room wearing a nightie, lathered in a nice layer of my vanilla lotion, and my hair blow-dried in its usual style, I felt more like myself.

As I settled back into my bed and turned on the TV, ready to end the night with a few episodes of *Supernatural*, I noticed another text from him.

I'm glad you're with your family and in a safe space. I hope this situation gets resolved soon. Let me know if there's anything I can do to help. —Hunter

There was an attachment under his text.

Here's my schedule. —Hunter

We have Horror & Cult Classic Cinema together. I'll be in the west side Monday morning. Would you like a ride to school? —Hunter

My eyes widened with glee. I could rarely get Anna or Layla to watch horror movies, so I added this elective knowing I'd be all alone. The professor cancelled the last class due to a family emergency, which meant our first class of the semester would be this coming Monday. I was happy Hunter would be there too.

I can't believe you're in this class!! Do you actually enjoy horror movies or was this the only elective that worked with your schedule? —Gabby

Also, yes to the ride! —Gabby

Clearly adding distance between us wasn't an option, considering how often I'd be seeing him moving forward. But as long as I didn't act on the attraction, everything would be fine, right?

Love horror. It's my favourite genre. —Hunter

I'll pick you up at 10 a.m. Is that okay? —Hunter

Yes, that's perfect. Thank you so much 😊 —Gabby

What did I say about the T-word, sweetheart? —Hunter

I giggled, picturing his stern, serious face. God, he was cute, and sweet, and handsome, and gentlemanly. The whole package, really.

Don't forget my house plant and baked goods. —Hunter

Wouldn't dream of it, pretty boy. —Gabby

You keep calling me pretty and I'm going to develop a complex. —Hunter

I'm surprised you don't already have one, Mr. Star Quarterback. —Gabby

You keeping tabs on me? —Hunter

Yes. I've memorized all your stats, watched all your game highlights, and practically worship the ground you walk on. I'm your number one fan 🖤 —Gabby

He could sense the sarcasm. I'd never watched a single game of football in my life.

Oh, yeah? What's my jersey number? —Hunter

Whoops, caught me there. I went on social media to stalk Josh's profile. I distinctly remembered him posting pictures of the football team in their uniforms two weeks ago. I could grab his jersey number from there.

But before I could do that, I got sidetracked by the series of pictures Josh posted Thursday afternoon that I must have missed. The first shot was a few boys from the football team running down a hallway. The second shot was him passing the ball to another player. The third shot was a candid moment in the locker room, the boys conversing and laughing.

My mouth fell open when I zoomed in on Hunter, leaning against one of the lockers.

Mid-chuckle. Hair mussed. His bare chest glistening with sweat.

I finally got a good look at that snake tattoo, spanning from his left wrist to his shoulder, the reptile wrapped around his swollen muscles.

But the star of the show was the silver barbell glinting in his right nipple.

I was going to pass out.

Hunter Saint Warren had no reason to be this filthy hot.

How had this man flown under my radar for this long?

Another text popped up from him.

That's what I thought, you little liar. —Hunter

Never thought I'd like being referred to as a *little liar*, but I could just imagine him saying two words in his deep voice. It only heightened his sexual appeal to me.

Once I got his jersey number, I typed a quick reply.

Nine!! —Gabby

Too late. I know you had to look it up. —Hunter

So much for being my biggest fan. My heart is broken. —Hunter

How do I mend it 😳? —Gabby

Come to my next game and wear my jersey. —Hunter

I blinked. Okay, so he had a bossy and demanding side.

I was totally here for it.

That's it? —Gabby

For starters. It'll take more than that to get back on my good side. —Hunter

Tell me what else I need to do. I'm willing to put in the work. —Gabby

Don't worry. I'll make you work hard for it. —Hunter

Oh my God.

He was flirting with me and I was enjoying every second of it.

Can't wait 🖤 —Gabby

Who knew you had such a polite side? A complete one-eighty from the heathen who was planning a man's funeral last night. —Hunter

Hey! I'll have you know I'm actually a very good girl. —Gabby

Oh, baby, I know how much of a good girl you can be. — Hunter

But I like your devilish side too. —Hunter

I threw my phone on the bed and covered my mouth, shocked. He did not just say that to me. Fuckity fucking fuck. And here I thought of keeping things between us *platonic*.

Luna's head peeked up at my reaction, her eyes narrowed.

"Luna," I whispered. "I'm in big, big, big trouble."

Hunter had to stop flirting with me. I had to put an end to this. Otherwise, we'd be fucking before the end of the semester. And I didn't want him to just be a notch in my belt, which was the usual case for all the men who entered my life. Not to mention, mentally and emotionally, I wasn't in the right headspace to start something—short-term or long-term—while my current predicament hung over my head like a sword.

Nor was it fair to start something with someone when you weren't able to give them your one hundred percent.

Luna went back to licking her paw, deeming my crisis unimportant, and watching TV. Meanwhile, I chewed my lip, nervously reaching for my phone again.

Of course you do, considering you were so quick to indulge me 😜 —Gabby

Also, speaking of last night... —Gabby

Just want to make sure we're cool? —Gabby

Why wouldn't we be? —Hunter

Well, I hope the fact that we kissed (which was obviously a one-time thing) doesn't make things weird in the future. — Gabby

Hunter read my message. He didn't reply right away. One second turned into ten. Ten seconds turned into thirty. When it was nearing a minute, my insides roiled over. Should I have not said that? I wanted to establish a boundary, but now I was second-guessing myself.

Nothing's weird. We're good. —Hunter

Relief sank into my bones. Satisfied, I sent him another text.

Okay, good! It was just a kiss and it meant nothing because we're friends, right? —Gabby

I could see the three dots indicating that Hunter was typing for quite some time.

Finally, my phone pinged again.

Exactly. —Hunter

Huh. I expected more than a one-word reply, but as long as we were on the same page, that was all that mattered.

I'm going to bed now, but just wanted to say that you didn't deserve what happened to you today. If you find out more information about the situation, please let me know. I'd like to be there for you. —Hunter

As a friend, of course. —Hunter

He really was so perfect.

I will! **** for everything. Good night, Hunter 🩶 —Gabby**

He understood that the ****** were a replacement for the thanks and he didn't reprimand me.

Sweet dreams, Gabby. —Hunter

I put my phone down, the lull of sleep pulling at my body. I yawned and settled more comfortably under the covers. Luna curled against me and within minutes, I knocked out.

That night, I fell asleep with a smile on my face.

And I dreamt of Hunter for the first time in my life.

CHAPTER 7
No More Time Wasted

ＨUNTER

I never realized that once I had a singular taste of my obsession, the need to touch her again would continue to surmount inside of my core like ivy, climbing through the rungs of my bones and weaving tightly around my skeleton like a caressing lover, needing the warmth only my addiction could provide.

It's what drove me this Monday morning to rush through my routine, eager and so very elated to be in the same vicinity as Gabriela. She was warm, the sun personified, and I felt cold and lonely without her presence, like the Earth at night. If I wasn't careful, this girl would construct herself into the depiction of my goddamn ruin.

And like a fool, I would let her.

She already had me wrapped around her pretty, manicured fingers. The kicker was that she had no idea how ruled I felt by the need to pursue her, to be near her.

Meanwhile, she'd actually friend-zoned me Saturday night.

"Okay, good! It was just a kiss and it meant nothing because we're friends, right?"

Her text gutted me. It was more than just a kiss for me. I was tempted to tell her that friends weren't supposed to know the way you taste. But I bit my tongue, not wanting to scare her with my intensity.

It took a lot of courage to put myself out there, to talk and flirt with her freely when I rarely did that with anyone. My life was meticulously composed of school, football, and my friends and family. I didn't have time for distractions or girls.

But I was making time for Gabriela, who'd been marathoning inside of my skull from the second I laid eyes on her four hundred and twenty days ago.

My dad always told me that when you found a woman who spoke to something deep within your foundation, it was your duty to hold onto her, to make her realize you were the man to treat her right, and to rearrange the world in a way she desired and needed.

I wanted to be that man for Gabriela.

My nerves were ever present, but my excitement blanketed most of them by the time I pulled into the driveway of her childhood home at exactly 10:00 a.m.

There was also a grain of guilt tumbling in my system due to the fact that I lied to her.

Firstly, I wasn't supposed to be in the West Side this morning. In fact, I was in my apartment downtown and drove all the way back here just to give Gabriela a ride. She didn't have a car and I wanted an excuse to see her again.

Secondly, I didn't have the same Horror & Cult Classic Cinema class with her...until she sent me her schedule Saturday night and I frantically logged onto the university's portal before the drop deadline and found an open seat. It was the only way I could mirror her schedule, even for a day, without compromising all my core classes.

I was so desperate to be near her that I'd subject myself to a genre of movies I otherwise avoided. And now that I knew she wouldn't be living across from me, courtesy of the break-in situation, I had to improvise ways to constantly be in her orbit.

Sharing a class and driving her to school every Monday was one way.

I'd spent so much time thinking about Gabriela. I only wished that now, with my efforts, I spent even just a small fraction of that time on *her* mind. Beggars weren't choosers, so I'd take any morsel of attention she threw my way.

I shot Gabriela a quick text that I was outside and placed my phone back into my pocket.

Seconds later, Gabriela emerged from the front door.

I swallowed at the sight she created as she descended the porch steps like a little prima donna, her usual short height hiked up a few inches by her booted heels.

A little black dress that was suited for a business meeting was poured over her body, sheer stockings with tiny black hearts covered her legs, gold jewelry was layered on her person, red lipstick was painted on her mouth, black cat-eye-shaped sunglasses were perched on her dainty nose, and a black velvet headband dotted with pearls sat over an immaculate side part, while the rest of her long red hair billowed freely behind her like a flag.

Fucking hell.

She was stunning.

I ran a hand over my mouth, utterly mesmerized. So much so that I forgot to step out and open the passenger side door for her.

Gabriela opened it herself, popping her head in the car first, her mouth curled in a big smile like she was so happy to see me. "Good morning, pretty boy."

Whenever she called me pretty boy, I melted on the inside.

"Morning," I rasped, the proximity of her presence overloading my senses and her delicious fragrance wafting over me like a welcoming hug. "How are you?"

She slid into the leather seat effortlessly, depositing her structured designer bag on the floor. "I'm good. Yourself?"

Amazing now that you're here. "Good."

"This is for you." Gabriela angled herself towards me and extended the offering in her hand. She was holding a little bouquet of three red roses. "It's not exactly a house plant, but I cut these fresh from my garden this morning. I baked you some blueberry muffins as well. They're in my bag. I figured you could snack on them during our class."

My infatuation sank deeper into uncharted waters, a place no woman had ever ventured before. I watched Gabriela helplessly, unable to make her understand the kind of emotions she invoked within me.

"Thank you," I murmured, my voice thick as I reached for the bouquet. I'd never been given roses. This was unexpected and caught me completely off guard. Gabriela was so goddamn cute. "That was very kind of you."

Tension drummed between us when our fingers brushed and caused a spark. The same kind I experienced right as she led me onto the dance floor Friday night.

"M-my pleasure." Gabriela sucked in a sharp breath, removed her sunglasses, and tucked them in her dress's neckline. "It's the least I could do for you."

Ignoring my pounding pulse, I placed her bouquet in one of the cupholders. I'd have to find a way to preserve it. My older sister, Heidi, was always drying her flowers. I could ask her, but that would mean giving her ammo to tease me about my crush.

"Just a fair warning, my papà has one of his men trailing after me for safety reasons. I hope that's okay." She let loose an awkward chuckle. "If you see a black sedan tailgating you, it's him."

"That's okay. Appreciate the heads-up." I put the car in reverse, placed a hand on her headrest, glanced over my shoulder, and backed out of the driveway. When I turned to face the front, I spotted her eyeing me. "Did you have time to get your morning coffee?"

"No." She shook her head, then bit her lip. "You look really good today."

My cheeks turned hot with a blush.

"So do you," I returned and touched the lapels of my blazer. "I'm having a late lunch today with my mom at some fancy restaurant, hence the suit. I make it a point to take her out for a meal once a week."

"How sweet. Are you close to your mom?"

"Very. I have a small family, but we're tight-knit."

She smiled fondly. "Same."

When my gaze swivelled to Gabriela, I was drawn to her fingers drumming against her thighs in beat with the song playing on the radio. "You changed your nail colour."

Gabriela frowned like I said something strange. Was I not supposed to notice that, let alone point it out? The blush on my face turned brighter. Fuck.

"Yes, I did. Yesterday."

"Why black?" I liked it, but I wanted to know why she picked it. I craved learning about how her pretty mind worked.

Gabriela inched a sly look my way. "To match the colour of my dark soul, Hunter."

I chuckled, surprised. "You don't have a dark soul, Gabby."

"But I do," she insisted, sitting up straighter in her seat. "My grandma occasionally calls me a witch because of my affinity for all things horror and spooky."

"I can tell." This girl soberly added an elective class about horror movies and my obsessed self followed suit. I hoped I didn't regret my decision. I hated scary movies. But not as much as I hated not being near her. "When did this fascination start?"

"Can't exactly say why or how, but around the time I was a kid. Halloween has always been my favourite holiday, much to my family's chagrin." She shrugged. "I can't help but gravitate towards darker things. As a result, my bookshelves are filled with paranormal romances, gothic lore, and all sorts of encyclopaedias of creepy stuff. Oh, and I like to listen to true crime podcasts in my free time."

"Jesus." I laughed. "No wonder you were contemplating murder the night we met."

She laughed with me. "Hey, I wasn't *actually* planning on committing a crime!"

I side-eyed her and drawled, "Sure."

She lightly punched my arm playfully in retaliation and I grinned wide. I felt like I was living in a fantasy. Finally talking to my dream girl. Finally driving her around. Finally being in her presence. I thanked my lucky stars, liquid courage, and Shaun's push for inciting me to finally make a move on her.

"Now that I've divulged my tastes, what about you?" she quipped. "What do you like to read, watch, and listen to?"

I floored the gas as I entered the highway, glancing at my blind spot and putting on my flasher. I noticed the inconspicuous sedan with her guard gaining speed on us, trailing behind like a shadow. "I like reading classics and Greek mythology. I tend to watch a lot of action movies. And I listen to a lot of the rap that plays in the locker rooms, and the rock bands from the early 2000s that I grew up on."

"Any favourite songs?"

"Plenty." I plucked my phone with one hand, keeping the other on the wheel. "Here. Go through my playlist and put on something."

Gabriela snatched my phone with grabby hands. "Passcode?"

The night I first saw you. "Zero, seven, one, nine."

After unlocking my phone, she browsed through my playlists and selected an old favourite of mine, the music blaring through the car with a prominent bass. Gabriela ran a hand over the dash in appreciation. "What type of car is this? I like it."

"A Jaguar. I got it last year." A sheepish smile graced my lips. "It was a gift from me to me."

Gabriela giggled. I loved that sound. "Good for you. One should always treat oneself to something nice and extravagant occasionally."

I'd been able to buy it from the generous trust fund my dad set up for me before he passed away. The car was a tribute to him. We'd both wanted one. At least now one of us got to drive it.

"Cars are my guilty pleasure," I admitted, switching lanes to take the next exit. They were my dad's as well. Some of his sports and vintage rolls still sat in our family home's garage. "What's yours?"

"I wish I could drive," she mumbled in an afterthought-like manner. And I almost said, *I could teach you*, but that would appear too desperate. I needed to maintain some form of decorum around this girl and not show her all my cards at once. Gabriela turned her head my way, grinning, and I saw a peek of the gem on her canine. Remembering how I ran my tongue over it as I devoured her mouth Friday night sent a rush of heat down my spine. "As for my guilty pleasure, I have a weakness for overpriced coffee, bags, clothes, shoes, skincare and makeup products, and the list goes on. I'm a firm believer in treat-yourself culture. Life is short. Buy the things that bring you joy. Do you agree?"

"Absolutely." We chatted some more until my ride rolled to a stop in Le Petit Moulin's parking lot. I unbuckled my seatbelt. "I figured we could grab some coffees to go before our class. What would you like?"

Gabriela appeared pleased at my idea. "I'll have a small mocha."

She reached into her purse for her wallet and I grabbed her wrist, halting her movements with a gentle squeeze. "No. Stay here. I'll be back."

I meant it when I said I never let a woman pay when she was out with me. Gabriela must have remembered that tidbit because she looked like she wanted to say something, probably protest, but I quickly left before she could get another word in.

The same woman from Saturday—Elsie—served me. I asked her to add half a dozen donuts to my order, selecting the chocolate-dipped ones Gabriela said she liked.

When I slid back into my car, Gabriela sat pensively, gazing at her black nails.

"Here you go." My voice coaxed her out of her thoughts and I handed her the mocha and pink box containing her donuts. "Careful, the coffee's hot."

"You got me goodies." Gabriela gasped, face morphing into that of a kid on Christmas. Her joy was so infectious, I couldn't help but smile at her reaction. "I'm going to devour these during class. I might…share one with you."

I chuckled, putting on my seatbelt.

"What did you get yourself?" she asked, taking a sip of her mocha, then puckering at the scalding temperature.

"A black coffee. Like your soul."

She laughed at my joke. It slowly faded as she leaned closer to the center console, studying my working hands as they removed the lid from the extra cup of water I'd ordered. "What are you doing?"

I submerged the short stems of the bouquet into the cup.

"Preserving my roses," I said proudly and placed my temporary, makeshift vase in my car's cupholder. "There you go."

That should keep my bouquet hydrated until I got home.

Noting the sudden tense silence, I peered up at Gabriela and froze, every muscle in my body thrumming with alertness. She was so close, I could see all her individual lashes as they fluttered in time with her breathing cadence, could see the unnamed emotion passing through her blue depths, could see the way her elegant neck worked with a swallow of whatever words she'd managed to fashion on her tongue before drinking them down and whispering a simple, "Oh."

As we stared at each other, the feeling flickering through my chest could only be described as hope.

Was it inexorable to believe there was a possibility that somewhere in the future, this girl could be mine in every sense of the word?

Corralled in this space together, with our thoughts floating beside one another, mine transparent and hers unknown, even the impossible seemed possible. I liked to believe that all this wait before she and I intertwined was for a reason. The universe conspired to make this happen, to take control, and to give me a small reward for all the sleepless nights I'd spent thinking about this one ethereal goddess of a woman.

"We should probably get going," she said softly with a benign smile, moving away and forcing her body to settle back into the leather seat. "Before we waste any more time."

Before we waste any more time.

Because I'd already wasted enough with my fears and insecurities.

No longer would that happen again. Though we were friends for the time being, I was going to do everything in my power to show Gabriela that I could be *more* for her...should she ever want me in that way.

CHAPTER 8
Hold My Hand

GABRIELA

Vesta University had one of the most beautiful campuses in the city. Various buildings for various studies spanned the streets of downtown Montardor, rich in their magnificent architecture, cobblestone pathways, and vibrant in their lush greenery and fountained parks.

Hunter parked his car a minute of a walk away from the arts building, where the Horror & Cult Classic Cinema class took place. He offered me his arm when my heel stumbled on the cracked pavement and with my hand resting in the crook of his elbow, we ferried to our destination. His leather messenger bag was slung over one shoulder and he held our coffees in a takeaway tray, while I held my purse and the box of donuts. Silence reigned between us as we enjoyed the September morning sunshine and the view of our landscape.

The realization that I wasn't fond of silence but didn't mind it with Hunter struck me again. I liked our silences. They were gentle and companionable. No words were needed to fill them. I also liked this newfound friendship we formed. Deciding not to act on the attraction I felt for him was the right choice. It wouldn't be easy, but I was determined. He was extremely handsome, but like an expensive flower bouquet, I could appreciate the beautiful sight and fragrance without needing to actually touch it.

The fact that we both agreed that our kiss meant nothing eased my mind.

As we entered the class—a giant auditorium with a large screen framed by red curtains, a podium for the professor, and cinema-style seats—a few people who arrived earlier craned their heads to stare at us.

We were a bit overdressed, but most business students at Vesta University frolicked in similar attire as ours. It was what happened when you were in and out of business classes, team project meetings, presentation preparations, networking events, or even returning from your day corporate job to attend school in the evenings. I always thought it was important to dress immaculately because if you looked good, you felt good, and you'd most likely perform good too.

Alongside me, my pretty rich boy swanned into the room like an unbothered prince amongst paupers, over six feet of pure muscles donned in a designer suit and his delicious cologne guaranteed to turn every woman within a ten-foot pole radius feral.

Hunter was so dapper and it came to him naturally.

We both wordlessly agreed to take seats in a back row. As we ascended the stairs, he put a gentle hand on my back to guide me ahead of him, and the touch practically *seared* me.

"Sweetheart," he purred in my ear from behind, his warmth radiating off of him in waves. "Now's a good time to tell you that your middle-aged guard is following us but doing a poor job at blending in."

"Is that so?" I threw a glance over my shoulder, welcomed by his broad chest. The height difference was killing me. I'd always had a weakness for tall men. I had to peer around his frame to catch sight of Oscar— one of Papà's men—disguised in a tracksuit reminiscent of something you'd see a boy band member wearing in the '90s. The backwards cap and overexaggerated swagger only made him stand out. "Well, fuck."

Hunter chuckled. "Fuck is correct."

"Just ignore him. He'll sit further away but keep an eye on us."

"Noted." Hunter waited for me to sink into a seat before he sat in the one beside mine. He placed a hand on my knee and brought his mouth near my ear to whisper, "Are you doing okay? Have your dad or Josh found out anything more?"

The only thing I could focus on was how big his hand looked against my smaller thigh and the heat of his lips so close to my skin.

"I-I'm fine," I stuttered. "There have been no leads, but I'm sure this will get resolved soon and I'll be able to move around freely, sans bodyguard." I tried to muster a smile and nudged him with my elbow. "And move back into my apartment so we can resume being neighbours."

"I hope so, Gabby," he whispered sincerely. "Fingers crossed."

I was saved from saying anything more when the professor—Dr. Richmond—entered the room, booming a loud greeting for the class.

We drank our coffees and I ate my donuts while Hunter tucked into the blueberry muffins I baked for him as Dr. Richmond orated on. He gave an introduction to himself, the class's curriculum, and his expectations for this fall semester. Every class, we'd watch a movie, have a discussion at the end, and our assignment was a short essay on said movie, completed in teams of two. The final dissertation, worth thirty percent of our overall grade, was the only solo paper. The workload was easy-peasy, lemon squeezy. I had a good feeling about this class.

Once the lights shut and the screen turned on to play the movie—one I'd both seen twice in the past and enjoyed—that *good feeling* quickly morphed into panic.

I could hear Hunter's soft breathing. I could smell his addictive scent. And I could feel his strong arm brushing mine on the shared armrest between us before his muscular thigh pressed against my right one as he shifted in his seat.

Shit.

I was all too aware of him and the darkness only amplified every sense. So much so that my sanity felt like a ribbon unfurling and falling down a steep edge with no purchase, drifting into the ether.

Instead of paying attention to the movie, my mind replayed moments from Friday night.

Us on the terrace.

Us on the dance floor.

How Hunter went from this sweet, good boy mischievously bantering with me to this nasty, bad boy kissing me with a salacious quality. If it weren't for the fact that we were in public, would we have crossed another line?

"Say please *like a good girl...And I will."*

God, I think we would have.

Hunter didn't kiss like a gentleman and based on the way he talked... he wouldn't fuck like one either. Which was exactly what I liked. A man who could take control and pound me into submission until I could barely walk the next day. I wondered if he was a gentle or rough lover. If he was quiet or a dirty-talker. Then I wondered what position he liked best and how he felt about being ridden.

No, no, no. Bad Gabriela. Stop it. You're friends and not the kind with benefits.

After the mental pep talk to wrestle my thoughts back to a more chaste route, I risked a glance to my right, where Hunter sat.

And frowned.

Why did he appear so rigid?

Was something wrong?

Not wanting to be the asshole who talked during movies and ruined it for everyone else, I flipped open my notebook to a blank page. On the top line, I scribbled the words: **Are you okay?**

I discreetly slid the notebook and my pen in his direction.

A borderline imperceptible jolt shook his body at my interruption during an engrossing scene, and his head snapped my way, eyes wary.

I chin-nodded towards my stationery.

With nimble fingers, he grabbed it and read my message.

I watched him scrawl a deft response and hand it back to me.

The first thing I registered was his handwriting. It was elegant, sophisticated, and cursive. The kind you'd find in old romantic letters. I closed my eyes briefly, hustling aside the imagery of romantic letters from Hunter running rampant in my mind.

Then I read his message.

No, I am not.

My stomach flipped with concern. In less neat handwriting than his, I replied: **What's wrong?**

The notebook was passed back to him. He swallowed, the tip of my pen barely poised against the paper as though he was debating whether or not he should reveal his woe. Eventually, with a resigned flourish, he wrote some more and slid the notebook my way.

I hate horror movies. I've never liked them.

For a few seconds, I was absolutely speechless.

He hated horror movies? He never liked them?

What in the ever-loving fuck was he doing in this class then?

Instead of replying, I just stared at him, confusion etched in my features. Hunter stared back, miserable. It was then that I realized he was rigid from *fear.*

Clearly, he was being sarcastic Saturday night when he said via text that this was his favourite genre.

Shaking my head, I penned: **Hunter, why would you pick this class?**

He cringed visibly at the gruesome scene on the screen and plucked my pen, writing back: *It was the only elective that fit with my schedule. I also thought it would be a great way to overcome my dislike for these kinds of movies. Completely regretting it now.*

Tenderness swept through me. It was admirable of him to take a class on a subject he didn't like for the sake of conquering his aversion to it. I may be a seasoned horror-movie-loving fiend, but I sympathized with him. His feelings were valid.

I added in the notebook: **I'm proud of you for doing this. I promise, before the end of the semester, you'll actually enjoy these movies.**

He simply wrote: *That's what I'm counting on.*

We went back and forth for a few minutes. Whenever our fingers touched as we passed the pen and notebook, a heady buzz rocked through my veins.

A jump scare popped on the screen and the whole class, including Hunter, reacted jarringly. I just giggled. He glared at me good-naturedly and I rolled my lips into my mouth, attempting to stop my laughter. Hunter wrote another message. So far, we used up three pages in my notebook.

You're enjoying this, aren't you?

Just a little bit.

I'm reconsidering our friendship.

I pretended to pout and give him my best puppy face expression. His lips tipped up at the corners in a mild smirk, like staying fake-mad at me was just too hard because I was that adorable.

Do you want to hold my hand? Will that make you feel better?

I meant the words in a half-teasing manner.

I didn't think he'd actually take action.

Hunter slithered his hand over my lap and presented me with his awaiting, upturned left palm. It was darker than mine and callused with deeper grooves. I wondered about his destiny and how long we would remain in each other's lives. For a short while or for a long time?

Knowing he'd want to continue talking through notes, I slid my left hand in his.

Hunter braided our fingers together and gave a gentle squeeze.

My breath hitched.

It was just holding hands. No biggie. I'd held his hand on Friday as well.

So why did my insides feel warm and fuzzy when he drew an absentminded circle on the back of mine with his thumb, almost softly and reverently?

I glanced down at our joined hands and went over the moment from his car, watching him try to preserve the bouquet I gifted him. I'd cut those flowers from my backyard on a whim, minutes before he arrived to pick me up. I was certain he'd throw them away at the end of the day. They were just from my garden, not fifty-dollar roses from a florist. But the way he handled those little blooms in his big hands with utmost care and this happy gleam in his eyes like he had every intention of keeping them alive, I all but swooned.

The rest of the movie droned on, but I couldn't focus on it. The invisible patterns Hunter drew on my hand with his thumb fully snagged my attention.

By the time the movie finished and the class discussion wrapped up, I felt like a live-crackling wire, everything beneath my skin sizzling from his mere touch.

When Dr. Richmond finished explaining the take-home assignment and told us to send him an introductory email with our paired teammate and student IDs, I shot out of my seat, jostling Hunter and dropping his hand. I packed my belongings and swung my purse into the crook of my elbow, then lined behind the row of students trying to exit the auditorium.

Flustered, I couldn't get out of here—or catch my breath—fast enough.

If Hunter sensed the shift in my mood, he didn't say. Instead, he stood behind me as we descended the stairs, solid like a rock and emanating his usual warmth.

"Is now a good time to ask if you'd like to be paired with me?" he whispered into my ear with a playful edge.

It was a no-brainer that we'd work together. We only knew each other in this class.

"Of course." I pasted a fake smile on my face, trying to mask the constant *badump, badump, badump* in my chest. Far from composed, I felt unravelled in a way I'd never had before. "I'll email the prof. Just text me your student ID, okay?"

"Okay, but—"

"My next class is in ten minutes. I'll see you around." I kept smiling as I sauntered forward in a dismissive manner. "I appreciate the ride this morning, Hunter."

A crestfallen expression fell over him and I felt horrible for cutting our interaction so short, but I couldn't stay here any longer. He nodded and returned blankly, "Right. Have a good day, Gabby."

Oh, this hurt. I swallowed. "You too."

On my way out of the auditorium, I collided with the back of a guy who was also exiting. An *oomph* noise escaped me as I recoiled back a step.

Dressed in a black T-shirt, white ball cap, and simple blue jeans, he peered over his shoulder, his mouth parted like he was about to say something rude.

But he froze the second he saw me.

I paused too, the colour leaching from my face.

It was like looking into a broken mirror, the jagged lines showcasing different moments in our relationship—the good and the bad—scattered across a timeline of three years, when we belonged to each other before inevitably leading to the one that caused the damaging crack in the first place.

My next lungful of air was painful and caused my eyes and throat to burn with anger.

He was a ghost of my past.

He should have stayed there, never to return.

For he knew my wrath—and my papà's—wasn't one he wanted to court.

"Hey," he said nonchalantly, like we were acquaintances and this was just another silly little day where we crossed paths. "It's good to see you, Gabby."

Then Franco Morelli, my ex-boyfriend who shattered my heart many moons ago, continued walking ahead like he didn't turn my entire day to shit.

CHAPTER 9
Three Red Roses

HUNTER

N ow that I'd officially moved out, I made a promise to my mom that I would spend every Wednesday night back at home with her and my older sister, Heidi.

Mom claimed the house was lonely without my presence and I understood those words were rooted in her abandonment and attachment issues. She loved her children dearly and wanted the best for them, yet seeing her little birdies leave the nest wasn't an easy feat. Especially with my dad no longer here. I knew that was why Heidi still lived at home, but it wouldn't be long before she was gone too.

During dinner, we discussed Heidi's new job at an accounting firm and the start of her CPA studies, followed by my schooling and my upcoming games. The Panthers were doing great. Coach Turner was convinced we were bringing the championship trophy home this year.

After dinner, I did the dishes, Heidi tidied up the kitchen, and Mom picked a movie for us to watch. Not horror, thankfully. I didn't think I could stomach another one so soon. I'd filled my quota for the month, a laughable concept since I still had two more classes remaining for September and a total of eleven until the end of the fall semester.

When the movie came to an end, I pecked both Mom's and Heidi's heads. "Good night. I'm exhausted and going to bed. I'll see you both in the morning."

It wasn't a complete lie. I was tired and would go to bed soon, but after I took care of something first. Heidi gave me a frown accompanied by a quizzical expression that said *I'm-not-buying-your-shit-Hunter.*

Exactly fifteen minutes after I barricaded myself in my old room, two knocks on my door broke my focus.

My fingers paused on my laptop's keyboard, halfway through my research. I didn't even have the chance to say, "Come in," before Heidi barged inside like she was a queen and this was her dominion.

I rubbed my forehead.

What was it about siblings and lack of boundaries?

Granted, I loved my sister, but couldn't a guy get some privacy to figure out how to preserve the bouquet he received from the girl he liked without being interrupted?

"What are you doing?" Heidi demanded nosily, crossing her arms and coming over to where I sat by my desk. She peered over my shoulder to stare at my screen.

So much for secrecy. I gestured to the paper cup filled with water and my three roses sitting close to my laptop. "Gabriela gave these to me today. I'm trying to find a way to keep them forever."

The confusion on Heidi's face morphed into glee. "Aw, Hunter," she gushed, cupping my cheeks with one hand and squeezing like she used to when I was a kid. "That's so nice of her."

My sister and I were close, four years separating us. I tended to share everything with her. All my wins and all my losses. Heidi was a great listener and advice giver. I trusted her judgement more than anyone else's in my life. She was well aware of my crush on Gabriela and had been rooting for us since the start—since the moment I returned from Josh's party awestruck and told her about the pretty girl who caught my attention.

Yesterday, I confessed to kissing Gabriela on Friday and then adding the same elective as her on Saturday. Heidi broke out into a cheer routine, and afterwards teased me for being whipped. I let it slide because it came with the territory of being an older sister.

"Yeah." I flicked my gaze back to the search results on my screen. "I'm thinking of making resin bookmarks with the rose petals. One for her and one for me. She's a bookworm, so I figured…"

I trailed off, but Heidi understood, squeezing my shoulder. "That's an amazing idea, Hunt. Here, let's watch some tutorials to better understand the process."

We did exactly that and I took notes with a fountain pen on one of my dad's old notepads. Later on, we placed an order online for all the supplies. Heidi promised to help with this creative project. Since I'd only need two out of the three roses, my sister said she'd take the last one and turn it into pressed flower art, saying that I could frame it in my apartment if I wanted to. And though it would only add to my *whipped* status, I wasn't completely opposed to the suggestion.

"Gabriela's going to love the bookmark," Heidi said, gently stroking the petals of the roses before heading over to take a seat on my bed.

I closed my laptop and spun around in my chair to face her. "I hope so."

"Now tell me what's on your mind." She crossed her legs and steepled her hands around her right knee. "You've been relatively quiet throughout the entire evening, and I know it's got nothing to do with school or football."

Heidi and I had the innate ability to see through each other. Lying or suppressing our feelings never worked. I combed my fingers through my hair and grasped my nape, the day's frustration ebbing away until the only thing I felt in my muscles was a dull resignation. "She wants to be friends, Heidi, and I want more."

Compassion stitched over her visage. "Hunter…"

"I can be that for her. But I do not want to be stuck in the friend zone forever." I'd spent over a year longing for her that a little bit of wait wouldn't kill me. Though the possibility that there may never be *more* for us just might. "Heidi, she doesn't mind that I'm introverted and more of a homebody. She even invited me to her association's upcoming mixer and promised to hang with me by the sidelines because, well, you know I'm not fond of crowded spaces."

"I see," Heidi echoed softly, pleased.

"There's something about her that just feels different, you know? She's kind, she's sweet, she makes me laugh, and though I've only known her for a short amount of time, it feels like I've known her forever. Maybe I'm getting ahead of myself, but I want to take a chance on her and I want her to take a chance on me too. I don't think it would be like…the last time."

And that was truly the crux of it all.

I had one ex-girlfriend, Ginette, from sixteen to eighteen years old. She treated me like garbage. The worst part? I let her for so long until I realized it wasn't fair to me. We met in high school during detention. Me, for being late. Her, for causing a ruckus in the music room. She played the trombone in the school's band. I'd seen her perform a few times and thought she was cute. It took me forever to gather up the courage to ask her out. Much to my delight, she was quick to say yes. Ginette was outgoing. I was comfortable in my little bubble. I thought it was normal for opposites to attract. Therefore, I assumed she liked me for *me*.

I couldn't have been more wrong.

After the honeymoon period was over, she became rude and acted like I was a nuisance no matter how hard I tried to just be there for her like a good boyfriend. We broke up because I found her cheating on me with my teammate.

Turned out, she only dated me for what I represented: a status symbol due to my position as the quarterback of the football team. I was her ticket to high school fame. Ginette hadn't cared about me as a person. It was a superficial relationship. And she'd been quick to point out during our last fight that I was too introverted for her taste, still too emotional over my dad's death, and that the only good quality I possessed, besides my looks, was my dick.

Ginette said I made it so fucking easy to be cheated on—that I deserved it.

After that confrontation, I remembered feeling like I was having an out-of-body experience when I left her and proceeded to puke my guts out in the nearest trash can, overwhelmed by all my painful emotions.

My dad's passing took a huge toll on me. I lost my best friend and my hero at a very young age. It turned me into a sad, withdrawn kid. The only time I felt alive was when I was on the field. Football was my sole remaining connection to him. Things got better when I entered high school because it was a fresh start. I made friends and learned to be a little bit more confident. But Ginette's nasty words were like an arrow straight to my chest. As if I were worthless because I couldn't become the extrovert she wanted overnight, couldn't turn off my grief like a faucet, and couldn't be anything more than a notch in her belt.

I'd come a long way since high school. Every now and then, my old insecurities roared to life until I pushed past them again. Though I still wasn't overly extroverted, I liked the person I was today after putting in years of work into myself. Reading self-help books, engaging in talk therapy, and having good friends like Josh and Shaun had gotten me here.

After my breakup with Ginette, I subjected myself to celibacy and then to some meaningless one-night stands for a while. I realized by the time I turned nineteen that emotionless hookups and casual dating weren't for me. I'd always been a one-woman type of man. But unfortunately, I turned too self-conscious post-Ginette, overanalysing and overthinking every little detail. It was like I'd become my own worst enemy.

That was why it took me so long to pursue Gabriela and why Friday night felt like such a breakthrough. It allowed me to rid myself of a mental shackle holding me back from the thing I desired most.

Gabriela was like a breath of fresh air compared to my past.

She didn't care about football, didn't know my jersey number, didn't know anything about my stats. Being Vesta University's star quarterback didn't matter to her.

If anything, it felt like she could like me for *me*.

I wanted her to see me the same way I saw her.

I wanted her to adore me the same way I started adoring her.

I wanted her to want me, plain and simple.

Heidi's voice sliced through my train of thoughts, stern but filled with a smile. "Hunter, you're my little brother and I'm biased, but I mean it when I say that you're wonderful and Gabriela will see it soon enough. And if she doesn't, it's her loss." She shrugged. "A year ago, you couldn't even imagine yourself being on speaking terms with her. You found the courage to make the first move and that was brave of you. Regardless of what happens in the future, I'm very proud of you."

This was my sister's way of telling me to count my wins. "Thanks, Heidi."

"You've taken a step in the right direction. Now trust the process. Let the universe do the rest and continue to be patient. It will all unfold the way it should and remember that everything happens for a reason. It's no coincidence that you and Gabriela are finally seeing each other, even if it's just as friends. And if I'm being honest, you don't give flowers to someone you don't care about. My guess is, based on what you've told me about your conversations, she's developing a soft spot for you. She may not know it yet, but I promise you, one day she will." There was a knowing glint in Heidi's eyes. "It won't be long before you realize I was right all along."

I smirked. "You just love to gloat, don't you?"

"It's the truth." My sister laughed and stood up, heading to my door. "Relax and get some rest, Hunt. You've made good progress with her. That's what counts." Heidi propped her hand on the doorknob. "Oh, by the way, Jaden is coming over for dinner Wednesday night."

"Sounds good." I debated whether I should say anything else before going ahead and asking the difficult question, "How are things between you and Jaden?"

Her shoulders deflated and her eyes grew sad. "We're fine."

Heidi and Jaden started dating when they were eighteen years old. They were together for six. Last year, he had an accident that caused him to lose his memories. He barely remembered his own family, including my sister. He hadn't been the same since the tragedy and neither had Heidi. It hurt me to watch my sister lose her spark and her zest for life. Now she spent every waking moment going through the motions. Go to work, come back from work, and cater to Jaden. On a fucking loop. She was stuck in survival mode. No matter how much my mom and I explained to her that she was barely living, Heidi refused to acknowledge the situation at hand.

Jaden may never remember their past.

And Heidi couldn't forget theirs.

Or the man who used to mean to her as much as Jaden did.

"You know I'm always here for you, right?" I walked towards her. "We're a team. We've got each other's backs. You can talk to me, Heidi. Whatever you need, I got you."

"I know and I love you for it. But really, I'm okay, Hunter."

I'd start believing it when I saw it with my own eyes.

"Fine." I wrapped her up in a bear hug. "Love you, too."

"Don't forget to buy a ticket to the mixer." She wagged her finger in a warning sign. "This is your chance. Make the best of it."

I would.

I had no intention of giving up on Gabriela until I gave it my all.

Heidi left and snicked the door shut behind her.

Before I went to bed, I searched up the meaning of red roses in particular, wondering if there was a deeper meaning to her gift.

Apparently, the blooms symbolized devotion, romance, passion, and true love.

One gifted rose meant love at first sight. Three gifted roses meant *I love you.*

My heart pounded.

Gabriela couldn't have known any of this, right?

If she had, why would she give me three roses?

And why red ones?

Yellow ones were for friendship, according to the online search engine.

I mean, maybe all she had in her garden were red roses.

But fuck, I hated that I was getting excited over something simple like flowers.

She probably just cut those red roses from her garden without putting much thought into it and I was the fool lying in bed, staring at my ceiling, a stupid smile on my face, drifting from every moment we'd shared so far, and hopelessly wondering how long it would take before the soft spot she held for me to develop into *more.*

That night, I fell asleep after purchasing a handful of paranormal romances and adding a few true crime podcasts to my queue.

And I dreamt of Gabriela, the way I consistently have for the last year.

CHAPTER 10

Unlovable

GABRIELA

Wednesday evening, I met up with the girls at Anna's place. We were sitting in the living room with our laptops and an abundance of food surrounding us. Anna made pães de queijo , I made cannoli, and Layla made her late Pakistani mother's pulao recipe.

We ate and talked while doing our schoolwork. Layla was researching peer-reviewed articles for her upcoming assignment. I was finalizing some graphs on Excel. Anna had already completed her weekly readings and was now working on our bustiers. And Michael—Anna's five-year-old brother—was curled up next to Layla's side on the sofa, his small arm thrown across her middle and his head tucked against her shoulder as he watched cartoons on the TV. He had no homework and was only here for Layla, whom he kept shooting bashful glances at when he thought she wasn't looking. It was adorable. Michael had a crush on her. Last year, when Layla and Josh became official, they'd come over for dinner and Michael had smacked Josh's crown jewels with his Light Saber until the latter choked with pain. Then Michael had bawled his little heart out because he couldn't believe that he was losing Layla to Josh.

I might have filmed the entire thing on my phone. It was a core memory. One I might decide to play at Josh and Layla's inevitable future wedding.

Once sleep started pulling at Michael's eyelids, Anna carried him upstairs to bed after he gave us all hugs and helped him through his night routine. Minutes later, when she returned, I figured now was a good enough time to drop my bomb of a news.

"So, I saw Franco two days ago while I was leaving my Horror & Cult Classic Cinema class," I casually announced while closing my laptop and diving for my bowl of pulao.

Layla's head snapped away from her laptop screen in my direction, pure disgust flashing on her face. "Oh my God. What?"

"Ew," Anna spat, a hard gleam in her hazel eyes as she paused her embroidery work, one hand gripping a thread and needle, the other one holding the bustier. "Why is that asshole back in the city?"

Franco moved to New York to live with his father shortly after our breakup when we were eighteen. As far as I was concerned, he'd dropped off the face of the Earth.

"I have no clue," I said bitterly. "But he had the audacity to say 'It's good to see you, Gabby.'"

Like the fucker hadn't left me with a handful of issues, anxiety, and so much trauma.

Layla shook her head angrily. "What a piece of shit."

Anna punctured her needle with excessive force into the fabric. "He needs to stay away from you if he knows what's good for him. Otherwise, he won't like what Layla and I do to him."

I loved my best friends and how they were always so ready to fight for me. When Franco broke my heart all those years ago, Anna and Layla broke into his old Camry to dump fifty pounds of pink glitter everywhere. Until it looked like a unicorn puked all over his car. It was a funny form of revenge and even without witnessing Franco's reaction, I just knew he had a bitch fit.

"I appreciate the unwavering love and loyalty," I responded. "But Franco isn't worth it."

I wished I'd understood that when I was fifteen years old. Instead, it took me three years to figure out we were far from compatible. We had some good moments, but the bad ones completely overshadowed them.

An old memory struck me—one I tried my best to suppress over the years.

The fight that ended Franco's and my relationship.

"Fuck, now I can't even talk to other girls?" Franco scoffed, pacing his room while I sat on his bed like a child getting scolded for doing something bad. Which was ridiculous. I shouldn't feel guilty for bringing up the fact that I saw him getting all cozy with Gertrude at yesterday's party. "Ma dai! Gabby, you're too much."

"You weren't talking to her," I retorted, trying to rein in my temper. "You were flirting with her. There's a difference, Franco. You were seconds away from kissing her and you probably would have if I hadn't caught you!"

"You're imagining it. It was a harmless conversation."

Please don't tell me this jackass is actually gaslighting me? *"Don't talk to me like that! I know what I saw! If you don't want to be with me, just say so! But don't fucking cheat!"*

"Cheat?" He barked out a laugh, throwing his head back and staring at the ceiling as though he was trying to find patience to deal with me.

I seethed. "Yes, cheat.*"*

"You're fucking crazy," he blazed, getting in my face. "Talking to someone isn't cheating!" His spit flew as he spoke and I had to rear back to prevent it from landing on me. "Did you see me with my tongue down her throat? With my dick dipping inside of her?"

Fuck him and that nasty-ass visual. I was so over him. He'd done nothing but cause me heartache for the last year. Franco and I might have had a sweet start, being childhood friends turned to lovers, but our ending was going to be sour. And though I was an individual quick to accept my flaws, he was not. He had a penchant for flirting with every other girl but his girlfriend now that he'd become the captain of the soccer team. Well, count me out. I was done with this playboy behaviour. I never signed up for it. Nor would I stick around for him to make a mockery of me.

"*That's it!*" *I hopped off his bed and tried to skirt around his tall frame. He blocked my path. I hated when he threw his weight around and reminded me that I was small and defenceless compared to him. I used my elbow to nudge him aside and it worked. I quickly headed for his door while hollering, "We're done. Go to Gertrude. Put your tongue down her throat. Your dick inside of her too. I no longer care,* stronzo*!*"

"*Gabriela, get back here!*"

On my way out of his room, I grabbed the paperweight action figurine I gave him for his sixteenth birthday and shot it against the hallway wall, smashing it to pieces. If I had more time, I'd have destroyed every gift I'd given him to celebrate our relationship.

But I was too focused on the tears stinging my eyes. I had to get out of here fast. I couldn't let him see me cry.

"*Gabriela!*" *Franco bellowed, his wrenching shout almost causing me to pause. "Don't walk away from me!*"

"*You don't get to tell me what to do anymore!*" *I enunciated, stomping down the stairs. "Fuck you, Franco!*"

His thundering footsteps followed mine. "Fuck you, Gabriela!" *He grabbed my shoulder and turned me around forcefully, razing, "You don't get to finish this!*"

The vein in his temple was throbbing and I had this murderous urge to pop it with a pin and let him bleed to death.

"*I can do whatever I want! I've had enough of you treating me horribly!*" *I yelled back. "First, it was verbal abuse and now you're emotionally cheating on me too? I'm so over your shit. You wasted my time, Franco. Three years of my life. Down the drain." My face reddened as my voice cracked. "If I could go back in the past, I'd never accept that first date or say yes to being yours.*"

It was the first time I vocalized these thoughts, mostly because it took me a really long time to realize that abuse wasn't always physical. It came in many forms, including the verbal one Franco doled out. If he played a bad game, he took it out on me. If he received a bad grade, he took it out on me. If he had a bad day—he also took it out on me. I was his metaphorical punching bag and somewhere along the way, after all these blows, I was deflated and empty.

Who could blame me for fighting back and finally putting my foot down?

Franco recoiled from my words like they were a physical lash. Like his disgusting behaviour never occurred to him. Even now, he stared at me as though I was a liar.

I supposed bad people never saw themselves as villains.

That was Franco's issue.

He thought himself godly, untouchable, and infallible.

Proving him wrong and kicking him off his high horse would be my greatest retribution.

As he soaked in my words, it slowly transformed his expression into a furious scowl that told me he was readying himself to rip into me. I braced myself, leaning back on the balls of my feet.

"Now here's a reality check for you: you're an attention seeker and loving you is exhausting. Do you hear that, Gabriela? Loving. You. Is. A. Fucking. Chore. You want the world to revolve around you and God forbid I have a life outside of your desires. Like shit, spending time with other people—talking to other girls—is not a crime. Yet you constantly make me feel like an asshole for not being there for you twenty-four seven. I used to be willing to deal with your tantrums, your mood swings, your goddamn neediness, but now I'm done. You're unlovable. You're worthless. And you're a bitch with only two redeeming qualities. Your tight pussy and your blowjob skills," he said frostily, every syllable driving into me like icy pin pricks. "You were a waste of my fucking time too. I obviously wasn't thinking straight all those years ago when I asked you out. If I knew better, I'd never have bothered. Girls like you are only good for one thing. My bad for mistaking you one step above a whore."

The tears I tried to halt coursed down my face, a hot and angry waterfall blurring my vision until Franco was nothing but a faded silhouette.

If he'd driven a knife into my back, it would have hurt less than this.

Bitch. Unlovable. Worthless.

Two redeeming qualities. Tight pussy. Blowjob skills.

One step above a whore.

I pushed him back with all my strength until his back collided against a wall with a prominent crack. "Fuck you, Franco!"

Franco couldn't hide his wince, but he watched me with coldness. "A puttana *never likes being reminded of her place, huh? Get lost, Gabriela, and don't ever darken my doorstep again."*

"Rot in hell, disgraziato.*"*

Hating myself for letting him tear into me and for ever loving this vile human, I pivoted around and ran away, my breathing laboured and my broken heart thudding inside of me.

When I arrived back home, my parents were in the living room, and I told them that Franco and I had split amicably while trying to wipe my tears. I didn't tell them about the hurtful words we'd exchanged, knowing it would break Mamma's heart and Papà wouldn't hesitate to teach Franco a lesson.

Afterwards, I locked myself in my room and had a panic attack.

Luna found me a minute later. My sweet girl licked my tears and made her soft purring noises to calm me down. I clutched her to my chest and spent the rest of the evening muffling my sobs in my pillow.

The next day, Franco was gone, having surreptitiously boarded a plane to New York.

I never forgave him for all the jabs he'd thrown my way.

I never would either, my blood concocted from my mamma's grudgeful nature and my papà's burning temper.

Franco would find more penance from the devil than me.

Even after two years, his egregious words were imprinted on my soul. Though I tried my best not to let that uncouth moment define me, some days it was harder than others. Unfortunately, it had affected all my forthcoming romantic relationships and flings. I didn't know how to make it stop. It was like a merry-go-round with a shattered console, no stop button in sight.

"Gabriela?" Anna's gentle voice belayed me back to reality and far away from my innerving musings.

I cleared my throat, glancing at both my friends with faux ennui. "Yes?"

They both exchanged a worried look that scored me. "You zoned out. Are you okay?"

"Oh." My fingers were still holding the spoonful of rice, halfway to my mouth as that horrid memory plagued me. "I'm fine. Just thinking."

Taking a bite, I tried to focus on the delicious spicy flavours on my palate and not the way both girls' faces fragmented with deep concern.

After an eternity of silence that caused my stomach to churn, Layla finally spoke up, "You didn't deserve what he did to you."

I knew it, but it was still nice to hear it out loud again.

"Anything you need, you let us know, all right?" Anna reached forward to squeeze my wrist in a gentle, *we're-here-for-you* manner.

I swallowed the lump around my throat, mustering a curt nod.

I hated thinking and talking about Franco, which was why I avoided telling Anna and Layla for two days. But these were my soul sisters. I couldn't hide my emotions from them. Nor did I want to. We told each other everything, no matter how trivial or crucial, and worked through it together. It was the beauty of knowing each other since childhood. We were one another's ride or dies.

"Also," Anna started somberly. "How are you doing with the whole break-in stuff, Gabby?"

I'd texted the girls this past weekend, letting them know what happened to me. Right away, they both stepped up to take turns driving me to school when my guard couldn't and promised to spend their free time with me so I was never alone, extremely worried for my well-being. So far, Papà and the Remingtons had looked into the situation but found nothing that would help them get to the bottom of this mystery.

"Physically, I'm okay. Mentally? I'm feeling disturbed. There have been no updates whatsoever, even after Papà rummaged through the security footage with the Remingtons. The only thing they know is that it was an unidentifiable man wearing all black—hoodie, jeans, face mask—who entered the building when the security guard was away, around the same time we were having brunch. The last thing the cameras captured was him entering the stairwell. No doubt, it was him who broke into my place. All the personnel have been interrogated. Papà said it wasn't any of them, so we're back to square one." I sighed, frustrated. "I also don't know who could hate me enough to do something like this."

Layla and Anna exchanged a glance, and the latter mumbled to me, "You don't think it's Franco, right?"

I blinked, the wheels in my mind turning.

I hadn't considered that possibility.

"It wouldn't be far-fetched to assume," Layla insisted. "Someone broke into your place four days ago and your ex-boyfriend, who loathes you, suddenly makes a reappearance after being out of the picture for years. That's extremely suspicious."

Fuck.

They did have a point.

"Despite the bad blood between us, do we really think he'd go as far as to taunt me like that?" I chewed my bottom lip. "That's too crazy, even for him, right?"

Their matching frowns spoke volumes.

Though Franco hadn't been physically abusive, he was proficient at wielding insults to strike me down. It would be just like him to use a Shakespearean quote to spite my intelligence, since I wasn't a classics reader. He'd hated the fact that all I ever read was contemporary romance books. Once when we were seventeen, he'd been ranting about the fact that he missed a game-winning goal and I made the mistake of telling him to calm down...so he retaliated by angrily cracking all the spines of my paperback novels to get back at me. I remembered becoming a blubbering, crying mess. And he replied that he was doing me a favour—that I was an airhead for reading books with unrealistic expectations for men.

God, I hated him.

It was a plausible theory that Franco was behind this—after all, it would be very diabolical and fitting for him to call me a bitch—but I wasn't fully convinced.

"Swear to us that you'll tell your parents what really happened between you two," Anna beseeched, pulling her long blond waves into a messy bun on top of her head. "Let your dad look into Franco to see if he has any connections to this ordeal."

"Please, Gabriela," Layla supplicated. "Don't rule him out until you know for sure."

There were over four million people in the city and it could be anyone. However, if we were to narrow down the search, Franco was a good place to start.

With a resigned exhale, I concurred, "Fine. I'll tell them."

The sooner we resolved this intruder situation, the better.

Because what if there was a next time and the damage was more than just hateful words scrawled across my wall?

CHAPTER 11

Crushing On You

GABRIELA

A dull ache yanked at my muscles as I shuttled home from Vesta University, transported in my guard's car like a prized possession being couriered from one destination to another. After a long day of classes and a late afternoon meeting with my WIB team to ensure everything was set for our upcoming event, all I wanted was rest from my exhaustive day, from the paranoia that followed me around like a shadow, and from the bickering happening downstairs between my parents on the phone, which I steadfastly chose to flout.

The first thing on my to-do list was giving my Luna some kisses before hopping in the shower. I let the hot water rule my stiff body into relaxation and did some breathing exercises while inhaling my eucalyptus essential oil.

When I finished scarfing down a plate of Mamma's pasta after my shower, I got an impromptu text from Hunter.

We hadn't spoken since I rudely dashed out of the classroom Monday afternoon and though I wasn't avoiding him, I'd felt a slight noose tightening around my throat the longer we went without communicating.

Not only because we had an assignment due next Monday that we needed to get started on ASAP, but because…I missed him.

It was the first time I felt too much in my head, unable to start a conversation with someone. There was something about Hunter that twisted my insides into knots. I'd never experienced anything like this with another individual.

When I read his text, a smile à la cat who ate the canary style blossomed over my face.

I bought a ticket to your mixer. —Hunter

I replied quickly.

Are you serious? —Gabby

You asked me to come. —Hunter

Are you reneging now? —Hunter

Don't say yes, sweetheart. You'll break my heart. —Hunter

Filled with surmounting giddiness, I fell back on my bed, resisting the urge to kick my feet with a squeal as I texted him back.

Wouldn't dream of breaking your heart, pretty boy. —Gabby

I'm happy you bought a ticket. I can't wait to see you 🩶 — Gabby

Do you promise to hang with me so I don't get lonely hiding in the corner? —Hunter

Yes, I promise. —Gabby

Good girl. —Hunter

I promise I won't drink beer either. —Hunter

I almost dropped my phone on my face.

Oh my God. I couldn't believe he'd actually said that to me.

Hunter wouldn't drink beer, in case I decided to kiss him again. My heart nearly danced out of its ribcage from the gravitational pull his words had on me.

My goodness. I insisted on us being friends, but now I was beginning to feel like we would cross a line soon.

And enjoy it too.

My long silence prompted him to send me another text.

What are you doing right now? —Hunter

Freaking out and trying to convince myself that we're a bad idea?

But goddammit, I'd like nothing more than to have Hunter's taste in my mouth again, to marvel at his thick hair coursing through my fingers, to feel his muscular body under my roaming hands…

Biting the inside of my cheek, I messaged him back something very *friendly.*

Nothing. Just finished eating dinner. Now I'm debating whether I should continue watching Supernatural or try a new show. You? —Gabby

Icing my shoulder. —Hunter

What happened? Are you okay? —Gabby

Brutal game tonight, but at least the Panthers won. —Hunter

I'm sorry to hear about your shoulder ☹ —Gabby

Congratulations on winning the game!! How are you going to celebrate? —Gabby

With you. —Hunter

I choked on my saliva, shocked by his boldness but also loving it.

My biggest fan was supposed to come to my game today and mend my broken heart, but you failed to show up. So you owe me. —Hunter

I should really try to keep up with the university's football schedule. I had no idea there was a game tonight.

I'm sorry, I didn't realize that was today! How can I make it up to you? — Gabby

Please don't say something dirty because I will literally match your freak. I'm hanging by a thread. Don't test me, Hunter.

Take a walk with me tonight. —Hunter

My mind and libido were evidently not in consonance with each other. Instead of adding distance between us, I did the complete opposite by further integrating myself into his vicinity.

I would love to ☺ —Gabby

Good. I'll come pick you up in half an hour? We can take a stroll and discuss the assignment. —Hunter

Sounds perfect! —Gabby

See you soon. —Hunter

Thirty minutes were more than enough to get ready. I searched through the dense cluster of black velvet hangers in my closet, muttering to myself. Piqued with curiosity, Luna padded over.

"I have nothing to wear, Luna!" I groaned, throwing a pile of outfit choices onto my bed.

My cat tilted her head, blinking her yellow eyes and silently reminding me that I had plenty of clothes.

"Yeah, yeah, I know," I grumbled. "Don't look at me with that judgy look." I picked her up and placed her on my bed. She protested with a sharp *meow*. "C'mon, help me pick something before he gets here."

With fall around the corner, I always found myself reaching for outfits that were gothic or dark academia inspired. My colour palette occasionally deviated from its usual shades of black and red to include a bit more of earthy browns, moody greys, and shadowy greens. Anna always drilled it into Layla's and my noggins that the world was your runway and every day you should dress to impress. Therefore, even if tonight was a casual stroll, I'd be lying if I said a wee part of me didn't want to hear Hunter's mellifluous voice complimenting me because I looked like a ten out of ten.

"I'm feeling black thigh-high socks, black faux crocodile skin loafers, grey plaid miniskirt, and…" I held up two tops against my chest, letting

Luna decide. She evaluated both before pawing at the black, full-sleeved mockneck. "This one it is." I kissed her head. "Thank you, baby."

I got dressed in record time, put my hair in a loose braid, layered some dainty gold jewelry, sprayed my signature fragrance, and by the time I finished my makeup by swiping my red lipstick on, Luna was trying to climb me, sensing that I was about to leave soon.

"Do you want to come with us?" I asked her.

Luna meowed in agreement.

My cat and I both had separation anxiety. I couldn't leave her alone for too long. Nor did she deserve to be subjected to Enzo and Lucia's soap opera unfolding downstairs. That was cruel even by my standards.

"Okay." I slung on my crossbody bag with my necessities—aka wallet, keys, gun, and a mass market paperback—and grabbed Luna's black carrier tote, lifting her inside of it after putting on her harness. "There you go." Hunter's text came through, letting me know he was outside. "He's here, Luna. Will you be good and behave tonight?"

Luna rubbed her face against my chest, giving me that soft, innocent expression that never failed to melt my heart. She was grateful I was taking her along for the ride.

When my parents still lived under the same roof, heated arguments and explosions were the norm, something that unsettled both of us. Therefore, I'd often strap Luna into a harness and sneak out of the house so we could walk to the nearby woods and escape the contemptuous environment at home. My furry companion loved exploring new places with her four-beat gait, especially woodland where she could scavenge the area like a crow in search of carrion. A handful of times, she'd brought me disturbing gifts in the form of dead birds or small mammals. I'd tried to curb those tendencies, but she was a creature of habit, bound by her predatory nature.

"Mamma, I'm going out!" I called out as I descended the stairs. "I'll be back late."

"Where are you going?" she countered from the kitchen, irritation coalesced in her tone, obviously stemming from Papà's goading. They'd been on the phone for over an hour and I was pretty sure he'd been prying information about Neal. And Mamma, who loved making Papà jealous, was more than happy to divulge.

"Um, on a walk with a…friend."

"Which friend?"

Here goes nothing. "A boy from school."

Mamma poked her head out into the hallway and waved a brownie-batter-coated spatula at me, her eyes wide and gleaming with excitement. The last time I mentioned anything about a boy was when I first started dating Franco ages ago. "What did you say—"

"Oscar will follow us. I'll be safe. Don't worry. Love you!" I shot her some air kisses and hurried out the front door before she could speed after me.

Like any typical mother, Mamma would want to be introduced to Hunter and when she saw him—every inch of his tall, muscular frame, expressive eyes, and long black hair—she'd tell me that I was a foolish girl for not locking him down pronto.

Hunter was already waiting for me by the passenger door of his steed. A thick palm coasted over the door handle, ready to open it when he saw me tear down the front steps like the hounds of hell were nipping at my feet.

He was devilishly handsome in an ethereal manner, cloaked in a collared dark coat that emphasized his allure, looking like a vampire lord on tenterhooks anticipating his long-awaited beloved.

The pallid sunlight flirted with the evening sky, casting blocks of shadows over his stature, leaving him half illuminated and half concealed in secrecy.

My feet truncated the distance separating us until I was able to catapult into him, throwing my arms around his broad shoulders in a loutish hug.

"Hi!" I gushed. "I'm so happy to see you!"

Hunter caught me effortlessly around the waist, carting me up his body so he could bury his face in my neck. He tightened his hold on me like he'd needed this just as much as me. My fragrance effused off my skin and melded with his in harmony.

Time could stop right here and I'd be content to have this as my final moment.

"Hi," he breathed softly. "I'm so happy to see *you*."

Luna, not liking being squished between us, voiced her displeasure with a sharp sound that had us rearing back. Hunter winced and I remembered his tender shoulder. I shouldn't have held on to him so tight. The apology on my tongue frittered away, though, as he glanced down at my cat with gentleness. "And I'm so happy to see you, Luna."

Luna agreed, closing her eyes as he stroked his fingers under her chin. Seeing him give her affection turned me to putty.

"I hope you don't mind that I brought her," I commented. "Luna loves walks."

"The more the merrier." He opened my car door like a gentleman, smiling. "Shall we?"

I belatedly noticed that we unintentionally matched, seeming like a perfect, blended unit. We were both accoutred in shades of black and grey fabrics, alongside my Nebelung cat with her grey pelt.

"I brought you donuts, by the way," Hunter informed as soon as he slipped into the driver's seat and turned on the ignition, the Jaguar humming to life underneath us. "Chocolate-dipped. Your favourites."

My face fell, guilt pelting me. "But I didn't get you anything."

He placed the familiar pink box from Le Petit Moulin in my lap. "Your company is gift enough, sweetheart."

Oh, I was really swooning now.

"Though maybe you can save one donut for me." His eyes twinkled as he slid on his seatbelt.

I pursed my lips jestingly. "Maybe I'll save two for you."

Hunter released a low, husky chuckle. "Deal."

This week alone, I'd eaten more donuts than I had in the last season, but I'd never complain, considering the thoughtfulness behind his gesture.

Franco rarely got me anything that didn't require begging. In fact, he used to go so far as making fun of the fact that I had a sweet tooth— claiming that it was childish—since he preferred savoury treats like a grown-up. Fucking prick.

Meanwhile, here was Hunter, indulging me without me having to ask him.

One boy from my past made me feel like 'too much' and one man from my present made me feel like it was an honour to be in my presence.

As Hunter drove us to our destination, I couldn't stop staring at his profile.

Two realizations sank in.

Firstly, against my better judgement, I'd developed a crush on this man.

Secondly, despite my current circumstances, *this* was the most at peace I'd ever felt in my life.

CHAPTER 12

Perfect Just The Way You Are

GABRIELA

Hunter chose a beautiful location for our walk, near a popular canal in the city with a vantage view of the Basilica, which was nestled at a high altitude amongst the darkened sky like a beacon.

Gothic revival architecture surrounded us and the cobblestone path we walked on bore vintage street lamps, food vendors, and buskers. A group of opera singers belted out a haunting rendition of "Caro Mio Ben" that had us doing a double take to watch the performance. Luna's head peeked out of the tote carrier, mesmerized by the magnificent melody.

A peaceful moment of silence befell us as we strolled and ate our donuts, observing the city's arresting landscape. Hunter stopped at a stall to grab us caramel apple teas, taking a minute to converse with the jolly old fellow making our drinks. You could tell a lot about a person by the way they treated those in customer serving roles and I really liked how nice Hunter was with everyone he encountered.

I hadn't realized they still made men like him. Kind. Sweet. Gentlemanly. It felt like they were scarce, or perhaps it was just my bad luck that I had the tendency to encounter the Lord's most diabolical creatures.

"What's got you smiling?" Hunter asked, handing me my tea after giving one to Oscar, who thanked him before retreating back a few paces to give us privacy.

That every man I've met before you has probably been a gremlin.

"Nothing." Still smiling, I mouthed, "Thank you," since I wasn't allowed to say it aloud, courtesy of his silly rule.

He playfully narrowed his eyes at me in a scolding manner and mouthed back, "You're welcome."

We continued walking. "I'm glad you asked me out tonight. I really needed to get some fresh air after the day I've had."

"Do you want to talk about it?"

I shrugged. "Academically, everything is fine. Personally? This whole"—I shot a glance over my shoulder to reassure myself that Oscar was still there—"*paranoia* stemming from the break-in is really doing me in."

"I get it," he sympathized and tried to give me an encouraging look. "I hope they find the culprit soon and deal with them accordingly." Then he frowned. "Please tell me you're carrying protection when you step out of the house."

My head swivelled around to make sure no one could hear us before I inserted slyly, "Don't worry, pretty boy. I've come prepared."

Hunter smirked. "What have you got on you, huh?"

"My Luna, my trusty gun, and my latest read about a centuries-old werewolf who finds his witchy mate in a treasure hunt and is currently going feral for her."

Hunter let loose a throaty chuckle. I loved that sound. "Are you serious?"

"Mhm." I skipped a little to keep up with his long-legged strides. He slowed his pace to match mine. "A girl's got to be prepared for anything."

"So your cat to scare away the intruder, your gun to kill him if he gets too close, and your book to read after you finish the job?"

I tilted my head and pretended to jokingly ponder it. "I mean, when you put it like that...that was my logic, yes."

His broad shoulders shook with his laughter. "You're something else, Gabriela."

"I'm going to take that as a compliment, Hunter."

"You should." He grinned. "It is."

I placed my hand in the crook of his elbow and peered up at him. "How am I doing on mending your broken heart? Am I forgiven yet?"

"That depends on whether or not you'll come to my next game?"

I nodded eagerly. "I'll do my best. And if I can't come, then I'll try to make it for the one afterwards. I promise."

He extended his pinky finger towards me.

I hooked mine with his and squeezed.

"Good." Hunter didn't let go of my finger, our hands swinging between our bodies as we walked. "I'll be sure to get you a jersey with my name on it."

A burst of colourful confetti shot inside of me when he finally released my pinky, just to fully weave his fingers with mine. I'd been intimate with men in the past—partaken in some of the raunchiest activities—but something as simple as holding hands with Hunter was making me blush.

I felt breathless, similar to the moment right before the swift drop on a roller coaster, my pulse skyrocketing high.

We were friends.

But now I was harbouring a crush on him and it felt forbidden.

He felt forbidden, akin to the fruit in the tree of knowledge. And just like Adam and Eve, I wanted to bite into him, sink my teeth into his flesh and unravel all of his secrets and taste all of his desires, while avoiding punishment for breaking my own rules.

I blew on my tea and took a sip, trying to ease my nerves and collect some composure. "How was your game today?"

Hunter squeezed my hand and drew an invisible half-moon on the back of it, like he was unable to help himself. "I scored two touchdowns."

My eyes widened. I knew enough about football—mostly through hearing Josh talk about his games whenever I hung out with him and Layla—to understand that touchdowns were coveted. "Wow. That's like twelve points, right?"

"Huh, so you do know a little something about my sport." Hunter smiled almost bashfully before mumbling, "Yeah, that is twelve points. We ended up winning thirty-five against twenty-seven."

"Hunter, that's really amazing."

He shrugged like it was no biggie. "It was a team effort."

"I bet you're a wonderful captain."

My compliment caused the high points of his cheek to pinken the slightest bit. He cleared his throat and took a sip of his tea. "What makes you say that?"

It wasn't poised in an accusing manner but rather in genuine curiosity. It reminded me of his tone when he'd asked me why my choice of weapon was a gun and why my choice of nail colour was black. Almost like he wanted to learn the inner workings of my mind on a deeper level.

We came to rest by a barrier, the canal's dark water rippling beneath us.

"Well, you have this calm energy about you that I imagine helps put the team at ease. From the short time that I've known you, I can tell you're the type of person who's always ready to help others, which means that your teammates probably feel comfortable coming to you with any issues. Moreover, Josh is always boasting about your impressive football stats. So in other words, you're steady, trustworthy, a gifted player, and I'd say that all of these qualities make you a great leader. On and off the field."

Hunter appeared stunned. "That is the nicest thing anyone has ever said to me."

My throat felt inexplicably tight with the way he was staring down at me in awe and gratitude. "I'm just being honest."

"I know." Something indescribable flashed across his face, hesitation maybe, before he said, "I scored one for you…A game-winning touchdown."

It was my turn to be stunned. "What?"

He smiled wistfully and glanced at the water, almost avoiding my perplexed gaze. "I thought you came to the game—I thought you were in the crowd, watching me, and I was trying to impress you."

This was too much for me to process. My mind raced a mile a minute and my heart clenched almost painfully from his words. He thought I was there. He scored a game-winning touchdown to impress me. Oh my God. "Hunter..."

Realizing that he'd revealed a little too much about *his* inner workings, he reverted to his teasing self, giving me a suave wink to downplay his admission. "No worries. I can do it again when you come to my next game."

"Make it three touchdowns," I rallied, but my voice was thick, unlike my usual flirtatious tone. "I'll be really impressed then."

"Deal." Hunter chuckled and Luna swivelled her head in his direction. She meowed for him and he gave her gentle scratches.

"I'm surprised," I said. "Luna barely takes a liking to anyone new."

He looked proud of himself. "I'm flattered."

"Do you have any pets?"

"None currently. But my dad did have a ball python from his collegiate years. He passed away from old age when I was a kid."

"Is that why you have a snake inked on your arm?"

"Yeah," he rasped. "I've always been fascinated with them and they're revered in many cultures as symbols of protection, guidance, transformation, and eternal rebirth. I have another one tatted on my right thigh."

Just imagining that tattoo on his muscular thigh made my insides flutter. "I know nothing about snake lore, but that sounds very interesting."

He let go of my hand a bit regretfully, after giving it a final squeeze because Luna kept pawing at him, desperately wanting to be cradled. He pulled her out of my tote and she relaxed once she was in his strong arms.

"Do you have any tattoos?" he asked me.

"Just one." I pushed my hair behind my shoulders and flashed him the small cursive *R* behind my ear. It was the same one as Layla and Anna. Our moms were friends before our births and gave us middle names that meant Queen in our respective cultures. Mine was Regina, Layla's Rani, and Anna's Reina. "Me and my best friends got these when we turned eighteen to honour our middle names."

Hunter bent down at the waist to peer at my tattoo. "It's beautiful, Gabby."

I preened. A mirthful expression twisted his features. "What is it?" I asked.

He smirked. "I'm just thinking that without the added height of your heels, you're a tiny little thing. Like a precious doll."

"Hey—I'm five-foot-two!" I retorted. "Not *that* short."

"I'm six-three, sweetheart. I've got more than a foot over you," he mused, swiping a thumb over my cheek in a featherlight caress. "You're definitely short by my standards."

More warmth suffused my face at the proximity and touch. "Is that a problem?"

"Nah, I think you're fucking cute."

I bit my lip. "Ditto."

Hunter's blue eyes flared wide, his full lips parting at my compliment.

My cat chose that exact moment to leap out of his arms and onto the bench next to us, spotting a butterfly. We gasped and I quickly caught her leash before she went too far, stopping her attempt at preying on the insect. "Luna!"

She gave me a mildly annoyed glance.

Hunter chuckled and I huffed an exhale. "Sorry about that."

"It's all good."

We sat down on the bench, caging either side of Luna. I caressed her back, unsure what to say next. Hunter was perched forward with his elbows on his thighs, his joined hands hanging in the open V of his spread legs. His eyes kept flitting from my cat to me...namely the bare skin exposed between the hemline of my miniskirt and the tops of my black thigh-high socks.

Unmistakable heat unfurled inside of me and I crossed my legs, causing my skirt to ride up higher. Hunter's stubbled jaw clenched and a muscle popped in his cheek. That heady, borderline feral expression was one of the hottest things I'd ever seen.

One thing was for certain: our attraction towards each other wasn't going away anytime soon. The more he complimented me, the more he held my hand, and the more he gave me this *I-want-to-be-inside-of-you* look, it was only a matter of time before we dipped into uncharted waters.

His eyes rose to mine with a hint of a challenge. As if he was waiting for me to admit this whole 'friends' thing was a lie. That there was only one way it would end between us. With sheet-clawing sex and our bodies purging this stark tension.

"Show me the book you're reading?" Hunter asked, breaking the silence, and I nearly shivered from the gravel in his voice.

I felt like I was going to disintegrate under the pheromones and the heat he was emanating from sitting so close to me. Fuck, he was incredibly sexy.

I reached into my purse and handed him my paperback. "Here."

Hunter thumbed through my book. "What is it that you like so much about these books?"

I'd never been asked that question, but the answer came to me easily. "The escapism. I love getting lost in fictional worlds. Sometimes, I feel like I've lived thousands of lifetimes because I read. You're never lonely if you have the comfort of your favourite characters."

Hunter reclined against the bench, lounging his arm along the back of it, his fingers close enough to play with my hair. "That's a nice way of putting it. I hadn't thought of it from that point of view." Then he weighed the paperback in his hand and added, "But you know what's not nice? The fact that you've dog-eared these pages. It's a crime, Gabby. A complete blasphemy."

A boisterous laugh burst out of me. I had to clamp a hand over my mouth to tame it as I scared some passersby. "Guilty. Since I always lose my bookmarks, this is my go-to method to remember where I last left off. Sometimes, I'll even dog-ear my favourite scenes."

The corners of Hunter's mouth tipped up in a mischievous smile and he went back to skimming through my book before I realized what I'd confessed. Shit. The last thing I wanted was for him to read the part where the crazed werewolf finally fucked his fated mate on a new moon.

"No!" I giggled, lunging for him. "Give it back to me!"

Hunter fended me off with an arm, falling on that exact scene. His eyes went wide with delight and a disbelief-laced chuckle escaped him. "So these are the kind of heroes you like, huh? Filthy and obsessed with their heroines?"

"Yes, I love my unhinged book boyfriends," I replied shamelessly, nearly climbing onto his lap to rip out my book. We play-wrestled for a few seconds, laughing. "Thief! I want my property back now!"

Luna screeched between us, getting squished by our tomfoolery, and the noise distracted Hunter enough that I was able to steal my book back.

With a fading chuckle, he asked, "Which one is your favourite boyfriend?"

"Blasphemy," I parroted his own word and gave a haughty flick of my chin. "And I can't choose. I love them all."

"But if you had to choose," he insisted, his pointer finger looping around a lock of my red hair and tugging lightly. "Which one?"

I should have batted his hand away, but I liked his touch too much. "Let me think. This is a hard decision."

"Uh-huh," he drawled, stroking his spare hand over Luna's back as she rubbed herself against him. "And while you take your sweet time thinking about your hard decision, just know that I'm making plans to steal your cat since she likes me so much." He gave her a forehead kiss and she closed her eyes in joy. I almost passed out from the cuteness of it all. "Isn't that right, Luna?"

"You really want to mess with me when I have a gun?" I deadpanned.

He tsked. "You don't scare me, shorty."

"Smart-ass." I harrumphed, but the grin on my lips betrayed me.

"Clock's ticking, doll. I want my answer."

Damn. I couldn't even pretend to hate him calling me *doll*. It rolled off his tongue in a filthy and sinful manner.

"Fine." I leaned my elbow against the bench, placing my face in my palm to appear casual and denote the butterflies in my stomach. "One of my favourite book boyfriends is this vampire who waited a thousand years for his fated mate. One night, after he finished showing her his castle, she told him she's never stargazed because she's from the city and you can't see them there. The next day, the hero took it upon himself to set up a picnic for her and they spent hours staring at the constellations. It was a simple gesture but extremely thoughtful. Acts of service are clearly my weakness. Plus, I've never gone stargazing, so that scene lives in my mind rent-free."

Hunter's expression softened. "You're a romantic."

"I am." There was no point denying it. "And yet I'm not really a relationship girl."

"Why?"

I gave him a white lie. "There's a lot on my plate. Balancing a relationship with my demanding academic life would be difficult."

That couldn't be further from the truth. After Franco and his cutthroat words, I was afraid of letting anyone too close to me. What if they found something within me that they didn't like—a deal-breaking flaw—while I'd fallen head over heels in love with them? I didn't think I was strong enough to handle that kind of rejection, let alone put my heart back on the line. Maybe in a few years, a man would enter my life and change my mind.

Maybe I'd be willing to take a chance on love again.

But right now, that was a slim possibility.

Sometimes it felt like Franco had stolen everything I possessed until my well had dried up, with nothing left to give.

Hunter appeared like he wanted to call bullshit on my lie. Ever the gentleman, he simply whispered, "I see."

I turned the tables on him, leaning closer until we were almost tête-à-tête. "What about you? Is there a special someone in your life?"

Hunter gazed at me with an unnamed emotion, giving Luna a final stroke before she padded over to me for a snuggle. "No. I haven't dated in a really long time. Not since high school."

"How come?"

He shrugged, continuing to twirl a lock of my hair around his pointer finger. "My ex-girlfriend, Ginette, cheated on me with my teammate. I had trust issues for a while."

I opened my mouth. Closed it. Opened it again. Shook my head, shocked. *Why would she do that to him?*

Hunter saw the question on my face. "I guess I wasn't enough for her," he stated plainly, but there was a sad edge to it that made me ache.

My heart broke for a young Hunter.

How devastated he must have felt to be faced with a cheating girlfriend whom he probably loved with his whole heart.

"Well, screw her. You didn't deserve to be treated that way," I defended. "I think you're perfect just the way you are."

The finger playing with my hair froze and the atmosphere charged with an electrifying energy. It felt crackling and tangible.

When Hunter's left hand reached for mine, his fingertips grazing my knuckles, a final cog clicked into place. No matter how much I tried to run away from the possibility of us, it would catch up to me. One day, I wouldn't be able to avoid this connection that continued to pulse between us like a living heartbeat and flow through my veins like ambrosia.

Hunter's fingers braided with mine in a manner that was quintessentially ours and he smiled tenderly. "I think you're perfect just the way you are too, Gabriela."

CHAPTER 13

In Too Deep

GABRIELA

The next two weeks trickled by expeditiously.

Mamma and Neal, boyfriend number sixteen, broke up. He ended it with her via text message like a total asshat. She was currently sulking and Papà walked around with his chest puffed out like a self-satisfied, arrogant man who'd conspired with the universe to get exactly what he wanted. I wouldn't put it past him to not only get on his knees and beg God to free his ex-wife from the shackles of a younger man, but also threaten the men she dated to help speed up the process. Enzo Bellafiore was relentless in his pursuit when he wanted something, and the truth was that he never stopped wanting his Lucia. He wouldn't rest until he made her his again.

My guard, Oscar, still followed me around everywhere like a shadow. I often checked over my shoulders wherever I went, worried that the culprit who'd vandalized my apartment lurked close by. We were nowhere near finding them. But thankfully, there hadn't been another disturbance since that first one. I was beginning to wonder if someone played a one-time prank just to scare me. Or if that said someone had gotten the wrong home.

Eventually, I also gathered the courage to tell my parents about the real reason for Franco's and my breakup, including the fact that he was conveniently back in Montardor after all these years. They were livid.

"Say the word and I'll lodge a bullet into his skull, Gabriela," Papà had offered, fuming. "No one is allowed to hurt my daughter."

"No." I'd shaken my head, pleading. "I don't want that."

I deemed it better for Franco to live with the guilt of his actions. He'd always been the kind of person to act like nothing bothered him, while internally detonating. I had an inkling that how he treated me secretly haunted him. However, if Franco really was behind the break-in, all bets were off. I wouldn't stop Papà. He'd have free rein to do as he pleased with my ex-boyfriend.

Academically speaking, things were progressing without a hiccup. Despite the stress of the situation that should have mentally crippled me, I persevered, staying on top of my game. All my readings, assignments, and class projects were completed in a timely manner. Nor did I miss a single WIB student association meeting, always present with my notes and financial projections. We were all set for our mixer in a few days and halfway done with the preparations for our next event, a networking affair featuring respected panellists from behemoth firms.

I also saw Anna and Layla often. We sometimes carpooled and they hung out with me if we had a mutual break on campus, rarely leaving me alone. And if they couldn't be next to me physically, they were constantly populating the group chat with texts, demanding I provide updates on my whereabouts every hour. I appreciated their concern and support more than I could convey in words.

With every passing day, the sunken claws of paranoia retracted from my pierced skin and I felt like I could breathe a little bit better. I continued marching through my day-to-day with more confidence in my step, knowing I was well-protected and surrounded by people who cared for me.

And then there was Hunter.

Regardless of his busy schedule, he sought me out whenever possible, under the guise of ensuring that I wasn't alone, even though Oscar always hung nearby. But deep down, I knew it was because he wanted to be around me. The same way I wanted to be around him.

On Mondays, he drove me to school and bought me a mocha and chocolate-dipped donuts. In return, I gave him roses from my garden. Sometimes one, sometimes two, sometimes three. They always seemed to make his day a bit brighter, his entire demeanour coming to life as though he was anticipating receiving them all week. One of the most endearing qualities he possessed was wanting to preserve the blooms, like he was a man who cherished any gift. No matter how small and trivial.

"This is my favourite part of Monday," he'd said last time, placing the bouquet in his car's cup holder.

I'd put on my seatbelt. "Receiving flowers?"

Hunter had shaken his head, confessing in a raspy tone, "Seeing you."

My heart had clenched inside my chest.

He'd traced the blush on my cheeks with the back of one knuckle before skimming a strand of my hair behind my ear.

Unable to stop myself, I'd also confessed, "Mine too."

On Tuesday and Thursdays, he always drove me back to my parents' home, even if he had to stay behind after his classes and football practices ended.

"You know you don't have to wait after me," I'd told him, playing with the ends of his hair as he parked his car in the driveway. "I'm sure you have better things to do."

The brief glance he cast me practically said *nothing is more important to me than you.*

My breath hitched when he caught my wrist and placed a butterfly-soft kiss on my fluttering pulse. "Though you have Oscar, I'll sleep better if I drive you myself and see you enter the house, Gabby. Let me keep doing this for you. If not for your sake, then mine."

My goodness. He was extremely sweet and I could never deny him when he implored in such a gentle tone.

On Wednesdays during our break, we worked on our weekly Horror & Cult Classic Cinema assignments. Hunter still held my hand during class, but he was less jumpy and more engaged, actually beginning to enjoy the films.

One particular weekday evening, in the midst of painting my toenails, I'd gotten a text from him. It was a list of the top ten scariest movies in the last decade.

Do you want to watch these with me? —Hunter

We can have a movie night at my place sometime soon. — Hunter

I was so proud that he'd overcome his previous aversion to this genre. In fact, I liked how much he looked forward to our weekly class. For those three hours, we were sucked into another world, passing messages through my notebook, eating treats, and holding hands while watching a horror flick.

I capped my red nail polish and texted him back.

Yes, I'd love that! —Gabby

Will you let me hold your hand? —Hunter

Hunter had held my hand figuratively and literally since the moment we met on the terrace, helping me, driving me, being there for me in any capacity…and it was only fair I returned the favour.

Of course, pretty boy. – Gabby

What are you up to right now? —Gabby

I'd seen him a handful of hours ago, but I still missed him. Oscar drove me back home today and I listened to songs from Hunter's playlist to keep me company in his stead.

Icing my shoulder again. Practice was rough. —Hunter

He attached a picture of an ice pack sitting over his broad shoulder.

You? —Hunter

I hope your shoulder feels better soon! —Gabby

And I just finished doing my nails. —Gabby

I sent him a picture of my sparkly crimson toes.

Free feet pics in this economy? I'm a lucky man. —Hunter

I chuffed out a laugh, loving his humour. Luna sidled up next to me on the floor, peering at my phone screen as I typed a text. Like she just knew it was *her* Hunter on the other end.

You're right. How foolish of me. That'll be $100. —Gabby

Less than a minute later, my phone pinged with an email notification, an automatic deposit into my bank account of exactly one hundred dollars by Hunter.

I sputtered, eyes widening in disbelief.

OMG, I was kidding!!! —Gabby

I'm not. —Hunter

Next time, I want to see your toes painted black. —Hunter

Just like your soul. —Hunter

God, help me. I adored our banter and flirty text messages.

Your wish is my command 🖤 —Gabby

Also, Luna says hi! —Gabby

I sent him a selfie of Luna and me.

Look at that. It's my favourite girls. —Hunter

My favourite girls. There weren't enough words to encompass what I was feeling in this moment. I responded with another selfie, this time a closeup of Luna's adorable face, and replied:

She says you're our favourite too. —Gabby

And on the weekends, if I wasn't hanging out with the girls, Hunter and I went on walks along the canal with Luna. That was when I learned he'd started listening to true crime podcasts and reading paranormal romances.

"Are you serious?" I'd asked him, surprised, while he fed Luna a cat treat.

He'd sent me an assessing look. "Why would I lie to you?"

It was true. He had no reason to. "Which podcast are you listening to?"

He'd told me and I'd brightened. It was the same one I'd been listening to as well.

"And what romance book are you currently reading?"

His mouth had formed into a teasing smile. "That's a secret for now."

My ex-boyfriend belittled and made fun of my hobbies and interests, choosing to keep me subdued so he felt better about the fact that he had little to none outside of soccer. And here was Hunter, choosing to embrace my passions in hopes of better understanding me.

The affection I felt for Hunter continued to grow on a daily basis. I knew I was screwed when I started keeping track of time based on when I last saw him and when I would see him again. Never in my life had I felt this way for another person.

Only Hunter.

Anna and Layla reminded me that it was okay to harbour a crush on him and break my own self-imposed rules, yet I still had my reservations.

But regardless of trying to keep him at arm's length, I was failing drastically when all I wanted was to be near him. Hunter made it so hard to stay away from him and keep things platonic. He made me laugh. He made me smile. He made me feel safe. I was a needy girl and he filled a void inside of me, whether he realized it or not.

This man tumbled into my life during a dark period and helped me weather the storm.

He was steady and solid, like a lighthouse providing me shelter in a tumultuous sea that was threatening to consume me whole.

I craved his presence in ways I was only now beginning to acknowledge.

And it scared me.

For all my inability to be alone, the thought of being tethered to someone after the last one cut me to shreds was a frightening thought. Even though I knew Hunter would never willingly hurt me.

When Hunter pulled up into my driveway, my mood lifted. When Hunter texted or called me, my grin was enormous. When Hunter's hand threaded with mine during our walks and classes, it was like a shot of gold rushing through my veins. When he was next to me, I was happy. And when he wasn't next to me, I was less happy.

He was like the sun and I flourished under his warmth.

There was a part of me that looked forward to seeing how this connection of ours would blossom and another part of me that worried that my past would catch up to me and ruin everything.

The night before the mixer, I got a text from Hunter just as I turned off the lights in my room and settled under the covers.

Can't wait to see you tomorrow, doll. —Hunter

It wasn't the first time he'd told me that he couldn't wait to see me, but it was the first time strong anticipation built inside of me, like the moment before a flurry of fireworks.

I feared that if we ever lost this friendship, I'd slowly wither away.

And with that thought running in my mind, in the darkness of my room, broken by a wedge of light seeping through my parted curtains from a full moon similar to the one from the night on the terrace, I texted him back two words:

Me too 🤍 —Gabby

CHAPTER 14

Jealous Pretty Boy

GABRIELA

By the time the mixer rolled around, I was a giddy mess from the excitement surrounding our event and at the thought of finally seeing Hunter after two days.

I specifically picked a hunter green silk minidress with a built-in bra, square neckline, and rhinestone straps. I did my makeup as usual with my signature red lips, added girandole diamond earrings, styled my dark red hair in loose curls, and wore matching platform heels to complete my look.

I never dressed to impress a man, but I'd be lying if I said I wasn't looking forward to Hunter's reaction. Whenever we were together, he often checked me out, appreciating my fashion choices before telling me how good I looked.

His compliments turned me to mush. I was smitten with him.

Now I was at MacGregor bar with my team, the mixer just having begun twenty minutes ago. We weren't packed like a can of sardines yet, but students were beginning to trickle in. Hera and I stood by the bar, nursing virgin mojitos and talking to some freshmen. They came over to us sheepishly after spotting the sticker name tags on our dresses stating our names and positions on the team. Though this wasn't a formal networking event and more of an opportunity for the student body to get acquainted with our faces and mission statement, we took the time to answer their questions about our upcoming events, our workshops, and how they could hopefully join the team.

But I was sidetracked and my eyes kept flitting over to the doors, waiting for my friends—including Hunter—to arrive.

When the freshmen left, Shaun broke away from his group of friends and prowled towards us, looking every bit like royalty in his crisp white button-down and black trousers moulded to his tall and muscular physique, his blond hair artfully styled and his blue eyes gleaming with their natural charm. The Jacobsens were prolific and old money, well known across Montardor and hearty investors at Vesta University. Everyone knew their name or at the very least their son, the captain of the school's prestigious hockey team.

And he was only here for one reason tonight.

Hera.

Shaun barely had to weave through the crowd. It parted for him. I wondered what it felt like to walk around like you had the entire world in the palm of your hand, ready to bend backwards at the snap of your fingers.

"Hey, girls," he greeted us smoothly, giving me a customary hug first. Then he enveloped Hera in a lingering one, going as far as kissing her cheek too. "Incredible job tonight, sweetheart."

Hera's green eyes widened, her face pinkening slightly.

"Thank you." She squeezed his shoulders before pulling away slightly, keeping her hands on him. "We've sold out every ticket tonight. I'm optimistic that this buzz will help for our next event as well."

"I'm sure it will." Shaun tucked one of her dark strands behind her ear, eyeing her gold dress and black heels with a deft gaze. He fingered the chain of riviera diamonds around her neck. "Nice necklace."

Hera was the definition of elegance and grace, but her usually polished composure slipped the slightest bit, alongside an almost shy chuckle, at Shaun's flirty tone. "I wonder who gave it to me."

Shaun smirked, a deeply satisfied noise rumbling in his throat. "Must be someone who likes you a lot."

Just then, Cade—Josh's brother and Shaun's best friend—entered our fold, towing along Ella, his girlfriend, and Darla and Dacia, all besties of Hera. The group exploded in lively greetings. They were a tight-knit crew and I knew them because we ran in the same circles since Hera and Layla were cousins.

As per usual, the girls and I gushed over each other's outfits and took an innumerable number of selfies. I hoped Anna and Layla would reach us soon. They texted me half an hour ago that they were on their way. I didn't want them to miss out on all the fun.

I'd just bought another virgin mojito when Ella sidled up next to me. "As your friend, I feel the need to tell you there's a particular girl in this room who keeps giving you the stink eye."

I stopped sipping my drink, my brows going high. "What?"

"On your left. Ten o'clock."

Discreetly, I cast a glance in that direction.

My entire demeanour turned frosty.

Of course.

Morgan.

I'd done my best to ignore her when the team arrived earlier to set up the venue for our event. The best solution to handle her agitating self was to treat her like a fly in the room, annoying but irrelevant to my existence.

To make it worse, Taylor was here tonight too. He was playing billiards with some boys and she hung onto him like arm candy.

"That's Morgan." I sighed. "She hates me."

Ella recoiled back, her unique sectoral heterochromia blue-brown eyes widening. "Why?"

"Jealous that I got the position on the team she was vying for and probably for other reasons unbeknownst to me."

Ella rolled her shoulders back and adjusted the hemline of her black leather minidress, the chunky gold bracelets stacked on her wrists jingling with the motion. "Want me to set her straight? She'll never look at you with that crooked sneer ever again."

I loved Ella. Truly. She was loyal to her core and a bit scary if you got on her bad side. Without hesitation, she'd teach Morgan a lesson, but

I didn't want to cause any drama. "I appreciate you, Ella, but it's okay. She's not worth it."

"Okay, but if you change your mind, the offer still stands."

The rest of the girls announced they were going to join the long queue for the bathrooms. I didn't need to go, but Ella said to them, "I'll be there in a minute."

She walked over to Cade. He was sitting on a bar stool, a drink in his hand, and just admiring Ella with this intense look. Kissing him, she murmured, "Be back soon."

"Don't take too long, *mo chuisle*," he murmured back, squeezing her hip.

Ella and Cade had been dating since they were sixteen years old. They'd briefly experienced a separation but remained strong as ever after getting back together last year. They were the kind of couple that gave off ride-or-die energy, like their entire universe started and ended with each other.

Once the girls were gone, Cade and I chatted in their wait. He was a fellow bookworm, so we started exchanging book recommendations. He urged me to add two new mystery thrillers to my to-be-read list and I was in the midst of turning him into a paranormal romance convert when a shadow fell over us.

The newcomer was none other than Morgan.

My face pinched in irritation.

She had a hand on her waist and a coquettish expression on her face. "Hi, I'm Morgan," she introduced herself, ignoring me. "And you are?"

"Not interested," Cade retorted in a bored tone.

I snorted and hid the sound with a fake cough.

Morgan glared at me, but Cade's comeback wasn't enough to deter her. She'd always liked the kind of guys who posed a challenge—the ones who were already in a relationship. "Cute. So that's how you want to play it, huh?" She chuckled and honestly, I was genuinely appalled by her audacity and inability to read the room. "I saw you watching me and figured I'd make the first move."

"I wasn't watching you." Cade was offended that someone would even suggest he had eyes for anyone but Ella. "Like I said, I'm not interested."

Morgan wrapped her claws around Cade's thick forearm and batted her lashes. "At least tell me your name."

Cade's gaze hardened at her touch. I was about to tell Morgan to fuck off, that this one was taken, and his girlfriend wasn't afraid to cut a bitch or two.

But I didn't have to say a peep because said girlfriend happened to reach us at that exact moment, cold fury wrapped around her frame.

Cade barely hid his smirk, knowing what was coming.

The saccharine smile carved over Ella's lips was an indication that she was going to make Morgan regret ever touching her man.

"Hi, Morgan," Ella drawled in a voice filled with pretty venom. "We haven't met yet. I'm Ella."

Morgan threw her a dirty look, like Ella was interrupting something. Hah. I only wish I had popcorn with me to really watch her fall off her high horse. "Uh, okay?"

Dacia, Darla, and Hera sidled up behind Ella. It was worth noting that my president seemed nervous at Morgan's unprofessional behaviour. And based on all the girls' faces, they definitely heard Morgan hitting on Cade.

"Do you like having fingers, sweetie?" Ella asked.

Morgan didn't catch the hint or remove her hand from Cade.

"Yeah," Morgan threw back with an attitude. "Why?"

"Then I suggest you stop touching my boyfriend before I break your fucking hand," Ella snarled. "And I promise you, I can make it *painful*."

Morgan jerked back with mortification, releasing her hold on Cade. He picked up a bar napkin and wiped his arm like a petty king.

"Excuse me? How dare you talk to me like that?" she snapped.

"I'll talk to you however I want." Ella used her pointer and thumb finger to flick Morgan's forehead. "Now shoo."

Unshed tears welled in Morgan's eyes and she glanced at Hera for help, all the toughness leaving her. Her mind finally computed her unprofessional act as a colossal fuck-up.

135

But Hera stood stony-faced, disappointment radiating from her as she regarded Morgan like an elementary teacher would a naughty child. Darla and Dacia didn't look impressed either.

"I'll speak to you in the office on Monday, Morgan," Hera said with a calm tone that emphasized she felt anything but.

I bet Hera was regretting hiring her right about now.

Morgan swallowed and backed a step before Ella reeled her in at the last second with a fistful of her sleeve. "While I've got you here, I also want to add that if you ever stare at Gabby with another dirty look, I will follow up on my threat. Understood?"

Morgan was seconds away from wailing and I couldn't help but feel a little bad, even if she brought this upon herself. I glanced over at Taylor. He watched this entire scene with confusion, like he hadn't even realized that she'd left his side. The prick couldn't be bothered to come over here and make sure she was okay. But maybe he didn't care because they weren't exclusive, given the fact that she was over here shooting her shot with Cade.

"Fine." Morgan shoved off Ella's hand and muttered something inaudible under her breath before stomping away.

The second Morgan was out of earshot, Ella's tough-as-nail demeanour melted away and she was all over Cade. "Are you okay, *querido*?"

"I'm okay. She was pushy but harmless." Cade yanked Ella into his embrace, murmuring with a hint of amusement, "Thank you for saving me, Ellie."

The girls and I laughed.

Cade was a mob prince down to his core. He certainly didn't need anyone to save him, but I reckon he enjoyed watching his girlfriend go all territorial over him.

After the laughter subsided, Hera's regretful eyes crossed over to mine. I once told her that I found Morgan vindictive. It always made the team uncomfortable when Morgan would demean me with a verbal jab when I was talking during our meetings. Last month, Hera had to pull Morgan to the side and explain that her behaviour wasn't okay or tolerated amongst the team. It subdued Morgan temporarily, but she still glared at me whenever we were in the same room.

I think Hera was beginning to realize the ridiculous extent of Morgan's unprofessionalism and misplaced dislike for me. Especially because I'd never done anything to her.

I shrugged, voicelessly letting Hera know that I was fine.

"Cade," Hera addressed him after clearing her throat. "My team is always respectful and courteous, and they're well aware that their actions tonight are a direct reflection on the association. Everyone was supposed to be on their best behaviour for tonight's mixer. I…I don't know why Morgan acted that way with you."

"You don't have to apologize, Hera." Cade shook his head. "It's not a big deal. I'm okay. She probably just drank too much."

"Probably," Hera echoed as an afterthought.

A few hours ago, Hera gave the whole team explicit instructions not to drink to the point that we became drunk or tipsy. That wasn't acceptable for a night like this, regardless of the venue and the nature of the event. Everyone who bought a ticket was given a free voucher for one drink— unless, of course, the attendees wanted to buy more drinks themselves.

But Morgan didn't look drunk or tipsy to me.

Plus, she said Cade had been staring at her—a complete lie. His eyes had never once strayed from Ella, except when she left to go to the bathroom. Maybe Morgan's dislike for me drove her to interrupt my conversation with a guy that she thought I was interested in—I obviously wasn't into Cade—just so she could shit on my parade and attempt to prove that she was the better option.

It would be quite like her character.

Ready to move past this Morgan fiasco, I checked my phone again. The latest texts in my group chat with the girls had my shoulders sagging in disappointment.

Layla's car just had a flat tire and we're stuck in the middle of a busy road. —Anna

We called insurance, but we're not sure if we'll make it in time.

137

—Anna

We're so sorry, Gabby. —Anna

If we weren't so far away, we'd walk to you 😞 —Anna

They sent me a selfie of them in the car with sad pouts, looking glamorous as ever.

I saw their location, confirming that they were nowhere near the bar. At least help was on the way. That filled me with relief.

I sent them my own selfie with a matching sad pout.

Please don't worry about it and stay safe 🖤 Keep me posted with updates! —Gabby

Also, WOW! You both look stunning 😍 —Gabby

Right back at you! You look hot as hell 🔥 —Anna

Is Oscar there, btw? —Anna

Yes, he's hiding in the corner of the bar, pretending to be incognito. I'm here with Ella, Darla, Dacia, and Hera. —Gabby

Okay, good. We'll let you know about our new ETA as soon as possible. Please keep texting us throughout the night so we know you're fine. Miss you! —Anna

PS: Tell the girls we say hi! —Anna

I will! Miss you both 🖤 —Gabby

I placed my phone into my heart-shaped clutch and focused my attention back on my friends, trying to salvage the rest of my night. Although Morgan's rude interruption and Layla and Anna's flat tire put a damper on my mood.

Also, where was Hunter? He said he would be here tonight.

Unless…he reneged.

No.

He wouldn't do that to me. Not without good reason.

Shaun, who'd momentarily left our group, rejoined and convinced everyone to play a game of Never Have I Ever. Our side of the bar erupted with jokes and laughter, and it helped take my mind off everything else. I was halfway through my second virgin mojito when an odd prickling sensation spread down my back.

Oscar was still in his spot, far away so that he wouldn't draw attention but still close enough to see me and any looming threat.

Reluctantly, I threw a glance over my shoulder.

And froze.

Franco entered the crowded bar with two guys I didn't recognize.

He appeared laid-back as he trawled the room. The second he spotted me, a frown marred his forehead, followed by a rude twist of his lips that set me on edge. I hadn't seen him since our first Horror & Cult Classic Cinema class. My guess was that he arrived right before class started and left the second it was dismissed to avoid another run-in with me.

Now he took inventory of everyone around me with newfound curiosity.

I didn't like it.

At all.

What if Anna and Layla are right? What if he's the one who broke into my place? What if he's here tonight to watch me?

Though this bar was a hotspot for students and our mixer had gained a lot of notoriety amongst the university populace, I wasn't sure why Franco would willingly show up to our event when he was far from a feminist and closer to a misogynistic pig.

My ex-boyfriend's presence exacerbated my low spirits.

Suddenly, a lump lodged itself in my throat and everything in the background blurred until the only sound in my ears was a low buzzing similar to a hornet's nest.

Excusing myself from my friends, I moved over to a stool and faced the bar wall lined with bottles of liquor, trying to control my surging anxiety. My eyes inexplicably stung. I was suddenly overwhelmed. Despite my need to constantly be surrounded by people, I had the urge to tear out of this place like a bullet and go somewhere where I could actually breathe.

As if manifesting him, a hard body pressed against my back, strong arms caged me on either side, and tanned hands came to rest next to my paler ones on the bar top. A soft kiss was placed on my crown. "Hey, sweetheart. I'm sorry I'm late."

All my panic fretted away in a singular whooshing exhale.

Hunter's familiar voice and cologne grounded me.

Without preamble, I spun around and threw my arms around his form, hugging him with all my might, my face practically mashing in his corded neck, where his pulse hammered under the graze of my red lips. "Hi, pretty boy."

Sensing that my greeting wasn't charged with my usual enthusiasm and feeling the light tremor running through my body, Hunter's arms wrapped around me.

"What's wrong, Gabby?" he murmured with so much gentleness, it nearly undid me. "I was stuck in traffic, but I tried to get here as fast as possible."

"Nothing's wrong." *Now that you're here.* "I just missed you. I'm glad you came."

"Of course I did." His chest vibrated with the sound of his deep voice and I felt the reverberations against my skin. "You asked me to."

Hunter uttered those words in a way that stated he would go anywhere I asked him, no matter how close or how far away. Even if it were the depths of hell, the ends of the earth, the heights of heaven.

Pulling back from the embrace of this man who was built like a beast but behaved like an angel, I observed my accidental lipstick stain on his neck with satisfaction.

I should tell Hunter about the mark, but I felt possessive over him. I didn't want it wiped off. I liked knowing that a part of me—even temporarily—was on him.

"Are you ready to hide in a corner with me?" I asked softly.

"Yes." Hunter smiled before cupping a hand under my jaw and tipping my head back so our gazes connected. "You look so beautiful tonight and I'm jealous of all the men eye-fucking you in this room."

I sucked in a breath through my parted lips, my hand tightening around my drink.

Guess I wasn't the only one feeling possessive tonight.

With his admission, another line was blurred. I didn't have it in me to re-erect it. It would be inane, when it was obvious we were close to departing the friend zone.

"I..." Could barely formulate a sentence.

Heat sparked in his gaze as it roved over my body with appreciation. "I'm getting a drink." He chin-nodded to my near-empty glass. "You want another?"

"N-no." Though the filthy look he perused my entirety with left me parched. "I'm good. What are you having?"

A bastardized smirk, filled with corrupt promises, spread over his mouth. "Certainly not beer, doll."

Fuck, I loved this flirty side of Hunter.

Everything about him turned me on. The luscious black hair that was pulled back tonight in a low bun at the nape of his neck, a lone strand trickling down his face. Those bedroom blue eyes and full lips drenched with wicked intent. That straight nose with the little scar on the bridge and that chiselled jaw just begging to be bitten. And that inked body of his that was Olympian in nature, harbouring thick, quilted muscles, poured in a mouth-watering combination of black pants, black dress shirt, black shoes, with his signature silver chain around his neck and Cartier timepiece on his wrist.

Hunter Saint Warren was an aphrodisiac and I wanted to savour every lick of him down to the core like a greedy goddess desperate for her fill.

I was afraid I'd never stop feeling this hunger until I had a bite.

In a vain attempt to stop undressing him with my eyes—although he didn't mind as he seemed to be doing the same thing to me—I questioned, "How was your game?"

"Great." He signalled over a bartender, pulling out his voucher. "Though it would have been better if you came, you little heartbreaker."

"I'm sorry, Hunter. If I didn't have to be here early to prepare with my team, I'd have been there, cheering you on."

"I know and I don't hold it against you." Hunter swept a few strands of my hair behind my ear, his thumb caressing the shell of it. An unexpected frisson chased down my spine. "You're forgiven."

141

I clutched his wrist before he could pull away, pressing my cheek into his palm. "Did you bring me a jersey?"

"Mhm. It's in my car." Then he leaned down to whisper, "What are you drinking?"

The four words fanned over my lips and I found myself licking my bottom one. "Virgin Mojito."

Hunter didn't let go of me but angled his head just enough to tell the awaiting bartender, "I'll have what she's having."

While the bartender made his drink, his brows furrowed as he ran his hand down my neck, down my shoulder, down my arm, until he reached my formed fist and unclenched it, weaving our fingers together.

A deep sense of tranquility curled into my ribcage, right next to my beating heart.

"Why are you so tense?" he rasped. "Are you sure nothing's wrong?"

I didn't want to lie to him, but I wasn't sure if I should speak to him about Franco. But deciding that honesty was the best policy, I ripped the Band-Aid and told him the truth. "My ex is here."

His jaw clenched. "Taylor?"

Taylor hadn't even crossed my mind. Our arrangement was short-lived and barely had an impact on my psyche. Not like Franco. "No—well, he's here too, but that's not who I'm talking about," I said. "My ex-boyfriend from high school. Long story short, we had a really bad breakup. I haven't seen him in years and now he's suddenly back. I hate him."

Hunter's beautiful face morphed into a scowl. "Who is it?"

"His name's Franco. He's here with two guys and talking to a bunch of girls." I tilted my head towards the left, where he was gathered with the rest. "White T-shirt, blue jeans, backwards ball cap."

Hunter's drink arrived and he took a sip while subtly shooting a glance in the direction of Franco, sizing him up.

"Fuck, Gabby, you dated that?" Absentmindedly, his fingers squeezed mine tight enough that I had to caress my fingers slowly down his veiny forearm to get him to alleviate his hold. Cursing under his breath, he softened it. "Sweetheart, you could do so much better. You're a motherfucking ten and he looks like sloppy leftovers."

I guffawed, my mood lightening. "Please, you're amazing for my ego."

"I'm being honest," he grated with so much conviction and disgust on my behalf. I smiled and rubbed a hand against his clenched jaw in hopes of getting him to relax. "You're beautiful and he's a weasel. Why would you ever give him the time of day?"

It was the third time I'd heard Hunter call me beautiful and the compliment never failed to make my insides melt. I'd never been praised like this and though I wasn't completely a vain woman, it was nice hearing it.

"Thank you," I said, despite his rule regarding the T-word. "Trust me, Hunter, I've asked myself that question a hundred times. But he was my first relationship. We dated from fifteen to eighteen, and my frontal lobe wasn't as developed as it is now. That's my only excuse."

The furrow between his brows smoothed and he let loose a puff of air, nodding in understanding. He finished his drink rather quickly and placed it on the bar top. "You want to get out of here?"

Technically, Hera said we only had to be present tonight for two hours and I'd stayed longer than that, so I was good to leave.

I threw a cautionary glance at our surroundings.

My friends were distracted with their game and Oscar was busy staring down at his phone.

And Franco?

His piercing gaze ping-ponged between me and Hunter as if he were trying to comprehend the dynamics of our relationship.

Fuck him.

He had no right to stare at us. No right to spear even the slightest of interest our way.

I wished I could flip him the bird.

But that would be unbecoming in public.

Therefore, I did the only thing I could—the only thing I wanted to—right now.

I grabbed Hunter's hand again. "I thought you'd never ask."

CHAPTER 15

Pegasus & Red-Stained Lips

HUNTER

Soft wind sifted through my sunroof as I drove my Jag down the road, the moon hanging high and bright, chasing us to our destination.

My obsession's eyes were closed, a gorgeous smile on those red lips as she basked in the feeling of the breeze caressing her hair, her manicured nails pushing her strands out of her face and behind her ears.

Gabriela was so precious to me and she didn't even know it.

Whenever I saw her eyes light up with happiness and her entire demeanour shift with excitement at seeing me, this urge to build a haven and safeguard her in it beat at my chest. To ensure that no one got close enough to harm her in any way. But to leave the door unlocked so she could flit in and out as she pleased, knowing she could always return to me.

How was it that I'd lived my whole life until last year without realizing a girl like her existed—one who felt cut from a different cloth but stitched by the same red thread?

We hadn't known each other for a long time, but it felt like I'd known Gabriela forever. Like she was a missing piece from a puzzle I'd been trying to complete for ages.

These last two weeks, I spent every possible waking hour by her side if I wasn't pulled away by my classes, practice, or a football game. I'd gotten so used to her presence that she'd become a part of me—a vital organ I wouldn't be able to live without if she were ever eviscerated from me.

She had so much power over me and she didn't even know that either.

Whenever we were together, I felt possessive over Gabriela in a way that turned my vision red with jealousy. I hated seeing other men stare at her in a manner beyond platonic. Their appreciative once-overs set my teeth on edge. I wanted to be the only man with the privilege to gaze at her. The only one who deserved to command her attention.

I knew it was unhealthy to think this way, but I couldn't stop myself.

And when she mentioned her ex-boyfriend at the bar, that jealousy tunneled through my system like a drug tenfold more potent than anything I'd ever consumed.

He'd touched her, kissed her, fucked her.

I wanted to go over there and punch him in his goddamn face.

I'd always been level-headed, but Gabriela was tearing me apart with longing, yet simultaneously soothing me with her sweetness whenever I was with her.

I had her with me, but I didn't have her in the way that counted.

As all *mine*.

Over the last few days, I'd come to realize that these feelings may not be one-sided. There was a strong possibility that Gabriela felt them too. Why else would she flirt with me? Touch me at every opportunity? Give me those tormented *I-need-you-inside-of-me-Hunter* eyes? It was fucking ruining me.

I needed some concrete answers that *this* was reciprocated. Otherwise, I may just go moon mad like one of those werewolf heroes from her paranormal romances that lost their shit when they couldn't have their fated mates.

And yes, I binged every book she recommended, including the one with the thousand-year-old vampire waiting centuries for his bride.

Entrenched in my musings, I belatedly noticed Gabriela's index finger skimming across my clenched knuckles on the steering wheel.

Goosebumps erupted on my skin at her touch.

"Why are *you* so tense?" she demanded in a sultry voice that hit me below the belt.

I wondered what her fingers would look like cascading down the hard planes of my torso before disappearing under my waistband to grasp my cock.

I bit back a groan. "Not tense."

Just doing everything in my power to avoid picturing what we'd look like fucking raw on my sheets with you tied to my bedframe like a naughty little bad girl.

Those blue eyes shot to me and then to the surroundings blurring in her passenger window, noting the night sky and the trees lining the road on either side. There were no cars going down this route. It was devoid of life except for us.

"Is this the part where you drive us to a ditch and kill me?" Gabriela mused.

My throat tightened uncomfortably. "I'd never hurt you."

The atmosphere in the car shifted from playful to downright dark. I didn't mean for the words to resound with such fervour, but I meant them regardless.

Gabriela's hand slid over my thigh like an olive branch, squeezing gently. "I was kidding, Hunter. I know you'd never hurt me."

I glanced at her, needing reassurance. "Yeah?"

She smiled in that way that made my heart explode. "Yeah."

A complete sucker for her, forgiveness would always be available where she was concerned. Especially when she teased me in what she deemed a harmless manner. Instead of voicing that out loud, I grasped her hand and brought her knuckles to my mouth for a kiss.

Her breath hitched.

Gabriela didn't pull away, letting me shower her soft skin with kisses as I drove. I couldn't stop touching her now that I held her hand. If she'd let me, I'd adorn her with my affection day and night.

"Where are you taking me, pretty boy?"

She'd been such a good girl, sitting in her seat while I told her to trust me.

I rewarded her patience. "Someplace you'll like. I promise."

"Will anyone else be there?"

"Just us, sweetheart. I'm far too greedy to share the sight of you when you look this stunning."

The magnitude of my statement encumbered her, a small sputter leaving her pouty lips before she went fundamentally speechless. Heavy silence punctured the veil of our blissful confab and I inched her a glance, making sure she was fine.

Gabriela stared back at me, eyes flickering with an unnamed emotion. "Hunter…"

Was she not used to hearing how stunning she was? Or—worse— did she not know?

There was no way a girl like her looked in the mirror and didn't realize that she was the epitome of beauty.

Still, I made a mental note to remind her more often how perfect she was to me.

"We're here," I announced before she could say anything more, gravel crunching under my tires as I pulled into a secluded parking lot attached to an old property my family owned. We used to come here all the time during the summer. It was our staycation home. Most of my prominent childhood memories were tied to this place. After my dad passed away, I rarely made the trip. It was too painful.

But it was one of the few places where you had a quintessential vantage point if you wanted to stargaze.

Gabriela frowned. "Where are we?"

"My humble abode." I unbuckled my seatbelt. "Well, one of them. I inherited it once I turned eighteen. It belonged to my dad."

I stepped out of the car and rounded the front to open Gabriela's door.

She ambled out, her head thrown back in awe as she registered the two-storey cottage-style home, shipshape lawn, and wrought iron fence. "This is incredible."

147

I grinned as I pulled out a wicker basket and blanket from my trunk.

When I reached her side, she finally asked, "What are we doing here?"

I offered her my arm. "Having a picnic."

She saw the items in my hand and put two and two together. The cutest smile spread on her face. "Oh."

"Shall we?"

Gabriela tucked her hand in the crook of my elbow and we started walking. I was mindful of her high heels and slowed my strides so she wasn't shuffling after me. I unlocked the gates and we rounded the dark house, heading for the backyard portion, a vast land that faced a spectacular lake.

We passed the wooden deck and the four-season porch, coming to a halt by the edge of the property, where the sound of the rippling water mingled with the crickets in a soothing lullaby.

If you tilted your head back, the scenic sight of the galaxy would greet you, its black tapestry scattered with millions of little stars.

Gabriela watched with acute fascination as I unrolled the blanket on the grass, got down on my knees, opened the wicker basket, and laid out the offerings. A bottle of sparkling juice, a charcuterie board with cheese, crackers, and fruits, and her beloved chocolate-dipped donuts from our favourite bakery.

She had her picnic and she had her stars.

This was the closest I could get to recreating one of her favourite book scenes.

I hoped I did her fantasy justice.

"Hunter." Gabriela's voice wavered at the end as her eyes bounced from where I knelt, lighting two citronella candles to keep the insects away, and towards the stars with astonishment. "I can't believe you did this. I… It's so perfect."

You're perfect. "Come join me."

Gabriela grabbed my outstretched hand and I directed her onto the blanket. She lowered herself in a graceful flourish, then curled into my side like a kitten and kissed my cheek with gratitude.

My heart lurched in my chest, yearning for hers in a cosmic way.

Vision veiled with stardust, all I wanted in this moment was to cup her face and kiss her lips like oxygen wasn't a necessity. I wanted to hug her until her bones, heartbeat, and soul mended with mine in a singular entity.

The depths of feelings I possessed for this girl should have scared me, but I embraced them with openness. If this was what falling entailed, then I was ready to be immersed in the sensation as long as the end result was making her mine.

I couldn't convey these thoughts to Gabriela yet, but I wished that tonight would be a turning point for us—that she'd be willing to take a chance on me.

I wanted her to understand that I was playing for keeps.

Mesmerized by the stars above, Gabriela let out a beatific sigh. "Look at the sky, Hunter. It's beautiful."

I never took my eyes off her. "It is."

She continued watching the stars while I traced her features with my eyes and memorized every detail so it was etched in my mind for years to come.

Her stomach grumbled on cue.

I chuckled.

She smiled sheepishly. "Sorry. I haven't had dinner and I'm starving."

"Eat." I hedged the charcuterie board her way. She picked at it quietly while I popped open the bottle of sparkling juice, poured it into two cups, and handed her one. "If you want something else, let me know. The kitchen inside is fully stocked and I can make you anything you'd like."

"You can cook?" Her brows hiked up right before she popped a few berries in her mouth.

"I'm no chef." I brought the cup to my lips for a sip. "But yes, I can fend for myself."

Impressed, she cocked her head. "What's your specialty?"

"I can make a mean grilled cheese sandwich," I replied. "Do you cook?"

"Yes, and I can make a *mean* lasagna." She grinned and wiggled her eyebrows. "When I can finally move back into my apartment, I'll make you some."

Now I was picturing Gabriela flouncing around in my kitchen bare ass naked, save for a little apron, and the lustful image had my blood rushing south. Fuck. What I wouldn't give for that scenario to be a reality.

"I'd really like that," I said. "How are you feeling with the whole, you know, situation?"

"I'm doing fine. As fine as one can be in my shoes." She leaned her head against my shoulder. "I appreciate you asking and constantly checking in on me."

It was the least I could do. I wrapped my arm around her shoulders and she burrowed her lissome figure into my side, seeking warmth when the strong wind blew towards us. I had an extra blanket in the basket, but I was afraid that if I gave it to her, she wouldn't need the heat of my body. "You think Oscar told your dad that you're missing?"

Her bodyguard was probably losing his mind since we'd made a quick escape from the bar, but Gabriela insisted she didn't want him following. Not tonight. She said she felt safe enough lately to escape his overbearing presence for less than a handful of hours.

"God, no. He's probably terrified of telling him that he was distracted with his phone and didn't see me slip out of the bar," Gabriela said. "But I did send my parents a text in our group chat that I'm hanging out with you. They know I'm in good hands and probably alerted Oscar by now."

They know I'm in good hands.

I was honoured to know she felt safe with me.

I'd protect her with every fiber of my being.

"I'd never let anything happen to you," I rasped.

"I know," she murmured with a lopsided smile.

Fuck, I wanted to kiss her so bad. I was about to do it, but then she turned her attention back to the sky. "It's so peaceful here."

I searched for the particular stars that were supposed to be visible tonight. Spotting what I was looking for, I pointed at it. "I think that's the constellation Pegasus, named after the winged horse from Greek mythology."

"Wow…" she trailed off and I marvelled at the way her face morphed with wonder. Her head snapped my way and she nudged me with her elbow. "Hey, Hunter?"

"Yes, doll?"

"You mentioned enjoying Greek mythology and I know nothing about it." Gabriela clasped my hand, the pulses at our wrists touching each other. "Tell me one of your favourite stories."

The fact that she wanted to learn more about me the same way I thirsted to learn more about her made my heart glow like a hundred fireflies trapped in a jar.

I reflected for a moment, wondering which story would appease her romantic heart. Perhaps she'd enjoy the renowned myth of Hero and Leander. "I have one, but it has a tragic ending."

"Most beautiful things do," she said wistfully. "Hit me with it."

Clearing my throat, I started recounting the tale, "Hero, priestess of Aphrodite—the goddess of love—and Leander, a young man, fell in love and had a secret relationship. They lived on opposite ends of the Hellespont Strait. Every night, he swam across it to be with her. And every night, Hero lit a torch in her tower to help guide him towards her." I mapped the curve of Gabriela's soft jaw with my pointer finger, tipping her head back so I could gaze into her blue eyes. "Their relationship bloomed during the warmer months, but when the weather got colder, they agreed to halt seeing each other until spring. But one winter night, Leander saw the torch lit in Hero's tower again. Desperate to see his beloved, he tried swimming to her. Halfway through his journey, a gust of wind blew out her light…And Leander lost his way, drowning. Legend has it, when Hero saw Leander's dead body in the water, she threw herself from her tower to be with him for all eternity."

A gasp escaped Gabriela. "*No.*"

"I told you it was tragic."

Her bottom lip stuck out almost sullenly. "That's incredibly sad."

I kissed her forehead, inhaling her vanilla and red roses scent. "Hero and Leander's myth has been culturally referenced many times over the years."

"I can see why," Gabriela muttered. "It must be the forbidden love aspect."

I toyed with the ends of her red hair. "Mhm."

"What got you interested in Greek mythology in the first place?"

I glanced at the water before us, glistening like a dark bejeweled surface. "My older sister, Heidi, had a best friend named Donovan. He used to read a lot of classics and mythology. When I turned ten, Don gifted me a comprehensive book on Greek mythology for my birthday. I must have read that book from front to back at least twenty times. Along with my dad, Don was one of the male figures in my life that I always looked up to."

Gabriela smiled. "How sweet."

"After my dad died, Donovan sort of stepped up," I said, "He'd come to all my football games and take me out to pizza parlours afterwards the same way my dad did. He'd watch action movies with me every week, without once seeming bothered to be spending time with his best friend's kid brother."

"I'm glad you had someone like that in your life." Gabriela squeezed my hand. "Donovan sounds like a great person."

"He is." Donovan was one of the most honourable men I'd had the privilege of knowing. Which was why him leaving the city years ago was such a harsh pill to swallow. He was no longer part of our lives, but he'd left his mark on me and Heidi, and it was something I'd always be grateful for. "Do you ever feel like you were born missing something because you were meant to find it later in life? I feel like I never had a brother because I was meant to have Donovan as mine."

The same way I felt like I was missing Gabriela my whole life without even realizing it…and here she was, in the flesh, the living personification of all my desires and dreams.

Gabriela's face softened. "Yes. That's how I feel about Anna and Layla. Though I'm an only child, I never felt like I didn't have siblings because I had them since childhood. They're my found family. We may not share a drop of blood, but they're my sisters in every way that matters. I'm lucky to have them."

"They're lucky to have you too." I glided my fingers through her hair and she shivered when my knuckles grazed her back. Feeling bold, I added, "And so am I."

The particles of the air hovering between us charged with an electrifying energy. Gabriela appeared angelic under the glow of the stars, and her eyes gleamed characteristically with desperate need. My expression no doubt mirrored hers.

I was about to lean over and fuse her mouth with mine, but she broke the heady eye contact and glanced down at our joined hands instead, biting her lip.

Dejectedness swirled in the pit of my stomach.

Did Gabriela not feel this deep connection pulsating whenever we were in the same vicinity?

There were times when I thought Gabriela wanted more with me but was holding herself back, hiding behind the guise of being friends. If I weren't so perceptive where she was concerned, making it my goddamn mission to study her, I may have missed the signs.

But they were there.

I didn't know what was holding her back, but I intended to find out soon.

Instead of vocalizing those thoughts, I dug into the wicker basket for the gifts I bought her.

A football jersey, a novel, and a rose-petaled resin bookmark.

"Here." I plucked them out and placed them into her lap. "For you."

Surprised, Gabriela let go of my hand to unravel the jersey and traced the number nine with her fingers. "You got me your jersey."

"I said I would, Gabby." I'd never break a promise to her.

"Oh, and a book." She flipped it around to face the front, her eyes flaring in recognition. It was one of her favourite stories—the same one with the vampire lord and his mortal bride that inspired tonight's date. She thumbed through the pages, gasping. "Hunter, you annotated this?"

Was that the wrong thing to do? I'd gotten into the habit of annotating my books because of school in order to be prepared for assignments and I occasionally did the same with the books I read for leisure.

She assessed me with an indescribable expression and heat smattered across my face.

"Yes," I admitted. "I highlighted my favourite passages and left notes in the margins regarding my thoughts."

I enjoyed this book, even though I initially read it with the sole intention of better understanding Gabriela. I wanted to know what it was about this romance story that stood out to her so profoundly. Four hundred pages later, I got it.

It was the attentiveness of the hero. His ability to constantly prioritize the heroine. To give her everything she could possibly want and need, to communicate eloquently and validate her feelings, to shower her with all the attention she'd never received, and to simply worship her as she was a gift from the heavens that he'd treasure forever.

Gabriela Regina Bellafiore wanted to be treated like a goddess, to be the center of her lover's universe, to be someone's damnation and salvation in one.

God as my witness, if she'd give me the chance, I'd cherish her for all of eternity.

"Hunter, this…" She shook her head, oscillating between shock and awe. "I've never received anything so lovely and thoughtful. I can't believe you read this book. I can't believe you brought me to stargaze. I can't believe you—" She paused when the bookmark I'd carefully nestled between the pages fell out. Grabbing it, she studied the crushed rose petals and gold flecks glittering in its clear surface, her expression of appreciation growing even further. "Is that—"

"I made it," I rushed out. "From the roses you gifted me."

Gabriela's gaze fastened on mine, brimming with a myriad of emotions that spoke to something deep inside of me.

I held my breath, anticipating her response like a man gone to battle waiting weeks for a letter from his beloved. Desperate to read her written words. Desperate to hear her lilting voice in his mind. Desperate for the anchor only she could provide.

"Why?" she whispered almost challengingly. "Why did you do this?"

Without looking away from her, I said in a ragged voice, "You know why, Gabriela."

Gentle fingers caressed the stubble on my jaw before cupping my cheek. I leaned into her touch, letting her see all the reverence painted on my face.

"I like you," I confessed in a murmur and let my thumb stroke over her cheek. "I think I've liked you since the first moment I laid eyes on you over a year ago, when I knew nothing about you...except for the fact that you were the most beautiful girl I'd ever seen."

Gabriela's hypnotizing eyes widened at my admission.

My heart thundered in my chest. "It's the truth."

One second, she stared at me like I was unreal.

The next second, she closed the distance and stamped her mouth to mine with a needy sound that caused heat to scorch my insides.

A groan climbed up my throat.

Our lips parted and our eyes met for the briefest second as though acknowledging that we'd been foolish to assume this wouldn't happen again.

Then our mouths collided once more like magnets, harder and needier.

Her kiss tasted sweet and of something that was uniquely Gabriela. I practically devoured her lips with my demanding kisses and frantic licks. Her tongue swept against mine almost teasingly, a languid erotic dance that set me aflame.

I felt dizzy and breathless from what the hot little minx was doing to me, wrenching open my ribcage, gazing into my heart, making room for herself, and slowly settling there like I was something to be possessed and owned.

For Gabriela, I was.

Wholly and unequivocally ready to be made hers.

I wrapped my fingers against that slim column just the way she liked and clenched lightly, relishing her sexy gasp. Gabriela's fingers twisted in the collar of my shirt, holding me hostage, as if I had any plans to ever escape her clutches.

Hook, line, sinker, this siren had ensnared me.

Using my arm, I curved it around her back and dragged her astride into my lap without once breaking our lip-lock. Her weight against me was divine, namely when she sat against my bulge, giving an experimental buck of her hips like she wanted to feel me inside of her.

I was losing control, at the end of my sanity rope. I needed to know what she wanted from me. Some kisses. A few fingers. My tongue. Or my dick pounding away inside that tight little pussy.

Right now, I was game for all of it.

Fisting her hair, I jerked her head back but kept my hold on her neck. "I'm barely hanging by a thread." I panted. "What are we doing?"

She was panting too. "Being *friendly*."

I nearly growled, slapping her ass and inciting a half moan, half sob from her. "Don't play with me, Gabby."

"Why?" She squared her arms around my shoulders and leaned in for another sensual kiss, nearly sucking the soul out of my body. "I thought we were friends, Hunt."

We were the furthest thing from friends and based on her playful tone, she knew it too. But it seemed she enjoyed toying with me. Fucking brat.

"Friends aren't supposed to know the way you kiss, touch..." I nipped her bottom lip. "Or taste."

"Maybe," she mumbled seductively. "We're the kind of friends who do."

I let loose a deep groan when she planted hurried kisses down my jaw and along my neck, stopping momentarily to bite me before soothing the sting with a lick. I was in heaven and hell all at once. "Fuck, tell me what you want from me while I'm still thinking straight, baby."

Judging by the way her breath hitched, she liked it when I called her *baby*.

Gabriela raised her face back to mine, lips pulled into a wicked smile and her bewitching gaze glittering as if all the starlight was sucked out of the sky and reflected in her depths. "I want you to stop thinking and kiss me, pretty boy."

CHAPTER 16

Starlit Tryst

GABRIELA

Hunter didn't need to be told twice.

Swimming with thick lust, his half-mast eyes closed right before his mouth latched onto mine with the hottest groan ever.

The sound of nature echoed around us—the whistling wind, the rustling trees, the volatile waves—as we kissed with an aggressive quality stemming from weeks' worth of pent-up sexual frustration. His tantalizing cologne and taste kept my senses company like a newly acclimated lover. My fingers left his stubbled cheeks and delved into his long hair, removing the band holding it together so I could knuckle fistfuls of his black strands.

I held him to me as we made out hungrily. The moans that left me when his tongue twined with mine should have embarrassed me, but I was far too turned on to care.

Hunter's big palms travelled south to grip my writhing hips, helping me grind against him, rewarding me with the kind of auditory experience filled with delicious pleas and groans that I would remember the next time I was alone and naked in my bed, playing with myself to the thought of him.

Hunter emitted a soft, hoarse noise when I tugged his bottom lip between my teeth before we went back to kissing like the world around us was ending.

I seemed to affect this man on a cellular level, the same way he seemed to affect me like no one in my past ever had. I practically vibrated the second he entered my orbit, helplessly drawn to him.

He was my moon and I was his tides.

This night was magical and our kisses cathartic, erasing all the lines I drew around me like a protective circle. My walls down and my emotions bare for him.

If Hunter looked into my eyes right now, he'd see inside my soul.

He'd see everything that I wanted and everything that stopped me from going all the way with him. And yet, against my better judgement, here I was, allowing myself to be gathered in the cradle of his strong arms like I was the cynosure of his world.

"Gabriela." He panted ever so lightly when we pulled away to breathe, our mouths joined by a ribbon of saliva. The tip of his tongue flicked over the tiny gem on my canine and I gasped, my own breathing laboured. "Is a kiss all you want?"

I couldn't even lie if I wanted to. "No, I want…more."

"Be specific."

He was going to make me spell it out.

Damn me if I didn't love it when he got demanding.

"I want you to touch me." My arms tightened their hold around his shoulders as I ground our cores together to make him understand what I meant. The gesture elicited a rough grunt from his throat. "Please. Even if it's only for tonight."

The hand holding and stolen glances weren't enough to tide me over until the next sunrise. I needed this—*him*—so badly.

If Hunter was bothered by the fact that I said *only for tonight*, he didn't comment on it. Though the slight narrowing of his eyes spoke volumes. My heart and soul were no longer a currency I bartered with, unfortunately.

My body was the only thing I was willing to give.

If Hunter wanted it, he could have it.

Against my lips, he murmured, "Why, baby?"

God, the word *baby* in his deep, husky voice was so perfect. I could listen to it on an endless loop. That and *sweetheart* and *doll* and every other term of endearment he bestowed upon me.

"You know why," I mumbled, my face flushed with warmth.

He'd already given me so much tonight with the picturesque date, plucked straight from my dreams. The picnic, the presents, the stars. It was everything to me. I'd cherish this night even when I was old and grey, remembering that there was someone, once in my life, who'd given me something so monumental.

This beautiful man had treated me so kindly and I was still processing the magnitude of this action. I would probably continue to do so for days to come.

Ending the night by giving in to this insane attraction that had been budding since the moment on the terrace many moons ago would be the cherry on top of the cake.

And maybe it was selfish of me to ask for a little bit more, but I couldn't help it.

Especially when I knew Hunter was on the same page as me. I could feel the evidence of his growing arousal between the juncture of my thighs. It was thick, hard, and from what I felt, so fucking *big*.

He wanted this just as bad as I did.

"Tell me." He dropped pecks along my jawline until he reached the skin behind my ear, where the cursive **R** tattoo for my queen moniker was inked. He kissed it and whispered in my ear, "I want to hear you say it, Gabriela."

I was unravelling at the ends like a loose ribbon. I wanted him. I needed him. There was no more lying, no more hiding. He had to know the truth.

"Because"—I choked on a moan when he bit the skin at the underside of my jaw and tilted my head back, granting him access to my neck so he could continue showering me with his intoxicating kisses—"when I'm lying in my sheets at night, it's *you* I think about as I touch myself." He

159

froze and I grasped his face, letting him see the sincerity in my expression. "And I always come so hard, Hunter." I brushed his lips with mine. "Every. Single. Time."

The atmosphere shifted with something utterly carnal.

I had a split second to witness the darkening in Hunter's eyes and the clenching of his jaw before he flipped us over in a smooth movement. I landed on my back and he hovered on top of me, pinning me under the weight of his muscles.

"Fuck, baby," he growled, drinking my gasp with a hot kiss. "You want to hear a secret?"

I wanted to hear all his secrets. "Y-yes."

His stubble tickled my cheek as he dragged his lips across my skin before positioning them at my ear to avow, "I do the same every night, fucking myself to your memory before falling asleep and dreaming of you."

My head spun with the imagery of Hunter's naked, mouth-watering body stretched in his bed, the sheets bunched around his waist, his cock wrapped in his fist as he fucked himself earnestly.

I yanked on his hair until his face rose above mine once more, his barrel chest bowing with his inhales and exhales.

"Show me," I said. "I want to see."

The glow from the citronella candles eliminated some of the shadows on his face, and his eyes widened at my request. A feral quality overtook his features right before he kissed me hard like a man who'd reached the end of his rope.

His deep groans and my soft moans melted together in a chorus that rivalled the song of the crashing waves beyond us. I felt like I was drowning underwater with only Hunter as my lifeline. I held him tight, my legs wrapped around his waist and my heels crossing over his back. His hands twisted in my hair as he sipped from my mouth greedily, his hips rocking between mine in a motion that made me see stars behind my closed lids, my very own constellation ignited by this extraordinary man.

My body was on fire and my clit throbbed, every thrust of his bulge against my thong-covered pussy pushing me to a new precipice. My restless fingers dove for the buttons of his shirt, undoing them in record time.

Hunter pushed away enough to allow me to rip his black dress shirt down his arms, his muscles flexing with the motion. When he sat back on his knees, the candles momentarily flickered as a light breeze sailed past before they settled into their full flame and allowed me to stare my fill.

I raised myself on my elbows and blinked a few times, my jaw falling slack.

Oh. My. God.

Tan skin stretched across thick and defined muscles formed from years of athletic training. That silver barbell nipple piercing was the hottest thing I'd ever seen. It was begging to be licked and sucked by yours truly. My eyes continued tracing the creases of his six-pack, ignoring the urge to map the indentations with my tongue before honing in on his brawny arms. Specifically the left one, tatted with the realistic-looking snake wrapping from his wrist all the way to his broad shoulder. It was so vivid, beautiful, and otherworldly. And then my eyes strayed down to the prominent V of his hip bones, remembering he mentioned having a thigh tat. My heart pounded at the beginning peeks of dark ink disappearing into his low-slung pants. I had to physically hold back from undoing his button and zipper to unveil the rest...and finally have my first look at his cock too, which I had no doubt was just as wonderful as the rest of him.

With his desire-fueled eyes fanned by long lashes, his black hair falling down to his shoulders in thick waves, and his herculean body kneeling before me, he oozed sheer animal magnetism and appeared larger than life. Like a sex god crafted straight from my romantic tales, he overshadowed everything in our surroundings until all I saw was *him*.

Hunter was a masterpiece.

Never in my life had I come across a man of this calibre, his physicality only a shard composing his overall magnificence. Though I'd only been acquainted with small parts of it, I knew it was his heart that made him all the more beautiful to me.

"Like what you see?" he murmured after a few seconds of me ogling him.

I sighed and mapped my hands over his chest, relishing the shiver coursing through his frame. "Yes. You're the most perfect thing to ever exist, Hunter."

"No." He grabbed my hands with both of his and brought my knuckles to his lips for a kiss filled with gratitude and longing. "*You* are the most perfect thing to ever exist."

It was a shame I'd lived two whole decades before stumbling across a man who was a combination of genuinely sweet, thoroughly mindful, and filthy hot. Now I had this need to wrap Hunter up in my arms and never let him go...And it sucked because he wasn't mine to begin with. Still, I pretended he was for tonight and bantered back, "Guess we'll just have to agree that we're both perfect and call it a truce, huh?"

Hunter smiled and drew my hand over his cheek like he was famished for my touch, nuzzling my palm lines. "Guess so, doll."

How was I ever going to protect my heart around him?

When Hunter bit the pad of my thumb in a playful, wolfish way, I was reminded of the faint ache in my core needing to be satiated. Using my free hand, I roved it down his washboard-worthy abs until I palmed his tented groin with intention.

A groan rumbled out of him.

"Take it off, pretty boy," I urged softly. "And let me see how you fuck yourself."

With the grace of a feline, Hunter moved fluidly to cover my body with his, the chain around his neck winking in the darkness and grazing against the swells of my breasts. "You first. Show me how you play with your little pussy, Gabby," he ordered, stealing a quick kiss. "And if you finish with my name on your lips, I'll give you a reward."

Fuck, he had no business being this sexy.

"What if I forget to say your name?" I arched a saucy brow, testing him.

"If you don't follow my rule, you don't get to see anything." His hands wandered down to the hemline of my dress. "But you're a good girl. You'll do as I say, won't you, baby?"

Oh, I feared I'd be anything this man asked of me. A good girl or a nasty slut. I was so gone for Hunter that I'd give him anything he desired.

Only for tonight, I reminded myself. "Y-yes."

"Now take this dress off, Gabby. I want you naked."

I realized putting on a show was kind of our thing. Whether in private or public. And unbeknownst to Hunter, I had a little bit of an exhibitionist streak.

I licked my lips. "Help me?"

Again, he didn't need to be told twice. Some part of me wondered if he had a side—along with his dominant one—that fancied being told what to do.

Hunter dragged my minidress over my thighs, my hips, my waist, my chest, until he was able to pull it off in one swoop. He was so gentle with me. As if I were made of glass and a special gift that he had to handle delicately.

Now that I was practically naked except for my thong, Hunter froze. If it weren't for his faint breathing, I'd think he was a marble statue.

"Fucking hell," he finally whispered, entranced. His palms drew over the curves of my body like a potter appreciating a fine creation. "Every inch of you is so goddamn beautiful. You're divine, Gabriela."

I swooned. I was in good shape, took care of myself, and loved knowing Hunter appreciated my efforts.

"Like what you see?" I returned, taking both his hands and moulding them to my jutting breasts.

"Oh, yeah." Hunter groaned, feeling the shape and weight of me in his hands. He used his thumbs and pointer fingers to toy with my pebbled nipples. It was my turn to moan. "How does it feel to be one of God's favourites?"

An unexpected chuckle burst out of me, broken by my choked whimper when he pinched my nipples and tugged. "G-great, actually. Thanks for asking."

He grinned roguishly as he recalled our past exchange. It seemed eons ago, instead of a handful of weeks. Even then, I think I knew that our story was just beginning. The kiss on the dance floor wasn't the end. It was the catalyst that pushed everything into place.

Souls at the mercy of fate, Hunter and I were meant to intertwine— to be in each other's lives for as long as the universe deemed fit. And hopelessly, I wished it were for a long time coming.

"When did you get this?" Hunter thumbed my heart-shaped belly ring.

It was a spur-of-the-moment decision. "When I turned eighteen."

He bit his bottom lip. "It's cute. I like it."

"Look at you lavishing me with compliments. Careful or you'll inflate my ego to astronomical levels."

"Can't help it. I like everything about you. Even the parts I have yet to learn."

I sucked in a sharp breath, caught between excitement and fear. That statement sounded serious, like this wasn't *only just tonight* for him. I knew Hunter felt something for me—the same *something* I felt for him, but this wasn't a forever thing. We needed to have an expiry date. Because I wasn't a long-term girl. Not anymore. And I'd never want to hurt him by giving him false hope.

I readied myself to speak, but the words evaporated when Hunter brought two fingers to my lips and dipped them past the seam.

"Suck, baby."

I swirled my tongue around his digits before sucking hard, my own lust spiking when his strong body jerked from my touch.

Spellbound, I watched him drag his wet fingers in veneration down my chin, my neck, the valley between my breasts, and down my stomach until he paused at the edge of my hunter green thong. "I love this colour on you."

"I wore it because of you."

Hunter dropped a low *fuck* under his breath. "Did you wear the dress for me too?"

I nodded, suddenly feeling shy. "Yes."

"Good girl," he rasped, sounding like he'd make me sorry if the answer were anything but. "Raise your hips for me so I can take off this soaked little thong."

My heart beat erratically as I obeyed his command. Hunter's fingers tucked into the sides of my thong and slowly drew the material down my legs, ensuring that it didn't snag in my heels. Then he split my knees apart and pushed my thighs back until I was obscenely splayed open for him on the blanket.

His blue eyes devoured my most intimate flesh, his mouth parting in amazement like he'd never seen anything like me. His finger lazily slid over my mound, outlining the neatly trimmed landing strip. "I wondered if you were a real redhead."

I trembled when he dipped his finger into my slit, coating it with my wetness. "I-I'm real."

"Hm, that you are." He sucked his finger into his mouth. "Fuck, you taste so good, Gabby."

I was wetter than I'd ever been and we'd barely gotten started. "Hunter, I want…"

He knew what I wanted.

It was written all over my face.

Him.

His lips. His tongue. His fingers.

But the dark smirk on his face let me know he'd torture me before giving me what I really wanted.

Hunter grabbed my right hand and brought it over my pussy. "Play with yourself, doll. Put on a show for me."

I was having an out-of-body experience. Like this moment between myself and the man who embodied all my fantasies never occurred and it was all a figment of my imagination.

The candles lit up our small bubble almost in a sacrosanct manner, shining just enough light for me to see my fingers dance over my wet pussy, collecting my arousal.

Keeping my eyes riveted on Hunter, I touched myself, rubbing my clit and moaning as lust built in my core and zinged through my veins like liquid fire. "Oh, God."

"My name, baby. Otherwise, I won't give you what you want." Hunter circled one veiny hand around my throat in a primitive, domineering way. "And we both know you need me to eat your sweet cunt like it's my goddamn job."

"*Hunter.*" I moaned as his other hand got busy tweaking my nipples, alternating between pinching and slapping the rosy peaks. I liked a little bit of pain with sex. Hunter knew it too, based on the way he licked his lips in hunger, watching pleasure wash over me.

Eyeing my pussy as I rubbed circles around my throbbing bud, he growled, "Do you only touch your clit, Gabriela?"

I shook my head, pinching my clit lightly. "S-sometimes I like to ride my hand." I whimpered. "Or use dildos."

Hunter's nostrils flared, the hand collaring my neck tightening. "Yeah?"

I bet he'd like seeing me use my toys.

"Y-yeah." I bit my lip to tame my sounds, my orgasm surmounting.

"Put a finger in your pussy." His deep tenor dripped with arrogance and control that just did it for me. "Fuck yourself."

"I want you to fuck me with *your* fingers."

Hunter grabbed the underside of my tit in a rough squeeze and tutted. "Don't demand like a brat. *Ask* like a good girl, Gabriela."

I closed my eyes and whispered, "*Please.*"

"You want me to finger your cunt, little doll?"

"Tongue it too," I added shamelessly, pausing my fingers on my clit long enough to say, "I also got tested recently and I'm negative. Please, Hunter. I'll do anything to feel your mouth on me."

"Fuck," Hunter cursed, his tongue peeking out to lick his bottom lip like he'd been dreaming of tasting me…and I'd just handed him the golden ticket to the lotto. "How can I deny you when you beg so sweetly?" He grabbed my hands and made me cup the back of my knees, demanding, "Hold yourself open for me. Good girl. Just like that, Gabby."

Every cell in my body shook with anticipation as I observed Hunter lower himself between me, his face lining with my pussy and his big palms skating over my inner thighs, making sure I remained spread for him like a feast.

His warm breath fanned over my swollen flesh and I released a breathy noise, unable to take any more waiting. It was so hot the way his face darkened with lust, the way his jaw clenched, the way his stormy eyes collided with mine.

"If I do something you don't like, tell me. I'll stop," he said. "And if I do something you like, tell me so I *don't* stop. Understood?"

I swallowed. "Yes."

Hunter's tongue flicked out and the flat of it glided slowly between my slit, tasting my cum like I was the finest meal at a five-star establishment before settling on my clit with a low, satisfied growl.

I jerked with a whine and my entire body arched under the stroke of his tongue, my heels coming to rest on his broad shoulders.

Hunter chuckled lazily at my reaction and scooped handfuls of my ass, dragging me closer to him and canting my hips for his ministrations. I rose on my elbows, the angle giving me the perfect view as he got straight to work. He began with slow flicks against my clit, gauging my reaction. I moaned in encouragement. Emboldened, Hunter increased his pace, licking me like a ravenous man, making my core clench and my toes curl.

"Hunter." I whimpered on a particular swipe of his tongue. "M-more."

"You like that, sweetheart?"

A breathy moan and my feet digging into his shoulders were my reply. I loved having my pussy eaten and Hunter was doing a great job at making me lose my mind. My orgasm crested again.

But suddenly, he stopped.

I nearly wailed from frustration.

*Why, why, why…*I wanted to come so bad and I wanted to come *now*.

Hunter raised his head and met my half-assed glare. "Then tell me," he grated, lips and chin glistening with me. "Say the words." He kissed my clit. "Am I pleasing you?"

167

Oh, this one might have a praise kink. Just like me. "You're doing amazing, baby."

He liked being called baby too, it seemed.

Hunter's mouth fell back on my pussy, gratified with my statement. The air erupted with filthy pussy-eating sounds and his appreciative hums, blending with my needy moans. He was so vocal when he licked and sucked, like this wasn't only for my pleasure but his own too.

He was fully enraptured in the task, maintaining heady eye contact and showing me just how much he was enjoying my cunt.

"Hunter." I gasped when his finger breached my opening. "Keep going. *Please.* You're such a good boy. *My* pretty boy."

He. Fucking. Moaned.

My praise had him thrusting two thick fingers inside in a controlled and unhurried pace, fucking my pussy in tandem with his tongue, hitting all my spots. I cried out, knuckling the strands at his crown and tugging like a leash, practically riding his mouth like a wanton slut. "Yes. Yes. Yes."

If he dared to stop now, I was never going to forgive him.

He had no intentions, though, if the heated glint in his eyes was any indication. He roved his free hand over my stomach and breasts until it locked around my throat again like a manacle, the possessive clench enough to cause my exhale to stutter.

I was on cloud nine.

It was ironic how Hunter had Saint as a middle name, yet pleasured me like a deviant god whose sole existence revolved around bringing me to orgasm.

The combination of his heathen tongue, sinful fingers, and stubble rasping against my pussy was skyrocketing me to a new height. I fisted the picnic blanket underneath me as he kept polishing my clit and caressing my inner walls like a man on a mission. My mind buzzed with the sounds of my squelching arousal, Hunter's masculine groans, and my sobbing pleas.

I was there.

Right there.

And suddenly, it happened.

I came long and hard on a screaming moan. "*Hunter.*"

The release was so powerful, I no longer remembered where I began and where I ended. Distinctly, I felt Hunter withdraw his fingers from my contracting flesh and suck them into his mouth. His tongue went back to collect the evidence of my earth-shattering orgasm from my pussy and inner thighs. And his voice reverberated against me in something praise-like, but I was far too gone to register the words.

I was panting, slowly floating back to reality with tears leaking from the corners of my eyes. Completely sated and spent, I lay before him, throbbing. The cool breeze fondled my flushed skin like a balm and I unwove my fingers from Hunter's hair.

Feeling his devilish smile on my pussy, I opened my eyes just in time to see him kissing my skin in worship.

"Good girl." *Kiss.* "You followed my rule." *Kiss.* "I'm so proud of you."

My pulse was showing no signs of slowing down, fully enamoured with this man and the affection he doled out. I wanted so desperately to call him mine, even though I knew it wasn't meant to be. Yet I couldn't help but imagine a world where we were together—a world that wouldn't get ruined by my shortcomings and flaws.

"I've never seen anything more beautiful than you coming." He crawled over my body, peppering kisses as he journeyed up, pausing momentarily to kiss my nipples tenderly as though apologizing for his earlier rough treatment. God, I adored him. Hunter cupped my face and stared down at me, softness flickering in his eyes. "Thank you for giving me the honour."

I wanted to cry. No man had ever cared to put my pleasure above his. And no man had ever beheld me the way Hunter did. Like I was the center of his entire being.

I opened my mouth to speak, but no sound emerged.

There weren't enough words in the language to communicate what I felt in this moment.

Right now, I was unarmed with no control. Hunter had all of it, whether he realized it or not. He'd altered me in a way where I would never be the same again. First with his kiss, second with his kindness, third with his sweetness, fourth with his ability to always be there for me, and fifth with his need to please me in every way a man could please a woman.

Everyone else would pale in comparison to this once-in-a-lifetime individual, who was warm like the sun and shined bright like the stars in the sky above us.

Brushing his wet lips against mine, Hunter asked in a heated voice, "Have you ever tasted yourself?"

I blushed. "No."

He grabbed my jaw in a possessive grip, parted my lips, and kissed me sloppily, letting my flavour infuse between our palates. A soft noise rumbled in the back of my throat as our tongues twined in the nastiest, sexiest kiss of my life.

I feared I was completely addicted to Hunter.

He wrapped his arms around my body and we continued exchanging wet kisses. My fingers trickled over the skin of his muscular back, massaging him. I'd never felt smaller or so protected from the harms of the outside world. Resting in his strong embrace came with the sensation of invincibility, like nothing could ever come close to hurting me. Not if I had him by my side.

"Since I was a good girl, can I have my reward now?" I asked as he planted small kisses all over my face in adoration, breaking another one of my walls. "Please, Hunter. I want to touch you too."

"Gabby, I need you to know that while I'm grateful the night led us here, I didn't bring you here with any ulterior motive. I just wanted to make you happy with something you never had before." He kissed my cheek. "I don't want you to feel obligated to give me anything because I gave you something."

I smiled, knowing that was the absolute truth. He was just that kind of person. He'd give but rarely take anything in return. That's why I needed to do this. "I know, but let me anyway?"

"Whenever you smile at me like that…there's nothing I wouldn't give you," he said, taking my hands and putting them over his bulge. "Go ahead. Touch me, sweetheart. I'm all yours."

I'm all yours. I'm all yours. I'm all yours.

I loved hearing those words from him. The serene atmosphere rang with notes of eagerness as my fingers undid his belt buckle.

"You should know." He grunted a little when my hand dipped under the waistband of his black briefs. "I've imagined this moment a hundred times in my mind, but nothing comes close to—*fuck*—baby, you're going to kill me."

My fingers had closed around his long, thick, and pulsing cock. Eyes wide and lips parted, I stared at him in shock. I knew it was going to be big.

Just not *this* big.

Holy shit. Sex with this man would be phenomenal once I adjusted to his size.

A bead of pre-cum was gathered over his flared head and my thumb swiped over it, watching his eyes roll back into his skull from my touch. "My God, Hunter. You're huge—"

Suddenly, a feminine shriek boomed through the air, cutting off my words and causing us both to flinch. "Get away from her, you asshole!"

Then another one chimed in, "We have a taser!"

Next thing I knew, a bejewelled pink bag smacked Hunter's head and he groaned in pain, falling on top of me, while I let loose a bloodcurdling scream.

CHAPTER 17

Just Friends

GABRIELA

I wanted to crawl six feet beneath the ground and never return to the land of the living.

Currently, we were inside Hunter's home, gathered on the ground floor, where the kitchen, dining, and living room were amassed together in a beautiful open concept. I barely had the chance to admire the rustic décor accented with gorgeous hues of browns, greens, and golds because I was too focused on the four unwelcomed guests watching Hunter and me with hawk eyes.

Embarrassment pinkened my cheeks. Mustering a mild glare, I cleared my throat with intention. They had the decency to avert their gazes and pretend like the ceiling and floor were more interesting than anything else happening in this moment.

"Does it hurt?" I whispered to Hunter, dabbing the cold compress against his bruising temple as I stood between the parted V of his legs.

He was sitting on a kitchen bar stool, his hand resting on the small of my back.

"I'm okay, sweetheart," he replied.

The *sweetheart* had Layla and Anna gasping in unison.

Josh and Sam—a really good friend of the boys' and another player on the football team—didn't attempt to hide their shit-eating grins.

I groaned internally.

Josh was the first to break the awkward silence, combing frustrated fingers through his dark hair. "If your little stunt"—he aimed narrowed eyes at Layla and Anna—"costs us the championship trophy, I'm never forgiving you girls."

Both my best friends broke out into rambling explanations slash apologies.

Long story short, Layla and Anna finally arrived at MacGregor after I left. Oscar came up to them, freaking out and saying that I'd disappeared into thin air. The girls panicked, thinking the same intruder who broke into my place had kidnapped me. Because I always shared my location with them, they decided to track me down in an attempt to save me. They texted Josh about the situation, who just happened to arrive at the bar with Sam. Then all four of them, alongside Oscar, decided to hop on a rescue mission like my personal brigade.

The girls reached the property first. They heard my screams—which they realized afterwards was me orgasming loud enough for the entire neighbourhood to hear—and followed the sound until they found us in the backyard. Thinking that Hunter was my kidnapper and attacking me, Anna smacked her sturdy rhinestone bag across his face, causing him to fall on top of me from the unforeseen swat.

Then Layla proceeded to actually tase him.

It was only when they rolled over his big, heaving body with kicks and feeble punches that they realized *who* it was and *what* was happening between us.

They'd interrupted my most romantic date, saw me in my birthday suit, and nearly knocked out Hunter cold. Their regret was palpable, but the damage was already done. I'd put my clothes back on quickly and shoved Hunter's limbs into his dress shirt, right as the others reached the premises.

Under different circumstances, I'd find the entire thing comedic.

Safe to say, my post-orgasm happiness had exploded to smithereens, replaced by shame and anxiety.

Clearly, my parents hadn't alerted Oscar that I was with Hunter. Otherwise, we may have been able to avoid this whole situation.

"Josh, it's okay, they were just looking out for Gabby," Hunter spoke in a gravelly voice, coming to the defence of his so-called assailants. "I'm fine."

"Do you think you'll be fine for the next game?" Sam countered.

Layla and Anna shrank when Josh stared at them pointedly. Hunter was the university's star quarterback and a vital part of the team. The Panthers were on the brink of a championship and tonight could have jeopardized the entire thing.

My shoulders sagged, understanding both sides.

My best friends truly were the most loyal and ride-or-die girls, and I really did love them. No matter what, they'd always have my back. But I also sympathized with the boys' situation. They'd been running on a high this season. They couldn't afford to lose Hunter right now.

"Yeah." Hunter grunted a little when he straightened his posture, his muscles probably still feeling the effects of the tasing. "I just need a good night's rest and I'll be back in top shape by tomorrow."

"I'm still having a doctor come look at you," Josh said. "That's not even up for debate."

Hunter sighed. It was futile going against Josh's wishes.

"We're really so, so, so sorry, Hunter," Anna said despondently and Layla nodded, chiming in, "If we'd known it was you with Gabby, we wouldn't have acted the way we did. Will you please forgive us?"

"I also should have alerted our friends or texted you both that I was leaving the bar with Hunter," I admitted. "I'm sorry again, girls."

I'd already apologized a multitude of times on our way into Hunter's home, but I felt like I needed to say it again.

"No harm, no foul." Hunter waved off Anna and Layla. "Don't worry about it anymore. Please."

Then he smiled at me in that sweet manner of his and I smiled back, wanting to kiss him badly but knowing we had an audience that would shower us with a million questions about our relationship status.

To be honest, we hadn't discussed where tonight left us and I was afraid to even ask Hunter. I'd planned to, after I gave him an orgasm, but that obviously got cut short. Were we still friends—but now with benefits? I was a mix of nerves.

"See, Josh? Hunter forgives us." Layla wrapped her arms around her boyfriend's waist. "Now will you forgive us too?"

Josh ran a hand down her back and cupped her hip possessively over the fabric of her maxi dress. "You tased my best friend, *mo chroí*."

"It was an accident. Plus, who gave me the taser to begin with?"

Josh did, for protective reasons. He was a mob prince and Layla was his girl. He had to ensure her safety first and foremost. The glove compartment of Layla's car was stacked with all sorts of weapons like pepper spray, knife, gun, and of course, the taser she used on Hunter.

"Touché." Josh's stern exterior melted when she peered up at him through her lashes, giving him that soft look that he could never resist. "Fine. You're both forgiven."

Layla pressed a kiss to Josh's clean-shaven jaw.

"Now that that's resolved, who wants a drink?" Sam asked, rummaging through the liquor cabinet and pulling out an unopened bottle of Irish whiskey and spiced rum.

We all agreed in unison. Not to be dramatic, but I needed an entire bottle to myself to drown out my woes.

I kept tending to Hunter as the others busied themselves with searching for glasses and chasers, their backs to us.

"I'm so sorry," I whispered to Hunter, stepping closer to him.

"It's okay, Gabby." Hunter stroked a thumb over my cheek. "I'm sorry we couldn't finish what we started, but you have to admit that this is a funny story to look back on."

"You getting hit and then tased till you almost pass out isn't funny to me." I pouted and laid a kiss on his bruised temple. "I...I don't like the thought of you hurt."

I was grateful we had this time tonight, but I greedily wished we could have gone all the way.

Hunter was about to speak when Josh swiftly turned around and said, "What do you guys want to drink—*oh*."

Like I'd been touched by fire, I jerked away from Hunter.

Josh squinted at us, the wheels in his mind churning. Only the girls figured out we'd been on an actual date. But they didn't tell the boys. The latter were under the impression that Hunter and I were just hanging out. Hell, I had been under that impression too until I saw what he did for me.

And the last thing I wanted was Josh opening his mouth and asking if I was getting it on with his best friend.

Masking my anxiousness, I shimmied a hand down my dress in a guise to straighten out any wrinkles from the silky material. "I'll, um, have a whiskey."

"Same," Hunter grated, his hands flexing on his hard thighs like he was stopping himself from reaching out and reeling me back into his embrace, our audience be damned.

It wasn't lost on me that we were behaving very affectionately and all our friends took note, but no one said anything. It only added to my nervousness for when they would ask. How would we react? What would we say? All these thoughts ping-ponged inside my skull and made my head spin.

Josh slid us our whiskeys, Sam prepared two Cuba libres for Anna and himself, and Layla nursed a non-alcoholic drink, topped with a maraschino cherry. We did a quick cheering motion and proceeded to joke about the circumstance that brought us together.

For the next half an hour, we proceeded to talk about all sorts of subjects and the tension ebbed away from my coiled muscles with every passing minute. Layla was sitting in Josh's lap, and Anna and Sam stood a respectable distance from each other but kept exchanging heated glances when they thought the other one wasn't looking.

As for Hunter and me?

His presence on the kitchen stool next to me was a searing brand poking into my side, the intensity of his gaze making me feel like a guilty, diminished version of myself. I tried my best not to stare at him, but it was impossible.

When I did, he was giving me this borderline hurt and confused expression as if he didn't understand why I was suddenly acting standoffish, since I'd been all over him less than an hour ago. That look inflicted a wound on me, one that slowly suppurated under my skin. I almost succumbed and grabbed his hand to reassure him that everything was fine.

But that would invite questions we couldn't answer yet, especially when we'd barely discussed anything amongst ourselves.

Swallowing the lump burning in my throat, I let my tousled hair fall over one shoulder, erecting a curtain between us. As if that would keep my emotions hidden, my heart protected, my mind at ease.

The attention was thankfully diverted from Hunter and me completely when Josh started drizzling noisy kisses along Layla's bare shoulder while she sipped her drink, hiding her lovestruck smile. Layla was a bit more demure and discreet with her affections, but Josh didn't care about PDA. If he could shout it from the rooftop that Layla was his for the world to know, he would one hundred percent do it. He was so whipped for her, it was endearing.

"Get a room," Sam said what we were all thinking, mockingly rolling his eyes.

A girlish laugh burst out of Anna, but she quickly tamed it by biting her lip.

Sam's mischievous gaze snapped her way, raking her figure from head to toe almost hungrily. Anna looked every bit the beauty queen she was, her makeup flawless, her pink halter dress poured over her sculpted body, and not a single strand of her blond bombshell waves out of place. The only thing that was missing from her person to really complete the imagery was a crown, a sash, and a sceptre.

Sam wordlessly told her that he found her drop dead gorgeous.

Without looking away from her, he picked up a crystal glass from the counter and took a sip of the rum and Coke, his stance calm and collected but his energy flirting with something untamed.

Anna's hazel eyes flared slightly and she murmured, "That was my drink."

Dark amusement tinged his smirk. He used a thumb to rub over his bottom lip, where her lipstick stain—previously stamped on the glass's rim—was now smudged over his mouth like an indirect kiss. "Was it?"

There'd always been a strong tension between Sam and Anna, woven from the moment they first laid eyes on each other. Despite them trying to play it cool whenever they encountered each other, I knew better.

Sam didn't come here tonight on a rescue mission to be a saint.

He was only here for Anna.

And unfortunately, for the moment being, Anna wanted nothing to do with men…and Sam wanted everything to do with her.

Regardless of her reservations, it didn't stop her from peering his way at every opportunity. With dirty-blond hair, alluring green eyes, and a lone dimple that peeked out whenever he smiled, he was extremely handsome. I couldn't fault my best friend for finding him irresistible.

The sensation of a familiar palm drifting over my bare thigh disrupted my train of thoughts, arousing goosebumps and fomenting tension anew. My back straightened like an arrow.

I refrained from casting Hunter a glance.

But his hand paused on my knee and upturned in wait.

Almost beseechingly.

Almost asking me to accept him and claim him as mine in front of everyone.

The connection that joined us, forever pulsating in the background, began to thrum as fast as my heartbeat…and because I couldn't deny this man, I slid my hand over his and he braided our fingers together in a worshipping clasp.

Relief echoed through the chamber of my soul and I exhaled, feeling calmer. *Steady* and *solid*. Because of my lighthouse.

That feeling was short-lived.

Josh, deciding that he was done giving Layla smooches, propped his head up from her neck and fixated on Hunter and me. "So," he drawled. "Was this a date? Did you two finally get together and—"

"No!" I suddenly snapped before I could fully process what I was saying, running purely on the fear caroming in my system. "I-it wasn't a date. We're friends. We were just hanging out. It's not like that between us and…"

I regretted it the second I uttered the sentences.

Because next to me, Hunter froze, a ghost-like expression misting over his face. A mixture of surprise, disappointment, and—more prominently—betrayal swam in his blue eyes.

I hated myself for being the cause of his pain.

He dropped my hand like it was a scorching touch rather than something that anchored us both.

A sense of foreboding crawled down my spine like an eight-legged creature.

Josh and Sam frowned at Hunter in confusion.

Anna and Layla eyed me in disbelief.

And I sat there, trembling under the weights of their stares. Incapable of defending myself. Incapable of salvaging the situation. Incapable of doing anything but anticipating the verdict; Hunter's gavel-pounding reply that would determine the outcome of our relationship moving forward.

Finally, Hunter broke the heavy silence, speaking with a blank voice, and his words nicked me like tiny blades. "She's right. It's not like that between us. We're just *friends*."

CHAPTER 18

Not The End Of Us

GABRIELA

It had been three days since I last saw Hunter.

Three days since the shitshow where my friends caught us.

And three days since Hunter opened any of my texts.

Safe to say, my anxiety peaked to a new high and a heavy block of guilt rested on my chest. I hadn't realized how accustomed I'd gotten to Hunter's presence that not conversing with him for a mere seventy-two hours felt like a drought. All my feelings of elation from Friday dried out like the desert.

My goodness, Gabriela. He spent time planning a romantic stargazing night for you. He gave you his football jersey, an annotated copy of your favourite book, and a handcrafted bookmark from the roses you gifted him. And you told that man and everyone in the room who was listening that you're only friends? No wonder he hasn't replied to any of your messages.

Just picturing Hunter gently peeling away petals from the roses and inserting them into a resin bookmark with glitter, reading a paranormal romance book with a pen and highlighter so he could write his thoughts in the margins, and packing food in a wicker basket to bring on what I now know was a date—where he recreated one of my favourite book scenes— made my heart clench.

Oh, God.

I couldn't believe I'd actually hurt him.

I regretted my hasty words. He didn't deserve that.

I had to talk to him so he knew where I was coming from. Once I explained to him my feelings and thoughts on why I didn't want to pursue a romantic relationship, he'd understand. He wouldn't fault me for it, right?

I hoped everything could go back to normal once he heard me out.

Since he hadn't responded to my texts, I hadn't expected him to come pick me up today. Therefore, Oscar drove me to school. But my guilt grew tenfold when I realized Hunter didn't show up to our Monday morning Horror & Cult Classic Cinema class.

I missed him.

I missed him so much that it felt like a limb had been wrenched out of me and now I was aching, bruised, and bleeding all over.

I missed his easy smiles, his husky chuckles, and his princely demeanour. I missed the way he'd wrap me up in a big hug that felt like a warm awning in a torrential downpour—safe, secure, and sheltering. I missed the way we could talk about anything and everything under the sun, our easy camaraderie feeling like something I'd been needing all my life without realizing it.

And now I lost it.

Panic sweltered in my frame. *No. No. No.* I was going to fix this. One way or another. I couldn't lose Hunter. And if I had to show contrition for my mistake and spend time making amends, then I would do so.

I was willing to pay any price to keep him in my life.

"Gabriela, I asked you to dice the onions. Not…butcher them."

Mamma's voice yanked me out of my daze. I stared down at the cutting board in horror. I'd gotten carried away with my knife. The onions were chopped into various cuts, far from uniform and ranging from strips to mince. I winced. "Sorry, Mamma."

She rubbed a hand down my back. "Are you okay?"

My brows furrowed as I grabbed another onion from the basket and started chopping again, making sure to dice it properly. "Why wouldn't I be?"

"You've been pensive for the last few days." She stirred the pot on the stove next to me. We were making dinner together. "Don't think I haven't noticed that a certain boy didn't come to pick you up this morning. Did something happen between you and Hunter?"

I had the tendency to share a lot of things with Mamma, treating her like a confidante and telling her about all my crushes growing up.

Though for some reason, I remained tight-lipped regarding Hunter, sharing nothing beyond the fact that we were friends and he was doing me a solid by picking and dropping me back home during this difficult period. Papà discreetly ran a background check on Hunter and begrudgingly approved of him. And Mamma finally introduced herself to Hunter last week, catching up to us before I could convince him to speed out of the driveway. Of course he charmed her and she practically swooned. Like mother, like daughter, I guessed.

Now she also approved of Hunter and spent her free time pestering me for details about our relationship. If I chose to date again, she'd want me to pick a guy like him.

Shaking my head, I tossed the onions into a pan with olive oil. "I think I hurt him."

"In what way?"

"Remember when I texted you and Papà on Friday night that I was with Hunter?"

"Yes."

"Well…he planned a romantic night for us."

Shocked, she demanded a rundown. Sparing her the scandalous details of our hookup, I relayed the rest, including the part where Anna and Layla bulldozed through our date at the end.

Mamma laughed while simultaneously tutting at their antics. "You have good friends, Gabby. I'm proud to know those girls would go through hell and back for you. But *Dio mio*, I cannot believe that sweet boy got hurt. At least he was okay afterwards."

When she noticed I remained quiet, partly from shame and partly because even talking about Hunter brought a pang to my chest, she squeezed my shoulder affectionately.

"Here's the thing," she said. "While your relationship with Hunter has been morphing, you've been toeing this line between friends and lovers. Never having discussed being more, I don't fault you for telling everyone that you are just friends. Your reaction was valid. So was Hunter's. Sometimes, we say things we don't mean in the spur of the moment and regret them later." She shrugged. "And it's okay because we're humans. Mistakes happen. But now I suggest you talk to him honestly, Gabriela. He'll understand your point of view." An impish smile curled her lips. "Plus, I've seen the way that boy looks at you. He's so smitten, it's adorable. I promise you he'll stop whatever he's doing for the sake of hearing you out. Chances are, he's hurt and tucked himself in a corner, waiting for you to reach out to him. Communication is the foundation of all strong relationships. Remember that."

Mamma was right, except... "That's the problem. Hunter hasn't opened any of my texts. He didn't even show up to our class today. How do I talk to him if he's not responding to me?"

Her expression fell for a split second before resolve stamped on her face. She went back to stirring the pot, thinking. "He still lives in the apartment across from yours, right?"

"Yes, why?"

"Well, if there's one thing I've learned from Enzo"—she enunciated Papà's name with a sneer—"it's that the way to a man's heart is through his stomach."

I grinned. "Is that how you wooed Papà? By cooking for him?"

She added more salt to her pot and dragged out an exasperated exhale. "Partially. But my point is, I think you should bring Hunter a peace offering. Men never say no to food. It's one of their vices."

I supposed that wasn't a bad idea. Hunter did enjoy the blueberry muffins I baked for him to pair with his black coffee every Monday morning. And though he wasn't answering his phone, I doubted he'd deny me if I was at his door with a tray of my famous lasagna and all the humility I possessed. "I'll take your word for it."

"Good. Cook him something nice and bring it to his place pronto. You'll have him eating out of the palm of your hand in no time," she said.

"And once you make up, for God's sake, invite that boy over for dinner. I want to get to know my future son-in-law properly."

I actually laughed at her absurdness. "Baby steps, Mamma. I'm not even sure yet if he'll forgive me. Marriage isn't even on the table right now."

I didn't have the heart to tell her that Hunter and I would only ever be friends. Nothing more…Right?

"When I was your age, I was already married and a mom of one."

"Yeah, that's because you and Papà forgot to use a—"

"Gabriela Regina Bellafiore!" she barked. "You will not finish that sentence!"

I only laughed harder. It was the truth. Nonna confirmed it herself one night after one too many glasses of wine. She also said that I was the biggest blessing in their lives, so I never felt bad about being 'unplanned.'

"Okay, okay, fine!"

She harrumphed, smacking a spatula against my rump chidingly. "I'm just excited for you. It's been years since you've dated anyone and I want you to experience some joy. I can tell Hunter makes you happy. You always smile brighter whenever you come back from seeing him. Why not explore this a little more?"

"I…I don't know, Mamma."

"Let me ask you this: do you like him?"

That was a no-brainer. "Yes. Very much. He's perfect. Like all of my book boyfriends wrapped into one."

"There you go," she said smugly. "If you take a chance on him, Gabby, I don't think you'll regret it. I have a good feeling about this one."

I swallowed toughly. "I'll think about it."

I wouldn't. My mind was made.

Even though there was a small voice in the back of my mind telling me that I was kidding with myself if I thought we could remain platonic and *just friends*.

Mamma huffed. "And if he ends up being like Franco—which I doubt—then don't worry. Know that Enzo will deal with him."

Papà approved of Hunter as my friend, but accepting him as more would be a stretch. No man was good enough for his little girl. He hadn't even liked Franco. The only reason why I was able to date him was because Mamma reminded Papà that there was no stopping young love and that I deserved to be with whomever I wanted. In hindsight, dating Franco was the worst mistake ever. But at least my papà wasn't the kind of overbearing where I wasn't allowed to do anything without his permission.

He exerted control where necessary but was lenient when it came to me making my own life choices. Even if they weren't always the greatest. But that's how you learned, right?

"Thank you for giving me your advice." I rose on my tippytoes to kiss her cheek.

She hugged me. "Anytime, *cara mia.*"

The fragrant aroma of tomatoes, spices, and herbs wafted in the air as we spent the next few minutes preparing our pasta. Just as we were about to start plating dinner, the front door banged open and then slammed closed.

Mamma and I jolted with surprise.

Enzo Bellafiore strolled into the house like a high court second-in-command returning from battle, an angry expression fixated on his face as his thudding footsteps closed in on us.

Something was cataclysmically wrong. I stayed mum, watching him slip into the kitchen with the faint smell of gunpowder clinging to his dishevelled black suit.

Mamma chose to poke the bear. "Well, well, well. If it isn't the guard dog entering through the doggy door like he owns this place. Didn't you see the mat in the front? It says 'Everyone is welcome, except for annoying ex-husbands.'"

I pinched the bridge of my nose, anticipating the onslaught of bickering.

Barely fazed by her barb, Papà folded his lean body into a chair and reclined back, eyeing her infuriatingly. "Ex-husband? Must have missed the memo, considering you're into draining my bank account like you're my current wife. Last I checked, you bought three new pairs of designer shoes on my credit card, Lucia, and I didn't complain one bit. So are you going to rein in the attitude and welcome me home or keep acting like I'm a parasite?"

Mamma bristled. "This isn't your home, Enzo."

"It used to be." He tilted his head, staring at her like he was enjoying watching her squirm. "*You* used to be."

A blush tainted her cheeks and she cocked a fist on her apron-clad hip, snapping, "What do you want? Have you come here to be fed scraps?"

He smirked with the sinister edge of a mob man. Papà was one of the best shots in the city and could take out anyone within the blink of an eye. No one dared to push his buttons. Except for Mamma. He loved it too, always letting her get away with it. "Some respect, for starters, would be great. But I'll settle for a glass of your finest wine, *principessa*."

"If you think I'm going to—*oh*." Mamma's eyes bugged out of their sockets as she swayed towards him. "Enzo, you're bleeding."

Papà opened his suit jacket, retrieved his gun, and carefully placed it on the table. "Now you care, huh?"

True to her words, he had a streak of blood smattered on his left temple. "Papà," I whispered meekly. "What happened to you?"

"I'm okay," he reassured and I went over to him with a clean washcloth. I dabbed at the blood. "I'm here to tell you that I've handled the situation."

I paused, suspicion sinking into me. "What?"

"He's gone. The one who taunted you. I killed him." Papà gripped my wrist. "No one will ever hurt you on my watch," he said vehemently. "*Te lo prometto.*"

The washcloth fell from my hand and Mamma gasped behind me at the news.

A sense of peace punctured through the worry that had accumulated for weeks. I closed my eyes, fighting back the sting in them and thinking about all those times that I spent frightened of a potential bad outcome and never truly feeling relaxed because of this situation.

"Truly?" I swallowed. "Is it really over?"

"Yes. Starting tomorrow, you can return to your apartment. We'll double up the security in your building and Oscar can still shadow you if it helps you feel safer. But you're free now, Gabriela."

I hugged him tight. "Thank you so much, Papà. I love you."

"You never have to thank me for protecting you. It's my job, kiddo." He kissed my head. "I love you too."

"Who was it?" Mamma asked, shuffling closer.

Papà scowled. "Maverick. The security guard. Turns out, he had a vendetta against our daughter."

I froze.

What? Maverick was responsible for the break-in?

"He wasn't happy that you rejected him, Gabriela. The asshole had an extra set of keys and snuck into your apartment when you weren't there. We installed new cameras on your floor last week and caught him on tape today, walking out with a bag of your spare…undergarments." Papà coughed and looked away, awkward. "When Vance and I tortured him, he confessed that he started a lucrative side hustle where he sold your belongings—alongside those of other women in the building—online to men who are into that kind of thing…I'm so sorry all this happened to you, *cara mia*. You didn't deserve it."

I was wheeling between feelings of humiliation, fury, and shock. Maverick was stealing other women's and my lingerie and selling it to creeps online? What. The. Hell. Every now and then, I'd notice a missing thong from my drawers and thought I was going crazy.

To top it off, the motherfucker actually had the audacity to break into my place and scare me because I rejected him?

It was very sad and disheartening that some men couldn't take no for an answer. The lack of respect for women was astounding.

Call me cruel, but I was glad he was gone. Papà was a ruthless man, soft only with me and Mamma, so I knew he gave Maverick the ending he deserved.

"Good riddance," I spat. "Did he say why he wrote that messed-up quote on my wall? I didn't peg him as someone who read Shakespeare."

"No," Papà said right as Mamma placed a glass of wine before him. Her thank-you to him for protecting me. "He denied writing it and unfortunately, prior to your break-in, there were no cameras in the corridors of the units." It was an older building from the '70s in a vastly safe neighbourhood. There hadn't been a need for cameras beyond the underground parking lot, ground floor, and staircases, as I'd been explained in the past. Clearly, the lesson was learned and new upgrades were installed. "But the CCTV footage showed him breaking into other women's apartments enough times today for us to conclude it was him vandalizing your wall. For what it's worth, he did beg for mercy and apologized for stealing from you, but I still gutted him like a fucking animal."

"As you should, Enzo." Mamma poured two more glasses of wine. One for me. One for her. "I'm so relieved the threat is gone. Our baby is safe and that's all that matters."

"I'm not a baby anymore," I muttered, taking the glass from her.

"You'll always be our baby, Gabriela." She kissed my head too. "Since this is settled, we should all celebrate." She gave Papà a sidelong glance. "Enzo, how can we ever repay you for all that you've done?"

"Kiss me," he replied to her.

My eyes widened in disbelief as they scurried from one parent to another. It wasn't a secret that they squabbled. Mamma antagonized Papà and he responded, but never so brazenly. This was a new development. I didn't know what to make of it.

"Enzo," Mamma said warningly.

"If you won't kiss me, then at least stop going on dates with losers."

"Who I date is none of your business."

"You are my business, Lucia," he said with a smoky voice. "You'll always be."

"Whatever." Miffed, Mamma rolled her eyes, but there was something on her face that spoke of pleasure. I quietly sipped my wine, trying to assess their back-and-forth from every angle like I was a cameraman in a sitcom so I could call Nonna later tonight and give her a rundown. She was going to freak out.

Papà picked up his wine glass and gave Mamma one of his striking smiles. "Now, I've had a long day and I'm hungry, so come feed your dog some scraps, *principessa*, and we'll celebrate tonight's victory, yeah?"

After setting the table and saying grace, we ate while discussing my semester. The night ended with us playing a few rounds of Go Fish. It was a picture of domestic bliss. My heart glowed, content and lax for the first time in weeks.

Before going to bed, I called Nonna and we chatted about my parents. She was ecstatic to hear about their exchange and asked me to call her back with any other updates. We also made plans to meet up later this week. Furthermore, I even texted the girls in our group chat that they found the culprit and the situation was resolved. They cheered for me.

Unable to help myself, I opened my conversation with Hunter and the high that I was riding up until now evaporated like mist.

He still hadn't seen my texts.

Trepidation gnawed at my stomach like a hungry beast.

It was one thing for him to be hurt, but…he couldn't hate me, right?

Hunter, please, please, please, don't hate me.

I despised that I'd turned into a wrecking ball packed with fret, swinging like a pendulum with no end in sight. There was a restless energy building inside of me and the longer we went without speaking, the more I feared it would spread like wildfire.

I'd take Mamma's advice and visit him in person with my own olive branch.

Then Hunter and I would be okay.

We had to be.

This wasn't the end for us.

I fell asleep with that mantra playing in my head.

My dreams were filled with Hunter, his passionate kisses, and a map of bright stars shining in the night sky above our heads.

CHAPTER 19

Just Yours

GABRIELA

I was officially moving back to my apartment.

When I was getting ready to leave, Mamma cried at the threshold and Papà stood with a stony face, trying to hide his emotions. Though we'd still see each other, I knew it wouldn't be the same. I was going to miss them terribly. In the weeks I spent living here, I'd seen a change in my parents. Our dinner and game nights were fun again, the way they used to be before their messy divorce, and their communication with each other had improved drastically. Like they were owning up to the faults that tore them apart in the first place. During my time back home, Papà dropped by often and despite Mamma's raillery, I knew she liked having him in her space. Missed it, even. We all still had a multitude of issues to wade through, but dare I say, we felt whole again.

How crazy that this semblance of peace in our home arose from such a disturbing chapter in my life. If the break-in had never occurred, I wouldn't have moved back and witnessed the small growth between Mamma and Papà.

Oscar drove me back to my apartment after a bittersweet farewell with my parents. He ushered boxes with my belongings up the elevator and I did my utmost best not to cast a glance at the door in front of mine when I entered my place.

I thanked Oscar for everything he'd done. He responded with a crooked smile and a pat on my head, saying it was nothing and that I was welcome to call him if I ever needed help.

With the threat gone, a huge weight was lifted off my shoulders. A younger guard had replaced Maverick, someone Vance Remington personally selected, and a bit more muscle was added around the building.

Anna and Layla arrived at my apartment just as I was putting my clothes back into my closet. They came bearing cake and a white box tied with a pink bow.

My jaw hung open when I unwrapped my gift, presented with the prettiest black bustier with gold chain detailing. "Oh my goodness."

"Do you like it?" Anna queried from her seated position on my bed.

"I *love* it. Are you kidding me?" I spun around to face the mirror, holding it against my chest. "This is stunning, Anna. I'm going to wear it at the Halloween party, and I'll pair it with my new miniskirt and heels."

Anna approved with a cheeky smile. "You're going to look so hot."

"Thank you, thank you, thank you. I'm obsessed with it, Anna," I gushed, absolutely enamoured with her creation. "Layla, did you already get yours?"

She nodded. "Anna gave me mine before we came over. It's cream-coloured, with beautiful pearl embroidery." She showed me a picture on her phone. "I'll wear it to the Halloween party as well."

"Yes, then we'll match!" I threw myself at Anna, hugging her with all my might and pushing us until we fell backwards on the bed with giggles. "Can't wait till you establish your own label and we can have wardrobes filled with your designs."

Not wanting to be left out, Layla ambushed us too. We were a tangle of limbs and laughter before settling on our backs and staring at the chandelier on my ceiling.

"What are you going to do about Hunter?" Anna questioned after a quiet moment.

"Has he replied to any of your texts?" Layla commented.

"He hasn't even opened them." I sighed. "I didn't mean to hurt him. I just…"

"It's fine, Gabby." Layla swept my hair back from my face reassuringly. "Just talk to him like your mom suggested. Everything will work itself out."

"I hope so." My chest twisted. "I don't want to lose him."

Anna raised herself on an elbow, peering down at me with knowingness. "You like him a lot, huh? Admit it."

I couldn't even deny it. "I've never liked anyone *this* much in my entire life."

Shocked gasps erupted from either side of me. I wasn't kidding. None of the boys from my past held a candle to Hunter. In such a short amount of time, my feelings for him ran so deep, I feared there was no bottom.

No one had ever treated me—cared for me—like Hunter.

Not even Franco.

But being friends with Hunter was the only way to ensure he stayed in my life. A romantic relationship wasn't in our cards. I was too scared. Too messed up from my past. I had many insecurities and fears that I hadn't worked through. I felt like I was doomed to screw up this good thing between us. Doomed to fail all of Hunter's expectations.

"For what it's worth, he definitely likes you back just that much— if not more," Anna said. "It was so obvious on Friday night. He kept watching you with this soft, possessive expression. I don't think he realized it himself."

That's what made this all the more painful. "I know he likes me too."

"Just a couple of weeks ago, you were saying that you'd never act on this attraction," Layla teased.

I chewed my lip before casting them both a meaningful glance. "I won't be acting on this attraction. I…I'm going to apologize to Hunter for hurting his feelings, but I'm going to make it clear that the only possibility in our future is remaining friends."

My best friends' faces fell. "Gabby…"

"I don't want to hear it. Please." My shoulders drooped. "I'll keep you both posted on what happens tonight."

After eating cake, the girls helped me clean up my apartment. We dusted, broomed, and vacuumed. Every inch was spick-and-span by the time we finished. They left afterwards and then it was just me and my Luna. She was happy to be back home, resting on her favourite spot by the windowsill in the living room, neighbourhood-watching like a judgy old lady.

I was currently in the kitchen, preparing a lasagna for Hunter.

Just half an hour ago, I'd heard shuffling in the hallway and looked into my peephole, butterflies swarming in my stomach at the sight of him entering his own apartment. It was Tuesday, which meant he probably finished football practice, if the duffel bag slung over his shoulder was anything to go by.

I hoped he opened the door when I knocked. Otherwise, I was going to be crushed.

While the lasagna baked, I hopped into the shower, mentally going over my speech to Hunter. There was so much I needed to say, so much he needed to hear. I hated to admit that I was nervous. This discomfort snaking in my belly was newfound and I was ready to put an end to it.

Would he be excited to see me? Or would he be annoyed?

I contemplated every possible scenario as I got ready in record speed, throwing my hair up in a loose bun with a few tendrils framing my face. I even went as far as to put on some makeup and don my red lingerie-style dress. I was pulling out the big guns for this apology.

"Are you ready to see Hunter, Luna?" I cooed to my cat, who bounded over to me when I unlocked our apartment door. I reckoned she missed him too. He'd become a fixture in our lives and being apart from him was doing no favours to either of us.

She meowed in agreement.

With the dish in my hands and Luna beside me like my trusty sidekick, we crossed the five steps separating our home from Hunter's.

"You can do this, Gabby," I muttered to myself before I fell apart like a weakly built house of cards.

I knocked tactfully on his door.

Fifteen seconds later, Hunter opened it.

And when I was finally face-to-face with him, my knees buckled and every thought, every sentence, every word failed me. My mind was a blank canvas of pure serenity in the presence of the man who shushed all my demons.

His familiar cologne wafted over and I inhaled, letting it travel through my lungs and ebb away the remaining anxiety in my body.

Hunter's blue eyes widened a fraction like I was the last person he expected to see. He quickly composed himself until he appeared austere. Even his clipped "Hi" was cold.

It gutted me a smidge, but I still persevered, my speech jovial as I said, "Hi! How are you?"

"I'm fine." He crossed his arms over his chest and leaned against the doorframe, looking absolutely delicious in a plain black T-shirt and lounge pants. "You?"

"Great!" I said a little too chirpily and internally winced. "We're, uh, neighbours again. As promised, I made you some lasagna."

I extended my olive branch towards him, but he didn't grab it.

Instead, his dark brows pulled into a frown. "You're back?"

"Yes." I gulped and decided to respond to his unspoken question. "It was Maverick. The security guard. He…He's been dealt with accordingly." *Dead*, to put it simply, but we had other neighbours on this floor and I wasn't about to air out my dirty laundry. "So I was allowed to return home."

"Ah," he drawled as if he wanted to ask me more but was refraining from doing so. "I'm glad to hear that. You're feeling okay?"

I'll be okay once we deal with the weirdness stacked between us.

"I am." I nudged the dish higher in an attempt to get him to acknowledge it. "Here you go. It's still warm. I hope you enjoy it."

"Thank you." He accepted the dish from my hands and our fingers brushed. Hunter's Adam's apple bobbed at the touch, the only indication that he was affected, but his expression screamed impassiveness.

He turned around to deposit the lasagna on his entryway credenza, then returned to the threshold. I squandered down my bout of sadness over the fact that he didn't invite me in.

I didn't know how to deal with him when he appeared so closed-off.

Luna padded closer to him, sensing the shift in the air, and rubbed herself against his leg with a purr. He smiled down at her and I was instantly jealous that my cat got one of his charming smiles. It wasn't fair.

Eventually, my cat trotted down the hallway, giving us privacy.

"Are you feeling okay?" I asked hesitantly. "You didn't come to class on Monday."

I missed having you there. Holding your hands. Passing notes. Sharing donuts.

He let loose a long, bone-weary sigh. "Yeah, about that, I had to take my mom to the hospital. She cut her hand while cooking. It was deep enough that she required stitches. I spent the entire morning with her, then rushed to my classes in the afternoon. These last two days have been crazy busy for me. I'm sorry I didn't tell you beforehand that I couldn't make it to our class—or pick you up."

I was relieved that he didn't skip our class because he was ignoring me, but still sad to hear about his mom's predicament. "I'm so sorry, Hunter. Is your mom doing okay now?"

I was torn between wanting to give him a hug and maintaining my distance because the frosty barrier he'd erected around himself was making it impossible to throw my arms around him.

"She is," he said curtly, like he was in a hurry to wrap up our conversation.

I wanted to speed back to my apartment this very second, but I promised myself I wouldn't leave until we addressed the pink elephant in the room. "Hunter, about Friday night—"

"What about Friday night?" He stiffened.

Fuck it. I slowly stepped closer, approaching him like he was a wounded animal and I needed to be cautious. I placed my hand on his forearm. "I wanted to apologize if I sounded rash. When I told everyone that we're just friends, I panicked and didn't know what to say."

"Are you embarrassed of me?"

I flinched, my mouth parting open. "Why would I be embarrassed of you?"

"You tell me, Gabriela," he whispered, his tone ringing with thinly disguised hurt.

"No," I whispered back, horrified. "My God, Hunter, no. I would never be embarrassed of you. What gave you that impression?"

"The way you were so quick to dismiss the possibility of us." Blue eyes filled with pain rose to mine and his jaw clenched. "You let go of my hand, put distance, and acted like being with me was so goddamn abhorrent in front of everyone."

I wanted to cry.

I knew I hurt him, but I hadn't realized how much until now.

"I'm so sorry, Hunter. I didn't mean to hurt you. That's the last thing I'd ever want." I shook my head and squeezed his forearm, willing him to understand. "I thought we were on the same page that Friday night's hookup would be a one-time thing. That's why I told them it wasn't a date—that we're just friends. Not because I'm embarrassed of you. That couldn't be further from the truth." My voice cracked as I murmured, "I…I adore you."

Hunter jolted back, surprised by my admission, before springing forward like he could no longer contain himself. He wrapped his arms around me and yanked my body into his, the familiarity of his embrace swiftly making me feel warm and protected. His heartbeat thumped fast under my palm, letting me know that he was far from the unaffected exterior he'd tried to portray.

"You adore me?" he rasped, his face alight with wild intensity.

The tension between us could be cut with a sharp knife.

I only managed a subtle nod.

Hunter leaned down until mere inches separated our lips, like I possessed some gravitational pull over him and he was helpless to obey. "Then why?" His tone was raw. "Why do I always feel like you want more with me, but then purposely hold back?"

I was not the least bit surprised that he was perceptive enough to pick up on that trait. I did hold back. With everyone. But he was the first man in a long time who made me want to break my own rules. Where Hunter was concerned, I wanted to throw caution to the wind and erase all of my carefully drawn lines, the ones that kept my heart safe and sound. "I don't date, Hunter. At all. I never wanted to give you false hope that there could be a future for us. Yet somewhere along the way, I think I did. And you'll never know how sorry I am about that."

His eyes were unruly, brimming with an emotion I couldn't decipher. "Give me a good reason," he gritted out. "Don't feed me some bullshit excuse about your academic life not giving you enough time to be with someone. Tell me what's causing you to retreat, baby."

Because I'm unlovable and worthless. Because my only redeeming qualities are my tight pussy and blow job skills. Franco's venom seeped into my veins once more as his taunting voice replayed in my mind like a chant, a reminder that I was damaged goods.

I was self-aware enough to know that it wasn't healthy to allow those thoughts to hold any power over me, but it was hard not to fall victim to my ex-boyfriend's tirade—the one who shaped me into the kind of girl who became afraid of loving.

For me, loving meant the possibility of losing. Someone could glimpse my inner workings, choose to be with me for a bit…before growing tired because they found me exhausting…and inevitably walking away after weaponizing all my flaws against me. It was too much to bear.

"I'm sorry," I croaked. "I can't, Hunter. I can't be with you like *that*. I can't be what you need and deserve."

"What are you trying to say?" There was a frantic gleam in his eyes.

"I want to be friends, Hunter. Just *friends*."

At least that way, I can keep you. At least that way, I won't lose you.

Hunter dropped his arms and took a big step back like I seared him, agony and despair slashing over his features. "I don't want to be friends, Gabby. I want to be yours. Just *yours*."

Pain pulsed through my entire being like a round of bullets was fired into my skin. I was a fool to believe that we could make it past all of this and come out unscathed on the other end.

"I think I've liked you since the first moment I laid eyes on you over a year ago, when I knew nothing about you…except for the fact that you were the most beautiful girl I'd ever seen."

197

His vulnerable words from Friday night echoed in my mind, adding more salt to the wound. My eyes stung with tears.

I saw all our past interactions in a different light and figured out, a little too late, that everything Hunter did, he did not only because he was a good person, but because he was slowly falling for me. From driving me around, to reading my favourite romance novels, to bringing me meaningful gifts, to sending me all sorts of sweet texts, to spending every spare moment in his day with me, and so much more.

It was all because he wanted to be mine.

Taking my silence as an answer, Hunter's eyes shut on an exhale.

"I'm done," he murmured with finality. "I'm done chasing after someone who doesn't want me, and I'm done feeling like I have no worth beyond a casual hookup."

Shocked by his words, I couldn't formulate my thoughts into sentences.

"I'll stay out of your way." He withdrew past his threshold, his knuckles white from how hard he clutched his door. "I'll sit far away from you during Monday's class and I'll email you my parts of the assignments every week. I trust that you'll do your part as well and send the completed versions to Dr. Richmond."

I willed my mouth to speak, my insides churning with so much anguish. "Hunter, *please*."

He gave me a wry smile, his eyes downcast. "It's okay, Gabby. It's not your fault that you don't feel the same way. I get it, trust me. No hard feelings." His voice was hollow. "Have a good night."

Like the gentleman he was, he didn't slam the door shut in my face, rather closed it with a soft click. Somehow, that made me feel worse.

I came here to fix things, to earn his forgiveness, and to remain friends.

Instead, I ruined everything.

I'd been so afraid of losing him…yet I lost him regardless.

And I'd been so afraid of rejection that when I came to my senses a moment later, I realized that was exactly what I did to Hunter.

Numb but still aching, I padded back to my place in a trance, Luna in tow.

The only sound in my ears was my rapidly beating heart splitting in two.

I had no recollections of turning off the lights and climbing into my bed.

All I remembered was bawling my eyes out over the fact that I broke the heart of the sweetest man I'd ever had the privilege of knowing. I made him feel unwanted and unworthy, while all he'd ever done was make me feel cherished and important.

My pillow remained wet by the time the sun rose and signalled the start of a new day.

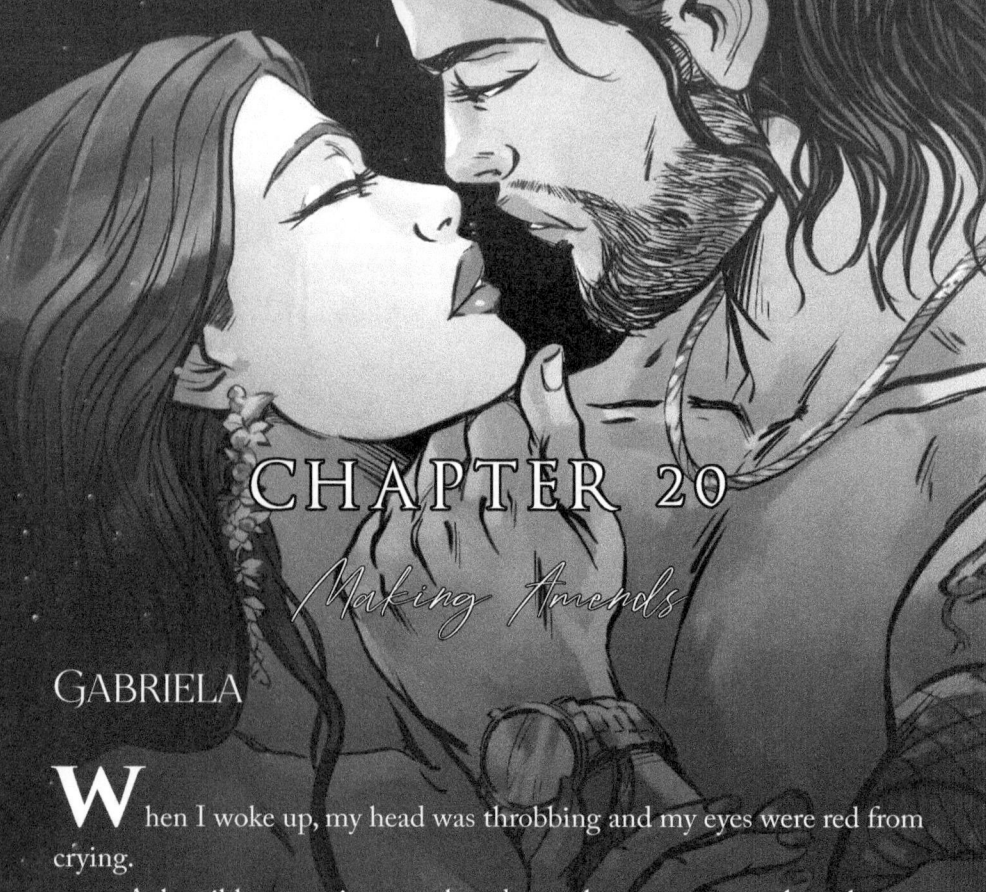

CHAPTER 20

Making Amends

GABRIELA

When I woke up, my head was throbbing and my eyes were red from crying.

A horrible sensation enveloped me that not even a hot shower, caffeine, and a thick layer of makeup could fix. I resigned to my fate: skipping the entirety of my classes and spending the day curled on the couch with Luna, wallowing in my misery. My furry companion knew something was wrong. She gave me worried glances and settled herself on my chest, hugging and purring softly.

It was mental torture, spending hours self-reflecting and replaying yesterday's scene from the hallway. The stark hurt on Hunter's face, the stoic demeanour that melted the second I confessed to adoring him, the pure yearning when he held me in his arms, and the resolute voice when he told me that he was *done*. I kept going over our interaction, dissecting where I went wrong and essaying on how I could have prevented the catastrophe so we ended up with a different outcome.

Yet I knew the only way we'd have a different outcome was if I wanted the same thing as him. To be together. To be his. To let him be mine.

A painful chasm widened inside my chest. Sitting down and ruminating alone wasn't doing me any good. Therefore, I gathered the courage to finally text the girls about the disaster that occurred last night. They were sorry to hear it and wanted to help me navigate through my inner turmoil. Before I knew it, our conversation quickly turned into a makeshift therapy session.

What is your heart telling you right now? —Layla

That I can't lose him. —Gabby

Even though I feel like I already did. —Gabby

And I hate myself for hurting him. It was never my intention. He means so much to me. —Gabby

Do you want to be with him? And not just as 'friends'? —Anna

Be honest with yourself, Gabby. —Anna

I closed my eyes and put my phone down.

The writing had always been on the wall and I was purposely not wanting to see it because the possibility of my past catching up to me and all my shortcomings was too strong. To Hunter, I was perfect. Selfishly, I wanted to remain that way in his eyes, not wanting to taint the image with my romantic relationship flaws. I thought that staying friends could keep us in the safe zone, but we'd long since left that territory. It was evident that after last night's exchange, I had nothing left to lose.

And if I was being honest with myself, then yes, deep down in my soul, there was a part of me that craved to be more than friends with Hunter.

Sure, I had issues and fears about falling in love. Sure, my ex had hurt me in bad ways. But none of that should stop me from taking another chance on myself, on Hunter, and on the possibility of us, right?

For so long, I kept a chain locked around my heart, never allowing anyone access to the real me. All because I was afraid of getting burned again.

But what was life without a little bit of risk?

If there was anyone who would take good care of me, it was Hunter.

In his own ways, I realized that Hunter, over the last few weeks, had been showing me with his actions and words that he was capable of treating me the way I deserved. Whether it was driving me to and back from school. Whether it was taking me on a long walk to get a reprieve from my situation. Whether it was taking an interest in my hobbies. And everything else in between. He was always there for me.

I never stood a chance against this sweet, beautiful man with a heart of gold.

The night on the terrace was the catalyst that pushed everything into place. Our meeting was no coincidence. Fate had been conspiring, orchestrating its magic from the beginning by throwing us on the same path. Now I needed to trust what the universe had in store for Hunter and me and right all my wrongs by undoing the unintentional hurt I caused him.

Mamma said good communication was the foundation of any strong relationship, so I was going to be brave and talk to him again. Even if it was the last thing I did.

Because I refused to lose him without a fight.

The time alone with my thoughts awarded me more mental clarity and after what felt like an eternity in a quandary, what I needed to do became abundantly clear.

Picking my phone up after another hour of self-reflection had passed, I sent my reply to the girls.

Yes, I want to be with him as more than friends. —Gabby

The truth is Hunter makes me happier than ever and I can't keep letting the past hold me back, right? I know in my heart that Hunter will never hurt me and only have my best interest in mind. —Gabby

It was liberating to admit it.

I could practically feel both my best friends' pride beaming from my phone's screen.

Atta girl! —Anna

Now we're talking! —Layla

We can all agree he's the furthest thing from that asshole Franco. Hunter's a safe bet, Gabby. —Layla

I have a feeling that he'll give you everything you deserve. Take a chance on him, Gabby. You won't regret it. —Anna

I was so glad I had this conversation with Anna and Layla. I'd just needed to confide in them and make more sense of my thoughts. The verdict was that Hunter was a walking-talking green flag and I would be foolish to let him slip through my fingers. Especially when I harboured such deep feelings for him, no matter how hard I tried to fight those emotions.

I owed it to both of us to give us this chance. We would be good for each other. Now I just had to tell Hunter that I was sorry, that I would do anything to make things right between us, that I wanted him the same way he wanted me, and that if he took a chance on me, he wouldn't regret it.

Which meant I needed to see him *stat*. No more pity-party. I had to talk to him and if cornering him after his football game was the only option, so be it.

I love you, girls 🩶 I can't thank you enough for hearing me out. —Gabby

We love you, too 🩶 You never have to thank us for listening to you! —Anna

Or offering advice! What else are sisters for? 🩶 —Layla

Now…What are the odds that we can go watch the Panthers' game today? —Gabby

I knew there was one in less than three hours. I hoped to make it.

Leave it to me! I'll get us tickets :) —Layla

It was decided. We were going. I rushed back to my room to get ready, where I spent an hour overthinking my outfit before settling on a short leopard print dress, red pumps, and my faux fur red coat since the temperature had dropped now that fall was upon Montardor.

Layla arrived to pick me up an hour prior to the start of the game.

"Hey, Gabby." She smiled when I slid into her car. "How are you feeling?"

"Better than I did this morning. You?" I leaned forward to give her a hug. "By the way, you look gorgeous."

She wore an elegant white coat—with Josh's football jersey underneath, no doubt—and matching white gloves embellished with pearls, her dark hair falling around her shoulders in loose waves.

"Thank you. So do you." Layla hugged me back. "And I'm doing okay." She started driving, heading towards the school's stadium. Anna wasn't carpooling with us since she was in the west, choosing to drive herself so Layla didn't have to do a detour. "Except for the fact that my dad is suspicious and thinks I'm sneaking around with a boy behind his back."

Well, shit.

After her mom's passing, Layla was all Marco Antonelli had left. As a result, he'd turned even more overprotective and overbearing. He would never accept her relationship with Josh, whose family was tied to the underworld. It wasn't that Layla couldn't date—she just couldn't be with a mob prince whose values and etiquette her dad deemed beneath him. According to his strict rules and moral compass, the daughter of a strait-laced Italian businessman would never mix with the son of a notorious Irish kingpin.

Layla had managed to keep her dad in the dark regarding her one-year-long relationship with Josh. Last year, Josh bought a brownstone so Layla could occasionally spend the night with him. But she'd always lie to her dad, saying that she was sleeping over at mine since I was close to campus.

When the time came, I truly hoped her dad was accepting of their relationship.

If he subjected them to his wrath, Anna and I promised to help them elope if it came down to it. They loved each other in that rare, genuine, *you're-it-for-me* type of way and people like that deserved to have their happily ever after.

"What did you tell him?" I inquired.

"I told my dad that I wasn't. But after tonight, I won't stay at the house for a while. I can't risk him finding out about Josh. I'm going to remain with him in the west side to ease his suspicions."

Josh was going to be devastated that Layla wouldn't be spending time in their shared home, but ultimately he'd understand.

"Everything will work itself out," I promised. "Don't worry, Lay."

The Panthers were on the cusp of another win.

We were down to the fourth quarter and the scoreboard showed that Vesta University was in the lead with six points. The entirety of the fast-paced game, a lump felt lodged in my throat. The Panthers were playing ruthlessly and strategically, but the rival university was desperately trying to catch up to them. There were a few close calls where the opposing team almost hurt Hunter. My heartbeat galloped and I might have cursed loudly at the players, much to Anna's and Layla's chagrins when I drew unnecessary attention towards us in the bleachers.

I couldn't help myself. This game was extremely important for him and the team. A win before the upcoming finals would be a huge confidence booster and I hated seeing anyone try to injure Hunter before the championship.

I thought that our last exchange may jeopardize Hunter's performance, considering how wounded he'd been when he closed the door on me. But thankfully, he was killing it tonight, a complete beast on the field.

Though I'd heard Hunter was a gifted quarterback, it was another thing to actually witness him work his magic as he expertly created plays throughout the quarters that put his team ahead of the opponents.

His latest one put the ball in Sam's hands, who crossed into the endzone for a touchdown. The crowd cheered loudly. His teammates jumped on him in celebration, and there was a brief instant where his head swivelled in our direction, scanning through the bleachers for a specific someone.

Anna.

Sam lifted the football in his hand and shot her an air kiss with the other as if telling her he scored that one for her. He had his helmet on, but I could just picture his usual mischievous smirk.

"I think he likes you," I stated the obvious.

Anna's back straightened in alarm and she tried to adopt a blank expression like she was uninterested in his attention. She composed herself quickly by tightening the sash of her light pink coat, crossing her thigh-high boot-clad legs, and resting her hands in a steeple around her knee. She was dressed like a supermodel about to sashay on a catwalk, not a football game attendee. "No. He can't like me." She cleared her throat. "He doesn't even know me."

But he wants to, I silently thought. Saying it out loud would only cause Anna to withdraw into her shell before she could make sense of whatever it was she felt for Sam.

"Fine. How about he thinks you're pretty?" Layla amended with a knowing smile. "Josh told me yesterday that Sam asked him if you're single."

Confounded, Anna's lips parted like she wanted to say something, but she choked down whatever it was and turned back to the game. It was clear she was mulling over Layla's revelation.

The latter leaned into my right side and asked, "Are you sure you don't want to hitch a ride back with Josh and me?"

The game would be over in a handful of minutes and though I could carpool with them, I knew Layla needed privacy to talk to Josh.

Plus, I needed to talk to Hunter too. If everything went according to plan, I'd be going back home with him.

"Positive," I hollered back over the noise of the boisterous crowd.

There were a few seconds left on the clock and the cheering was growing in decibels as the Panthers took possession of the ball again. My gaze was perpetually fixed on number nine, watching Hunter run across the field with the football while simultaneously dodging tackle attempts from the rival team. For a man of his robust stature, he was surprisingly fast and agile, like a sleek predator as he crossed the remaining yards that would bring him into the endzone.

With three seconds left, Hunter scored another touchdown that caused the entire stadium to erupt in a deafening roar as the Panthers secured another victory.

His teammates jumped all over him with gleeful shouts and the cheerleaders danced with their pompoms, fuelling the crowd's screams.

Pride slammed into my chest.

When Hunter removed his helmet, he huffed from the exertion of the final push, his hair sticking to his face and neck with sweat. A glorious smile was carved over his face as he soaked in his surroundings.

He'd never looked more beautiful to me.

As he walked towards the bench, he paused briefly, his eyes travelling over the crowd until they found what they were looking for.

Me.

My heart twisted in its cage.

Right this instant, I wished I could tell him how proud I was of him, how apologetic I was for last night, how hard I was going to work to fix my mistake and give us the chance we both deserved.

The hallway in the athletic complex was buzzing with the excitement of tonight's win. Anna had to skedaddle right after the game since she'd received a text from her mom, asking her to pick up her little brother. Now Layla and I leaned against a wall before the men's locker room. The game had been over for almost an hour. I alternated between observing the coaches and players congratulating each other on their way out and resisting the urge to nervously bite my nails. The footsteps resounding against the linoleum floor mirrored my thumping heartbeat as I waited, to no avail, for Josh and Hunter to finally emerge.

"What's taking them so long?" Layla tapped her foot in impatience. "Even the athletic staff has left."

"Maybe Josh got distracted singing a ballad in the shower?" I supplied.

One time I went over to their home and while Layla was preparing dinner for us, Josh was in the shower after a long day of work, belting out a semblance of a romantic song at the top of his lungs for ten minutes. It was loud enough to deafen everyone in the neighbourhood. And wake the dead.

But if Josh ever acted silly, it was only to make Layla laugh. When they'd met, she'd been a sad version of herself and all he wanted was to bring her happiness.

Layla scoffed, but the small smile on her face was proof of how much she loved him and his off-key singing. "If he were singing, we'd all have heard it by now."

I chuckled. "True."

Layla's phone lit up with a call from her dad. Her entire face leached of colour. "I have to get this."

"Go ahead."

She picked up the call and walked down the hallway to a quiet area.

At that exact moment, Josh strolled out of the locker room, wearing a comfortable hoodie and sweatpants combo, his dark brown hair wet from his shower, a duffel bag with his gear slung over one shoulder, and his brown eyes gleaming with smugness from his win. "Hey, Gabby."

"Hey, Josh, congrats!"

He threw his arm around my shoulders in a quick, brotherly hug.

"You did well."

"Thank you." He grinned. "I'm beat now. Can't wait to go home and celebrate with my girl." His head poked around. "Speaking of, where is she?"

"Over there." I chin-nodded down the hallway, where she seemed to be locked in a heated conversation, clutching the roots of her hair. "Listen, just a heads-up, she's talking to her dad."

An unusual dark expression swept over Josh's features. "Ah, I see."

Obviously, Layla's dad was a sore subject. He knew that Marco Antonelli would never accept their relationship—never accept *him*.

"Anyways." He swiftly shook off the grey cloud looming over him, hoisting the strap of his bag higher up his shoulder. "We need to talk."

I arched my brow. "About what?"

"About Hunter."

Just hearing his name caused my chest to clench. "What about Hunter?"

Josh tucked his hands in the pockets of his pants. "In case it wasn't fucking obvious, he likes you. A lot. That date he planned on Friday night? It was his way of showing it to you. Though it's not my place to say this, I really think you should give him a chance. Hunter's a great guy, Gabby. One of the best. I swear, he'll treat you like a princess."

My throat was uncomfortably tight. Josh wasn't saying anything I didn't already know. "I'm aware, Josh. Believe me, I want the same things as Hunter."

Josh perked up like he wasn't expecting me to say that. Another arrow of guilt pricked my skin. I must have done a great job convincing everyone on Friday night that there was no future for Hunter and me beyond friendship. "Okay, great. My job here is done."

"That's actually why I'm here tonight. I want to talk to Hunter. I'm hoping it's not too late to fix things."

"It's not," Josh insisted. "Hunter's been a mess these last few days. He's still got it bad for you."

I didn't like knowing he'd been a mess. The need to assuage his pain pulsed through me like a command. I needed to see him. Now.

"He's in there, by the way." Josh angled his head in the direction of the locker room. "There's no one left except for him." He shrugged. "You know, if you wanted to talk to him or something."

Or something.

He meant us kissing and making up.

That was definitely on the agenda, once Hunter and I sorted out our feelings.

"Thanks, Josh. I appreciate it. I'll see you and Layla soon." I hiked a thumb towards the locker room. "I'm going to go talk to Hunter."

As my feet carried me towards my destination, I heard Josh say, "You're welcome. Have a good night."

"You, too."

"Oh—wait a second!"

"Yeah?" I glanced at him over my shoulder, with my hand on the locker room door.

"In case you need further evidence of how whipped my best friend is for you: He never had Horror & Cult Classic Cinema to begin with. He only switched into that class after you sent him your schedule. Hunter was willing to put himself through hours of torture if it meant spending time with you, Gabby."

CHAPTER 21

Fangirl Behaviour

HUNTER

My tired muscles relaxed under the spray of the warm water.

I watched suds disappear down the shower drain as a sense of calm finally filtered through my system after the adrenaline from today's game. The team had played exceptionally. So had I, despite the state of my mind. Everyone was riding on a high from our win. Coach Turner had never been prouder as he gave his usual talk post-game. I didn't want to get overly cocky and confident before the finals, but we all had a strong feeling that the championship trophy was finally coming home to the Panthers.

Now everyone left and I was the last one in the locker room, needing time alone to untangle the mess that was my head. I felt like a wreck on the inside. It didn't matter that I played the best game of my university career. Not when all I could focus on was the red-haired beauty sitting in the bleachers.

I assumed my eyes were playing tricks on me. That she was a mirage.

But there she was, in the flesh, and I couldn't comprehend why she'd shown up after making it clear last night that she only saw me as a friend.

The painful reminder had me gnashing my teeth until my jaw hurt. But I was grateful for the ache elsewhere than in my goddamned heart—

the stupid organ that brought me nothing but torment since I'd first laid eyes on Gabriela. I wished I could carve it out of my chest and throw it away.

This yearning was tearing me apart and I just wanted it to stop.

But like a masochist, I kept replaying the moment she sliced me to ribbons with her words. She never meant to give me false hope for a future. She couldn't be with me *like that*.

While I foolishly confessed wanting to be just hers.

In the midst of my self-loathing, over the pitter-patter of the water, I heard the locker room door swing open and then a soft click. My shoulders stiffened and I raised my head, wiping back the wet strands sticking to my face.

Maybe Josh had returned to pester me again and ask if I was okay for the tenth time. I appreciated his concern, but I was not in the mood to tolerate his or anyone else's presence.

As I hedged a glance over the shower stall, I seized with tension.

Through the steam rising around me, I managed to decipher the silhouette of my obsession, leaning back against the locker room's door.

Most of the lights were shut, save for a handful of fluorescent ones in the changing area that lent some faded illumination near the shower stalls. But it was enough to confirm that it was *my* Gabriela.

She appeared dazed before her head snapped up.

Her gaze unceremoniously connected with mine.

A slow-burning heat erupted in my core. My pulse pounded embarrassingly fast, the way it always did when she was near me. I wanted to know why she was here and what I needed to do so I could be a man worthy of her.

My moral compass was nonexistent where she was concerned, for I feared that I wasn't above doing whatever it took to make her smile and laugh. To make her *mine* if she allowed it. As a queen to my humble kingdom, I would give her access to my everything. She only needed to reach out and claim me. I was hers for the taking. I had always been. And though I never considered myself to be a gluttonous bastard, I greedily wished she'd be willing to give me a little piece of her heart in exchange for all of me. I would cherish it—her—until the end of my time.

There were a thousand things I wanted to say, yet I couldn't speak a single word.

My luring siren became more visible by the second as she waded closer.

Her indelible beauty struck me once again.

Those blue eyes of hers always reeled me in with their power like I was a pirate lost at sea who'd finally found his beacon of hope. Those red lips held me hostage like a man whose only task in life was tasting her kiss, and that toned body with gentle curves that belonged on a painting in a museum taunted me like a forbidden fruit.

Gabriela was exquisite and I was sick out of my mind with need for her.

In my trance, I opened the shower stall's door, an invitation clear as day.

Suddenly, we were mere inches apart as she came closer. I could practically taste her exhale with my inhale, her signature vanilla and red roses fragrance funneling through my lungs like a drug.

Her hypnotizing gaze fell over my muscular body in rapture, following the water rivulets glistening down my skin. Lust formed on her features as she eyed the snake tattoo wrapped around my right thigh before gasping when she registered the sight of my thickening cock.

I didn't bother hiding myself. She already saw all of me.

And though Gabriela may not like me the way I liked her, she couldn't hide that she was insanely attracted to me.

It was my curse, it seemed, to fall for women who only cared about my outer appearance. But that wasn't entirely true with Gabriela, was it? She cared for me immensely. Just not the same way I cared for her. This was all *friendly* for her while I'd strayed too far in the romantic realm of things.

Quietly, we watched each other through a thin curtain of steam and water. Words were insignificant for this moment crackling with pure thrill and anticipation.

A few water droplets landed on her cheek and I was helpless to reach for her, thumbing them away and stroking the softness of her skin. When she leaned into my palm like she'd missed my touch, giving me this look that fucking unravelled me, I lost what small control I had left.

"What are you doing here, little doll?" My voice came out guttural but coated with layers of my undeniable longing. "Besides torturing me with what I want—and what I can't have—so fucking bad, hm?"

Her eyes closed and she let loose a breathy noise as though my words landed like a shot straight into her sternum. I hated the wrongness of it, wanting to ease her discomfort. "I…"

I leaned down until our foreheads touched and our lips were a hairbreadth away. "Talk to me, baby."

Gabriela's eyes snapped open, swimming with conflicted emotions. "You were never in that class to begin with…You only joined because of me."

I expected her to tell me that she was here to further push her friendship agenda, not state that she somehow figured out my secret. I wasn't even embarrassed that she now knew the truth.

"Haven't you realized by now that I'm obsessed with you?" I confessed. "That I would do anything to be next to you—anything for you to acknowledge my existence?" I wrapped my hand around her neck, her pulse hammering under my thumb, and dragged my open mouth across her cheek, until I reached her diamond-earring-adorned lobe. "I saw you four hundred and forty-seven days ago and you've never left my mind since. You fucking live in there, Gabby. I go to sleep dreaming of you. I wake up thinking of you." My lips grazed the shell of her ear. "And I spend every hour in between like a pathetic fool trying to talk to you, to be next to you, to just please you as though it's my life's sole purpose."

Gabriela jerked back, blue eyes flaring with intensity as she watched me. Her hands rose to cup my cheeks. "You're not pathetic, Hunter. Far from it," she said firmly. "The truth is that there aren't enough words in any language to properly encompass what you are, but I can say with conviction that it's nothing short of perfect."

She leaned up on her toes to stamp her mouth to mine in a kiss that heated my blood and pulverized all my resolve to stay away from Gabriela.

I'm undone, I thought. *I have no defences against her. I'm an open vault and she can take anything and everything from me. So long as she keeps coming back. So long as she never leaves me alone.*

I kissed her back with equal fervour, sipping from her roughly like a thirsty man wandering barren lands and finally finding sustenance. Gabriela's fingers plunged into my wet hair. With the hand still clasped around her neck, I dragged her deeper into me, plastering her fully clothed body to my naked one.

"You can't say shit like that to me. You're killing me, Gabriela," I growled against her lips between short, passionate kisses, squeezing her ass and neck for emphasis. The soft whine she released drove me mad. "Did you come here to pick up where we left off Friday night?"

Gabriela panted like she'd run a marathon, pulling away just enough to gaze at me. The water had drenched her high ponytail, her lashes, and her fur coat. The heavy-lidded look on her face, coupled with flushed cheeks and a kiss-smeared red mouth, was extremely sexy. I remembered it from three nights ago. I had memorized it like a sacred scroll, including the taste of her pussy on my tongue, the sounds of her needy moans, and the feel of her hands on my body, pleading for more.

"N-no. I came here to talk to you. I want to mend what I broke, pretty boy."

That term of endearment wrenched at my heart. "I don't want to talk right now."

I didn't want to hear her apologizing for not being on the same page as me. We couldn't help who we liked or when our feelings weren't reciprocated. I made peace with it. From the very beginning, I was in too deep. While I wished I could be enough for Gabriela to forgo whatever it was that was holding her back...I wouldn't hold it against her.

"No?" She arched a daring brow. "Then what do you want right now?"

"For you to end my misery and take off your coat," I found myself saying, my voice low and pressing. "I want to see what you're hiding underneath."

215

I couldn't think of anything else truthfully.

Gabriela's slow smile was hot as hell. "Fine. I'll play by your rules. Let's pick up where we left off Friday night." She dragged a manicured finger against my bottom lip. "But after that? We're talking. Whether you like it or not."

There was something different about Gabriela today. She was determined and bold, an unspoken resolve sketched in the lines of her frame. Unlike the shy and nervous neighbour who knocked on my door last night reeking of guilt and regret.

In this moment, she appeared like she wanted something for the taking and that thing was *me*.

Hope bloomed in my chest. I squandered it quickly. I shouldn't dwell on the possibility of us being more than whatever it was that we were now. But goddammit, she was lassoing me back into her orbit with just one look.

I forced myself to stay quiet and see how this panned out, retreating two steps so my back was once again immersed under the water and I had a better view of the show she was putting on.

Chin held high and fire burning in those blue eyes, Gabriela watched me sultrily as she opened her fur coat and let it tumble past her shoulders, over the crooks of her elbows, and down her wrists until it landed in a heap on the floor just outside of the shower stall with a flourish.

Leaving her in red heels and a short leopard print dress with a joke of a neckline that showcased an ample amount of cleavage and was so tight I could see her nipples, hard like diamonds, poking through the fabric.

Fucking hell.

By the time she toed off her heels, pushed aside the straps of her dress and let it shimmy down her body, revealing smooth expanses of that moonlight skin just begging to be marred with love bites, I was rendered speechless.

I dragged a palm over my mouth, muttering a curse under my breath. "Keep your panties on."

She paused with her fingers tucked in the sides of her crimson thong. It barely covered her cunt and was damp with arousal. "Why?"

"So I'm not tempted by that pussy." I fisted my cock, picturing my length running over her slickness. "I don't want to see it and if you dare show it to me, I will be reddening your ass in punishment, doll."

I could tell Gabriela wanted to defy my command just to see my reaction. Just to see if I would actually follow through with my threat. "Maybe I want a spanking."

"Frankly, you don't want a spanking—you *need* one for being a tease and having the brattiest little pussy I've ever had the pleasure of licking." I rolled my bottom lip into my mouth, choking the tip of my cock with a groan. "But we both know you'd enjoy me slapping your ass until you're a horny, wet mess, and I'm not ready to reward you yet."

"You're a killjoy."

"Call it whatever you will," I rasped. "But I haven't had a moment of peace since you sashayed into my life like you goddamn own me."

"Serves you right. I haven't stopped thinking about you either since that night on the terrace."

I hissed in a breath. "Is that so?"

"You live in my mind, too," she said bashfully. "All the time, Hunter."

Her admission weakened and strengthened me simultaneously. "Gabby," I begged. "Get in here. Now."

So I can touch you, kiss you, hold you, convince you that I'm worth a shot.

Gabriela slinked back into the shower stall and let the door slam shut behind her, locking it for good measure.

Then it was just us.

Two mortals permeating the air with their desire, their hearts beating jaggedly but in unison like we possessed the same whole.

Curving an arm around her waist, I tugged her under the spray until the water rained down on us both. Gabriela gasped and anchored her hands on my shoulders. "Now what, you bossy man?"

"Don't act like you don't like my demanding side."

"I love it, Hunter." Water cascaded down her face and washed away some of her mascara and lipstick, revealing piecemeals of her natural beauty. With or without makeup, she was stunning to me nonetheless. "So very much."

I twisted my fist around her ponytail twice and yanked her head back, causing her to release a delicious, faint whimper that I drank in with a crude kiss. Lust sizzled under my skin, bubbling over like lava and scouring away the dejection from last night. A feeling of righteousness settled into my gut. I could finally breathe again.

Everything in my world felt aligned now that her lips were on mine again.

Right where they belonged.

"You still owe me, you little heartbreaker. You came to my game, but you didn't wear my jersey. Instead, you wore a silky dress that leaves nothing to the imagination," I said huskily against her mouth. "It's a good thing you didn't remove your coat in the bleachers. Otherwise, I'd have been off the field mid-game to pummel my fist in the faces of those leering men."

"I'm sorry for not wearing your jersey, baby. Let me make it up to you." Gabriela started mapping her sensual kisses down my chin, jaw, and neck until she reached my right pec. She flicked the silver barbell with the tip of her tongue before sucking my nipple in a wicked manner. I grunted. Every inch of me was an erogenous zone under her tongue and I needed her to lick me all over like an ice cream cone. "Since I am your number one fan."

"Yeah?" My voice was thick with need. "So get on your knees and show me your fangirl behaviour, sweetheart."

CHAPTER 22

His Favourite Groupie

HUNTER

Stifling a groan, I watched in acute fascination as Gabriela trailed her lips down my body, ruining me one kiss at a time.

My nerve endings were on fire. She paused to nuzzle my stomach muscles and lick the beginning of the serpent tattoo under my right hip bone before she lowered herself to a kneeling position in front of me. Those blue eyes of hers were packed with zeal as she grasped my dick. "Is this how all your fangirls show you their appreciation?"

I trembled under her touch. "I've never had a girl appreciate me like this."

Stunned, Gabriela whispered a shell-shocked, "What?"

My face warmed with a blush. In the past, I'd had sex and gone down on women, but no one had ever sucked me off. This was a first. I was glad I saved it for her. "You heard me, Gabby."

Gratification zinged through her expression and she smiled. Did she like that I'd never received a blow job? And fuck, why was I so excited over her reaction?

"Good. I like that I'm the only one who gets to show you how amazing this will feel."

When she gave my length a slow pump from root to tip, I bit back a moan. The sight of her ruby red nails wrapped around my cock and the exhales from her lips fanning over my heated skin had me losing my mind. I flattened my hands against the tiled wall above her head to stop myself from gripping her hair and stuffing her mouth full of my inches. And while I was a gentleman outside of the bedroom…Gabriela would soon learn that I was nothing but a dirty motherfucker when it came to delivering and receiving pleasure. "Stop torturing me and put me in your mouth."

A sinful glint flashed in her eyes. "Say *please* like a good boy and I will."

She threw my own words back at me—the same words I said before kissing her on the dance floor. "Please, baby. I need you so fucking bad."

My reward was my living fantasy's tongue skating out to taste my flared head in an experimental lick. I choked back another moan, ensuring that I didn't draw unwanted attention towards us in case any passerby lingered outside of the locker room. Gabriela dipped into my slit to collect the pearly drop of pre-cum with an appreciative hum. "*Mm.* I love the feel and taste of you, Hunter."

A myriad of sensations coursed through me and all she'd done was lick me. Overwhelmed, I screwed my eyes closed. *This* was what I'd been needing all along. Gabriela. On her knees. Her hands, lips, tongue, all over me.

Clearly not liking that I wasn't giving her my undivided attention, a small tut rang in the air. "Keep your eyes on me or I will stop, *principe.*"

Speech failed me. I couldn't ask her what *principe* meant. Only obey as I stared down at her with a clenched jaw and water trickling into my eyes, obscuring my vision.

But not enough to avoid witnessing the sheer magnificence that was Gabriela Regina Bellafiore looking half celestial-sent and half Tartarus-risen. An angel and a witch wrapped in a silky red bow. The smug smirk on her lips told me she knew exactly what kind of chokehold she had me in.

"Just like that," she praised. "And don't try to be quiet. I want to hear all your sounds. I love your voice, Hunter."

Then the hot little minx ruined me forever, licking the underside of my cock before sucking more than half of me in one swoop, her hands working in tandem to cover the rest. Fuck, fuck, fuck. "*Gabriela.*"

When her head started bobbing up and down, I could no longer control the loud groans rumbling out of me. I nearly went cross-eyed at the pleasurable clutch of her mouth and the way my saliva-coated cock shuttled in and out of those scarlet lips. Was this really happening? Was the girl of my dreams actually servicing me on her knees? I threw my head back, pleading, "Keep going. Don't stop. Please, please, please. Feels so good. Feels so perfect. *You're* perfect."

I never knew anything could feel so earth-shatteringly right.

Tears rolled down Gabriela's cheeks, stained black from her mascara. My girth was too thick and my length too long, but she kept going like a trooper, enjoying herself even. As her hand played with my aching balls, I felt the telltale signs of my impending release.

I held back from coming, wanting to prolong it.

Gabriela pulled off my cock with a *pop*, her gasp echoing loudly over the sound of the rushing water. I almost cursed at being denied my orgasm, but my retort died in my throat when she continued jacking me off. I feared my own fist would never do it for me. Nothing would, except for her.

"Hunter, I want you to fuck my mouth."

Every line in my body tensed with her demand, my arousal spiking higher. Fuck, I wanted that too. Removing my hands from the wall to frame her face, I gazed down at her in affection. "I don't want to hurt you."

"You won't," she insisted, angling her head enough to place a kiss in the middle of my palm, turning me to mush with her gesture. "I want you to experience this. If it becomes too much for me, I'll tap your thigh twice. But I do enjoy being dominated and I'll love every second of you forcing your cock down my throat like you hate my guts."

My nostrils flared and my head spun with the imagery of face-fucking Gabriela. Her words were like a trigger, causing my fingers to make fast work of removing the tie from her ponytail. I knuckled handfuls

221

of her red hair and yanked her head back so she was forced to stare into my narrowed eyes, a hot whimper susurrating behind her closed mouth.

"I adore you. Please don't forget that. Even if I get a little rough, I still respect you." My next inhale juddered in my chest. "And I swear to stop if it gets too much for you."

She grinned. "I know, pretty boy."

With the level of trust established between us, I brought one hand down to cup her chin, gently prying her jaw open by dipping my thumb between the seam of her lips. She watched my every move with keen interest. I shivered when she flicked her tongue against the pad of my finger. "You really are the most beautiful thing I've ever seen, Gabby."

With the submissive way she knelt, her wine-coloured strands tumbling over the swells of her breasts, and the way the water sluiced down her porcelain skin like she was a centerpiece in a fountain, she resembled a venerated goddess.

My goddess of victory.

Tenderly, she cupped my wrist and kissed the web of veins there. "Likewise, Hunter."

Please, God. Let me have this woman for keeps. I'll provide her with everything. An abundance of smiles, laughs, happiness, and memories to be cherished until the day we both die.

Fisting my cock, I guided it towards her awaiting mouth. "Take me in, baby. Give me a taste of my sanctuary."

Gabriela obliged, widening her jaw. I pushed into her, warm wetness encasing me like an aphrodisiac. Her gaze never once wavered from mine as I pumped my hips, giving her more of my length. Not a single gag reflex in sight. "Ah, *fuckkk*," I spat, so fucking turned on and impressed with her ability to take me with such ease. "You okay?"

She jerked her head in a semblance of a nod, her *yes* muted by my cock.

Ever so slowly, I withdrew until just my tip was poised on her tongue before rocking back in. I kept the pace steady. Getting us both used to the sensation. Loving the way her lips moulded over my thickness. Shaking from the pleasure building at the base of my spine.

The thoughts in my brain slowly quieted until I was reduced to the singular feeling of her mouth hugging my cock like it was her best fucking friend as I sawed in and out of her. There was no way I would last longer than a handful of minutes. Especially when her throat relaxed all the way through, allowing me to slot the last few inches inside of her, my balls resting against her chin and her nose pressed to my pubic bone.

It was obscene how such a small mouth was stuffed full of my fat cock.

The visual and the tiny moans vibrating against my skin destroyed any finesse I had remaining.

Finally, I face-fucked Gabriela.

My hips pounded my cock into her mercilessly. I breathed like a goddamn bull, my fingers digging into her hair like a pair of reins to hold her head in place for my cruel treatment.

God help my little doll because she enjoyed it, despite the tears cascading down her cheeks and the thick stream of saliva pooling down her chin, dripping onto her shaking tits. Gabriela's nails raked against the muscles of my ass and gripped me tighter, urging me silently to give her more.

I fucking would.

I'd disrespect that mouth like it was a fuck toy until my cum leaked out in a white mess.

And because I was such a good fucking boy, I'd scoop it up with a kiss and spit it right back on her pussy so her tight little hole didn't feel neglected.

I had a feeling she'd spread her legs wide open to receive my offering.

"You're a good girl, Gabriela," I praised on a growl, thrusting like a madman. "Allowing me to use you like a nasty slut after I scored three touchdowns for you." *Thrust.* "Getting down on your knees like a sweet groupie." *Thrust.* "Looking like a filthy little doll with your mouth crammed full of cock." *Thrust.* "Once I finish coming, I'll make a meal out of you." *Thrust.* "I fucking promise."

Gabriela's eyes rolled back, an approving moan blasting against my length. She wanted me to return the favour. I couldn't wait. Now that I knew she got off on a combination of praise and degradation, I'd use it to my advantage.

The shower stall resonated with my deep grunts and the glugging noises of my cock sloshing in her mouth, all marrying together with the sound of the water beating down on us.

My pace was unruly as I neared my peak. "Fuck, baby." *Thrust.* "I'm almost there." *Thrust.* "Should I spill in that talented mouth or paint your gorgeous tits with my cum?" *Thrust.* "Choose now before I make the decision for you."

Gabriela dug her nails into my flexing ass, pinning me with sharp eyes that dared me to disobey her. She wanted me in her mouth. That was exactly what she'd get.

With less than half a dozen thrusts, I finally came on a guttural groan that seemed dragged out of the recesses of my soul. I nearly went blind from the powerful release, my fingers tightening in Gabriela's hair as I filled her mouth.

I'd never come this much or this *hard* in my life.

Panting, I watched Gabriela, completely obliterated by her.

No other woman would ever hold a candle to her.

She was it for me.

Now and forever.

"Don't swallow it yet," I commanded harshly, my fingers feathering over her cheeks in reverence. "Keep me in your mouth."

Before she could question my motive, I lifted her into my arms and boosted her ass onto the metal grab bar on the wall adjacent to us. Gabriela's hands clutched it on either side for better balance, her legs spreading wide and ready for what I promised.

I ripped the red thong down her legs like it had personally offended me, baring that soaked pussy for my feasting eyes. Swollen, pink, and dripping with arousal. It was practically begging to be spanked.

So I slapped it.

Twice.

Gabriela jolted with a whimper.

My hand shot out to squeeze her jaw and I crowded her, our naked chests gliding. "Are you on birth control?"

She nodded, eyes going hazy with more lust.

"Good." My tongue licked her bottom lip. "Now spit in my mouth, doll."

Gabriela tilted her head and parted her lips. The hottest moan escaped her as she dribbled my own cum into my eager mouth. *"Mm, Hunter."*

A light tremor coursed through her body as she watched me get on my knees in front of her. My hands skimmed over her inner thighs before my thumbs roved over her slit and parted her sex for my ministrations.

With my eyes on hers, I spat on her pussy.

The salacious act had Gabriela releasing a half gasp, half moan.

Our essences mingled together beautifully. My seed and her nectar. An elixir that beckoned me until I was ruled with the absolute need to lick the entirety of her pussy from tight hole to throbbing clit like a famished man. I did just that, groaning at her arousal mixed with me and wanting to go to Church to thank the Lord for making this flawless creation. "It's unreal how fucking delicious you are, Gabby. I haven't stopped thinking about this pretty pussy since I first tasted it. I want to lick it, suck it, slap it. Spend the rest of my life buried between your thighs like my only source of nourishment comes from here."

"Hunter." She panted, tits rising and falling with every breath. "Please. I need you."

"Yeah?" I taunted, the tip of my tongue teasingly swiping over her clit. "How badly do you need me?"

"So bad that I can't think straight." She squirmed and I threw her legs over my shoulders. "Please, Hunter. Make me come."

She earned it after all, for performing like the dirtiest of sluts straight from my godforsaken fantasies.

I stopped playing around and went for broke, eating her out like *I* was the groupie and flicking her clit with my tongue until the movement was a blur. She stared down at me in astonishment, the most porn-worthy moans tumbling out of her. I chuckled lazily against her wet flesh and plunged two fingers knuckles-deep into her pussy, finding the erogenous spot and abusing it until her pleasure-stricken cries grew in decibel. They were loud enough for anyone outside of this room to know that she was getting the tongue-fucking of her life. "You like that, baby?"

"Oh my God." Gabriela screamed and it was music to my ears.

"Never been called God, but I accept the title." My tongue continued to remind her everything it was capable of doing until she writhed in my hold, her feet digging into my back and her fingers twisting in my hair with intent. Gabriela's walls tightened around my fingers and her pussy rode my chin and lips, leaving a glistening trail. She engulfed all my senses. Her taste. Her scent. Her touch. Her goddamn needy noises. I spanked her pussy and enjoyed her throaty moan before sucking her clit into my mouth, loving the taste of us. "Fuck, you're almost there, hm? Dirty girl. I want you coming all over my mouth."

It didn't take long for Gabriela to reach her orgasm. A couple more seconds of my fingers and tongue working her pussy, and she exploded with her head thrown back, screaming, "*Hunt!*"

My little doll. My goddess of victory. My fucking ruin.

She was beautiful when she was in the throes of passion.

"Gabby." Her pussy spasmed and her body quivered from the strong release. I kept lapping at her arousal. "Mm. So fucking good, baby."

Pressing frantic kisses, I chased my way up her mound, her stomach, the valley between her breasts and paused when I reached her mouth. Gabriela huffed, a glazed look in her gaze.

Silently, we stared at each other for three heartbeats.

You blew my mind, she said with her eyes.

There's no one like you, I returned with my own.

Gabriela wrapped her arms around my shoulders and drew me in for a kiss. My fingers slipped over her wet skin and grabbed her waist as my tongue entered her mouth. She hummed, enjoying our taste.

My hardened cock slid against her throbbing cunt. We moaned together.

Gabriela bucked her hips, demanding more. "Fuck me. I can't take it anymore. Please."

"I don't have a condom on me," I said regretfully between intoxicating kisses and grinding. Nor did I want our first time to be here. I'd plan it out properly. Roses. Candles. Silk sheets. She was a romantic at heart and deserved that at the very least. Not a fast, hot fuck in a shower stall where I'd have to cover her mouth to ensure we didn't get caught.

A sobbing moan escaped her. "I don't care."

"You should. Don't let me pump any more cum in this tight pussy," I growled, nipping her bottom lip. She mewled. "I'm supposed to be a gentleman." I slapped her cunt twice to hear that needy whimper I was addicted to. "Even though I'd like nothing more than to fuck you hard like you're my filthy little plaything."

Gabriela licked the water droplets from my collarbone and drew soft kisses to my ear, where she whispered, "I want to be your filthy little plaything, *bello*."

"Fuck, sweetheart. *Fuckkk*." My vile curses rang in the air when Gabriela grabbed my cock and rubbed it over her folds.

"P-please, Hunter."

She was prime for the taking after all this foreplay. I could screw her fast and rough in several positions. Gabriela would love every second of our dirty fucking. The brazen imagery played in my mind. Yet I still held back, gritting my teeth. I was determined to give her the perfect first time. Something that proved to her I was in it for the long run. That she mattered enough for me to go the extra mile. "Gabby..."

Gabriela fluttered those long lashes and gave me a coy look that nearly shredded my resolve, moaning when my cock caressed her swollen clit. "W-will you give me just the tip?"

Denying her anything physically hurt. Built with the inherent need to cater to her, I was torn between two options. But I realized this could end in a way where we both received more pleasure without going all the way.

Decision made, I dragged Gabriela down. Once her feet hit the floor, I swiftly spun her around and she grabbed the metal bar for leverage when I hiked her ass in the air with an arm under her hips.

Then I cracked my palm against the slippery skin of her left ass cheek. "Stop acting like a brat and behave."

Her surprised gasp resounded in the stall.

The energy between us stirred with more wickedness. Gabriela waited for further instructions with bated breath, her posture submissive.

Grasping a fistful of her hair, I yanked and she cried out, her back plastering to my front. "I'm not giving you *just the tip* because you're too gone for me right now. If I give you even an inch, you'll impale yourself until your little cunt is full of me and we're fucking like animals. Even though that's what we both want. Isn't that right, baby?" I whispered darkly in her ear and she moaned under her breath. "However, since you've been such a good girl, I'll give you some relief." A soft *yes, please* left her with a sigh. "Spread your legs." When she did as I asked, I fisted my heavy length and brought it between her legs, tucking it right under her pussy. Arousal dripped over my shaft instantly. "Squeeze your thighs and lock me in. *Ahh*—fuck, just like that." I brought my left hand to clutch her tit and my right hand over her clit before licking the shell of her ear. "Now rock your hips and fuck my cock like it's one of your toys. Give me a preview of how you'd do me, doll."

"My God. You're nasty." Gabriela leaned her head back against my chest, gazing up at me with passion-filled eyes. "I love it."

"Tell me I'm a good boy for keeping myself in check around your hot little pussy."

She cursed like she couldn't believe I'd said that. We both knew I was far from a good boy in her presence. But that's what she liked. "You're a good boy, Hunter." She kissed me and I groaned. "My little saint."

I was about to show her how much more unsaintly I could get.

"Get to work," I ordered, pinching her nipple before giving her tit a quick swat. "I need something to tide me over until I can really fuck you, Gabriela." I slapped her clit for good measure too, relishing her whine. "And I will fuck you. Make no mistake. This will happen."

With my oath echoing in our enclosure, Gabriela clenched her legs and started snapping her hips, the rhythm nothing short of maddening. I moved with her in unison, my lap meeting her beautiful ass with every thrust. The wet glide around my cock was pure magic, her pussy enveloping my length like it never wanted to let go. My deep groans and her girlish moans were amplified over the sound of the rushing water. I gauged her reaction through the thin veil of steam as I strummed her nipples and clit, getting her ready for another orgasm. As our bodies collided, we half kissed and half breathed into each other's mouths, eyes locked on one another. The slick tunnel of her thighs, the warmth of her throbbing flesh, and the grind of her clit against my shaft were too much.

I murmured all sorts of dirty talk in her ears as we climbed our peak.

"Goddamn, look at you, being so friendly *and letting me fuck these gorgeous thighs, baby. It's the least you can do after driving me wild for more than a year. There's still a long way to go before I forgive you, you little heartbreaker, but you'll repay me when the time comes. On your back. Legs in the air. Screaming my name as I pound your pussy six ways to Sunday."*

"Did you lock the door? Of course you didn't. You want someone to catch us, don't you? Bet you'll come ten times harder from being watched like the exhibitionist that you are, sweetheart."

Before we tumbled over the edge, I collared Gabriela's throat with my hand, giving her that dominant side she loved, and rasped, "Make this pussy come before one of my teammates returns and sees that I've got my hands full of the hottest slut. Do it before I have no choice but to keep treating you like you're nothing but my favourite fuck toy, Gabriela."

"*Hunter.*" A scream, muffled by my palm, tore out of her mouth as she finally came, eyes squeezed shut in pleasure.

Unable to hold back any longer, I hurtled over the edge with her. My bellow was muffled against her jaw and my cum splashed all over her inner thighs, pussy, and stomach.

Still trembling, I clutched her like she was my lifeline, layering kisses anywhere I could reach—her lips, cheeks, forehead.

My voice was ragged from pleasure when seconds later, I confessed in her ear, "I've never seen you as just a friend. Always as the woman I want to be owned by—the one I want to treat like a queen, Gabriela."

I finished by kissing the **R** tattoo behind her ear.

CHAPTER 23
Heart-To-Heart

GABRIELA

The quiet that followed our mutual orgasm and Hunter's confession was laced with tender harmony. A flurry of goosebumps ignited on my flesh, having everything to do with the beautiful, protective man standing behind me, pressing his kisses into my skin while his arms bracketed me like I was an anchor in the midst of a tumultuous storm.

Unexpected tears stung my eyes. I wanted to tell him that I returned the sentiment—that I was ready to be owned by him too. Yet my tongue felt glued to the roof of my mouth as I kept going over his fervently spoken words, my heart glowing warm.

All my walls crumbled to smithereens like the ruins of an old castle until I was a skeletal version of the old me before being resuscitated from Hunter's touch like a phoenix rising from a pile of ashes.

When he proceeded to wash me with utmost care afterwards, soaping my body and shampooing my hair in a soothing lather, like he marvelled at every strand of my hair and every line of my figure, an abundance of affection for Hunter unravelled inside of me, grander than anything I could contain in my frame.

Without a doubt, that was the most intimate shower of my life. We hadn't had penetrative intercourse and it still rivalled all my past experiences with other men by a long stretch.

I couldn't recall another human ever gazing at me with such innocent wonder and stark longing. Like I was punishing him by not letting him be mine. Like he was eternally grateful for every second spent together, regardless of the outcome. It made me hate myself a little for putting him through any sort of pain, when he'd only ushered joy into my life since our meeting on the terrace. It made me want to wrap Hunter up in my arms and safeguard him from any harm, though he was bigger and stronger than me.

Our companionable silence did not come to an end when Hunter turned off the shower and carried me out of the stall. He proceeded to pat my skin dry with a fluffy towel and massage his lotion into my lax muscles. No man had ever taken his time with me before, during, or after sex. Except for this one. And we hadn't even gone all the way.

There was a lump in my throat as I watched Hunter go about the task with a concentrated frown on his face. I sensed that he needed this quietness to refuel himself before we actually talked.

I also wondered if he was afraid that speaking would shatter the magic of the moment.

Belatedly, I wondered if that was why I was also silent.

By the time he finished combing out my wet hair and brushing a kiss in the curve where my shoulder met my neck, I couldn't help but grasp his stubbled cheeks and lay a kiss on his lips. It was filled with all the things I had yet to tell him.

Hunter sighed against my lips, eyes still closed.

"I'll be right back," he murmured almost vulnerably. "Please, don't go anywhere without me."

Oh, Hunter. I wouldn't even if I could.

Overcome by the tightness in my chest, I simply nodded.

Hunter trudged towards the sinks and mirrors to give me privacy to dress. I imagined him repeating the same post-shower routine on himself as I put on my clothes, sans panties, because those were a dripping mess, and contemplated how to best broach the topic of us.

It was the entire reason for me coming to his game tonight and I wasn't leaving until I mended what I foolishly broke yesterday.

My belly fluttered with nerves when Hunter re-emerged. He wore a pair of black pants and a white dress shirt that was half-buttoned haphazardly like he'd hurried with dressing himself to ensure I was still here.

His clothes clung to his strapping form, the material translucent where his skin was still damp and highlighting his big muscles. I couldn't believe I'd seen him bare and had my hands and mouth all over him. My God, I was going to dream of that thigh tat. I wish I'd taken the time to lick the entirety of it with my tongue before I sucked his cock.

"You waited," he breathed, relieved.

A pang travelled in my chest. Did he actually think I would bail?

I supposed I'd given him every reason to believe so.

My eyes rose to find his beseeching ones, waiting for me to break the spell we seemed to be under. A hint of fear lurked in his depths. I wanted to set him at ease, my own heart twisting in its cage as I beheld this perfect man who was fairy-tale handsome like a gallant knight in shining armour, besotted with the princess he thought he couldn't have.

"Of course, Hunter." I flexed my hands by my side. "I have something to say. Will you listen to me?"

His back straightened with attention and he nodded.

"I came here tonight to talk to you—to apologize for last night. I never meant to hurt you. Not when you mean so much to me. I hope you can forgive me for making you believe otherwise." I inhaled deeply and cut straight to the chase. "And I want to try being more than friends. I want to take that chance with you. If you'll still have me."

I barely finished speaking before Hunter was suddenly in front of me, cupping my face and staring down at me with hope. "Are you serious?"

"Yes."

"What does 'more than friends' mean to you? Because I won't settle for being just your fuck buddy. I'm not some dirty secret to be hidden behind closed doors. I know my worth and I deserve more than that." His thumb roved over my cheek. "So do you, Gabby."

"I don't mean as a fuck buddy." I cleared my throat, glancing away for a brief second before meeting his blue eyes again. "I want us to date... To eventually become boyfriend and girlfriend."

Exhaling, Hunter dropped his forehead to mine. I physically felt the relief penetrating through him. "You'll really give me a chance?"

"Yes. If there's anyone who's going to be good to me, it's you." I ran my hands over his back in a gentle caress. His bunched muscles relaxed under my touch. "Just please be careful with me. For all my bravado, I am delicate."

Admitting it out loud was freeing since I knew Hunter would never weaponize it against me. I'd tried my best to pick up my pieces after Franco. Some days, I felt whole. Other days, I felt like a teddy bear with its stuffing torn out.

"Baby, I'll treat you like glass if it means I can keep you with me. I'll never let anything or anyone hurt you, including myself." He dusted his nose against mine. "All I want is the opportunity to show you how good it can be between us."

He'd already shown me how good it could be between us and for once, I wasn't scared.

"Okay. First date this weekend?" I said teasingly but thoroughly meant it.

"On one condition."

"What?"

"You let me plan it. From start to finish."

I loved a proactive man. "Deal."

Hunter's smile was so radiant and infectious. It incited my own. "Fuck, is this really happening? I feel like I'm dreaming."

I pinched his butt and an amused sound erupted from him. "See? Not dreaming."

He shushed my chuckle with a claiming kiss that left no room for argument. Simply the understanding that we were two individuals who were finally taking the chance that we owed ourselves.

"Are we moving too fast?" I couldn't help but ask.

"If anything, we've been moving too slow. I've been pining over you for more than a year, Gabriela. Give me some credit. I want you. I've wanted you from the first second I saw you at Josh's birthday party, looking like the most beautiful girl in the world. I wondered about your name, about the things you liked." He kissed me again. Like he couldn't stop himself. Like I was just that addictive. "I also wondered about the feel of your lips, the taste of your skin." His voice took on a husky edge. "And there's a part of me that likes to believe that you've wanted me and wondered about these things too. At least from the moment we crossed paths again on the terrace."

"I have," I admitted as Hunter laid kisses along my jawline, my fingers curling over his shoulders. "I meant it when I said you haven't left my mind since. I think about you all the time. You make me smile, you make me laugh, you make me feel at peace. Doesn't matter what we're doing—watching a movie, taking a walk, or simply texting each other. You ease my anxiety and quiet the demons in my mind. When I'm not with you, I count the hours until I can see you again. And when we're together, I want to make every second last because I'll miss you so much when we say good night." Remembering his words from the shower, I added softly, "I need you to know that I see you, Hunter. It may have been later than when you saw me, but I acknowledge your existence. I see it, I feel it, and it's so precious to me. *You're* so precious to me."

A small noise rumbled in the back of his throat and Hunter crushed me in his arms. His mouth pressed to my forehead and he held it there, breathing me in. "Fuck, baby. What are you doing to me?"

Exactly what you're doing to me. "It's the truth, Hunter."

"What made you change your mind from last night to now?" he asked and I sensed that a part of him gnawed over the fact that I may be pitying him.

He was far from a charity case. I'd make sure moving forward that he never felt unwanted or unworthy.

To me, he was everything and more.

"Honestly?" I grasped his face, loving the feel of his trimmed stubble against my palms. "I grew tired of denying myself the thing I want most—you. I spent all night crying over how I lost you when I could have had you—in the way we both want—and I no longer want to keep self-sabotaging. Please know that anytime you've felt like I've retreated, it's never had anything to do with you and everything to do with my own issues."

"Your ex?" he guessed bitterly.

I nodded.

"Okay, I'll take it. Whatever you're able to give. It'll be enough for me."

I could feel him wanting to say *for now* but holding back.

"At the end of the day, I just want to be with you—to keep making you smile and laugh. Whenever you're ready to talk about your fears, I'll be here to listen without judgement and help you work through them."

"I adore you," I murmured, kissing him.

He kissed me back. "I adore you, too."

After a few seconds, Hunter tightened his arms around me and hesitantly said, "It wasn't easy for me to put myself out there. I took a gamble and was glad that it paid off, especially when I realized how easy it was to talk to you without feeling like I was making a clown out of myself. You have no idea how fast my heart pounded with excitement whenever we talked, whether in person or through texts. For all my confidence, there was a part of me worried that you wouldn't want me the way I wanted you. I'm not one to flirt or chase after girls, but I bent those rules for you, and I don't think I've ever been as happy as I've been these last few weeks with you. Gabriela, there aren't enough words to convey how much joy *your* presence brings me. You're like a ray of sunshine. You brighten my world. And you were the first person to make me feel like I could be my raw self and you'd accept me as is—and you did." He kissed the tip of my nose. "You're not the only one who's been hurt in your past. So have I. But I'm willing to work through those issues if you're willing to do the same. I'm just like you. I have insecurities, but…we'll figure it out together, okay?"

His speech left me a little shaken up but relieved too. "Deal," I replied, my voice laden with emotions. "Also, what are you insecure about? You're basically perfect."

Hunter's Adam's apple bobbed, his features imploring. "I'm glad you think so, but I'm really not, Gabby. I'm human, just like everybody else, and I'm more than my physical appearance. Having my entire worth reduced to just that one singular, superficial aspect has left me with more bruises on the inside than I can count on two hands."

My expression fell and my mind wandered to his bitch of an ex, wondering if she was responsible for birthing these so-called bruises inside of him. If she was, she'd better pray she never came face-to-face with me. "I'm so sorry. For what it's worth, though you're drop dead handsome, the most beautiful part of you isn't your physical appearance." I placed a hand on the left side of his chest, gazing at him knowingly. "It's your heart."

We spent enough time together for me to quickly come to that conclusion.

The most powerful thing about Hunter was his heart and how he wouldn't hesitate to take the shirt off his back for someone in need. People like him were rare and I was finding myself growing more and more possessive of him, a sick and twisted part of me wanting to hide him from this traitorous world and keep him safe in my lair, where no one could ever hurt him. Not even myself.

Hunter smiled. "Thank you for saying that."

My answer was to kiss him for what felt like the hundredth time in the last hour.

"Last chance to get away from me before I sink my claws in too deep," I jokingly warned. "Do you really want to do this? You might realize I'm awfully needy once we start dating."

"Good." He picked up my hand to kiss the back of it. "I want you to need me."

I turned to putty but tried my best to put on a serious expression. It was more playful than anything, really. "I mean it, Hunter. I need attention like oxygen. I may wither away without it."

It was a bit dramatized and Hunter chuckled. "I'll shower you with all the attention you need. There will be no withering away on my watch."

"I also like to cook and bake in my free time, so your fridge might be overstocked with pasta dishes and blueberry muffins."

"Only an idiot would complain." He arched an eyebrow. "I, however, won't. You have free rein to do as you please in my kitchen."

Smart man. "And I don't drive, so you'll have to chauffeur me everywhere."

"Baby, I'll chauffeur you to the ends of the earth. Wherever you go, I'll follow." Amusement twinkled in his blue eyes. "What else?"

"My cat and I are joined at the hip. I like to bring her with me wherever I can. Will that be a problem?"

He scoffed. "Please, I adore Luna. I'm well-aware that you're a package deal."

"Good." I tapped my chin mock thoughtfully. "Well, I think that's it for now."

"If you're done trying to scare me away from dating you"—Hunter slung his duffel bag onto his shoulder and offered me his hand—"I'd like to take you home, Gabby."

I smiled, twining our fingers together. "All right. Take me home, Hunter."

CHAPTER 24

GABRIELA

Hunter invited me and Luna over for dinner and to watch this week's horror movie so we could complete our weekly assignment. I'd barely eaten today, heartsick with yesterday's events, that I finally felt my appetite returning with renewed vigour after our shower and talk.

I needed to get ready and rush over to his place, but the first thing on my mind was texting the girls in the group chat the second I crossed my apartment's threshold.

Guess who officially has a date this Saturday? —Gabby

They read my message immediately. I could see Anna and Layla typing while I put my damp hair in a quick braid, the smile on my face barely wavering. It seemed to be plastered there from the minute Hunter and I left the locker room hand in hand.

Oh my God!! —Layla

This is so exciting!! —Anna

I cornered him in the locker room and we had a really good conversation 💜 I don't know where we'll be going for our date, but I'm looking forward to it! —Gabby

I purposely omitted the part about what occurred in the shower. I figured I'd give them the whole rundown when I saw them in person.

I'm glad tonight paid off and you guys were able to patch things up 🩶 —Layla

So happy for you, Gabby. You deserve this 🩶 —Anna

Thank you both 🩶 —Gabby

Also, brunch this Sunday? We're going to want to hear all the details! —Anna

Seconded! —Layla

Brunch on Sunday sounds good! Can't wait 😊 —Gabby

Btw, Josh peered over my shoulder and read our convo. He says congrats. Now he wants to go on a double date. —Layla

I told him we're not crashing your first date but that we could all hang out another time. He proposed bowling. Obviously, he wants a rematch. —Layla

Josh and I had a competitive streak and we both enjoyed bowling. I beat him the last time we played. He'd been sulking like a sore loser ever since.

LOL sounds like a plan. —Gabby

Let's invite Sam and make it a triple date. —Layla

?? – Anna

I gasped at the last two texts, in the middle of shimmying on a pair of small black shorts and Hunter's gifted football jersey.

Sorry, Josh stole my phone and typed that out. He says there was a lot of tension between Sam and Anna this past Friday night. He thinks they both want each other and we should help their courtship by putting them in the same room. —Layla

Tell your boyfriend he's lost his marbles. —Anna

The only tension present on Friday night was Gabby and

Hunter's. —Anna

There's nothing going on between Sam and me. —Anna

Anna was getting defensive. But we'd all be lying if we said there hadn't been something between them. However, I didn't want to add more fuel to the fire by saying anything that might bother her. Layla clearly didn't get the memo because her next text had my eyes widening as I put on a pair of fluffy socks.

In that case, if Josh invites Sam, maybe we can invite Darla, Dacia, or Hera? What do you think, Gabby? I feel like he could be their type. —Layla

Huh? Was that actually Layla or did Josh steal her phone again? Anna started typing. Then stopped. And started again.

Not Hera because Shaun's going to have a fit. But definitely Darla or Dacia. —Gabby

You're right. Shaun will probably have my balls. Let's set him up with Dacia. I think he's got a soft spot for tall, leggy blondes. —Layla

That one hundred percent was Josh, playing matchmaker as usual. Finally, Anna's text arrived.

Does Dacia like Sam? —Anna

I rolled my lips into my mouth, surprised. For all her avoidance regarding Sam, maybe she did care a little…

Not in the romantic sense, but if she spends more time in his presence, she definitely will •• What's not to like? He's a catch. Six foot four, rich, hot, and the list goes on. —Layla

Why, does that bother you? —Layla

You sound jealous, Anna. —Layla

If you want Sam all to yourself, all you need to do is come on our triple date. —Layla

I was laughing now, padding over to the kitchen to pour food into Luna's bowl. It was merciless to allow Josh to unleash his craziness on the group chat, but I was too curious to hear Anna's reply. Therefore, I let this play out for a while longer.

Why would I be bothered or jealous when I don't want him? —Anna

Liar!!! —Layla

So is that a yes or no for the triple date?? —Layla

You're insufferable, Josh. —Anna

I'll take that as a yes and be sure to tell Sam that you're looking forward to seeing him 😌 —Layla

A few seconds later, another text came from Layla.

Josh abducted my phone and shut me in the bathroom while he texted all of that ^ I'm so sorry, Anna. —Layla

You give him too much free rein. It's time to tighten his leash. —Anna

Oh, believe me, I know. Tonight, as punishment, I'm going to tie him to the bedposts like a prisoner. —Layla

No, stop! He's going to love that! —Gabby

You're probably right 😕 —Layla

We said our good nights in the chat and then I picked up Luna in one arm, her bowl in the other, and strategically shut off the lights with my elbow. When I stepped out into the empty hallway, Hunter's door was already ajar, anticipating our arrival.

Luna squirmed and I placed her on the ground while I locked our apartment. She instantly walked over to Hunter's home and I followed suit, pausing briefly at the door when I beheld the most adorable sight.

Hunter and Luna.

Bare-chested and only wearing low-slung sweatpants, he was petting my cat, who happily snuggled into his arms with her eyes closed like it was her safe space.

"Hi, Luna," he cooed, smiling. "I've missed you."

She tried to climb him, her paws shifting on either side of his neck in a hug. He returned it, his palm coasting down her back in a caress. She meowed and he rested his cheek against her head gently. "Yes, you've missed me too, huh?"

Was it possible to feel your heart being mended, one stitch at a time? Hunter had always treated me so sweetly, but seeing him do the same—relentlessly and effortlessly—whenever he encountered my Luna? It healed a broken part of me.

Franco had constantly ignored her, despite her loving nature.

Yet Hunter always embraced my cat with open arms and doted on her.

"She has missed you," I said upon entering, placing Luna's bowl on the floor next to the console table and snicking the front door shut.

Hunter's blue gaze warmed, seeing me in his jersey. "Well, if it isn't my two favourite girls. Welcome home."

I loved the sound of *my two favourite girls* and *home* a little too much.

Keeping his eyes on me, Hunter gently lowered Luna to the ground and she headed straight for her bowl. That was my cue to skip over to him and throw my arms around his neck in a hug. As if I hadn't seen him in days, not mere minutes. "Hi, pretty boy."

"Hi, doll." He kissed my lips. "My jersey looks even better on you than it does on me."

I doubted anyone could look as good as Hunter in this jersey. But I played along, giving him a little twirl. "Right? I look so cute."

"That you do." He chuckled at my cheekiness and reached for my hand, weaving our fingers together. "Come. Let's have dinner. You must be hungry."

I was famished.

Later, I'd ask him for a tour of his apartment. I never got a chance to properly see it, considering the last time I was here was under not-so-ideal circumstances. The swift glance I shot at our surroundings concluded that Hunter had impeccable taste.

The kitchen was illuminated with mellow light from the stovetop and votive candles sitting on the island counter, awarding the space a cozy and romantic ambience. The smell of herbs and citrus drew my attention towards a simmer spot, perfuming the air with a scent that was quintessentially autumn. I loved that Hunter took the time to make his space into an actual home with these touches.

"Do you usually light candles?" I commented.

"Only when I'm expecting a beautiful girl to come over." He smiled at me conspiratorially before his eyes wandered to Luna eating near the foyer. "Girls," he amended.

Be still, my heart. "Charmer."

"I aim to please," he repeated the same words from the night of Shaun's party.

I fought the urge to squeeze Hunter in my arms and plant kisses all over his face. "What's for dinner?"

"I'm making you a grilled cheese sandwich. My specialty." He pulled out a few ingredients from his fridge, including a familiar red dish. "And I'm having your lasagna." He cast an apologetic glance my way. "I didn't get to try it yet."

"That's okay." I gave him a reassuring grin. "I hope you enjoy it."

"I know I will."

When Hunter stood in front of the kitchen counter to prepare my dinner, I decided I wanted to watch him do so.

I hugged him from behind and pressed my cheek to his muscular arm.

My *principe* was an endless hearth, providing warmth and shelter, and I'd been cold for too long.

Hunter dipped his face to lay a kiss on my head and then went about his task. Meticulously slicing fresh sourdough bread, spreading generous dollops of his homemade garlic butter on each side, caramelizing onions, and gathering a mixture of three cheeses, followed up by bundling the sandwich and dropping it carefully into a hot pan. Next to it, tomato soup was being reheated in a pot on the stovetop.

When he finished plating my food, I was close to a marriage proposal.

This man could cook, clean, drive, dress nice, and give me mind-numbing orgasms? He was too good to be true. I felt like the luckiest girl in the world, given the privilege to experience him.

"Thank you for making me dinner." I peered up at him with—no doubt—hearts in my eyes, accepting the plate from his hands.

Hunter beamed. "You're welcome, Gabby. Grab a seat. I'll be with you in a moment."

While he heated up two slices of my lasagna for himself, I boosted myself onto a bar stool by the kitchen island. His laptop sat on the granite surface, the screen open and displaying an instalment of the true-crime podcast I'd recommended to him. I gasped. "I've been meaning to listen to this week's episode. Have you already started it?"

"Not yet." He came to sit on the seat beside mine with his own plate and two glasses of water for us. "I thought we could listen to it together as we ate. I took notes from the previous episodes and I have some theories I'd like to share with you."

"Are you officially a true-crime podcast convert now?"

"You've turned me into a fan."

Hunter taking a sincere interest in my hobbies filled me with immense happiness. This particular podcast was created by a local woman in Montardor, about a girl who'd gone missing during a Halloween party. It was no secret that I loved spooky affairs and it appeared that I'd successfully coaxed Hunter to the dark side as well. "This is the best news I've heard all day."

He smiled and took a sip of his water. "More than hearing I only joined that blasphemous class because of you?"

I could practically hear the blush in his voice, but thankfully no hints of self-deprecation.

"The *second* best news, actually." I lovingly grazed a hand over his jaw. "Knowing what I know now, all I can say is thank you. For joining that class, for having the courage to tell me how you feel, and, I suppose, for seeing something worth pursuing in me."

Hunter's eyes narrowed a fraction. He didn't know the full story, but he understood that my ex did a number on me. Enough for me to run away from commitment, to fear love except in platonic forms, and to not always see myself in a good light. For the most part, I was confident. But there was a tiny nugget within me that felt unworthy because of my past. It was the only logical explanation for my self-sabotage and though I knew it sucked to still feel this way, at least Hunter wouldn't judge me for my flaws.

We were all a work in progress and masterpieces took time to build. I just hoped Hunter stuck around long enough to behold me in my finest, nonpareil form.

"If I ever see your ex again, I won't be responsible for any damage I do." His gaze glimmered with a dark quality. "Fuck him for making you feel less than stellar. I don't care what you've been led to believe, but you're worth it, Gabriela." He drew a knuckle down my cheek. "Give me enough time to prove it to you."

I kissed him in reply.

Luna joined us as we started eating. Hunter sighed at the first bite of my lasagna, his powerful jaw working as he chewed. "This is the greatest thing I've ever eaten, Gabby."

I'd just taken a bite of the sandwich, my own taste buds singing at the flavour of garlic, cheese, and warm bread. "Funny, I was just about to say the same thing to you. This is the greatest grilled cheese and tomato soup I've ever had, in my unbiased opinion."

He chuckled, his eyes crinkling endearingly. "I guess this means we'll have to cook for each other more often, eh?"

I would love that. "I guess so, Hunt."

We continued eating and listening to the podcast, comparing our theories and reacting to the plot twists in this episode.

In the midst of it all, I was struck with the realization that perhaps this was how real love should feel like. Calm, easy, and fun. Not the version I had with Franco, which felt like a dark thorn prickling into my side, creating a wound that got infected and festered with pus, bringing forth nothing but hardship and misery.

I imagined this was how the beginning of truly falling in love with someone felt like. And oddly enough, the thought didn't scare me as much as it would have weeks ago before I met this wonderful man under the light of a full moon.

Once dinner was complete, I insisted on washing the dishes while Hunter dried. Luna sat by our feet, listening to us talk about anything and everything under the sun with a curious expression.

Afterwards, Hunter gave me a tour of his apartment. Black, navy, dark wood and copper accents comprised the colour palette. The furniture and décor were sleek, masculine. Moreover, I made a mental note of what books rested on his shelves so I could binge a few. He started reading paranormal romances because of me and I wanted to immerse myself in his favourite literature too.

Finally, we stood in his hallway, appraising the framed photos lining the wall like an art museum. There were various shots of his family, a testament to how much he loved them. His mom, Hannah, and his older sister, Heidi, were beautiful in a modelesque manner. And his dad, Kyle, had harboured a classic handsomeness that you didn't always find in today's world. The genes in this family were stunning.

My favourite picture was the one where Hunter was five years old with a bright, toothy grin on his adorable face and cradled in his dad's arms, holding on to a ball python.

"You're so cute!" I said. "Now I see where you get your good looks from. You're literally a carbon copy of your dad. You have the same blue eyes and long hair."

Hunter's eyes shone fondly. "He used to call me his twin."

I clasped his hand in mine. "Will you tell me something about him? A memory, an anecdote, anything you wish to share."

He stared at the picture and mulled over my request. "My dad was the most amazing person I knew. He was my best friend and my hero. Some men are mama's boys, but I can safely say that I was a daddy's boy."

My face softened at that last tidbit.

"You know when you're asked that question as a kid, 'What do you want to be when you're older'? My answer was always my dad. He taught me how to play football, how to be brave, how to stand up for myself, how to be kind, and so many other things. Some people on this earth feel like they're heaven-sent angels, and I was convinced my dad was one." Hunter draped an arm around my shoulders, roping me into his side. I hugged him back, sensing he needed comfort. "I aspire to be at least half the man he was. Growing up, I mimicked everything he did." He smiled wryly. "I even went as far as wearing my hair just like him. My dad had great hair and always took care of it. During chemo, when it began to fall out, I knew it pained him. He remained optimistic that it would grow back one day, once he got better. So I got this idea—something that I believed would bring him joy—and started growing out mine. Eventually, it was long enough that Heidi and my mom took me to a hairdresser. We chopped off my strands, sent it to a professional perruquier, and she made a wig from the hair. I'll never forget the look on my dad's face when we gifted it to him." Hunter released a bone-weary sigh. "He cried and…only got to wear it for a day before he passed away."

My eyes welled with tears and my chest tightened with awe-like emotions.

Hunter's gaze was fixed ahead on a particular photo of him with hair way past his shoulders and curled next to his dad on the sofa, glancing up at him with unabashed hero-worship. The latter looked tired and weak, a far cry from the strong, robust man in the previous shots. But he still had the most radiant smile. As if even cancer couldn't dim his spark. Kyle Warren must have been a lovely man.

"I'd do anything to have him back," Hunter said. "Grief really is like a shadow that follows you constantly. Some days you see it. Some days you don't. But you always feel its presence. I don't think one truly stops mourning a dead parent, though it does get easier with time." He stared down at me and jolted, his expression melting. "Oh, baby." He kissed the tear trailing down my cheek. "I didn't mean to make you cry."

"I can't help it. I'm sad for you." I sniffled. "I'm so sorry you lost him. For what it's worth, regardless of whether you chose to have a storied career in football or follow in his footsteps and become a lawyer, your dad would be so proud of the man you turned out to be, Hunt."

He wrapped me into his arms for a tight hug. Despite him trying to appear unaffected on the outside, I noticed a light tremor course through his body. "Thank you, Gabby."

"What did we say about the T-word?" I playfully bit out, my voice muffled against his bare chest.

His smile feathered over my hairline. "All right. Enough walking down memory lane. Let's go put on that movie, hm?"

"Are you going to hold my hand through it?"

He chuckled. "Yours and Luna's."

My insides warmed. "Sounds good."

Hunter cupped my face, stroking his thumbs over my cheeks. "I appreciate you asking me about my dad."

"I liked hearing about him. Anytime you want to talk about your memories, I'll lend an ear." I toyed with the silver chain around his neck, not meeting his eyes. "I want to be there for you in every way possible."

A strand of his hair escaped from his low bun and fell across his face. I pushed it back, and he grabbed my hand and kissed my palm lines. "Likewise, Gabby."

The future may be uncertain, but I looked forward to what the universe had in store for Hunter and me.

I hoped it was nothing but good things.

CHAPTER 25

Hunter's Goddess Of Victory

HUNTER

A three-beat knock, hesitant in nature, rapped against my front door.

I paused in the middle of spraying my cologne, brows drawn. Was that Gabriela? Hope sparked in my chest. I finished buttoning my black dress shirt and beelined it out of my bedroom.

It was Friday evening and the grand opening of Josh and Cade's joint venture, an old establishment that once belonged to their dad, now renovated into a high-end nightclub for the reveling populace of Montardor. Our entire group of friends and teammates were going as a show of support. I offered to drive Gabriela, but my sweet neighbour insisted on meeting me there, choosing to hitch a ride with her friends. She left me on edge after sending a selfie that barred the lower half of her face and torso.

I couldn't glance away from those crimson lips curved in a smirk, like she knew exactly what kind of effect she had on me, and the plunging neckline of her short, form-fitting, sequined red dress. A diamond necklace collared her slender throat and from the middle of it, a singular thread of jewels trickled down the valley of her plump breasts like a short leash.

I had the unfathomable urge to tug at the end of her necklace and make her crawl to me on all fours like a submissive brat.

Underneath the filthy shot, she had the audacity to text me:

If you're a good boy tonight, I'll let you unwrap me 🤍 — Gabby

No choice but to fuck my fist in the shower, I'd been counting down the minutes ever since, excited to see Gabriela again after missing her for the last forty-eight hours.

Maybe she changed her mind, I thought on my way to the front door. Maybe we could go to the club together. Of course, after taking a quick detour that involved my mouth, my fingers, and her tight-as-fuck pussy. I wanted to kiss her lips until they were all pouty and leave my marks all over her skin so when we walked into the club, every motherfucker with a hard-on for Gabriela knew she was *mine*.

But the second I swung open my apartment door and saw the person on the other side, my face fell.

It was my sister.

Dressed in her corporate work attire with an overnight bag slung over her shoulder, she stood blank-faced, head down, and completely drenched from the rain, the ends of her dark hair dripping a puddle next to her shoes.

"Heidi?" I mumbled warily.

Her eyes snapped up and that blank expression shattered, kaleidoscoping in many shades of distress and helplessness. "Hunter?"

I didn't ask her what was wrong. Simply opened my arms. Heidi immediately rushed in, hugging me and trembling. From the cold rain or whatever was haunting her, I didn't know. "Are you okay?"

"N-no," she croaked. "I'm sorry for dropping by unannounced. I…I need to be somewhere that doesn't remind me of Dad or Jaden."

My rough exhale fanned against her forehead and I rubbed her back in comfort. "You never have to apologize. My home is your home. Stay here tonight, all right?"

I had a spare room that I converted into a guest bedroom in case Mom or Heidi decided to sleep over.

She pulled away from my chest and sniffled, registering my ironed dress shirt and how it was soaked from her hug. "Oh, are you going somewhere?" she asked and I nodded solemnly. "I-I didn't realize. I'm sorry for encroaching on your plans."

I held her tighter. "You're not a bother, Heidi. I'll cancel and we can stay in, hang out like old times."

"I couldn't possibly ask you to do that. Please go." She wiped the tears from under her eyes. "I'll spend the night here, if that's okay, and be gone in the morning. I just want a reprieve from"—her gaze darted away briefly—"everything."

If there was anyone who deserved a break, it was my sister. Sometimes, Heidi reminded me of a lonely leaf blowing in the blustery wind. Forcefully flowing with the current, nothing holding her down, and living life on everyone else's terms. Her own wishes be damned.

"Do you want to talk about it?" I already knew her answer. Nonetheless, there was no harm in asking.

Heidi shook her head. "No, but thank you for offering." She took off her shoes and her sopping blazer, a cloud of sadness looming above her. "I'm going to take a shower and then relax. Do you mind texting Mom to let her know that I'm here?"

"I will." I stuffed my hands in my pockets. "Listen, if you want to invite a friend, feel free to do so."

Maybe if she asked one of her girl friends to come over, it would help take her mind off whatever was plaguing her thoughts—whatever caused her to leave work and rush here, rather than home or Jaden's.

"I just want to be alone."

I didn't want to leave Heidi alone, but I also knew that if I stayed here, she'd only withdraw deeper into her shell. She might even put on a fake mask and act like she was fine for my sake, when she was actually withering on the inside.

So I relented. "Whatever you prefer. I'm going to be out late, but I'm just a phone call or text away. Don't hesitate to reach out if you need anything. And if you want the space to yourself tonight, I can crash with a friend after we leave the club."

"That won't be necessary." She seemed to be in better spirits than seconds ago as she slid a sly expression my way. "Is Gabby going to be there tonight?"

"She will." I combed my fingers through my hair. "Oh, I also forgot to tell you that I have a date with her tomorrow."

A genuine smile broke across Heidi's face. "Hunt, I'm so happy to hear this."

"Yeah, yeah, I'll tell you all about it this weekend, okay?" I turned her around with my hands on her shoulders and practically marched her down the hallway towards the guest bedroom before she could begin the onslaught of sibling teasing. "Now go shower and unwind. You've earned a restful evening."

"You're the best brother."

My throat tightened, upset that her quiet words sounded like she felt undeserving. "I know, Heidi. You tell me all the time." I opened the guest bedroom door and gently nudged her inside. "Remember to contact me if you need anything while I'm gone."

Her chin quivered with a wobbly grin. "I will."

I left her and headed for the kitchen to plate her dinner. I scooped up a hefty amount of a chicken casserole I attempted today, cut a thick slice of a chocolate pie I purchased from Le Petit Moulin, and poured a glass of water. I also pulled out a few snacks from the pantry and placed everything in a mishmash on the kitchen counter, hoping Heidi would feel hunger if she saw the food laid out. Otherwise, I feared she'd skip a meal and go straight to bed, wallowing in her sorrows.

Afterwards, I changed my damp dress shirt into another clean black one and returned to the guest bedroom. The sound of the shower running reverberated on the other side of the adjoining bathroom door. I knocked on it and hollered, "Heidi, I'm leaving. There's food on the kitchen counter for you. Please eat and stay warm tonight."

"Thank you! Love you!" Her voice was faded, but I still heard it.

"Love you, too!" I whirled around to leave but paused when I spotted her unzipped bag thrown carelessly on the bed.

Her personal items jutted out.

Including a familiar old journal I hadn't seen in years.

Suddenly, I understood the reason for her mood.

Against my better judgement, I picked up her journal and gingerly flipped through the pages containing the pressed flowers.

Daisies.

Hundreds of them.

Given to her by Donovan, once upon a lifetime ago.

This was what haunted Heidi on an unhealthy basis. Guilt. It ate at her bit by bit, keeping her up at night. Wondering if Donovan was okay, wondering if he had everything he needed, wondering if he was alive.

She was unable to ghost the memory of the young man who fell in love with her.

And by the time Heidi realized how her best friend felt, he was long gone.

Club Azul was situated in one of the busiest boulevards of downtown, a nightmare if you were looking for parking. When I arrived, Josh, Shaun, Sam, Cade, Nico and Nate—two more friends of ours—were already waiting at the front doors, waving me over. Josh and Cade conversed with two burly bouncers, giving them some sort of instructions. The rest of the club line seemed annoyed that we got to skip ahead. I congratulated the boys and greeted everyone else. Ella, Darla, Dacia, and Hera were here, too. Huddled together and shaking from the windy weather in their glittery outfits and heels.

Unfortunately, the other girls hadn't arrived yet. Namely Gabriela, whom I was desperate to see.

The crowd inside the club began to thicken once we entered. Upscale interior composed mainly of royal blue with black velvet booths greeted us. A wide circular backlit bar rested in the middle of the scene, a handful of bartenders managing the patrons. Blue lights illuminated the fountain walls, and crystal beads hung from the ceiling, giving the space an underwater allure.

We were escorted to the biggest booth in the room with a vantage view of the dance floor, two hostesses sashaying after us for bottle service. I asked for a Reine D'Or, recalling that it was Gabriela's choice of champagne. She'd mentioned it once in an off-handed comment and I wanted to surprise her. Once the liquors, chasers, non-alcoholic drinks, and garnishes arrived, we cheered to Josh and Cade's accomplishment.

Then I pulled out my phone to text Gabriela, unable to wait much longer.

Where are you, sweetheart? —Hunter

Her reply was instant.

Almost there ☺ We're just looking for parking! —Gabby

I can't wait to see you. —Hunter

Same 🤍 —Gabby

Eventually, the boys and I left the girls to their own devices and walked over to the bar with our drinks, where athletes from Vesta University's football and hockey team were congregated. I barely paid attention to the ongoing conversations, my thoughts on Gabriela...before my attention veered towards Josh.

My best friend appeared on edge.

When he threw back three shots in succession, I grasped his shoulder and leaned close so no one else heard me. "You okay, man? Something wrong?"

It wasn't like Josh to brood. I was smart enough to know his sunshine persona was sometimes a way to hide the miscreant underneath. He rarely showed his dark side, a wolf in sheep's skin, but tonight he looked on the verge of unleashing it.

"Layla," was his clipped response before he downed another shot.

Ah, that explained his demeanour. I spoke to him yesterday in between classes and he said she wouldn't be staying in their shared home for the foreseeable future—a fact that pissed him off. Something about

Layla's dad being suspicious and her wanting to lie low until his overbearing attitude blew over. I was certain Josh understood her reasoning, but it still hurt him.

My best friend deserved to be loved in the light, not hidden away in the shadows. Even though Layla treated him like the apple of her eye, Josh probably ached at the thought that she wasn't able to claim him in front of the whole world.

"It's going to be okay, Josh." I wished I could offer him more concrete reassurances. "Give it a few days and she'll return home. Things will go back to normal."

He scoffed, brushing a frustrated hand through his dark brown hair. "I doubt it, Hunt."

As if he manifested his beloved, she walked into the club at that exact moment with Anna by her side.

Josh stared at Layla, brown eyes glimmering. He made no advances, wanting her to make the first move. Dared her, even, as he took a languid sip of vodka straight from a bottle, never glancing away from her.

Layla puffed out a breath and whispered something to Anna. They both sauntered in our general direction.

We weren't the only ones watching their approach. Cory, one of the guys on the hockey team—who was clearly drunk out of his mind—made a show of leaning back to leer at Layla, catcalling, "What I wouldn't give to tap that ass every single night."

He said it loud enough for everyone in our vicinity to hear.

Including Josh.

Layla paled and Anna threw Cory a scathing look. The boys in our circle all paused, shocked at the hockey player's audacity and—quite frankly—temporary insanity. Everyone knew Layla was Josh's girl. I was about to smack some sense into Cory before Josh drained the bottle, dropped it on the bar top with a decisive thud, and met the offender's eyes with murder in his own.

We only had seconds to brace ourselves before chaos ensued.

That infamous Remington temper surfaced and Josh lunged for Cory.

He slammed him face-first onto the bar, disorienting him before dragging his head up with a handful of his hair and introducing his fist to his nose. His jaw. His cheeks. Anywhere he could reach. "Talk about my girl like that again." *Smack.* "I dare you." *Smack.* "I'll make you regret ever existing, you goddamn waste of space."

The clubgoers around us gasped and screamed, scampering away as the fight broke out. The music was loud, the bass thumping, yet none of it hid the sound of glass shattering when Josh smashed the bottle against Cory's head, pieces flying like shrapnel.

Along with the other boys, I jumped in to stop the situation before blood spilled all over the floors. But our attempts were half-hearted, knowing Cory had it coming. Josh was like a man possessed, successfully pummeling the hockey player into a whole new realm. By the time Nico and Nate pulled away a bleeding Cory, and Shaun and I tore away a heaving Josh, Cade had ushered over two bouncers. They picked up a slack Cory and dragged him out.

The party resumed as if nothing had occurred, the DJ jesting with the crowd and proceeding to put on a few throwback tunes.

Blood streaked Josh's right temple and a few speckles had landed on his white dress shirt. He looked unhinged. Like a beast. Breathing unevenly and head swivelling around in search of Layla.

Sam had been holding back both girls to stop them from getting hurt in the brawl. The turn of events visibly shook them.

Wordlessly, Josh snatched Layla's hand and started dragging her to the second floor of the club, away from everyone's prying eyes.

Anna made a move to follow her, but Layla cast her a meaningful expression, mouthing, "I'll be fine."

"Are you okay?" Sam leaned down to murmur in Anna's ear.

The beauty queen glanced at his face in a trance-like manner and nodded meekly.

"You look exceptionally beautiful tonight," he complimented.

Anna, who was previously holding on to his tattooed arm with a death grip during the fight, loosened her grip and stepped back, panicked. A blush rose on her cheeks. "Thank you. I-I should go."

Before I could stop her and ask where Gabriela was, Anna strutted away quickly, Sam's compliment having unbalanced her. She joined her friends in the designated booth and entirely avoided the heat of Sam's stare.

"Have you thought of ever asking her out?" I asked him. "You obviously like her."

Sam ran his tongue over his teeth before taking a pull of his whiskey. He kept watching Anna with a lazy smirk. "I will. One day."

Now with Cory gone, things returned to the status quo. Without a doubt, there wouldn't be charges pressed tonight, unless he had a death wish. No one wanted to court the Remingtons' wrath.

I continued conversing with the other boys, but my gaze kept bouncing around the club, rummaging for Gabriela. Her friends were already here, so where was she?

I was about to text her again when I heard a female voice next to me, bordering on a shrill, "*Hunter?*"

I peered to my left.

And my heart rate kicked up.

Ginette.

My ex-girlfriend.

She was here with two of her friends, giggling with drinks in their hands.

"Hi!" she chirped, scanning me appreciatively. "I thought I recognized you."

Immediately, I shrank back a step and froze.

It was like I'd been thrown back in time, warped in a nightmare. We were high schoolers again and I was standing in the music room with her as she tore me to shreds with her cruel words. Like I wasn't a human being with feelings, but a puppet for her to play with.

After our last explosive encounter, I never expected to see this ghost from my past. Over two years had gone by. Why was she saying hi to me? Why was she acting like we were old acquaintances and not exes who ended on horrible terms?

"You look really good, Hunter," she praised and I hated the lewd hint in her tone, like I was still just a vessel to her with no soul, my outer shell the only thing composing my worth. "But what are you doing here? This is far from your scene."

A sense of humiliation washed over me. My mind played her old jeering tirade on a loop. All the healing I did since our breakup seemed to unravel when my mouth opened to speak and speech failed me. There was an acerbic taste in my mouth that amplified with every beat of my heart.

"Cat got your tongue?" she said with her usual mean girl energy. "Then again, you were always a man of few words. Too quiet for your own good."

I couldn't believe I'd ever loved someone like Ginette.

I couldn't believe I gave the right parts of me to someone so wrong.

Remembering my therapist's advice from eons ago, I pushed through the pain roiling in my stomach and stood my ground.

"Don't," I gritted out angrily. "Don't fucking talk to me, Ginette."

The venom in my retort shocked her since she only remembered me as a quiet and passive boyfriend who always put up with her shit. Ginette flinched, finally having the gall to be embarrassed. "Excuse me? What the hell is your problem—Oh my God!"

A body knocked into Ginette from the back, causing her to stumble and spill her drink onto herself. The fruity concoction stained her white dress in an ugly hue.

Ginette screeched.

"Oops, sorry!" came the not-so-sorry voice of Gabriela, who blazed into the scene and threw her arms around me possessively. She pressed a kiss to my lips and claimed me in front of everyone before I could blink. My girl then proceeded to shoot Ginette and her posse a mock innocent expression. "I didn't mean to do that. Total accident on my part."

It wasn't an accident and I didn't feel bad for Ginette.

I placed my hands on Gabriela's hips, lassoing her deeper into me.

Her familiar fragrance and the curve of her body set my heart and mind at ease.

She tamed all my anxiety, set all my demons quiet.

They didn't exist when she was near me.

Ginette glared at Gabriela while her friends dabbed at her soaked dress uselessly with napkins from the bar. "You did that on purpose."

"Did I?" Gabriela drawled almost menacingly. "Prove it."

Ginette couldn't. She and her friends looked like they wanted to fight Gabriela. That would never happen on my watch. No one would lay a single finger on her.

"I promise you, I'm the last bitch you want to mess with," Gabriela taunted further, almost baring her teeth. "Now turn around, walk away, and never, *ever* speak to Hunter again. Otherwise, I'll make you sorry for even breathing the same air as him."

I was stunned. No one had ever stood up for me. Not the way Gabriela had, without batting an eye. She would make Ginette pay. If not with her barbs, then with that trusty gun of hers.

Realizing it was futile to argue with Gabriela and perhaps sensing the weight of her threat, Ginette and her friends backed off after a few more colourful words aimed in our direction.

I didn't spare them another glance, my undivided attention on the red-haired beauty in my arms.

She was all that mattered to me.

"Hi, baby." I cupped her face, gazing down at her with affection. "You made it."

"Hi, Hunt." She kissed me again. "Did you miss me?"

I nodded vehemently. "So much."

"I missed you, too."

She might as well have shot me in the chest with an arrow. Her statement of missing me was just as powerful as her statement of adoring me.

"That was your ex, huh?" she asked bitterly. *The one who cheated on you*, I heard the silent accusation in her tone.

"It was."

"I heard what she said to you and when I heard you say her name, I put two and two together." Her face scrunched like she sucked a sour candy. "Serves her right to have her drink spilled over that abomination of a dress."

I laughed. "You defending me was very sexy. Thank you," I said playfully. "My hero."

She nuzzled my lips, smiling. "I'll always defend you. No one is allowed to hurt you, Hunt."

My heart felt like it would burst. "Right back at you, Gabby."

She wove her fingers with mine, brought our joined hands to her mouth, and kissed my knuckles.

Gabriela looked stunning tonight. Her hair flowed down her back in loose curls. Her makeup was flawless. Her ears were adorned with jeweled earrings. Her feet were thrust into strappy heels. And that red sequined minidress and diamond necklace tempted me yet again. My mouth salivated with the need to lick, suck, and bite her flesh.

God, she was perfect.

My little doll. My bewitching siren. My goddess of victory.

I would do anything for Gabriela Regina Bellafiore.

"Are you ready to go hide in a corner with me?" she murmured, knowing me so well.

"No." I stroked a knuckle down her cheek. "I want to dance with you first."

Surprise lit her eyes, morphing them into a warm, tropical blue. "I would love to dance with you."

For so long, I'd wanted to hide from the world and blend in with the crowd.

But Gabriela made me want to stand out and be seen.

As she led me to the dance floor, I realized this was where I was always meant to be. Every lesson, every obstacle, and every heartbreak were preparing me for this moment—to be next to this strong-willed, big-hearted, amazing girl that I was falling for in every sense of the word.

CHAPTER 26
Gabriela's Principe

GABRIELA

Club Azul vibrated with an energy fencing on recklessness and lust, the atmosphere perfumed with the scent of gyrating bodies and heavy spirits. The mirrored fountain walls gave glimpses of Hunter and me as I ferried him to the dance floor.

I would never get over the stature of this man. Even in my heels, he remained enormously taller than me, making me feel petite and protected. When his big palm coasted over my hip and landed in the curve of my waist, I basked in the possessive grip. He let everyone in our surroundings know that I was his. Anyone who dared to approach me would have to reconsider. My pretty boy had a jealous streak and I looked forward to fanning the flames of that fire.

Especially now that I knew underneath his gentlemanly exterior lay a filthy animal—the kind that liked to pleasure his woman and fill her with cum in the most primal manner.

Reaching the center of the dance floor, I dragged my hands over his black dress shirt, enjoying the expanse of his strong, quilted muscles, and clasped them at the nape of his neck…before teasingly raking the tips of my nails against the skin of his scalp.

Hunter shivered.

He always reacted like argil under the adroitness of my touch.

It made me feel powerful as though I was his maker and he my submissive mortal lover. But we both knew that subservience only stretched so far before he was ready to dominate me like *I* was his creation, his commands curling around my bones like the sweetest of chants.

And I loved this side of us, wanting to explore its depths over the course of the next few weeks as we courted one another.

Hunter wrapped his arm around my back and placed his other hand on my derriere, carting me into his body until my softer curves moulded to his hard planes and there was no space left between us.

Watching each other, we swayed to the provocative beat thrumming through the veins of the club like a living heart, enticing my own to beat in the same frivolous rhythm.

"Are you feeling okay?" I mumbled against his mouth. "After seeing her?"

I bumped into a friend from school when I reached the club and got sidetracked catching up with her near the coat check. Eventually, when I slid inside the main room, Josh had already grabbed Layla after wreaking mayhem, Anna had hightailed it to the booth with the rest of our friends, and a brunette was chatting up Hunter. Jealousy had boiled inside of me. I marched in their direction with the intention of staking my claim. Little did I know she was far from flirting with him. Hearing her throw condescending remarks at Hunter turned me livid. I was proud of him for telling her off, but I couldn't help inserting myself into the situation in hopes of ending her bullshit.

I fucking hoped his ex-girlfriend had the worst night ever. I'd ruin her dress all over again if given the opportunity to teach the cheating bitch a lesson. Hunter deserved so much better than a girl who had treated him callously.

He never told me the full story of what occurred between them, and I decided that I would ask him about it later tonight.

"I'm fine." He dropped his forehead to mine. "And I don't want to talk about her. She's irrelevant."

I ran a finger over his stubbled jaw. "And what do you want to talk about?"

"You." He kissed me, stealing my breath. "And how you are, once again, the most beautiful woman in the world."

Hunter calling me beautiful in that husky voice would never get old. The compliment plated my insides like gold. "And *you* are the most beautiful man in this world."

My pretty rich boy. My tender *principe*. My sweet undoing.

I hoped he realized that there was no comparison.

He was one of a kind.

Hunter Saint Warren was God-tier, in a league of his own. Possessing the kind of beauty and strength that would have enticed women in the past to write waxing poetry and lyrical songs about him. Had I honed my prose, I may be tempted to write verses about his blue eyes, reminiscent of glaciers. His defined jawline with a rough terrain of black stubble. His inky strands, tousled and untamed, falling down to his broad shoulders, like a hero from olden tales. And his small scar at the bridge of his nose, its story still unsung, that only added to his charm.

"You're flattering me." Hunter spun me around, keeping us moving to the sensuous music.

"I'm being truthful." Leaning my head back against his chest, I raised my hand to toy with the edge of the silver chain looped around his neck. "Do you doubt me?"

His mouth poised at my ear as he whispered, "Never, baby." He trailed kisses down my neck. "Fuck, this dress will be the death of me."

"Not what I'm wearing underneath?" I asked coyly.

He groaned. "Don't torture me, Gabby."

"But you love it when I tease you."

"Mm, that I do." I felt the deep rumble of his voice at my back before it slowly travelled down and sank in my core. "Am I being a good boy so far?"

"Yes, you are." He'd be unwrapping me later tonight. "Though if you want to get on your knees and further prove that good boy status, I wouldn't be opposed to it."

"Fuck." He manacled my throat and angled my head to snatch a kiss that turned me breathless. "On top of being a brat, you're pure trouble."

"You like the kind of trouble I bring, *principe*."

"Tell me what that word means," he pleaded. "I've been meaning to ask you for two days now."

"It means prince." I cupped his jaw. "In my mother tongue."

Blue eyes awash with shock peered down into mine. "You think I'm princely?"

"I don't think—I know," I affirmed. "You're gentle, dignified, selfless, and kind. What I like most about you is how you'd do anything for the people you care for. A better man does not exist."

Hunter released a low noise in his throat like my words slayed him. He tightened his arms around me and tucked his chin in the crook of my neck, breathing in my scent with an audible inhale. "My God, I adore you. I used to dream of a time when I could hold you just like this. When I could kiss you like you belong to me. When I could talk to you freely and learn how that pretty mind of yours works. How is it that the universe knew exactly what I wanted and needed and delivered you to me like a gift? I look at you and feel like all my prayers have been answered."

Oh, Hunter.

In this instant, luxuriating underneath the veil of those beautiful words, I felt undone in a way I couldn't properly convey. My pulse fluttered fast like the beating wings of a bird trying to free itself from a cage, and everything screamed within me to clutch this man to my person and never let him go.

"You're obsessed with me, aren't you?" I teased, trying to bring some light-heartedness to a moment that felt charged with enough emotions that tears stung my eyes unexpectedly.

I took it back. The thing I liked most about Hunter wasn't his mannerisms but his honesty. It was the most handsome part of him. How he was so truthful, not a single lie woven on his tongue. He spoke from his soul and meant every word.

"Yes." He kissed the heart-shaped earring in my lobe and I closed my eyes. "I covet you."

It was decided. I would do anything and everything to keep him.

I no longer cared what was engraved in my palms. I would rewrite fate until he was mine forever. There was no better individual out there matched for me.

Only him.

It was an insane thought to have perhaps, when we'd known each other for such a short time, but my atoms vibrated like they'd been right next to his when the universe was created and the cosmic feeling was evidence enough for me.

Filled with the urge to turn around and witness his expression, I did as instinct called me to and confessed, "I covet you, too."

The smile that blossomed over his face was radiant.

I wanted to feel it on my lips, so I kissed him.

He tasted like whiskey, sinful nights, and the first rays of sunshine filtering through sheer curtains, caressing your skin first thing in the morning.

"Sweetheart," he whispered. "I'm already yours for the taking. Don't you know?"

I did know. He once asked to be mine and now I gladly accepted. Only a fool would reject him. And I was no longer going to squander our precious time. We deserved each other.

"Yes," I whispered back. "In case I didn't make myself clear, I'm yours too."

This was exclusive. There would be no one else for me and no one else for him.

I could practically see the elation funneling through his system at my admission. His eyes glowed and his mouth curled in a heart-stopping grin. "Good."

We traded kisses and watched each other under the gleam of blue strobe lights, dancing in a sea of bodies to the tune of our beating hearts. The world around us blurred until it felt like it was only him and me, fully surrendered to this connection of ours. Past budding, now in full bloom.

Was it possible to feel your heart physically being stolen?

I felt like Hunter finally snatched mine and I let him oh-so-easily, with no defences or armour. As though it had been waiting for him all this time.

"Have you had enough?"

We'd been on the dance floor for twenty minutes. Far from the shadows, we were straight in the limelight. Hunter wasn't only doing this for me but for him as well. To help chip away another layer of the shy and introverted exterior that made him want to hide. But I didn't want him to push himself to stay longer than necessary.

"I like this. Dancing with you. Being seen with you." His lips plumed over my cheek in another kiss. "We'll do this again, yeah?"

"Yes, we will." I latched onto his hand and squeezed. "Come. Let's go mingle with our friends before I drag you to a dark corner and have my wicked way with you."

"You promise?"

"I promise."

We joined our friends in the booth. The volume of our group and the lack of space made it so we were a bit cramped in terms of seating. I had to sit in Hunter's lap. When he threw an arm around my waist, holding me to him possessively again, the girls sent me smug smirks. No one shot ribbing comments, choosing to go with the flow. Like seeing Hunter and me together was a daily occurrence. And funny enough, it felt natural being with him in front of everyone.

Hunter and I were meant to wind up here. I'd just taken some time to see it. But now we were on the same page.

"I ordered you a bottle of champagne," Hunter murmured in my ear.

My eyes widened in surprise. I reclined until my back was fully pressed to his front, canting my head to the side to stare up at him. "You did?"

He pushed a red lock behind my ear. "You mentioned yesterday you were looking forward to celebrating tonight. I figured Reine D'Or was the best way to go. That's your favourite, right?"

I loved how he paid attention to everything I told him. "It is. I can't believe you remembered."

"I remember everything about you like it's my goddamn career, Gabby."

I couldn't mask the crazy smile curving my lips. "Stalker."

"Temptress," he returned, his hand delving just under the hem of my dress to squeeze my upper thigh. "Driving me absolutely crazy. From the top of your head to the tips of your manicured toes. I just want to take a bite out of you."

"Who's stopping you?" I batted my lashes. "Certainly not me."

He grinned wolfishly. "Careful, doll. I'm trying to be a gentleman, but you're making it really hard."

I bit my lip and shifted discreetly, feeling his bulge pressing against my ass. "Oh, something's hard all right."

Thankfully, none of our friends could hear our conversation. The music was deafeningly loud in the club and everyone was caught up in their own bubble. Drinking. Laughing. Partying. No one paid any attention to us.

"Are you going to do something about it?" Like a deviant, he grazed the shell of my ear with the tip of his tongue.

I shivered in his arms.

Unbeknownst to Hunter, I was so far gone for him, I'd lick the champagne off his cock if he so much as asked me to. "That remains to be seen based on your behaviour for the rest of the night."

"Take me to a dark corner," he commanded when I ground against him under the guise of shifting into a more comfortable position. "Have your wicked way with me."

I didn't need to be told twice. I wanted him all to myself, far from the prying eyes of the world. Hoisting up from his lap, I extended a hand. "I know a place."

Hunter swung the unopened bottle of champagne in one hand and grabbed my hand with the other. "Lead the way, sweetheart."

CHAPTER 27

I Am Yours

GABRIELA

Before the renovations and grand opening of Club Azul, this old establishment was once dilapidated, far from boasting its current swanky interior, and used primarily for mob business amongst Vance Remington's close circle. When I was a little girl, Papà would often bring me along if Mamma or Nonna couldn't watch over me. If Josh was here as well, we'd play with my dolls or his toy cars in the hallways while meetings were being conducted in the main offices. Sometimes we'd even play hide-and-seek. We often giggled like naughty children when the bodyguards tasked with watching over us went absolutely insane if they couldn't find us for long stretches. All to say, I grew up here and knew this building's structure like the back of my hand, including most of the guards present tonight.

Taciturn types, they observed us mildly as we mounted up the stairwell leading to the second floor. It was off-limits for patrons, but not for us. Some of them sent me nods of acknowledgements. Others sized up Hunter. These mob men had long memories and short tempers. They were always on the lookout for threats.

I had to give it to Hunter; he didn't cower under their hostility. Cool, collected, and composed, he even chin-nodded in salute to those who cast him menacing glances.

"Don't mind them," I said once we reached the landing of the second floor. It was dimly illuminated with the same blue-light fountain walls from downstairs. The music still echoed above, but it was more of a faint thump. "They didn't frisk you, which means they're trusting Josh's and my judgement and trying not to be overly rude."

None of the guards wanted to upset us because that would inevitably piss off Papà and Vance.

"Well, even if they did, I've got no weapons on me, so we're in the clear." A sly gleam entered his eyes. "Though it just occurred to me, now that I'm dating a mob princess, I should probably learn how to wield a gun."

"I heard nothing beyond you calling me a princess." I curled my arms around his neck and kissed his lips. "Say it again."

"Nah. I'll say it again when you've earned it." He slapped my ass and kneaded the flesh with greedy hands. I gasped. "Preferably on your back with your tight little pussy full of me."

My thong dampened. It never stood a chance around this dirty-talking man. "You're no fun."

"Oh, baby." He nipped my bottom lip and soothed the sting with a lick. "I have the rest of the night to show you just how fun I can be."

"I'm counting on it." I winked at him and dragged him down the hallway. There was a spare room at the end that I recalled rarely being occupied. I hoped Josh and Cade hadn't gotten rid of it during the renovations.

On our way there, we passed the door for the main office where the Remingtons discussed their dealings and, quite audibly, heard Josh's gruff voice on the other side, pleading, "*Come home. Just come home to me.*"

I ached, feeling for both of my friends. Hunter pretended not to hear it too. It wasn't our place to say anything. Josh and Layla needed to wade through their emotions together without any external intervention.

Thankfully, the door of the spare room was unlocked—otherwise, I'd have used my bobby pin—and gave way with a single twist of my wrist. Inside, everything was as I last remembered it. An old leather couch, a coffee table housing an ancient ashtray, and a wooden desk and chair chucked in front of the large window with dark curtains.

Hunter followed after me and closed the door, then engaged the lock with a prominent click. I moseyed over to the window and pushed open the curtains even further, allowing moonlight to bathe every available expanse of the room in a beautiful silvery hue.

When I looked over my shoulder, Hunter watched me with hunger. Even his blue eyes appeared sterling from here. His barrel chest bowed with a deep inhale and exhale, his attention on me with riveting intensity. "Have a drink with me?"

My feet carried me back towards Hunter before he finished his request. If he was in my orbit, my natural instinct was always to go towards him. "Yes."

He popped open the champagne and curved an arm around my back, tugging me deeper into his warmth.

Wordlessly, he tilted the bottle at an angle for me to receive the first sip and I let the bubbly flow through my parted lips, its taste—sweet, crisp, and citrus—dancing on my palate.

A stray drop trickled down my chin and neck.

Before I could wipe it, Hunter leaned down and licked it with the flat of his tongue.

A tremor wracked through my body at the impish act. He traced the trail back to my lips and kissed me passionately with a satisfying hum. It was so hot. My mind spun, my blood heated, and by the time he pulled away and rasped a *"Delicious,"* against my wet mouth, I was weak in the knees.

"Me or the champagne?" I asked coquettishly, my finger tugging his bottom lip, silently letting him know I wanted more of his kiss. More of his debauchery. More of him.

He smiled rakishly, his black brow arching. "What do you think, Gabriela?"

Me.

Always me.

I was the most delicious thing he'd ever tasted.

Without breaking eye contact, he took a sip of the champagne straight from the bottle, his lids growing half-mast. I watched in sheer fascination as his Adam's apple rifled up and down in that corded neck with his hearty swallow. Beautiful. Such a beautiful, suave, and rugged man. If I could sink my claws into him and never let go, I would.

Another wave of jealousy, this one stronger than the one that burned downstairs when his ex touched him, ignited inside of me like an inferno.

No other woman would have him.

Ever.

Only me.

The tension in the room ratcheted up.

The scorching look in his eyes was enough to set my skin aflame.

There was a tingling sensation running through my body, like he had touched me everywhere with a single glance. Each lungful of air was ribboned with his addictive scent, the champagne, and something utterly sexual.

"Now that you've brought me to your dark corner," he drawled, "what would you like to do?"

I backed away from him slowly, grazing my nails down his chest suggestively. "Play a game with me?"

"What game?"

I crossed over to the dartboard hanging on the wall and plucked the handful of darts resting on the floating shelf just underneath. "This," I said. "Have you played before?"

Hunter walked over to the wooden desk facing the dartboard. "I have."

I gave him a saucy look. "I'm thinking we add some stakes."

Hunter smirked and perched his big body on the desk. He spread his muscular legs and took a swig of the champagne in an indulgent manner, appearing like a dark warlord finally retiring to his chambers after a long day, ready to spend the night with his lover. "What are these so-called stakes?"

My God, he had this natural charm that made him look so incredibly sexy without even trying. It was his aura. The way he was the right amount

271

of confident and playful, and yet still so in touch with his vulnerable side. And with the moonlight streaming through the window, highlighting the edges of his frame, I couldn't help but run my gaze over him in appreciation for the tenth time tonight. His black hair was left loose and tousled, the ends brushing those broad shoulders. His powerful body was poured in all black—shoes, pants, and dress shirt, with the top three buttons undone to reveal the silver chain around his neck and the sleeves rolled up his forearm, showing his watch and the snake tattoo wrapped over his tan skin.

The cherry on top of the cake was his expression.

It dripped with sinful promises.

And I was the promisee on the receiving end of them all.

"We'll play seven rounds. If your dart lands on double, triple, or bullseye, you get to ask a question. Anything is fair game," I started. "And we have to answer truthfully. However, if your dart lands on a single, you don't get to ask a question. How does that sound?"

"Sounds good, but you should know"—Hunter's smirk turned arrogant and his blue eyes flashed mischievously—"I have excellent aim and I plan on coaxing all your secrets, Gabby."

"Maybe I'll coax all your secrets instead," I challenged.

He placed the bottle next to him on the desk and reclined back on his palm. "Maybe." He patted his muscular thigh in a beckoning motion. "Now come here, doll."

With the darts in my hand, I sashayed towards him. I loved the way his features darkened as he took in my high heels, the bare skin of my legs, the sway of my hips, and ended his journey at the neckline of my halter dress, lingering a little too long on the curve of my breasts and the diamond necklace trickling in the valley.

Hunter hissed in a low breath when I sat on his lap, the thickness of my ass meeting his bulge. To tease him, I pretended to adjust my position like I was trying to get comfortable. Then I peered up at him innocently. "You want to go first, *mio principe?*"

"Call me that again."

"Only when you've earned it." I drew a ruby nail along his bristly cheek before squeezing his jaw and bringing his face down to mine, our lips a scant inch from each other. "Preferably on your knees with your face buried between my thighs."

"You don't want to play *this* game with me, Gabby," he warned, his breath washing over my skin like a caress.

"Oh, but I do." I flicked my tongue over his bottom lip. He moaned, parting his lips and waiting for me to deepen the kiss. Except I proceeded to pat his cheek almost condescendingly, biting back my smile. "Take your turn, Hunt."

Shaking his head like he was planning on making me pay later, he picked up a dart from the pile. Weighed it in his hands. And shot it nonchalantly.

It cut through the air swiftly and landed on a double bullseye.

I gaped, dumbfounded. "Excuse me, what?"

Behind me, I could feel his chest vibrating with a low chuckle. "I told you that I'm an excellent shot."

I thought he was being pompous about his aim. I didn't think he'd actually hit double bullseye on the first try. I mean, come on, who gets *that* lucky? I guess it was naïve of me to assume otherwise. Hunter was a star quarterback. Of course he'd be a skilled marksman.

I was plagued with the knowledge that he'd win, I'd lose, and he'd walk out of here with more of my secrets than I with his. Not fair.

"Fine. I'll get you back." I harrumphed and picked up a dart, squinting with concentration. As if I was going to hit bullseye next. Hah. "Just so you know, I will win."

"I'm sure you will." Hunter smiled around the champagne bottle's rim and took a swig. "What does the winner get?"

"Bragging rights." My voice came out breathy when he slid his hand over my waist and let it rest underneath my belly button. "A-are you trying to distract me so I miss?"

He grinned roguishly. "Is it working?"

Yes, goddammit. "No."

His answer was to steal a kiss and turn my face towards the dartboard wall. "Go ahead. Shoot. Show me what you got."

I tsked. "I don't like men telling me what to do."

"Good. No one should be bossing you around." His voice purred against the side of my neck before he started layering his kisses along my sensitive column, pressing them into my skin with the softness of a feather. "Except for me. You love it when I tell you what to do, hm?"

I closed my eyes, enjoying the brush of his warm mouth. "You're my exception, Hunt."

His sharp intake of breath conveyed his contentment. "And you're mine, Gabby."

I liked that we were each other's exceptions.

Carefully raising my arm, I angled my head to better gauge my shot and threw my dart. It sailed straight into a single. My shoulders sagged. Bummer. "All right. Ask me a question."

There was a beat of hesitation. I glanced over my shoulder. A grim press of his mouth welcomed me. "Tell me…something about your ex. Something that you disliked about him."

My face scrunched up slightly. Talking about Franco was never fun.

Hunter was about to learn that he was a million times the man my ex could ever be.

"All right." I gathered my thoughts and Hunter waited patiently. "Well, I met Franco when we were kids. He lived down the street from my childhood home and we grew up together. One year into us dating, I saw sides of him I never saw before when we were just friends. It's like high school and his familial issues changed him—brought out the worst in his character. He…He used to be the nicest guy I knew and then over the course of three years, he became verbally abusive and an emotional cheater. In his mind, I think I morphed from the girlfriend he was supposed to love to a fictitious punching bag." I laughed humourlessly. Hunter stiffened. "He started flirting with other girls while we were still in a relationship. When I called him out on it, the manipulative asshole accused me of being needy and imagining things. He also had the tendency to take all his anger out on me. Never physically, but his verbal jabs hurt the same. Anything that went wrong in his life—a bad grade, a bad game, a bad day, he found a way to make it my fault." I sighed. "All I ever wanted was to love and support him. And you know what I got in return? Franco hurting me, bruising my pride, and calling me a whore. He said my only redeeming qualities were my pussy and blowjob skills."

"Gabby," Hunter choked out, his arms tightening around me. "I'm so fucking sorry. No one is allowed to call you a whore. No one is allowed to hurt you. You didn't deserve it. Tell me you know that. *Please.*"

"I know," I whispered into the stillness of the room. I must be progressing in my healing journey since recounting this story didn't fill me with pain.

I was okay.

Franco no longer had any sway on me and that was extremely liberating.

Hunter laid a shaky kiss to the crown of my head as I said, "You know what pisses me off the most in this entire ordeal?"

"Tell me." His voice was barely above a snarl.

My breath hitched in my throat at his furious expression. Fury on *my* behalf. It made me even more tender for him. "Franco used to shit on my reading tastes all the time. Said I was a loser for reading romance books because they gave women unrealistic expectations for love. During one of our fights, he went as far as yanking out all my favourite books from my shelves, cracking their spines and ripping out the pages. Basically damaging them beyond repair. I cried myself to sleep that night."

One of my biggest regrets was allowing Franco to treat me like shit for as long as he did. I should have put my foot down and stood up for myself much earlier. It was like my kindness and love allowed him to forget who I truly was—the owner of a loaded gun.

Franco also forgot that he was dating the daughter of a mob man and sometimes I wish I'd tied his scrawny ass to a chair and played Russian roulette with him, just to watch him pee his pants. Fucking *stronzo*. Why did he have to come back to my city? Why couldn't he just rot in hell?

I was pulled out of my musings when Hunter framed my jaw with one hand and craned my head back to gaze into his tormented eyes. "I've never considered myself to be a violent man, but the thought of anyone hurting you fills me with rage. I want to put my hands on that fucker and teach him a goddamned lesson."

The confession curled through my skeleton like incense, warming my bones with its bloodthirsty nature. "My little saint," I murmured. "How wicked of you."

"It's the truth. I want to end anyone who has any ill intentions towards you, doll."

"When I saw you on that terrace, I thought you looked like a knight in shining armour from a fairy-tale romance." I smiled. "Now I'm beginning to think I've pegged you all wrong. Maybe you're more like the morally grey villain."

"Whatever I am," he murmured, brushing his lips against mine, "I am yours."

My heart melted.

I should be afraid of the depth of feelings I possessed for him, but I wasn't.

For once, I was ready to fully embrace whatever the universe threw our way and fall for Hunter, knowing he would always catch me.

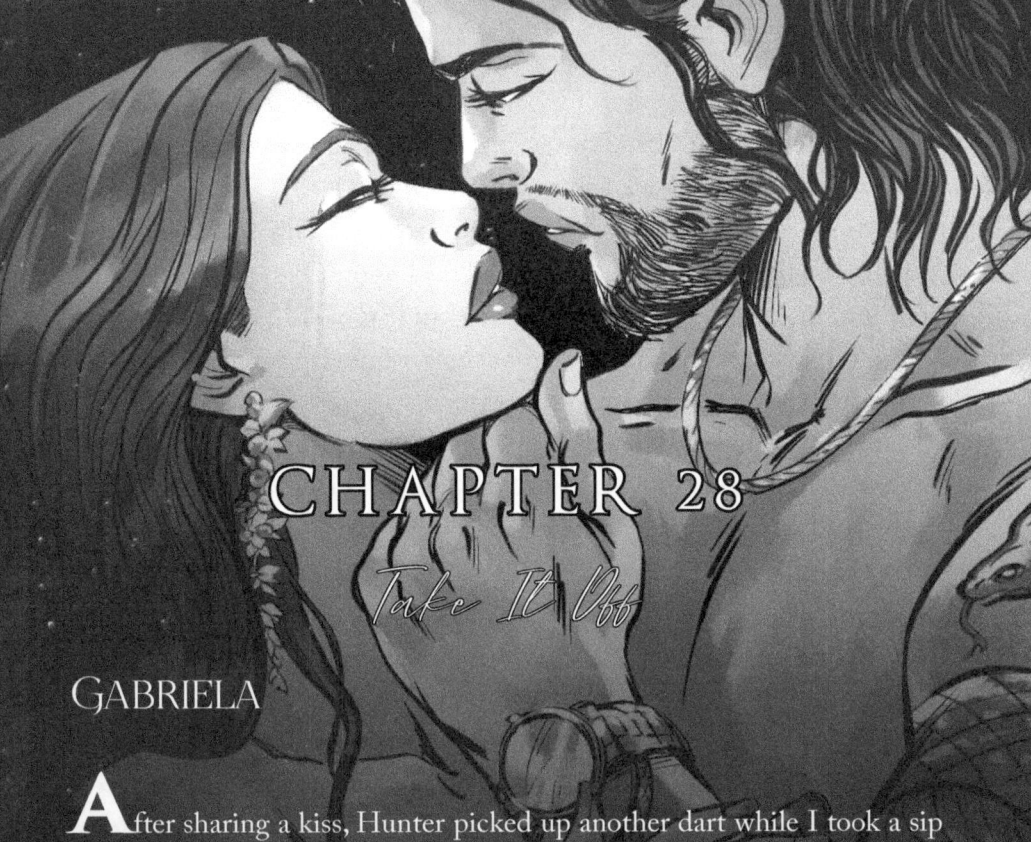

CHAPTER 28

Take It Off

GABRIELA

After sharing a kiss, Hunter picked up another dart while I took a sip of the champagne to mask my erratic heartbeat.

He threw the shot expertly and it landed on a triple.

I gave him a stink eye.

Hunter laughed throatily, his eyes crinkling endearingly. Fuck, he was a sight for sore eyes.

"Whatever. I'll win this round. Just wait and see." But when I shot my dart, it only struck a single. I resorted to giving Hunter my best puppy-dog expression, sticking out my lower lip to really drive the message home.

He let out a fake-exasperated huff, but the smile playing on his lips betrayed him. "Fine. You can ask me a question. Even though I scored higher this round."

A little squeal eked out of me, and I turned around in his embrace and squared my arms around his neck. My happiness was contagious; it caused his smile to morph into a wide beam. "Okay, so. I want to hear about your ex, too. Tell me something you disliked about her."

Seeing her tonight didn't put a damper on Hunter's mood and that was a win in my book. He was over her and I had nothing to worry about.

Hunter slid his hands over my waist. "I'm going to need more champagne if I have to talk about Ginette."

Since my pretty boy's hands were occupied, I only had one option. Taking a sip of the champagne, I opened my lips over his and let the liquid pour into his mouth. He drank it with a crude groan. I loved that sound. It only served to remind me of our hot shower foreplay, when he drank his cum straight from my mouth like a heathen.

"More," Hunter pleaded.

"No." I pecked him. "After you tell me about her, *bello*."

"And what does that word mean?"

"Handsome," I murmured. "A term of endearment in Italian quite fitting for you."

Blue eyes swirling with a heady concoction of desire and reverence pinned me on the spot. Like he was seconds away from chucking aside our game to give us both what we really wanted. But he was waiting for the right moment.

"Handsome, huh?" He ran his hands over my hips. "I'll take it."

"Knew you'd like it." I tucked aside a lone strand of his hair behind his ear. "Give me my story, *bello*. I'm waiting."

He pondered for a few seconds before speaking. "Ginette was…a piece of work. That's the nicest way I can put it. She was in the school band, a trombone player, and I thought she was cute. I asked her out and we dated for less than two years. I learned the hard way that she never really liked me—only what I represented. A popular jock who would be her ticket to high school fame. In the beginning, she was nice to me, but it was all an act. Halfway through our relationship, she turned horrible, acting like I was an inconvenience and speaking to me in a condescending manner. I didn't see the red flags until much later because I always saw her through rose-tinted glasses. It took me a long time to understand that someone you love shouldn't treat you that way. And despite her shitty treatment of me, I continued doing everything in my power to be a good boyfriend. I just wanted to please her, make her happy. However, by the end of it all, it became obvious that Ginette hated everything about me. During our final fight, she said I was a boring introvert, still too emotional over my dad's death, and that the only good quality I possessed was my dick. The worst part? She said I deserved to get cheated on—she boasted about sleeping with my teammate like it was her biggest accomplishment. I left the room in so much pain and puked my guts out in the nearest trash can." It was Hunter's turn to chuckle without humour and my insides clenched with agony for him. "I guess Ginette and Franco were similar in that manner, huh? Both of them diminished our worth to something so trivial."

They really were. Those two idiots would be perfect for each other.

"I hate her," I seethed. "What a bitch."

I wanted to go back downstairs and dump an entire bottle of liquor over her. Or kidnap and drag her useless ass to one of the Remington warehouses and do some damage. Like Hunter, I wasn't violent by nature, but I would do anything for the people I cared for.

"Oh, I think she knows just how much you hate her. That display by the bar was all the evidence she needed."

"Good," I said, annoyed by the thought of his rude ex-girlfriend. "I want to hurt anyone who hurts you too, Hunter. How dare she treat you so cruelly? I'm so sorry. You didn't deserve that either."

"It's okay, baby." He rubbed his palms up and down my arms soothingly. "I did therapy for a bit and I'm fine now."

"Can't believe we both had shitty exes," I grumbled and sipped the champagne. "Hey—I have an idea! Maybe for our date tomorrow, we should partake in a fun activity. Go to an axe-throwing range and pretend their faces are the targets. Wouldn't that be so therapeutic?"

Hunter threw his head back in a full-belly laugh. I grinned, proud of myself. His laughter felt like an achievement. I reckon I was the only girl who made him laugh this hard.

Unable to help myself, I smacked noisy kisses all over his lips and cheeks. I was feral for him. I wanted to squeeze Hunter in my embrace and never let go.

"Yes," he said in the midst of me planting pecks on his modelesque cheekbones. "That would be therapeutic."

"Thank you for indulging in my crazy." I hoped he knew that I wasn't kidding.

"I love your crazy," he said. "But who cares about Franco and Ginette, right? We have each other now and that's all that matters."

He was right. "And as we agreed, we're basically perfect, so it's really their loss."

In the moonlight, his eyes glittered like precious diamonds. "Exactly."

There was a feeling in my gut telling me this was going to be good. Us. Together.

"Hunter." I cupped his cheek and he did that thing where he turned his head enough to kiss my palm. I swooned. "I want you to know that you have more substance than your physical appearance and being a star quarterback. You're chivalrous, you're kind, you're loyal, you're smart, you're a good friend, and you have the wonderful ability to set those around you at ease with your calming energy. Anyone who spends more than ten minutes in your presence will agree. I'm sorry Ginette never bothered seeing the incredible human being on the inside." I pressed a hand over his heart. "Like I said before, *this* is the best part of you."

Before I could blink, he plastered me to his chest for a hug and buried his face in my throat. "Fuck, Gabby." He kissed the hollow in my throat almost frantically. "You have no idea what those words—what *you*— mean to me."

If the thumping beat of his heart against my chest and the way he held on to me was any indication, I was beginning to understand just how bad he had it for me.

Hunter may have fallen for me first, but little did he know that I was beginning to fall for him too.

I laid my cheek on top of his head and combed my fingers through his soft hair. "I adore you."

It was the simplest way to convey what he meant to me.

Hunter's voice was muffled against my skin, but I heard it all the same. "I adore you, too."

We continued our game, sharing champagne and sweet kisses in between. One of my darts finally landed on a double and Hunter's on a single. Though I suspected he purposely missed so I could win.

"Tell me a dream of yours," I asked softly. "Something you want to accomplish in the next fifteen years."

He tucked his chin against my collarbone and tightened his arms around me. "It's cheesy."

I squeezed my hand over his tattooed forearm. "I won't judge."

"I want a home, a wife, and kids. I want the kind of family I was in growing up before my dad passed away." He skimmed the tip of his nose against the side of my neck, inhaling my fragrance and stopping to kiss my pulse. "And I just want to live a good life with them and have my happily ever after. That's it."

Why did that make me teary? "That's beautiful, Hunter." I leaned my smooth cheek against his stubbled one. "I hope you find your happy ending."

"I will." He kissed my cheek. "And so will you."

Bliss settled over me.

We played another round and I hit a single. Hunter hit the outer bullseye.

"Say something in Italian."

I shivered from the rough timbre and the way the pads of his fingertips glided over the bare skin of my thighs, eliciting a flurry of goosebumps. "What do you want to hear?"

"Anything you want to tell me."

The words formed on my tongue before I had a chance to stop them. *"Penso che mi sto innamorando di te."*

Hunter's lips parted, awed. "What does that mean?"

I smiled around my white lie. "You're so cute."

He smiled back. "Likewise, doll."

We played another round while drinking. The bottle was now halfway empty and a light buzz pumped through my veins, stemming from Hunter's champagne-stained kisses and the feel of his muscular arms caging me in their fortress. I was in my own little slice of heaven, the faded beats and lyrics of an R&B song from the club faintly echoing through the room.

Hunter won the current round and I felt like a sore loser.

Wanting to mess with him a little, I leaked a steady stream of champagne down the front of his black dress shirt. He jolted and I fake-gasped. "Oops. I didn't mean to do that. You should totally take your shirt off now that it's all wet."

Smirking and seeing right through me, Hunter undid his buttons with calculated slowness. He dropped his shirt on the desk and let me have at him.

Straight away, my fingers swirled over the snake coiled around his bulging muscles. It was ethereal. Whoever inked it did a fantastic job. "I love your tattoo. I want a similar one."

"Yeah?" he said gruffly. "Where would you get it?"

"Undecided for the time being." My fingers waterfalled over his chest and abs. "Tell me about your piercing?"

"Didn't I win this round?" He arched a brow. "Shouldn't I be the one asking the question?"

"Indulge me." I rained kisses down his neck and over his right pectoral, pausing to flick the tip of my tongue over his silver barbell. "Please."

"Gabriela," he moaned long and low as I licked and sucked his nipple before tugging at the piercing very lightly with my teeth. "You have to stop. Or this game will end with more than bragging rights."

I pouted. "What's the point of getting a piercing like this if you don't want it appreciated?"

"It was a dare." He panted when I sucked a hickey on his neck. "I lost a bet and Josh made me do it."

"Remind me to thank Josh the next time I see him."

"Don't talk about Josh when you're kissing me," he growled.

"Jealous?" I whispered in his ear, sucking the lobe.

"*Yes.*" He slapped my ass and I yelped before he spun me around between his legs and tucked me back onto his lap like it was my personal throne. He swallowed my small giggle with a dirty kiss and breathed harshly into my ear, "Let's finish this, Gabby."

He must have been too horny to complain about the fact that I grabbed a dart when it was supposed to be his turn. Or maybe he was indulging me again. That seemed to be his motto where I was concerned.

Just when I started to throw my dart, Hunter's palm glided under my dress and over my inner thigh.

Then his agile fingers collectively brushed over my thong's gusset.

My dart didn't sail towards the board, falling to the ground with an embarrassing clatter instead.

You've got to be kidding me...

Miffed and flustered, I elbowed Hunter lightly in his stomach. "C-cheater! You did that on purpose!"

He chuckled, eyes twinkling with mirth. "What did I do?"

"Don't try to play innocent!" I spun around in his hold with narrowed eyes. "You knew I'd miss my shot if you touched me like that!"

"Touch you like what?" he egged on, mapping his palms over my waist and ribs. His thumbs rubbed half-moons an inch away from the underside of my breasts.

"You know what I mean." His touch scalded me through the red sequin fabric. I felt hot and needy for him. "You distracted me so I'd lose this round."

"Guilty. What are you going to do about it?" he demanded, leaning forward to peck my lips. "Punish me, Gabriela?"

"Would you like that?" I countered, feeling his cock rubbing against my thigh. "Being punished?"

His hands slipped under my hem to grip my hips. "Every minute that you fail to show me what you're wearing underneath this dress is punishment enough," Hunter gritted out through clenched teeth. "You're a brat, baby." He delivered a stinging slap to my ass. "You knew exactly what that picture would do to me."

Hunter stole another kiss from me like a thief. I felt drunk in a way that had nothing to do with the champagne and everything to do with this sinful man's essence. I'd barely scratched the surface of him and I was dying to peel back his skin and see if any part of me was tattooed over his heart, the way he was slowly beginning to etch over mine. "Tell me, pretty boy. What did that picture do to you?"

Thick, raspy, and far too sensual, I barely recognized my own voice.

Hunter fanned his heated words over my lips like a silk-wrapped threat. "It made me fuck myself in the shower to the thought of playing with your tits and screwing your pretty pink pussy raw, little doll."

A dam broke inside of me and I lunged for him, clasping his jaw and stamping my mouth to his with a desperate moan. Under the glow of the moonlight, we kissed with an aggressive zeal. I rubbed my thighs, needing friction, and pressed closer to him. Grabbed fistfuls of his luscious dark hair. Dipped my tongue into his mouth.

In response, Hunter clutched my throat, the diamonds from my necklace digging into my skin, and continued making out with me with deep strokes of his tongue. His other hand came up to squeeze my breast and he dragged hurried, hungry kisses down my neck and straight into my cleavage. My mouth parted on another broken moan as he took his time licking and kissing the swells of my breasts. "Fuck, I bet I can make you come just from sucking these gorgeous tits, Gabriela."

"W-we have a game to finish, remember?" Panting, I yanked his head back and forced him to meet my gaze. His own was tempestuous, swimming with wickedness and arousal. "If you win, I'll let you have more than bragging rights."

Hunter would win. It was inevitable.

He licked his bottom lip. "Be specific. What can I have?"

"Me. In any way you want."

Wordlessly, he grabbed the last dart and shot it.

It landed on another bullseye.

The atmosphere in the room filled with salacious tension. I mentally tallied up our points. He won our game by a landslide, having reduced his score to zero.

"Well, no surprise here, you win—*oh*." I flinched when a stream of champagne cascaded down my bare back.

"Looks like your dress is ruined," Hunter said matter-of-factly. "You should take it off, Gabriela."

My heart skipped a beat. "Take it off yourself, baby."

CHAPTER 29

Diamonds & Champagne Kisses

GABRIELA

Just as I glanced over my shoulder to see if he'd obey my breathy command, Hunter began licking the trail of champagne beading down my back with his tongue, tasting my skin all the way up to my nape.

Then, with a simple tug of his teeth, he unravelled the tie holding up my dress, letting the front of it fall down to my waist.

I shivered as my pebbled nipples were exposed to the cool air in the office.

Hunter whispered against my lips, "I know where you should get your tattoo."

"Where?" I replied, extremely turned on.

"Right here." His fingers glided down my spine. "It would look so sexy on you."

I trembled under his touch. "If I go to the tattoo parlour, will you come with me?"

He spun me around so we were face-to-face again. "I'll definitely come." The double meaning didn't go unheard by me. Hunter tipped up my chin with a finger. "Have I been a good boy tonight?"

"Yes."

"Can I collect my prize now?"

I nodded, biting my lip.

Hunter pushed the dress down my hips until the shimmery fabric pooled at our feet and I was left in nothing but my jewelry, thong, and high heels.

"Gabriela." He ran a hand over his open mouth, captivated by me. "You are a goddess."

I'd never forget the way Hunter looked tonight with his heart on his sleeve, his blue gaze alight with emotions, and his naked muscles bathed in the moonlight.

He beheld me like I was the personification of a holy grail.

I cupped his face. "Which one do I remind you of?"

I remembered Hunter telling me he had the tendency to associate mythological characters with the real people in his life growing up.

"Nike," he rasped. "The goddess of victory. She was worshipped by those who wanted to win any war, any competition." He leaned forward to press a kiss over my beating heart. "Often, she was depicted with wings and a gold wreath."

"Why her?" I thumbed his cheeks as something soft unfurled in my chest at the thought of him referring to me as a goddess who personified triumph.

"For one, I imagine her winged self to be swift and hard to catch, similar to you." The slow curling smile on Hunter's lips melted me further. "I've been secretly trying to grab your attention for over a year now, to no avail. You're an elusive target." A blush glazed my face and Hunter kissed my cheeks, tasting the warmth with a pleased sound resounding in his throat. "And from the moment we crossed paths again on that moonlit night, you've turned this desolate man infinitely victorious. Did you know I haven't lost a single game since you entered my life?" His mouth danced over my jaw, dropping more kisses as I shook my head, shocked. "You want to know why, doll?" *Kiss.* "It's because I worship you like a religion." *Kiss.* "You're the sweetest victory I've ever known." *Kiss.* "You're my treasured obsession, Gabriela. One I'll continue to show my devotion to until I die."

My eyes closed on a sigh, never having heard such a devout, honest, and romantic statement. Hunter had destroyed me. One kiss, one touch, one word at a time. Butterflies swarmed in my stomach and arousal seeped between my thighs, pooling in my thong. The room drummed with sensual potency and before I knew it, I found myself begging, "Then show me how you worship, *mio principe*."

Hunter's manicured stubble grazed my skin as he feathered kisses down my neck with a barely contained groan. "Fuck, there are so many things I want do—and say—to you that are downright immoral, but I shouldn't…"

"I want to hear these things."

"Too disrespectful. I'm a good boy, remember?"

I almost chuckled at him playing the good boy card. "You're not capable of disrespecting a woman, Hunter."

"Outside of the bedroom?" He tucked two fingers on either side of my thong and dragged the lace down my legs, letting it fall at our feet alongside my dress. "No." He gazed at my bare pussy as though it were a succulent meal, his jaw flexing. "Behind closed doors? If she was into it… Well, that's another story."

"You know I'm into it, Hunt." The light degradation combined with his praise just did it for me. "So let's hear it."

"You looked beautiful in that expensive dress, baby," he started with a tone that was pure honeyed sin, pressing his forehead to mine. "Like a hot little slut who'll bend over for the right price and let me eat her tight cunt until my face is drenched in cum."

Oh. My. God.

I sucked in a sharp breath.

"But you're even more beautiful naked, wearing a diamond necklace that looks more like a leash than anything else." His tongue licked along my seam, parting my lips. He didn't kiss me, though. Simply poured the onslaught of dirtiness straight into my mouth. "Bet you'd let me tug on it while I disrespected the fuck out of that mouth with my cock." He seized the end of my necklace and *tugged*. "I'd even hand you my black card before we started…as an apology for inevitably spilling my cum all over that gorgeous face, doll."

My eyes widened in awed disbelief, a craving for the exact thing he described building in my core. Now all I could imagine was me on my knees and him looming above me, face-fucking me like a handsome, filthy prince demanding his due.

While I hadn't worn the necklace with that intention, I was ready for him to use me any way he deemed fit.

Taking my stunned silence as encouragement to keep going, Hunter picked up the champagne.

I didn't anticipate his next move.

Hunter slowly dragged the head of the expensive bottle over my wet slit to collect my arousal. "And you've got the prettiest pussy, don't you? Too soaked and too empty for its own good." The glass rim rubbed back and forth over my pussy like a tease, a foreign sensation that kept me frozen under a coat of lust so thick, it nearly suffocated me with need. "I want to fill you up." Gingerly, he thrust an inch of the bottle neck into my opening. "Do you want me to give you something to ride or do you want to choke on my cock, princess?"

I'd momentarily lost the ability to form a coherent sentence, gasping in lieu of giving him my reply when he thrust another inch inside of my pussy.

And Hunter ate the sound with a racy kiss, my fingers curling into his broad shoulders. I couldn't believe he'd done that. Couldn't believe he was still doing it, inserting a third inch in my tight hole. Couldn't believe how much I was loving it, my hips shamelessly bucking. "H-Hunter," I finally chastised, my voice shaky but playful. "N-none of that was very gentlemanly of you."

He withdrew the champagne bottle while I nearly cried out at the loss and brought it between us, evaluating the glistening mess coating its neck. His devilish tongue snaked out to lick at my juices before he took a sip of the expensive liquor, keeping his lusty stare fixed on me. "Wearing a dress that messes with my sanity and rubbing your ass all over my dick during a game of darts isn't very ladylike of you either," he said with an arrogant but seductive grin. "Nor is stripping down to your birthday suit in a locked office with the man who's dying to fuck you. Act like a bad girl and you'll get treated like one, Gabriela."

God, I wanted Hunter to treat me like a bad girl. "What's stopping you?"

Smirking, he fisted the hair at my nape and craned my head back. "I asked you a question. Decide, sweetheart, before I make the decision for you."

After a sexually charged beat, I whispered, "Both."

Hunter's blue eyes flared and he jerked slightly, excitement winding through the lines of his body. The hold around my hair loosened as I began kissing my way down his muscular frame, worshipping every inch I could reach like he was *my* religion, making sure to flick his nipple piercing just to hear that rough moan of his that I loved so much. My goodness, he was decadent. Comfort and sin wrapped around my senses. All at once.

Before I could come to a knee in front of him, Hunter haphazardly threw his dress shirt down so my bare knees didn't touch the floor.

"Have you been dreaming of this?" I undid his belt buckle, lowered his zipper—the sound magnified in the quiet room—and reached into his black boxer briefs to take out his cock. It was hot, veiny, long, and so thick in my palm. I fisted him from root to tip slowly, marvelling at its sheer magnificence.

"*Yes.*" Hunter groaned gutturally. My clit pulsed. I could feel my arousal trickling down my inner thigh. Widening his legs, he perched back against the edge of the desk and gripped it on either side, his knuckles turning white from exertion. "Haven't stopped thinking about it since you first took me in your mouth, Gabby."

"Me neither, *bello.*" My tongue lolled out to lick along his balls and the underside of his cock, smiling at his reaction—the curses and groans escaping him—before lapping at the pearly drop on his plump head. To me, his taste and scent were sublime. And though I'd only sucked him off once, I knew I wanted to do it again not only for him but because bringing him pleasure also brought *me* pleasure. "You're the biggest I've ever seen and I love that I have you all to myself."

His hand enclosed around the end of my necklace, gently yanking at the diamonds like a rein. "D-didn't realize I was signing up for such a greedy girlfriend."

Girlfriend. My heart soared as our gazes clashed. Hunter slipped up, but he wasn't taking it back, based on the hard set of his jaw. He meant it. The title was mine to take. We hadn't spoken about official labels yet, but this moment cemented what we were to one another.

"Possessive, too." I spat on his length and massaged it with two hands, peering up at him through my lashes with a saucy expression. "You're mine, Hunter."

It was his turn to stare at me in awed disbelief, blue eyes soft, chest heaving with his breaths. Oh, he was so smitten with me, blushing the second I claimed him as mine.

"Good. That's all I ever want to be," he said with a raw edge, struggling and failing to keep himself in control as I jerked his cock. With a shaky hand, he reached into his back pocket for his leather wallet, flipped it open, plucked out his black card…and dropped it on my lap. "There. Spend to your heart's content. Drain me of every cent. I don't give a fuck." He grunted, throwing his head back when I sucked his tip with light pressure. "Just please let me feel your mouth again, baby."

Who was I to deny him when he begged so nicely—when he laid his entire fortune at my feet?

With a deep breath, I got to work, licking and sucking his eight inches like he was my favourite candy. Getting myself reacquainted with the familiar feel of his thickness stretching my jaw. Getting myself hornier with every cheek-hugging pull and watching his taut stomach muscles flex, his face transforming with dark lust, his hands misbehaving as they ran through my hair, slapped my swaying tits, and tugged on my diamond necklace in a pleading motion to not pull away until his cum was painted all over me. "Mmfuck. You're driving me crazy. God, I love this mouth. Love it so much, baby."

He made me so hot that I didn't have a choice but to dip my hand towards my pussy. I rubbed my slit. Played with my clit. Thrust a finger into my opening. All while I sucked him off. His dick seemed to grow even thicker under my affection, along with the volume of his beastly groans. He was close. I could feel it. It wouldn't be long before he came.

His expression was feral as he watched me gobble up his inches without a gag reflex and finger myself like a fiend. "Gabriela," he growled when I gently scraped my teeth along the vein pulsing on the underside of his shaft, giving him the roughness he so enjoyed. "Put another finger in your pussy." I did. "Another." Again, I obeyed, my moan muffled around a mouthful of cock. "Fuck yourself the way I would." I rode my hand eagerly. "Yes, just like that. Mm. You're dripping all over my shirt like a slut. Go ahead. Keep making a mess. I'll lick you clean after I get mine."

My eyes rolled back, awash with pleasure.

Hunter let me control the pace, refraining from grabbing my head and crudely pumping his shaft inside of me like a fucksleeve. Even though he wanted to. *Badly.* Instead, he was content enjoying the show, his tumultuous gaze bouncing from my stuffed pussy to my stuffed mouth. He couldn't get enough of me. He'd never have enough of me, my poor pretty boy. I had him wrapped around my fingers.

Sweat began to perspire on his skin. I wanted to lick him all over, taste the salt on my palate, and cover him with hickeys and teeth marks. It was a rapacious thought to have, but I was rarely in my right mind where Hunter was concerned. It was his fault. He'd made me completely addicted to him.

When Hunter raised his hand to clutch the hair at my crown and used it to yank me off his cock with a prominent *pop*, I cried out in protest, glaring and pouting.

He was well aware that he ruined my fun, the sexy smirk on his lips a telltale sign. He tugged on my necklace again, not letting me retreat too far. "Beautiful little brat," he rasped, his breathing choppy like mine. "You like my cock that much?"

I panted. "Obsessed with it—with *you.*"

A rough, amoral sound escaped him. He loved hearing my statement. "Do you want a drink, Gabriela?"

That was what I was vying for. His cum overflowing my mouth. Assuming his dominant streak needed to hear it aloud, I tongued the droplets of cum trickling from his engorged tip and said, "Yes, please."

Hunter picked up the champagne again, a quarter of the bubbly remaining, and gave it a swirl.

Realization didn't dawn on me until he tipped the bottle and a slow stream of amber liquid poured down his thick cock and into my awaiting mouth. "Open wide, doll."

My shock misted away and pure pleasure seeped through my pores. The champagne mixed with the taste of Hunter was a delicious combination. I swallowed as much of it as I could, while some of it leaked down my chin, my neck, and my breasts.

"Good girl. Drink every drop of champagne." He groaned. "Before I make you drink my cum."

I sipped every bit of the liquor with greed, humming in delight. Then I licked the remaining beads on his cock and sucked him into my mouth again, taking him all the way to the back of my throat with practiced ease. Hunter growled and continued pulling on my leash as my head bobbed and my fingers went back to working my pussy. "Fucking hell, Gabby. *Fuckkk*. Get ready. I'm going to disrespect that face soon."

We came seconds apart. I whimpered, my body arching under the intensity of my orgasm, and Hunter groaned ferally, his face tightening and his seed pouring into my mouth.

Cristo, he was beautiful in the throes of passion. I watched him, mesmerized.

Hunter drew his length out of me and his fist shuffled down his wet inches quickly, cum ribbons spraying over my face like an artist painting white strokes on his canvas.

Grinning wickedly, I stuck my tongue out to collect a few spare drops.

I was a horny mess of saliva, cum, and champagne. But Hunter gazed at me like I was the centerfold of his universe. And though I'd been the one to service him, I'd never felt more powerful when I saw his big body sag back against the desk with loud huffs. Knowing I'd reduced him to a mess filled me with pride.

My fingers smeared over the trail of cum sliding down my cheek and shoved it past my lips, tasting more of him. "Did you enjoy that, *bello*?"

"Very much." Through his ragged exhales, he ordered, "Give me your hand."

I withdrew my fingers from my sopping pussy. They shone with arousal. Hunter caught my wrist and lowered himself enough to suck my digits into his mouth with a dirty moan, his eyes closing as he relished my taste. "Mm." His tongue swirled between my fingers, down to my knuckles. "I could live off the taste of you. You're divine, baby."

My breath hitched, the vain creature in me satisfied. "So are you."

He smirked around my fingers, drawing them out of his mouth with a prominent sound. "Do you like wearing a man's cum on your beautiful face, doll?"

Good Lord. It was always the quiet ones, huh? "Only yours."

"Correct answer." He plucked out a few tissues from the napkin box sitting on the desk and cleaned the cum off my face gently. He smiled at my wonderstruck expression. "C'mere. Give me a kiss."

Hunter helped me stand up, my legs shaky. "You owe me a new necklace."

"You'll put my card to good use," he jested. "I know it."

Roping me into his arms, he kissed me passionately like he'd been starved for my lips—like we hadn't been kissing all night long already. We moaned as our tongues met in a languid, erotic dance. My hands dived into his hair and clasped his chain, holding him to me, and his hands mapped all over my naked body.

I couldn't take it anymore. I was losing my mind, clawing at the walls like an animal desperate to be let loose from its cage. "Fuck me, Hunter. Please. You know I'm on the pill."

"I got tested weeks ago and I'm negative too. I haven't been with anyone since I laid eyes on you."

My gaze widened. He'd been celibate for over a year? "Why haven't you been with anyone else?"

"I couldn't bring myself to touch, let alone look at another woman, because you're it for me." He gazed at me intently. "You're the only one I want, Gabriela. Don't ever doubt it."

He spoke vehemently and assuredly, leaving no room for argument. I'd never question this man's yearning and devotion for me. It was right here, in the flesh.

Grabbing the backs of my thighs, Hunter hoisted me up and my legs automatically twined around his waist. He turned us around and deposited me on the desk. "And as much as I want to be inside of you, our first time won't be on an office desk. You want romance, Gabby. To be wined and dined properly," he murmured, dusting the tip of his nose against mine. "You want to be taken back to a nice room with silk sheets and candles, where you can be fucked hard and rough. Wholly devoured until there's nothing left of you. I'll give you that soon, but right now…let me fill you up in other ways."

Tingles shot down my spine as Hunter placed a hand on my neck and gently reclined me back until I was raised on my elbows with my legs splayed open on the desk, my heels resting right at the edge. He parted my thighs wider, stared at my bare pussy, and whispered a "*Fuck*" like my beauty was too much for him.

The desire pooling in my gut never had a chance to cool down. Its flame only rose in ferocity. It spread through my system and burned under my skin, making me crackle like a live wire everywhere he touched me.

The nerve endings in my body chanted a hymn that solely belonged to *mio principe* and when he used the champagne bottle to pour the last sip over my body, I moaned his name—a half plea, a half demand—as the droplets trickled down my breast, stomach, and just shy of my mound like glittery confetti. "Hunter."

He lowered himself to cover my body, snatching another kiss like my lips were his kryptonite and he couldn't stay away. Those drugging kisses of his trailed down my jaw and towards my ear. "Do you want me to disrespect you a little more, sweetheart?"

"*Yes.*"

He smirked and his tongue forked out, drinking the champagne from my skin like it was liquid gold, blazing a path to my wet cunt. "Hot little sluts like you love to drive a man wild, hm?" He licked the drop running over my hip bone with a hungry sound. "Prancing around the club like a gorgeous dicktease, knowing every man in the room's got a hard-on for you." Sucked a love bite on my waist. "But I'm the only one who gets to have all of this, huh, baby?" Nipped my mound playfully. "I'm the lucky motherfucker who gets to please you until you're screaming loud enough for everyone to know what we're doing behind closed doors." Then the head of the empty bottle parted my slit and mingled with my wetness. "Now keep your eyes on me while I stretch your pussy with this champagne bottle like it's one of those toys you love so much, doll."

Fuck, he was such an alpha.

Like a good girl, I kept my eyes on Hunter as he inserted one inch, two inches, three inches, and fuck the entire neck of the empty champagne bottle into my pussy. My back bowed at the welcomed intrusion, my toes curled in my heels, and my breath caught in my throat…until he started slowly sliding the makeshift toy in and out of my snug channel. The cold glass against my warm arousal only heightened my desire in a way I couldn't fully comprehend or explain. I just knew that I needed him to keep going. "Oh my God."

His eyes darkened at the sight of my pussy stretched and leaking arousal on the glass surface. His free hand came to tweak and slap my nipples the way I liked, while his other kept thrusting the champagne bottle inside of me like it was his cock.

"More, Hunter." Gasping moans slipped out of me. My walls clenched around the impromptu glass dildo. Hunter lavished my breasts with attention and I pushed them together for him, facilitating his access as he alternated between licking and sucking each of my hardened peaks. "Please."

"You're beautiful filled to the brim, Gabriela. Like a filthy little plaything showing her favourite footballer some groupie love." His fingers rubbed my clit in time with the bottle's thrusts, caressing the very spot inside my pussy that turned me cross-eyed. The prominent veins along his forearm would be enough to make me come, if not for that sinful crooning voice. "I want you to picture something. Your scumbag ex. Walking in on us. At this very moment." The tip of his tongue traced one nipple before he gently bit and tugged, a retaliation for the way I'd treated his piercing. "The shock on his face when he sees you, naked in the moonlight, getting your wet pussy fucked with the kind of champagne bottle his loser-ass could never afford." He repeated the same treatment on the other nipple. "Then he freezes when he realizes it's his ex-girlfriend making all that noise as she gets done by a real man. Franco hears your loud moans and feels shocked, embarrassed, and angry. You were always the best thing he ever had and now? He probably cries himself to sleep every goddamn night, knowing he lost a fucking ten while I get to have you for keeps."

I panted louder. Spread my legs wider. Canted my hips to chase every thrust.

"We'd give him the show of his life, baby. He'd never be able to fuck himself again without remembering how stunning you look creaming over a bottle that's no doubt twice the size of his puny dick."

I gasped and writhed.

Hunter chuckled lazily, blowing on my nipples. "And right as you're about to orgasm, like a coward, he runs away with his tail between his legs, knowing he could never treat you like me." Hunter bit my neck. Right over my pulse. A claiming mark. "I'm sure Franco never dropped a single penny on you. Unlike me. I'm stacked up and I'll spend it all on you as long as it keeps you satiated, doll."

The. Mouth. On. This. Man.

He was nasty, feeding me images of my useless ex-boyfriend finding us like a cuckolded bitch, and I loved it.

God, my body on fire. "*Hunterhunterhunter.*"

He stared down at me almost angrily, an undertone of his hunger. "Fuck." The same fingers that had been rubbing my clit skated over my lips. "What I wouldn't give to feel your mouth wrapped around my dick again."

Despite the cobwebs of desire clouding my mind, I managed to plead, "D-do it." I sucked his fingers into my mouth. "Fill me here too, Hunter."

His nostrils flared. "Yeah?"

I nodded. "Do it while you do me."

Hunter withdrew the champagne bottle from my drenched pussy and brought it between us. "Taste how delicious you are, Gabriela."

Grabbing the bottle with a shaky hand, I licked it as he directed, keeping my eyes on him as he shed his pants and briefs. They joined my discarded dress and his shirt.

Stripped down to full nakedness, I was hypnotized by the picture he created—all muscles and smooth tan skin inked like a work of art. The snake tattoos on his left arm and right thigh seemed to come alive as he shifted towards me, the silver nipple piercing glinting in the light. Pure strength. Flawless beauty. And completely untouchable.

Hunter looked every bit the incarnation of the wicked sex god I claimed him to be, ascended from dark lands and roaming the mortal realm in search of his lover.

Me.

Despite his name, there was nothing saintly about this man.

Underneath his formal attire and football uniform was a heathen who loved seeing me undone. He brought out my demon side, the one whose limits of depravity were fictitious, and played with it like he was a master puppeteer holding the very strings of my being.

I never wanted to escape his clutches.

Be it hell or heaven, I wanted to be next to Hunter Saint Warren.

"Good girl," he praised when he saw I polished the bottle and manoeuvred my body around till I lay sideways, placing me flat and center on the surface of the sturdy wooden desk. "Now lay your head back and relax. I'm going to enter you gently and if it gets too much, tap my thigh twice, all right?"

I could only muster a nod, excitement momentarily robbing me of breath.

Hunter balled up his discarded dress shirt and positioned it under my head so I was comfortable. Then I watched him climb onto the desk with the sleekness of a predator, that strong body of his half shadowed and half illuminated in the moonlight.

As he grabbed the backs of my knees and brought them to my chest, folding my body in half and leaving my pussy open for him, my vision was blessed with the sight of his thick cock dangling above me.

And his ass...

It was muscular and biteable, the kind you could bounce a quarter off. I gave in to the urge to grab it with both hands and squeeze. "This ass deserves to be on billboards."

Hunter could make millions as an underwear model.

He laughed low and deep. "Funny. That's the same thought I have whenever I see yours." With his knees on either side of my head, his hand clasped underneath my chin. "You ready for me, Gabby?"

I had sixty-nined before, but never reversed like this. Anticipation expanded in my core. "Yes."

His thumb parted my lips. "Open wider for me." I did as Hunter asked and he dipped an inch of himself slowly inside of me. He groaned, inserting more of his inches into my mouth. "Ah, *fuckkk*. Twice was enough to ruin me, baby. Twice was enough for me to know that I'm going to need to feel your mouth wrapped around my cock forever."

I relaxed, letting him fully bottom inside of me in just a few more strokes.

Hunter trembled above me from the pleasure, hands caressing down my torso. "You good?" he asked huskily. "Tap me once."

I slapped his ass.

He choked out a strangled sound, having meant his thigh. Oopsies. Could you blame me, though? "Devious girl."

My smile stretched around his thick girth.

Hunter leaned forward to cover the rest of my body with his and brought his mouth just shy of my cunt. His warm breath blew over my slickness and he dipped a finger across my sensitive slit. I shivered and heard the unmistakable sound of him sucking me off his finger, the moan that followed afterwards downright immoral. "I really could eat you out all day, princess."

Hunter fell over my pussy and went straight for my clit, flicking it in quick spurts of that talented tongue. Two fingers entered my opening at the same time, working in tandem to drive me wild. I whined and moaned. My hips tried rocking in time with his thrusting fingers, yet were pinned beneath his strong weight.

My eyes widened when Hunter pulled his wet fingers out of my pussy and trailed them towards my puckered hole.

"You ever taken a cock here, doll?" He rimmed it teasingly and lifted his hips enough to free my mouth so I could speak. A stream of saliva cascaded down my chin.

I gasped. "N-no, but I—"

"Good." He swiftly shoved his cock back inside my mouth with a rough pump that had my eyes watering. His satisfied smirk plumed over my flesh. "You'll take mine. I'll fill every goddamn hole in your tight little body until you forget about any fucker who came before me."

My head swam with unspeakable lust. Dirty and raw like Hunter's smoky tone, it trickled through my veins like a match, setting me on fire.

Hunter pistoned his hips, shoving all his inches into my mouth with no finesse. My tongue laved over his cock and I sucked him like my life depended on it, the walls of my throat flexing around his thickness. I grabbed onto his outer thighs and ass for purchase, raking my fingernails over his skin, leaving marks that were akin to the ones he left indelibly on my soul.

His masculine groans reverberated against my sensitive flesh as he ate me out with zeal, my own moans not too far behind. He dipped the tip of his thumb into my ass…And the champagne bottle returned, its neck fucking my pussy in sync with his tongue flicking over my engorged clit in a blurring motion. Every hole of mine was filled by him.

I was losing my mind, my body going into overdrive and wracked with a myriad of sensations travelling from the tips of my toes to the top of my head, causing my heart to pound fast and my arousal to drip onto the table.

When his gravelly voice said, "You're so wet, so tight, so mine, baby. Mm. I want your pussy to make a mess all over my face. Do you think you can be a good girl and do that for me?" I knew I'd never be the same again.

I was convinced that he had always belonged in the tapestry of my destiny—that the lines in my palms had always been stitched with his name.

The air in the office was decorated with our desire-fueled sounds and the smell of sex. Our mutual orgasm began to crest. There were no thoughts. No inhibitions. Only this sweet surrender as we pleasured each other.

"Fuck, you're close," Hunter all but snarled over my throbbing cunt. "Me too." His pace grew jerky as he sloshed his cock in and out of my mouth, while never leaving my clit alone, and switched out the champagne bottle for three fingers, hitting my G-spot in the perfect rhythm. "I want you to swallow every drop like the nasty slut you are, Gabby."

It didn't take long before I exploded with a muffled scream.

Hunter lapped at my arousal, coming down my throat with a deep groan.

I made sure to drink down every bit of him.

After a few seconds, Hunter grunted as he pulled his softening cock out of me and rolled over to the side, giving me space. He carefully balanced his big body so he didn't fall off the desk.

We were both panting and a mixture of twisted limbs, but I could have lain here until the end of time.

That was so much fun. I wanted to do this with him again. And again. And again.

Hunter dragged his wet fingers over the cum seeping from my mouth and fed it back to me. I licked and sucked his digits clean, tasting both our releases.

Then he braided our fingers and brought my knuckles to his lips for a kiss.

I lifted myself on one elbow and caught Hunter's blue eyes and sated expression. His body glistened lightly with the exertion of our activity and strands of his black hair stuck along his forehead with sweat.

The gentle smile slowly curling over his mouth had my heart swooning.

"Gabby," he grated. "Are you okay?"

I nodded.

"Talk to me," he said when I watched him silently with a possessive look, rubbing his palm over my thigh in a soothing motion. "What's on your mind?"

That you're so handsome, so perfect, and so very mine.

Still heaving from that powerful release, I smiled. "That this is one sturdy desk."

Hunter's entire face morphed with amusement and he laughed my favourite laugh.

CHAPTER 30

My Happy Ever After

GABRIELA

Saturday afternoon, at exactly twelve on the dot, a knock echoed on my apartment door. I placed the magazine I was reading on my coffee table and stood up from the living room sofa. Luna's head swivelled away from the TV and in my direction. She eyed me judgingly as if she knew I was leaving her with *Supernatural* reruns and to be cat-sat by Anna.

Because I finally had my first official date with Hunter.

We returned from Club Azul at 2:00 a.m. and spent fifteen minutes making out in the hallway between our homes. Neither of us wanted to part ways for even a few hours. By the time we pulled away, our lips were kiss-swollen and our hearts had never been happier.

"I had a great time tonight," he'd mumbled.

"Me too. I can't wait to see you again."

"Be ready by twelve." He'd pressed a kiss to my forehead. "I'll come pick you up."

"Where are you taking me?"

"It's a surprise." He'd smiled cheekily at my pout. "But we'll be out for most of the day."

"Fine." I'd nuzzled my nose against his. "Good night, Hunt."

"Good night, Gabby."

"Just so you know, I'll be dreaming of you tonight."

And all the things we'd done in the moonlit office.

Warm fuzziness had splashed over Hunter's face at my admission. He was so cute. I couldn't help but peck his mouth a final time when he'd whispered back with innocent wonderment, "I'll be dreaming of you, too. Like I always do."

I'd entered my home feeling like I was walking on cloud nine. A big smile stayed on my face as I took a shower and went about my night routine. Just like I predicted, once I'd fallen asleep, my dreams were filled with Hunter.

That was ten hours ago.

I was dying to see him again, the nail-biting anticipation surmounting.

"Do you want to come say hi to Hunter, Luna?" I cooed and she leapt down from the sofa, following my footsteps.

I walked into the mirrored hallway, taking a moment to appraise my reflection. My hair was pin straight, not a single strand out of place, with my cat-eye-shaped sunnies resting on my head. I wore a black blazer dress, black lace stockings, and black knee-high boots. Pearls adorned my earlobes and I wore a matching Vivienne Westwood necklace around my throat. The love bite Hunter sucked highlighted the side of my neck. I couldn't find it in me to cover the mark with makeup. I liked how it looked and I didn't care who saw. My ensemble was complete when I grabbed my red vinyl coat and small red Lady Dior bag that Mamma had gifted me last Christmas.

When I swung open my door, Hunter stood at the threshold looking dapper and quintessentially prince-like.

Long black hair tied at the nape with a single ruckus strand escaping the fold and lingering near his temple. Blue eyes shining with happiness. Smiling lips surrounded by trimmed stubble. He was as handsome as ever. And because my pretty rich boy actually knew how to dress well, Hunter wore polished shoes, ironed black pants, a white dress shirt, and a crisp grey melange coat that was masculine and elegant. His silver chain and watch glinted under my entrance light as he stepped inside, a bouquet of red roses in his hand. "Good afternoon, doll."

I slinked straight into his arms. "Hi, long time no see."

"I know, right? Feels like I haven't seen you in ages," he joked, kissing the apple of my cheek. "These are for you."

"Oh, Hunter, I love them." I grabbed the roses from him. Red was my favourite colour and roses were my favourite blooms. I liked that he paid attention to all these details. "Come in. I'll put these in a vase and we can get going."

I heard Hunter sweet-talking to Luna and her purring in response, while I filled an empty glass vase with water in the kitchen sink. Upon my return, I saw him sitting on the foyer bench with my cat in his lap.

He caressed a hand down her back. "I also brought you a gift, Luna."

She rubbed her head against his bicep.

Arranging the flowers on my console table, I asked, "What is it?"

"Remember how you told me you've been meaning to get Luna a new collar?" Hunter smiled. "I hope you don't mind, but I got one for her."

He pulled out a small velvet box from his coat pocket and plucked off the lid to reveal a cat collar. It had a red strap encrusted with rhinestones and a gold heart-shaped pendant with *Luna Bellafiore* engraved at the front and my phone number at the back.

I watched Hunter, stunned.

A few weeks ago, during one of our commutes to school, I told him the kind of collar I intended to get Luna. He took notes and delivered exactly as I envisioned.

There weren't enough words in any language to explain how amazing Hunter was. I clasped his face and planted a series of closed-mouth kisses on his lips. "Thank you." *Kiss.* "Thank you." *Kiss.* "Thank you." *Kiss.* "It's gorgeous."

Pink tinged the tops of his cheeks in an endearing manner. I loved that I could easily make this strong man blush.

"You're welcome." He glanced at Luna, who kept pawing at his shoulder, telling him she wanted his attention too. "Want me to put it on, sweet girl?"

Luna meowed like she was saying *yes*.

We removed her old collar and once her new one was on, she eyed herself in the mirror and, dare I say, even preened a little. Just like her momma.

"You look so cute, girl," I hyped her up, bending down to stamp a kiss on her grey pelt. She leaned into my affection with closed eyes. I loved her with my whole heart. "Anna will be here in less than ten minutes. Be good for her, okay?"

"Ready?" Hunter asked when I rose, standing up as well.

I grabbed my coat and purse again. "Ready."

He perused me with keen interest. "You look beautiful, Gabriela."

I did a small three-sixty spin to showcase my outfit. "You like?"

Grabbing my hand, he brought my knuckles to his lips for a kiss. "I *love*."

My breath caught in my throat and I blinked quickly, feeling unbalanced by the four-letter word. He was showing his appreciation for my clothes as usual, yet a small part of me couldn't help but wonder if there was another underlying meaning to the sentiment.

We bid Luna goodbye, locked my door, and headed downstairs to the underground garage.

Hunter absentmindedly drew half-moons on the back of my hand with his thumb. It was such a simple thing, but it made my heart race.

He helped me slide into the passenger side of his Jaguar. Once he sat in the driver's seat and the car roared to life, Hunter's hand crept back into mine like it was the most natural thing in the world.

Like we were two halves of one whole.

My fingers squeezed his, trying to convey my innermost thoughts, and he took that as his cue to bring my knuckles to his lips for another kiss, before shooting me a dopey smile that I reciprocated.

Hunter drove with one hand. We cruised down the highway and the sun shone bright, enhancing my mood. Though I suspected my lifted spirits mostly had to do with him. After a moment of companionable silence, he hedged, "What are you thinking?"

That if I allow myself to dream bigger, you'll start to feel like my very own happily ever after.

"Nothing. Just how much I love being driven by you."

"Yeah?"

There was something incredibly sexy about him behind the wheel, driving such a powerful car with smoothness and sheer confidence.

"Mhm. Who needs a license when you have a hot neighbour to drive you around?"

"Neighbour, huh?" he volleyed back playfully. "That all I am to you?"

No, you're beginning to feel like everything *to me.*

"Yup." I popped the P at the end, my tone teasing. "Why, do you want to be more?"

He shook his head with a smile, mouthing the word brat under his breath. My shoulders shook with a silent chuckle. We both knew how much he adored me.

My eyes veered towards his dashboard. He was driving a respectable hundred kilometres an hour. Unable to help myself, I blurted, "Does your sports car go any faster?"

"Of course it does." He tsked. "But I'm not driving recklessly while you're seated next to me, Gabby."

I was pleased that my safety was always his concern. Still wanting to toy with him, I muttered a low, "Pussy."

Hunter cut me a brief glance before a depraved smirk touched his lips. I watched as he floored the gas, hitting one-sixty within seconds. My breath whooshed out, my body plastering against the leather seat from the high speed. "I guess you are what you eat."

I burst into a giggle.

The look in his eyes said he loved that sound.

Then he lowered the speed back to the highway limit. In a quarter of an hour, we reached a cute brunch spot I'd been meaning to check out. We were seated at a bistro-style table next to the window, overlooking a scenic sight. A waitress came to take our orders and we decided to share a salad and try their popular Croque Madame sandwiches.

We washed everything down with a drink—iced mocha for me, black coffee for Hunter—and powdered sugar beignets, while chatting about the latest true-crime podcast we were listening to and narrowing down the list of horror movies we wanted to watch before the end of the month. It was a delicious meal. I tried to grab the bill, but Hunter beat me to it. "What did I tell you, Gabby?"

I gave him a rueful expression. "That you never let a woman pay when she's out with you."

"Exactly." He wiped the remnant sugar from my bottom lip and kissed me. "Now let's go. We have another place to be."

Hand in hand, we crossed the parking lot towards his car.

"Thank you for the meal, Hunt."

"Thank you for the company and conversation, sweetheart."

Hunter started driving again and I busied myself with gazing into my compact mirror, swiping another coat of red lipstick. Throughout the journey, Hunter gave me soft, possessive glances. My heart glowed warm.

Before I knew it, we arrived at our next stop.

Currently, we were standing inside one of my favourite places in the world.

A bookstore.

"So what's the plan?" I asked. "Did you need to pick up some titles for your new shelf?"

The last time I was at his place, I saw the bookshelf he'd set up in the living room, right next to the TV. It was barren and in desperate need to be filled with colourful spines.

Hunter plucked a basket at the store's entrance and tipped my chin up with his leather-gloved hand. "The plan is for us to grab the books *you* want to read and to replace all the ones your asshat of an ex damaged."

I almost stuttered back a step. "What?"

A furrow pinched his brows. "I'm sorry Franco ruined your books and shamed you for your reading taste, Gabby. Being a voracious romance reader doesn't make you a loser. Fuck him for making you feel that way."

My exhale stalled as I oscillated between shock and contentment. How did one even reply to such a thing—to such a thoughtful gesture?

In two months, Hunter had shown me how a woman truly deserved to be treated. He was attentive to every aspect of my life, catering to all my wants and needs without me ever having to ask him.

Hunter didn't make my life harder. He made it easier by simply being in it and living alongside me.

I didn't care that we were in a bookstore surrounded by a milling crowd. Didn't care about any unwritten PDA rules. Nothing could have prevented me from rising on my toes to plant a gratitude-laden kiss on his lips.

Hunter was a once-in-a-lifetime individual. I meant it when I said I wouldn't allow anyone to steal him from me. He was mine, mine, *mine*. I'd do anything to protect this man who I was beginning to fall for hastily, knowing that I was safe with him. He would cushion my fall with his strong arms and that expansive heart of his, filled with so much tenderness.

He kissed me back softly, like I was as delicate as the red roses he gifted me.

I realized quickly that this was what I had been missing my whole life.

This was what none of the past men ever gave me.

Romance. Kindness. Thoughtfulness.

"How many books can I get?" I murmured when we broke apart.

He appeared ruffled, my kiss tilting him off his axis. So adorable. I wanted to keep smooching him and never stop. "As many as I can carry, Gabby."

I fought the Cheshire Cat grin twitching my lips. "And we both know you can lift a hefty amount."

"That's right." Turning me around, he tapped my ass in a quick swat. "Now go do some damage."

He didn't need to tell me twice.

I dragged him into the romance section. Hunter waited patiently as I piled one book after another into the basket. He evaluated each title with interest. "This looks good." He picked up a fantasy novel, weighing the thick paperback in his hand. "Have you read it already?"

"No," I replied. "Do you want to read it with me?"

"Like a book club?" He smiled and I nodded. "Sounds good to me."

I was happy that he wanted to read this. No one else in my immediate circle read fantasy romances, and I liked that Hunter and I would have something that was just ours.

We moved over to a shelf housing a particular paranormal romance series that I was fond of. "Technically, I already have these books…but these rebranded covers are super cute."

He shrugged. "So? Get the new editions. Grow your collection."

"Really?"

He raised his eyebrows. "Do I look like I'm bluffing, Gabriela?"

I wrapped my arms around his waist and gazed up at him, blinking innocently. "Okay, I'll get them all since you insist."

Hunter puffed out a laugh and kissed my forehead. He saw through my façade. I wanted these books and he was here to indulge me as always.

"Let's play a game," I told him as I stacked the entire series in the basket. We were already at forty books.

A sly look crossed his face. "What kind of game?"

I nudged him with my elbow. "Not that kind of game, you pervert. We're in public, for heaven's sake."

"As if that would stop you, you little exhibitionist," he whispered in my ear.

I blushed and whispered back, "Hey, you don't see me kink-shaming you!"

"I would never shame you." He kissed the tip of my nose. "I like your kinks."

I tightened the sash of my red coat around my waist, giving my hands something to do before I climbed him like a tree and pecked my red-stained kisses all over that handsome face. "Do you have any I should know about? For research purposes, of course."

He smirked. "Tying you up to my bed and fucking you like a dirty little doll."

An old granny happened to walk by next to us and she squeaked upon hearing that tidbit. Oops. I supposed we weren't as quiet as we thought. She scurried away, scandalized, leaving Hunter and me alone in the aisle.

When the coast was clear and our embarrassed chuckles subsided, I said, "Throw in a blindfold and I'm game, pretty boy."

His blue eyes danced with amusement. "Cool. It's a date."

I bit back a squeal. I loved this banter between us. It was refreshing and a reminder that dating should be fun and easy-going, right?

"Now back to what I was saying." I edged him into an Arts & Crafts aisle. "Let's pick a hobby-related book for each other, something new for us to try, with only one minute to spare on the clock."

Hunter perked up at the challenge. "Okay. I'll set a timer."

The second he pressed the start button on his phone screen, we darted down the aisle on separate ends with swift excitement. My eyes scanned through the titles. Woodworking, glassblowing, gardening, birdwatching. It was past the forty-second mark when I fell upon a mandala colouring book.

I knew Hunter's shier disposition and the events from his past had given leeway to his mild anxiety. The front page of the book claimed that colouring mandalas was a stress-relieving activity that helped promote mindfulness and relaxation. With the end of football season looming close, a championship to win, and a fast-paced academic schedule, I figured this would be an optimal hobby.

The alarm on Hunter's phone went off and we met each other halfway. I panted from having run in my heels and Hunter's own chest bowed with quick breaths. "What did you get me?"

I held up the colouring book with a beaming grin. "Ta-da!"

He scooped it from my hands, impressed. "This looks fun, Gabby."

I knew he'd like it. "What did you get me?"

Hunter passed me a guide on diamond painting, parroting my, "Ta-da!"

I flipped through the pages. "Right up my alley. Good choice." I stared up at him, hopeful. "Maybe we can get some supplies next week?"

He'd need colouring pencils too if he didn't already have them at home.

For our second date, I was thinking something laid-back at my place, watching a horror movie while we worked on our respective art.

"I'm down." He wrapped an arm around my shoulders, drawing me deeper into his chest. "Is there anything else you want to get from here?"

"Nope. I have everything I need."

"C'mon, let's get these checked out."

But on our way to the cash register, I spotted a comprehensive Greek mythology encyclopedia and placed it in the basket along with my other books.

Hunter gave me a surprised look. I winked at him.

He'd done such an amazing job immersing himself in my world of interests that it was only fair I do the same for him. I'd start with this and eventually work my way through the other classic tales he liked to read.

While we waited at the end of a long cue, I burrowed myself into Hunter's side and rested my head on his chest. His arm was still draped around my shoulders.

"Do you mind?" I asked him after a few seconds.

He frowned, perplexed. "Mind what?"

I'd always liked to hug and cuddle. But Franco hated that, calling me an attention seeker. "That I'm clingy."

"No." Hunter squeezed my body closer like he couldn't get enough. "I like it. Cling to me all you want."

Enamoured, I peered up into his handsome face. "I really like you."

My sentence transformed Hunter's entire face. He practically lit up, lips parting and eyes widening with glee. He tried to play it off like it was no big deal, but I saw through it.

Hunter waited so long for me to say those words. I wished…I wished I'd started falling for him over a year ago, like he had for me, when we first locked eyes at Josh's birthday party.

If I'd just paid more attention to him, we could have been dating long before now, I thought regretfully.

"Is that so?" he asked, not in a way that stated he needed reassurance, but more in the playful manner of his I was coming to love.

"Yes."

"What a coincidence." His nose skimmed over my cheek before he brushed a kiss on my blushing skin. "I really like you, too."

Nothing more needed to be said. We were finally on the same page. I'd caught up to Hunter and now our real story could begin.

I listened to the gentle pitter-patter of his heart as we waited for the line to advance.

Fifteen minutes later, we walked out of the store with bags filled with books and a cloud of bliss surrounding.

I'd never felt happier in my life.

Hunter wasn't kidding when he said he planned an entire day for us. This was easily the best date ever. Food, books, shopping, and good conversations really were the key to my heart.

Presently, we were at a mall in a formal menswear boutique. Hunter needed to pick up a suit he'd had altered. As he spoke to one of the employees, I wandered around until a row of ties caught my attention.

Amongst the neat display, there was a hunter green one and a light blue one. The latter reminded me of the exact shade of my boyfriend's eyes.

Thankfully, he had his back to me, still in discussion with the employee, so he didn't see when I quietly purchased the two ties and hid them in my purse.

"I'm parched," I told him when we stepped out of there.

"Let's get you something to drink, doll."

He directed us towards a coffee shop in the food court, where he proceeded to buy me a hot chocolate with whipped cream and sprinkles. The barista eyed Hunter flirtatiously and I burned with jealousy. It was unlike me. I'd never felt territorial over my ex-boyfriends or flings. But Hunter was different.

He was beginning to feel like my forever.

And the energy inside of me bordered on unhinged. I wanted to mark him as mine in a way that was visible to the entire world. So every onlooker knew to keep their interest to themselves.

Would he consider getting a tattoo for me—something that said 'I belong to Gabriela'? I sipped my hot chocolate almost furiously on the bench as I pondered, Hunter sitting beside me. Or maybe I should go Josh's route and make Hunter wear a ring with my name on it?

No, stop it, Gabriela. Your crazy possessiveness might spook him.

Or…he might love it.

"What are you thinking about?" Hunter teased as if watching my thoughts play out on my face in real time. I practically chugged down half of my drink to avoid telling him. "You really are addicted to chocolate, huh?"

"And you're addicted to me," I countered in a singsong tone.

"I can't help it." He kissed me and sucked the whipped cream from my top lip. "You smell good, look good, and taste good. I just want to take a bite out of you."

"You're insatiable." But secretly, I loved his answer. It tamed the green-eyed monster inside of me. "Didn't you have enough last night?"

Earlier, Hunter's hair came undone from his low bun and since I liked him with his hair open, I'd stolen his hair tie and worn it around my wrist. Now when he leaned into my space, those tousled strands brushed my neck and I shivered, right before he confessed in my ear, "I'll never have enough of you, Gabby."

I wouldn't have enough of him either. "Good answer."

He chuckled and the deep sound poured through my skin and bones until I was certain Hunter would always be ingrained inside of me.

Drink finished, he ushered us to our next destination without telling me where we were headed. But realization dawned on me as my favourite lingerie store neared.

Noting my inquisitive stare, he offered, "We're going to replace all the things that creep Maverick stole from you and get you anything else you want, all right?"

My jaw slackened. "Are you serious?"

He tugged me into the store. "I never joke when it comes to you."

He didn't need to buy me new lingerie, but I didn't protest. While I could take care of myself, a part of me understood that Hunter liked taking care of me. *Craved* it, even.

Plus, when we entered the store and a salesgirl handed Hunter a pink basket for my shopping, I was hit with a bigger realization: I was just like my mamma. She liked being spoiled and spending Papà's money…and I liked being spoiled and spending Hunter's.

And if my pretty, rich boy's kink was dropping a couple thousand on me, then who was I to deny him?

Like a good sport, Hunter walked beside me with a confident gait, taking in the half-naked mannequins with racy lingerie, the racks with silky gowns, and the displays of colourful soutien-gorges. I needed to stock up on a combination of things. Maverick, the asshole, not only stole my thongs, but my favourite teddy and babydoll from my armoire.

"You should get that." Hunter chin-jerked at a red lace nightie that left nothing to the imagination.

I cast him a cunning glance over my shoulder as I placed it in the basket. "Done."

He watched me heatedly. I continued filling the basket with more lingerie. His expression said he'd like nothing more than to see me in every piece. Before he ripped it off my body with his teeth like the animal I knew him to be.

"You planning on buying the entire store?" he quipped after twenty minutes of me picking up one item after another. His tone was far from reprimanding.

Oh, Hunter, I have a knack for shopping and you have a black card with no limit. That's a lethal combination.

"Would you oppose?" I shot back.

"I'm not in the business of saying no to you, sweetheart."

He'd let me have anything, wouldn't he? Including every bit of his heart if I demanded it.

"Careful." I walked backwards while facing him. "That's a lot of power you're giving me."

"You've always had it." His eyes glittered with an unnamed emotion. "There's no doubt there, Gabriela."

Hunter had so much power over me too.

If he saw inside my mind, he'd know just how much space he occupied. More than I'd ever allowed another. And as vulnerable as it left me, I wouldn't change it for the world.

On our way to purchase my items, we passed by a BDSM-inspired accessories stand, housing furry handcuffs, small leather crops, flogs, and so on.

Blue eyes trained on me, Hunter's gloved hand passed over a blindfold, reminding me of our future date, before sliding it into the basket with a wink in my direction.

I bit my lip, my heartbeat almost jackhammering.

Though we'd had plenty of foreplay, I couldn't wait until we properly consummated our relationship. The truth was I wanted him to tie me up and fuck me like his groupie slut. In fact, it may be the only thing keeping me going at this point.

After checking out, Hunter clutched the handful of pink bags in one hand, placed his other one into mine, and led us out of the store.

My serotonin levels were at an all-time high. Perhaps this first date was a bit unconventional by some standards, but Hunter tailored it exactly to my wants—letting me shop to my heart's content and spend the day with my favourite person—and that was all that mattered.

I brushed my fingers along his jaw, turning his head towards me. "Thank you, baby. For everything."

Pleased at the term of endearment, but trying to play it stern, he said, "What did I say about the T-word?"

"How will I ever convey my appreciation then?"

"How about you give me a private show—model that red lace number—when we get back home," he rasped, painting the words against my lips. "And I'll call it even."

My breath hitched and he smiled victoriously, kissing me.

But the only thing I could focus on was him saying *home*.

He probably didn't mean to imply that his home was my home.

But that's how I took it.

My heart filled with immense warmth.

The sun was beginning to set, the canvas of the sky marred with strips of blue, purple, orange, and pink as Hunter drove us back home. Or I *thought* he was driving us home until he pulled into a deserted parking lot of an old plaza, past opening hours, so all the stores were closed and we were the only car in sight.

Confused, I said, "What are we doing here?"

Wordlessly, Hunter turned off the car, unfolded out of his seat, and rounded the front to come to my side. He pulled open my door and unclicked my seatbelt. "Hunter?"

He drew me out of the car gingerly. "I know we've had a long day, but there's one more thing I want to do."

I cupped his face with one hand. "What is it?"

He turned his head enough to kiss the inside of my palm before grabbing my wrist, bringing it between us, and…dropping his car keys inside my hand. "You're going to drive."

"E-excuse me?"

"You said you wanted to learn." He caressed a knuckle softly down my cheek. "And I want to teach you, Gabby."

No one ever had the patience to teach me how to drive. I sat in the driver's seat a total of two times. First with Papà, but he freaked out when I accidentally ran a stop sign. Second with Mamma, but she clutched her seatbelt with her eyes screwed shut, praying under her breath like I was going to drive us into a ditch. Mind you, we'd only been driving around the residential streets of our neighbourhood. Both times lasted a total of ten minutes. I had my permit, yet I never moved on to the next phase after my parents' reactions. It deterred me. Killed my confidence before I even had the chance to give this new skill a decent shot.

And here was Hunter, wanting to help me overcome my fear. "Are you sure? You won't be scared sitting next to me?"

He smiled like I was being silly. "Not at all."

Before I knew it, I was in the driver's side of his Jaguar. Hunter helped me adjust all my mirrors, including bringing my seat forward because I had shorter legs. Excitement mixed with dread bloomed within me. I held the steering wheel with a death grip, the car still in park. "Hunter, what if I do something wrong—what if I wreck your car?"

He clicked his seatbelt on and said smoothly, "That's what insurance is for, baby."

My pulse thudded faster at his reassurance.

Hunter placed a strong palm on my bare thigh, squeezing lightly. "Just promise me you'll be careful."

I nodded eagerly. "I promise I'll be careful not to damage your car."

He shook his head. "I don't care about the car. I care about *you*. I want you to try to be as vigilant as possible for your own safety, all right? We'll take it easy for our first lesson. Do a couple turns, practice your stops, and check your blind spots. Get you comfortably oriented in the driver's seat. Sound good?"

It sounded amazing.

Hunter's trust in me caused some of my fear to evaporate. I started the car as he instructed before shifting gears and beginning to drive slowly. We spent the first fifteen minutes going around the parking lot until I felt a bit more confident behind the wheel. I couldn't believe I was doing it—driving again without a scolding adult. Hunter was patient and calm, praising me for the simplest of turns and stops. "You're doing amazing, Gabby."

My throat was dry. "Really?"

"Really. You've got this." He pointed forward. "Now I want you to exit the parking lot."

He didn't say the lesson would actually include driving on the road. A nugget of trepidation nearly had me chickening out. But Hunter's sheer belief in my ability had me agreeing with a feeble, "Okay."

I wouldn't take this opportunity for granted. I wanted to learn how to drive and be good at it.

The apartment building was ten minutes away. I figured that was where he was trying to lead us with his quiet commands. *Stop here. Take a right. Now take a left. Keep going straight.* Hunter was giving me another layer of confidence by teaching me that I could drive us home.

"Am I still doing well?" I asked anxiously after two more minutes of driving.

Funnily enough, I expected myself to be super stressed. But I was okay, despite my palms being a bit clammy.

There was a silver sedan driving a far enough distance from me in the rearview mirror. It never got too close, though I kept worrying that they were silently judging my slow driving. Especially because they seemed to be taking the same route as me. Maybe my nervous observation just stemmed from my first real time on the road. It wasn't a big deal.

"So far so good. You're driving the speed limit, you're doing your full stops, and you're constantly checking your blind spots," Hunter said. "You're not a bad driver, Gabby, or incapable of learning. Just like everyone who starts off, you need a bit of practice and you'll be a pro in no time."

There went my heart, further softening for this man.

Finally, I pulled into our apartment complex, narrowly missing the sidewalk's curb. Hunter pretended to ignore my sheepish glance. He meant it when he said he couldn't care less if his car got scratched.

I was his only priority.

Hunter had a designated numbered spot in the outside lot and in the underground garage. He asked me to park in the former. That almost made me ill. What if I hit someone's car?

Thankfully, the spots on either side of his were empty, giving me a wide berth to slide his sports car between the white lines.

I was trembling when I shifted the car into park, like a shaken-up bottle of a carbonated drink about to pop off.

"Want to practice how to parallel park?" Hunter asked when I turned off the car.

I threw him a horrified look.

He laughed. "I'm kidding. Lesson for next time."

"Hunter," I groaned. "I can't believe I did that. I'm literally shaking."

He grabbed my hands from the steering wheel and braided our fingers together, ebbing away the last of my queasiness. "See? That wasn't so bad. You did a wonderful job, Gabby." He kissed my knuckles one by one. "I'm so proud of you."

My heartbeat returned to its usual cadence. "It was scary at the start, but you set me at ease."

"I'm glad to hear it. Two bad experiences shouldn't stop you from trying again. I'll keep giving you lessons and before you know it, you'll have your license in no time."

"You're a patient teacher. Thank you for the driving lesson and for an incredible first date. I had fun."

I leaned forward to kiss him.

"I had fun too," he murmured in the space between our mouths. "I always do when I'm with you. And you don't have to thank me. This was nothing."

That's the thing. It wasn't nothing.

It was *everything*.

Hunter's way of showing affection was quiet, but his gestures were grandiose, whether he realized it or not. He was single-handedly raising all my standards. Hell, he was my new standard.

My ex-boyfriend only ever tried to burn my wings.

Meanwhile, Hunter helped me soar to new heights.

We kissed for what felt like an eternity, our hands roaming everywhere they could reach. Neck. Jaw. Cheeks. Hair. Tugging each other as close as we could with the center console between us.

I couldn't stop kissing him. Feared I never would. Hoped I never had to.

The inside of the car echoed with the sounds of our wet lips and our gentle moans.

The sky was effortlessly blue, like Hunter's stunning eyes, and the sun dipped into the horizon when we parted ways…only to join our foreheads together. My exhales were his inhales, and his exhales were my inhales.

"How do you feel?" he murmured.

I feel see-through, like the fabric of my soul is lace and you see every rip and tattered edge and choose to cherish all the imperfections instead of shunning me for not having mended every flaw.

319

I feel celebrated by you, like I'm worthy of being put on a pedestal.

But most of all... "I feel whole, Hunter."

My *principe* smiled at me with his entire heart, coating every fissure in my soul with gold, making me feel like a masterpiece. "So do I."

And right then, another rare sight occurred.

An anomaly at this time of the year.

A dragonfly danced over the windshield, capturing our attention.

The good omen reminded me of the first time I saw one with Hunter when we'd just exited Le Petit Moulin, our story having just begun.

It felt like a sign from the universe. Like it was telling me that everything would be fine and it was okay to dream bigger.

Because the beautiful man sitting next to me might just be my happily ever after.

CHAPTER 31

Hero & Leander

GABRIELA

The past seven days flew by in the blink of an eye. Midterm season was nearing its end, so we were busier than ever. I had two written exams and three assignments to hand in from Monday to Thursday. Hunter's schedule was just as hectic. As a result, we saw each other sparsely, save for our Horror & Cult Classic Cinema class, the two times Hunter drove us to Vesta University in the morning, and the one evening walk we took around our neighbourhood Tuesday night.

Safe to say, I couldn't wait to see Hunter again.

I missed him so much.

Luna missed him too, occasionally wandering out into the hallway and pawing at his door with soft meows, trying to urge him out, without realizing that he wasn't there. My poor baby. I had to give her cat treats to assuage her until Hunter could return and give her the cuddles she demanded.

Wednesday afternoon, he sent me a text before his football practice. I read it while rushing from one classroom to another.

Whatever plans you have on Friday evening, cancel them. — Hunter

I texted back, in the mood to banter with him.

Sorry, me and Luna are busy 😕 We're doing our nails, putting on face masks, and watching Supernatural reruns. —Gabby

That was a lie. We had no such plans.

I'm actually offended that I wasn't invited. —Hunter

Girls' night 🌙 No boys allowed. You have cooties! —Gabby

Did you think I had cooties last week when you sucked my cock and I licked your pussy in the club? —Hunter

Speechless, I abruptly stopped in the middle of a busy hallway leading to a large auditorium. Passersby bumped into me with mild annoyance before I moved over to lean against a wall. A goofy smile smarted my lips at his response.

I definitely didn't think he had cooties then.

Hunter took my lack of reply as a no.

Didn't think so. Now back to what I was saying. Cancel your plans on Friday. You're busy with me. —Hunter

Officially seven days of being my boyfriend and you think you can boss me around, huh? —Gabby

You love being bossed around. But only by me. Remember? —Hunter

Oh, did I ever. That heated hookup in Club Azul would remain a lifetime highlight.

Fineeeee. What are we busy with, pretty boy? —Gabby

You're my plus-one. We're going to a fundraising gala in the city. I get an invite every year and I want to take you. —Hunter

An opportunity to get all dolled up and wear a cute dress? I would never pass that.

I would love to go with you 🩶 —Gabby

There's one problem though… —Gabby

Tell me, baby. —Hunter

I really did love it when he called me *baby*.

I don't have a dress for the occasion 😖 **—Gabby**

We both knew I was bluffing. I had an entire wardrobe filled with dresses and I could certainly find one fitting for a black-tie event. If not, Layla and Anna would let me borrow one of theirs.

I'll leave my card on your console table tonight. Get yourself whatever you want. —Hunter

You're the best 😊 **—Gabby**

I know. You can repay me by sitting on my face Friday night. —Hunter

I fought the crazy grin threatening to take over my face. I adored this man to pieces. There was no denying it.

It's a date 🩶 **—Gabby**

And that was how I found myself at Anna's place, forty-five minutes before Hunter arrived to pick me up. The girls wanted to help me get ready for the gala and offered to cat-sit Luna for the night. They seemed to be just as excited as Mamma that Hunter and I were finally dating. I also wasn't fooled—this was a chance to quiz me about what happened last weekend at Club Azul.

Since our brunch got cancelled last minute, I was all too happy to divulge the details now.

"So you're saying," Anna began with a lilting voice, brushing my cheeks with pink blush. "That while the rest of us were dancing the night away, you two were doing the nasty in the office upstairs?"

I met both their gazes in Anna's vanity mirror, nodding earnestly. "Yup."

They burst into chuckles.

"I will never look at a dartboard the same way ever again," Layla mused, running a straightener through my red hair. "Or a champagne bottle, for that matter."

Honestly? Me neither.

"Platonic, my ass," Anna tittered, switching the blush compact for a shiny highlighter one, dabbing the product on the high points of my cheeks. "You've been lying to yourself this whole time."

"I really have." I could openly admit it now. "It was foolish of me to assume that we could only ever be just friends. Especially when I feel this way about him. I'm glad I snapped to my senses before it was too late."

I could barely fathom the thought of losing Hunter forever because of my self-sabotage.

The girls smiled. It had been two years since I took a chance on someone, and they were firsthand witnessing how Hunter melted the icy layers I built around my heart to keep myself safe.

"And how is it that you feel about him?" Layla prompted, adding the finishing touches to my hair.

I lowered my gaze to my fresh set of sparkly crimson nails. I felt a lot of things where Hunter was concerned. I was doing my best to untangle and make sense of those feelings, but the bottom line was that I liked him. A lot. "Like he could actually be the one."

They gasped loudly.

"I'm serious. I know this is still new, but the kind of connection I have with him? I'm convinced it's once in a lifetime. That's the best way I can explain it. I...I don't think there's another man out there who'll treat and care for me—and Luna—the way Hunter does."

"We're so happy for you," Anna said.

"And proud of you," Layla added. "You and Hunter are going to be good for each other."

Talking to them about this felt like coming full circle. "Thank you, girls. For listening and for helping me get ready."

"What else are best friends for?" Anna's hazel eyes gleamed as she gauged my reflection in the mirror. "Now go get dressed before your hot date arrives."

Knowing Hunter's punctuality, I practically raced to Anna's gigantic walk-in closet.

Yesterday, I went on a last-minute shopping excursion to pick up a gown courtesy of Hunter's card. I even left one of the ties I bought him in his locker with a note saying, **Make sure you wear this tomorrow so we match, xo**.

The gown in question was a strapless, mermaid-style, hunter green silk number with matching gloves that stopped above my elbows. I wore the ensemble with six-inch heels and complementary jewelry. The centerpiece was my necklace, a white diamond snake coiling around my neck, its head and tail meeting against a large teardrop emerald resting between my collarbones.

With my pin-straight hair parted to the side and flowing down my back, my makeup perfected with a sharp winged eyeliner, and my favourite shade of blood red on my lips, I felt beautiful beyond words.

I couldn't wait to see Hunter's reaction.

My best friends cheered when I stepped out and I did a three-sixty spin, preening a little extra for them. Choruses of praise rang in the air and I soaked it all up. Layla proceeded to marinate me in a cloud of perfume while Anna finished zipping up my dress the rest of the way. Afterwards, I was subjected to a hundred pictures so we could capture the perfect shot for me to post tonight on my social media.

With less than a handful of minutes remaining until Hunter's arrival, we descended the stairs and met Michael on the ground floor, his arms full of Luna, who appeared all too happy to be hanging out with her younger sibling.

"Wow, Gabby," Michael said shyly and I bent down to kiss his cheek with a loud *mwah*. He handed Luna to Anna and scurried off with a toothy grin to half-hide behind Layla, his favourite person.

"I hope you all have fun tonight." I pouted. "But not too much fun without me."

They laughed. Layla palmed Michael's hair affectionately. "You know we won't."

"I'll come pick up Luna in the morning, all right?" I said, giving my sweet girl some chin scratches.

The doorbell rang on cue.

My best friends gave me shit-eating grins.

Anna jerked her chin towards the door. "Go answer. Don't keep him waiting."

When I opened the door and crossed the threshold, my exposed skin pebbling under the fall night with only a faux fur shawl to keep me warm, my boyfriend waited at the bottom step with a large bouquet of red roses.

For a few heartbeats, we simply gazed at each other.

Blue eyes cascaded down my body, committing every detail to memory.

My own eyes drank him greedily like he was a mirage that would disappear.

Tonight, Hunter appeared the embodiment of a classy hero from my favourite romantic tales, with an indomitable presence and courting his most-awaited beloved. Dashing as ever, a crisp black tux was poured over his muscular frame and he had omitted the bowtie for my gifted hunter green tie instead.

We matched perfectly.

He extended his hand.

I grabbed it.

He helped me descend the remaining steps, keeping his eyes on mine like he was voracious for the sight I created.

"You're beautiful," he said huskily, drawing my knuckles to his mouth for a kiss. I shivered, feeling the touch of his lips seep through the thin material of my gloves. "The most beautiful, Gabriela."

I touched his cheek with affection. "So are you, *bello.*"

He kissed me, warm and sweet, smiling against my lips.

"These are for you," he whispered, handing me my roses.

"Thank you." If he kept at this pace, my entire apartment would be filled with roses and no place to walk. Not that I would ever complain. "I love them."

He guided me closer. "Ready to go? We have an audience."

I peeked over my shoulder and, true to his words, four curious heads—Anna, Layla, Michael, and Luna—were spying on us through the window. The second I caught their stares, they scampered behind the curtains with sheepish laughter.

"Yes, I am. Whisk me away, Hunter."

HUNTER

The fundraising gala was held at a pristine hotel in the heart of downtown Montardor, the inside already droning with a panoply of suits and gowns.

After handing over my keys to the valet, a doorman held open the door for us and I escorted Gabriela inside, my hand skimming down her back until it rested at the small of it. My possessive gesture didn't go unheeded by my date. I wanted everyone within a ten-foot radius to know she belonged to me. Just as I belonged to her.

Gabriela didn't mind my caveman tactics. The playful wink, coupled with her small smirk, was proof enough. She liked my territorial side as much as I liked hers.

Upon entering, a number of people greeted us.

From the corner of my eye, I spotted Morgan Huxley and Taylor Prescott. The former glared at Gabriela. I gritted my teeth. My girlfriend, thankfully, remained unbothered. My teammate, finally noticing his date's improper behaviour, turned his head in our direction with confusion to inspect what had her undivided attention. Taylor's family, similar to mine, also rubbed shoulders with the affluent individuals present here tonight. Therefore, I often saw him at events like these. But we seldom conversed off the field and I wasn't about to engage in small talk now. Taylor smiled at me and I gave him a nod of acknowledgement, albeit glacé in nature, and turned to Gabriela.

"What would you like to drink?" I asked.

"Champagne, please."

My nostrils flared at her teasing expression. Indubitably, I would never forget how much my girl enjoyed champagne.

I snagged a flute from a waiter walking around the foyer and handed it to her with a kiss on the cheek. "How does it feel?"

"How does what feel?" she returned, daintily sipping her drink.

I curved a finger around the shell of her ear, pausing to touch the long diamond earring adorning her lobe. "To once again be the most beautiful woman in the room."

The grin that broke over her face reminded me of the first rays of light touching the dark sky when the sun broke over the horizon. "I'll never get tired of hearing you call me beautiful."

"Good. I'll never get tired of saying it." I kissed her bare shoulder. "Let's go find our seats, hm?"

The minute we entered the banquet hall, I recognized a few of my dad's old entourage. The Warren family remained a name on the guest list every year, for we were generous with our donations and my dad had once conducted business with more than half of the people present in this venue. Gabriela and I paused to shake hands and speak with some of my dad's friends. They reminisced over past anecdotes that speared a flurry of nostalgia—any mention of Kyle Warren did—and asked about my studies, my football season, and the stunning redhead hanging on my arm.

Gabriela was a natural, charming the men and stroking their egos. They, in turn, told me that I was a lucky bastard to have scored such a smart girl.

I wasn't even going to deny it.

My goddess of victory was a million-dollar vision to behold in that green dress that wrapped around her tight little body like a clingy lover, her silky hair waterfalling down her back, and all those jewels—especially that impressive snake necklace—glinting under the light of the massive chandeliers above us.

My mouth watered. What I wouldn't give to taste her *right now*.

I wanted to drive us back home so I could tie her to my headboard and fuck her thoroughly, all night long, the way we both desperately needed.

But that would have to wait. This wasn't just a formal date, but a glimpse into my world. I wanted Gabriela to see this facet of my life so she knew what to expect moving forward. Sometimes, I had to attend these events, and I would like her to come with me whenever possible.

There wasn't a single doubt in my mind that Gabriela would seamlessly fit into this part of my world.

We ate a three-course meal, we mingled with our friends present tonight—Cade, Ella, Darla, and Dacia—and now we reached the auction portion of the evening.

My palm coasted over Gabriela's thighs, wishing her dress had a slit so I could touch her bare skin…and feel the heat between her legs. I bet I could make her come in a room full of people with a few brushes of my fingers and some dirty words hushed in her ear. My little exhibitionist would enjoy the hell out of that. But I supposed that wouldn't be very cultured of us, considering our friends were seated at the same table.

Gabriela broke away from her conversation with Darla, sensing I needed her attention. "What is it, Hunt?"

"When the auction begins, I want you to tell me what you want," I said. "I'm going to get it for you."

A sibilating inhale whistled through her parted mouth. "Really?"

"Anything, doll." I punctuated my statement with a peck to her lips.

My sassy neighbour smiled excitedly. "Okay."

Then her eyes trekked over something beyond my shoulder and the happiness drained out of her demeanour.

I followed her line of sight.

My jaw clenched.

Franco.

Her ex-boyfriend.

He wore the standard waiters' uniform, planted behind the empty bar. His own expression was slightly dumbfounded and uncomfortable. Like he'd been watching me and Gabriela interact for quite some time now and didn't like what he saw.

My neck bore a visible red lipstick stain from when she'd kissed me earlier.

Even from far away, I could tell he zeroed in on the mark and hated it.

Good.

Fucking prick. I wanted to go over there and punch him into oblivion. Hurt him for how he hurt my Gabriela with his disgusting words, a shaft of trauma I knew she still carried. And though a physical altercation wouldn't eradicate the past, it would give me satisfaction to see his nose bloody and broken.

Had we been in a secluded spot, far from the prying eyes of the public, I would have done it. Last week, I meant it when I told her I wanted to teach him a goddamned lesson.

Gabriela snapped her face away from Franco, dismissing him like he was shit at the bottom of her six-inch stilettos. Unworthy of even being seen by her. Insignificant like a dust mote floating in the air.

I was proud of her and showed it by draping my arm around her shoulders and kissing the side of her head. She closed her eyes on an exhale, leaning into me.

"You okay?" I asked.

"Yes. He doesn't matter and he can't hurt me anymore. I have you now."

My chest swelled with pride at her progress. She was healing. "You'll always have me, Gabby."

The last week was gruelling in terms of studies and football. But despite the multiple stressors, it had been one of my best ones yet.

Because I finally had Gabriela. She was mine in every way that mattered.

Heidi and my mom were stoked that we were dating now. They were eager to meet Gabriela and I promised them I'd arrange a time for us to have lunch or dinner. I just wanted to run the idea by my girlfriend first. Not because I thought she'd be spooked out that we were moving too fast, but as a courtesy.

I was confident in her feelings for me.

I may have fallen for her first, but it was clear she was falling for me too.

"I adore you," she murmured our three-word confession.

Heart racing, I murmured back, "I adore you too."

The auction began shortly, yanking our attention to the front stage, where a charismatic woman in a gold dress spoke from the helm of a podium, starting with the usual introductions.

The first item was unveiled and the bidding process ensued. I treasured the exhilaration in Gabriela's eyes as she watched the scene unfold. When an item she wanted was up for grabs, she whispered in my ear and like a dutiful boyfriend, I outbid everyone in the room.

A wine-tasting tour.

A pair of tickets to an upcoming pop star's concert.

A signed hockey jersey from one of her favourite players on the Montardor's Ravens.

And then came an arresting painting, a beautiful rendition of Hero and Leander. It depicted the priestess in her light tower, watching her mortal lover swim to her before tragedy fell upon them. Save for a single **R** signed at the bottom of the anonymously donated canvas, the artist was unknown.

Gabriela gasped and clasped my wrist, giving me a pleading look. "Hunter, I want it. Please. It'll mean so much to me."

I'd have bought it without her even asking me. It was a tangible piece of our history.

The auction started at a mere five thousand dollars. I raised my paddle with my bid.

Gabriela waited with bated breath.

"Five thousand dollars for Mr. Warren," the auctioneer said in the microphone with an upbeat tone. "Anyone else for—"

"Ten thousand dollars," Dacia bid out loud, raising her paddle.

I remained calm, upping my bid to, "Fifteen thousand dollars."

"Twenty-five thousand dollars." Dacia tried to appear her usual ice princess cool, but I caught the subtle hint of worry in her frame.

Unfortunately for her, I would be taking this piece home. "Fifty thousand dollars."

The auctioneer's voice sparked with jubilance. "Wow. Fifty thousand dollars. Does anyone want to top that? Going once, going twice—"

Darla frowned and grabbed her sister's wrist, speaking to her in a quiet tone. Dacia mumbled back something inaudible. I was ready to up my bid as high as needed, but it was too late. The Hill sisters missed their window and I was declared the recipient of the painting.

"Sold! For fifty thousand dollars to Mr. Warren."

The little squeal Gabriela emitted filled my insides with pure joy. I grinned as she turned my head towards hers for a series of kisses. "Oh, Hunter." *Kiss.* "Thank you." *Kiss.* "Thank you." *Kiss.* "Thank you."

"You're welcome, Gabby. It was my pleasure."

Gabriela ran her fingers over my stubble in adoration. I knew how much she liked the trimmed beard I sported. "God, you're so handsome." She planted kisses all over my jaw. "And sweet. And cute. And I can't wait to go home and show you my appreciation, *bello mio.*"

Fuck, I melted at her praise even as I chuckled at her cute aggression. "Is that so?"

"Yeah. We have other plans for tonight, don't we?"

Like her sitting on my face for starters.

I kissed her again. "Yes, we do, baby."

CHAPTER 32
Teaching A Lesson

GABRIELA

After the auction came to an end, I was ready to call it a night and head home with Hunter. But we lingered a little longer, talking with our friends by the bar and trying to pretend like we weren't moments away from tearing the clothes off one another.

The energy between us crackled with tension. It was nearly tangible. I could practically feel its tendrils weaving themselves around every muscle and bone until I reverberated with need like the plucked strings of a guitar.

I wanted Hunter so bad that every fiber of my being ached.

He evoked a fever within me and the only remedy was his touch.

I felt like Hero from the painting, hooked with breathless anticipation by her tower's window as she waited for Leander. Counting down the minutes till she could take him into her arms and lose herself in the throes of their passion.

God, he looked so fucking good in that tux, with his black hair tousled and his mouth tainted just the barest hint of red from my lipstick. I branded him so everyone in our vicinity knew he was mine to kiss, mine to touch, and soon, mine to fuck all night long.

"Gabby?" Hunter hushed in my ear, the breath fanning across my cheek almost causing my knees to buckle with the weight of desire pressing onto me.

We'd barely touched in any sort of sexual manner, save for trading some sweet kisses throughout the night, and I was ticking like a bomb. Ready to explode at the mere scent of his delicious cologne ribboning around me, at the faintest rasp of his stubble against my skin, at the way he uttered my name like a filthy caress.

The fact that he bought me all the items I requested from the auction in that confident, *I'll-cater-to-all-your-demands* type of way was just the cherry on top of the cake. I appreciated that he went the extra mile for me, namely to procure that stunning painting.

What affected me most wasn't that he fulfilled my materialistic wishes, but rather the thoughtfulness behind his gesture. It seemed that my happiness was *his* happiness too.

"Yes, Hunt?" I glanced up at him with a soft smile, loving the way his eyes flared and washed over my face in an awestruck manner. Like he couldn't believe I was real. Like he could stare at me all day, all night, and still not have his fill.

How many women were recipients of such a look? I'd never been until Hunter, and I considered myself fortunate to experience this kind of veneration. It was lovely and heart-warming, but on a deeper level? It altered me in a cosmic way.

"You've been awfully quiet." He curved an arm around my waist and dragged me closer to him. "What's on your mind?"

I'd zoned out momentarily, withdrawing from the conversation circling in our group as I daydreamed about Hunter. "You."

He grinned. "Yeah?"

"Mhm. I'm thinking about all the things you bought me, including where I'm going to hang the painting."

"What's the verdict?"

"Either the wall above my bed or in my spare room." I tilted my head, thinking. "Except the latter is a bit of a mess. Maybe once I clean it up and turn it into a proper home office, I could potentially place it there."

My voice rose a fraction towards the end of my sentence and Dacia heard the last bit of our exchange.

Her head swivelled in our direction and determination crossed my friend's face.

"Speaking of the painting," Dacia started matter-of-factly, pushing her blond hair behind her shoulder. "How much do you want for it?"

The question was aimed at Hunter. "Pardon me?"

"A hundred thousand?" she spurred on, waving her hand flippantly in the air, the impressive carats on her diamond rings catching the light. "A quarter million? Name your price."

My brows hiked up. Dacia was a lover of arts, a collector of sorts. But I didn't realize she wanted the painting badly enough that she'd be willing to fork out such capital.

Did it also have a significant meaning to her?

I noticed she hadn't bid on anything else during the auction. Yet the second the Hero and Leander painting was revealed, she picked up her paddle with a vengeance. I almost asked her if there was a particular reason why she gravitated towards that art piece. If it was truly important to her, I'd ask Hunter to relinquish our purchase and give it to Dacia for the same amount he bought it for.

I didn't have a chance to say anything because Hunter chuckled and shook his head. "Absolutely nothing, Dacia. I'm not selling it to you."

Something akin to resignation flashed over her features. "Is there no way I can change your mind?"

"No. The painting means something special to me—to us." He glanced at me pointedly. "I can't give it to you."

She shrugged and sipped her drink to show her unaffectedness. "All right. That's fair."

Cade and Shaun called Hunter over, where they languidly leaned against the bar.

Franco was working the other side of the bar, but his attention kept jerking towards us as he prepared drinks. The unhealed version of me would have probably done something petty. Make out with Hunter in front of him so he'd have a direct view of the show. Insult him like he'd insulted me all those years ago. Or even ask him if he'd ever gotten all the pink glitter out of his Camry.

Yet the version that was slowly healing didn't want to give him the satisfaction of a reaction. I was ignoring him. Not because I wanted to pretend like our past never occurred, but because Franco Morelli simply wasn't worth it.

"I'll be back." Hunter dropped a chaste kiss on my temple. "I'm going to speak with them for a bit, and then we'll leave."

"Promise?"

"Promise, baby."

Hunter walked away, leaving me with the girls. In the middle of chatting about the upcoming Halloween party, I noticed that Dacia was a bit disconnected. As if her mind had wandered elsewhere.

I slid closer to her, taking a swig from my champagne flute. Not wanting to be the reason for the damper in Dacia's mood, I felt called to explain to her why the painting meant so much to Hunter and me. My soft heart couldn't stand seeing the people I cared for being upset in any capacity.

"Before Hunter and I officially got together," I began and Dacia's eyes veered my way, holding, "he took me on a date—but at that time I didn't realize it was actually a date, though that's beside the point—and we stargazed for the first time and saw the constellation Pegasus. Since he has an interest in Greek mythology, I asked him to tell me a story— whichever one he wanted to share—and he told me the tragic tale of Hero and Leander. When I saw the painting at the auction, it felt symbolic. That's why I wanted it. Something tangible that represented a small slice of our relationship."

Dacia smiled with understanding. "That's really sweet, Gabby."

I was glad she thought so. Still, I added, "But if the painting has any sort of importance to you, please tell me, and I'll let Hunter know."

Maybe she knew the artist. Maybe she was an avid collector of their work.

There was something wistful in her expression. "It's of no importance to me. I thought it was pretty and wanted to add it to my collection. That's all." She squeezed my shoulder reassuringly. "You deserve to have it. Especially given the reasoning behind it."

The event dwindled down and the girls ended up leaving before midnight, Cade and Shaun in tow.

Hunter was engaged in a conversation with one of his dad's old friends and I didn't want to interrupt, so I texted him that I was headed for the washroom. I wanted to freshen up and reapply my lipstick.

When I finished and stepped out into the empty hallway, secluded and far away from the banquet hall…a surprise awaited me.

It caught me so off guard that for a moment, I just stood there.

Completely shocked.

Franco pinned me with perplexed brown eyes, hands stuffed into the pockets of his black pants. "Hey, Gabby."

I blinked. *Is this really happening?*

"Can we talk?"

I almost gawked at him. It definitely wasn't my imagination. He really stood before me, his voice loud and clear.

Somewhere between then and now, Franco must have gone nuts if he thought I would actually speak to him after all this time. Fucking twat.

I squished down the old memories trying to burst free from the figurative box I shoved them into all those years ago. I hated how he appeared so blasé. He tore me to shreds and stomped on my teenage heart until it was a pulverized mess. He barely had the decency to treat me with respect when I'd been his good childhood friend before becoming his girlfriend, and that should have counted for something. So how dare he speak to me like he had any right?

I'd always deserved better than him.

Gritting my teeth, I side-stepped my ex-boyfriend, hell-bent on continuing to pretend like he didn't exist.

Franco's hand shot out to grab my wrist, halting me.

I bristled and tried tugging my arm free. "Let go of me, Franco."

He yanked me towards him.

This was the closest we'd been in three years. And my heart began to beat fast, not in a *I-have-butterflies-in-my-stomach* manner, but more in a *get-me-the-hell-away-from-this-asshole.*

"You're not going anywhere until you hear what I have to say," he clipped. "I've had three years to think about what happened between us, three years to—"

"Franco, respectfully, shut the fuck up," I growled. "Even the sound of your voice is grating. I'm literally developing hives as you speak. Let. Me. Go."

"Fuck, Gabriela!" he whisper-shouted, attempting to keep his voice down so no one witnessed his clown behaviour, but failing regardless. "I just want to say—"

"What part of you thinks you deserve to be heard after everything that transpired between us, *stronzo?*" I snarled, finally managing to tug my arm free. But now it hurt from the force of his hold. "We said all that needed to be said three years ago. Now fucking get lost!"

"I'm sorry!" he barked, losing all composure.

I reared back.

Never did I expect this bullheaded individual to give an apology.

"I'm sorry, all right?" he spat, face reddening. He shoved a frustrated hand into his hair. "I just wanted to tell you I'm sorry, Gabriela. For everything."

Apparently, Franco took my shocked silence as a green light to continue talking. "I never wanted to hurt you, but I did. You'll never know how sorry I truly am. I regret the things I did and the callous words I spoke," he heaved, and much to my disbelief, I saw the so-called regret in his eyes. "Back then, I was troubled and highly insecure. My parents' divorce impacted my mental health more than I'd like to admit, and having a girlfriend who was…infinitely smarter and charming than me messed with my ego."

All I could do was stare at him, speechless.

"Instead of cherishing and loving you the way I should have, I treated you like garbage. You were right to call me out on it. What I did to you has haunted me for three years. I hate that I ruined us. And you'll never know how many times I wished I could just pick up the phone, call you, and confess these things."

Tears stung my eyes unexpectedly, some of it stemming from anger, but most of it because I loathed the fact that I actually felt bad for him. "So why didn't you?"

Franco's eyes shut and he dragged out a long breath. "The day we had our fight, your dad came over to my place an hour later and told me to leave the city. He said this was the only mercy he granted me. That I was lucky he wasn't doing more damage for having broken his daughter's heart."

All this time, I assumed that I did a decent job of muffling my sobbing cries after I returned home from our fight. I didn't think my parents suspected that I was lying when I told them that Franco and I broke up amicably. They believed me so easily, their calm demeanours barely giving them away.

But hearing Franco's confession, it was clear that Papà had heard me at the very least. Knowing that I wouldn't tell them the truth, he must have gone over to the Morellis to confront my ex-boyfriend. And like the loving father that he was, he took matters into his own hands and delivered justice, sending Franco far, far, far away from Montardor, where I would never have to set eyes on him and relieve that pain.

"Why are you back?" I said drolly, though I didn't feel any ounce of amusement. "Why now?"

His posture sagged like a deflated balloon. "I never got along with my dad, you know this, and living with him in New York was hell. But a few months ago, I found out my mom was sick. She's terminal, Gabby. She doesn't have much time left. I got in contact with your dad and begged him to let me return for her sake."

Oh.

That hurt to hear. For all of Franco's faults, Mrs. Morelli had treated me like the daughter she never had. She was an angel and I never understood how she gave birth to a devil of a son. "I'm sorry to hear about your mom, Franco."

He kept staring at me with this expression I couldn't decipher. "Your dad had conditions. Mainly that I was supposed to stay away and never talk to you. I tried at first, when I saw you in that class. I tried again, when I saw you at MacGregor. But seeing you tonight, I...I knew I had to apologize."

On one hand, I wanted to forgive Franco, but I wouldn't sincerely mean it. And on the other hand, I wanted to scoff at him, turn around, and never look back.

The past couldn't be erased and every wound he mauled upon my being like the lash from a whip? I had to do the work—*I* had to be the one to heal myself.

His apology did nothing for me. It would never justify the way he treated me. Only give an explanation for his behaviour. While I understood the latter, I didn't condone his actions.

"*Perdonami*, Gabriela." Franco took a sizable step in my direction. "That's all I want. Your forgiveness."

"You can't have it," I stated firmly. "Thank you for the explanation, but there's no redemption for you in my book, Franco. You'll always be a villain to me."

Franco's eyes darkened, not liking that response. For him to have expected me to bend over backwards and accept his apology said volumes about his piss-poor character development over the last three years. He may be sorry, but he still hadn't changed much. He was still the guy who hurt me.

"Maybe I can change your mind." He forgot the concept of a personal bubble and entered mine. I slid against the wall, further from him, but he managed to clasp my face and raise it to his, ironically using his strength to overpower me. Just like old times. "God, you look so pretty tonight, Gabby. I couldn't keep my eyes off you. The truth is I never got over you—"

"Franco, let go of me!"

He kissed me.

On the mouth.

My frozen state only lasted two beats before I thawed and registered the range of audacity this idiot possessed.

A sharp cry escaped me and I shoved at his chest with pounding fists.

He wouldn't budge, gripping my face harder.

So I raised my leg and kneed him where the sun didn't shine.

"Fuck!" Franco wrenched out in pain, withdrawing enough to cup his crotch. Thunderous footsteps echoed against the marble floor, approaching us. "What are you—"

A strong fist thwacking against Franco's jaw cut off the rest of his sentence, whipping his face to the side and causing his body to crash to the floor.

Hunter.

I gasped.

Then my boyfriend was all over Franco, grabbing him by the scruff of the neck and throwing him against the wall. "You fucking piece of shit," he snarled, sending his cocked fist sailing forth, a crunching sound resonating in the hallway. "How dare you touch her?"

Oh my God.

My head spun like a tilt-a-whirl ride from the sudden switch of Franco apologizing, to Franco kissing me, to Franco now getting beaten.

Hunter smacked my ex like he was a punching bag, effectively breaking his nose and doling out a few generous bruises that would blossom blue-purple soon. Franco whimpered, trying to defend himself, but he was no match for Hunter's strength.

For once, he was overpowered.

A bitter part of me relished seeing how the tables turned. It wasn't so nice having your will stolen from you and being unable to fight back, huh?

After the fourth punch, I sprang into motion and grabbed Hunter's elbow. Enough damage was done. "Hunter," I pleaded hoarsely. "Stop. Let him go. He's not worth it."

Hunter's eyes flung to mine. A chaotic energy unlike anything I'd ever seen before swirled in his depths.

I remembered him telling me that he wasn't a violent man, but I was his exception.

The thought of anyone hurting me made him want to teach the offender a lesson.

Right now, Franco was the recipient of all that rage.

And while I loved knowing Hunter would always rise to my defence, we were still at an event and anyone could walk by and chance upon this scene.

I couldn't risk Hunter getting in any trouble.

"Please, my love." I grazed his jaw, hoping to ease him out of the cloud of fury surrounding him. His chest bowed with his ragged breaths; gaze fixed on my lips. My insides twisted. I could only imagine how he felt seeing Franco's mouth on mine. "Let's just leave."

Hunter's gaze shuttered for a split second as he snapped out of his angry trance from my soft, coaxing words. He let Franco's body drop to the ground like a sack of potatoes.

"I'm only going to say this once." When Hunter addressed Franco again, there was an eerie calm to his tone. "You don't come near her, you don't talk to her, you don't touch her, and you sure as fuck don't kiss her. Cross those boundaries again and I'll make you regret ever having the privilege to breathe the same air as her. Understood?"

Franco wheezed, a hand covering his bleeding nose and mouth. "F-fine."

My shoulders drooped with relief. I wasn't worried about Franco reporting an assault because I would send Papà and every Remington man to hunt him down like an animal. He knew that with certainty. But I was worried about the cameras in this venue.

Hunter dismissed Franco and faced me. His hand trembled as his knuckles grazed over my cheek in his signature manner. "Are you hurt?" he said harshly. "Tell me."

"I'm not." I entwined his fingers with mine and drew him away from Franco. "I'm okay. Take me home, Hunter. Please?"

We'd been having such a good time and I despised that this one moment wrecked it all. But I was still adamant on salvaging our plans.

Hunter grabbed my face and his thumb swept over my lips, wiping away my lipstick with a tortured expression.

He couldn't stand the thought that Franco had his lips on mine.

I couldn't either.

The hunger glinting in his gaze let me know that before the end of the night, Hunter would ensure that his touch and kiss were the only thing I remembered.

He would eradicate every man from my past until he was the last one standing.

CHAPTER 33
Filthy Little Plaything

HUNTER

The red haze veiling my vision slowly dissipated with each grain of sand trickling through the fictitious hourglass in my mind. I drove us back home, shoulders bunched tight with the last tail end of my anger.

My jaw clenched as I replayed the scene where I went to search for Gabriela, once my conversation with one of my dad's old friends came to a conclusion.

The only thing on my mind was taking her back to my place so I could make good on every promise. My control started slipping from the moment I saw her in that form-fitting green dress. I wanted to tear it off her body and fuck her all night long—against the wall, on the floor, in my bed—until the world around us blurred to nothingness and we were reduced to the singular feeling of bliss that always erupted when we came together.

I was practically salivating with the need to command her, taste her, ruin her sanity the way she had ruined mine, and counting down the minutes before I could pull Gabriela into my arms again.

Imagine my goddamned surprise at finding her in an empty hallway with her ex-boyfriend.

I prided myself on being level-headed.

But seeing another man kiss *my* Gabriela?

I. Fucking. Lost. It.

The bastard had the gall to touch her like he had every right in the universe and for that reason alone, I wanted to break him. If Gabriela hadn't stopped me, I wondered if I'd actually have ended the fucker.

The inhale I sucked through my gritted teeth juddered in my chest, barely easing the ache rooted there.

I glanced at Gabriela sitting in the passenger seat, brows knitted into a frown as she furiously typed away on her phone.

Before sliding into my Jag, she'd wiped her lipstick and applied a fresh coat of crimson red, effectively eliminating all traces of Franco's kiss.

But it wasn't enough.

The jealous—downright territorial—side of me needed to lay claim on Gabriela. Touch her, kiss her, fuck her in a branding, *there's-no-going-back-from-here* type of way. Until all the men from her past were specks and I was the only thing she saw, felt, and fucking adored.

Before dawn broke over the horizon, I needed to ensure that my treasured obsession realized that I was her everlasting fit.

My flesh, my muscles, my bones, my thrashing heartbeats.

It was all for *her.*

I was brought into this world, given breath, solely for Gabriela Regina Bellafiore.

A slim finger skimmed over my whitened knuckles in a familiar manner, drawing my attention away from my troubled musings and back towards the center of my universe. "Hunt?"

I didn't say a word. We were almost home. My body heaved with the anticipation of what was to come.

The blue in Gabriela's eyes brimmed with vivaciousness. "I texted Josh. He's going to look into the cameras. See if there's any evidence of what happened. If there is, he'll make it disappear. Don't worry."

Truthfully, my only concern was beating Franco Morelli to a bloody pulp and nothing could have stopped me. Except for my girl. "I'm not worried, Gabby."

She bit her bottom lip before licking it. I was going to nibble on that mouth while I fucked her from behind, collaring her throat and seating myself so deep in that pussy she'd forget where we began and where we ended. "Then what are you feeling? I can't get a read on you and I'm nervous. I want to make sure you're okay and—"

I cut off her rambling by grabbing her gloved hand, bringing it to my mouth for a kiss, and placing it on my lap. Right where she could feel my weighty erection pushing against my suit pants. I was ready for her. "That's what I'm feeling, Gabriela."

"*Oh.*"

"Once we cross the threshold of my apartment, I'm going to fuck you," I rasped, my eyes drinking in her beautiful face, the pulse in her neck, and her chest, rising and falling with her breathing. Her tits looked like they were seconds from spilling out of the low neckline of her dress. My mouth watered. My cock hardened further. I nearly veered my car to the side of the empty highway and took her right there. "You know that, don't you, baby?

A needful sound clawed at the back of her throat. "Yes."

"Good." I was itching to get my hands on her. "Fuck, if your dress had a slit, I'd put my hands between your thighs and rub your sweet little clit to orgasm. Get you nice and ready for what's to come."

The night was young and dark above us, but the lampposts on either side of the street as I exited the highway, bringing us less than five minutes from home, seeped their illumination through my sunroof and windshield, erasing the shadows painting Gabriela's face and showing me the sharp slice of excitement that sparked over her features.

Those red lips with the pretty Cupid's bow parted—one heartbeat, two heartbeats, three heartbeats—and pressed back together when a decision was made, causing her to lean over the center console.

She was so close that all I could smell was her delicious vanilla and red roses perfume.

"Maybe not me, but we can certainly make sure you're ready," Gabriela hushed and that devilish tongue peeked out to trace the shell of my ear. I grunted, so fucking turned on. Her silk-gloved hand gave an experimental squeeze over my tented bulge. "What do you say, *bello*?"

Fucking hell.

"You're playing a dangerous game," I warned, though I wasn't opposed to it. Not when I knew that sucking me off and catering to that kink of hers would result in me getting to play with the wettest, juiciest pussy on Earth. "People might see us."

We'd just arrived at a red light, a single car packed with college-aged men waiting next to mine. All they had to do was stare out their windows and they'd see my date with her hand over my dick.

But that was exactly what she wanted.

The thrill stemming from the taboo nature of this act.

And Gabriela knew well enough that I wasn't one to deny her anything.

"So?" Her lips quirked up in a wicked smile as she removed her right hand's glove, letting the silk drop on my dashboard with a flourish. My nerve endings sparked with anticipation. She undid my belt buckle and lowered the zip in record time, the sound amplified in the quiet car. Though it wasn't as loud as the heartbeat rushing in my ears. "Let them see what a slut I am for the hottest football player in the city." Her breasts pressed against my chest as her mouth kissed my lobe, whispering, "Let them see me thanking him for beating the shit out of my useless ex-boyfriend."

There she was.

My hot little vixen.

I hissed in a breath when her bare hand slid under the waistband of my briefs and pulled out my hard cock. My hands tightened on the steering wheel and my eyes drooped at the pleasurable clench of her fist as she jerked me once from root to tip, her thumb catching the pearly drop and smearing it over the flared surface. "Fuck, Gabby."

She tutted under her breath, glancing at me coyly through her lashes. "My, my. How long have you been like this, hm?"

I choked out a half groan, half laugh, but there was no humour in it. "Since the moment I laid eyes on you tonight."

"Aw, my poor pretty boy." Her melodious voice was laced with a mixture of mock condescension and pure poutiness. "I'll make it better."

God, she was a brat. Fuck me if I didn't love it.

Screw it. If we were really doing this, we might as well go all the way.

I raised a hand to clutch her chin. "If you don't finish me off by the time I park this car, I will punish you," I said in a dark tenor. "And, Gabriela? You will swallow every drop." I jerked her face closer until our lips brushed. "Now get to work, doll."

Her blue eyes burned. The side of her that basked in my dominance was satiated. So was the side of hers that liked to defy me.

The light turned green.

I floored the gas.

Gabriela's head descended onto my lap, accepting the challenge.

The first flick of her tongue against my skin was shiver-inducing. The second flick was ecstasy. And when she finally sucked my tip into the warm cavern of her mouth with a little whine—like she got off on blowing me, a rough growl ripped out of me. "*Fuckkk.*"

This girl was going to be my end.

Her mouth swooped down, taking an impressive amount of me despite being in such close quarters. My groans were guttural, marrying with her small hums. She wasted no time driving me crazy, head bobbing as she sucked gluttonously, her tongue serpentine-like around my shaft, and her hands playing with my balls, leaving not a single bit of me unappreciated.

Never in my life would I forget the sight of her red lipstick staining my cock, her tits rubbing against my muscular thigh, and her snake diamond-emerald necklace winking like a thousand stars under the blurring streetlights.

God-fucking-damn.

There was no one like Gabriela.

On a cheek-hugging withdraw, she paused to kiss my tip and flash me a smile, the little rhinestone in her canine glinting. "You like my mouth, *bello?*"

"Love it, baby."

"So tell me." Her soft exhale washed over my wet skin and I cursed. "I want to hear it."

How could I forget? We both got off on the praise.

Gabriela's mouth fell back on my cock with a hearty suck and my eyes nearly rolled back into my skull.

"*Gabriela.*" I removed one hand from the wheel and placed it on the back of her head, clutching fistfuls of those long red strands. "So good. You're doing amazing. Don't stop. *Please.*"

The threat—or promise, really—of my punishment and the figurative timer she was working with fueled her to blow me like she was making a statement. No other woman could get me this heated. Only her.

The inside of my sports car filled with the sloppy noises of her mouth hoovering my cock and the nonsensical words I panted.

I was close.

So. Fucking. Close.

My little doll was loving the ever hell out of this moment.

Soon enough, I was pulling into the darkened underground garage of our complex. I couldn't recall the last five minutes of the ride back home. How I managed not to crash. How I managed to maintain my coordination. How I managed to keep it together.

Until the moment I shifted into park and groaned a deep, "I'm coming."

She swallowed every drop with a zealous moan, satisfied with herself for having reduced me to a baser self, stripped of my usual restraint.

I breathed unevenly, my chest rattling with the heady concoction of lust, yearning, and residual fury. She drew off my softening cock with a *pop*, unable to conceal the smug expression nor her own laboured breathing. "I did as you asked, Hunt."

I grasped her neck and yanked her to me, loving the way she gasped under her breath and the way her eyes went half-mast with desire.

"No, you didn't." To prove my point, I licked the spare drop of cum lingering near her lips and fed it back to her with a salacious kiss, groaning when our tongues twined. "Do you know what that means, sweetheart?"

She would be punished.

But we both knew that word was synonymous with reward in Gabriela's vocabulary.

A soft sigh stuttered out of her. "Yes."

We barely made it to my apartment.

I nearly took her on the hood of my Jaguar when we stumbled against it during our kiss.

I nearly took her in the elevator, my finger millimetres from pressing the *stop* button so I could hike the skirt of her dress above her waist, tuck her thong to the side, and bounce her on my dick.

And I nearly took her in the hallway between our homes, feeling like a raging beast driven solely by his primal instinct to fuck its mate. Bend her forward. Pin her down. Eat that pussy from behind. And pound into her tightness six ways to Sunday.

I'd never been this way, spiralling with fierce need for another until Gabriela.

The sexy little redhead kept testing my control by kissing me the entire journey it took us to reach my door and saying teasingly against my mouth, "Right here, Hunter. Take me right here. You know you want to."

Fuck, did I ever.

Yet I managed to keep some semblance of composure as I shoved us into my apartment, locked the door, and threw off my leather gloves in a surrendering motion.

Then it was just Gabriela and me.

Our heavy breathing.

Our fast-beating hearts.

Our ramping desire, misting the air between us.

Wrapping my left hand around her neck, I dragged her towards the full-length mirror resting against my foyer wall and turned her around to face the front.

Gabriela's hands reached out to brace herself against the surface, blue eyes going glassy with lust at my manhandling. She watched us quietly—hypnotized by the picture we created.

We were fully clothed, but our need for each other was painted nakedly upon our faces.

I leaned down, pressed the side of my face against hers, clenched her throat, and murmured darkly, "You see these lips?" Using my right hand, I wiped my thumb over her plump bottom lip. "They belong to me. No one but me will ever kiss you again, doll." I smeared the rouge on my thumb over her fluttering pulse. "You see this? It beats for me. Same as mine does for you." I punctuated the statement by giving her jaw a quick nip. "Only *you*." She moaned low when I roughly pushed down the neckline of her dress, cupping a handful of her tit. "These nipples? Pebbled for me." My hand made fast work of her zipper and pushed the dress's silky material past her hips, letting it pool on the floor. My hand mapped down her torso, past her belly piercing, and stopping over her mound. The entirety of my hand covered her cunt and I squeezed it prominently. "And this bratty little pussy? Fucking dripping for me." I slapped it. Gabriela moaned again. "You remember that the next time you wander out of my sight and some asshole decides to corner you." I tilted her head back with the hand still around her neck. She peered up at me, heavy-lidded. "Tell him you've already got a man who owns you."

I wasted no time kissing her hard.

She kissed me back, reciprocating my ardour.

"Is that so?" She gasped when I bit her bottom lip and tugged. "Didn't realize I was signing up for such a possessive boyfriend when I agreed to date you. Maybe I should reconsider. Your bossy nature might be an issue for me."

She loved to play with me.

And I loved to play back.

"I paid for everything you're wearing tonight," I grated, spinning her around to face me and tightening my leash around her throat. "I own it all, including you and that sinfully gone expression on your face." I slapped her ass. She cried out. "So I've earned the right to boss you around and you're going to stop pretending like being told what to do doesn't get you hot, baby."

Gabriela enjoyed it when I took charge.

Lucky for her, I wasn't planning on handing her the reins anytime soon.

"Now strip," I commanded against her red lips. "I've got a pussy to eat."

Gabriela's arms lunged to vine around my neck and she stamped her mouth to mine in an impatient kiss, her moan barely muffled. She climbed my big body like a feral kitten, wrapping her legs around my middle, and I groaned at her enthusiasm. As we exchanged wet kisses, I spanked her ass in reprimand. For she'd disobeyed me by not removing her soaked thong.

So I ripped it off her in one clean swipe.

She whined into our kiss.

I smirked, giving her my tongue.

We made out almost angrily, stumbling against the foyer walls as we eagerly clawed at each other. I removed my suit jacket and she tackled my tie and dress shirt with vigour. Piece by piece, my clothes fell to the floor, joining hers, save for my suit pants, which were slung low on my hips, my hardened cock straining against my abs.

Harsh desire beat like drums between us, racketing up in intensity as we crashed into the foyer bench.

I sat long enough to shove two fingers into her slickness and gauge her reaction.

Gabriela threw her head back on a shaky scream, her sopping pussy easing my entry as I fingered her the way she liked. Stretching her. Preparing her. Giving her a preview of how good she was about to have it. The ends of her hair brushed my thighs and her tits quaked in my face. Naturally, I snagged a nipple, licking, sucking, and biting until my mark bloomed. "Oh, God. Hunter."

Her walls tightened around my thrusting fingers. I wouldn't let her come yet, refusing to renege on my promise of edging her.

I pulled out my drenched fingers and licked them clean, much to her protesting cry. "You think you deserve to come after failing to lick every drop of me, Gabriela?"

"Yes! *Please.*" Her frustrated, needy tone only made me grin as I slid forward, taking the brunt of the impact as we dropped to the floor. I'd punish her later then. Gabriela yelped with surprise when I flipped our positions so I was the one lying down and she was the one firmly seated atop my stomach muscles.

"Fucking come here," I growled, urging her forward by grabbing two handfuls of her ass. "Come sit on my face, you filthy little plaything. I know you want it."

Gabriela appeared dazed, her inhibitions swirling in the same lust-infused fog as me. There was a recklessness in the way her gloved hands dove into my hair for purchase and her knees quickly positioned on either side of my head, her pink, glistening pussy dangling just an inch above my mouth.

The sight and scent of it turned me on even more.

"That's it," I praised, hands clapping her perky ass. "Let's get you riding till you've soaked me, yeah?"

My breath fanned over her flesh. She squirmed above me, more than ready. "Y-you'll signal if I'm suffocating you, right?"

She weighed feather-like to me. There was no chance of suffocation. "Even if you do, there's no better way for me to go out, Gabriela."

Fear sliced through the desire in those hazy blue eyes for a brief second.

"Relax, doll, and enjoy the ride." I cut off whatever she was going to say by slamming her horny cunt onto my awaiting mouth. She whined and I grunted at the taste of her, flicking my tongue to collect her arousal before zeroing in on that pulsing clit.

Gabriela moaned, her hips giving an experimental buck from my chin to my upper lip. "*Hunt.*"

"Yes, Gabby, let me give you what you need," I rasped around the most delicious mouthful of pussy. Without delay, I got to work. Lapped the entirety of her slit. Sucked her clit rhythmically. Then thrust my tongue inside of her hole.

Gabriela whimpered like a spoiled princess, glancing down at me in pleasurable shock. Her thighs boxed my head and her fingers clutched my hair at the root, almost to the point of pain, but I loved it.

"Move your hips," I ordered, voice thick and gravelly. "Make a mess all over me, sweetheart."

Seeing that I was more than okay with her sitting on my face like a throne and hearing my encouragement, Gabriela sprang into motion. She rocked smoothly like a wave, getting used to the feel of her pussy surfing over me, and moaning as her clit got the right amount of pressure. Before quickly growing emboldened at my appreciative groans and rocking faster, engulfing the lower half of my face in arousal.

Fuck, yes.

My fingers dug into her thighs. Her taste melted on my tongue like sweet sin and her fragrance wrapped around my senses like heaven.

"Hunter," she choked out, grinding that shiny cunt over me. "F-feels so good."

Me too, baby, I wanted to say, but my mouth was currently occupied with her using it like a fuck pillow. My cock twitched against my stomach muscles. I could probably come from just this alone. Keeping one hand on her ass to hold her up, I grabbed my length with the other and jerked off.

The hallway rang with the melody of Gabriela's pleasure-stricken moans as she rode my lips and tongue, the squelching sounds of her arousal as I fucking ate that pussy like it was my dessert, and the occasional smack on her ass to get her to work those hips faster. To show me how badly she wanted it. To prove how slutty she was willing to get for her orgasm.

Gabriela's breasts bounced, back arched, eyes shut, and mouth parted as she moaned throatily.

"Mm, you're so sexy, baby." I groaned. "Fuck, look at you."

And she did, craning her head to the side, her gaze peeking open enough to see our reflection in the hallway mirror. It was obscenely hot. Me, lying prisoner underneath my girl, fisting my cock, while she knelt over me, body working desperately to seek her release.

"Eyes on me again." I gave her clit a series of flicks and sank my fingers deep into her ass. "I want you to watch me as you come."

"Hunter." She grabbed her tit and pinched her nipple. "I-I'm so close."

It took less than another minute for her to come in a beautiful explosion, screaming and yanking at my hair as she was swept under the current of a powerful climax. Groaning, I lapped at her arousal like it was liquid gold, relishing her essence and the little porn-worthy noises dropping from her lips as she kept grinding, slowly coming down from her high.

Gabriela eventually slumped backwards, landing on my chest, panting breaths falling from her lips. The satiated glint in her eyes was a telltale sign. She'd had the time of her life. "Oh my God."

I wiped the back of my hand across my mouth and licked my lips for the remnant of her taste. "Careful, Gabriela. You keep addressing me like that and I'll develop a god complex."

A light coat of perspiration glowed on her moonlight skin. She tossed her hair behind her shoulders and chuckled airily—almost sheepishly—in post-coital bliss. "I wouldn't oppose, pretty boy. I'd say you earned it after that performance."

I knifed up in a sitting position and she gasped before I grabbed the back of her neck and silenced her with a dirty kiss.

She sucked on my tongue like a man-eater.

I stood up and carried her down the hallway leading to my room.

Tossing her in the middle of my king-sized bed, I rasped, "Let me show you in all the other ways I can be godly, little doll."

CHAPTER 34

His Treasured Obsession

GABRIELA

"**A**nd how exactly are you going to do that?" I panted, rising on my elbows.

My mind was slowly returning back to Earth after that sense-numbing climax. I didn't realize that sitting on Hunter's face could make me come *that* amazingly.

I wanted to do it again. Soon.

Hunter's lips, covered with a sheen of my arousal, tipped up into a smirk. "For starters, by tying you to my bed and fucking you raw and deep. Just like we both want." He shed his black pants but tossed his leather belt onto the bed. A foreshadowing for later. "Then if I feel like it, I'll take my belt to your ass until you're seeing stars and screaming my name loud enough for everyone on this floor to hear."

I craved it all. "I want everything you have to give. Please, Hunt."

"Such a good girl—so obedient—when you want something from me, hm?" he mused, the low, husky laugh that escaped him only making me wetter. "Now scoot towards the headboard and grab the bars."

Eager to do his bidding, I gave a sensual display of slowly rolling over on all fours and crawling towards his slatted headboard, knowing he had an eyeful of the ass he wanted to spank.

Eat and fuck too.

I smiled when he dropped a rough groan. I removed my emerald silk gloves, turned back around, grabbed the bars, arched my back, which jutted my breasts, and spread my legs enough to give him a teaser. "What next, *bello*?"

His gaze devoured me like I was a feast. "You will be the end of me, Gabriela."

There was a vulnerable edge to his words, even though they were echoed with passion.

"No," I said with conviction. "We're each other's beginning, Hunter."

Pleased with my response, he headed over to his nightstand and retrieved what appeared to be silk red ropes.

My heart sped, excitement and nerves knotting together in my belly. I took a brief moment to allow my gaze to wander in his room. Like the rest of his apartment, the inside bore sleek furniture with blue and black accents. The curtains were already pushed wide, a generous amount of moonlight flowing in. But he still went ahead and lit the three candles on his nightstand so we'd have more illumination.

Hunter climbed onto the bed with the swiftness of a predator who'd finally cornered his prey after months of stark craving.

A rare burst of shyness ignited over my skin, raising goosebumps as I was subjected to his intense perusal. He saw me naked before and I knew I lived up to all his fantasies, but I still felt the need to ask him, "Is this what you'd picture for four hundred and fifty days?"

"Four hundred and fifty-eight days," he corrected, widening my thighs to accommodate his herculean frame, his knees keeping me open like a makeshift spreader bar. "I've wanted you—*needed* you—for that long. You have no idea how many times I've imagined this moment." His slightly callused palm slithered over my torso before wrapping around my throat, right above my snake necklace. "And nothing comes close to the real thing." He leaned down, the muscles in his arms shifting in a manner that made the serpent tattoo on his skin appear like a living, breathing entity. "I'm going to ruin other men for you tonight." He brushed his lips against mine, plume-soft. "I won't stop until I've wrecked every inch of you, Gabriela."

Hunter's possessiveness was laced with a sweetness that I was drawn to like bees to honey. It turned me to taffy, my limbs malleable underneath him, a puppet for him to bend, move, and use to his will.

He did just that, expertly winding the silk red ropes around my wrists and the headboard, the hold harbouring a luxuriating feel as the ties skated against my skin, keeping me poised for his ministrations.

"Do it. I'm yours," I exhaled like an incantation and Hunter inhaled it in the fictional space separating our mouths, bodies, and hearts. "Fuck me like you own this pussy. Pin me down, pull my hair, slap my skin. Anything you want. Just don't stop."

It was hard to tell if Hunter's groan was from my words, from the way his thick cock grazed against my wetness, or from a mixture of both. "But if you do want me to stop, tell me and I will. Without question. I'm as much at your mercy as you are at mine." His hands roved down my shackled arms and over the curves of my body, pausing at my waist. "There aren't enough words to describe your beauty in any language. You're sublime, Gabriela."

The heat between us didn't dim with his utterance. It simply added another beautiful layer to our relationship. A reminder that with all the praise and degradation singing between us when we were intimate, I could always be grounded in the knowledge that, above all, I would always be a venerated goddess to Hunter Saint Warren.

I kissed him to convey my unspoken thoughts. He kissed me back, tasting them, accepting them, and keeping them safe in the cradle of his golden heart. "I adore you."

"And I adore you." He drew his mouth to my jaw for more kisses. "Remember to keep your eyes on me. I want to watch your face as you take my cock for the first time."

He was such a gentleman on a daily basis that sometimes I forgot what a seductive alpha lurked underneath his designer suit, football gear, and Prince Charming smiles. It only made me slicker when he spoke to me in that raspy voice, bossing me around like I was his…which I was. With every breath, every heartbeat, and every atom in my body.

Hunter was a gift from the universe—a recompense for my patience after all the hardships I'd endured in my past—and I accepted him wholeheartedly.

I was drenched in arousal to the point where it trickled down to my puckered hole. Hunter swiped his fingers over my slit and smeared my slickness over the length of his shaft before dragging the underside of it over my folds, coating himself further. Pearly essence beaded at his plump head in an erotic picture that left me parched. And when he worked his fist down his cock from root to tip, slapping it against my pussy and letting a drop of cum fall onto my clit, I burned with immeasurable heat.

It felt like an eternity before Hunter guided himself to my entrance.

"Breathe," he demanded and his thumb pried my bottom lip from where my teeth held it captive. "I'll go slow in the beginning until you get used to me. All right, sweetheart?"

He stroked my chin, waiting for my reply. I was riveted by the size of his massive dick, finally registering that I was going to have *all* of that inside of me. Swallowing, I asked something that I should have long ago, "W-what if we don't fit?"

"We will." Hunter pressed a hand above my mound to hold me in place and worked the first inch in. He groaned. I whimpered, tugging at the restraints. But I didn't want to go anywhere. I wanted to stay here, pinned under his muscular weight and impaled by his thickness. "You're so wet—so ready for me. Look…" He shoved a pillow underneath my hips, lifting them so I could watch exactly where we were joined, and slid a second inch. "See how perfect we are together? You were made for me. Same as I was made for you."

"*Hunter.*" I emitted a moan as my pussy stretched to accommodate his third inch, the sight of his cock sliding into me marvellous. He was right. We were perfect for one another. I was panting, sweating. He wasn't even halfway in and my entire skin felt electrified, like I would combust in less than a handful of touches. "*Ohhh.*"

359

"I know, baby," he replied softly, gripping my waist and giving me a fourth inch. "Feels so good, hm?" A whine tore from my throat at the fifth inch. "You're doing amazing." Sixth inch. "Letting me fuck my tight pussy." Seventh inch. "Such a well-behaved slut." His fingers slid into my mouth, muting my whimpers. "Completely bound and gagged." Finally, the eighth inch that allowed him to bottom inside of me. "And now full of your man's cock." He closed his eyes on a deep moan, fully undone. "Fuck, I knew you'd fit me like a glove. You're beautiful like this. So. Goddamn. Beautiful. Gabriela."

My hands pulled at the silk ties, my pussy squeezing him like I never wanted to let go. I could feel his heartbeat pulsing inside of me and I released a muffled noise of pure need.

We fit undeniably well. Two missing pieces finally slotted into a puzzle, rendering the *objet d'art* complete.

He was thick and long enough to make me squirm. Thick and long enough that my fingers dug half crescents into my palms. Thick and long enough that I was stretched and filled to the brim, aching with the rapacious need for him to just *thrust, thrust, thrust* into me until the only thing keeping us sane was the rhythm of our dirty fuck.

Hunter trembled above me as if holding back from thrusting was physically hurting him, but he didn't move. He was being patient for me and savouring this rare first time.

There was nothing quite as exquisite as us, like this.

He withdrew his fingers from my mouth and replaced them with his gentle kiss.

"Gabriela," my beloved, the handsomest in the world, whispered softly against my mouth. Black hair tousled. Chiselled jaw clenched. Tattooed skin glimmering with sweat. Nipple piercing gleaming under the candlelight. Blue eyes reminiscent of stormy seas fastening me under their depths. He was wondrous. I sucked in a deep inhale when his hand rose to cup my cheek, thumb caressing my high point delicately. "Are you okay?"

Now that I'd grown accustomed to his size, I sighed a "Yes."

Hunter slammed his mouth onto mine. We alternated between kissing passionately and breathing in each other, while his wet fingers voyaged towards my swollen clit and played with it. "You like the feel of me inside of you, baby?"

I moaned. "I-I love it, Hunt."

A gratified sound rumbled in his chest. "Nothing compares to the feel of being inside of you. You're so warm, slippery, tight. I'm addicted to you and we've barely gotten started," he said raggedly, kissing the **R** tattoo behind my ear. My heart pounded faster at his confession. "I'll need this every day till I die. I'll go insane without it—without you."

"Me too." I'd lose my mind without him. I was thoroughly ensnared in his web. Hunter clutched the undersides of my tits and licked and sucked my nipples. "P-please move. I want to feel you."

"Call me your love again."

Something foreign moved inside my heart at his request. "Please, my love. I need you."

"I need you too, my love." He churned his cock deep inside of me, the deep groan that ignited from his throat melding with my soft moan. "All the damn time."

God, this man.

What was he doing to me?

I'd never stood a chance against him and all his affection. He'd successfully broken down my barriers and every attempt to keep things platonic. I felt myself falling for him with every passing day...but now it was evidently clear that I was already halfway in love with him. And I embraced the emotion with open arms.

If there was anyone worth loving in this lifetime, it was Hunter.

"I'm going to move now." Hunter gripped my hips. "Tell me if it's too much."

I nodded, unable to string together a sentence.

For a moment, Hunter simply rocked in and out of me. Pulling out till just the tip kissed my entrance before pushing back until he was seated to the hilt. I couldn't stop staring at his glistening, fat cock pushing into my small pussy. It was incredibly sexy.

The outside world melted and curled away like a parchment lit on fire. Leaving just us in the moonlight with the glorious sensation of

Hunter's slow and deep thrusts, chipping away the remaining vines that kept my heart shielded from the very feelings he wrought within me.

Everything he was doing to me wasn't enough. If anything, I wanted… "More, Hunt."

He threw my legs over his broad shoulders and somehow went even deeper.

My gasp melted into a long moan, his cock hitting a spot that had previously only been caressed with his fingers and one of my toys. *"Mmfuck."*

Hunter smirked devilishly. This debonair man of mine who constantly flirted with a wicked edge appeared like a tattooed sex god between my legs, full lips parting enough for his tongue to peek out so he could lick his thumb and bring it down to my clit, rubbing it in that expert way of his that made a coruscation of constellation dance behind my lids. "Like that, doll?"

My next orgasm began to crest already.

"Mhm." Though I enjoyed being tied, I couldn't help myself from unconsciously yanking at my bonds, wanting to cup his face and kiss him everywhere, wanting to sink my nails into his powerful thighs, wanting to clutch at his back and feel every muscle in it shifting as he screwed me in a way that was more akin to lovemaking. "You're fucking me so well. I'm so full, *bello.*"

My praise washed over him with a feral quality.

"Fuck, baby. *Fuckkk.*" His barrel chest bowed with an inhale and his thrusting increased slightly in pace, but he still held himself in check. I needed him to unleash the entire extent of his depravity and fuck me like a brute. He threw his head back on a particular hard thrust, that corded neck of his just begging to be bitten. "I can feel you tightening. You're going to come again, aren't you? Just from this?"

The squelching sounds as our flesh met grew in decibels. Unashamed, I mumbled out a shaky, "Y-yes."

He smirked darkly and slapped my clit. "I'm going to fill this slutty little hole with so much cum, you'll be leaking me for days, princess."

That nearly sent me over the edge. "Hunter!"

"You've got permission. Come all over my cock," he growled, strumming my body like a maestro. "Give me something good to lick, Gabriela."

A choppy moan broke past my lips right as I was swept under a current of bliss. Right before my eyes shut, I caught Hunter's awestruck expression, loving the way I clenched around him.

My goodness. I was right. Sex with Hunter was phenomenal...and we'd only gotten started.

Panting, out of my mind, and floating somewhere on cloud nine, I barely registered the loss of him.

My confusion morphed into a mixture of disbelief and delight when I realized he'd crawled down my body to replace his cock with his tongue, fucking my still spasming pussy like a greedy boy whose sole purpose was licking me clean.

"*Fuck yes.*" Groaning, he tasted my orgasm with aggressive enthusiasm, looking like the sexiest thing ever lying between my splayed thighs. "That's what I'm talking about, baby. So fucking good."

I whined, canting my hips against his face, smearing my juices all over his chin and lips. Freaky bastard. He was going to make me come a third time.

Before that could happen, Hunter rose and licked his drenched fingers. I didn't even have a chance to draw in a centering breath when he rasped, "Seems to me like you've adjusted, doll."

That was the only warning I got.

Hunter grabbed my neck in a primitive hold and rammed all eight inches back inside of me.

I screamed.

Then he started pounding into me the way we'd both been wanting it from the beginning—fast, deep, and so fucking rough, pure ecstasy rushed through my veins. My breasts bounced under the force of his swift thrusts. Unintelligible sounds and his name coursed out of my lips.

"Louder, Gabriela." *Thrust.* "Tell everyone in this building who's fucking your tight little pussy." Thrust. "Let them hear what a good girl you are for me."

The headboard banged against the wall in consecutive thumps.

The melody in the room crashed together like ocean waves. Soft and jarring. My feminine screams of pleasure—alerting all our neighbours who was fucking me—marrying with Hunter's brutish grunts, and the fleshy smacks of our bodies colliding over and over again. A symphony I would remember for many moons to come.

His voice rang in my ear like a dark lullaby. "You look stunning taking my cock, baby."

There was nothing saintly about the way Hunter wrecked my pussy. His tempo was merciless, a reminder that he was a star athlete at the start of his prime with stamina for days.

I'd never felt smaller, sheltered, and protected as I did right now, beneath him while he took me like a raging beast. His big body covered mine and he clenched my throat, cutting off my air supply momentarily. Knowing I loved breath play. Knowing it would make me come so hard for him.

I tugged at the ropes but was still rendered powerless in the face of his beautiful, angry lust.

He loosened his chokehold enough to kiss me sloppily and twine his tongue with mine. The way he bounced his cock in my cunt was animalistic and unyielding.

The sheets beneath us susurrated with our hot fucking and sweat beaded over our bodies. I was spiralling, on the verge of another climax, and Hunter was determined to give it to me. Words failed me, but my eyes sought his, frantic and needing, the question swimming in my gaze.

"Gabriela." He snarled against my mouth. "Come for me."

It only took another half dozen thrusts before I came with a shout, my orgasm rushing out of me. "*Hunt!*"

He went wild, somehow managing to fuck me harder, deeper, faster, prolonging my release until I fell limp underneath him, all my senses overwhelmed, murmuring pleas.

"We're far from done, doll." Without pulling out of me, my pretty boy undid the silk ties and picked up my slack, tired body. He seated me upright in his lap and wrapped his arms around my waist. My arousal pooled between us and seeped over my inner thighs. Dazed and still coming down from my high, I squared my arms around his neck and kissed him lazily, running my fingers through his sweat-slicked hair.

Hunter started ramming into my pussy from below with teeth-chattering upstrokes.

"*Hunter,*" I screamed, throwing my head back. Loving the feel of him in this position. "S-so deep."

His dark laugh curled around my bones like smoke. "And you're taking it." *Thrust.* "Every inch." *Thrust.* "We both know you love that I'm this big and this deep inside of you." I cried out in euphoria, scratching at his back to hold myself steady as he pounded away. "So show me what a good little slut you are, Gabriela, and let me fuck *my* little pussy." *Thrust.* "Let me own you the way you need, baby."

His dirty talk—tailored to my perfect liking—and fueled me on. I bounced on his cock and held on to him tighter, shaking in his embrace. The crying moans tumbling out of my mouth only made Hunter hungrier for me.

"Good girl," he growled and slapped my ass, the sting giving leeway to a delicious burn I basked in. His finger trailed into my arousal and scurried to my back hole. My eyes widened. He dipped his finger the slightest bit. Enough to drive me wilder. Enough to make me aware of what he wanted soon. "Can't wait to fuck this peach of an ass, sweetheart. You'll let me, won't you? 'Cause you're mine to touch, fuck, and love, hm?"

"I am." I cupped his face and met him thrust for thrust, the bed quaking under our lust. "*Amore,* come inside of me."

His deep moan wrapped around my core and clenched. "Filthy little plaything. Want my cum in that gorgeous pink pussy?"

"Y-yes." I rode him harder and faster. "Fill me up."

My demand washed over Hunter like a magic spell, transforming his already hard fucking to downright ruthless, frantic, and driven purely by his undeniable yearning for me. "Fuck," he groaned, shoving his cock into me until the only thing keeping me alive was his vicious thrusts. I exchanged breaths and open-mouthed kisses with him, our lips clashing the same way our bodies did. "You're everything to me, Gabriela."

Oh, Hunter. I'd do anything for you. Give you my heart, my soul, my everything, should it bring you even the smallest amount of happiness.

"You're everything to me too, Hunter," I tried to say, but my statement may have gotten lost in the passion-filled cocoon surrounding us, every ounce of my focus pulled towards the way he was making me feel—mind-addled and like the only girl in the world.

We stared at each another, caught in a trance. This was making love. A rougher version of it. But ours regardless. And based on the glint in Hunter's eyes, I could tell he'd never done this before either.

This was a piece of us that no one else had ever deserved, except for one another. It was humbling to share it with someone who understood me so profoundly and perhaps even in ways that I myself may not know yet.

Hunter peeked at my inner workings and put every layer of me on a pedestal so I could shine like the brightest north star in his sky.

It wasn't long before he made me come again.

Screaming, I nearly passed out as pleasure tackled my already sensitive flesh.

Hunter switched positions, tossing me around onto my front, then coming behind me again. His muscular, inked forearm curved around my waist and hiked me up till I was raised on my knees, ass up and face down. He grabbed his forgotten leather belt with his other hand and skimmed the flat of it against my skin tauntingly.

I clawed at the sheets when his wet tip glided through my swollen pussy and rubbed teasingly against my clit. "Hunter—*Ahh.*"

He slapped my ass with the belt. "How many times?"

I couldn't even see straight, let alone understand what he was asking. "W-what?"

"How." *Slap.* "Many times." *Slap.* "Did I." *Slap.* "Make you come?"

Though mathematics was my forte, I struggled to recall anything right now—including my name. "I…"

"Four." He looped the belt around my neck and used it like a rein, raising my head enough for me to see our reflection in the dresser's mirror before us. "And I'm going to make you come a few more times, baby. Now keep your eyes on me while I fill your bratty little pussy with my cum."

Hunter thrust back into me, bottoming in a smooth stroke.

I moaned, keeping my eyes trained on our reflection. "Oh, God."

"That's right, little doll." He tugged on the leash. "Pray to me."

Hunter's hips punched against my shaking ass as he fed every inch of his cock into my dripping pussy. He made me cry out for him like he was the very creator of my universe and his fingers remained on my clit, his belt keeping me positioned exactly like he wanted.

At his mercy.

He continued to show me in all the ways he was godly and his dirty words kept fondling me like a cool balm in the midst of our heated fucking.

"Gabriela, you're such a good girl for giving me a wet pussy to play with."

"You're my entire world, doll."

"Every day, every hour, every minute. I've longed for you. You were worth the wait, my love."

He'd done it.

He had successfully ruined everyone for me until he was the only one I saw, felt, and wanted now and forever.

"Hunter." My voice was hoarse as I begged him to never stop his worship of me.

Hunter covered my body with his, his front pressing to my back and his chin tucking between my neck and shoulder. He let go of the belt and his hand came to grasp my jaw. Without easing his vicious pace, he turned my head enough to snatch a kiss. "Baby, you're going to make me come so fucking good."

I kissed him back, panting, "I-I'm there."

"Let go." He groaned. "Come with me, Gabriela."

It took a few more strokes before we came together, limbs intertwined and sweat dripping on each other. He poured his seed deep within me, moaning with me at the sensation. My arms gave out and I fell forward while Hunter pulled his softening cock out of my pussy, his cum leaking in its wake.

"My treasured obsession, I would do anything for you—anything in the world." His mouth dragged over my spine as he planted one kiss after another. "You're it for me. My person. The other half of my soul, Gabriela."

Oh, Hunter.

Why did that make me want to cry?

He turned me onto my back, leaning down to kiss me unhurriedly and gently as though time was ours forevermore.

It was in that delicate moment of soft kisses, holding on to each other as we lay in the moonlight with our hearts on our sleeves…that I realized it happened.

I fell in love with him.

And Hunter Saint Warren made it so easy.

CHAPTER 35

Couple Era

GABRIELA

I was over the moon.

It had officially been two and a half weeks since Hunter and I started dating—since I assumed the role of his needy, territorial girlfriend whom he adored—and I genuinely didn't remember the last time I smiled or laughed this much.

I never realized how much happiness I was actually missing in my day-to-day until Hunter. I loved everything about us and how we seamlessly fit into each other's lives like we were always meant to be.

He showed me in many ways how committed he was to us.

Every day, he arrived at my doorstep with a smile and a kiss. Well, two kisses. One for me and one for my Luna, who officially recognized him as her daddy. And Hunter accepted the title with open arms, doting on my furry companion with cooed words, cuddles, and cat treats. He even proofed his apartment into a cat-friendly zone, bought her catnip toys, a princess-style cat bed complete with ruffles and a canopy, and a cat tree. That way, she'd be comfortable whenever we went over to his home. She was spoiled beyond means. Just like her momma.

Hunter's generosity knew no bounds.

He drove me to school even on the days when my classes began before his, and he always made pit stops at our favourite café to grab us coffees and chocolate-dipped donuts for me. And I, on my end, always brought him homemade baked goods. I couldn't help myself. My love language was acts of service and I wanted to cater to him in any way possible.

Two weeks ago, we sat side by side in the auditorium classroom, holding hands as another cult classic horror movie played on the big screen. Hunter didn't flinch at the jump scare, simply watched the movie with an engrossed quality—I was so proud of him for getting over his fears—while polishing off the blueberry muffins I baked fresh for him that morning.

I pulled out my notebook, flipped it over to a blank page, wrote a message, and passed it to him.

By the end of the year, I'll be adding 'private chef' to my résumé with the amount of cooking I do for you.

Hunter read it in the midst of a gory scene before plucking my pen and replying back in a neat cursive scrawl.

I'm very grateful, doll, and I love everything you make for me.

In fact, I'm wondering when my sweet little neighbour will be inviting me over for dinner?

The praise washed over me like a drug. He made me so giddy with a few words.

How's this upcoming Friday?

It's a date. He wrote.

What's your favourite cuisine?

I'd whip up whatever he requested because *I* was just that whipped. He wrote his reply and slid me my notebook back.

Anything you make for me, but I have a fondness for Italian.

When I peered at him, face warming with a blush, Hunter simply bestowed a butterfly-soft kiss on my cheek. We went back to watching the movie, our hands twined together, and a sense of tranquility floating between us.

And regardless of when I ended my classes or work meetings, Hunter always stayed back until I finished so he could drive me back home. Technically, I could hitch a ride with my best friends, but I knew how much Hunter cherished the task of taking care of me.

"You don't always have to wait for me," I'd cajoled one time when I stepped out of my evening finance class and saw him waiting for me in the hallway, leaning against the wall with his hands in his trouser pockets.

Hunter had this upper-class, rich-boy quality to him that just did it for me. It rang in the way he carried himself, in the way he dressed, and in the way he smelled. To me, he was the crème de la crème of Montardor's high society. Confident, charming, and the right amount of cocky when the situation called for it.

Even now, with the lines of fatigue sketched in his face from his long day, he still appeared suave and deliciously alpha in a tailored coat and dress shirt, and that welcoming smirk on his face that never failed to make my heart thud in response.

"And I've told you before that I prefer to drive you myself." He stroked a knuckle down my cheek. "I don't like going home if you're not there, sweetheart."

I cupped his face and rose on my tippytoes to kiss him. "Okay then."

Plus, I enjoyed commuting with Hunter. Time spent conversing with him while listening to his music playlists was something I looked forward to every day and every evening, similar to how people looked forward to their first cup of coffee in the morning to get their day started and their cup of nighttime herbal tea to unwind before bed.

I didn't know when it happened, but Hunter became the key to my smooth circadian rhythm and I feared that without him my entire cycle would be amiss.

"Okay then," he parroted playfully. "Speaking of home." He fished out a key from his pocket. A red heart charm hung from its end. "Here. It's a key to my place in case you and Luna ever want to come over, whether I'm there or not." He attempted to play it casual by shrugging. "I want you to know that you can come and go as you please."

He's telling you his home is yours too, Gabriela.

My heart twisted in my chest. I gently grabbed the key from him. "Oh, no." I couldn't even feign a nonchalant demeanour as I joked, my voice layered with thick emotions that gave me away. "Do you have any idea what you've done? Luna and I are basically going to camp at your place starting now. Good luck trying to get rid of us."

Hunter wrapped an arm around my waist and lassoed me into his chest, soft blue eyes searching my face. "I never want to get rid of either of you." He tipped my chin up with a leather-gloved hand. "I want your print all over my home. I want my sheets to smell like you, my shelves filled with your books, my kitchen stocked with your favourite foods. Every inch of you over every inch of me. Do you get me, Gabriela?"

What a fool I'd been, thinking we could ever just be platonic.

We were always meant for so much more.

After Franco, I jumped from one fling to another, trying to fill the void in my chest, to no avail. I thought I was content living like that—I thought there wasn't a single man out there who could fit my standards.

Now I wondered if the universe had left an empty space beside me, not because there wasn't anyone to fill it, but because it wanted me to wait for divine timing. It was slowly pushing Hunter into my orbit so he could arrive at the perfect instant and take his rightful place.

King of my heart.

How I adored this blue-eyed, dark-haired, gentle beast of a man.

"Yes," I whispered. "I get you."

His answer was to kiss me in the middle of a crowded hallway.

After that, I put Hunter's key to good use just days later.

Friday evening was our date night and I went to his home earlier to begin preparations while he was at football practice. My boyfriend arrived just in time to find me in the kitchen, wearing the red lace nightie he bought me and red oven mitts with hearts on them, holding a baked lasagna in my hands.

"Welcome home, *bello*," I said with a mischievous smile, placing the dish on the counter. "You're just in time for dinner."

Hunter dropped his duffel bag on the floor and prowled, his expression dark and hungry. Wordlessly, he picked me up, plonked me onto the island counter, pushed my legs wide—causing my lingerie to hike to my waist—and settled himself on a bar stool.

"H-Hunter?" I squeaked out in surprise.

He wrapped his arms around my thighs, jerked me forward, and slapped my bare pussy hard. "Hush, doll." His tongue dragged along my slit, parting me open. "I'm eating."

I moaned and writhed and screamed as he made a meal out of me.

Hunter ate my pussy until I nearly lost my voice.

But he wasn't done there.

He dragged us into the shower. We were a tangle of wet limbs and white-hot need, kissing and groping each other. Once the soap washed away, Hunter turned me around to face the tiled wall before dropping to his knees behind me.

He buried his face in my cheeks to eat my ass.

"Hunter!" Eyes wide, my hand reached out to clutch at a fistful of his hair…whether to stop him or to keep going, I didn't know.

The answer became apparent when he thrust two fingers into my slick pussy at the same time and curled them against my G-spot. Coupled with his tongue licking my puckered hole, a foreign sensation I suddenly found pleasant, I was now in heaven.

Oh, God. I…I might need this all the time.

"Mm, you like that, don't you?" he crooned, his misbehaving tongue relentless.

My *yes* came out garbled as I fell apart, vision dancing with stars.

I had a few seconds to brace my palms against the wall when Hunter stood up, lined his tip with my opening, and bottomed inside my pussy in a smooth go.

I whimpered.

"Tell me I'm a good boy, Gabby," he rasped, gripping my hips and thrusting into me with a vengeance, our skins smacking together in a cacophony with the shower water.

"S-such a good boy, Hunt."

He groaned, going harder and faster. "Play with your clit, baby. I want you to come with me."

Once we finished, Hunter drew me out of the shower and patted my skin dry with a warmed towel. He followed it up by putting lotion on me, combing my wet hair, and slinging his clean football jersey over my body.

We reheated the lasagna and ate before migrating over to the living room with Luna, who decided to park herself in her princess-style bed. Hunter put on a romantic comedy that I selected and then he sprawled over the large sectional sofa in grey sweats—the sluttiest thing a man could wear, in my humble opinion.

I lay on top of his muscular frame, my legs on either side of him, and my arms folded over his chest with my chin resting on them.

"Is there a reason why you're staring at me and not watching the movie?" he inquired, running his hands down my back.

I couldn't help it. He was so handsome. My finger traced the shape of his smiling lips. "You're more interesting to look at."

"Yeah?" God, I loved it when he blushed.

I stole a kiss. "Yeah."

His smile morphed into a grin. He tucked a wayward red strand behind my ear and his thumb and forefinger rubbed my lobe in a manner that practically made me purr like a kitten.

"What are you thinking of?" he mumbled after another quiet moment of me counting his lashes and wondering why it took me so long to notice this beautiful human.

"How I wish I'd met you before," I said. "Before Franco. Before all the others…" I could have avoided all that unnecessary heartache. But then again, without all those trials and tribulations from my past, I wouldn't be who I was today. And I did like what I saw in the mirror every day. The human experience was all about learning from our mistakes and evolving into the best versions of ourselves, right? "It's unfair that our story began less than a handful of months ago."

"We needed to grow apart into who we were meant to be before we could be where we are today." Hunter smoothed away my frown with his thumb. "I'm not bitter that I laid eyes on you more than a year ago, but only got my chance with you now. Everything happens for a reason. All that matters is that we found our way to each other. We're young, Gabby, so don't worry. We have our entire lives to continue writing our story."

When he put it like that, the gloomy sky clouding my thoughts cleared away and gave leeway to a rainbow that brought forth lots of hope.

We did have all the time in the world to write our story and though I had read hundreds of romance novels in my two decades on Earth, I knew without a doubt that ours would always be my favourite love story.

"Just so you know, you're all my favourite book boyfriends wrapped into one."

"Coming from you, that is the highest of compliments." He smiled. "Do I eclipse your vampire lord book boyfriend?"

I smiled as well, all too happy to declare, "By a million percent."

"Well, that's good to know. Felt like I was fighting for my life trying to impress you at times," he jested and kissed me.

I giggled against his lips. "Consider me impressed."

We barely watched the movie. I yapped about anything and everything under the sun—random subjects and things that were important to me—and Hunter listened patiently, inserting a comment here and there to encourage me and validate my feelings.

When I let out a yawn, he grabbed the remote, turned off the TV, and kissed my forehead. "My bed or yours tonight?"

He stood up with me clinging to his front like a baby koala. I didn't want to let go of him. Not even for us to cross back to my apartment. Moreover, he had a king-sized bed that was bigger and much comfier than my queen.

"Yours." I planted sleepy kisses all over his face as he trod down the hallway.

Hunter entered his room and climbed into the bed. "In we go."

I landed on my back with him on top of me. Immediately, I noticed the glow-in-the-dark stars taped to his ceiling.

In the shape of the constellation Pegasus.

"Hunter, what are these doing here?"

"You said you didn't like to sleep in the dark," he explained, getting us under the covers. "I installed them last week. But I can turn on a nightlight for you as well, if you'd like?"

My expression softened. "No, this is perfect."

Lying on our sides facing each other, we kissed until we grew lethargic and eventually fell asleep wrapped in each other's arms.

My love for him continued to grow every hour that we spent together. He wormed his way into my heart and now I was never letting him leave. He was stuck with me. Forever.

Sooner than later, I'd be introducing him to the Bellafiore bunch as my boyfriend. Nonna was the first one to hear about Hunter. I called her when I went over to my childhood home, while my parents bickered and set the table for dinner.

"Nonna, I miss you," I told her as a greeting when she picked up.

Her smoky laugh welcomed me. "*Ciao, piccola.* I miss you, too. I'm sorry I can't be there tonight. I already had plans with the book club ladies and Arlene's on her way to pick me up."

I perched against the half-moon table in the hallway, twirling the antique rotary phone's cord around my finger. "That's okay. The only thing you're missing is Mamma and Papà's argument." But she could probably hear it in the background. They were noisy as hell. "Anyways, what book are you currently reading?"

"Another monster romance." She pretended to sigh like she was annoyed. In truth, she was growing fonder of the genre, thanks to Arlene. "About an alien and his marriage of convenience bride."

"Ooh, I'll have to add it to my to-be-read list." I laughed. "Sounds like fun."

"Fun my ass." She scoffed, but we both knew she didn't mean it. "Anyways, Gabriela, will I be seeing you soon?"

"Yes, you will. I'm hoping we can all do dinner next week. I want to introduce you guys to someone."

"Oh." She sensed the hint of excitement in my voice. "Who is this someone?"

I barely managed to tame my big grin. "A boy that I really, really like, Nonna."

"Is he Italian?"

"Nope. But he does have some Irish in him."

"Bummer. It's a no from me."

"Nonna!" I complained good-naturedly, nearly stomping my foot. "You haven't even met him yet. He's perfect and so handsome. Like a real-life Prince Charming."

She laughed at my dreamy tone. Obviously, she was joking and pushing my buttons. Her own husband, my late grandfather, whom she loved dearly, was Irish. When they married, he changed his surname to Bellafiore as a token of love for Nonna, making us all the Bellafiores.

"All right, send me a picture of him through the app you put on my cell phone," she said. "I'll be the judge of this so-called Prince Charming."

"Okay!" I perked up and cradled the handset in the crook of my neck, while plucking my cell phone from my skirt pocket. I quickly sent her a series of pictures I captured of Hunter while he did mundane things like driving with his sunglasses on, sitting on the sofa watching a movie with my feet in his lap, playing with Luna. Including a screenshot of that one picture from Josh's social media, where Hunter stood in the locker room post-game, unaware that he was being photographed with the rest of his teammates, body glistening with sweat, his tattoo and silver nipple piercing on full display.

Nonna would appreciate the last shot.

"*Mamma mia!* They still make them like that?" she hollered. "Gabriela, he's stunning!"

I giggled. "Isn't he? I really, really like him, Nonna."

"You already said that," she teased. "And does he 'really, really like you' back?"

"Yes. He adores me. Practically kisses the ground I walk on. He's so good to me. No one's ever treated me like him. He picks me up every morning for school, buys me my favourite donuts, brings me flowers, watches horror movies with me, reads my romance books, dotes on Luna and he…He's my comfort person."

And I'm so in love with him.

I hadn't told that tidbit to anyone else yet. Not even my best friends.

I wanted Hunter to be the first person to hear it and I was waiting for the right moment to confess. There were many times that I wanted to and yet, the second I opened my mouth, my words died on the tip of my tongue, nerves getting the best of me.

"Men like that are a rare breed, Gabriela."

"I know. That's why I'm holding onto him. He's never escaping my clutches."

She laughed, probably thinking I was kidding. "I'm happy that you found your person. You deserved to be loved right."

"Thank you. It means a lot to me."

"Arlene's here, so I got to go, but set up a date so we can meet him soon."

"Okay," I said. "I love you, Nonna. Have fun with the book club ladies. Tell them I said hi!"

"Love you, Gabriela, and will do."

In the upcoming days, Hunter and I fell into a routine. We went out for walks despite the temperature dropping. He usually bought me a hot chocolate to keep me warm. We also went to cat-friendly cafés with Luna so we could study and work on our assignments. Luna always sat in Hunter's lap, glancing at him with love, and he snuck her little treats. And sometimes in the evenings, when we didn't want to stay cooped up at home, we drove around aimlessly, listening to his playlists, until we found a clearing where we could gaze at the stars. Hunter even signed me up for driving classes so I could get my license. He encouraged me to practice on his Jaguar and I did, feeling more confident behind the wheel with every session.

Mere days into our relationship and I was glowing. Not to mention that I felt calm and relaxed, my system at ease from its usual anxiety.

I guessed that's what happened when you were in a healthy relationship with a man who didn't drain your cup, but rather filled it and uplifted you into a higher version of yourself.

Hunter was my sanctuary.

I never feared him judging me. He indulged my chatty, clingy self like it was the highest of honours. And I loved him even more for that.

One day, we were hanging out at my place, sitting before the coffee table in my living room with snacks surrounding us as we worked on our respective hobbies. Hunter had coloured a total of one mandala before Luna came over and demanded her daddy's attention. I continued with my diamond painting activity until I got the brilliant idea of using my colourful rhinestones to bedazzle my current romance book's cover.

In the middle of sticking a golden rhinestone, I hedged, "Hunter?"

"Yes, doll?"

"If you could read one book for the rest of your life, what would it be?"

He pondered over my question, while dangling a cat toy in the air for Luna. She leapt up excitedly, pawing at it with a meow. "Does a picture book count?"

I shrugged. "Sure."

He grabbed Luna and she snuggled up to him, purring. Tonight, a black bandana was tied over the top half of his head, keeping his hair away from his face. He looked incredibly hot and I barely managed to keep *my* paws off him.

"In that case, my family album. I'd go through every picture from start to finish, and reread all the anecdotes my parents scrawled behind each memory."

Oh, that was so sweet. "That's lovely, Hunt."

"I'll show it to you when you come over." He winked. "You know, when you meet my mom and sister."

I was glad that we were both at that stage in our relationship where we wanted each other to meet our family members. Some may say it was too soon, but it felt right for us.

"Can't wait." Another rhinestone went on my book cover with meticulous precision. "Next question: if you could listen to one melody for the rest of your life, what would it be?"

"Your voice."

My eyes widened and my heartbeat pounded. "Eat one meal only?"

"Anything you cook for me."

I swooned and drew my finger over the faded scar, barely visible, on the bridge of his nose. He told me a couple nights ago that he got it as a kid, having fallen off his bike. "Revisit any one memory?"

"When I saw you on that moonlit terrace."

I swallowed the lump in my throat. "Me too."

"Yeah?" He pressed his forehead to mine. Luna was snuggled between us. "Why is that?"

So I could fall in love with you all over again. "Because until then, I don't think I'd ever seen a more beautiful man."

Hunter's face softened.

He fused his mouth to mine, pouring all his unspoken feelings and emotions into our kiss.

The next day, when I got home from seeing Anna and Layla…Hunter was already there, courtesy of the key I gave him so he could come and go as he pleased too. Candles were lit, music hummed in the background, and my dining table was set with takeout food from my favourite Middle Eastern restaurant.

"Well, this is a surprise." I took off my coat. "Hi, pretty boy."

"Hi, baby." Hunter crossed over to me, Luna resting in his arms. "How was your day?"

"Good." I kissed him, lingering longer than usual. "How was yours?"

"Good. I actually have another surprise for you."

"Oh?"

"Close your eyes." I did and he grabbed my hand.

If any other man had asked me to blindly put my trust in them, I would never. But Hunter? I'd follow him to hell and back. As long as I was with him, I didn't care.

He tugged me down the hallway and we entered a room. Hunter let go of my hand to flip some switches. "Okay, open."

For a moment, I was speechless as I soaked in my spare room.

He converted it into a safe haven for my bookworm heart.

Black floor-to-ceiling bookshelves spanned two walls, stocked with all my romance titles from A to Z. A matching work desk with my bedazzling kit sat on the surface and a small velvet heart-shaped sofa lined the other walls. An art deco lamp, a leopard print rug, and fairy lights completed the newly renovated space.

And the pièce de resistance?

The Hero and Leander painting that Hunter bought from the auction now mounted on the wall above my sofa.

"I asked Anna and Layla to keep you busy for a few hours while I built the furniture and organized everything according to your taste." He cleared his throat, a nervous blush smattering his cheekbones. Luna wiggled out of his hold to investigate the room herself. "I know you mentioned wanting to renovate this room, so I hope I did your vision justice."

"Hunter, I…"

"Do you like it?" He held his breath.

"Like it?" I repeated, shocked. "I love it! Are you kidding me?"

Hunter's relief was palpable when I beamed and jumped him, my arms and legs wrapping around him. I smothered his face in gentle pecks and he chuckled, tightening his arms around me. "Thank you. Thank you. Thank you. I can't believe you did this for me. I'll be spending all my time here."

"What did we say about the T-word?"

"Shh." *Kiss.* "Let me." *Kiss.* "Express." *Kiss.* "My appreciation." *Kiss.* "I love this room." *Kiss.* "So much, Hunter."

"I'm glad you do," he replied. "Figured you needed your own reading nook and a place to let your creativity thrive."

I fall in love with him more and more and more every day. What will I ever do without him? He was becoming an integral part of me, like a vital organ, and I couldn't fathom the possibility of ever losing him.

"Where have you been all my life?" I whispered.

It was perhaps one of the most important questions I'd ever asked.

His eyes crinkled at the corners endearingly as he grinned. "Right here in the city."

If I knew he existed even before Josh's birthday party, I'd have scoured the entirety of Montardor to find him. "You'll never know how much I regret not striking up a conversation with you those four hundred and sixty-three days ago. If I could go back in time, I would change it all."

"I wouldn't." Hunter shook his head. "I told you that I like our story and how it's written. Don't beat yourself over the past, baby. We're exactly where we are supposed to be."

I pressed my forehead to his. My red hair curtained around us, blocking the outside world until we were in our own little bubble. "And that's all that matters, right?"

"Exactly."

I could give Hunter a million thank-yous and a million gifts in return for all the abundance he brought into my life in such a short period. Yet I wanted my love to be the most powerful thing he received because I knew, at the end of the day, that was all he ever wanted.

All of me. In my rawest, truest form, loving him the way he deserved.

I almost told him right there and then how much I loved him. But Hunter, sensing the weight of my intense gaze as I watched him and came to the realization that I would do anything for him, recognized that words were insignificant to convey the magnitude of what I was currently feeling in this moment.

"Come on, Gabriela." He ushered us out of the room, Luna right behind. "Let's eat before our food gets cold."

As the days went on, I realized that while Hunter's love was quiet and comforting, it was also encompassing in its grandeur. Like the spring season filled with life after a barren winter. Like the gust of a strong wind blowing past you, plastering your clothes against your skin in a hug. Like the first shot of espresso in the morning, awakening all your cogs and preparing you for a whole new day of adventure. And like an ever-flowing current of water against rocks, softening even the harshest of surfaces.

I felt it all the time in my veins, in my muscles, in my bones. It sat inside of me like a peaceful entity, strengthening me with its pillars, raising me to unimaginable heights.

I wrote down these things in a personal journal, never wanting to forget the feelings he invoked within me. Not today, not tomorrow, and not for decades to come. Maybe one day, long after we passed, someone would find my penned words tucked in the safety of these papers and learn that to be loved so effortlessly like this was possible.

It was jarring how quickly my heart went from an inhabitant in my own chest to suddenly walking outside of my body in the form of Hunter Saint Warren.

And it was humbling—almost painful—to witness. Any hurt directed at me, I could withstand. But hurt directed at Hunter? It would ache differently. All I wanted now was to protect and shelter *mio principe* from the harms of this wretched world. If I ever told him that, he would smile, shake his head, kiss me, and tell me I was being worrisome for no reason.

But he didn't understand that if he was no longer in this world, I wouldn't survive.

It was getting harder and harder to live life and not tell Hunter how much I loved him. There were moments where I wanted to…but an invisible zip kept my lips sealed shut. I was overthinking. Too much in my head. Continuously waiting it out for the right time.

I even came close to telling him on Saturday night, after a double date with Layla and Josh, when we were on our way home.

The weather was gloomy and cold, a light drizzle falling from the sky. Hunter let me drive, saying it would be good practice. Both our phones had died, ironically, so we were listening to the radio—an old favourite Beyoncé song playing in the background—while we conversed. Less than a mile away from home, the car released a flapping sound, followed by the unmistakable crunch of something. My fingers tightened on the wheel and I braked, peering at Hunter with confusion and fear rooted in my sternum. "Hunter?"

He gazed out his window, muttering a curse as he found whatever he was looking for. "Sounds like a flat tire. I think you drove over a patch of glass. There's a flurry of broken beer bottles lining the sidewalk and road."

I felt horrible and guilty. "I'm so sorry."

He tutted and grabbed my chin. "Don't apologize. It's not your fault. Plus, it's extremely dark out, so it's not like you could have seen the mess. I didn't either." He stroked his thumb over my jaw, noticing my panic. "Hey—it's okay. Relax, Gabby."

My shoulders deflated as I shifted the gear into park. "But I feel bad."

"And I'm telling you not to," he said. "This car doesn't have a spare tire, so you'll have to drive closer to the curb and park. Since we're less than ten minutes from home, we'll walk and then I'll call the insurance company."

The flat tire was worse than either of us expected. A new screeching sound echoed in the five seconds it took me to line the car with the curb. Great. The earth should open right now and swallow me whole. I was never driving his or any car ever again.

"Gabby." Hunter unbuckled his seatbelt. "Whatever you're thinking, stop it."

I unbuckled my belt too, shame pelting at me from different angles. "What?"

"Baby," he murmured. "These things happen to beginners and veteran drivers. It's okay. It's not a big deal. This is part of the driving experience. Please don't berate yourself or let this stop you from driving again."

"I gave your car a flat tire. You're not mad at me?"

Franco would have cussed me the fuck out if I'd done that to his Camry.

He cupped my face. "I could never be mad at you."

"You don't hate me?"

He frowned, mildly disturbed that I would think that, but perhaps understanding that in my previous relationship, I would get chided for the smallest of mishaps. "What I feel for you is the furthest thing from hate."

Butterflies swarmed in my stomach. "Yeah?"

Hunter pecked my lips softly. "Yeah."

He was looking at me like he was in love with me. It undid me.

Telling him that I loved him after giving his car a flat tire probably wasn't a good idea. Nor would it be my finest moment. So once more, I kept those three words locked in the safety of my heart.

Hunter stepped out of the car and came to my side, opened my door and extended his hand for me. I accepted it and handed him his keys. But then my heel broke and I stumbled forward with a yelp.

He chuckled, breaking my fall before I could face-plant into the ground.

"I got you." My boyfriend swung me into his arms in a princess-carry style. "You're okay."

I wrapped my arms around his neck, gazing at him with heart eyes. "My hero."

"All your book boyfriends wrapped into one, huh?"

I nodded and he kissed my forehead. That singular gesture made me so warm and protected. Hunter was the strongest of shields. He would always keep me safe.

As if the turn of events couldn't get any more disastrous, the dark sky above us pulsed with a flash of lightning and the rain turned from a drizzle to a torrential downpour. Hard sheets of water bounced off the ground.

Hunter started walking down the sidewalk leading to our apartment complex.

We were soaked in seconds.

Our eyes met and we shared a laugh. Getting caught in the rain should have annoyed me. Except all I could think about was how this was the most romantic moment of my life.

"Hunt, put me down." I pushed away the red locks sticking to my neck. "I'll walk."

"You mean limp, considering your heel is broken?"

I tucked my face in his neck and kissed the droplet of rain travelling down his jugular. "Yes."

"I want to carry you home tonight." Hunter laid his cheek gently against my head. "Just let me, sweetheart."

God, I love him, I love him, I love him.

"You'd do it, wouldn't you—walk miles in the cold rain and bring me to safety?"

"Yes." His deep voice rumbled against my skin. "You're my whole world, Gabriela. I need to keep you protected."

Tears stung my eyes. One escaped and trekked a path down my cheek. I prayed Hunter didn't notice and that it mingled with the rest of the raindrops on my face. "You're my whole world too, Hunter."

CHAPTER 36

Grim Reaper & His Angel

GABRIELA

Midterm season came to an end. Things slowed down slightly before they inevitably picked back up since there were six weeks remaining in the semester. The Panthers were entering the semi-finals, so Hunter had a lot on his plate, and I wished I could do something more to alleviate his stress besides making him daily fresh meals and giving him massages when he got home. Hunter wasn't needy by any means—except for my affection— and he never once complained about all he had to do. Even when he was tired, he continuously made time for Luna and me, his two girls.

Like tonight for Halloween.

Cade and Josh were hosting a party at the Remington manor with their trusted close friends and teammates, and I'd been looking forward to it all week long.

I somehow convinced Hunter to go dressed up as a grim reaper. His attire was all noir, save for his signature silver watch and thin chain, and his hair was half down and half up in a low bun. Moreover, he even let me paint a black-and-white skull on his face. He looked hot—scary hot—and I couldn't wait for him to devour me.

As soon as we arrived at the party, Hunter's friends dragged him across the room for drinks and I beelined it to Anna, Layla, Ella, Darla, Dacia, and Hera.

The entire place was atmospherically dark, save for the strobe lights flashing on the makeshift dance floor. Thankfully, we weren't packed like a can of sardines tonight and there was enough space to move around without getting hit by a flailing limb or inhaling a gross combination of BO and alcohol.

Ella and Layla outdid themselves with the décor. A mélange of spooky-themed garlands and spider webs hung from the ceiling, jack-o-lantern pumpkins dotted every available surface, black roses sat in large vases, and a photobooth was set up in the corner of the room that the future sisters-in-law were hogging as they took an innumerable number of shots before the camera.

The rest of us girls were gushing over each other's outfits. Every year, Anna, Layla and I wore matching costumes. Last year we did the *Totally Spies!* and this year we dressed as angels, donning the bustiers Anna sewed for us. Layla was in all white, with a long maxi skirt and kitten heels. Anna was in all pink, with a short skirt and thigh-high boots. And I was in all black, with a micro-miniskirt and stilettos featuring gold snakes that wrapped all the way up to my ankles. We wore wings that matched our respective colours and dare I say, along with Ella, Darla, Dacia, and Hera, we were the best dressed in the vicinity.

In the midst of all our chatter, laughter, and dancing, my eyes wrested over to Hunter.

In my biased opinion, he was the handsomest grim reaper to exist.

I was doing my best to keep my clingy behaviour at bay. Yet all I wanted was to go over there and have my wicked way with him.

Apparently, I wasn't the only one who thought he looked exceptional. Many stares veered in his direction and strayed longer than needed. Men and women alike. I guessed it couldn't be helped. Still, it made me want to bare my teeth at the onlookers.

One was brave enough to have the audacity to approach him. I recognized her from school. She was in my finance classes.

Tina.

Fucking Tina.

She was a nice girl, but now that she'd encroached on *my* Hunter?

I saw red.

Was I having indigestion or was my chest actually tight from jealousy?

The emotion was so foreign to me until Hunter came along. Now I felt it whenever he gave his attention to others. I wanted his eyes on me and only *me*. It was a maddening thought, but I didn't know how to stop my possessiveness.

"Um, Gabby, are you okay?" Anna asked when I stopped dancing, frozen like a statue.

I forced my gaze away from Tina and towards my best friend. The rictus tilt of my mouth and the lunatic glint in my expression had her wincing.

"I'm peachy," I replied, eye twitching.

Tina put her hand on Hunter's forearm. I wanted to shout at her, '*Go away. He's mine!*' But that wasn't very cultured, right?

Layla eased away from the other dancing girls and stepped closer to me and Anna. "What's going on?"

I downed my remaining drink in a single gulp. "Does anyone know any quick, effective methods to kill and not get caught?"

I didn't have my gun on me. Maybe I could borrow one from Josh and Cade's stash? A single shot between the brows should do the trick. Oh, or poison! That would probably get the job done more discreetly.

My best friends shared a concerned look.

Layla cleared her throat. "Is everything okay at home?"

Anna followed my line of sight and caught on. "Gabby," she chided. "You're not murdering Tina for touching Hunter."

"I didn't say I was!"

"You're thinking it." Anna sighed. "It's written all over your face."

Layla chuckled but tried to mask the sound with a cough. "Listen, Tina probably has no idea that you guys are dating. And for what it's worth, it seems like Hunter is breaking the news to her right now."

I snapped my attention back in their direction.

Sure enough, Hunter said something to Tina and she hedged him an apologetic expression. Before replying and inclining her head towards me.

Whatever it was, it caused Hunter to laugh my favourite laugh.

Tina finally backed away and blended into the crowd.

"I'll be right back," I mumbled to Anna and Layla, already crossing the distance towards Hunter.

He met me halfway, a knowing smirk on his lips. "Hey."

I placed my hands on my hips and schooled my features into my best scowl. "Don't 'Hey' me after I caught you red-handed!"

Hunter raised his red Solo cup for a swig. "Caught me doing what?"

"Laughing with Tina!" I growled. "Why don't you go back to her? You know, since she's sooo funny."

His broad shoulders shook with laughter. "Are you actually jealous?"

"No," I said defensively, though we knew I was a territorial little bitch. I crossed my arms over my chest. "But I thought I was the only girl you laughed with?"

Hunter kept chuckling at my sullen tone. He hooked an arm around my neck and drew me into his body. "Get over here."

I pounded feeble fists against his muscular chest, mock-glaring at him. "I don't want your pity hugs."

"What about my kisses?" He planted one on my forehead, my nose, and my cheeks. "You want those?"

Did I ever. I was so weak when it came to Hunter. "Why'd you let Tina touch you?"

It was irrational since *she* touched him and not the other way around. I just had this inherent need to rib Hunter. The mischievous way he grinned told me he saw right through me.

"Sorry, baby," he apologized like a good sport. "I told her I wasn't interested—that I have a girlfriend. She was embarrassed and said she realized exactly who it was, since you were glaring daggers at her. That's what made me laugh." His mouth travelled to my ear, murmuring, "You have nothing to worry about. The only woman I want touching me is you."

The green-eyed monster inside of me quieted down. "Kissing you, too?"

"Mhm." He nodded. "I'm yours and you're mine. Remember?"

"How silly of me to forget." I grabbed his face and pecked his mouth. "We should probably ditch the party and go home. Wash your arm of all the Tina germs."

"Is that the only reason why you want to go home?" he purred, his voice sending shivers down my spine.

No, it wasn't. I wanted to fuck him tonight. "Well, we could make a stop at a tattoo parlour. Get that ink we talked about." I still wanted a snake down my spine to match the snakes on his arm and thigh. "I'm thinking we get you something that says 'Gabriela's Pretty Boy'—you know, to make it clear that you belong to me."

He arched his brow. "And where shall I get this tattoo?"

I batted my lashes coquettishly. "On your dick?"

Another laugh burst out of him. "That might be quite painful, but I'd do it for you, Gabby."

Of course he would. He'd do anything for me.

"I'm kidding—I mean, about the location," I swiftly amended. "Anywhere you want will do."

"Cool. Now enough talk about tattoos." He walked us backwards, his hands on my hips. "I want to dance with my girl."

HUNTER

There was a sense of déjà vu as I led Gabriela to the middle of the dance floor, an ocean of gyrating bodies surrounding us, reminding me of the first time we did this. Except now we weren't putting on a show.

This was for us alone.

I spun her around and pulled her back to my front. She gasped under her breath and it quickly morphed into one of the giggles I loved so much. That sound evoked the feeling of *home* inside of my chest. My arms came around her waist, my hand still holding my drink, and I swayed us to the beat.

Once upon a time, my introverted self would have never willingly inserted myself onto a dance floor, much less partied. But that was then and this was now. Gabriela didn't outright say it, but the beam on her scarlet lips echoed how proud she was of me. At moments like these, I too was proud of my growth and the work I put in. Gabriela once told me we were all works in progress, and every day was one step closer to your masterpiece. I'd come a long way. I liked this version of myself and I wouldn't have been able to find it without her.

So much in my life had changed since Gabriela walked into it.

I wouldn't have it any other way.

"What are you drinking tonight?" She leaned her head against my shoulder, moving her hips sensually to the rhythm.

"Just a soda. Since I'm driving and you don't kiss boys who drink beer."

Her smile was laced with nostalgia. "Good call."

I tightened my arms around her. Our bodies were glued together, yet I wished I could somehow get closer to her. Sink deep into her skin. Anchor myself into her soul. Reside in her heart and never leave that space vacant.

For I had fallen in love with Gabriela Regina Bellafiore.

It didn't happen instantly, rather in small increments over the span of weeks. I think I fell in love with her smile first—the way she laughed and grinned during our banter. Then her eyes—the way they watched me with soft possession whenever I was doing something mundane like driving, opening her car door, carrying her belongings. Then her voice—the way she sounded when we talked about anything and everything under the sun, especially when we lay together in bed. Then her kindness—the way she always complimented and made me feel so warm, the way she cooked and baked for me, the way she fussed over me to make sure I was okay, the way she always held my hand. And her demeanour—the way she remained positive even during one of the greyest periods of her life and how she never failed to be there for her loved ones.

I wanted to tell her I loved her. I wanted to tell her so bad, but I remained tongue-tied, an invisible force keeping those three monumental words at bay.

I'd already made myself vulnerable before her. She owned so much of me. Maybe a part of me was afraid that if I said *I love you* out loud, it would change the perfect pace we had going. Though I was certain she was halfway in love with me, I wanted to be certain that she was in this *all the way* before I poured my heart out.

"How does it feel to be watched by everyone like you're the most beautiful girl in the world?" I whispered in her ear.

She inched me an amused expression and tucked her winged back deeper into my chest. "You haven't seen every girl in the world, Hunter. You can't know if I'm the most beautiful."

"I don't need to see all the girls in the world. You've been my definition of beauty since I first laid eyes on you, baby."

The amusement on her face shattered and was replaced by something solemn. She whirled around in my embrace and gently stroked my bottom lip with her thumb.

Fuck, she's so lovely. All I want to do is keep her safe.

"And I don't need to see every man in the world to know that the most beautiful one is standing right before me. I adore you with every fiber of my soul." She searched my gaze. "Thank you for patiently waiting for me. Being with you is one of the greatest honours of my life…and the fact that you no longer want to blend in with the crowd fills me with so much joy. You're one of a kind, Hunter, and you were made to stand out. I'm so glad you've finally seen it."

Her confession robbed me of speech momentarily.

I could only watch her beseechingly, my heart pounding.

Somehow, I found the will to utter in a thick voice, "It's because of you. You made me want to be seen, Gabby."

She grinned, the little gem on her canine winking in the light. "What a pair we make, huh?"

"The perfect one."

"I need you to kiss me, Hunter."

We'd finally come full circle. "Say *please* like a good girl and I will."

"Please," she whispered like it was a prayer, brushing her mouth to mine.

Unlike our first kiss, which was packed with urgency and carnal desire, this one was softer and slower.

We made out like we had all the time in the world. Her arms vined around my waist, pressing us close. Hand clutching her neck, I kissed her passionately. My tongue licked her mouth with deep strokes, and needy sounds clawed up Gabriela's throat. I bet if I pushed my fingers between her thighs, I'd find her pussy soaked.

I drew my kisses down her neck, pausing to decorate love bites on her porcelain skin. Gabriela tilted her head back, giving me more access. "H-Hunt, let's leave. I can't wait anymore. I want you."

"We've only been here for thirty minutes, doll." I nipped Gabriela's bottom lip, goddamned hungry for her. "We leave now, everyone will know it was to fuck."

"I don't care," she moaned into our kiss. "Please."

Fuck, I could never deny her. I'd been sporting a semi since she walked into my apartment looking like my wet dream in her Halloween costume. Everything about her had me salivating. The black angel wings on her back. The gold serpents on her heels and the one coiled around her neck. The obsidian-painted toes, courtesy of that one time when she sent me a feet picture and I jokingly requested she do black like her soul next. The criminally short black leather skirt that did fantastic things for her legs but was one slip away from baring her perky ass. The matching bustier revealing flashes of her flat stomach and the heart-shaped belly ring when she moved. The red-glossed lips with her dark red hair curled loosely the way I loved.

She looked every inch like my fallen angel from Shaun's party all those weeks ago. Roaming the Earth. Tormenting me with her seductiveness. Reeling me in with the sinful curl of her mouth.

I'd already had her this morning when she woke me up with her mouth on my dick. I came down her throat with rough, sleepy groans. She crawled up my body, kissed my lips, and told me in an innocent tone that my breakfast was ready. A steaming mug of black coffee and four heart-shaped fluffy pancakes rested on my nightstand table, with a generous dollop of whipped cream and sprinkles. Instead, I flipped Gabriela onto her back, spread her thighs, and ate her out first.

Now I was raging with the need to take her again. This time outside on the hood of my Jag and cater to that exhibitionist streak of hers.

I was so addicted to my little doll. I would never have enough of her.

Based on the way she watched me—packed with heat and wickedness, she wouldn't have enough of me either.

"You win, sweetheart. Wave goodbye to your friends so we can leave."

"What—ooh!"

I picked her up and slung her over my shoulder, fireman style. She squealed. Her skirt rose up enough to bare the ends of her cheeks. I spanked her ass, barely resisting the urge to bite it, before dragging the hemline back to its original place. For now. "Say bye, Gabby."

She waved and blew air kisses to her girls as I walked us out the front doors of Remington manor.

CHAPTER 37

Masked Fantasy & Moonlit Rendezvous

HUNTER

A moonlit night welcomed us when I stepped outside. Cars lined the circular driveway, but I'd parked further out by the edge of the woods in a secluded area for *this* very reason. The air fringed with notes of recklessness and our ramping lust as I neared our destination. Far into the distance, crows cawed, a dog howled, and the wind picked up in ferocity.

I felt half-moon mad like the men from her paranormal romance novels. Battling with their primal instincts. Wanting to pin down their mate. Dying to fuck their pretty pussy until it was overflowing with seed.

"Hunter…" Gabriela's shaky voice called out from over my shoulder as my sports car came into view, gleaming under one of the lampposts dotting the perimeters of the estate. "What you did back there? That was very caveman of you."

I smacked her plump ass before rolling her body down mine, keeping my arm securely around her waist until her feet touched the ground. "Stop acting like you don't like that side of me, Gabriela."

Her blue gaze swam with desire. "I love it."

I fused our lips together. Gabriela kissed me back frantically, her hands jerking my black leather jacket over my shoulders. I helped her take it off and she threw it senselessly on the hood of my car without breaking our lip lock. She tackled the buttons of my black dress shirt next, running her hands greedily up the hard planes of my torso once I was bared to her. When she reached for my belt buckle, I snatched her hands, whirled her around, and plastered her back to my front. She gasped. I brought my lips to her ear. "Do you want me to fuck you?"

She nodded, her breathing a hint uneven.

I switched to grip her hands in one and brought my other to squeeze her jaw. "Use your words."

My dirty angel whimpered, rubbing her ass against my lap. "I want you to fuck me, Hunter."

"Are you wet for me?"

"Y-yes."

"Let me see." I released her and she swayed before I caught her hips. "Bend over and grab your ankles."

"Say *please* like a good boy and I will," she joked.

"Don't be a brat." I spanked her. "Bend. Over."

She pouted at me over her shoulder but did as I ordered.

Slowly, she dipped forward, running her hands over her body sensually before her manicured fingers wrapped around her ankles. The tits that spent all night being propped up by her black bustier were no match for gravity, her pink nipples slipping out to give a teasing peek. "Like this?"

That breathy, taunting tone just did it for me.

I shoved up her skirt, letting it belt around her waist, and ripped her black thong down her legs, baring the globes of her ass.

"Good girl." I spread her cheeks apart to see the red jeweled silicone plug I thrust into her puckered hole with a hearty amount of lube right before arriving at the party. I grazed a finger teasingly over the topper and down her crack. "How does it feel?"

We'd been stretching her ass nice and steady for the last two weeks. I bought her a variation of plugs, increasing in size every so often and never allowing her to wear one for longer than the recommended time frame.

Soon enough, she'd be able to take my cock up her tight hole like a pro. Knowing my horny, *game-for-anything* girlfriend, she'd enjoy the hell out of it too.

Tonight was the first time she wore one of the plugs outside of our homes. I wanted to make sure she was okay while indulging in her kinky side.

"It feels good," Gabriela murmured. I tore off my leather gloves and my bare fingers grazed over her wet slit. She whined. "And like we have our own naughty secret."

I smirked, thrusting a finger into her pussy and grasping a handful of her left cheek in a rough squeeze. "When I win my championship, I'm going to fuck this tight little ass. You know that, don't you, baby?"

"*Yes.*" Her pussy squeezed my finger. "I'll let you."

Fuck, she was so gone for me, uncaring of our surroundings. We were in a shadowed corner but still out in the open for anyone who came down this path to see her spread open like a needy slut, with a jewel up her ass and her boyfriend's finger in her cunt. "Of course you will." I slapped her wet flesh. "'Cause you're my filthy little plaything. Mine to fuck, mine to break, mine to mend, yeah?"

Gabriela moaned choppily. "All for you, *amore mio.*"

I adored it when she called me her love.

But I selfishly wanted her to be *in love* with me the way I was in love with her. However, I was a patient man. I'd wait as long as needed—even eternity—for her to get there.

"Stay like that," I demanded, slapping her ass again just to watch it jiggle beautifully. I lowered myself to my knees behind her. "I want to eat some pussy."

"Always so hungry, *bello.*"

"Only for you, doll. Been in this mood since you stepped into my apartment looking like all my dreams wrapped in a pretty black bow."

Since you stepped into my life for the first time, looking like all my prayers to the universe had finally been answered, Gabriela.

I savoured the moan that escaped her when I kissed her clit before giving it a teasing lick. "Slutty little angel, I'm going to devour you whole." I thrust two fingers knuckle-deep and pumped earnestly, curling against the spot that always made her cry out, her thighs shake, and her pussy clench like a vise. "By the time I'm done with you, you won't even remember your name."

"D-don't ever be done with me, Hunter."

My heart stuttered at her vulnerability. "Never, baby." Her cunt released a squelching sound when I popped out my fingers and pushed them straight into my mouth, going cross-eyed at the taste of her. So fucking good. "I'm keeping you forever."

My thumb pressed into the jeweled topper of her plug—the discreet button of this sex toy—and it vibrated to life at a low intensity. Gabriela yelped in surprise, nearly toppling forward. She caught herself with her palms flat on the hood of my sports car.

I chuckled darkly and grabbed her hips to steady her.

Right before shoving her pussy onto my ravenous mouth.

Loud moans fell past her lips as I ate her from behind like a buffet with coarse sounds that seemed dragged out of the deepest recesses of my soul. Nothing had ever tasted as succulent as my goddess of victory. She was candied sin melting on my tongue.

"*Hunterhunterhunter.*"

Her chanting my name only made me wilder and more determined to make her come quickly. In any other circumstance, I would have edged Gabriela. Licked her folds. Kissed her inner thighs. Rubbed her slit. Without zeroing in on where she really wanted. But we didn't have time for that. I needed her to come quickly so we could fuck the way we'd been anticipating since the moment we got to this party.

I alternated between drawing circles around her clit with my tongue to jabbing at it in a blurring motion that had Gabriela bucking her hips. She reached back to grab a fistful of my hair at the crown, while I screwed my tongue deep into her opening, gathered her pussy juices, and returned to swirl on her clit. Her moans turned into screams when I increased the intensity of the toy's vibrations, sawed three fingers in and out of her drenched pussy, and pinched her nipples. Each one of her nerve endings was on fire as she climbed to a new high, stimulated in all her erogenous zones. "Mm. You're so fucking hot and delicious. Be a good girl and come all over my face, Gabby."

She exploded with a shout and squirted all over my mouth and chin. "Hunter!"

That's what I'm fucking talking about.

I licked at her arousal like a man obsessed, drowning in her essence. My fingers dug into her ass, devouring her cunt as promised. Gabriela kept crying out, clawing forward for purchase. Her legs couldn't hold her up anymore. Her body was shaking from the remnants of her orgasm. And she had a beast between her thighs who couldn't stop eating her out.

Like a puppet with its strings cut, she slumped over my car's hood. If I hadn't been clutching her, she'd have fallen to the ground. She was huffing from the pleasure I unleashed on her flesh. "H-Hunt, please."

But I kept licking and sucking her clit, rushing her to another orgasm as she sob-moaned, tremors wracking through her frame.

Ripping the thong stretched around her ankles, I wiped my chin and mouth of her fluids and stood up, pocketing the tattered lace.

Shivering in the moonlight from her two releases, my little goddess looked like a defiled innocent angel. Her black wings crooked, her skin flushed, and her hair sprawled around her like a river of blood. When I stroked my knuckles down her cheek, her glassy blue eyes fluttered open and her red lips parted.

I took it back.

This was no innocent angel.

She was a sultry witch who'd woven her spell around me so deeply, I was never escaping her clutches.

Nor did I want to.

I covered her body with mine and kissed a path from the crook of her neck to her ear. "Have I tired you out already, Gabriela?"

She sighed as I licked the shell of her ear with the tip of my tongue. "W-who's Gabriela?"

I chuckled lazily, turning her face my way to kiss that intoxicating mouth. "I did say I would make you forget your own name."

"Mm." She kissed me back. "You also said you would never be done with me."

I hiked a brow and undid my belt buckle; the sound amplified in the quiet night. "Do I look like I'm done with you?"

"No." Her breathing quickened when she saw me pull my belt out of the loops. "You look like you're just getting started."

Our gazes connected and the world slowed.

Eyes were the windows to our souls, and there was a brief moment where I felt like she could see straight into mine and read the writing on the wall. *I'm in love with you. I'm so fucking in love with you, Gabriela, you're the beginning and end of my universe.* And foolishly, I felt like I could see straight into hers and read the same thing.

Though that was probably wishful thinking on my end.

But there was no denying the pure softness sitting in plain view for me to see. Hidden behind it were threads of *hope*. The possibility of her falling in love with me existed right there in the flecks of her blue eyes.

Gabriela Regina Bellafiore was my first real love.

She would be my last love too.

I prayed that I could be both of those for her as well—that I could soon tell her what she meant to me. Since I couldn't say it with my words for now, I would say it with my body.

"I am, Gabby." Without wasting time, I tied both of her hands at her back with my belt and wrapped a hand around her throat, using it to bring her body upright. "I'm just getting started with you."

Excitement zinged through her muscles. She loved being bound. Communicated exactly that with her stare when she glanced at me over her shoulder. "Are you going to make me beg?"

I smirked and unzipped my pants, then reached into my briefs for my cock. I gave it a long stroke from root to tip. Prolonging the torture. Massaging the bead of pre-cum onto my skin. Making her mentally count the seconds until I was inside of her. She released a breathy noise, tilting her hips and searching for friction—for me. "Yes. You beg so prettily. Get to it."

She whined when I dragged the head of my length through her wet folds and tapped her clit teasingly. "Pleaseplease—"

I slammed into her in one smooth thrust.

A moan erupted from Gabriela and mingled with my deep groan.

"*Fuck.*" I screwed my eyes shut and fought not to come too quickly. But God, her walls clenched my shaft in a stranglehold and the vibrations from her sex toy felt heavenly on my flesh too.

"H-Hunter, stop torturing me."

"Only when *you* stop torturing *me.*" I tightened my hold on her neck. "How am I supposed to move when you're squeezing me so tight? Been fucking you every day, every night for the last two weeks and I still can't get over how you clamp up around my dick like it's the first time." My fingers smoothed over the front of her pussy, feeling where we were joined. "You've got me addicted, baby."

"I-if you don't start fucking me, I'm going to scream."

"Scream away." I slapped her clit. "We both know you get off on the thrill of getting caught." I pulled out till just the tip poised at the opening of her cunt. My length glistened with her arousal. "Do it loud enough that we garner an audience, doll. I'd like nothing more than to fuck you in front of every fucking man who thinks he's got a chance with *my* smoke show."

I punched my hips forward and drove myself inside of her in a crude thrust. Before pulling back just as quickly and leaving her wet cunt with the need to be filled.

Gabriela threw her head back on a frustrated howl. "*Hunter.*"

She was a daddy's girl, entirely used to getting everything she wanted. I always indulged the spoiled princess, but tonight I wanted to play with her. Tug her leash a little. Remind her that I held all the cards and she was at my mercy.

I smirked and drew a finger over her slit, collecting her arousal. "You need me balls deep inside this needy pussy, Gabriela?"

She sucked my digit when I pushed it past her lips, her *yes* muffled.

"Tell me why." It was taking everything inside of me not to pin her down and just *thrustthrustthrust* into her like a madman. "Tell me why you need me."

I wanted to hear the magic words. The same ones she whispered in my ear last night when I was fucking her deep and slow, the closest I could get to making love to her without saying it aloud.

"I'm your slut." She panted when I toyed with her clit. "*Sono la tua troia, amore mio.* So fuck me like it, please."

There wasn't a single drug in the world that could compare to the ecstasy that unfurled in my veins at hearing her dirty talk to me in Italian.

"Yes, you are." Achingly slow, I thrust back into her, inch by inch, watching my shaft disappear into her snug channel. The most obscene, sexy sight would forever be her small pussy stretched around my fat cock. Gabriela moaned loudly. "My slutty little angel who needs to have her pussy fucked raw, hm?" I pulled out. "All the damn time." And thrust back in. "When I first saw you, I thought you were a good girl who fancied sweet, vanilla sex." Her body jolted on a particular hard, fast, deep-seating thrust. "Not a bad girl who needs it hardcore to keep her appetite satiated."

Gabriela got tired of waiting for the dirty, rough fuck I promised.

She took matters into her own hands and started moving while I held still, manacling her throat and fisting her hair. *This* was why I loved driving her to a tipping point. She turned shameless in her pleasure and I got a front row seat at her ass bouncing in my lap with eagerness, using my cock like a fuck toy and moaning salaciously. "Feed me, *bello*. Fuck your filthy little plaything."

My nostrils flared.

God-fucking-dammit.

I gritted my teeth and choked her, cutting off her air supply momentarily as I started pounding into her with merciless strokes. The wet, fleshy smacks of our sexes echoed in the atmosphere. Tears leaked from the corners of Gabriela's eyes. Her mouth opened on mute cries. Her breasts spilled free of the bustier and quaked with every pump. Her tied hands clenched and unclenched unconsciously, like she was desperate to touch me.

I caught piecemeals of our reflection in my car's windshield.

The way we fucked under the moonlight was nothing short of animalistic.

I brought my lips to her ear and said harshly, "Open your eyes." *Thrust.* "Look at you." *Thrust.* "You're always beautiful, Gabriela." *Thrust.* "But most beautiful when you let me pound into you like a fuckdoll." *Thrust.* "Fucking stunning, baby."

She watched, entranced at the sight we created. I licked at the lone tear leaking from the corner of her eye and kissed the apple of her cheek without losing our pace.

"S-so are you," she returned on a whimper. "The most stunning, Hunt."

My chest cracked wide open. She wasn't talking about my physical appearance. Rather my heart, my mind, my soul. It was all hers for the taking.

I belonged to her.

"Fuck, Gabby." I tugged harder at her hair and her neck arched. I buried my face against it, painting my words against the slender column. "You never have to be jealous when I'm this obsessed with you."

When I'm this in love with you.

Another sobbing moan slipped out of her when I slapped her clit in time with my thrusting. "G-good. 'Cause I was going to kill Tina tonight."

I let go of her hair to squeeze her jaw till her mouth popped open and drizzled spit into it. She moaned at the taste. "Crazy little mob princess."

She kissed me sloppily, meeting me thrust for thrust. "You're mine."

"Yours," I vowed.

The blustery wind spread its fingers through our surroundings and caused the leaves in the forest beside us to rustle loudly, but it didn't drown the sound of our lovemaking.

I held Gabriela down by the nape of her neck against my car's hood and slammed even harder into her, sweat trickling into my eyes. My balls slapped against her clit rhythmically. Her pussy fluttered around me. She was nearing her peak. I pressed the button on the butt plug and increased the intensity of the vibrations. She cried out louder. The sensations were incredible and I clenched my teeth, holding back from coming.

Gabriela moaned, overwhelmed and overstimulated. "Moremoremore."

She was living her best life, tied and pinned down for my use. Small *uhs*, *ohs*, *yeses*, and *Hunters* escaped Gabriela. I loved how unabashedly vocal she was in her pleasure as I thrust ruthlessly. "You going to come for me, Gabriela?"

"*Yes.*" She went to her tippytoes when my cockhead rubbed against her G-spot. "*Fuck yes.*"

"So soon?" I teased in a gravelly tone.

"Mhm."

"No." *Thrust.* "Not yet." *Thrust.* "You don't come till I say so."

But did she listen to me?

No.

Gabriela came fast and hard, a girlish scream tearing from her throat.

Her pussy squeezed my cock and I pulled out of her before I could come.

She protested at the loss of me.

"Fucking brat," I growled, so fucking turned on by her and her defiance. I slapped her ass in two successive swats for good measure. My handprint bloomed on her skin. "You never listen to me, huh?"

Panting and basking in her orgasm, she barely heard me.

Right then, the skies above us opened up and rain drizzled. I undid the belt, freeing her hands from the confinement, unhooked the back of her bustier, and unzipped her skirt, peeling off the skimpy costume until she was left naked in her heels and dark angel wings. I removed my own wind-mussed dress shirt but grabbed my leather jacket before I flipped Gabriela around and hauled her into my arms.

She mustered the strength to wrap her legs around my waist and her arms around my neck.

Then I headed into the forest.

Moonlight broke through the canopy of trees overhead as I waded us deeper into the area so we'd have shelter from the rain…and to appease my girlfriend's fantasy of being fucked in the woods by a masked stranger. Naughty little doll wanted to be ravaged by her grim reaper tonight.

Gabriela never ceased kissing me, gentle pecks voyaging over my face. I groaned when she laved my corded neck with nips and love bites.

Miss possessive's hips kept undulating in a beat meant to destroy me, her glossy pussy glazing over the underside of my dick. She was desperate to have me back inside of her. "Hunter, I want you to come too."

I cursed when just my tip dipped back into her warm cunt. I went over a year without sex, but now that I'd had Gabriela? I couldn't fathom going a day without being inside of her.

"Soon." I threw my jacket on the ground, then dropped to my knees with her. "After I teach you a lesson."

"Now," she demanded when I lowered us, making sure her back and bottom were comfortably lying on the leather.

I tutted, pushing my black pants further down my thighs. Gabriela licked her lips, eyeing my thigh tat. She was obsessed with it. I spread her legs and pressed her knees down until she butterflied. Her pink cunt was swollen and drenched. "Patience, Gabriela."

She attempted a half-assed glare and grabbed my wet cock, giving it a stroke before guiding the tip back to her entrance. "No. Now—"

I spanked her cunt hard.

Gabriela whimpered, eyes widening in shock and…glee.

She loved being dominated. And getting spanked? Yeah, that got her hot as hell. My hand shot out to grab her jaw in a possessive clasp. "Listen to me and listen well." I snarled, slapping her flesh twice more. She mewled, back arching. "I've got a bratty little pussy to discipline and you've got a lesson to learn." *Slap.* "Remember that this is your fault." *Slap.* "You came before I gave you permission." *Slap.* "Did I give you permission, Gabriela?"

She met my eyes with defiance in hers. "No, but I did it anyway."

"Exactly." I brought my face down until our noses touched. Until I could count every individual lash and every grey fleck in her blue eyes, which appeared almost sterling under the shard of moonlight seeping through the trees above. "So show me you can follow my rules, and I'll make you come again. Understood?"

She rolled her eyes, but the taunting curve of her mouth betrayed her. She was loving this game. "Fine. Understood, you tyrant—*ahh.*"

I slapped her heavy tit. "Count with me. Twenty spanks and I'll consider you graduated as long as you don't come before I'm finished." I pinched her nipple the way she liked. "Now keep your legs open, baby."

I slapped her pussy and she shakily mumbled, "One."

Again. "Two."

She cupped the back of her knees tighter on my third slap, glancing down at where my hand met her pussy. "T-three."

I turned up the intensity of the butt plug for the remainder. Gabriela's body shook underneath me. "H-Hunter, I p-promise, I'll be a good girl. I'll do better next time."

"Yeah?"

The innocent façade was just an act. We both knew she couldn't be good—only bad—but that's what I liked. She nodded frantically. "I-I will."

"Liar." I slapped her pussy a fourth time. "Keep counting."

My girlfriend obeyed. By the time we made it to eighteen, she was breathing unevenly. Skin flushed pink. Red lipstick smeared. Mascara-stained tears running down her cheeks. She was a beautiful wreck and I needed her like the breath in my lungs.

The drops of sweat fell down my chest and onto her torso, mixing with the light rain sprinkling around us. Gabriela gazed through half-mast eyes, jerking then moaning when I slapped her pussy yet again. "N-nineteen."

"Fuck." I rubbed my fingers over her slit appreciatively, humming. "Your pussy's always so wet, so needy, so ready to play. Isn't that right, *bella mia?*"

She gasped, surprised.

I was learning her language. Had started not long ago. And based on the spark in her eyes, she liked knowing it and hearing the term of endearment.

"You're the reason I'm always like this—*you* did this to me." Her neck worked with a swallow. "Now you have to take care of it, Hunt."

"I will." I swore. "After this last one."

Gabriela braced for the final spank and I delivered, the noisy swat resonating in the darkness encasing us.

She moaned shakily, stomach dipping, thighs shaking. "T-twenty—"
I shoved back inside of her before she finished speaking.

Gabriela screamed and I groaned, enveloped in wet, hot, slippery heaven once more. "See, that wasn't so hard now, was it, doll?" I gave half a dozen shallow thrusts, toying with her clit and watching her pussy lips hug my cock on every withdrawal like they didn't want to let go. "All you need to do is listen to me and I'll reward you. It's that." *Thrust.* "Fucking." *Thrust.* "Simple."

"I-I'm going to come. I-I need to. *Please.*"

It was inevitable. She was asking for permission before she gave in to the sensations imploding within her core.

"Come," I commanded, my hands kneading the flesh of her ass to get as close to her as I thrust, not easing my tempo. "You deserve it for being such a good girl."

An undeniable ripple coursed through her body as she came. I drank in her soft noises with my rough kisses as she rode out her orgasm and clawed at my shoulders for anchor, swiping my tongue into her mouth to lick thoroughly, fucking it the same way I'd been fucking her pussy.

I held myself still inside of her and stopped kissing when our breaths ran sparse and she seemed somewhat calmer, muscles going lax from the four releases. I moved aside tendrils of dark red hair sticking to her temples from sweat. "I want you to do me a favour, Gabriela."

Head lolling back against my leather jacket and lids drooping, she panted a meek, "What?"

My hands grabbed the undersides of her breasts and lifted them to my mouth. I tongued, sucked, and tugged her nipples lightly between my teeth, knowing she got off on the pain. I raised my head enough to gaze into her eyes, swimming with a maelstrom of emotions. "I want you to come again." I licked a path from the valley between her breasts to the shadowed notch between her collarbones before continuing all the way up her throat, chin, and lips, where I paused to steal another kiss. "One more time with me."

She shook her head slowly, exhausted. "I can't."

"You can." My hands hooked around Gabriela's ankles and I brought them down on either side of her head, spreading that tight body in an illicit V. "And you will."

Then I started bouncing my cock inside of her tightness with renewed vigour—a brutal pace that left her breathless. My pelvis mashed against her clit on every thrust and her hands dug into my sides, refusing to let me go as pleasure built back inside of her anew.

"That's right," I growled, enjoying the way her tits swayed back and forth, the way her mouth shaped into an O with hoarse moans emerging, the way I was slotting even deeper in this debauching position. My naughty little angel was spread wide open, bent in two, with no choice but to receive my offering. I pressed the button on the sex toy again—the final setting—and savoured how the high intensity, coupled with our dirty fucking, unleashed mayhem on her body. She was going to come again despite saying otherwise and it was going to be so fucking good. "You take what I give you." *Thrust. Thrust. Thrust.* "And if I want you to come again?" *Thrust. Thrust. Thrust.* "You." *Thrust.* "Fucking." *Thrust.* "Will."

Nonsensical sounds of enjoyment tumbled out of Gabriela. There was something satisfying in my strength overpowering her when she craved it this much. I'd fulfill all of her fantasies in a healthy manner and protect her till the very end. She knew it too.

While I rutted between her thighs like a damn animal, she played with her clit, sucked and tugged on my nipple piercing like a greedy girl, and raked her nails down my torso, leaving pink scratch marks everywhere.

Red-hot lust nearly blinded my vision. I released her ankles and grabbed her throat in a rough squeeze instead. "Mm, you're already starting to tighten up on me, Gabby. It's the choking, isn't it, you beautiful brat?" I licked at the bead of sweat on my upper lip. "Or is it the feel of my cock in your pussy and the vibrating toy in your ass?"

"B-both!"

"Fuck." I snarled and covered her mouth with my hand, muffling her cries. She watched me with wide, impatient eyes. "If you keep moaning and screaming like this, someone will catch us and I won't be able to stop until I've filled your pink pussy with my cum." My pace grew jerky and the base of my spine tightened. "But that's what you want, huh? For everyone to see me claiming you as mine?"

She nodded, tears coursing down her cheeks.

In a deceptively soft and dark voice, I begged in her ear, "Can I come now, princess? I've been such a good boy—such a little saint for you."

I removed my palm from her mouth just in time to hear her scream, "*Yes!*"

Three thrusts later, we tumbled over the edge, coming together with shouts and expletives in the moonlit forest.

My cock twitched and poured inside of her ravenous cunt while she squirted again, coating my lower abs and the space between us.

Heaving, I landed on top of her, defeated by our mutual orgasm, and Gabriela sagged further into the rain-softened ground. My hands delved into her hair as we made out slowly and lovingly.

For mere moments, we simply lay and breathed each other in. The cool night air and the leftover trickle of rain were a balm to our heated skins. Gabriela sifted her fingers through my hair and I shivered, wrapping my arms around her in a hug, my face buried in her neck.

"Doll," I mumbled, blindly reaching between us to turn off the butt plug. "You okay?"

"More than good." She kissed my temple. "You?"

"More than good too."

The sight of her all ruffled and smiling tugged at my heartstrings. Her thumb smoothed over my mouth. I expected her to ask me to remove the toy or to clean her up. Instead, she whispered, "When did you start learning my language?"

Warmth suffused my face at her question. "I started taking lessons two weeks ago. I…I just wanted to feel closer to you."

An emotion I couldn't decipher flashed over her features. "Is that so?" I nodded, unsure what to say, and she cupped my cheek. "Tell me what else you've learned."

I leaned closer to kiss her lips. "*Ti…Ti adoro*," I said hesitantly. "*Sei bellissima.*"

I adore you. You're beautiful.

Gabriela didn't say anything, stunned.

I frowned. Did I pronounce them wrong? I learned some basic Italian, but mostly only memorized terms of endearment and praise because those were the most important things I wanted to shower my Gabriela with.

She urged me closer with the hand on my cheek and bestowed a featherlight kiss on my lips. "*Farei qualsiasi cosa per te, bello. Sono innamorata di te.*"

My heart pounded and I swallowed thickly. "I'm not that advanced, Gabby. What did you say?"

She caressed my jaw. "That's for me to know and for you to find out one day."

This would only make me more relentless in my pursuit to learn Italian, if simply for the sake of understanding the words the girl I was in love with spoke to me.

"Fine. Keep your secrets." I stroked a knuckle down her cheek. "But one day, I'll have them all."

"I'm sure you will."

I rose up on my knees and pulled my softening cock out of her. We both groaned at the sensation and watched my cum trickle out of her opening. Unable to help myself, I fingered it back inside. Gabriela closed her eyes on a blissful sigh, clutching my jacket on either side of her hips.

My chest shuddered, making more room for her presence, as if she wasn't already all that I saw and all that I felt. I didn't think there was a single fiber left inside of me that she hadn't already laid claim to.

I was all hers.

She was all mine.

And I wouldn't let anything change that.

Gingerly, I popped out the butt plug since she'd worn it for longer than I intended, and wiped her pussy with the pack of tissues I kept inside my leather jacket pocket.

Gabriela observed me with a gentle expression as I went about my task. I loved the aftercare part, where she relaxed beneath me and I could tend to her.

A crackling of branches drew our attention to the left.

We both stared at the path where we'd entered from. There was nothing but shadows and trees.

"Do you think... someone is there?" Gabriela hushed, rising to her knees.

Maybe one of the Remington guards heard the sounds of our activity and came to investigate. "If there was, they probably saw us and left."

"You're right." Her eyes wandered back to me—my chest in particular—and she frowned. "Oh, I left too many marks."

I grinned at her awestruck tone. Clearly, she wasn't mad about leaving marks, just that there were too many. "As if that wasn't your intention, Miss Possessive."

"Do they hurt?"

"No." I pecked her forehead, taking a moment to breathe in her familiar vanilla and red roses scent. "I'm okay."

I cleaned myself as best as I could and zipped up my pants. Then I dragged Gabriela into my arms and grabbed my jacket from the ground. "Ready?"

"Ready." Her arms and legs vined around me, and I walked us out of the woods. "I had fun, Hunt. Best party ever."

I laughed and she chased the sound with kisses all over my throat. "Me too, Gabby."

Now I just wanted to take her home so I could wash us properly, make her a hot tea, see our Luna, and tuck them both into bed.

The clothes we'd thrown in front of my car were a rain-drenched mess, but at least I had an extra football jersey and blanket in my trunk that Gabriela could use. I'd crank up the heat on our drive so she could get warm.

A ruby red nail drew between my pecs before she pressed a kiss to my sternum. "I'm sorry for marking you, Hunter."

"I'm not," I said. "But if you do want to apologize, let me hear it in your language."

As I neared my car, Gabriela bent her head and kissed each one of the scratches, taking her time and smiling in between. "*Scusa, bello. Perdonami.*"

Longing unfurled in my chest. I pressed her against the side of my Jaguar, peering down into her eyes. "Are you going to do it again?"

Understanding dawned in her gaze. "Yes."

"And why is that?" I rasped, touching my forehead to hers.

"Because you're infinitely mine, Hunter," she murmured. "You always have been, since the moment we laid eyes on each other."

You're infinitely mine, Hunter.

There weren't enough words to describe what that statement did to me.

I murmured back, "Finally, you caught on, doll."

CHAPTER 38

Bone Of Contention

GABRIELA

Friday afternoon, I was in the spacious WIB student association's office on the eighth floor of Vesta University's business school. Everyone was gone for the day, including Hera, who left a few minutes ago after handing me some cheques from our sponsors. I needed to pass by the bank before closing time to have these deposited, since we'd be using the funds to cater food for our upcoming event.

I was answering a last-minute email from my teammate, who asked if we had the budget to purchase customized USB flash drives to hand out during our next team bonding activity, when I heard the unmistakable sound of keys jingling on the other side of the office door.

A few seconds later, the door swung open and Morgan Huxley entered. My spine stiffened.

The particles in the room shifted to accommodate her infuriating energy. All the previous tranquility I felt was siphoned out. Now I was tense and doing my best not to glance away from my laptop screen.

I pressed send on my email while she headed for the desk opposite mine.

Of all the places she could have situated herself in, she chose the one closest to me…

Ignoring her, I opened up my spreadsheet with an overview of our upcoming expenses.

"Rude," she remarked with snark, throwing her bag loudly across the desk and stationing herself on the office chair. "You don't even say hi."

My temper flared.

Did she get off on being a bitch to everyone or was I the only one unfortunate enough to be subjected to her ire?

Since the mixer at MacGregor's, where she made a complete ass out of herself by hitting on Cade—while he repeatedly expressed his uninterest—and forcing Hera to berate her for her disgusting behaviour, Morgan had ignored me.

During our weekly team meetings, she gave me the cold shoulder, speaking to me only when necessary. Which was fine by me. Morgan and I would never be friends. She ensured that from the get-go. But that didn't mean I had to put up with her draining envy when I'd done absolutely nothing to her.

If me holding the financial coordinator position—the one she vied for at the beginning—pissed her off, then that was *her* problem. Not mine. I couldn't control people's treatment of me. Just my own reactions to their actions.

Even now, I was choosing to be the bigger person by tonelessly saying, "Hi."

Crickets chirped in the air.

Against my better judgement, I looked up from my spreadsheet.

And found her eyeing the cheques sitting next to my mocha cup with a grimace. There it was—that ever-present jealousy. Unbeknownst to her, she didn't have the guts to handle my position on the team. To remain angry over Hera's decision to place her in another role, instead of being grateful that our president had even found her worthy of being on the team, was beyond me.

I was going to stay quiet, but then her gaze veered over to the other item on my desk.

The rhinestone bedazzled fantasy book that Hunter and I were buddy-reading.

She scoffed. "What are you, five? Looks like a kid's arts and crafts project gone wrong. So fucking tacky." She shook her head. "That book sucked, by the way. The hero dies trying to save the heroine."

That's it.

My anger boiled over.

I slammed my laptop lid shut and stood up, the wheels of my office chair scraping back loudly.

She jumped in her seat, surprised.

I was tired of dealing with the Morgans and Francos of this world. Acting like I was beneath them. Acting like they could walk all over me. Acting like my kindness was a weakness. For some reason, I had the tendency to attract the most unhealed scums. Screw them.

I rounded my desk to the front and perched on it, crossing my arms over my chest. "I'm only going to ask you this once. What's your fucking problem, Morgan?"

Never once did I raise my voice at her. Alone or during our team meetings. Usually, I let her shitty behaviour slide because I couldn't be bothered. But if there was one thing I truly loathed? It was people with hater energy that was a disguise for their jealousy.

"What did you say to me?" Morgan drawled with a mean smirk in a vain effort to appear unaffected.

I caught the slight shake in her limbs. The wobbling of her chin. She was all bark, no bite. Confrontations weren't her style. Unfortunately for her, she had it coming.

"You heard me," I said through gritted teeth. "I refuse to put up with your animosity any longer. I'm tired of your bitchy attitude. Either you tell me what your fucking problem is, or I'll get your ass kicked off this team faster than you can snap your fingers." I edged forward, placing my hands on either side of the desk, my expression downright menacing. "And make no mistake—I can make that happen."

It was no secret that I was close to Hera. Our relationship wasn't born from being in the same student association. In fact, we'd been friends for years, given that she was Layla's cousin. Without a shadow of a doubt, if I told Hera the extent of Morgan's discomforting behaviour and comments towards me behind the team's back, she would kick her off without a second thought.

I mostly kept silent because I didn't want to cause any discord, least of all any disruptions in our team's dynamics. But that wasn't fair to me either. Now, if necessary, I wouldn't hesitate to wield the favouritism in my benefit and get this girl removed from the team. Even if it meant taking on more responsibility and filling in her role as well. And me taking Morgan's place would really suck for her. Being part of a student association during your academic career looked stellar on your résumé.

"You're threatening me?" Morgan enunciated each word like she couldn't believe I'd said what I said.

"About time, don't you agree? However, like I said, if you tell me what your problem is and we come to a truce, I won't spill a word to Hera about the rude way you've treated me for the last few months. Really, the choice is yours, Morgan. I'd pick wisely if I were you."

We stared at each other for a moment.

She watched me, appalled.

Clearly, she didn't think I'd ever stand up for myself, let alone have the balls to call her out. Maybe she didn't even realize what a bitch she'd truly been until now.

I kept my steady gaze trained on her, not backing down.

Morgan squirmed.

"I'm tired of making myself smaller so it's easier for you to digest my presence, Morgan. I'd rather you choke on me at this point than to put up with your bullshit any longer."

Morgan hadn't seen my bad side. I rarely showed it. My legacy was tainted with violence and bloodshed. Having grown up as Papà's daughter, I was acquainted with the darker side of life. That's why I chose to live as positively as I could, see the glass as half full, and always be kind to those around me.

But if I had to get nasty with Morgan…I would. It was overdue.

"You want to know what my problem is?" She leaned forward on her elbows and pointed a finger at me. "*You* are my problem."

"Yeah, yeah." I waved my hand dismissively. "You made that abundantly clear when you tried hitting on a guy I was talking to platonically, mind you. I know I'm your problem. I'm asking *why*."

Morgan's face flushed red, a combination of humiliation and anger. "I hate girls like you," she spat. "Who get their way with everything in life because of their pretty privilege. Any position you want, any man you want—really, *anything* you want. It's yours and you barely have to work for it. Opportunities naturally gravitate towards you and you have it so fucking easy, you don't even realize it."

Of all the things I expected her to say, this wasn't it.

I thought she'd say something juvenile like she hated the colour of my hair, hated how talkative I could be, hated the way I typed during our meetings—hell, even hated the way I breathed.

But not this.

I blinked out of my stunned state and mulled over her words.

And all I felt for Morgan was pity.

I wasn't just dealing with someone who was jealous, but one who was entirely too insecure in their skin.

Physically and from society's standards, Morgan would be considered gorgeous. She was tall and slim, beautiful-faced, and her long hair a pleasing light shade of brown. Begrudgingly, I would also admit that she was book-smart, even if critical thinking failed her in certain situations.

I didn't think Morgan realized her own worth. Otherwise, she'd know that she was also a recipient of this so-called pretty privilege. I also didn't think Morgan was surrounded by female friendships that empowered her. Because if she had been uplifted by the women in her life, I guarantee she wouldn't see others as competition.

Harbouring bitter feelings towards a peer whose only crime was occasionally existing in the same vicinity as you was…well, quite fucking sad.

"First of all?" I began, collecting my wits. "You think I'm pretty? Flattered. Second of all, Morgan, look in the mirror. You are beautiful *and* smart." My compliment caught her off guard and the venomous expression swiftly wiped off her face. "Unfortunately, I don't think this is something you see. Insecurities are normal. We all have them. But when yours start to negatively impact the way you view and treat the people in your surroundings, then that's a problem." She seemed uncomfortable with every passing second of my gentle-toned monologue. "Thirdly, you think I can have any man I want? Thank you for stroking my ego, but there's only one man I'm interested in and he's currently mine. Lastly, you are correct in saying that I can have any position I want. But that's because my GPA and work ethic speak for themselves. Hera knew I had the skills to thrive in this role and she picked me—not you and not any of the fifty candidates she interviewed—for a reason. It's nothing personal.

"And contrary to your belief, I don't have it easy. To insinuate that the only reason why I've had opportunities tumble my way is because of my looks? That's extremely rude and dismissive of the years of hard work I've put into my academic career. I get that you're pissed because this is the position you initially wanted, but hating me for something that was outside of my control?" I shook my head. "That's unfair and honestly? Very petty at your age. For the sake of the team, I'll be grateful if you kept your spitefulness to yourself. It would be a shame to lose you when you're so good at your role and do deserve to be here. But I'm not going anywhere either, so I'd appreciate it if we could come to an agreement. I also can't change who I am just to appease you, nor will I ever do that. I'm comfortable in my skin, and I hope you get to heal the parts of you that prevent you from being that too."

The only sound in the office was the heating unit's light droning.

Wide-eyed and parted lips, I rendered Morgan speechless.

I glanced down at my watch. Anna's class was ending soon and we were carpooling. She was driving me to my apartment first so I could get ready and then dropping me at my childhood home since Hunter was coming over for dinner tonight.

I was already anxious over him meeting my family for the first time, and I didn't want to waste my energy worrying over a resentful peer too.

Taking her silence as an answer, I packed my bag in record speed and strode towards the closed office door.

Morgan finally spoke up.

"I'm sorry, Gabby."

I closed my eyes. Those words did nothing to assuage the past. But I wasn't into kicking a woman when she was down. And this confrontation was Morgan's rock bottom, I could tell, from her barely audible voice, layered with guilt and something like self-deprecation.

Glancing over my shoulder, I gave her the olive branch she never once extended my way. I smiled weakly. "Water under the bridge, Morgan. I'm already over it."

I proceeded to walk out of the office with my head held high.

CHAPTER 39

Cat Out Of The Bag

GABRIELA

Anna dropped me off at my parents' home in the early evening.

I bounded up the porch steps with Luna's carrier in one hand and my new black purse in the crook of my elbow. I couldn't wait to show it to Mamma. She was going to foam at the mouth when she saw the structured crocodile skin patterned beauty with pretty gold buckles.

It was a gift from Hunter. One I found this morning sitting on my coffee table with a sweet handwritten note.

Good morning, doll.

You mentioned needing a new purse and I snooped through the wish list on your laptop last week. I hope you like it.

—Your pretty boy

Suffice to say, I didn't need a new purse, per se—I just wanted one—and as always, Hunter indulged me. I loved him. The note was now taped to my fridge with a heart-shaped magnet and I would cherish his gift forever.

Unlocking the front door, I entered my childhood home and called out, "Honeyyy, I'm home!"

Silence welcomed me.

420

I frowned as I toed off my red bottom pumps in the foyer and put on indoor kitten heels.

Opening Luna's carrier so she could roam freely, I hollered again, "Mamma?"

No response.

Huh.

That was odd.

I headed over to the kitchen to unload a bottle of red wine and a chocolate box from an actual maître chocolatier's shop for the special occasion.

I sent Mamma a text thirty minutes ago to let her know I'd be coming over earlier than anticipated. Mostly to ease my nerves and make sure everything was in order for tonight's dinner. It wasn't every day that your family met your boyfriend for the first time. This was a huge milestone.

I wanted Hunter to like my family. And more than anything, I wanted my family to love and accept him the way I had. I wasn't worried about the women in my family. Out of sheer excitement, Mamma insisted on preparing a three-course meal, Nonna made her famous tiramisu, and Papà? He was bringing his judgemental self and a loaded gun like a typical mob man.

Luna followed me when I ascended the stairs to the second floor in search of her grandmother. Mamma's car was in the driveway; therefore, she was home. Maybe she was busy getting ready and that's why she wasn't answering me. Regardless, I had every intention of barging into her room and smothering her with my affection. I hadn't seen her in ten days and I missed her.

A prickling sensation ignited goosebumps on my skin in a foreboding manner as I padded down the hallway leading to her bedroom. My instinct told me something was awry, especially when my hand closed around her doorknob and I heard an odd, dissonant *thump, thump, thump* sound.

With fear drumming in my chest, I shoved the door open.

And came face-to-face with every child's worst nightmare.

At first, I was frozen at the threshold, unbelieving.

Two seconds later, I actually registered the horrendous sight.

Mamma.

Papà.

Moaning. Dirty-talking. Having sex under the covers.

I screamed, horrified.

Their heads whipped in my direction and they screamed too.

I screamed louder, with Luna joining the chorus.

"*Cristo Santo!*" I wailed and covered my eyes, whirling around. "What have I done in my life to deserve coming home to this blasphemy!"

"Gabriela!" they yelled angrily in unison.

"Lord, forgive me for I have accidentally sinned by stumbling upon the most vomit-inducing scene!" I exclaimed, my voice booming. Blood pumped through my veins furiously as I stomped down the hallway. "Where's the bleach in this house? I need to forget ever having witnessed this immoral, extramarital act that will leave me scarred forever!"

I all but ran to the kitchen with Luna hot on my heels, fighting the urge to gag.

I was going to be sick.

God, please, just take me. Right now. I'm not one of your strongest soldiers. I don't think I can ever come back from this.

But God had other plans for me, so my only solution was uncorking the wine bottle I bought and pouring myself a healthy amount.

My cat meowed by my feet, eyes wide. She was judging her grandparents too.

"I know, Luna, I'm just as disgusted as you." My hand shook as I brought the wineglass to my mouth for a sip.

I hadn't even swallowed when the two culprits hastened down the stairs, their faces flushed. Mamma wore a silk robe in a hurry and Papà a pair of inside-out linen pants.

"Gabriela, *per favore*," Mamma cried, entering the kitchen. "It's not what it looks like!"

"It's exactly what it looks like," Papà retaliated, shooting Mamma a mild glare. At least he had the decency to send me a half-assed apologetic expression. "But we are sorry you saw that, *cara mia*."

"Apologize to your grandchild too."

Luna squared up, giving them the full force of her haughty gaze.

I tapped my foot impatiently.

Papà rolled his eyes and palmed his forehead. Mamma felt guilty enough to say, "We're sorry you saw that, Luna. There. Happy?"

Luna hissed.

And I was far from happy. Disturbed and wholly grossed-out was more like it.

In all the years that we lived together, I'd never once caught my parents in the act. In fact, most days I pretended that I was dropped on their doorstep via pelican and that was my birth story.

I took another sip of the wine to wash down the bad taste in my mouth, watching my parents over the rim of the glass. They squirmed, embarrassed.

The tension in the kitchen was so thick, you could slice it with a knife.

"What are you doing here anyways?" Mamma huffed, patting a hand over her disheveled hair. "You weren't supposed to arrive for another two hours."

"Oh, so it's my fault that I arrived early?" I threw back at her reprimanding tone. "Mamma, I texted you! But clearly y-you both were busy doing—ugh!" I narrowed my eyes and waggled a finger between them. "How long has this been going on? Explain yourselves."

Suddenly, no one could meet my accusatory stare.

The puzzle pieces finally clicked into position and I had a light-bulb moment.

Oh my God.

"This…This never stopped, did it?" Shocked, I shook my head. "All this time, you've both claimed to hate each other, and yet…"

In between all of Mamma's failed relationships, she and Papà never stopped being together. Not in the physical sense. Despite being divorced, it was obvious they fell back into their old habits like nothing had changed. They were still each other's one true match, no matter how dysfunctional. Even after twenty-plus years, their love never died. It was obvious they were still crazy for one another.

Deciding to be the adult in this situation, I swiped Mamma's car keys from the kitchen counter. "Let's go. I'll drive."

They both exchanged a concerned glance.

Papà asked, "Go where?"

"To church!" I yelled, half joking, but half meaning it. "You both obviously need a trip to the confessional. I'm sure Father Domenico would be delighted to help you cleanse your sins. Afterwards, you can renew your vows!"

Bewildered, Mamma sputtered, "C-cut it out! We are not getting married just because you caught us. It was a mistake. This slip-up won't happen again."

Yeah, right. Now I was certain they'd had more slipups than I could count on two hands.

Papà arched a dark brow in her direction. "You don't want to marry me?"

A slight hesitation on Mamma's part. "No, Enzo."

"Why not?" There was a note of unmissable yearning in his words and my previous anger softened at the edges. I felt bad for both of them. Mamma knew exactly who Papà was when she married him. The mob was part of his blood. Compromises and sacrifices were needed to make any relationship work. Somewhere along the way, they both forgot that fact.

Papà should have made an effort to reduce his long working nights, and Mamma should have communicated her feelings more.

"Please." Mamma scoffed, but there was no weight to the sound. "There are better men out there. I just need to keep dating until I find the one for me."

Well, shit.

I exhaled a long breath.

Not only were they crazy for one another, but they were both *plain crazy*.

At her statement, Papà went from her besotted lover to the ex-husband who loved riling her up. His posture straightened, his chest puffed, and he wiped the lovesick expression on his face with a casual hand across his stubbled salt-and-pepper jaw, his signature scowl taking its usual place.

Forget the confessional. These two needed couples' therapy to solve their issues.

"Hey, guys." I tried to defuse the situation before it escalated. "How about we pretend like this never happened? Hunter will be here in less than two hours. I'll start setting up the table and you can go get dressed. I promise, you'll love him. He's such a sweetheart—"

"What did you say, Lucia?" Papà drawled in a low voice. "You want to keep dating until you find *the one for you*?"

I rubbed my temple. There was no use pretending that a battle wasn't about to break out in this household. I already knew how it would go down: with kitchen utensils and a passionate screaming match. They were doomed to be together, just like Nonna said, and I should leave them to untangle their own mess.

"Yeah." Mamma crossed her arms over her chest. "That's exactly what I said."

"Even after your last boytoy ran away with his tail between his legs?"

Horror splashed over Mamma's features. "How would you know Neal ran away with his tail between his legs?"

Papà's silence spoke volumes.

She connected the dots, red-faced. "Are you…Are you telling me that you threatened Neal so he'd break up with me?"

Papà leaned against the kitchen doorway, entirely too relaxed for a man who was about to have his ass whooped. "I told him I'd kill him if he didn't break up with you and he pissed his pants like a pathetic fool. Is that the kind of man you want to date?"

Mamma inhaled long and sharp, then spat through gritted teeth, "Is this why every single man I date breaks up with me abruptly? Because of you?"

"We both know you only dated those men to piss me off. Luckily for you, it worked." Papà's chin jutted and he smirked arrogantly. "I've threatened every single boyfriend of yours since we divorced. If a hefty cheque didn't get the job done, then my fists did. Think of it, Lucia. If they really loved you, they'd never leave you, regardless of what I did to them. But they did and the truth remains that the only man who loves you with his entire heart, mind, and soul is me. *I* take care of you, *I* provide for you, *I* would die for you. You know it too. You're just being stubborn because it's easier than admitting that you want to give us another try."

Wow.

I almost wished I weren't surprised. Papà always appeared so blasé when Mamma got a new boyfriend. Now I realized it was because it didn't matter who she dated. Mamma would never sleep with them—like she'd sleep with him—and within sixty calendar days, her current boyfriend would kick the curb.

Papà had ensured it, in his own unorthodox way.

Mamma picked up a spatula from the utensil crock and whipped it in his direction.

"Enzo," she spoke with an eerie calm. "I'm going to fucking kill you."

"I'd like to see you try, Lucia. You love me too much to see me dead." Still, he backed away as she advanced towards him. "Just remember, I did this for us. You're mine and I've always been yours."

Fuming, she rounded the table while he scurried to the other side. "I'm going to butcher you to pieces for every tear I shed from heartbreak."

"With what, that spatula in your hand?" he goaded, but the smile on his lips told her everything she needed to know. He won. She lost. "Good luck. You can't even hurt a fly. Plus, if you kill me, you'll miss me too much. Who else is going to put up with your needy nature, *principessa*—"

Like a woman scorned, she pounced on him with a battle cry, spatula at the ready.

The doorbell rang that very instant.

"I'll get it!" I declared all too happily and got out of the kitchen before they started destroying things.

Luna strutted after me.

Neither of us was fazed. When both parents had lived under the same roof, this was a daily occurrence in our home.

I swung open the door with a bright smile on my face, already knowing who it would be. "*Ciao*, Nonna! I'm so happy to see you!"

My grandmother stood on the front porch with her cane and a dish of tiramisu in her hands. Behind her, a taxi exited. "*Piccola*, I'm so happy to see you too."

I hugged her, breathing in her homey smell. "You're here early. Not that I'm complaining." I smacked a noisy kiss on her wrinkly cheek. "I missed you."

"I missed you too." She smiled. "Your papà was supposed to pick me up in half an hour, but I had an inkling that something was wrong. Hence why I decided to come on my own."

"Your instincts are on point." I grabbed the tiramisu dish from her so she could enter inside with her cane. "Oh, I love your outfit. You look so cute."

She gave me a slow twirl, elated. "We match."

We both wore black dresses. Mine was form-fitting and down to mid thigh, coupled with sheer stockings that had little black hearts on them. Nonna's was ankle length and billowy. She accessorized with the cutest rhinestone crossbody purse and jeweled clips to keep her grey hair away from her face. And blood red lipstick, of course. That was a classic Bellafiore women staple.

"That we do."

On cue, a loud *vaffanculo* rang in the background.

"Nonna...do you still carry holy water in your purse? We have a bunch of sinners in this house."

Nonna shut the front door, locked it, and peered down the hallway to see a sliver of the chaos in the kitchen. Mamma and Papà went at each other's throats like dogs. A plate got thrown on the floor. Glass shattered. Curses were exchanged.

"Oh!" She reared back. "What's going on?"

"Okay, so basically..." I gave her the entire rundown in under thirty seconds. Nonna emulated the cross sign when I told her what I walked in on. By the end of my storytelling, she was shocked but not surprised at their antics.

"Now"—I flicked a glance towards the kitchen—"it looks like Mamma picked up a knife and she's going to stab him."

"She won't stab him," Nonna said. "Also, Enzo's like a cat. He's got nine lives."

"Yeah, well, if she does stab him, he'll be down to eight."

"Meh. A little bit of fighting is good for the soul."

"Shouldn't you be more concerned about your son's well-being?"

She shrugged. "He's a hellion, just like your grandfather was—may his soul rest in peace. Men like that deserve a good spanking every so often. Let your mamma berate him. Furthermore, she's doing it out of sheer pleasure, not anger." She waved her cane in their general direction. "Secretly, the part of her that fell in love with his dangerous side loves that he was crazy enough to sabotage her dates. They're just letting out some much-needed steam. Trust me, Gabriela. Their passion lies in their fight— it's how they thrive. They were like that even when they were young. But you, my child, are an angel compared to them." She patted my face lovingly. "That's because you take after me, of course."

I chuckled. "Of course I do."

She bent down to coo at Luna, who was pawing at her leg for attention. "Hello, my pretty little baby. My other angel who takes after me. How are you? Yes, yes, I've missed you too. I have some treats with your name on them."

While she rummaged through her purse for Luna's treats, I observed my parents over my shoulder. "Um, Nonna, they don't seem like they're fighting anymore." My eyes squinted in disbelief. "Ew. They're kissing now and oh my God, Papà is down on one knee, proposing to her!"

All three of us crowded into the hallway to watch the scene unfold.

"Yes!" Mamma cried out dramatically, a pool of broken glass surrounding them. "Yes, I'll marry you again, Enzo!"

The last hour leading up to Hunter's arrival was a rollercoaster of emotions. From the surprise at seeing the proposal, to congratulating my parents, to cleaning up the kitchen, and to mentally winding down from this ridiculous high.

Hunter would be here in ten minutes and Nonna decided it was time for a last-minute family meeting. We were all gathered in the living room. Mamma and Papà, showered and dressed to the nines, were sitting in the love seat. Mamma blushed and cast him side-long glances. Papà was displeased at Nonna summoning him against his will. But whenever his eyes connected with Mamma's, his face softened.

After years of fighting and denying their feelings, they were finally at peace and like teenagers in love.

Mamma also couldn't stop staring at the shiny five-carat rock on her left hand's finger. It winked under the chandelier's light in all its impressive glory. Apparently, Papà never stopped carrying around the diamond ring he proposed to her with more than two decades ago. Now it was back where it rightfully belonged.

Nonna sat in the armchair in front of them with Luna in her lap, and I was perched on the armrest.

"Let's set some ground rules before Gabriela's boyfriend arrives." Nonna hedged her cigarette holder in my direction and I lit her vice with a Zippo. She brought it to her lips for a puff. "Firstly, I want both of you *bozos* to be on your best behaviour tonight. This is an important occasion and none of you will ruin it with your theatrics"—she glanced pointedly at Mamma, then at Papà—"or your macho bullshit. Understood?"

He uncrossed his arms from his chest and stood up. "This lecture is entirely unnecessary—ow!"

Nonna whacked him on the shin with the end of her cane, glaring. "Shut up and sit back down, Enzo. I'm not done talking and you won't interrupt me again."

Papà killed for a living—had murdered men for simply staring at him the wrong way. Yet under his mother's scolding, he shrank back like a kid being grounded.

"Secondly, this is Gabriela's special evening." A plume of smoke curled out of Nonna's mouth. "We're all aware that you both have always had bad timing your whole lives. Getting engaged right now, of all days, was a choice. Nonetheless, here we are." She sighed. "With that being said, your engagement announcement will have to wait. I refuse to allow you to steal my granddaughter's thunder any more than you already have. This is her night. So no talk of rings or weddings. Understood?"

My parents had the gall to look embarrassed and simply nodded. It was good enough for me. I wasn't angry that they'd gotten engaged today, but I loved and respected Nonna's need to stand up for me. Tonight was about me formally introducing Hunter to my family as my boyfriend and I wanted that to be the key focus.

"Thirdly." She took another puff of her cigarette. "You've traumatized my granddaughter and great-granddaughter. I'm expecting them to be fully compensated for punitive damages. Gabriela, begin with the list of demands."

I stopped my mouth from twitching into a smile. I was having entirely too much fun. Mamma and Papà narrowed their eyes. Nonna hid her laugh with a cough.

"Number one." I opened my thumb from my closed fist. "Luna needs a new cat tree. The one in this home is old and worn out. Only the best for my girl."

It was the least my parents could do after putting us through years of their soap opera.

Papà ground his teeth. "Fine, a new cat tree for Luna. Easy enough."

"Number two." I stuck out my index finger. "I'd like you to go to couples therapy before you tie the knot again. That is non-negotiable. For the sake of all our mental health, you need to sort your stuff out."

"Gabriela…" he warned testily.

I stood my ground.

Mamma relented, placing a hand on her soon-to-be husband's thigh. "It's okay. We'll go."

"Excellent." I beamed and unfolded my middle finger. "Number three: Nonna and I are more than happy to be the bridesmaids at your wedding. However, Nonna says she refuses to wear bright yellow. According to photographic evidence from your first wedding, she says that the colour you picked for her dress made her resemble Big Bird from Sesame Street."

Mamma gasped. "It was a beautiful shade!"

Nonna tsked. "I looked horrendous, Lucia. Absolutely not."

"Fine." Mamma sulked, then perked up, glancing at Papà with adoration. "Maybe the colour palette this time can be pastels."

Papa kissed her cheek. "Whatever you want, *principessa*."

I cleared my throat to gain their attention before they started embarrassing themselves further by accidentally making out on the sofa. "Last demand." I gulped and Nonna patted my arm encouragingly. "I'd like a car."

Papa shot a *you're-kidding-me* look my way. "You want me to buy you a car when you don't even drive, Gabriela? Get your license first, then we'll revisit this idea."

"I'm learning how to drive—no thanks to both of you. I signed up for classes and Hunter takes me out for practice too. I'll have my license in the upcoming months if all goes well."

Mamma and Nonna were happy to hear it, especially the part where Hunter was teaching me. "Enzo," Mamma pleaded. "Please get it for her."

He scrubbed a hand over his face, knowing there was no use in arguing.

"Please, Papà. I want something red. Oh, and with a drop top." I glanced at my cat. "Luna and I really love fresh air. A convertible will suit us quite well. Right, baby?"

Luna meowed on cue.

"Seems you Bellafiore women exist solely to make demands out of me," he grumbled. "All right. I'll buy you a car. Is that all?"

I hid my smug smile at our successful negotiations. "Yes, that's all. *Ti voglio bene*, Papà."

Like the soft teddy bear that he was on the inside, he melted the second I told him I loved him. He was wrapped around my finger and I was going to have a brand-new car by the end of the month.

The familiar chime of the doorbell resonated through the house.

I instantly hopped off the armrest. "I'll get it."

Behind me, Nonna echoed again, "Remember what I said: best behaviour, everyone."

Everything in my universe seemed to right itself when I unlocked the front door and saw Hunter standing there.

He was handsome as ever in a white button-down, charcoal pants, polished shoes, and a black wool coat tailored to his muscular frame. His inky black hair was pulled back in a low bun. Due to the heavy wind, a few strands that couldn't be tamed tendrilled down the sides of his face artfully. His blue gaze drank me in with a hungry, *I-missed-you* quality.

He held three red rose bouquets.

"Hi." I gravitated towards him, opening my arms for a hug. "You made it."

"Hi, baby." He bent down to kiss my forehead, hugging me. "I did. Wouldn't miss tonight for the world."

"Are these for me?"

Hunter smiled and handed me a bouquet. "You know they are. For you, your mom, and your grandmother."

My sweet *principe*. "If you keep buying me roses at this rate, I'll have no more room left in my apartment."

"That's my plan." He tucked a strand behind my ear. "Then you'll have no choice but to spend all your time at mine."

I blinked. "Luna and I already do."

"Good." He kissed me again and murmured cheekily, "Let's keep it that way."

I bit my bottom lip to tame my goofy smile, but it was no use. I loved him so much.

"Come in." I tugged him inside. "They're excited to see you."

I towed us into the living room, announcing, "Hunter's here."

Mamma, Papà, and Nonna were already standing on their feet, anticipating us.

There was a beat where Hunter appeared anxious, but then he swallowed down his nerves and I watched him morph into his confidence, his broad shoulders straightening.

"Hello," he said warmly.

Mamma was the first to step away from the rest. She hugged him. "Hi, Hunter. Welcome to our home."

"Thank you for inviting me." He handed her a bouquet. "These are for you."

"Oh, my." She hedged him a teasing expression. "Such a gentleman. Gabriela, does he do this often?"

I nodded proudly and hooked my arm with his, my fingers gripping his bicep. "Hunter brings me roses all the time."

"How sweet of you," Mamma said. "These are beautiful, Hunter. Thank you."

Hunter's cheeks pinkened. "My pleasure."

Nonna approached Hunter with her cane, grinning. "And those must be for me. Unless you tell me they're for Enzo, in which case I'll be sorely disappointed."

He grinned as well. "They are for you."

She grabbed her bouquet and put her arms around Hunter, pecking his cheek. "It's good to finally meet the man my granddaughter has been obsessing over."

"Obsessing over, huh?" Hunter said, winking at me.

"Oh, yes," Nonna returned in her typical boisterous fashion. "She told me all about you during our last call." She mimicked a phone's cradle with her thumb and pinky finger, bringing it to her ear and mouth to imitate me. "*Nonna, he's perfect and so handsome. Like a real-life Prince Charming. I really, really like him.*"

"Hey, I do not sound like that!" I inserted, chuckling. Hunter chuckled too, pleased. I told him all the time how much I liked him, but hearing it from another important person in my life must fortify the fact. I didn't even mind being the butt of a small joke if it helped reassure him of my feelings.

"You do, Gabriela." She nudged Hunter with her elbow. "I don't think I've ever seen her this smitten before. It's adorable. You clearly mean a lot to her."

"For what it's worth," he rasped, "she means everything to me."

My heart raced.

Nonna's expression gentled. "Oh."

Behind us, Mamma pretended to swoon and faint.

Papà cleared his throat and unbuttoned his suit jacket, pushing the lapels aside as he shoved his hands into his pockets. A power move to purposely expose the gun sitting at his waistband.

I resisted the urge to roll my eyes.

"Sir." Hunter redirected his attention towards him, extending a hand for a shake. "It's nice to meet you again."

Papà eyed Hunter's hand with disdain, leaving it suspended in the air.

Hunter, thankfully, didn't balk under his scrutiny, waiting for him to acknowledge it.

Papà assessed him the way he did every man in my life and without removing the scowl from his face, he reluctantly grabbed Hunter's hand for a shake, making sure to squeeze extra hard.

My boyfriend didn't flinch.

"It was nicer meeting you the first time," Papà said with a shark grin. "When you were only my daughter's *friend*."

I glared at him.

"Enzo," Nonna said through gritted teeth. "*Stai zitto*."

Hunter didn't take offense.

Before Papà could further instigate Hunter, Mamma's falsely jovial voice interrupted in the background. "Dinner's ready, everyone!"

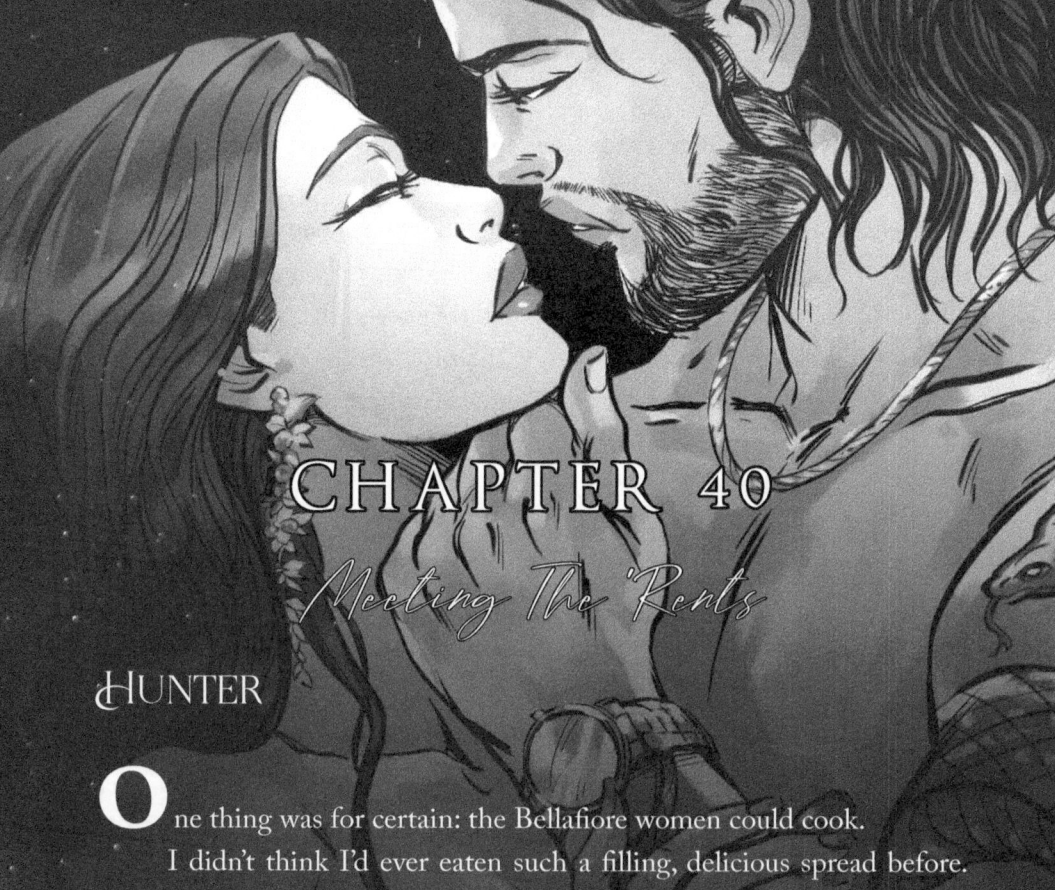

CHAPTER 40
Meeting The 'Rents

HUNTER

One thing was for certain: the Bellafiore women could cook.

I didn't think I'd ever eaten such a filling, delicious spread before. Between my girlfriend, her mom, and her grandmother, they kept adding more food to my plate till it was piled high, insisting I try *this* and *that* and *this*.

Luna was eating with us too, currently curled near my feet with her own bowl, pausing every now and then to glance up at me. We hadn't seen each other in over twenty-four hours. She missed me. Same as I missed her. I brought my hand down to pet her head and she leaned into my touch with a meow. How quickly she and Gabriela wormed their way into my heart. Now I couldn't imagine my life without either of them.

Dinner was far from a quiet affair. Gabriela's Mamma and Nonna peppered me with a multitude of questions. When was my birthday? What was my favourite colour? How many siblings did I have? What were my hobbies? How did I balance football and academics?

Naturally, they were extremely curious as I was the first man Gabriela brought home since the last fucker. I was all too happy to answer their questions and ask some of my own. I found that all three Bellafiore women

435

had a natural charisma to them—the kind that attracted people to them like bees to honey.

As an introvert, I sometimes struggled when silence sparked in the middle of a conversation, but I had nothing to worry about with this social bunch. There were no awkward pauses and they instantly made me feel like I belonged right there, sitting amongst their fold, at the head of the table.

By the time dinner was swept away and dessert was laid on the table, I'd successfully won over Mrs. Bellafiore's—or Lucia, as she demanded I address her—and Nonna's hearts.

"Was everything to your liking, Hunter?" Lucia asked, spearing a spoon into her tiramisu.

"Absolutely." I smiled at her and Nonna. "You're both wonderful cooks. Now I know where Gabriela gets her culinary skills from." My eyes strayed back to my beloved. "And beauty."

Gabriela grinned fondly and kissed my cheek.

Lucia placed a hand on her chest in an 'Aw' motion and Nonna nodded approvingly while sipping her drink. "No wonder our Gabriela is so smitten."

A loud throat clearing drew our attention towards the other end of the table.

Enzo Bellafiore spent the entirety of dinner glowering and going as far as placing his gun—barrel angled towards me—next to his charger plate. I didn't miss the subtle threat. Earlier, Lucia had demanded he put his weapon away and he ignored her.

He'd remained silent from the minute we sat down for dinner, letting the women steer the conversation while he evaluated me like I was a convict and not his daughter's boyfriend. Though perhaps those two terms were synonymous to the Bellafiore patriarch.

I didn't let that bother me much, knowing it would take time for a man like him to warm up to my presence. Plus, I'd been around his type of mob man for years now, courtesy of my friendship with Josh. I wasn't fazed or afraid. My only concern lay in proving to him that I deserved a fair chance.

No one would treat his daughter like I would.

"Hunter," Enzo's voice echoed with authority. "Do you know how to shoot a gun?"

Nonna grumbled under her breath, disguising it with another sip of her drink. Lucia discreetly palmed her forehead, muttering an inaudible prayer. Gabriela froze, eyeing Enzo. Even Luna, now sitting in my lap, lifted her head enough to stare at her grandfather's oddly timed question.

I smiled. "Are you offering to teach me, sir?"

His scowl deepened. "My daughter is an independent woman who can take care of herself, but I would feel better knowing she's with someone who could actually protect her. And judging from the ongoing dinner conversation, I don't know if you have what it takes."

Fuck.

That stung more than I'd like to admit.

Indirectly, he was saying that he wasn't sure I could be a part of their world. I wasn't raised like him, in the underbelly of Montardor's criminal empires. That much was obvious. But that didn't mean I couldn't protect Gabriela if the situation demanded it.

On cue, all three women and Luna glared at Enzo.

"Papà," Gabriela chided through gritted teeth. "That was extremely uncalled for."

I'd anticipated this exact behaviour from Enzo. I wouldn't let his words deter me. He was testing me, trying to determine if I was fit to be by his daughter's side, and I couldn't even fault him for it.

Sitting up straighter, I calmly took a sip of my drink before earnestly saying, "With all due respect, sir, I understand your concerns and they are valid. But I would appreciate it if you gave me a fair chance to prove myself worthy of being by your daughter's side." I exchanged a quick glance with Gabriela, who observed me with bated breath, before focusing back on Enzo. "I do know how to wield a gun. I've been going to the shooting range with Josh for the last week. Though I may not possess the kind of skills you do, which I understand come with years of experience, I can fend for myself. And Gabriela too. If ever she's in a distressing situation where she needs me, I'll move Heaven and Earth to be there for her—I'll do whatever it takes to ensure her safety, even at the expense of my own."

It got utterly quiet in the room.

Enzo never took his gaze off me, but the scowl misted away and gave leeway to a neutral set of features.

Wanting to assure him further, I quietly added, "We may have been raised in different worlds, but it doesn't change the fact that I'm with Gabriela now. Her protection and happiness will always be a priority to me. I would do anything for her. I am completely devoted to her."

Gabriela, Lucia, and Nonna appeared moved by my admission.

Enzo nodded, satisfied with my reply. "Good," he stated. "If that ever changes, I'll make you regret it."

I passed his test with flying colours and the relief was palpable in the room.

He inclined his wine glass in my direction in a brief display of truce.

I smiled and did the same.

And we resumed eating dessert.

"That went well, don't you think?"

The nervous bite in Gabriela's tone made me smile. "I'd say so."

She handed me a plate and I dried it with a washcloth. We were on dish duty, having insisted upon it, since Lucia and Nonna cooked. The rest of the Bellafiores had congregated in the living room with their glasses of grappa, awarding us a moment of privacy.

Gabriela rinsed another plate under the faucet, suds disappearing down the drain. "My family hasn't scared you off, right?"

"No." I leaned down to kiss her forehead. Her body relaxed under my touch. "I'm never letting you go, sweetheart. You're stuck with me."

How could I let you go, when I'm this *in love with you?*

Relief splashed over her face. "I was worried you'd change your mind after witnessing my papà's antics."

"I enjoyed having dinner with your family, Gabriela. Your mom and grandmother are sweet and made me feel very welcomed. I liked hearing their funny anecdotes and your Nonna's latest book review." We shared a quick chuckle. "As for your dad, I'm not worried. He'll warm up to me with time. I can't say I blame him for saying the things he said. You're his only daughter and he loves you very much. After the ordeal with Franco, it's only natural that he's extra cautious of whoever you bring home."

"You're right, he'll come around and then he'll grow to lo—" She suddenly paused, clearing her throat. "Like you the way I have."

Tonight was a big step, but I hoped Enzo came around to liking, if not at the very least, accepting me.

We washed our hands with soap and wiped them on a clean towel.

Gabriela broke the pensive silence. "Sometimes I forget that he's Vance's second-in-command. Though I grew up around this life, I wasn't always exposed to the bad side of it, usually kept sheltered for my own good. Despite me being aware of who my papà was, what he did, and how he made his money, I'd rarely seen his rude side since he's only ever been tender around his family. I suppose him questioning you that way caught me off guard—nor did I like it. But I understand where he's coming from and I just wanted to make sure you were okay, Hunter."

I loved that she worried for me, but she had no reason to. I was perfectly fine.

"I'm okay. Don't worry. Dinner went well and I had a good time." I cupped her face. "And I'm not going anywhere. Not even an army could pry me off of you, Gabriela. That's how deep I'm in, baby."

She smiled finally and covered my hands with her own. "And if you stray too far from me, I'll yank you back where you belong."

"I'm banking on it." I kissed her lips. "You look so beautiful tonight in your little black dress." *Kiss*. "And these heart-shaped earrings." *Kiss*. "And these sweet, red lips that I just want to keep kissing until I run out of air."

She giggled as I pressed one reverent kiss after the other.

Queen of my heart.

She was so goddamn lovely.

All I wanted was to protect and love her until my dying breath.

Now her hands were coasting down my sides, one pausing over my right rib…where I had the Pegasus constellation inked. We went to the tattoo parlour a few days ago to get our inks. Though she'd jokingly suggested I get 'Gabriela's Pretty Boy' the night of the Halloween party, the idea of our stars tattooed on my skin was more enticing to her. My skin was her canvas. Whatever she wanted, I would have gotten it. And in return, she got a stunning cursive and thin serpent tattoo down her spine.

"Shall we head back to the living room?" I asked. "They're probably wondering what's taking us so long."

"They definitely know you're in here stealing kisses."

I puffed out a laugh before stealing another kiss. "Guilty."

Gabriela filled two more grappa glasses for us. Hand in hand, we joined the others in the living room. An old vinyl played on a record, decorating the atmosphere with musical notes. Enzo, Lucia, and Nonna were locked in a discussion, so Gabriela and I headed straight for the large bay window. Luna was sitting on the sill to watch the neighbourhood.

Sensing our approach, she turned around and meowed.

"Hi, Luna," Gabriela cooed, caressing her.

But Luna appeared restless, pawing at the window and meowing. As if trying to redirect our attention to the street lining the Bellafiore home…

Where an unmarked silver sedan rested at the curb.

Narrowing my eyes, I glanced out the window with Gabriela.

"Who is that?" my girlfriend questioned in a thoughtful, quiet manner.

A shadow moved inside the car.

"Are you expecting anyone?" I asked.

She shook her head. "No—"

Gabriela didn't even get to finish her sentence.

Suddenly, the car pulled away with screeching tires and gunned it down the street.

Disappearing from view like it had never been there.

CHAPTER 41
Ghost From The Past

HUNTER

Saturday afternoon, I was at a packed MacGregor with Josh, Cade, and Shaun after finishing at the Remingtons' shooting range to grab a bite. I'd been spending more time there, perfecting my aim and familiarizing myself with different firearms. I credited years of football for honing my marksmanship skills, for I hit one bullseye after another at today's session.

There was a part of me that wished Enzo Bellafiore were there so I could make him eat his words from last week's dinner.

Weaving through the busy bodies of patrons, a waitress finally brought over our food and drinks.

Josh's phone pinged incessantly as we began to eat.

"You want to get that, Mr. Popular?" Shaun teased, popping a fry into his mouth.

Josh picked up his phone, unlocked his screen, and said, "Oh, it's the girls."

Cade perked up. "The girls?"

At his brother's inquisitive tone, Josh shrugged and plucked a straw, unwrapped it, and dipped it into his soda. "It's our group chat. Mine, Ella, Darla, Dacia, and Hera's."

"Excuse me, you have a group chat with the girls?" Shaun asked incredulously.

"I do," he quipped.

"Why are you in this group chat?" Cade appeared affronted. "And why aren't we?"

"Because I'm cooler and more fun than all of you combined?" Josh gestured at us with his drink before taking a hearty sip. "And I'm resourceful? Not to mention, they added me. Sometimes I even get invited to their hangouts."

Amused, I asked, "You're allowed at their girls' night?"

"'Course, I am." Josh shrugged like it was no biggie, while Cade and Shaun battled with their newfound jealousy. "I'm in charge of bringing the tea and cookies to their gossip sesh."

"Add us to the group chat," Shaun ordered. "We deserve to be there just as much as you."

Cade nodded, looking grim. "Agreed."

Josh raised his hands in surrender. "Listen, I'm not betraying their trust. If they wanted both of you there, they would have invited you."

"But you're there," Shaun spat. "How is that fair?"

Josh snickered. "To be honest, I earned my spot after all the labour I've done for them."

"What labour is that?" I inquired, slicing into my chicken cutlet with a knife.

"Well," he drawled dramatically, keeping us on edge. "There was that one time where they kidnapped me when I was high as fuck so they could break into someone's house and have me sift through their laptop for intel. Not to mention, my poor back was used like a stepping stone. Ergo, I've put in the work and deserve to be in the group chat. The rest of you have done nothing of the sort. Therefore, you aren't granted the honour of being there. Plain and simple."

I remembered Josh recounting that to me last year. It made me chuckle then and it made me chuckle now.

Cade and Shaun weren't happy. The latter cleared his throat and folded his arms across his chest, leaning back in his chair. "Fine. At least tell us what you talk about in this group chat."

Josh clicked his tongue and picked up his club sandwich. "Why? Afraid that they're talking shit about you guys?"

"Are they?" Cade hedged.

"Nah." Josh took a bite and chewed thoughtfully, dragging it out while both men stared at him in impatience. "But I will tell you this one piece of info. There's this guy named Idris that Hera recently met and I'm pretty sure they're going on a date soon."

Cade threw an alarmed glance at Shaun.

Who had completely frozen over.

I was about to say something when my eyes unceremoniously caught a figure leaving the back offices of MacGregor before blending into the crowd and heading towards the exit leading to the side alleyway.

It was a split second.

But I caught *him*.

I would recognize that face anywhere.

What were the odds that I would see him here, after all these years, on an unassuming weekend afternoon in a crowded bar, appearing like a ghost from my past?

I scraped my chair back and stood up, telling my friends, "I'll be back."

They called after me, but I was already power-walking after him. Afraid that if I wasn't fast enough, he'd slip through my fingers and disappear for longer this time.

The noise from MacGregor drowned in the background as my vision became laser-focused. My attention was solely on his broad back, cloaked in a long black coat.

As I flung open the exit door and sped after him, my heart pounded and the cold fall air nipped at my skin. The alleyway was deserted, save for an inconspicuous charcoal sedan.

I caught up to him right as he neared the car and hollered his name, "Donovan!"

He stiffened, pausing.

A hand went to his waistband, probably to cradle his gun, before he whirled around and pinned me with a wary gaze.

He stared at me like he was seeing a stranger.

It took three seconds for recognition to flash in his expression. "Hunter?"

I smiled and advanced towards him. "Hey, Don."

A slow smile spread across his face in reciprocation.

Donovan Shaw still had that larger-than-life demeanour and intimidating stature to him. Gone were the boyish features I remembered. Now they were refined with age. His brown eyes harboured steeliness, like he'd seen much of life and wasn't impressed, and he sported a short brown beard, a hint unkempt like his tousled hair. And that ever-present gangster swagger of his remained as he crossed the six feet separating us and dragged me into his arms for a brotherly hug.

"Hey, Hunt." He clapped my back once, strongly. "Didn't recognize you there for a moment. When did you get so tall, kid?"

We were the same height now. "Right about the time you left."

There was sorrow in his eyes, mixed with something bittersweet. Not a single part of me expected an apology. At the end of the day, Donovan had to do what was right for him, and if that was escaping the city and the memories of his and Heidi's past, then so be it. I wasn't one to hold a grudge.

"How are you?" he rasped, tucking his hands in his coat pockets.

"I'm good." I gestured back at MacGregor's exit door. "I was having lunch with my friends when I thought I saw you. Chased you down to make sure I wasn't seeing a mirage."

He cracked a rare grin I hadn't seen in years. "I'm surprised you spotted me."

He used to be the closest thing I'd had to a brother. I hoped he remembered that. "You're family, Don. I'll always spot you in a crowd full of people."

He reached forward to ruffle my hair the way he did when I was young. It brought back old memories of whenever I finished playing a game and he took me to a pizza parlour for my post-football treat.

"How are you?" Last I remembered, he left Montardor about five years ago. "What are you doing here?"

A muscle in Donovan's jaw ticked. "Had some business with Mac."

"Oh." I shoved my own hands in my pockets. "What kind?"

"He's getting old, wants to sell this joint, and I'm buying it off of him."

"Wow. Congratulations." MacGregor was one of the oldest Irish pubs in the city, with a long history and a loyal clientele. It was a smart and interesting move. "Does this mean you're back in the city?"

I didn't ask him where he'd been. If he wanted to reveal that tidbit, he would himself.

"Not exactly." He relaxed against his car and chin-nodded at the establishment. "Mac is still going to manage it until he's ready to retire and I'll be hands-off. Plus, I have other business to take care of."

Business that wasn't here, was what he meant to say.

Donovan looked like he wanted to say something else but was fighting against it. His jaw clenched. His fingers combed frustratedly through his hair. Eventually, he sighed. "How is she?"

In that instant, all I felt was sadness for both of them. He couldn't say Heidi's name and she never said Donovan's either. Not since he left.

"She's fine." I hesitated, then bit the bullet. "Still thinks about you."

Raw pain burst over his features.

Hearing those words surprised him. Did he really expect Heidi to forget he ever existed? It was evident that he hadn't forgotten her either.

Donovan swallowed roughly and shutters fell over his expression, rendering him a blank slate. He squeezed my shoulder in farewell. "It was nice seeing you, Hunt. Take care of yourself."

I hoped it wasn't the last time I saw him. "You too, Don."

"Do me a favour?" he asked as he opened his car's door.

"Anything."

"You didn't see me. As far as anyone is concerned, I was never here."

Meaning he didn't want Heidi or Jaden to know.

I respected his choice. "Understood."

We said goodbye and he drove away. Though despondency lingered, for the most part I was happy that I got to see Donovan again, even if it was under these circumstances.

On my way back into the pub, goosebumps erupted over the exposed skin of my forearms and an odd sensation slithered down my spine.

I turned my head to eye the busy street.

It was hard to tell with the amount of bustling traffic, but for a second, I could have sworn that I spotted a hooded figure watching me from across.

They retreated into an alleyway, blending with the rest of the passersby.

I chalked it up to my eyes playing tricks on me and went back into MacGregor.

CHAPTER 42

Glorious Victory

GABRIELA

In the two weeks leading up to the Panthers' championship, Hunter was busier than ever. If he wasn't occupied with school and football games—home and away—then he was spending that time with Luna and me. However, he was always so exhausted that our dates consisted of either hanging out at my place or his and often calling it an early night.

"Once all of this is over"—he yawned as we cuddled in bed—"I'll take you out on a proper date."

Though I loved a good party and an occasion to step out in my best attire, I enjoyed our cozy home dates immensely. There was something heartwarming in cooking for one another, watching TV with our Luna, working on our newfound artsy hobbies, and finishing the night wrapped up in each other's arms.

My lips skimmed his stubbled cheek, pressing a kiss on the high point. "And where will you be taking me?"

"Anywhere you want, Gabby." His tone was soft and tinged with sleep. He tucked his face in my neck and I tightened my arms around him, embracing him like I was his protector. Hunter might be bigger and stronger than me, yet oftentimes I found myself wanting to shield his pure soul from the eyes of this horrid world. Hunter hugged me back and I combed my fingers through his washed strands. I trimmed them the slightest bit tonight to remove any dead ends so his hair remained healthy as ever. "But I…I was thinking of taking you to that upcoming masquerade ball."

He must have overheard me telling Anna and Layla that I wanted to go. "Really?"

"Really." He nuzzled my skin with a series of lazy kisses. "I've never cared to go to these kinds of events until you."

Because I made him want to be seen. Tenderness unfurled in my chest. "I would be delighted to go with you."

"And you'll probably need a new gown so you can go shopping next week with my card," he rasped. "Make sure you buy me a tie, doll. I want to match."

I grinned. "Sounds like a plan."

"Gabby?" He was just about to doze off, slumber pulling at his lids and his deep voice slurring adorably.

When I was faced with this version of Hunter, I sometimes forgot that this was the same sinful, tattooed, alpha man who fucked me raw in various positions until I was screaming loud enough to have the neighbours knocking on our door, asking if we were okay.

"Yes, *bello*?"

"Tell me a dream of yours," he whispered. "Something you want to accomplish in the next fifteen years."

I asked him that same question weeks ago at Club Azul and his answer was imprinted inside of me. Gazing at the glow-in-the-dark Pegasus constellation on the ceiling, I pondered how to best say my truth. Finally, I whispered, "I want to be with you, Hunter. You're my happily ever after."

But he didn't hear me.

His body had gone slack as he succumbed to a peaceful sleep, his arms curved around my body as if he was worried I'd drift away from him.

I wished I could muster the courage to tell him how I really felt. How I loved him, how he was the center of my world, how he was my moon and I was his tides, forever gravitating towards him. But still, an invisible force kept the words rooted deep in my core. Maybe it was irrational, but I was aware that it was the overthinker in me—the one who wanted to do everything perfectly right. And most importantly, the one who wanted to give Hunter a love confession that he would remember for decades to come. This kind-hearted man had waited so long for me. It was the least he deserved.

I kissed Hunter's forehead and eventually fell asleep too.

A few days later, we were on our way to meet Hunter's family.

"I was right," I said as he pulled his car into a circular driveway. "You really are a prince."

The Warren mansion was colossal, located in a gated community on the East Side. An imposing residence that screamed old money and was straight out of a fairy tale, with a manicured lawn and hedges, limestone fountain, and spotlights leading up to the front stairs. There, both his sister, Heidi, and his mom, Hannah, awaited us with eager anticipation.

Hunter stepped out of the Jag and rounded the front to come to my side. He grabbed the flowers, the box of chocolates resting in my lap, and extended a gloved hand for me.

I ambled out in my six-inch stilettos and Hunter kissed the side of my head. "Ready?"

I dusted off my nerves and adjusted my red faux fur coat. "Ready."

Heidi and Hannah met us halfway, buzzing with quiet excitement.

We exchanged greetings and hugs. A fuzzy feeling settled in my chest as I realized that I was essentially meeting my future in-laws. Hunter belonged to me. He was my destiny. Therefore, it was imperative I made a good, lasting impression on the women who raised him.

They were a lovely and welcoming bunch. The daughter and mother duo could easily pass for sisters and had this otherworldly, classy, model-like, dark-haired beauty that I'd only seen in the pages of my fashion magazines. I told them they were gorgeous and they blushed. Heidi told me it was nice to finally meet the girl her brother had been pining over for a year, to which *I* blushed. And Hannah said that I was the first girl Hunter brought home, to which I cheekily replied that I would be the last.

They chuckled.

The Warren women proceeded to show me their home, old baby pictures of Hunter, and showered me with praise as we ate a fantastic four-course dinner. The vain creature inside of me ate up the compliments with a spoon. My future with them appeared bright. Our personalities meshed well and we'd already made plans to go get manicures and pedicures together next week.

"My goodness, you're so cute and tiny. I just want to wrap you up in my arms and never let go," Hannah said, snatching and squeezing me to her in a motherly gesture, right before we set up the table for dessert. I hugged her back, touched by her sweetness. She kissed my forehead. Hunter definitely got his affectionate side from her. "Like a doll."

"That's what I call her, Mom," Hunter chimed in.

"As you should," she told him and focused back on me. "You're beautiful, Gabriela. Tell me; do you take after your mom or dad?"

"Thank you." I smiled. "I get my height and my red hair from my mom. As for my looks, I'd say I'm a good mix between both parents."

"Is that so?" She beamed. "Well, I would love to meet them one day."

Everyone in the room sensed that it was a big step, but it was a step in the right direction nonetheless. "My family would love to meet you and Heidi too. Once football season finishes—" I cast Hunter a meaningful glance over my shoulder and rephrased, "Once *Hunter wins his trophy*, I'll set up a date."

"Once?"

"Yes. I've been going to Hunter's games and he's incredibly gifted. There's no one like him. The only outcome is his team winning the championship."

Her eyes twinkled with something like pride. "You're so sure of him, huh?"

I heard a double entendre in her words. "If there's one thing in my life I'm certain of, it's Hunter."

Including the love I harbour for him.

"Aren't you two the cutest?" Hannah gushed. "Hunter, I really like her."

Hunter watched us the entire time from his perch against the kitchen island counter, his strong arms crossed over his chest. There it was. That soft, possessive look that continuously did me in. "I really like her too."

In my mind, I practically heard the word *love* substituted for *like*.

Two days later, while Hunter was gone for an away game, I was out gown shopping with Anna and Layla for the masquerade ball after finishing an in-class assignment. I made sure to buy a matching tie and two half-face masks for Hunter and me.

Goods secured! —Gabby

I texted him a picture of my shopping bags the minute I set foot in his apartment, using the key he gifted me to let myself in. Hunter's signature cologne lingered in the air. I longed for him. Luna missed her daddy too. The moment she crossed the threshold, she wandered over to lie down on Hunter's couch...in the exact spot he always sat.

I joined her and snapped a picture of us, then sent it to him.

PS: Luna and I miss you 🤍 —Gabby

His replies came forty-five minutes later, after his football game came to an end.

I miss my girls too. —Hunter

Can I call you? —Hunter

Yes 😺 —Gabby

I picked up on the first ring and held my phone in a way so he could see Luna too. "Hi, pretty boy," I greeted. "How was your game?"

Usually, I tended to watch his away games on TV with the girls or on my phone if I was out and about. But I didn't get the chance today due to my other commitments.

"Hi, baby." He was bare-chested in a hotel room, with an ice pack over his shoulder, his torso half-propped up against a headboard. More longing unravelled inside of me. I wanted to be next to him. "Amazing. We crushed it."

I yipped with excitement for him. Luna reared back at the unexpected sound, and Hunter laughed happily. "Congratulations, I knew you'd win!"

"Thank you, Gabby." I loved the light blush on his face. "I'll be back home tomorrow. I can't wait to see you and Luna."

"We can't wait to see you either. When's the final game?"

"In three days."

"How are you feeling about it?"

Hunter had been confident all season long and I was relieved to hear he still felt that way when he said, "Like we're going to bring the cup home. I can feel it in my bones."

"That's the spirit." I sank deeper into his plush couch. "I wish I could have been there to see you play."

If possible, I'd have booked a last-minute flight to be at Hunter's game. He mentioned in the past that the away games were the toughest. At least on their home field, they had a boisterous crowd whose supportive energy fueled them on.

"I wish you could have been here too, but it's okay. You'll be there for the final game."

Nothing would stop me from attending it. "I will. There's no doubt, Hunt."

His eyelids drooped and he licked his lips, inching me a hungry look I was all too acquainted with. "How was your assignment today?"

I swallowed, the heat from his stare nearly scalding me. "It went well. A solid A+ if I do say so myself."

"Good girl." His husky words washed over me and I immediately knew the conversation was about to veer in a whole other direction. "Is Luna occupied?"

I slyly threw her a glance. She comfortably lay in her princess-style bed, dozing off. "Yes."

"I want you to go to my room, Gabriela."

My blood thrummed in my veins. I stood up. Biting my lip, I walked towards his bedroom. "And?"

"Now I want you to strip until you're naked and get under my sheets." I saw his own hand moving south, roving over those hard stomach muscles. "Show me how much you miss me by playing with your tight little pussy."

"You're filthy, *amore*." I stripped down to my birthday suit and did as my bossy boyfriend commanded.

"But you like this side of me, doll."

I shook my head, getting under the covers. "No. I *love* this side of you."

I love every part of you, Hunter.

Then we engaged in the hottest phone sex of my life.

Three days later, it was the big day.

The Panthers' final game versus a rival university and the night where I would tell Hunter how I truly felt about him.

I had it all planned out. After the game and the party Josh hosted, we'd return to my apartment. I decorated the whole place with balloons, a gold congratulations banner, and a makeshift indoor picnic with all of Hunter's favourite foods. I wanted to celebrate him—to make him feel as special as he was—and finish the night by making love to my star quarterback.

There was less than a minute left on the clock. The final quarter of the game was nearing its end. Breathless anticipation spread through the stadium crowd as the football lay in the rival team's hands. The Panthers had a small lead. But if the opposition managed to score now, it would be over.

"Please, please, please," I chanted under my breath, standing in the bleachers with Anna and Layla on either side of me. Heidi and Hannah were here too, a bit further down.

I was trying to remain optimistic. But as the clock trickled down, nervousness surged and expanded in my frame.

The tension was thick in the atmosphere.

Even from afar, I felt like I could sense Hunter's despair. He and the whole team had worked so hard for this very moment. They couldn't lose. They were so close to winning.

The coaching staff hollered something from the benches. The players on the field shouted something inaudible amongst themselves.

Then suddenly, it happened.

The center snapped the ball to Hunter.

With no other option, he decided to run it in himself.

The stadium erupted in cheers as Hunter crossed towards the endzone.

And right before the very last second, he scored a game-winning touchdown.

I thought my heart would burst out of my chest from sheer excitement.

The noise was deafening as the crowd roared to the rafters. The athletic staff exploded in congratulatory handshakes and the football players piled onto each other with excited shouts and cheers. Hunter was lifted into their arms and over their heads.

I snapped as many pictures as I possibly could of the surreal moment, making sure to zoom in on Hunter.

His black strands clung to his skull with sweat, droplets beading down his handsome face as he smiled with his boys.

That candid shot was now my lockscreen photo.

Pride like never before swelled in my chest. God, I was so happy for him. I just wanted to hug and kiss him right now.

As if he heard my call, Hunter broke away from the swarm. He hollered something over his shoulder to his teammates and jogged forward.

"Go!" Anna and Layla ushered me with smiles. "He's coming for you."

I didn't need to be told twice.

I exited the row and rounded the front of the bleachers when Hunter reached me. "Gabriela!"

"Hunter!" I threw myself into his arms with a squeal and he caught me, spinning me around on the field with his own laughter marrying with mine.

My legs went around his waist and my hands cradled the back of his head as our mouths fused together in a scorching kiss before I pressed tiny pecks over his full lips.

"You did it." *Kiss*. "You did it." *Kiss*. "You did it." *Kiss*. "I'm so proud of you, Hunter." *Kiss*. "Congratulations, my love."

A grin carved on his face. "Thank you, baby. I couldn't have done it without my lucky charm."

I smiled and pretended to play coy, pointing at myself. "Who? Me?"

He chuckled and kissed me again. "My goddess of victory, I told you. I've never lost a game since that faithful moonlit night." He stroked a knuckle down my cheek. "And now that I have you? I doubt I ever will."

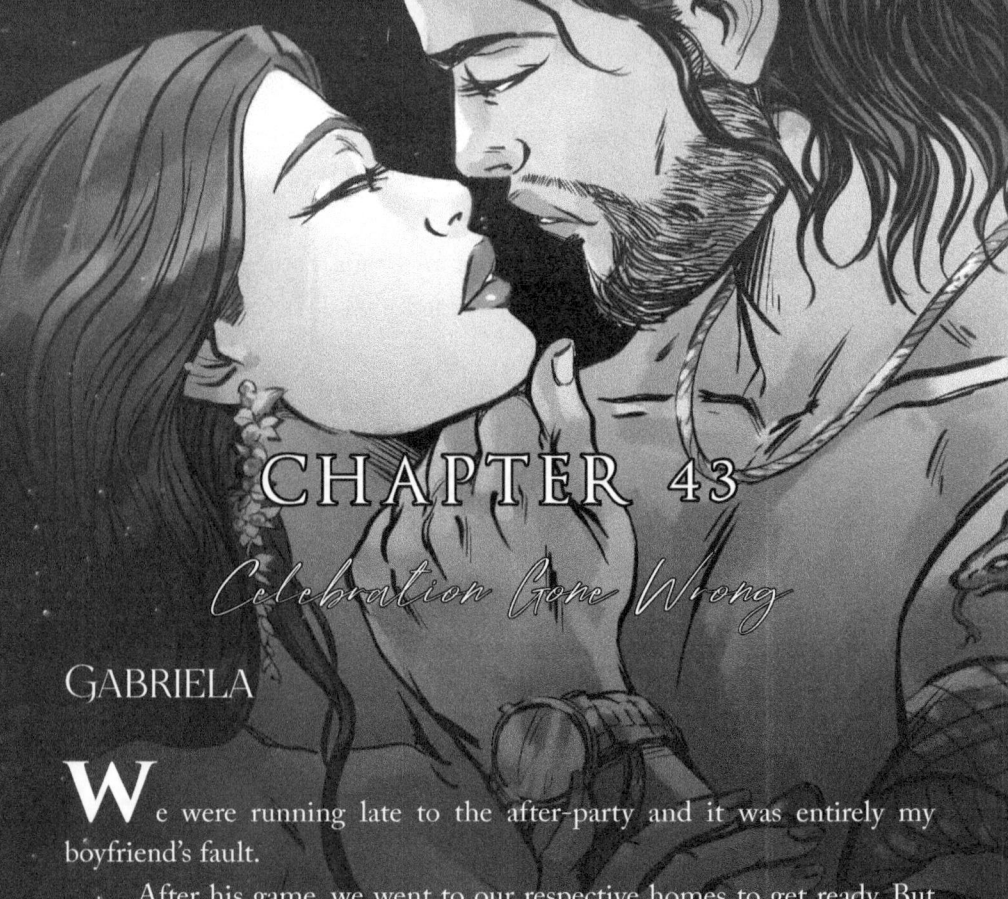

CHAPTER 43

Celebration Gone Wrong

GABRIELA

We were running late to the after-party and it was entirely my boyfriend's fault.

After his game, we went to our respective homes to get ready. But the minute I entered his apartment, all dolled up, Hunter was unable to keep his hands off me.

"Let's skip the party," he growled in my ear from behind, pinning my front to his door and trapping me in a fortress of muscles. He kissed my neck and nipped my bare shoulder. "We can have our own right here."

"T-the party is for the Panthers and you're the star player," I stuttered. "We can't not go, Hunt."

"We can if I say so." Impatient hands kneaded my ass, spanking it hard. "Especially when you wear a dress that messes with my sanity."

"You don't like it?" I teased. "Should I change?"

It was a blood-red, skin-tight, backless minidress with a giant bow on my derrière since my ass was a gift and he was going to unwrap me later tonight. I paired it with matching stilettos, a heart-shaped choker necklace, and wore my hair in loose curls.

"Don't you dare," he warned, dragging open-mouthed kisses down the healing serpent tattoo on my spine. I shivered. "You look beautiful. Fuck, I can't wait to have you all to myself."

"We don't have to be there for long, *bello*."

"One hour."

"Three hours."

"Two hours," he countered huskily. "Then you're mine."

My bargaining skills needed some help, but so did Hunter's compromising ones. Because the heated looks he cast me on our way to the party made it abundantly clear we wouldn't even last the hour.

Josh and Layla's brownstone was crawling with Vesta University athletes celebrating tonight's win by the time we arrived, twenty minutes late. Loud music, laughter, and cheers ribboned the ambiance. The second we crossed the threshold, Hunter was instantly engulfed by his teammates.

Anna and Layla grabbed my arm and veered me in the opposite direction.

My fingers unwove from Hunter's and I called out, "Find me later?"

He looked like he didn't want to let go of me. "I will."

It was Hunter's night and I wanted him to have fun with his friends before I stole him all for myself.

The girls hedged me into the main living room, where the rest of our friends waited. I hugged Ella, Dacia, Darla, and Hera, then a flute with sparkling apple juice and a chocolate-covered strawberry—courtesy of chef Layla—were thrust into my hands.

I munched on my snack while us girls chatted, pausing occasionally to congratulate the passing by football players on the win.

"Lay, I love what you've done with your home," Darla commented to our hostess, brown eyes glancing appreciatively at our surroundings. "You have impeccable taste. I'm especially partial to the grand piano. It really brings the place together."

Layla smiled, passing a hand over the skirt of her light-yellow maxi dress. "Thanks, Darla. Josh let me have full creative control. It took a few months to find all the pieces, but"—she too passed an admiring eyeful around their space—"I'm satisfied with the outcome."

"You should be." Darla tucked a black strand escaping her usual chignon back in place. "Dacia and I were talking about how we've got two spare bedrooms at our home that are in desperate need of a redecoration. Would you be up for the task?"

"I'm not an interior designer by any means, but I'm more than happy to help."

Our conversation came to a halt when Idris, another fellow student from Vesta University, joined our group to say hi to Hera and introduce himself to us. Hera met him recently and they were in the talking stage, so she invited him tonight. He was polite and had a charming demeanour. She genuinely liked him.

Idris said something that made Hera throw her head back in laughter.

Unable to help myself, my gaze darted towards the other end of the room, where a group of athletes popped open a champagne bottle in celebration, Josh naturally at the helm of it all.

Shaun stood amongst them.

But he wasn't participating in their shenanigans.

Instead, his cold blue eyes were fixed on Hera and Idris, the drink in his hand looking like it was seconds from shattering.

Truth be told, I always thought there was something between Hera and Shaun. The sweet smiles. The soft glances. The easy camaraderie. The… occasional flirting.

Right now, Hera didn't notice Shaun, completely riveted by Idris.

Eventually, Cade came to snatch up Ella because he was a needy boyfriend who couldn't be left alone for longer than fifteen minutes. Dacia, Hera, and Idris wandered off to stare at some artwork. Layla and Darla were still exchanging interior design notes, which left Anna and me alone.

My best friend pensively sipped her drink.

"I love what you've done with your hair," I said. It was in an updo, with tendrils of her blond hair framing her face. Glittery statement earrings hung down the sides of her neck and she wore a short sequin dress in her signature pink. "It's a vibe."

"Thank you." She smiled, but it was faint and I sensed her nervousness. "I wanted to try something new."

Anna used to enjoy socializing and being the life of the party, once upon a time. Now she only made the effort when it was an important occasion. Like tonight. She was doing her best to get reacquainted with going out and enjoying her life again.

I squeezed her hand to silently tell her that I was proud of her.

Her stiff posture relaxed and she squeezed back, letting me know she'd needed this reassurance.

Eventually, when her eyes steered over the other side of the room and held long enough, I followed her line of sight to see what had captured her attention…

And noticed Sam standing against a wall, talking to another football player.

As if he felt her gaze on him, his head turned slightly.

Anna's eyes flared and she gulped at being caught.

He gave her a half smile and a playful, acknowledging wink.

Taking a page out of Josh's matchmaking book, I inserted, "Why don't you go over there and congratulate him on the big win?"

"Why would I do that?"

"Because he just won a championship?" I supplied. "And because he's into you?"

And you're kind of into him too.

"He's not into me," Anna denied. "Like I said before, he doesn't really know me—"

"What are you girls talking about?"

"Nothing!" we said in unison when Josh ambushed us from behind and threw his arms around our shoulders.

"Where's my congrats? I just won a championship and I deserve to be showered in praise."

"Congratulations!" I said on cue. "Happy for you, Joshy!"

Anna, on the other hand, said, "My goodness, Josh. You're so humble. I wonder where you get it from?"

"From my daddy."

Anna rolled her eyes good-naturedly at his response and I snorted. Vance Remington was the furthest thing from humble. "Right."

"Keep antagonizing me and I'll call Sam over. Then you'll have to congratulate us both," he volleyed back, wiggling his brows. "Oh, by the way, I'm also here to assuage your fears."

Anna eyed him skeptically. "What fears are those?"

"Sam is not into Dacia—he's into you. So your jealousy streak can rest at bay."

Anna paled. "Wait, what are you talking about?"

"For your sake, I flat out asked Sam and he confirmed they're just friends." Josh shrugged. "And I did tell him that you would be up for a triple date with Layla, me, Gabby, and Hunter…if he joined."

Oh my God.

Josh had a death wish.

Anna took a deep breath and the bright grin on her face was akin to the one she wore when she won her many pageant awards. But underneath, she was bristling. Without breaking composure, she muttered through clenched teeth, "Josh, I'm going to fucking kill you."

"You can't kill me. I'm too pretty to die young. Let a guy live a little, why don't you?"

"I'm giving you a head start by counting to three. Run."

Obviously, Anna was kidding. She wasn't actually going to harm him. Nonetheless, Josh backed away slowly, raising his hands. "Listen to me, Anna. Experiencing emotions is a normal, healthy part of being a human. It's okay that you felt jealous. I, in fact, feel jealousy all the time when another man looks at my Layla. Makes me want to tear their eyes out. I don't always act on the impulse. I mean, maybe I have once. I'm only human after all. The point is, it's totally okay to be attracted to my friend and want to explore this—fuck!"

He broke out into boyish laughter when Anna advanced towards him. He practically ran over to Layla, interrupting her conversation with Darla, and used her as a shield to protect himself.

"I'm kidding! I didn't say shit! I'm just teasing you!" he yelled, still laughing. He was drawing a crowd. "Layla, save me! Anna's trying to kill me!"

As always, Josh found enjoyment in riling the people in his vicinity.

"Whatever you did or said, I'm sure you deserved it." Layla mock-sighed but still braced her arms back to protect him. It was comical. He was twice her size and towered over her, yet she was defending him. "Anna, I'm sorry on behalf of Josh. Will you please forgive him?"

"Only if he promises to stop trying to set me up with people," Anna returned as she neared them. She wasn't able to keep up the stern façade, though. The smile twitching her lips betrayed her. "And if you promise to tighten his leash."

"Done." Layla elbowed Josh. "Apologize, sweetie."

"It was a harmless joke." Josh pouted in a silly, sullen tone. "Fine, I'm sorry. I promise I won't meddle in your love life again. But don't come running to me when you need my help."

"Thank you." Anna placed her hands on her hips. "And congratulations on winning your trophy, Josh. You did great."

"See, that wasn't so hard."

"Don't push it."

"What's going on here?" Hunter joined our circle, wrapping an arm around my waist and tugging me into his side.

"Anna and Josh had a brief squabble," I informed. "It's all good now."

Hunter touched his forehead to mine. "Are you ready to leave?"

That husky, laced with lust, tone told me I was in trouble. I spared the party a deft glance. "We haven't been here for long."

His gaze darkened. "I did my rounds and had a drink with the boys. I'm ready to leave and celebrate with you." His mouth drifted to my ear, whispering, "I doubt we'll be missed. No one will notice we're gone, doll, and by the time they do"—his sentence ended on a low chuckle—"I'll already be deep inside your pussy."

My desire fluttered like a hummingbird locked in a cage, desperate to be let loose. "*Hunter.*"

Blue eyes drew to my mouth like a moth to a flame. "Say yes, Gabriela."

Why was I torturing us by prolonging the inevitable? Hunter was right. Everyone was having a good time. They wouldn't realize if we left early.

The pads of my fingers drew over his dark stubble and his jaw clenched, the lines of his body following suit. All those thick, tan, rippling muscles. At my beck and call. I couldn't wait to tear *mio principe* out of his clothes and ride him to kingdom come.

"Yes," I whispered. "Let's go."

We said quick goodbyes to our friends, under the guise of heading home because we were tired. They didn't call us out on our bullshit, their knowing smirks doing the talking instead.

Hunter didn't even put his coat on after helping me in mine. He draped his over his arm and tugged me out of the brownstone and down the empty sidewalk with the quality of a man running low on patience, his libido guiding his every action.

I would have laughed if I weren't in the same boat. My thong dampened with need and my hunger spiked to insurmountable heights with every passing second of his polished shoes and my heels clicking against the concrete ground.

"Move those legs faster, shorty," he teased. "I've got places to be."

"I'm trying," I retorted. "You're not the one jogging home in six-inch stilettos because your boyfriend is desperate to fuck you."

His throaty laughter only fanned the flames of my desire further. God, everything about him was a turn-on to me. "Guilty. You want to be carried, princess?"

I huffed, stopping. "How gentlemanly of you to finally ask."

He lassoed me into his chest. "You going to keep running that smart mouth once we get home?"

"Mm." I captured his bottom lip and tugged until he moaned low. "But you like my smart mouth. Especially when I let you disrespect it, *bello*."

"I'm going to fuck you hard, all night long." His hands inched under my coat and over my ass, squeezing. "You won't be able to walk tomorrow, Gabriela."

"That's what I'm counting on."

Before Hunter could effortlessly lift me into his arms, someone emerged out of the small alleyway in the middle of two houses and moved straight for us.

It all happened so swiftly.

I gasped and Hunter cursed.

Two angry words escaped the cloaked figure, ripping into the night with the force of a bullet, "*Fucking bitch!*"

And suddenly, a flash of silver glinted in the dark night as a gloved hand rose.

My scream got caught in my throat as Hunter's quick reflexes had him pushing me behind his body.

I stumbled against one of the parked vehicles along the street, setting off the alarm.

But not before I heard the unmistakable sound of a knife slicing in the air. Tearing fabric. Slashing through skin. And Hunter's disbelieving, painful, "*Fuck!*"

Terror slammed into my system.

"*Hunter!*" I screamed. "*No!*"

CHAPTER 44

Unknown Number

GABRIELA

I shakily reached for the gun inside my purse, but it was too late.

The attacker had already run off, disappearing into the darkness of the night.

I righted myself on wobbly legs and pushed towards Hunter's swaying frame.

"Oh my God. Oh my God. Oh my God." On the verge of tears, I grabbed fistfuls of his dress shirt and turned him to face me. My hands searched him vehemently. "Hunter? Where are you hurt? Show me!"

Under the flickering light of the streetlamp, his complexion was pale, his jaw was clenched, and his breathing was laboured as he brought trembling fingers to touch his bicep.

The white dress shirt was stained crimson with his blood.

Seeing Hunter bleeding undid me.

A sensation of faintness spread through my limbs. My heart pounded and the ground beneath me felt malleable.

He gritted his teeth, wincing. "I–I'm fine, Gabby. It's okay."

"Like hell you are!" I wailed. "W–we need to get you to a hospital!"

The car was still blaring behind us. I realized belatedly it was Layla's. The jarring noise, coupled with the fear lodged in my throat, turned my vision hazy. Four homes down, the door to Josh and Layla's opened.

Josh came down the stairs with car keys in hand, pausing for a split second when he saw us standing there, shocked and distressed. He ran in our direction. "What's going on?"

"Someone knifed Hunter!" While I panicked, Hunter was doing a better job at keeping it together. "They ran away in that direction!" I pointed down the dark street. "Josh, we need to get him to a hospital *right now*."

Josh cursed when he took in his bleeding best friend.

"I'm fine," Hunter said again, but it was a weak rasp. "No hospitals. Remember what you said before?" He aimed the question at Josh. "You don't involve the authorities with families like yours."

"Hunter, this is different," I begged. A brash mixture of fury and fright pumped through my veins. I couldn't believe it. Someone had hurt my Hunter. Someone made him bleed. "Please. We're taking you." I shook my head. "Josh, the attacker came out of the alleyway between these two homes and he was wearing all black, a hood and a mask covering his face."

"Gabriela." Hunter's hand rose to cup my cheek softly, his voice strained. "He…He was heading for you. That knife wasn't meant for me, baby."

I closed my eyes, fighting back tears.

Fucking bitch.

Without a doubt, those two words were aimed at me.

But why?

Who was it?

What did I do?

If Hunter hadn't pushed me out of the way, it would have been me bearing that knife wound.

Or worse.

Based on Josh's expression, it was clear this was deemed mob business. We wouldn't be taking Hunter to a hospital. It was too risky. Nor would Hunter allow us to drag him there.

Josh's mouth pinched into a grim line. He put pressure on Hunter's wound. "Let's go back to mine. We'll patch you up. I'll look through the cameras in this area and have my men sweep the neighbourhood as well. But we can't stay here in case the attacker returns. It's not safe."

It went without saying that the party was over.

Josh and Layla told everyone except for our immediate group of friends that there was a sudden family emergency that needed tending to. It incited everyone to leave, much to their chagrin. I couldn't care less about the damper on their moods. We were downtown with a million bars in short proximity. They could continue their festivities elsewhere.

With an armed member of Josh's personal security team, Hunter and I waited outside in the shadows, along the side of the house where we wouldn't be seen by the exiting people. And once they were gone, we went back inside.

Now Josh and Cade were giving instructions to a handful of the Remington guards in the living room, and the girls were helping Layla tidy up.

I paced in the hallway right next to the ajar bathroom door.

Sam and Shaun were cleaning Hunter's wound and stitching him up.

Earlier, I had insisted on mending him. It was my fault. He wouldn't have gotten hurt if it weren't for me. But my clammy hands kept trembling with the thread and needle, and all three men grew uneasy with my heightened emotions.

Sam had offered to do it instead, imploring me with a gentle tone, "Let me take care of it, Gabby. I've done this before."

I licked my dry lips. "I-I can do it."

"He's right, Gabby." Shaun was in the midst of helping Hunter out of his blood-stained shirt, shaking his head. "You shouldn't have to see this."

I was about to fight my stance, when Hunter inched me a levelled look that left no room for argument. "It's okay. I'll be fixed up in no time. Go wait outside for me. Please."

Ultimately, Sam and Shaun taking care of him was the right move. I wasn't in any shape to stitch him myself and would probably do a botched job with the shakiness in my hands. Plus, it wasn't Sam's first rodeo and Shaun's energy was probably more calming than my anxious self.

I adhered to Hunter's wish, but before they closed the door the slightest bit to award a semblance of privacy...I caught the damage.

A long, thin, angry slash down Hunter's bicep, the once flawless skin marred by the ugly imperfection. Blood poured out of the cut.

I closed my eyes, willing the sight away. My stomach churned and my throat tightened, an acidic taste extending on my tongue.

In a vain attempt to gather myself, I now rested against the hallway wall, my head lolling back and my eyes screwed shut. Inhale. Exhale. Inhale. Exhale. I concentrated on each breath, as if that would evade the bad thoughts creeping in my mind.

God, that should have been me. Not Hunter.

He didn't deserve to get hurt on my account.

I love him and I could have lost him tonight.

The realization weighed heavily on my chest, like a suffocating, taunting pressure.

I choked back a sob but was unable to hold back my tears. They steamed down my face like a river. I kept wiping them away. I didn't want Hunter to see me like this. I wanted to remain strong for him.

Fucking bitch.

Those two words looped in my mind like a broken record.

Now that the adrenaline slowly wore off, I replayed the moment in my head.

It was dark, the attacker appeared in a flash, and all their features were masked. There was no way Hunter and I could have identified them. Furthermore, I didn't know who it could be...but whoever it was, they had a vendetta against me. Saying I was the wrong person at the wrong time would be a fluke. Nothing in our world was a coincidence. It was also clear that I'd been watched for a long time, if the timely attack was anything to go by.

How else would they have known where I would be this very night? Chills rushed over my skin.

The Remington men stated that it might be one of my papà's enemies, someone he pissed off and they in return wanted revenge. Getting said revenge by hurting me—his daughter—wasn't out of the realm of possibilities.

There was a smaller voice in my head that said perhaps it wasn't someone who had beef with him. Perhaps it was someone from my past… like Franco.

I wasn't fooled by that sham of an apology the night of the gala. Given Franco's abusive past, it wasn't far-fetched to assume that he could be the so-called attacker.

And if it was him, then God have mercy. Papà would tear him limb from limb.

I told my theory to Josh and Cade. They said they'd have their men locate Franco just to be certain. They also insisted that I stay at one of the Remington safe houses tonight until they figured out who was behind this ordeal.

But Hunter offered his home instead—the same one on the city's outskirts where we had our first unofficial date—and I agreed. It was private, far away, and would keep me out of the limelight.

Despite the threat looming, it wasn't my well-being I was concerned for.

It was Hunter's.

I hated that he got hurt because of me—hated that he could have been fatally wounded if the attacker's slash had landed elsewhere.

What if it was his jugular, his head, or that heart I loved so fucking much?

I was spiralling, unravelling at the seams like a worn-out piece of fabric. It wasn't healthy to harbour these thoughts, but I couldn't stop the train wreck thinking once it began.

Hunter was still being stitched up in the bathroom and I was waiting outside for him, feeling helpless, worried, and bone-deep exhausted.

Right as I made the decision to knock on the door and see the verdict, my phone pinged with a series of incoming texts.

I pulled it out of my clutch, unlocked it, and my heart thudded.

The texts came from a number I didn't recognize.

And when I read them…

Everything inside of me wheeled to a temporary halt.

Did you like the quote I left on your wall? —Unknown Number

Here's another one for you. —Unknown Number

Love all, trust a few, do wrong to none…but you did me wrong, you stupid cunt —Unknown Number

Bitches like you are only good for one thing. —Unknown Number

I'll remind you of your place. —Unknown Number

CHAPTER 45

God Of The Sky

HUNTER

Gabriela was uncharacteristically quiet during the drive to my home.

We were sitting in the back of a bulletproof SUV, being transported to the location like expensive cargo, with a sleeping Luna in her carrier. Another Remington guard was currently driving my Jag, trailing a few paces behind us.

My right arm harboured a slight burn from the stitches and bandage wrapped around my wound. But I could still move and lift my arm if needed. The damage was minimal and the painkillers I swallowed lessened the ache. Sam and Shaun did a thorough job patching me up, ensuring that the scar wouldn't be botched during the healing process.

But I didn't give a fuck about any of that right now.

Not the wound. Not the stitches. Not the pain.

The only thing I cared about was the silent red-haired beauty sitting beside me in the backseat, tucked into my side, her head resting on my left shoulder and her fingers gripping my white dress shirt in a death grip.

She was scared.

An eerie calm pulsed around her like miasma.

Her mind was incessantly going over the reality of our new situation, and all I wanted to do was chase away her demons, for I was built with the inherent need to soothe her discomfort and make her happy.

I lifted her chin with a finger. "Talk to me, Gabby."

Her unfocused eyes blinked and met my worried ones. "Hm?"

"I don't like it when you get quiet on me," I whispered, mindful of the guards sitting in the front. I didn't want them to hear our conversation. "What are you thinking?"

"That I want them to kill whoever is taunting me." She exhaled, closing her eyes. "And whoever hurt you."

I could only imagine how devastated she must feel. From witnessing the knifing to the text messages from the unknown number. Unfortunately, one thing became crystal clear...

Her dad killed the wrong guy.

Maverick had been a creep who'd broken into her house to steal her things, but he wasn't the *actual* culprit we'd been looking for.

Which made this tenfold worse.

It could be anyone at this point. Her ex-boyfriend, her dad's enemies, and anyone in between. There were no leads, even though Josh, Cade, Enzo, and Vance were currently leading the witch hunt.

Regardless, whoever broke into her place the first time was still out there. Waiting. Watching. Working out a plan to finish the job. This whole time, she thought she was safe after Maverick was killed, going about her daily routine without a zilch of worry. And now we were back to square one.

It boiled my blood.

I once told Gabriela that I wasn't a violent man, but the thought of anyone hurting her made me want to teach them a lesson.

That still rang true.

I would be six feet beneath the ground before I let anything bad happen to her, even if I had to defend her with the barrel of my gun or the flesh on my body. I would be her weapon and her shield.

I was so goddamned in love with her that to remove her from my existence would be like wrenching a vital organ out of my person. I wouldn't survive without her.

She was the very breath running through my lungs, the very beat keeping my heart pumping, the very essence powering my soul. Without her, my life would be a colourless canvas with endless murky depths.

Gabriela Regina Bellafiore was the other half of me.

I would never allow anyone to hurt her, let alone take her away from me.

"Don't worry, sweetheart," I hushed, kissing her hairline. "They'll find the culprit. And in the meantime, I'm here and I'll take care of you. Always. You know that, right?"

And alongside me, the perimeters of my home would heavily be barricaded by guards, so if anyone dared to approach my property—and my Gabriela—there would be hell to pay.

Instead of answering me, she pecked my lips.

I felt the tremble in her body. It took every ounce of my strength not to unbuckle her seatbelt, drag her into my lap, and wrap my arms around her protectively.

I was strong enough for the both of us. Whatever demons haunted Gabriela, I would chase them away. No one would hurt her. Not one would ever lay a finger on her so long as I breathed.

She was my whole world.

I would keep her protected, sheltered, and cherished for as long as I breathed.

My private property came into view within seconds and we pulled into the lot, the other armed vehicles following suit. I helped Gabriela out of the car and she was mindful of my injured arm, steering away from it like it would combust at her touch.

Her dad stepped out of his car with two of his guards, Oscar included, and headed towards us, casting weary glances at the darkness surroundings like a threat would pop out mid-air.

"*Cara mia*," he began. "Are you sure you wish to stay here?"

"Yes, Papà. I told you; I want to be with Hunter. I trust him and the guards."

He appeared like he wanted to oppose but nodded instead. "All right. You'll stay here for the weekend until I can make other arrangements for you, closer to our home." A regretful expression flashed over his face, which he was quick to cover up with his usual scowl. "We'll find who did this to you and put an end to it. For real this time."

I concluded that his stoic demeanour wasn't because he was pissed Gabriela was staying here with me, but rather disappointment in himself. Enzo killed the wrong guy—never mind that Maverick deserved to die—and it gnawed at him.

Gabriela hugged Enzo. "I know you will. You always protect me."

In what I assumed was a rare display of affection in front of his men, he kissed the top of her head. "If you need anything—whatever it may be—I'm just a phone call away, okay?"

She smiled. "I know."

Then he gave a meaningful glance in my direction and said with a stony tone, "Thank you for protecting Gabriela. If you hadn't been there—" He cleared his throat, swallowing roughly. "Lucia and I are forever in your debt."

"You don't have to thank me for that, sir," I replied, reaching forth to grab my girl's hand. "I would do anything for Gabriela."

Enzo Bellafiore may have been wary of me at the beginning, but tonight was a turning point. He would warm up to me, slowly but surely. I was going to be his future son-in-law one day, so it was in his best interest that we got along.

If not for our sakes, then Gabriela's.

"Let's go inside," Enzo said, nodding at my home. "I want to see the layout and debrief the guards on the plan."

Enzo and the guards took an hour to analyze the indoor and outdoor structure, devising a strategic plan to ensure the entire property was secured, not to mention the various weapons they discreetly stashed in every corner of the house in case anyone broke inside. It was a slim possibility. They doubted that the same attacker from tonight would strike twice, let alone know where Gabriela was staying. But we wouldn't be taking any chances.

I locked the doors and windows once Enzo left after bidding us good night and lecturing us to call him if we experienced even the slightest suspicious activity. Josh had already hacked into the cameras lining the outside of the property, so we were covered on that end too.

I dragged in a deep breath as I walked down the hallway to find Gabriela. She'd put Luna to sleep in her princess bed earlier, cooing at her softly since the latter was a bit distressed, having been shuffled from her usual home to another.

Before we left to come here, guards had accompanied us to our respective apartments to help us pack our bags for the weekend. That's when I saw Gabriela had decorated hers with balloons, a banner, and all my favourite foods so we could have an indoor, cozy picnic to celebrate my win. She was so disappointed that her surprise was ruined. My chest twisted at the sight. I'd kissed her and reassured that it was the thought that counted.

Now I hoped to salvage some of our plans at the very least.

On my way to her, I paused by the bar cart to pour some whiskey in a glass with my left hand.

I found Gabriela in the dining room area, facing the floor-to-ceiling windows leading to the backyard.

She was fiddling with the new phone Josh gave her, since he kept her old one to monitor any incoming text messages.

I wrapped my arms around her from behind, ignoring the mild ache in my right one. "Hi, baby. What are you doing?"

"Hi." She melted into my embrace. "Just texting the girls to tell them that we're fine. They wanted to make sure we were settled in before they called it a night."

I kissed her temple. "You good?"

"Hm."

Gabriela seemed far away. Physically, she was present, but her mind seemed lost in another world. It worried me when she got quiet. I wasn't accustomed to her pensive self. I needed my playful, teasing girlfriend back.

"Look," I whispered in her ear. "It's our constellation."

Gabriela traced her fingers over the window's glass, glancing at the night sky. The stars were visible, including Pegasus.

"I finished reading the book on Greek mythology," she whispered back, leaning her cheek against mine. "The one you bought me."

Excitement zinged through me. "Yeah?"

"Yeah." A ghost of a smile touched her lips. "I know which God I would associate with you."

My glass halted halfway to my mouth. "And which one is that?"

She stared at me while I took a sip of my drink, eagerly anticipating her response.

Gabriela palmed my jaw tenderly. "Uranus. The personification of the sky."

A primordial God.

Father of the titans.

Something swelled in my throat. "Why is that your choice?"

"He helped form the foundation of the universe. Some even say he was the first to rule over the world." She traced her thumb over my lips. "And whenever I look up at this very night sky, I think of you. To me, you're the embodiment of all the stars and all the heaven I will ever know. You're my happily ever after, Hunt."

She'd slain me with those words.

I dropped my glass and it crashed to the floor, shattering to pieces.

Gabriela gasped, but the sound was quickly drowned when I grasped her face and stamped her mouth to mine in a passionate kiss filled with all the love I possessed inside of me.

Love for her.

Only ever her.

Gabriela moaned sweetly into the kiss when I thrust my tongue into her mouth and consumed her like she was my only source of nourishment. My soul fed off her kisses and thrived under the sheer magnificence of the confession she bestowed upon me.

She tasted like red roses, vanilla, and all fucking mine.

I wanted to make love to her.

Right. Now.

I was on the verge of telling her my true feelings when she pulled away and gave me a wry smile that made my insides clench. "Hunter, I want to tell you something."

I gazed into her beautiful blue eyes, my very own oasis lying in those depths. "What is it?"

"After this weekend, I think we should take a break."

CHAPTER 46

Ti Amo

GABRIELA

The sentence tore out of me like a bullet, ricocheting loudly in the stillness of the room.

I wouldn't take it back, though. I meant it and I had a good reason too.

At first, Hunter appeared confused. Dazed even. As though he was running the words back in his mind and couldn't make sense of them.

Then his eyes flared in understanding, his hands fell from my face, and he staggered back a step like I daggered him straight into the chest.

"What did you just say?" Heartbreak exploded over his face and the agony in his voice drove into me like a wrecking ball. "Gabriela?"

"Listen to me, please." I reached to grab his hands—to feel his warmth because without him, I was nothing but a cold shell. He let me braid our fingers together, but it did little to dissipate the pure shock on his features. "If the culprit isn't caught by this weekend, I…I think we should take a break until the situation is resolved."

A tremble rushed through his body. "I don't understand. Why would you suggest this?"

"Hunter," I pleaded. There was a frantic quality in his eyes as they searched mine for answers. "That knife was aimed at *me*. You're hurt

477

because of *me*. Your life is being upended because of *me*." I shook my head. "I can't risk you. If you're not in my vicinity, then you're safe."

His chest bowed with his uneven breathing. "And your solution is to break up so I'm not in the crossfire?"

"No!" I said quickly, horrified. But he let go of my hands and stepped back. "Not break up. Just…lie low and wait for the situation to blow over."

He chuckled humourlessly. "Absolutely not. I won't be parted from you."

He was half illuminated by the night lights seeping through the floor-to-ceiling windows and half shadowed by the darkness of the room. Even so, he looked larger than life. My god of the sky. A figure worth idolatry. The epitome of all my love and desire. I watched him in rapture and yearning. His corded neck worked with a difficult swallow when he raised his hand to shove his fingers into his black hair, pushing it back from his face and allowing me to see the full-fledged pain my words had caused him. And when I noticed the way his thick muscles strained against the white fabric of his dress shirt, namely the bloody stain on his bicep…I knew deep in my heart this was the right decision.

He was the most precious thing to me. I needed to ensure his safety above all else. Above mine too.

"Hunter, I could have lost you tonight," I said in a vain attempt to get him to understand my side. "Do you understand the magnitude of that? It would have *killed* me."

He crowded me in two steps, clutching my face with despair. "And don't you understand that I would gladly take a hundred knife slashes if it meant you're alive and well?"

My eyes stung with new tears and I got choked up, grabbing his hands on my face with my own.

The air around us simmered with emotions and the things we left unsaid. I had planned an entire romantic evening for us and though this wasn't how I envisioned things going, I couldn't hold back anymore from telling him my truth.

"Hunter, I'm in love with you." A newfound sensation of peace settled into my chest after the confession left my mouth. "I wish I could pinpoint the exact moment it occurred, but I realized now that I'd slowly been falling for you from the start. No one has ever treated me the way you have—no one has even made me feel like I was worthy of the kind of love you've given me. Hell, I didn't even know this kind of love could exist until you. From the minute we met again on that moonlit terrace, you've raised all my standards until you became the living embodiment of them." A lone tear trickled down my cheek as I stared up at him with all the humility and love residing within me. "I love you so much that I always want your face to be the last thing I see before bed, just so I can dream of you for the few hours that I'm not awake. I love you so much that I don't think I could go on a minute if you weren't here. And I love you so much that I would jump in front of a grenade if it meant saving you, Hunter."

Even on my deathbed, I would never forget the look on his face.

Pure awe mixed with disbelief.

"Don't," Hunter began vehemently, blue eyes shining with a sheen of moisture. "Don't talk like that. I don't want to exist in a world where you're not there, Gabriela."

"It's the truth. If something happens to you, I wouldn't make it to nightfall. That's why I need you to take a step back from me and heal if the culprit isn't caught soon. Tonight was a close call and it scared me more than I can ever convey in words, *amore mio*."

Hunter backed me against the window and laid his forehead to mine. "How can you say all of that and still think I'd be okay with taking a break—even a short one? Haven't I made it clear that it'll take an army to pry me off of you?" His lips hovered over mine, painting the words against my skin. "Haven't I made it clear through my actions that I'm so fucking in love with you that I'm never leaving your side, baby?"

More tears gathered in my eyes. "You love me?"

These past few weeks, I felt it. In his body language. In his words. In his touch.

But it was a whole other thing to hear the confession aloud.

My heart felt like it would burst from happiness, knowing that all my love was reciprocated too.

"Yes," he murmured in the small distance between our mouths. I pressed a hand against his chest, feeling his heart hammering. "I'm so goddamn in love with you that there's no end to *this*. You're etched deeply in the fabric of my soul, doll. And when I look at you, I feel grounded in the knowledge that you breathe and exist beside me, for you center my entire being. I love waking up and going to bed next to you. I love our drives where we listen to music and talk about anything and everything. I love taking walks with our Luna and spending time with both of you at home, watching horror movies and eating home-cooked meals. I don't want to live this life if you're not in it either, and I refuse to be parted from you when you're the other half of me, Gabriela."

My heart pounded and another tear fell down my cheek. "Hunter."

He wiped it away with his thumb, gaze never wavering from me.

In that moment, I felt like I could see his entire soul, reflecting all the truths from his utterance. Being chosen and loved by this magnificent man who treasured me beyond means healed the parts that my abusive ex broke.

Hunter Saint Warren beheld all the fissures inside of my armour, coated them with gold, gave me wings, and set me on a high pedestal, worshipping me like a goddess.

The universe knew exactly what I needed and delivered him right to me.

He was a gift and I would cherish him until we died.

Unable to string a coherent sentence together, I did the only thing I could.

I kissed him with all the passion and adoration coursing through my veins.

Hunter groaned, matching my fervour as always. Sipping hungrily and almost angrily from my lips like he couldn't have enough—would *never* have enough—of me. Chasing his hands down my sides until he grasped handfuls of my ass and hoisted me up. My legs wrapped around his waist and we stumbled back, clawing at each other like the only thing keeping us sane was this vivid connection that always sparked whenever we collided.

"Fuck," he rasped. "I need to make love to you. Right now."

"Y-yes," I pleaded between kisses and he walked us further into his home, his clipped footsteps echoing in rhythm with my erratic pulse. "Hunt, I *need* you."

Wordlessly, Hunter guided us into the living room. The lights were turned off, the curtains drawn, and the fireplace was on, casting a romantic, amber glow around the place.

He lowered us on a fur blanket before the warm fire. My back met softness. Hunter's mouth skimmed my cheek and came to a stop at my ear. "Remember what I said I'd do to you once I win my championship?"

I shivered at the heated, growled words. "Yes."

"Tell me."

I whimpered when he nipped my jaw and dragged kisses down my neck. "That you would fuck me."

"Exactly. So turn around and get on all fours."

My core tightened at his heady request. Licking my lips, I obliged, glancing at him over my shoulder and rushing out, "B-but we have to be mindful of your injury—"

Slap.

He clapped my ass with a firm palm and I gasped.

"You let me worry about that, baby." He ran his hands appreciatively over my derrière, fingering the big red bow gathered where my backless dress scooped down at the base of my spine. "Wrapped your tight little ass like a gift for me, hm?"

I let loose a half chuckle, half whimper when he swatted my ass again. "Yes, *bello*. You promised to fuck it, remember? I was just being a good girlfriend and giving you a gentle reminder in case you forgot."

"How could I forget?" Impatiently, he pushed my dress up and removed it in one fell swoop. Then he actually *ripped* off my thong like an animal. "Fuck, you're so wet." Before slapping my pussy and causing me to jerk with a moan. "And so goddamn gorgeous."

Hearing him appreciate my beauty never failed to boost my ego. "Love you."

"I'll never get used to hearing those words."

"Guess I'll have to tell you how much I love you until it sticks, huh?"

"Guess so, Gabby." I heard rustling as he stood up and used his foot to kick my legs apart, widening my stance for him. "Stay like that for me."

"What are you doing?" I watched him head towards the black leather sofa in the room. He rummaged through one of our overnight bags, pulling out a few things. My pulse nearly skipped a beat when I saw the familiar bottle of lube and another butt plug. "Oh."

His reply was a salacious smile as he undressed deceptively slow to give me the opportunity to soak in his gobsmacking physique.

Without a doubt, Hunter was going to work me down to my bones. We were going to have another all-nighter.

And I couldn't wait.

With his white dress shirt and black pants shed, he advanced towards me. Saliva pooled in my mouth as I observed his tan muscles bulge and ripple with every movement, taking in his cut torso, those powerful thighs, and that thick cock bobbing against his abs.

Tonight, I wasn't just fucking the man I was in love with or my tender boyfriend.

I was fucking the star quarterback, who just won a national championship.

The way he devoured me with his eyes stated that he wanted his pound of flesh. The very prize that was promised to him.

Me.

His goddess of victory.

I licked my lips when he kneeled behind me, feeling smaller and vulnerable under his robust stature. I'd already done the necessary preparations before we left for the party because I knew this was coming. My anticipation continued to surmount when he uncapped the bottle of lube and spread my ass cheeks apart, pouring the substance right where I needed it.

"Steady," he urged when he gently inserted the butt plug and I quivered underneath him with excitement. We'd been stretching my ass in slow increments with various girths. Therefore, my puckered hole gave way easily under the intrusion. I couldn't wait to feel Hunter there. "Good girl."

I breathed calmly through my nose at the full stretch, knowing this was just a preview, considering his cock was so much bigger. "I need you inside of me, Hunt."

My boyfriend rained kisses over my tattooed spine and yanked my head back with five fingers in my hair. I arched under his hold. His mouth feathered over the shell of my ear. "You want me to fuck this virgin ass, doll?"

I closed my eyes on a moan when he shoved two digits into my pussy, fingering me unhurriedly. "Y-yes."

"Beg me, Gabriela. Let me hear how much my filthy little plaything wants me to claim all of her."

That sexy, guttural tone wrapped around my clit and squeezed. My arousal trickled down to my inner thighs and I chased his thrusting fingers with eager hips, crying out when he hit my spot. "Please, please, please. Fuck me, Hunter—"

The rest of my sentence got lost in a squeal when Hunter unexpectedly flipped us over so he was lying on the furs and I fell astride on his lap. I gasped at the swift motion. "Oh, God."

"Your favourite one." Hunter gripped my hips and smirked devilishly. "Now ride me, sweetheart. Get me nice and wet for your ass."

Fuck, I loved when he got bossy and demanding. It never failed to make me hot.

His dick was nestled between the juncture of my thighs, my slick pussy coating the underside of it. A pearly drop of cum seeped out and I rubbed it into the plump head before lifting up enough to lodge his tip in my entrance.

"Go slow," he commanded, licking his bottom lip. "I want to watch your cunt split open over my cock."

Such a nasty fucker. I loved him to pieces.

We didn't assume this position often, but Hunter really enjoyed seeing me on top, wiggling and moaning as I took his long dick to the hilt before riding him like a cowgirl.

"Anything you want, pretty boy." I breathed and lowered myself onto him, loving the incredible feel of him filling me. Hunter cursed under his breath and eyed the space where we were joined, my pussy enveloping his length one inch at a time.

The sensation of him entering me was amplified with the toy in my ass.

I threw my head back on a whimper when he finally bottomed inside of me. Hunter responded with his own deep, masculine moan.

"You okay?" he asked, voice strained. He needed me to move, but I just needed a moment to savour us like so. I closed my eyes on a moan and put my palms on his chest for leverage, nodding.

His calloused hand snaked up between my breasts and wrapped around my throat. "Words, Gabby."

The clenching of his fingers grounded me. The snake tattoo on his arm appeared like it serpentined to life against the glow of the firelight. "I-I'm okay. You feel so good inside of me. You always do."

He agreed with a low hum. "Nothing has ever felt this right, baby."

Me and him.

It *was* the most cosmically veracious thing ever.

I grabbed his hand, kissing the lines engraved in his palm.

From the very start, this was our destiny. We were fated. Written in the stars.

Hunter helped guide me as I rode him. He kept one hand on my hip and the other around my neck like a leash. I loved his protective and possessive clasp.

We rocked in perfect unity like waves moving together in a vast body of water. He watched me in utmost fascination—the way my breasts swayed, the way my fingers dug into his chest, the way my face transformed under our lovemaking. He gazed at me the same way Leander did Hero in that painting he bought me. Undone and so in love with his woman.

"You're so beautiful, Gabriela," he rasped, glancing up at me in worship. "I can stare at you for all eternity and never tire."

The compliment bloomed inside of me like a midnight flower.

I kissed him, drinking in his coarse groans and praise, letting his essence bleed into my soul like ink words on parchment.

Shivers feathered down my spine. Blue gazes tangled and anchored each other. Senseless sounds fell past the seam of our mouths, growing in decibels. Making love to Hunter before the fireplace was the most romantic and erotic moment of my life.

It felt like all our cards were on the table. All our naked truths revealed.

We kissed and touched and mumbled all sorts of admissions.

I love you. I love you. I love you, Gabriela. Sei…tutto…per me.

I love you. Ti amo. So much, Hunter. With all my heart.

In the midst of making out, with my long red hair curtained around us and cocooning us in a blissful bubble, I reached completion, pulsing and echoing nonsensical words against Hunter's wet lips.

I held on to him, our skins glistening with sweat and our breathing harsh. With all my senses overwhelmed, I blacked out for a few seconds.

I returned to reality when Hunter drew soothing circles on my back. "How are you feeling?"

Face tucked in the crook of his neck, I smiled and grazed my lips against his flesh, tasting the salt from his perspiration. "Fantastic." I lifted my head enough to glance at him. "And like I'll never have enough of you."

A cocky smirk graced his lips. Fuck, he was so sexy. "Luckily for you, we're far from done."

He eased me off of him with strong, capable hands, his cock still hard and now shining wet with my arousal. We both groaned at the loss of him inside of me.

Hunter quickly switched our positions so now I lay on my back, with him looming above me. He studied my face with a nondescript expression and pushed aside the strands sticking to my forehead.

"Sometimes I look at you"—he brushed his mouth against my kiss-swollen lips—"and feel overwhelmed, grateful, and awed that you exist… and that I get to experience you, Gabriela."

Be still, my heart. "*Hunter.*"

"It's the truth." He laid soft kisses all over my face in veneration. "I love you so much. I don't know what I would do without you."

"I love you so much." I wrapped my arms around his neck. "And I don't know what I would do without you either, *amore mio*."

We sealed the sentiments with a long kiss. Hunter was rooted right here in my heart. Planted like a seed. Growing every day and taking up all the space until I was certain one day I wouldn't be able to remember what life was like before him.

Stormy eyes riveted on me, Hunter painted his kisses down my neck and breasts, shaping the undersides with his hands as he tongued my nipples and sucked them hungrily. His stubble abraded me in a pleasurable manner. My hands curled in his broad shoulders as plaintive whines spilled out of me. Hunter's smirk stamped down my taut stomach and paused over my mound, hovering a scant inch away from my swollen clit.

"Please," I begged him.

His thumb ran over my slit, collecting my wetness. "Please what?"

My fingers were merciless as they dove into his hair and tugged indicatively. And in case he didn't get the hint, my hips canted against his handsome face too. "Fuck my pussy with your tongue, *bello*. I need it so bad."

The reverberations of his dark, naughty chuckle against my sensitive flesh had me spiralling. "*Mia regina*," he tutted, grazing the tip of his nose against my clit as he inhaled my scent like an animal scenting its mate. "Always chasing her next orgasm. Always so greedy for me."

Hearing him call me *mia regina*—his queen—warmed my heart.

He was picking up my language quickly.

"You're no better." My pretty boy couldn't go a day without needing me either. I squirmed at the feel of his breath against my slit. "You're just as greedy as me."

His tongue flicked out to taste straight from the source, humming appreciatively like a sex fiend. "I'm worse, Gabriela. So." *Lick*. "Much." *Suck*. "Worse."

A thorough debauching of my pussy followed Hunter's self-awareness statement. He addled my brain and turned me into a knotted mess. I held on for the ride, my thighs boxing his head and my moans of abandonment adorning the ambiance. Hunter relished them, if the way he groaned hungrily against my slit was anything to go by.

It didn't take long for me to come, exploding against his relentless tongue and fingers.

While I basked under the onslaught of pleasure, Hunter licked his fingers clean and climbed up my body again, kissing me so I could taste myself.

"I'm going to fuck your ass now." Hunter reached next to us to grab a fallen pillow and brought it under my head for support. "If it hurts too much or you want me to stop, say the words."

"I will." But I doubted I'd want to stop.

Hunter dragged the bottle of lube and my favourite clit vibrator closer. I trembled when he used a forearm beneath my hips to raise my bottom half so it was draped over his thighs. The top half of me was comfortably snuggled in the furs.

Positioned like this, I was fully at his mercy.

Ever so slowly, Hunter popped out the butt plug and replaced it with two thick fingers. I liked his fingers there…and I liked it a whole lot more when the fingers of his other hand began to toy with my clit. Goosebumps ignited over my skin. I was splayed open for his use and loved that he was working my body so masterfully. "Mm. *More.*"

"You love it, don't you?" His tone was gravelly and sinful. "Having your ass and pussy stroked like this, baby?"

"S-so much." I panted, digging my fingers into the prominent veins of his forearms. "Can't wait until you're buried inside of me."

"You're so tight, so warm, so sweet for me, doll." A muscle jumped in his clenched jaw on a particular thrust of his fingers in my ass. "I can't wait to have my cock in here. Can't wait to fill you with more cum."

God, his filthy mouth. Lust careened through my core, making me wetter and hornier. I moaned as he dribbled more lube over my hole and massaged it in. "Please, Hunt." I rolled my hips. "*Now.*"

"I can never deny you when you beg me so nicely." He grabbed a hold of his thickness, already coated with my arousal, and dolloped another generous amount of lube so it was extremely slippery. He appeared so primal as he gave himself a few long strokes. It was hot. *He* was hot. My mouth went dry and my pussy practically fluttered. "Breathe, Gabriela. I want you to relax for me."

I inhaled.

His plump tip feathered down the split of my cheeks.

I gasped when he breached the tight ring of muscle. "Fuck."

Hunter groaned at the sensation, grasping my hips in a way where I would have finger-shaped bruises in the morning.

"Eyes on me." He petted my clit to alleviate some of the burn. "Watch me as I enter you."

And then he pushed in another inch.

My eyes widened, my back arched, my thighs shook, and my mouth fell open on a tortured whine. "*Hunter.*"

"You're being so calm and patient as I feed you my cock." He kissed my lips. "Such a good girl for me, Gabriela."

There was pressure as he continued sliding in. *Mio principe* was the only man to ever have me this way and he loved it. Those blue eyes kept me hostage, not allowing me to glance anywhere else as he fucked me. He wanted to see me break softly for him. Before stitching me back together with his love and affection. I didn't feel any staggering pain from this claiming. Just a sweet, bearable ache and relief that he was mine and I was his in every way possible.

"*Goddamn, Gabriela.*" His animalistic tone was like rock to a flint, sending sparks all over my body. "You're sucking me in so deep—so perfectly." He exhaled sharply as he stared at his thick cock, halfway into my asshole. "How do you feel, sweetheart?"

"Incredible." But nothing could have prepared me for the stretch and fullness. He was fucking huge. Incomparable to the toys. And yet, I took him like a champ, even getting off on the slight burn accompanied with this first-time entry. He paused for a bit, allowing me to adjust to his inches. One hand gripped my ass cheek and the other gripped my neck, pinning me down. The bunched muscles and the feral expression let me know just how much it cost him to physically stop himself from thrusting completely into me. "Give me more. I can take it."

"My needy girl." He groaned and rolled his bottom lip into his mouth, pushing another inch inside of me. "You're doing amazing."

His fingers resumed polishing my clit and I moaned, toes curling. Gingerly, my hand rose to cup his bristly cheek. He screwed his eyes shut, undone by my touch yet still keeping himself in check. "A-all the way in, Hunt."

My sentence severed the last thread holding him back.

Hunter snapped.

With a final thrust, he seated himself *all the way* inside of me.

We both groaned simultaneously, shaking and panting.

Hunter felt even longer, bigger, and thicker than ever.

His dick practically throbbed inside of me in tandem with my clit. "Play with yourself, Gabby," he growled. "I want to watch as I fuck your tight little hole."

My toy was lubed up and ready to go. When I brought it over my pussy, I moaned and tensed around Hunter's cock.

"Mmfuck." He bit his bottom lip and withdrew his shaft. Before thrusting back in, slow and steady. I whimpered and met him thrust for thrust. "There she is." *Thrust.* "My naughty little doll." *Thrust.* "Giving her favourite football player a wet pussy and virgin ass to wreck." *Thrust.* "Fuck. Just like that. Squeeze around my dick. Make me fill you with my cum. God, you're perfect. Doesn't this feel so good, baby?"

He was perfect. So. Damn. Perfect.

Extremely sensitive and unable to speak, I managed a nod. Thriving under his commands. Moaning as I played with my clit. And gasping from the pleasure of having my ass pillaged by Hunter's thick cock.

One of the things I loved about Hunter was even when he was losing control, I was still his first priority. He was never rougher with me than what I could tolerate and never putting his own release before mine. "Harder, *bello*. I want it."

"You want it harder?" he snarled. "I'll give it to you harder."

It wasn't a threat, but a promise, and he delivered.

Hunter's punching hips met my ass as he drove his cock faster inside of me. And I could do nothing but lie there and fucking *take*, *take*, and *take it.* The room rang with a chorus of my screaming moans, the crackling of fire, and the obscene sounds of our bodies slapping together roughly. Our lovemaking felt otherworldly. I was a liquified mess underneath him. I touched, tasted, smelled, saw, and heard only Hunter Saint Warren.

"Yes, yes, yes," I chanted mindlessly as another orgasm crested.

We made out sloppily before his mouth poised at my ear and his dark voice hushed dirty talk that set me aflame. "That's a good girl, letting me enjoy my reward after such a tough season." He wrapped his hands around my ankles, uncrossed them from behind his back, and brought my legs down by my sides, until my knees practically touched my shoulders, and my feet dangled in the air. I screamed at the new angle. His menacing and lustful gaze told me he enjoyed seeing my body folded vulnerably as he bore down harder. "Keep your legs spread wide for me. I plan on using your holes all night long, little doll."

My gaze was awash with disbelief and pleasure. It felt good. So. Breathtakingly. Good. "Hunter!"

Smirking roguishly, he held the back of my legs and screwed his cock even deeper into my ass. "You're the hottest groupie slut, Gabriela," he crooned in a sweet, husky voice. "Your ass is gripping me so tight." *Thrust.* "And your pussy is making a creamy mess." *Thrust.* "Fuck yourself with two fingers." Thrust. "Show me how good you squirt when I ride you deep."

Fuck, he was an alpha through and through. I did as he demanded. Two fingers in my pussy to rub my G-spot, one toy over my swollen clit, and a rock-hard dick tunneling in and out of my snug channel. All inching me closer to my precipice.

Our pace was wondrous. I could feel him *everywhere.* "Oh my God."

"Yours," he vowed.

"Yes." My god of the sky. My sweet ruin. My fierce protector. "*Mine.*"

Sweat rivulets ran down our bodies. Handprints blossomed over my ass from his spanks. Nails raked across Hunter's back as he loved me harder, drinking my moans with his sensual kisses. He played with my bouncing tits. Licking, sucking, tugging at my nipples. And when he collared my throat again and stared down at me with unadulterated gratification, it was evident he was seconds from coming.

"Don't stop. Don't stop." I moaned choppily. "I'm almost there!"

He panted, his black hair sticking to his temples from the exertion. "I'm right there with you."

"Come with me, pretty boy."

"Fuck, Gabriela!"

And mere seconds later, we came together. Hunter buried his face in my neck, groaning raggedly as he emptied inside of me, and I screamed loudly, my release splashing between us.

It felt like time rolled to a stop as we held on to each other in the aftermath of it all.

Finally, Hunter raised his head and we locked eyes. Disheveled hair. Clammy skin. Uneven breaths. We were a perfect mess.

"That was…" he trailed off, shaking his head. "I have no words."

I gave him a lopsided smile. "I know. Want to do it again?"

He puffed out a low chuckle. "Anything you want, Gabby."

"You're such a good boyfriend." I grinned, fingering the ends of his hair. "Always spoiling me."

"I would do anything for you, Gabriela," Hunter confessed, gazing into my eyes with so much love. "You're my everything." He kissed my lips. "Forever."

My everything forever.

Tears pricked my eyes and slowly streamed down my face. Hunter tenderly brushed them away with his mouth, hugging me closer to his chest.

"Thank you for cherishing and protecting me." I pressed a kiss to his wound, over the bandage on his bicep. "Thank you for seeing me four hundred and eighty days ago…and not giving up."

Hunter's mouth pulled into a heart-stopping smile and he whispered, "I love you, Gabriela."

"And I love you, Hunter."

Then my handsome prince proceeded to lay four hundred and eighty kisses all over my body to mark every day since he first saw me.

CHAPTER 47

Unexpected Turn Of Events

GABRIELA

The entire weekend with Hunter was nothing short of bliss.

If we weren't cooking courtesy of the fully stocked kitchen, watching old movies from the Warrens' impressive DVD and VHS collection, or hanging out with Luna, Hunter and I were wrapped in each other's arms, making love until the early hours of the morning.

I would never forget the feeling of his stubble rasping against my skin, the feeling of his intoxicating kisses, and the feeling of the honeyed words he fanned over my flesh.

"*I love you. I love you. I love you,*" he whispered endlessly in my ear, day and night, like the sweetest of lullabies, and I held on to him like I was afraid he was a mirage that would disappear—like he was a dream that was far from everlasting and I would wake up any moment, wishing I'd stayed asleep instead.

Hunter had unravelled me. Peeled back all my layers, glanced at my center, plucked the essence of my soul and shaped it in a way where he could tuck it in the space next to his own. All my walls were down, my defenses broken, and yet I'd never felt safer. Or adored, cherished, and worshipped like the very goddess he claimed I was.

By the time Monday morning rolled around, a permanent smile was carved on my face.

Somewhere between sunset and sunrise, I had decided that I was going to marry Hunter Saint Warren in this decade. It was inevitable. He was my person. The other half of me. Might as well put a 24-karat gold band on his finger and make him my husband.

"How long did you say you'll be gone?" Hunter asked, leaning against the hallway wall and watching me with softness as I put my shoes on.

I smiled. "I already told you."

"Remind me again."

We weren't gone yet and he already stared at Luna and me like he missed us. "Three hours. Long enough for me to pacify the women in my family. Then I'll come running back to you."

Mamma and Nonna were in shambles when Papà delivered the news about the attack on Friday night. They knew I was staying at Hunter's home this weekend, protected by him and a brigade of guards. Saturday and Sunday, we had two phone calls and they spent most of it crying. Mamma said she didn't spend eighteen hours in labour to give birth, only for me to be living elsewhere during one of the scariest times of my life. And Nonna said that since I refused to come back to my childhood home in the West Side, she was coming over here to camp in the courtyard with her cane and rifle, in case the attacker returned. She didn't trust the guards to get the job done and stated that she was a better shot than all of them—which, to her credit, wasn't a lie since Nonna was a badass. Both women also spent a long time showering Hunter with love and thank-yous, grateful that he protected me but still upset that he got hurt in the process.

"Promise?" Hunter uncrossed his arms and pushed off the wall, advancing towards me.

He was bare-chested and in low-slung black pyjama pants. We'd woken up an hour ago and all I wanted was to get back in bed with my warm, sleepy, pretty boy.

I wrapped my arms around him and pressed a kiss over his bandaged wound. "I promise, Hunt."

Oscar and another young guard named Craig were driving me back to my childhood home. Mamma and Nonna were desperate to see me in person, even if it was for a quick lunch.

I hated how Hunter's and my entire lives had been flipped over in an instant. And I *hated* that this occurred right as Hunter won his championship, the attack putting a damper on the high he was riding. Not to mention, our academic lives. We were putting a stop to attending school for this week. Both of us had already emailed the necessary personnel to let them know we had family emergencies.

I hoped seven days were enough time to catch the culprit.

There wasn't a single part of me that wanted to drop this semester when we were so close to the finish line, but if that was what it came down to for security purposes…then so be it.

I was trying to remain optimistic for the sake of both our mental, physical, and emotional health, yet there were no leads. Papà and the Remingtons were doing their utmost best to solve this in a timely manner so our lives could resume back to normal.

Though I had enough self-awareness to know that our lives would never be fully normal after this chapter.

Hunter kissed my lips, his warmth radiating off of him and seeping into me. "Come back home to me soon."

"I will. I promise."

At least he wouldn't be alone here. Hannah and Heidi were coming over to visit him in an hour. Plus, many of the Remington guards would remain on the property.

By our feet, Luna meowed. I picked her up. She blinked her big eyes at her daddy, sad at the thought of leaving him for even a short time, and pawed at him.

"You too, Luna," Hunter said, kissing her head. "And take care of your mommy for me, please."

She meowed in agreement before going into her carrier.

A knock on the front door let us know my two guards were ready and waiting for us.

"I love you." Hunter cupped my face. "Be safe, Gabby."

"I love you," I returned. "Don't worry. I'll be back before you know it."

He pecked my forehead. "I'm counting on it."

After squeezing Hunter's hand one final time, I stepped out of the home and headed over to the bulletproof SUV, where Oscar and Craig waited for us.

The backseat door was open and I climbed inside, Luna in tow.

I waved to Hunter before the door closed, the sound akin to the final nail being pounded into a coffin. My exhale was shaky. Through the tinted window, I saw Hunter watching the vehicle and the guards with hawk eyes.

As if trying to tell them silently: *Take care of my girls.*

I dragged my fingertips down the glass, tracing his silhouette. I was already counting down the minutes before I could see him again.

My bodyguards got in the front and minutes later, we pulled out of the driveway and headed down the deserted road that led to Hunter's home.

The sky was grey and the air smelled like a hint of petrichor. A rainstorm loomed nearby. I was uneasy and attributed it to the fact that I was parted from Hunter, my safety net, and not at the odd sense of foreboding curling in the car.

I reminded myself that I was armed. A loaded gun sat in my purse, a pocket knife was tucked in the upper-thigh holster hidden underneath my skirt, and I was wearing a gold locket Papà gave me on Friday night, a small tracking chip inside…so if anything went awry, they could find me.

I was okay.

I was going to remain okay.

Luna glanced at me, meowing. My sweet, furry baby. She was uneasy too.

I removed her from the carrier and brought her into my lap. She instantly curled against me and I petted her back, enjoying her soothing purrs.

"I gotta take a leak," announced Craig to Oscar.

Oscar, who was behind the wheel, shot Craig a scowl. "Hold it in."

"Can't," he said in an awfully annoying and holier-than-thou tone. "I'll piss my pants."

"Then you'll piss your pants."

"It'll stink up the car and then Princess in the backseat will complain to her daddy dearest that I ruined her little day trip."

Craig had nothing but audacity. Especially because he threw me a wink over his shoulder like I was going to find him funny. Ew. I knew to a certain extent I'd lived a sheltered life, but insinuating that I was a brat and using that as ammo wasn't a way to get in my—or the Remingtons'—good graces.

"Oscar, it's okay." I adopted a fake, sickly sweet smile. "Let the young *boy* relieve himself. It's not his fault he's not toilet trained yet."

That sobered up Craig and dragged a chuckle from my usually stoic, middle-aged bodyguard.

Craig glared at me. I shot him an air-kiss with my middle finger.

Oscar grumbled, "I'll pull over and you have less than a minute to do your business. Understood?"

Not waiting for a reply, Oscar drove the car to the side of the road and Craig flung open the door. To give him privacy, Oscar and I looked the other way while he did his thing.

Immediately, we heard a loud thump.

I jolted in my seat and Oscar cursed at the noise.

Craig's tall frame could no longer be seen.

Did Craig faint in the midst of peeing?

"Shit." My guard grabbed his gun. "Stay here, Gabriela."

Oscar stepped out of the car and I moved down the backseat so I could peer out the window with Luna.

And instantly regretted it.

Goosebumps erupted over my body, that sense of unease amplifying.

Craig was dead, a bullet lodged in his head.

Oscar saw it at the same time as me.

Our worried eyes connected through the window, a silent warning passing through us.

Oscar threw a fleeting glance at our surroundings as he rounded the front of the car. He opened the driver's door and barked, "We've been compromised. We need to head back. *Now.*"

Before Oscar could get inside, we heard the whistling sound of another bullet.

It struck him right in the throat.

My mouth fell open on a choked, mute scream, Luna following with her own hiss.

Oscar's body hit the ground with a jarring thud.

Teary and panicked, I scrambled forward to glance in the space between the two front seats. "No, no, no." Fear slammed in my gut. "*Oscar!*"

He was dead, lying in a pool of his own blood.

I began crying as I rummaged through my purse for my phone, needing to call Papà, freaking out because someone just killed the two guards who were meant to safely ferry me to my destination.

I never got to call Papà.

I never got to calm an anxious Luna.

Because my door was suddenly yanked open and I screamed, coming face-to-face with the same cloaked figure from Friday night.

He was in all black, with a gun in his hand.

His hood was up and a mask covered his expression.

All I saw were soulless dark eyes.

Before he yanked down the covering and unveiled himself.

Taylor Prescott hedged me a crazy, secretive grin. "Said I would remind you of your place, didn't I, you stupid fucking bitch?"

CHAPTER 48

A Losing Battle

GABRIELA

Nothing—and I mean nothing—could have prepared me for this turn of events.

My guards were dead and now my ex-situationship was blocking my exit, with a deranged expression and a weapon in his hand.

The same weapon he used to kill my guards.

I didn't understand *why* he was here or *why* he would do this.

The only thing I knew with certainty was that it was never Maverick or Franco.

All along, the culprit was Taylor.

The break-in, the stabbing, and the texts.

He was behind all of it.

My chest clenched with fright and my throat tightened.

I didn't want to engage with this motherfucker. So I clutched Luna to my chest and skirted down the seat. I could escape via the other side's back door and burst into a run. We weren't far away from Hunter's home. Barely three minutes away. If I screamed my lungs out, someone—anyone—would hear me.

I just needed to make it out and not catch a bullet.

Taylor quickly caught on and entered the car, cocking his gun against my head. "Ah, ah, ah. I wouldn't move if I were you."

I froze, the blood in my veins turning cold.

My brave Luna chose that exact moment to hiss and leap out of my arms, scratching the fuck out of Taylor's face. He howled and stumbled back.

She gave me enough time to lurch between the front seats to grab Oscar's fallen gun.

But I wasn't fast enough.

Five fingers wrapped around my hair and jerked me back *hard*, nearly breaking my neck with the force. I screamed as pain exploded along my scalp. Taylor's mouth came at my cheek, his breath sour and gross as he taunted, "What do you think you're doing, Gabriela?"

"*Fuck!*" Tears coursed down my face as Taylor yanked me out of the car by my hair. Like a fish out of water, I squirmed uncontrollably, crying and shouting, "*Let go of me, Taylor!*"

"You're coming with me," he growled. "We have a score to settle."

My back collided painfully against the road and my skin scraped as he dragged me towards an awaiting vehicle, the trunk already popped open.

The fucker was going to kidnap and do God knows what else with me.

My heart raced like it was trying to jump out of my ribcage.

Luna caterwauled, running after us, frantic to save me.

"*Help!*" Uselessly, I fought against his grasp, but I was no match for his strength, overpowered and hauled around like a weightless toy. I never stopped screaming, making noise in hopes that someone would hear and come to my aid. I never stopped digging my fingers in the back of his hands either, attempting to dislodge his hold, knowing at the very least I was breaking skin and his DNA would be under my fingernails. "*Help, help, help!*"

"Keep screaming, bitch," he threatened, appearing like a fucking monster. "No one's going to hear you."

When he smacked me so hard across the face, my shouts died and my cheek split from the knuckle rings he was wearing.

Pain like I'd never experienced expanded inside of me.

It felt like a whip flayed open the skin of my back, my face, and my scalp. I wished I were numb. Yet I felt every ounce of hurt ringing in my bones. To the point where I was seconds from passing out.

Luna managed to climb Taylor's body and swipe at his cheek in retaliation, cutting open his skin and leaving three long lines that were akin to the hellhound mark.

He cursed and loosened his hold on my hair. I managed to scramble free for less than a blink of an eye before he caught my ends and dragged me back.

At that moment, Luna scratched his eyelid.

The burst of pride in my chest at Luna's ability to disengage my attacker was swiftly squashed by fear when Taylor howled, "Fucking cat! Should have killed you the first time I saw you!"

He grabbed her body and flung her away. She landed painfully on the ground with a feeble meow that broke me.

"*No!*" A renewed sense of fight funneled through me. I screeched until I thought my lungs would collapse, struggling in his hold as angry tears blurred my vision. "Don't touch her, you fucking asshole! I'll kill you!"

"I'd like to see you try." He hauled my injured body in the back of his trunk. He was twice my size and strength, and yet I still tried, and tried, and *tried* in vain to escape through sobs and sheer perseverance. But Taylor kept shoving me back every time I managed to lift my bloody, bruised self up. The sadistic piece of shit was enjoying watching my futile attempts. "After today, you'll never be able to leave me ever again."

The last thing I remembered was a piece of cloth being shoved against my nose and mouth and Taylor's gleaming eyes staring me down as he suffocated me.

Then my body went limp and I fell into a dark abyss.

CHAPTER 49

Taken From Him

HUNTER

In the half an hour since Gabriela left, a sense of dread bloomed within me.

At first, I tried to ignore it and chalk it up to my attachment issues with her. I was obsessed and so damn in love with the red-haired beauty that I hated being away from her. We spent the entire weekend glued together, laughing, talking, making love, and simply existing next to each other like we were always meant to be.

And yet all the kisses, all the strokes, all the conversations weren't enough.

I feared even an entire lifetime with her wouldn't be.

I wanted eternity and beyond. I wanted to possess every smile, every laugh, every touch. I wanted to possess every facet that composed this beautiful, brilliant, star-powered woman. Even the ones she'd yet to discover about herself.

Gabriela Regina Bellafiore was my drug and I was a fiend for her.

It wasn't a healthy mindset, but I didn't care.

I was all about this little goddess of mine.

And because her well-being would always be my top priority, I could no longer ignore the foreboding prickling the atmosphere of my home in her absence. It perforated the air and wrapped around my throat like a noose.

As I emerged from my en suite, a fresh gauze applied over my wound, a towel around my waist, and another to dry my hair, my eyes drifted over to the digital clock on my nightstand.

It read 12:45 p.m.

Right about now, Gabriela should have reached her family's home.

I donned my clothes in record speed, then headed downstairs. My place was less bright without Gabriela's and Luna's presence. A few guards lingered inside as a precaution, prepping for my mom and sister's arrival.

They gave me silent nods of acknowledgement that I returned.

I'd left my phone on the console table. When I plucked it from the wooden catch-all bowl and unlocked it, there wasn't a single text or call from Gabriela.

Frowning, I opened another app to check her location.

And abruptly halted when I realized that it hadn't moved in the last forty-five minutes.

She was about a kilometer away, on the road leading to my home.

Did she and the guards encounter a car issue?

I called her. After a few rings, it went to voicemail. I called her again, pacing the hallway. Voicemail once more. I resorted to texting her.

Is everything okay, Gabby? —Hunter

Your location hasn't moved. Did something happen? —Hunter

Please call me back. —Hunter

I need to hear your voice. —Hunter

My texts were delivered but remained unread.

There was a sinking feeling in my core.

I glanced over to my right and caught one of the guards' attention. "Have Oscar or Craig contacted anyone regarding car issues?"

He appeared confused. "Not to my knowledge, sir, but I can ask the others."

Fuck. "Please do straight away."

While the rest of the guards inquired amongst themselves, I pulled up Enzo Bellafiore's contact information and sent him a text.

Hi, Enzo. Have you heard from Gabriela? I checked her phone's location and she hasn't moved in over half an hour. I'm worried. —Hunter

Three dots popped up, letting me know he was typing.
Then my phone pinged.

No. She should have been here by now. I'm calling Oscar. —Enzo

Fuck, fuck, fuck.

Something went wrong. I felt it in my blood, in my bones, in my fucking soul. I could either sit here and wait for the others to figure out what was going on, or I could grab my keys and head out myself to investigate.

My decision was made within thirty seconds.

"Sir, you have to stay inside!" one of the guards hollered as I fast-walked down the pathway leading to the driveway where my Jag was parked. "It's not safe to go out!"

I ignored their calls and unlocked my driver's door, getting in before they could stop me. The engine purred to life and I peeled out of the driveway with speed, heading to the location where Gabriela's car was stalled.

Some of the guards got in vehicles and trailed after me, but I was faster.

The thought of Gabriela in danger overshadowed the ache in my right arm as I drove, so much so that I could pretend for a moment that I hadn't been injured three days ago.

Panic rose in me like a tidal wave when a familiar black SUV came into view, parked on the side of the lonely road, with two doors open…

And two bodies on the ground.

No, no, no.

I threw my hazard lights on and stumbled out of the car, making sure to grab my gun from the glove compartment. My heart drummed fast and my breaths thinned as I walked with heavy feet, a figurative chain manacled around my ankles, slowing me down from viewing the train wreck.

My first and only encounter with death had been my dad.

I remembered seeing his corpse tucked in a casket, his expression peaceful. He'd still appeared full of life, like minutes from waking up after a long nap.

But nothing could have prepared me for witnessing *these* lifeless corpses.

There was nothing peaceful in their expressions. Their eyes were open in shock and their mouths parted, lying in a pool of their own blood.

So. Much. Blood.

I recoiled back at seeing a dead Oscar and Craig, bile rising in my throat.

"Gabriela!" I screamed for her, tossing a glance at my surroundings. The empty road and the forest lining either side of it. Frantically, I rounded the car to peer into the backseat as well.

But Gabriela was nowhere to be found.

Her purse lay open in the backseat, its contents—including her phone—scattered across the surface.

As if she'd left in a hurry.

No.

As if she'd been *taken*.

I felt like the walls around me were closing in.

No, no, no. She couldn't be gone, she couldn't be hurt, she couldn't be…

I couldn't finish the thought.

The very thought that Gabriela was no longer on this Earth was unfathomable to me. I refused to believe it.

Something inside of me cracked. I threw my head back on another mournful scream that boomed in the cold morning air like a desperate plea, "*Gabriela!*"

I needed to hear her voice. I needed to see her. I needed her in my arms. She had to be okay. There was no other possibility. Otherwise, I

504

would hold a grudge with every god out there, every star, every inch of the universe's tapestry for stealing her away from me.

In the midst of the chaos that was my mind, I heard a faint meow right as I was about to pull out my phone to dial Enzo.

Luna.

My head snapped to my left, watching with tormented eyes as Luna ran towards me, her gait a little slower than usual. Almost like she was limping. She came from the opposite side of the road, closer to my home and furthest from where the car was parked.

Her small cries cut me to the quick.

It struck me that she was probably headed towards my home to the best of her ability, in an attempt to alert us. And if any of the guards— or myself—had seen Luna arriving at the property, we'd have known something cataclysmically wrong had occurred.

"Luna." I knelt just as she reached me, her distressing sounds growing in decibels as she pawed at me. "It's okay. I'm here. I'm—"

My sentence died when I realized Luna's pawprints had blood on them. They left a red mark on my white dress shirt like a bad omen.

Trepidation rushed through my veins when I checked Luna for injuries. Physically, she appeared fine, but she released a pitiful noise when I touched her back leg, letting me know she was actually hurt.

When I tried to grab her, she ducked out of my arms with a sharp yowl and trotted across the road. Confused, I followed after her with a grim expression.

She kept circling an area across the road, beckoning me closer.

I froze upon seeing more blood smeared against the asphalt.

I stared at the sight with vengeance.

Please, please, please. Don't tell me that's Gabriela's blood.

To confirm my worst suspicions, Luna meowed and directed my attention towards the side of the road, where a familiar pearl bracelet mocked me.

It belonged to Gabriela.

My fingers shook as I picked up the discarded item, clutching it in my palm fiercely as if that would keep my anger and tears at bay.

Not too far away from her bracelet, there was another item.

A fallen, slim leather wallet.

I picked it up.

When I flipped it open to reveal a flurry of credit cards and a driver's licence…every breath, every heartbeat, every thought came to a standstill.

The photographed face of Taylor Prescott stared back at me.

My haunted eyes rose to Luna. Her gaze never wavered from mine.

She tilted her head as if silently confirming my question.

At that exact moment, two more things occurred.

Bulletproof cars rushed in on the scene, filled with Remington guards.

And my phone rang, Josh's caller ID flashing on the screen.

Numbly, I picked it up and brought it to my ear, not saying a word.

Josh did all the talking for me. "We know where she is."

CHAPTER 50

Finally Over

GABRIELA

I awoke to dampness and a blurry vision.

The first thing that welcomed me was a painful, splitting sensation travelling over my face like a fissure, where the skin of my cheek stung from Taylor's smack. It was followed by a deep-seated ache in my entire body. Every inch of me throbbed. My hands, zip-tied in front of me. My back, hips, and legs, from how I'd been dragged across the road. And in my head, from the newly pounding headache.

My senses were slower than usual as I struggled to take inventory of my new environment, my eyes barely registering a low ceiling. Four walls. Concrete ground. A faded light coming from somewhere to my right.

Where the hell was I and how much time had passed since Taylor kidnapped me?

I fought the sob choking its way up, trying to calm myself down and muster the mental strength to get out of this hellhole.

What did I do to deserve this? Why had my seemingly unbothered ex-fling—who broke up with me of his *own* volition—turn out to be a fucking psycho?

I may not know his reasoning yet, but I would find out. Sooner or later, I would escape or be rescued by Papà, the guards, and…

Hunter.

By now, he must have figured out that something wasn't right. My pretty boy must be going out of his mind with worry, trying to find me.

And Luna.

My sweet girl who fought so bravely for me.

The thought of my little family gave me more strength and resilience. Filled my cup anew. I wouldn't perish here. I was going to make it out alive because I wanted to continue building a life with Hunter.

And once I got freed?

I would fucking kill Taylor Prescott myself.

He wouldn't hurt me more than he already had.

I was my papà's daughter and Bellafiores never went down without a fight.

It took nearly all my energy to twist myself onto my right side with a barely suppressed groan. God, that hurt. My head swam and I closed my eyes, slowly counting to ten.

It was quiet in here—wherever I was—almost to a point where the stillness seemed eerie. When I opened my eyes, the blood-curdling scream I let out shattered that stillness.

Beside me, lying on her front, with her light brown hair fanned around her…was Morgan Huxley.

There was a bullet lodged in her forehead, a trail of dried blood stamped down the bridge of her nose.

And her eyes were open, staring straight into mine, as though seeing *through* me.

No.

No.

No.

The sob I tried to hold back burst free from my dry, cracked lips as I took in my peer's dead body. He killed her. The sick fuck actually killed her. I cried silently, my body quivering against the hard ground with the depth of my sorrow.

Morgan and I may have had our differences, but I was willing to bet on everything I owned that she had never done anything to warrant this kind of ending.

My tied hands attempted to reach for her.

But I wasn't able to, regardless of how close she rested.

Through a tear-stained gaze, I noticed a cross positioned against a mosaic-stained window, where the barest amount of light filtered in, and rectangular fixtures in the wall with dates and names.

All ending with Prescott.

Fuck.

We were in the Prescott family's mausoleum.

Chills spread over my skin. Acid burned in my throat. Nausea worsened everything.

Was this Taylor's big plan? Kill Morgan and me for whatever reason his fucked-up mind concocted and bury our bodies right here, where we couldn't be found, our families and loved ones searching until their hope ran out?

No.

I couldn't afford to think like that—couldn't allow those thoughts to pierce the already fragile veil keeping my mind from crumbling.

I was going to escape.

I wouldn't die here.

This wouldn't be my final resting place.

It may very well be Taylor's, though.

With *that* echoing in my mind like a final statement, I calmed just a bit. It wouldn't be easy getting out of here, but I was determined.

Seeing Morgan dead next to me only fortified that I wouldn't be Taylor's next victim.

Inhaling through my nose, I glanced down at my body. My clothes were still on, but my black opaque tights, underneath my skirt, had various rips and holes from when he'd hauled me and I tried to fight. The skin around my knee was scraped and when I shifted, I felt cuts pulling at my skin in various spots. I didn't sense any soreness between my legs, which meant the sordid asshole hadn't assaulted me while I was unconscious.

The relief I experienced grew tenfold when I realized that I still wore the necklace Papà had given me.

The one with the tracker.

Thank goodness.

My loved ones would figure out something was wrong—if they hadn't already—and I needed to keep myself alive.

Exhaling slowly through my nose, all my senses sharpened when I remembered I still had my pocket knife tucked in my upper-thigh holster. I could feel it as I shifted. Taylor hadn't realized that I had a weapon on my person. Otherwise, he'd have removed it.

I wasn't sure where he was or when he would be coming back, but instinct told me it would be soon. Working fast, I did my best to wriggle into position and reach under my skirt with my tied hands.

A sliver of victory blazed through me when I caught the handle of the knife, a keepsake my nonno left for me before passing away, and dragged it out.

A beacon of hope, the metal of the blade glinted in the dim light.

Anticipation rattled in my chest as I began slicing at the bindings, sawing back and forth until finally…they snapped and my hands were freed.

I didn't move a muscle, momentarily wracked with disbelief that *I did it.*

Just as I was about to sit up, a clatter near the entrance had me freezing like a deer caught in headlights.

I stayed put, joining my hands to give the illusion that they were still tied.

The atmosphere morphed with something sinister as Taylor entered through the mausoleum's opening. Hood down. Mask off. And a shovel in his hand that he propped against the doorframe, the end coated with grass and mud.

His presence made the space appear even smaller, tighter, inescapable.

A frisson travelled down my back.

"Oh, good." He approached me and lowered himself to a crouch. "You're awake."

His knuckles skimmed my cheek and I recoiled with a sneer. "Don't fucking touch me!"

The only man who was allowed to skim his knuckles down my cheek was Hunter.

Taylor's gaze hardened, a menacing smirk blooming over his lips. "You forget who's in charge, Gabby." He leaned in, his disgusting hot breath blowing over my skin. "*Me*. And if I want to touch you?" He pinched my chin between his thumb and forefinger. "I. Fucking. Will."

I squirmed, under the guise of being a damsel in distress. I didn't have the perfect angle to strike—yet—so I feigned helplessness, gripping the closed knife between my fisted palms. When the time was right, I was going to finish Luna's job and take his fucking eye out.

I'd never been a violent or bloodthirsty girl, but this was a turning point for me.

A dark chaos consumed my mind, its fingers spreading through my mainframe like a sickness. I would never rest until Taylor was dead. I grew antsier every second that he lived.

"Why?" I asked sharply. Taylor's brows rising stated that he was surprised at the lack of defeat in my tone. "Why do all of this?"

It was clear what I implied. My apartment break-in. Writing on my wall. Stabbing Hunter. Sending taunting texts. Killing my bodyguards. And everything in between that I might have missed. I wanted all the answers before he died.

Taylor combed his fingers through his hair, a bitter chuckle escaping him. "Why?" He pinned me with wide, angry eyes. "*Why*, Gabriela?" he thundered on. "You dense fucking bitch! Because I love you!"

I blinked.

To say I was flabbergasted would be an understatement.

Through my thinly concealed fury, I replayed his words.

Then I burst out laughing.

My full, belly-deep laughter triggered Taylor.

"Stop laughing!" he barked, backhanding me exactly in the same spot as his previous strike. "I love you and you wanted to break up with me! You did this! You drove me to this! You're at fucking fault!"

That sobered me, the last strains of my chuckle dying. "You love me?" I snarled incredulously. "Last I remember, you're the one who ended things by sending me a text saying you'd found better! With *her*!" I jerked my head towards Morgan's dead body, growling, "So now I'm supposed to believe you taunted, stalked, and kidnapped me because you love me? Get a grip, you fucking gaslighting lunatic!"

He stood up with an angry roar, kicking aside the shovel on the ground like a petulant child not getting his way.

"She was just a distraction!" he screamed, the vein in his neck popping. "A way to get over you! A way to get back at you!"

"What the fuck are you talking about?" I spat through gritted teeth.

But Taylor barely heard my question, pacing the length of the mausoleum while mumbling some bullshit to himself. He was such a different version than the smooth-talking jock I met over the summer. The one who conducted himself in such an easy-going manner, like he took nothing in life too seriously. The one who acted like he was on board with the idea of a friends-with-benefits situation since he didn't want any attachments.

Obviously, that was all a façade. *This* was the real him.

Taking advantage of his silence, I pushed myself into a kneeling position, still keeping my hands close together to give the semblance that I remained tied up.

I calculated the proximity to the mausoleum door. If I slashed my knife anywhere across his face or jugular, that would buy me enough time to flit past the doorway. I hoped that if I kept running without stopping—without getting caught again—eventually, I'd come across some Good Samaritan who could help me.

"Taylor?" I prodded again when he didn't answer. "What are you talking about?"

He stopped pacing and cut me a sidelong glance. "At first, it was casual between us. We both agreed to keep things physical. But then I fell for you. I was getting ready to ask you to be my girlfriend…right before I saw your texts."

He might as well be speaking gibberish. "What texts?"

His face reddened as if he was frustrated that I wasn't getting it. "The last time we fucked, you left your phone on my nightstand and went to the bathroom. Your phone kept vibrating with texts. I'd seen you put in your passcode enough times to know what it was. So I went through it—specifically your group chat with your bitch-ass friends."

Another wave of fury swept through me. This motherfucker had the audacity to encroach on my privacy and call my girls bitch-ass friends?

"You wrote that you were bored with me. You told them that I was a lousy fuck and that you were going to end our arrangement soon—that you were trying to find the best way to let me down gently without hurting me!" He blazed on. "And the fucking cunts encouraged you! As if I wasn't the best fucking thing to have happened to you!"

My God.

Taylor Prescott was delusional.

I was about to correct him and say that the best fucking thing to have happened to me was Hunter, when he yanked out a thick wad of something from his jacket's pocket and practically threw it on the ground between us.

I flinched at the motion.

And when I saw what that *something* was?

My heartbeat rushed faster.

Printed pictures of Hunter and me.

Hundreds of them.

From our first interaction on the dance floor the night of Shaun's party...to last Friday night when we'd been celebrating the Panthers' football championship at Josh and Layla's home.

Some of the shots had perfect resolution. Others were blurry, captured quickly to avoid getting caught. All of them were taken in discreet angles and always when Hunter and I seemed wrapped up in each other, the outside world faded.

There was no way for us to have realized we were being photographed, let alone watched.

The shot that made me nauseated was the one from Halloween night. Hunter and I had just finished making love in the woods when we heard a noise nearby. I naively assumed it was one of the guards patrolling the area, who got too close to us before retreating.

But no.

It was Taylor, *stalking* us from the very beginning.

My haunted gaze rose to his and he gave me a glare. "You wasted no time, did you? The minute I ended it with you, you hopped on the next available dick."

My nostrils flared. "So let me get this straight. You decided to end things with me by using Morgan to get back at me? But then you get mad that I didn't give a shit and—"

"Yes, you fucking bitch! You were supposed to care!" he spat, throwing his arms up in the air. "Not move on with my captain and search for each other's tonsils on the dance floor! You fucked up by kissing him, Gabriela. So I broke into your apartment with the spare key I had made to leave you a warning...and you failed to heed it." His voice pitched low to a baleful level. Of course the English major would use Shakespearean quotes as taunts. Fucking classic. "And not only that, but you actively dated Hunter after telling me you weren't a relationship kind of girl. Watching you fall in love with him made me hurl! It should have been me with you! Not him! If I had a proper opening and you weren't being surveilled by a guard, I would have punished you weeks ago."

I seethed as the puzzle pieces clicked into place. Had my parents not taken the precaution to protect me, had Oscar not been guarding me, had Hunter not been there for me twenty-four seven...this sick fuck would have hurt me a long time ago.

All this time, Taylor feigned nonchalance whenever we were in the same vicinity, giving off the impression that he didn't care that I was with Hunter since he broke up with me. But really, he was bubbling with anger on the inside and planning revenge. "Now what's your big plan? Spend all your free time stalking me from the shadows so you could what? Stab me to death? Profess your undying love? Win me back in your own fucked-up way? Tell me!"

My sentence ended on a screaming note.

Taylor pinned me with flinty eyes. "Yes, I stalked you. Yes, I love you. And no, that knife wasn't meant for you." His jaw clenched. "It was for Hunter. You're mine and he touched you—he *sullied* you. Which meant he couldn't go on living. My only regret is that I missed the mark."

I wanted to vomit. "You're fucked up, Taylor. Never in a million years did I think you'd turn out this way."

A cruel laugh rumbled out of him. "You made me this way. Like I said, it's your fucking fault."

I turned my head when his spit flew too close to my face.

"Had that idiot bodyguard of yours not stepped out to take a piss, I'd have resorted to shooting the tires. Either way, we would have found our way here. My PI spent all weekend searching for you. Hiding out in a safe house was a good idea, I'll give it to you. But there's nowhere you can go where I wouldn't find you, Gabriela."

He said it in a creepy sing-song manner that amplified my bloodthirst.

I licked my lips. It beckoned Taylor closer. Good. I needed him in arm's length for what I was about to do. "If Hunter and I were your main targets, why kill Morgan? What role did she play in this?"

"She was collateral damage." He shrugged like this news was no biggie—like his lover wasn't lying dead next to me by his own hands. "Sure, she was a good fuck, but too clingy for my taste. I was going to end it with her soon anyways. What I didn't expect was for her to show up at my home unannounced today. She caught me going through the pictures in my room and had the audacity to say I was fucking crazy for stringing her along while being obsessed with you. Claimed I should be locked up in an asylum for stalking you." He chuckled like this situation was actually funny. "She was trying to give you a call to warn you, but I caught her as she walked away. Never expected her to be a fighter, but she fought me for a total of eleven minutes. At first, I was just going to tie her up until I dealt with you and Hunter. But then...I realized she was a loose end." The amusement slipped off his face in the flash of a lightning bolt. "And loose ends always have to be disposed of."

I shuddered, a sharp pang travelling through my chest. Poor Morgan. I imagined the pain and shock she must have felt at discovering that the guy she was seeing was deranged. Right before he killed her. She didn't deserve this. At all. And even though we rarely saw eye to eye, she still attempted to call me.

Now we'd never be able to mend what lay broken between us because she was dead.

"There's a special place in hell for men like you," I spewed at Taylor. "You're a fucking piece of shit."

"And you're mine," he stated matter-of-factly. "But I no longer want to fuck you now that Hunter's had his dick inside of you. Which leaves me with only one choice." His face darkened. "I have to kill you…and myself."

If I could go back in time, I'd never give this psychopath the time of day. The fact that I slept with him made me sick to my stomach.

He crept close and I firmly gripped the blade in my hand, readying myself.

Just a little bit closer…

Taylor crouched in front of me again and clasped my face with a dirty palm. A ragged sound erupted from my lips. "I dug us both a grave. Our final resting place won't be in my family's mausoleum, but six feet beneath the ground, right next to each other, where our bones can lie together until the end of time."

The visual burned like a hot ember in my chest.

Fuck this man.

He couldn't die fast enough.

At least I had him right where I wanted.

I smirked once, cold and cruel, and whispered against his mouth, "You're mistaken, Taylor. Our final resting place won't be next to each other and you were a *lousy fuck*. We were together a handful of times. It's not my fault you romanticized it and fell in love, you delusional moron."

His eyes flared with shock. "You fucking—"

"And today won't be my last day on Earth. But it will be yours," I growled and moved fast, slashing my knife across his face. "This is for hurting my Luna!"

I got him right in the eye and down across his cheek.

Blood instantly sprayed out of the cut and some of it landed on my white turtleneck. He screamed and fell back on his ass in a dramatic flourish, clutching his face. "*Fuck!*"

His bellow shook through the mausoleum and I leapt up on my unsteady feet. Whirling around, I dashed away, adrenaline pumping through me. Taylor staggered behind, howling in pain.

When I almost reached the threshold and felt the heat of him at my back, I quickly grabbed the shovel he'd discarded earlier and turned around. "And this?" I spat. "This is for Morgan!"

I whacked him *hard* with all my might.

The sound of metal meeting flesh and bone crunched loudly in the air.

Taylor screamed again and fell back a few steps, bending over to brace his middle.

Satisfied that I'd disengaged him enough, I darted forward.

It must have rained. The manicured green lawn beneath my feet was wet and slippery. We were in a large clearing—maybe the backyard of Prescott Mansion—and willow trees lined the perimeters. Between the spaces, I could make out a wrought-iron fence and a street beyond it.

Run as fast as you can, Gabriela. All you need to do is get there, drag yourself to the other side of the fence, and get help. You can do it.

I ignored the protesting ache in my body as I pushed myself to a sprint, gnashing my teeth when I saw the grave to my left.

"Come back here!" he yelled. "Gabriela!"

How did he manage to gain on me with his injuries? He must be moving on pure adrenaline. Determined, I also kept running. Despite everything in me wanting to collapse right here, right now.

An arm circled around my waist. I was lifted into the air.

I turned feral, screaming, kicking, clawing at his hold as he dragged me back.

His heavy pants hit the top of my head and a knife pressed against my throat.

"You never listen, do you?" he grunted while I struggled. "We're meant to be together. The sooner you accept it, the fucking better."

He threw me to the ground. I landed right next to the grave. Every nerve ending in my body cried out. I was beyond exhausted and yet I still managed to crawl backwards and away from him. "Go to hell, Taylor!"

"I am." He was gruesome, every bit the depiction of a monster, with sweat-matted hair and blood running down his eye and sunken cheek. "But I'm taking you with me, Gabriela."

Sobs spilled out of me as I retreated on weak limbs. I'd lost my own knife in the scuffle and had no weapons to use against him. Taylor was purposely taking his time trekking forward, the sadistic side of him basking in my fear.

"I'll slice your throat first," he announced. "I'll do the same to myself and join you. Don't worry, baby. It'll all end as it was meant to be. You and me. Together. Forever."

His words filled me with revulsion.

I didn't want to die.

I wanted to live.

I wanted to grow old and grey with my friends, with my family, with my Hunter.

Just as I had that last thought, Taylor's body was tackled to the ground by another taller, bigger, and much stronger one.

Hunter.

As if my mind summoned the man I was in love with, he appeared like a mirage.

There was a brief second where our eyes connected, despair and torment radiating off of Hunter as he studied me. Soaked, in my bruised and bloodied state. There was relief in his gaze that I was breathing, but the volatile glint in his blue eyes overshadowed it.

The picture I created filled him with a violent rage.

He was going to make Taylor pay.

My body sagged under the knowledge that I was safe. I wouldn't have to fight my battle on my own anymore.

Not a sound was exchanged between Hunter and me.

But I knew what was coming next regardless.

Lightning sparked and thunder clapped in the sky right as Hunter flipped over a caught-off-guard Taylor.

He got on top of him, robbed the knife from his clasp, and threw it far away from his reach.

The grey skies above came down in a torrential downpour as Hunter's hand closed around Taylor's throat and another cocked a gun at his head. He deadpanned, "Any last words before I introduce you to your maker, you piece of shit?"

"F-fuck you." Taylor attempted to spit at him, but his saliva drooped down the sides of his mouth. He turned blue under the chokehold and tried to buck Hunter off, to no avail. "L-let go of me. She's mine."

Hunter's anger skyrocketed.

"She was never yours." He glared down into Taylor's last eye. "And now I'm going to kill you for what you did to her."

I'd never seen Hunter like this.

Gone was the gentleman with the princelike demeanour. This was my protector, who mercilessly drove his fist against Taylor's face with an unruly expression that should have worried me. Yet only satiated the bloodlust churning within. The one that wanted to see Taylor get a dose of his own medicine.

Hunter could have easily ended Taylor with a bullet to the head. But as the rain poured down in harder sheets, plastering his clothes to him like a second skin, and lightning lit the sky, illuminating his skyrocketing anger…I understood that he was not only possessed with the need to avenge me, but grief for what I'd endured.

He wanted Taylor to suffer in his final moments.

Hunter pounded on Taylor until the latter stopped squirming, succumbing to the wounds I'd dealt and the current strikes Hunter laid on him without missing a beat. *Thwack. Thwack. Thwack.* The chorus of Hunter's punches mixed with Taylor's feeble wails.

I shifted on all fours, wincing at the throbbing pain in my muscles, and crawled towards Hunter.

Taylor was reduced to a bloody pulp, barely moving except for when Hunter's fist collided against his face, his head jerking in whiplash.

"H-Hunt," I said hoarsely, placing a shaky hand over his forearm, squeezing. "S-stop. Look at me."

The trance gripping him slowly misted away at my touch and the sound of my voice. Sucking in a large inhale, he turned to me, bubbling with emotions. Rage was the most prominent one. It simmered underneath the pain he experienced at my disappearance and at my current visible wounds.

"Let him be," I whispered.

"Gabriela." He closed his eyes, a shiver threading through his body when my hands grabbed his jaw and drew him closer to me. He moved away from a limp Taylor and wrapped his arms around me.

"I know." I rested my cheek against the cold of his soaked dress shirt, hugging him back. "I know."

Warm drops fell against my forehead.

His tears.

My throat tightened.

"I almost lost you," he croaked, heartbreak laced in his tone. "Gabriela…"

Words were insignificant for what had transpired.

"Hunter?" I mumbled. "I want you to close your eyes for me. Just for a moment." I licked my bloodied lip and tasted a metallic tang. "Please?"

Confused, he did as I asked.

With his gaze shuttered, I glanced over at Taylor.

He was alive, even with a bloodied face, weak body, and broken spirit.

Hunter wasn't like me, born into a world of violence, death, and bloodshed. Regardless of the fact that he wholeheartedly meant it when he said he'd kill Taylor, I couldn't let him live with this burden. I didn't even want to gauge what it would do to his mental health down the line, knowing he took a life, even if it was in my defense.

And I also meant it when I said I'd kill Taylor Prescott myself.

So taking the gun Hunter had abandoned, I brought the barrel to Taylor's temple with a shaking hand and made sure to look him in the eye.

There was no silencer.

The bullet pierced loudly in the atmosphere.

Hunter's body straightened at the sound and his eyes flew open.

Surprise, disbelief, and finally understanding dawned on him.

He cursed and tugged me deeper into his chest.

I melted into his embrace, listening to his heart rapidly pumping beneath my ear.

It was over.

It was finally over.

A second later, my world turned pitch black.

CHAPTER 51

A Shell Without Her

HUNTER

Despair like I'd never known before coursed through my veins as Gabriela collapsed in my arms.

My world went as grey as the sky above and my sanity crashed to the ground.

"Gabriela!" I panicked, palming her head and gently tilting her back. She was slack in my hold. "No, no, no. Open your eyes. *Please*."

Raindrops dotted her porcelain skin. Once flawless, it was marred with a bruise on her cheek and a small vertical split on her bottom lip that caused another surge of fury within me.

"Please." Cradling her cold body against mine, I begged her. God. The universe. Anyone who would listen to me. My own tears mixed with the rain, falling on her forehead. "You can't leave me."

If you leave me, Gabriela, I'll wither without you. A shell of a man with no purpose, roaming the earth endlessly in hopes of being reunited with you again. I love you. I love you. I love you. You're my other half. I just found you. Don't leave me lonely.

With a shaky hand, I pressed my fingers over her pulse, feeling it thrum faintly.

An iota of relief bled through. *She's alive. She just fainted. She needs medical help.*

I lifted her into my arms and stood up on legs that felt like cement. Taylor deserved to die a thousand deaths for what he did to my Gabriela. I didn't know what motivated him to do all of this. The *whys* and *hows* would remain unknown until she woke up. And God forbid, if she didn't…

No.

There was no outcome in which she didn't survive. She was my soulmate. We were meant to live our lives together until the very end.

I ran with Gabriela in my arms, crossing the lawn of the Prescott property. My Jag was parked haphazardly on the other side of the iron-wrought fence. I arrived here with some guards. While they demanded entry into the residence, I'd heard a distant but potent feminine shriek that I would recognize anywhere. I didn't think. Just acted on pure instinct by climbing over the fence and beelining it straight for the source before anyone could stop me, let alone catch up to me.

The scene I stumbled upon—Taylor looming over Gabriela and stating he'd slice her throat—would haunt me for years to come.

Fuck, the thought of arriving any later and finding Gabriela in a pool of her own blood, throat cut open by that insane motherfucker, made me want to howl in pain.

My panting and the heartbeat rushing in my ears were so loud that I almost missed the open gates and the harsh voices resonating in the air. I abruptly halted at the silhouettes of Enzo, Cade, and Josh, guns out and threatening demeanours in place.

A brigade of Remington guards circled Prescott staff members. Enzo had a gun cocked against the head security guard's head, barking instructions.

"Enzo!" I shouted raggedly.

His head craned to see where the sound came from and he stiffened, the way only a father who loved his daughter would after searching relentlessly for her whereabouts.

The fear sketched over his features spoke volumes. He thought the worst.

"She fainted." I wheezed, crossing over to him. "Needs medical help."

"Go!" Josh ushered us, failing to hide his wince upon seeing Gabriela's injured state. "Take her to a hospital. Now."

"Where's Taylor?" Cade demanded.

"Dead," I said low enough that no one except for us four heard. "She killed him." After he terrorized and hurt her. "His body is by the mausoleum."

Cade clutched Enzo's shoulder. "Go, Enzo. Josh and I will handle the rest. Don't worry."

Enzo didn't need to be told twice. He caressed a shaky hand over Gabriela's face, crestfallen. "I'll drive," he said. "Put her in the backseat of my car."

I nodded and Josh took my keys from my pocket, saying he'd drive my car over to the hospital once this was settled.

At Enzo's SUV, we draped Gabriela across the backseat and I got in with her, positioning her head over my lap. Enzo dove for the driver's seat.

The tires screeched as he gunned it for the nearest hospital, less than five minutes away.

All I could do was sit here helplessly, holding Gabriela and hoping she woke up soon.

My prayers were answered.

The moment we arrived at the hospital and Gabriela was laid onto the stretcher, she showed signs of waking up, right before she was wheeled into the ER.

The figurative noose wrapped around my neck slowly loosened. They were performing tests on her right now and all I could do was wait for the verdict in the hospital's waiting room.

The antiseptic smell lingering in the hospital made me sick, but not sicker than the faint traces of blood on my soaked dress shirt.

Gabriela's blood.

I screwed my eyes shut, attempting breathing exercises that unfortunately did nothing to calm me. I needed to erase the scene of her bruised and bloodied. Purge it from my mind like it had never existed. I cursed Taylor Prescott's wretched soul. I hoped he was burning in hellfire right now—hoped he never knew peace since he was so quick to try to rob me of mine.

I ached for Gabriela. I wanted to hold her. To feel her softer curves against my hard planes. To feel her spirited heart beating against my skin. To feel her cheeky smile tucked against my neck as she lay on top of me, clutching me like I was her very anchor to this reality.

Tired and weary, my head lolled back against the wall. Two of Enzo's trusted guards were here too, keeping watchful gazes on me. The rest were outside, monitoring the hospital entrances for any threats.

Given that Josh and Cade were still stabilizing the situation at Prescott Mansion and trying to figure out if Taylor was acting alone or in cahoots with anyone else, Enzo wanted to minimize the risk by only having me, him, and Lucia at the hospital. Nonna was back at their family home with Luna, desperately waiting for news.

I remained optimistic that Gabriela would be okay. She would smile for me again. She would laugh for me again. She would whisper the words *I love you Hunter* against my lips before she kissed me again.

Gabriela Regina Bellafiore breathed life into me and I wasn't going to lose her.

I had mere months with her and I wanted a lifetime.

I wanted now and forever.

It wasn't going to be easy to eradicate the memories of today. But I would be her pillar, standing beside her as she built herself back up stronger than ever. We were going to heal from this.

Footsteps clicked against the linoleum flooring.

My head snapped up in the direction of the newcomer.

Enzo lowered himself into the chair beside me, extending a cup of black coffee in my direction. "Here. You look like you need this."

"Thank you," I rasped, taking it. "What did the doctors say?"

It had been over an hour since they took her in. I wasn't immediate family. Therefore, the only people allowed near her were Enzo and Lucia.

He crossed his arms over his chest and reclined back. "They said she most likely fainted from exhaustion and dehydration. She's stable now. Her vitals are looking good and they did some bloodwork. None of her cuts are deep enough to require stitches and her bruising will take time to heal. She doesn't appear to have a concussion, which is good news. They want to monitor her for a bit longer." He cleared his throat. "She fell asleep after the doctor left. You can go wait in her room if you'd like. Lucia and I will be heading to the cafeteria for a bit."

All the nervous energy tangled up inside of me slowly evaporated with my next exhale. "Good." I sagged in my chair, tears of relief stinging my eyes. I fought them back. "I'm glad to hear she's going to be okay."

I also appreciated them wanting to give me some privacy with Gabriela. I would head over to her shortly.

The empty waiting room was quiet, the only sound a wall-mounted clock ticking. I sipped my coffee, unsure what more to say to him.

Enzo appeared to mull over his next words. "Hunter?"

"Yes?"

"Thank you. For helping save Gabriela. Not once, but twice." Sincerity rang in his statement. "If you hadn't gotten there in time...I-I don't...Can't imagine." He stopped to collect his thoughts, sighing. "You gave her a chance to win her battle and she made it through because of you. So thank you from the bottom of my heart."

"Like I said the first time, you don't have to thank me for this, sir. I would do anything to ensure her safety."

He glanced at the floor, his head hanging between his shoulders. "I'm beginning to see that."

I shifted in my seat, uncomfortable. "I know I'm probably not the man you would have picked for your daughter, but I want you to know that I love Gabriela with every fiber of my being. She's it for me. If I have to spend the rest of my life to earn your blessing—to prove myself to you—I will—"

"You don't have to prove yourself to me, Hunter," he interrupted. "You already have. It's no secret that I can be overprotective of my daughter, but she's the most important person in our lives. We want her to be happy and protected. You've shown up for her in ways that no one else ever has. Now it's clear to me that you are the perfect person for her. *You* are the man I would pick for my daughter."

In this period of darkness, I found an ounce of elation in Enzo's sentiment. "Thank you," I managed to choke out. "I appreciate it."

In an unexpected fatherly gesture, he ran his hand over my hair. "Don't worry. Everything will be okay now, son."

Son.

Warmth sprang inside of me like a watered seed finally bursting free.

We exchanged a smile.

Then I got up, went to the designated room, and waited for the love of my life to wake up.

CHAPTER 52

Wherever you go I will always follow

GABRIELA

My eyes fluttered open to a peaceful stillness.

I was in a hospital room, having fallen asleep after a multitude of tests, my body giving in to the need to rest and recuperate now that I was in a safe environment.

There was a stale taste in my mouth, a needle injected in my skin and hooked to an IV, a faint soreness in my limbs…but at least I was alive.

When the cobwebs clouding my sleepy mind fully dissipated, I recognized a lone figure sitting on a chair in the corner of the room, arms crossed over his chest and gazing up at the ceiling, lost in thought.

"Hunter," I called out, croaky-voiced.

His head whipped in my direction. The disbelief etched in his features faded away and sheer relief replaced it. He pulsed of yearning as he perused me like he was trying to ensure I was real and actually here, not a figment of his imagination.

"*Gabriela.*" The tightness leaked from his bunched muscles as he stood up and advanced towards me.

His presence gave me all the strength I needed to roll out of the bed and try to close the distance between us, IV machine and all.

But he reached my bedside first and wrapped his arms around me, a shiver wracking through him. "I've missed you." His tone was ravaged. "I've missed you so much."

Mere hours away from this man felt like an eternity.

"I've missed you and I'm so happy to see you." My words were muffled against his shirt and I fisted the sides of it, keeping him plastered to me. He was never escaping my clutches. "I love you."

"I love you too." His mouth trembled as he dotted a fervent kiss on my temple. "I love you and I almost lost you. If I had been any later, I…I…"

I wouldn't be alive.

He didn't need to say it. That sentence hung over our heads like a sword.

"But you made it and you helped save me." I lifted my head from his strong chest to cup his bristly cheek. "No amount of thanking you will be able to convey my gratitude."

"I never wanted to hear you thanking me for something like that." He inhaled sharply. "The sight of you fighting for your life…" He shook his head. "It'll haunt me forever."

My expression fell. "Let's not dwell over the what-ifs any longer. I'm here and I'm okay. Let's focus on that, *bello*."

His eyes searched mine desperately and he cupped my face. "How are you feeling?"

"Sore." I sighed. "And in pain."

Hunter thumbed my bottom lip and frowned, perturbed.

"I look like a nightmare, don't I?" Without evaluating my reflection, it was obvious my hair was grossly matted to my scalp, my cheek harboured a bruise, and my bottom lip a cut. "How rude of me. You look handsome as ever and I've welcomed you looking like Frankenstein's monster."

He puffed out a chuckle, against all odds, but sobered up quickly, pinning me with impassioned blue eyes. "You could never look like a nightmare. Even battle-worn, you're beautiful as ever. I saw the damage you did to him before I arrived. I'm so proud of you, Gabriela."

I adored this man—who constantly validated, praised, and cherished me—to infinity and beyond. "Luna and I are the luckiest girls alive to have you, Hunt. Speaking of our daughter, how is she?"

I'd been worried sick about my cat. I hoped she wasn't lost right now. I couldn't handle that.

"Luna's okay. As soon as you were taken, she tried to head back in the direction of my home in what I'm assuming was an attempt to alert me or the guards. By the time I arrived on the scene, she trotted over with a limp and coaxed me over to a patch on the road…where I found your fallen bracelet and Taylor's wallet." Hunter's jaw clenched. "That's how I concluded he was responsible. Josh deciphered your location with the help of the tracker in your necklace and I came straight to find you. One of the guards took Luna to the vet. Her leg is sprained. They gave her some medication and put on a cast. It'll take her a few weeks to heal, but ultimately, she'll be okay. The last update I received was that she's at your family's home with Nonna, desperately waiting for you."

How I loved my Luna. Despite her own hurt and distress, instincts led her to find Hunter so I could be rescued. But I hated that she got injured. If I could go back in time, I'd slash both of Taylor's eyes and lodge an extra bullet in his skull. Fucking asshole. No one was allowed to lay a hand on my cat. Ever.

"I'm relieved she's okay. What she witnessed—" I swallowed down my growing ire. "I have no doubt it terrified her." I couldn't wait to go home and hug Luna. "You should have seen the way she fought him, Hunter. She nearly took out his eye. I was simultaneously scared for her but proud of her too."

"She's resilient and a warrior." He brushed a kiss on the side of my neck. "Just like her mommy."

I smiled.

Hunter scooped me up, being mindful of my IV, and sat on the bed, depositing me sideways on his lap. Instantly, my face tucked in the crook of his neck and I relaxed in his arms.

His hand cupped mine underneath, his thumb opening my palm and grazing over the lines. Namely my lifeline. We had many decades ahead of us.

Our usual companionable silence wouldn't last long, since I expected Hunter's incoming line of questioning. No matter my reassurances, he wouldn't rest easy until he heard the whole story. Had the roles been reversed and I stumbled upon a bloody and bruised Hunter, I'd have the same reactions and feelings as him. "Ask me what's on your mind, Hunt."

He leaned his head against mine. "Will you tell me everything that happened and why he did this to you?" he pleaded. "If you're okay to talk about it, I need to know. *Please*."

There was a part of me that wanted to spare him the gruesome details. But it wouldn't be fair to keep this from him.

My jaw clenched when I recalled the kidnapping. Waking up in a mausoleum. A deceased Morgan lying next to me. Taylor promising to kill me. Hunter showing up and beating him to a bloody pulp.

And me finishing the job by shooting Taylor dead like the piece of shit he was.

I never thought I'd take a life. But if given the chance, I'd kill Taylor a thousand times over. I would never feel bad about his death.

"Taylor did all of this because he was in love with me."

Hunter reared back, blue eyes burning with fire. "What?"

I grabbed the glass of water on my bedside table and washed down some of the bitter taste on my palate before continuing. "He ended our arrangement all those months ago, not because he wanted to, but because he went through my phone and saw my texts with Anna and Layla. The ones where I told them *I* was planning on ending it with Taylor. Prior to that, he was planning on asking me to be his girlfriend." Hunter was astonished. "It hurt his ego, to say the least, and so he ended it with me first via text and then hooked up with Morgan. He thought rubbing her in my face would piss me off. And when I remained unaffected through the entire debacle and moved on by kissing you on the dance floor...it pissed *him* off.

"He broke into my apartment the next day and left me that message on my wall. Taylor would have kept terrorizing me, but by then Oscar was on my case. You were always with me too." I swallowed. "I was never alone enough for Taylor to find an opening and strike. But, Hunt…he stalked us. In the mausoleum, he showed me hundreds of pictures he'd accumulated of you and me over the weeks. He watched from the shadows—including that time in the Remington woods—until the perfect time. And Friday night? He didn't just mean to stab you…He wanted you dead." I closed my eyes, shuddering at the reminder. "He was furious that I fell in love with you. That's why he kidnapped me. He was going to kill me and himself. He even dug a grave for us. Said our final resting place would be together."

Hunter was hardened stone against me, his anger growing exponentially. I rubbed my hands over his bunched muscles to alleviate his tension, but it did little to soothe him.

"If he wasn't already dead," Hunter bit out, "I'd kill him right fucking now." He used two fingers under my chin to tip my face up. "What happened when you left my home this morning?"

Hunter listened with intent as I explained to him how Craig and Oscar died. How Taylor yanked me from the vehicle and dragged me against the road to his awaiting one. How he cursed me out and stuffed me in the trunk. How I woke up in the mausoleum zip-tied, with a dead Morgan lying next to me. How Taylor revealed his fucked-up plans. How I fought him off for as long as I could before Hunter found us.

By the end of it, I felt better having confided in Hunter. The weight on my shoulders lessened.

"I'm sorry." Hunter burrowed his lips against my hairline in a shaky kiss. His body vibrated with the remnant of his fury and pain for me. "I'm so sorry you had to endure that. I wish I could remove this chapter from your life."

"I know," I whispered. "I'm just glad it's finally over."

"There's no way to have known it was him, Gabby, especially with the way Taylor acted so indifferent whenever we were in his vicinity. But it does baffle me that the culprit was right under our noses this whole time."

A harsh chuckle erupted from him. "Nothing you or I did to him was enough. I fucking hope he's rotting in hell as we speak."

"I hope he is too." I ran my fingers through the ends of his hair. "And I agree that nothing we did to him was enough, but he's dead now, so let's let bygones be bygones. It'll take time, but we'll heal from this. I promise you."

Though Hunter appeared calmer after all was said and done, I didn't miss the edges of darkness clinging to him. The memories of today might haunt us for the foreseeable future, but I was optimistic that we would overcome this part of our story together.

"Gabriela." He feathered his mouth over my tender cheek. "I want you to know that there's no reality where you don't exist and I remain whole. Had anything happened to you, I would have gone with you."

My heart thudded.

It was in that moment, as we locked gazes, that a specific realization dawned on me. Franco once said I was worthless and loving me was a chore. But with his words and actions, Hunter proved that couldn't be further from the truth—loving me was the easiest and most potent thing he'd ever done. The highest honour of his life. And if it was his final act, he'd go out with an almighty smile on his face.

"It's the truth." At my shocked silence, he laid his forehead to mine and simply breathed me in. "Wherever you go, I will always follow, doll."

I would do anything for this man—anything in the world to ensure his happiness and keep the light in his eyes.

I kissed him gently and expressed my devotion. "*Ti amo così tanto, bello.* You're my home. Wherever you go, I'll always follow you too."

There it was. That soft smile of his I adored so much.

A knock on the door interrupted us.

We moved away from each other to ensure there was a respectable distance between our bodies just in time for my parents to barrel into the room.

"Oh, Gabriela, you're awake!" Mamma nearly wailed, coming over to grab my face and kiss my forehead. "How are you feeling? Are you hungry? We brought food."

Right on cue, Papà deposited soups and sandwiches on a table. Smelling the savoury aromas, my hunger returned in small spikes.

"I'm okay, Mamma," I said. "And yes, I can eat."

She'd arrived at the hospital minutes after I was wheeled into the ER. She and Papà stayed by my side while the doctor and nurses performed tests and discussed the verdict.

Before I'd fallen asleep, she'd wept by my bedside. "We were so scared, *cara mia*. We searched high and low for you."

My chin had wobbled. "I-I was scared too, Mamma. I worried I'd never see you guys again."

"Oh, my baby." Her voice had cracked.

Seeing them in the flesh, a dam had broken. My tears wouldn't cease. The reminder that I could have died and never gotten to see them again was too much to bear. They'd taken turns hugging, kissing, and whispering well-wishes to me. I'd leaned into their affection, needing their comfort now more than ever. And somewhere between it all, slumber had called to me and I'd knocked out for an hour.

"Just so you know, once you're discharged, you're coming home," Mamma said now with maternal affection. "That's non-negotiable. I'll be nursing you back to optimal health."

I wouldn't argue. There was a part of me that wanted to be coddled and taken care of like a pampered princess after this godforsaken ordeal. "Okay."

Papà cleared his throat. "Can I have a moment alone with Gabriela?"

"Of course." Mamma combed her fingers through my hair. "We'll be right outside."

Hunter kissed my knuckles before heading out.

Then it was just Papà and me.

He pulled a chair closer to my bed. The dark circles under his eyes were a telltale sign that he desperately needed rest. He grabbed my hand in his callused one. "I'm so sorry, Gabriela. If I'd done a better job protecting you and gotten the right guy from the start, none of this would have happened."

Not expecting him to say that, I shook my head. "Papà, please. It's not your fault."

"You're the apple of my eye—my proudest achievement—and despite how much I've tried to safeguard you over the years…I failed you." His voice was thick, layered with emotion. "We almost lost you today. I would have never been able to forgive myself."

My face softened. No matter how much we bickered, I never doubted a day in my life that I was the most important thing to my parents.

"I'm asking you to," I pleaded. "Please don't berate yourself over this." I wiped away the single tear that leaked from the corner of his eye and drew him in for a hug. "You've always protected me and you always will. In the end, you guys found me, no? I survived and I'm fine. That's all that matters."

His big body shuddered, clutching me close. "*Ti voglio bene*, Gabriela."

"*Ti voglio bene*, Papà." I pecked his unshaven cheek and whispered hesitantly, "Will you tell me what happened after I fainted?"

I hadn't gotten the chance to ask Hunter and I wanted to save him from reliving the horror. I would never forget the look in his eyes when he found me. This day would always be branded on his soul.

I'd rather hear the recount from Papà.

His eyes briefly veered to the door, ensuring it was closed. "I arrived at the property with Josh, Cade, and our men. Hunter had you in his arms. We put you in the backseat of my car and I drove here." He sucked in a centering inhale, pinching the bridge of his nose as if to rid himself of the image. "The Remingtons' last text to me was that the situation is resolved. The Prescotts won't bother you, Gabriela. Not unless they know what's good for them. There's security footage of what their son did to you and the other girl."

My heart hurt thinking of Morgan. Dead. So young. "What about her family? Were they contacted?"

"She barely had a family. Her parents died years ago and she had no siblings, no aunts, no uncles. Only an old grandfather currently residing in a nursing home."

It wasn't fair. Morgan didn't deserve this. "I want to pay for her funeral." I gulped. "We didn't always get along, but she was my peer. She figured out what Taylor was about to do and tried to warn me before he killed her—"

535

Papà nodded in understanding. "I'm sorry she died and you had to see her like that. We'll give her a proper burial. Don't worry."

"Oscar and Craig too."

It was my fault they were gone.

"As you wish—"

Papà's sentence was cut off when another knock at the door interrupted us. The same middle-aged doctor who tended to me before stepped inside.

"Hello, Miss Bellafiore," he said, coming to my side. "How are you feeling?"

I shifted into a more comfortable position in my bed. "Tired and in a bit of pain."

"Understandable." He pulled off his stethoscope from around his neck. He did a quick examination. Checked my breathing, heart rate, eyes, and my head. "The good news is that your neurological assessment is normal and there's no sign of a concussion. Over the next few days, I'd like you to rest as much as you possibly can and take time off work and school to allow your bruises and scrapes to heal. For now, I'd like to keep you here a little longer and repeat some bloodwork. If everything looks fine, you can be discharged later today."

Relief poured into me. I couldn't wait to go home. "Sounds good."

He smiled and scribbled on a piece of paper. "Here's a prescription for painkillers and antibiotic ointment." He handed it over to Papà and a somber expression befell him. He cleared his throat. "And lastly, please don't forget to file a police report."

Papà and I shared a brief glance. We both knew I wouldn't be filing a report. Mob business was always handled discreetly. Plus, the Remingtons and Papà had enough corrupt law enforcement on their payroll. The Montardor Police Department wouldn't be getting involved in my case.

And the way I saw it?

Justice was already served by the time I lodged a bullet in Taylor's brain.

"Of course. We'll take care of dealing with the authorities," Papà lied and extended his hand to shake the doctor's. "Thank you. I appreciate all that you've done for my daughter."

CHAPTER 53
My Happy Ever After

GABRIELA

My outlook on life had significantly changed in the span of a day.

Today's tragedy made me vow to myself that I would never take anything for granted, that I would live every moment to my fullest, and I would always see the glass as half-full. If that meant I had to lean into my delusions and wear rose-tinted glasses, then so be it.

Once I was discharged from the hospital in the late evening, Hunter drove us to a pharmacy to pick up my medications and then straight to my family home. I nearly got whiplash from the two extremities I experienced within twenty-four hours. Being in the back of my kidnapper's trunk to now sitting shotgun in my boyfriend's sports car, one of his playlists running in the background. The old routine, so achingly familiar to us, soothed me like a warm cup of milk and honey.

The courtyard lights were lit when Hunter steered into the driveway. Some of Papà's guards loitered around the property. But for the first time in a long time, I wasn't stressed. There were no more threats.

I was as free as a bird breaking out of its gilded cage.

Hunter opened my door and extended his hand like a gentleman. I had two working legs, yet I didn't get to put them to use since he hauled me into his arms, princess style.

I yelped at the unexpected gesture. Then sank into his unyielding warmth. His fresh leather and black ice cologne, faint but ubiquitous, was a balm to my soul.

"I can walk the short distance to the front door, you know?" I teased.

"I'd rather carry you, Gabby. I'm about to be your personal butler, bodyguard, chauffeur, chef, and everything in between until you fully heal," Hunter informed.

"Will there be a bell at my nightstand to ring for you?"

We crossed the threshold of the Bellafiore residence. My family was somewhere on the ground floor, making arrangements for the upcoming days and probably whipping up a late dinner for us. But I wasn't hungry for food. I only cared to see my Luna.

Hunter already knew that. He ascended the staircase to the second floor, where my room was, wordlessly taking me to her. "No need for a bell. I'm going to be sleeping right here in your bed."

"My parents are okay with that?" I'd never had a boy stay for a sleepover.

But Hunter wasn't just a boy.

He was my future—my everything forever.

"Yes," Hunter said. Given how he handled today by coming to my rescue and beating the ever-living hell out of Taylor, it was a no-brainer that my parents were bending the 'no boys overnight' rule of theirs. "Even if they hadn't, though I respect them, I'd still find a way to climb to your window and sneak into your bedroom, Gabby."

It'll take an army to pry me off of you.

Hunter was a man of his words, after all.

"Good." I nestled my face into the crook of his neck. "I need you here, Hunt."

"Anything my girl wants." His arms tightened when he reached the second floor. "Just so you know, I'll be handcuffing you to me moving forward so you're never out of my sight again."

"Kinky. Guess we'll finally be able to break into those cuffs we bought from the lingerie store."

"Sounds like a date."

"Make me a grilled cheese sandwich and it'll be a *perfect* date."

Hunter smiled. "Your wish is my command."

He padded down the hallway towards my bedroom. It wasn't hard to know which door was mine, considering I still had a heart-shaped plastic doorbell stuck on it from my early tween years. I went through a phase where I was big on personal space and demanded both my parents ring me up before I determined whether or not I was in the mood to answer them.

Hunter shouldered open my already unlocked door. Bags with my stuff were piled onto my bed, courtesy of the guards who shuffled them over from Hunter's home to here.

But that was not what snagged my attention.

It was Luna.

Awake and perked up on her bed.

I got choked up seeing her.

Hunter put me down on my feet. She was just about to leap in my direction, cast on her hind leg and all, before I grabbed her.

Luna's paws went on either side of my neck and she snuggled up to me, meowing continuously to express herself. I felt it all. Her pain and her relief at finally seeing me. I shed more tears and she licked at my chin. I kissed her wherever I could reach. "Luna, I've missed you so much." *Meow.* "I'm so happy you're okay." *Meow.* "Thank you for helping to save me." *Meow.* "Yes, yes, I love you too."

My sweet girl, so affectionate in her nature, would not unlatch even as I attempted to pull back. She dug her claws into me, telling me in her own way that she wouldn't be letting me out of her sight either.

I sighed blissfully. "Luna won't let me go."

Hunter wrapped his arms around us from behind. "That makes two of us."

I turned my face to his, awaiting my kiss.

He delivered it. Soft and gentle as a feather, breathing life into me all over again.

The scars on our bodies and the wounds underneath our flesh would heal with time, but as long as we had each other, we would be fine.

Hunter helped me shower and changed my bandages. My once flawless skin bore enough marks for his expression to transform into a blend of helplessness and anger that said he wished Taylor were alive so he could kill him this time.

"I'm okay, *amore mio*," I reassured, grazing my fingers over his clenched jaw.

It did little to assuage him. He dressed me in a pair of loose shorts and his clean football jersey. I tried to hide my wince as my sore muscles moved. Hunter didn't miss it.

He dressed quickly in a pair of grey sweats and a white shirt, escaping my help when I tried to put a fresh gauze on his bicep. He did it himself. The unblinking stare and the grim pinch of his mouth said he was here to take care of me and in his presence? I really wasn't to lift a single finger.

"Go rest in your bed, sweetheart," Hunter murmured. "I'm going to make you a grilled cheese sandwich, then you can take your medications. All right?"

I kissed his cheek. "All right."

As instructed, I got into bed with Luna curled by my side. The warmth of my skin and the coldness of my pillows and comforter were a divine contrast, igniting a new surge of lethargy. I wanted to slip underneath and go to sleep. But instead, I plucked my retrieved cell phone from my nightstand and unlocked it to a multitude of messages. I answered the ones from Anna and Layla. Apparently, Mamma already told them what happened to me.

I texted them an update: I was fine, would be thriving soon again, and loved them dearly. It helped ease their worry a smidge. I promised to tell them everything tomorrow when they dropped by for a visit.

Later on, after my family came to my room to bid me good night and ask me for the hundredth time if I was all right, I ended it tucked into Hunter's side, my belly full of the grilled cheese sandwich he whipped up for me, drowsy from the meds, Luna settled into his lap, purring as he petted her, and an old rom-com movie playing on my TV.

"What are you thinking?" Hunter brushed his lips against my forehead.

I mumbled sleepily, "That there's nowhere else I'd rather be."

Than in the comfort of my principe's *arms.*

He kissed my skin. "Me too, doll."

I fell asleep with gratefulness ringing in my bones.

The next day, I felt well-rested but still in a bit of pain. The doorbell rang in the afternoon, signalling Anna and Layla's arrival. I waited for them downstairs in the living room and they entered with weary faces, a bouquet of flowers, balloons, and a get-well-soon basket.

My best friends' red eyes told me they'd been crying. It undid me. I opened my arms for a hug. "Hi, girls."

They rushed to me and we clung to each other like we were three pieces of a whole. In a way, that was exactly what we were. Each other's platonic soulmates. We ended up crying together and all I could do was count my blessings that I made it through yesterday's horrific events. I couldn't fathom the possibility of never seeing Anna and Layla again.

"How are you feeling?" Layla asked, sniffling.

I adjusted the throw blanket on my lap. "I'm feeling better today, but I'll be on painkillers and using antibiotic ointment for the next week."

"Your mom called us as soon as you were taken." Anna dabbed under her eyes with a tissue. "We were terrified, Gabby."

I could sense them wanting to probe more about the situation. They were holding back, afraid that it would trigger me. Sooner or later, they'd have to know. So I ripped the bandage and told them. They listened with undivided attention, their revulsion for what I went through growing by the second.

"This is all horrifying, to say the least." Anna grabbed my hand when I finished. "You were so strong and brave."

"We're proud of you for fighting off that monster, Gabby." Layla grabbed my other hand. "And so glad you're going to be okay. Please let us know if you need anything from us."

"We love you and we're always here for you," Anna added.

"I love you both." I really did have the best sisters. "I'll be staying at my parents' home for a bit longer. Maybe we can have a sleepover for old times' sake?"

They grinned. "Done."

By day three of being discharged from the hospital, I started to feel more like myself. There was a bounce in my step, my injuries hurt less, and I didn't have a single nightmare about Taylor. The lack of PTSD was another blessing. I was glad the asshole wouldn't have a hold over me even after his death.

But if there was one person I would think about, even after their death, it was Morgan. I wished she'd never gotten caught in Taylor's web. I wished she could have escaped him.

I wished she could have lived.

We rarely saw eye to eye, but it didn't change the fact that she had so much potential. She deserved to see it through, not be buried six feet beneath the ground.

My girls had been dropping by periodically to check in on me and to gift me all sorts of care packages stocked with all of my favourite things.

When Hera visited with Ella, Darla, and Dacia, I had to confess to her what really transpired. She was the WIB student association president and she probably realized that Morgan wasn't replying to any of her texts, let alone any work emails. The girls were shocked, to say the least, when I recounted the tragedy. Naturally, they swore that they'd be taking this to the grave. We couldn't risk anyone figuring out how Morgan, Taylor, and I were connected. Namely since it could jeopardize Papà and the Remingtons.

"We're so sorry, Gabby," Ella echoed. "If there's anything we can do for you, please let us know."

"Once the semester comes to an end, maybe we can plan a fun girls' night with Anna and Layla." Darla exchanged a glance with her sister, Dacia. "We can host at our place."

"That would be lovely." I'd need many girls' nights to recharge after this. I looked pointedly at Hera, who was pensive. "Hera, I'll be organizing Morgan's funeral."

She cleared her throat. "Can I help in any way?"

"Would you be okay sending our team the date and details of her service? I imagine they'd want to be present to pay their respects. And if you know the contacts of any of her friends…"

I barely knew anything about Morgan's life outside of the student association. If she had friends or not. A pet. Other engagements.

Hera nodded. "Of course. Leave that to me. I'll create a digital invite and forward it to the proper crowd."

And three days later, at Morgan's funeral, I was glad to see many faces outside of our WIB student association. Morgan may not have had much family, but at least she had friends who cared and would feel the loss of her. If anyone asked, the story we were going with was that Morgan died during a car crash and that was why her funeral was closed-casket. No one would know that I footed the bill for the funeral, that Taylor killed her, or that I was lying next to her in the Prescott mausoleum, where her body was retrieved from.

To the public, I was simply a peer here to pay my respects.

Hand in hand, Hunter and I walked to her casket and I gingerly laid my bouquet of blue hyacinths and white carnations on top. The florist said they symbolized heavy regret and that you wouldn't forget the person. My last message to Morgan. I prayed she found peace in the afterlife.

"Rest easy, Morgan," I whispered under my breath.

Hunter squeezed my hand.

Once everything wrapped up, we headed out of the cemetery, but I paused when I saw a familiar figure standing by a small tombstone.

Franco, with a bouquet of white roses in his hand.

His mother's favourites.

My eyes closed briefly, realizing Mrs. Morelli—the reason why he begged my papà to return to the city—had passed away.

As if sensing my presence, his head lifted. Our eyes connected for mere seconds. Blotchy-faced and red eyes, he appeared miserable. I gave him a meaningful look to wordlessly express my condolences. His reply came in the form of blowing out a long breath and an imperceptible nod.

I hoped I never had to see him again. Even though he hurt me in many ways, I didn't wish him ill. Only healing and peace from here on out.

Jaw clenched, Hunter pinned Franco with a frosty stare before continuing to direct me towards his car.

My current read, which was an alien romance courtesy of Nonna's recommendations, sat on the dashboard. I removed my nestled bookmark—the same one Hunter gifted me on our first unofficial date—and picked up where I left off while he drove.

I thought we were going home but was pleasantly surprised when he steered in Le Petit Moulin's direction. I could go for a mocha and a box of chocolate donuts. Elsie, the owner of the café, recognized us when we entered, offering a warm smile and throwing an extra slice of a raspberry-chocolate cake into our order. On the house, she said, which was very kind. I made a mental note to leave her a five-star review. The café was relatively busy at this hour, but we managed to seat ourselves in the same spot as the first time we came here.

Hunter sipped a black coffee and picked at the complimentary cake, watching me.

"What is it?" I asked after scarfing down half of my donuts like a hungry beast.

Hunter smiled. "Nothing. It's just good to see you regain your appetite and strength."

I smiled too, inching forward the two donuts I saved for him. "I couldn't have done it without the help of my personal butler, chef, bodyguard, chauffeur, and everything in between."

He chuckled when I quoted him. Licking his bottom lip, he rasped, "Will you take a walk with me today?"

It was an exceptionally sunny fall afternoon and we should definitely take advantage. Taking a walk was another way to infuse more normalcy into our lives again and we absolutely needed to resume our usual routine.

"I would love nothing more, Hunt."

The semester was nearing its end, with less than a handful of weeks left, and I still had many assignments and exams due. My professors, however, were very accommodating when I sent them an email with a doctor's note about my condition. Most said they wouldn't dock marks for participation and that I was welcome to finish my semester from the comfort of my home. Others offered me any necessary extensions. That way, I wouldn't fall behind and could finish this term with all my good grades intact.

A few days after Morgan's funeral, I was seated at the dining table with Mamma and Nonna. We were wedding planning over coffee and tiramisu, despite Mamma's earlier protests. They initially wanted a small, December wedding but considered pushing the date forward, given my situation. I promised them that I would be fully recovered by the time the wedding rolled around. I didn't want them to delay any more. They waited long enough to get back together and I didn't want to risk either of them getting cold feet. Plus, they'd started couple's therapy and things were progressing well. If anything, I was really excited for them to tie the knot again.

"It's decided," Nonna said, stroking Luna's back while shoving her glasses higher up the bridge of her nose, reading her notes. "We're going with pink for your theme."

Nonna was internally fist punching the air over not having to wear canary yellow again.

"Sounds good. I want an arrangement of hydrangeas on every table as the centerpiece." Mamma folded her fingers underneath her chin like a bench and dreamily gazed at the ceiling. "You think Enzo will agree to wear a pink tie?"

I jotted down *pink hydrangeas* under the *table centerpiece ideas* row in my notebook, suppressing my smile.

"I think that besotted fool would agree to pluck the moon from the sky and bring it to you if your heart so much as desired," Nonna supplied. "Really, Lucia, do you not know anything about the man you're marrying? My son would do anything for you. Wearing a pink tie included."

Said besotted fool chose that exact moment to poke his head through the dining room entrance, his expression instantly softening when it landed on Mamma. For a few seconds, they locked eyes and gave each other that secret smile of theirs. "There you are, Lucia. Feels like I've been searching everywhere for you."

"I'm here. We're wedding planning." Mamma blushed. "Enzo, how do you feel about pink?"

He frowned. "Is that your final choice?"

She nodded, hopeful.

He grinned wide. "Then I love it, *principessa*."

I almost rolled my eyes. Nonna pretended to gag. My parents hadn't stopped behaving like teenagers in love. No matter how much we ribbed them, this was preferred over their headache-inducing arguing.

"Gabriela?"

I put my pen down. "Yes, Papà?"

"I want to show you something." He hedged forward, slipping his hands in his pockets.

"What is it?"

"A surprise. Meet me outside and dress warm."

I donned a wool coat over my loungewear attire and stuffed my feet into fur-lined boots.

The front door was already ajar. I stepped out onto the porch…and my jaw fell open.

Sitting on our driveway, gleaming under the morning sunlight, was a dark red convertible with a big white bow on top.

"Papà?" I advanced towards the car. "Is this mine?"

"It sure is." He handed me the keys. "You said you wanted one, no?"

"Oh, thank you, thank you, thank you!" I hugged him tight. He chuckled. "I love it!"

He chin-tipped towards my new car. "I bought it for you and would have had it delivered last week, but your boyfriend asked to add some modifications."

Curiosity piqued, I moved around it to see these so-called modifications…and paused when I found them. Heart-shaped taillights and silver heart-shaped rims welcomed me.

Oh my God.

I was obsessed.

Dare I say in my totally biased opinion, this was the prettiest car I'd ever seen. I couldn't wait to obtain my licence in a couple of months and drive her around the city.

I shot a selfie of myself posing with my car and sent it to Hunter.

Look what arrived today!! I adore the modifications you made. You know me so well. —Gabby

He replied within seconds.

You're welcome, Gabby. —Hunter

Can't wait to experience life as a passenger princess. —Hunter

I snickered.

I love you 🖤 —Gabby

I love you too, doll. —Hunter

The rest of November trickled by within the blink of an eye. Little by little, life returned to normal. I regained my strength as the bruises, cuts, and scrapes on my body healed and the memories of that wretched day faded. Any spare time between work and school, I spent with my loved ones and doing things that brought me joy. Like bedazzling all the covers of my romance books. Taking long walks and watching scary movies with Hunter and Luna. Driving my new car with Hunter as the passenger princess and Luna our co-pilot. Trying new cat-friendly cafés in the city. Going out to bars and dinner dates.

I felt more like myself with every passing day, like a snake shedding its old skin and thriving in the new one. With every new outfit and every new layer of makeup, the Gabby from the kidnapping was erased and in its stead was the version I always wanted to remain—the one that loved to don her best for every occasion and go out with her friends.

But not because I was trying to fill a void in my chest with endless parties and drinks.

I was simply embodying my new motto: living life to the fullest.

And I did it all with Hunter by my side.

It was on the second weekend of December, after our semesters came to an end, that we finally went to the masquerade ball. I'd been anticipating this night for so long and it didn't disappoint.

The inside of the banquet hall dripped with opulence, glittery chandeliers hanging overhead, lit candelabras on numbered tables, the gentle strains of the orchestra playing on the dance floor, an array of expensive suits and beautiful gowns, and ornate Venetian masks covering the faces of the attendees.

Tonight, I was dressed as Nike.

Hunter's goddess of victory.

My white dress draped around my body in a Grecian-inspired fashion, my dark red hair fell down my back in waves, with a crown sitting on my head, and I wore gold wings to pay tribute to my namesake.

Safe to say, Hunter fell in love with me all over again when he arrived to pick me up, a dozen red roses in his hand and awe plastered all over his face.

I preened, giving him a twirl. "You like?"

He climbed the steps up to me as if the distance between us was too much to bear. "I *love*, Gabriela. You look exceptional." A kiss was pressed to my hand. "The most beautiful woman in the world."

As always, I ate up his praise like the finest of delicacies.

"You don't look too shabby yourself, *bello*." I danced my index finger down his tie. He wore a white one to match my dress. "The most handsome in the world."

In his tailored black suit, polished black shoes, and long black hair left open and tousled in an artful manner, he was all my book boyfriends wrapped into one. And tonight, he resembled a fallen angel prince, roaming the Earth with the sole intention of causing mayhem.

At my compliment, he smiled in that heart-melting manner of his.

When I placed a gold wreath crown on his head, Hunter's smile morphed into a wide grin that showcased all his straight, pearly white teeth. "To what do I owe this honour?"

Nike was known for carrying a wreath crown, her task to place it upon the heads of the winners of battles and athletic contests.

Hunter understood the symbolism.

"Whether it's a national championship or coming to my defense, you're always triumphant, Hunter. I could think of no individual more deserving of this crown." I slinked into his arms and peered up at him. "I also thought we'd match this way. Me, your goddess of victory, and you, my glorious victor."

He kissed me until I was weak in the knees before whisking me off to the ball.

Upon arrival, we did our rounds and exchanged greetings with all our friends.

We drank, we ate, and we danced the night away. Hunter ushered me off the dance floor, where Layla and Josh were still present. They were waltzing—or doing whatever was Josh's version of a waltz. He twirled and dipped her back, snatched a quick kiss and caused the nearby old ladies to swoon at his antics. Then he asked Layla to twirl him.

She laughed and did exactly that.

"It's all so arresting," I said to Hunter, holding my gold mask up to my face with the handheld stick as I surveyed the party.

The top half of Hunter's face was covered in a gold filigree mask that matched mine, except his was tied at the back of his head with a black ribbon. The bottom half of his face was exposed, showing off his manicured stubble and full lips. He grabbed two glasses of champagne from a waiter's tray. "I'm glad you're having a good time." He passed me one. "Step outside with me for a moment?"

"Yes."

On our way to the banquet hall's terrace, we walked by a quiet alcove where Anna stood in a shimmering gown and...Sam in front of her, half shadowed in darkness.

They talked about something in hushed voices, but Hunter and I didn't pause to acknowledge them, sensing that they wanted to be left alone.

The empty terrace opened up to a breathtaking view of a cliff to our left and crashing waves. Far in the distance, there was a lighthouse, gleaming under the fierce moonlight.

Hunter led us to the balustrade, where we deposited our glasses and masks.

549

A strong gust of wind blew past us. I shivered, shifting in my heels.

Hunter shrugged off his suit jacket, placed it around my shoulders, and wrapped his arms around me from behind. Warmth suffused my body and I pressed my cheek to my pretty boy's stubbled one, closing my eyes as I relished this soft moment and the wondrous sight before us.

It was akin to the Hero and Leander painting hanging on my home office's wall.

"It's so peaceful here. So beautiful." I shivered when another cold breeze swept against us. "And freezing."

Hunter laughed, his chest vibrating against my back with the sound. "I'm looking forward to winter. It'll be nice to finally relax and lie dormant after these hectic months."

My mind spun the imagery of a fireplace, hot chocolates, holiday movies, and cozied up with Hunter next to a Christmas tree. "I agree."

"We can do a weekend getaway at a chalet, if you'd like," he whispered against my temple and skirted his lips down to my cheek. The skin was healed, no longer bruised. He kissed it. "Invite our friends too."

"I would absolutely love that."

"I'll teach you how to snowboard."

"I can't wait."

We watched the scenery and sipped our champagne.

"What's on your mind?" Hunter rasped in my ear after a silent moment.

I angled my head to gaze into his eyes. They were almost sterling under the moonlit night. "That I want to marry you someday."

I remembered his dream from the night at Club Azul. Except he wouldn't have to wait fifteen years to see it to fruition. I would marry him tomorrow, if given the chance. I would give him the home he so starkly craved. And I wouldn't make him wait long for kids either, just after we graduated and started our careers.

"Do you want that, Hunt?"

"Yes," he replied quickly and I smiled at the speed of his answer, which caused him to blush a little. He was a perfect mix of cocky and vulnerable. I would never get over this man. "I want that too, Gabriela. So damn bad."

"I guess this means I have to catch the bouquet at my parents' wedding, huh?"

"Guess so." He cleared his throat. "Speaking of weddings… According to you, how early is too early to propose?"

I gave him a sly wink. "My, my, so eager to put a ring on my finger, hm?"

"If I had it my way, doll, you'd have been legally mine a long time ago."

That pleased the territorial monster inside of me. "Ditto."

My answer pleased him too, if the darkening of his eyes was anything to go by.

"Hypothetically speaking, where would we live?" I asked. "After we got married?"

I loved our apartments, but I always saw myself settling down in a nice house with a big courtyard and backyard for my kids to run around and play in.

Hunter tucked a strand of my hair behind my ear. "I suppose I always saw myself moving back to the East Side, where I grew up and have all my fondest childhood memories. There are lots of beautiful homes there. Good place to raise a family."

I looked forward to growing old with Hunter. We were in for a lifetime of fun, happiness, and memories we would cherish until the end.

I felt that in my soul.

"And hypothetically speaking, how many kids would you want?" I prodded.

"It's your body, Gabriela. As many or as little as you'd want to give me."

My heart pounded with excitement. "Good answer, *amore mio*. So marriage, a home, and kids? Sounds like a good plan." I kissed his lips. "You'll finally have the happy ever after you wanted."

"My treasured obsession." Hunter thumbed my cheek softly, smiling. "*You* are my happy ever after."

EPILOGUE

GABRIELA

Mamma and Papà tied the knot again on a gorgeous, snowy December day.

It was an intimate affair with close friends and family. Nonna, me, and Anna's mother—one of Mamma's best friends—acted as the bridesmaids, Vance Remington was Papà's best man, Luna was the flower girl, and Anna's little brother the ring bearer. We made sure to keep an empty seat in the front row to honour Layla's late mother, who'd also been one of Mamma's best friends.

Hunter was here with his family, looking dapper as ever in a black suit. Though he wasn't officially part of the groomsmen party—since Papà didn't want one, he still insisted Hunter wear a matching pink tie. Another olive branch. He wanted my boyfriend to feel like he was every bit a part of the Bellafiore family.

Hunter caught my eye when I stood at the front, next to the other bridesmaids.

"You look incredible," he mouthed.

Filled with giddiness, I mouthed back, "You too."

The ceremony passed by fast, yet not without the usual theatrics associated with our family. Mamma's vows were long and heartfelt, making Papà tear up. And his had Mamma full-on crying and swooning. Nonna appeared like she was over them and ready for a few glasses of wine.

When the officiator declared them husband and wife again, the place erupted in cheers as Papà and Mamma kissed.

"Finally!" Nonna grumbled jokingly next to me, but the grin on her face mirrored mine.

We were so happy for them.

The reception hall was decorated as per Mamma's instructions. Pink hydrangea centerpieces, a flurry of tealights, ornamental white trees, and rhinestone garlands to give the illusion of falling snow. It was a stunning winter wonderland.

Taking a small reprieve from my bridesmaid duties, I joined my friends at their designated table while Hunter went to his friends. The minute I sat down, I took a breath of relief. My feet were killing me. I was just about ready to remove my heels.

"They look so beautiful." Darla gazed at my parents as they now shared their first dance. "Like a fairy tale come to life."

Ella elbowed her playfully. "Your blond-haired, blue-eyed Prince Charming is right around the corner. Just you wait."

Dacia sipped her champagne. "I don't think Prince Charming is Darla's type."

Hera smiled cheekily. "So what is your type, Dar?"

"Well, since you asked…" Darla started listing her requirements on her fingers.

At that moment, Anna and Layla nudged me. "Look! Your mom's getting ready to throw the bouquet. Let's go!"

We all scrambled over to the dance floor. Dacia with less enthusiasm. She once said that she had no desire to get married. But she tagged along regardless.

Across the dance floor, I caught Hunter's attention.

The mischievous glint in his eyes said *you better catch that bouquet.*

I threw him an air-kiss.

"Ready, ladies?" Mamma called from the front, pushing aside her veil to glance at us over her shoulders.

"Ready!" we called back.

And when she threw it, I caught it.

Choruses of cheers and disappointed sighs rang in the air.

My friends congratulated me, but I had eyes solely for my Hunter.

I lifted the bouquet in his direction to let him know we were next.

He winked at me.

<hr/>

A few months later...

HUNTER

"**W**here are you taking me, pretty boy?"

A smile touched my lips as I drove down the long, empty road, struck with nostalgia. Everything was coming full circle.

"Someplace you'll like, Gabriela," I returned and my blindfolded girlfriend—soon-to-be fiancée—grinned, the tiny gem on her canine winking in the nightlight.

My sunroof was open, the summer breeze drifting in and fanning her curled hair. She looked mouth-wateringly gorgeous in a silky red number with a high-slit, nails and toes painted black like her soul, and diamond jewelry.

Seven hundred and thirty days later, she still took my breath away.

She always would.

The last few months were nothing short of a roller coaster, endless memories filled with the most blissful time of my life because she was by my side. And I looked forward to doing life with her until the very end of time.

Over the last few weeks, Gabriela dropped hints that she was ready to take our relationship to the next level: marriage. It was always our end goal and though we were young, I didn't see any sense in delaying the inevitable. I'd found my person, my soulmate, my best friend, my other half. I wanted to be with her forever.

Not to mention, our families meshed so well together. Mom and Heidi loved Gabriela to pieces. Lucia and Nonna had dropped the son-in-law title on me more times than I could count on two hands. And Enzo practically treated me like the son he never had and didn't realize he wanted until I came along. Sometimes he teased Gabriela that I was his favourite, which always ruffled my girlfriend's feathers.

Point being, I was ready to take our relationship to the next level as well…and I had an emerald ring sitting in my pocket to prove it.

Tonight, I was proposing to Gabriela.

As far as I could tell, she had no idea and thought we were on our way to a fancy dinner date. I did my best to keep it a secret—a difficult feat, since I never lied to Gabriela—and pretended like I had no idea of the numerous engagement rings she'd tabbed on her laptop.

A month ago, I went to the jewellers and picked out her ring. Last week, I went to Enzo and Lucia's home to ask for their blessings. They were ecstatic. So were Heidi and Mom. Anna and Layla were also in on the surprise, since I asked for their help with tonight's setup.

I pulled into a parking spot in my staycation home. The same place where Gabriela and I had our first unofficial date. It seemed like a fitting location for me to propose to her. And on the same day that I first laid eyes on her two years ago.

"Can I at least know where we are now?" Gabriela asked with impatience and excitement.

"Not yet." I turned off the car and unbuckled our seatbelts. "But in a minute."

She remained quiet as I rounded the car to come to her side, opened her door, and swung her into my arms. She laughed girlishly and clung to me as I ferried us to our destination.

The backyard was lit up with hundreds of fairy lights hanging around the trees and candles lining a path towards an awaiting picnic blanket, ice bucket with champagne, red roses bouquet, and all of Gabriela's favourite foods scattered on top.

And behind it all sat an archway made of red roses with marquee letters that spelled **MARRY ME** on the ground.

I gingerly placed Gabriela on the picnic blanket, facing away from me. "Open your eyes, Gabby."

Right as she removed the blindfold and turned around, I got down on one knee before her and opened the velvet box housing her ring.

She gasped, awestruck.

I grabbed one of her hands and placed it on top of my thumping heart. "Gabriela Regina Bellafiore, I'll never forget the first time I saw you. In a room full of people, you were the most beautiful woman I'd ever seen. I couldn't take my eyes off you. You left me speechless with this yearning to get to know you. And when I finally gathered the courage to seek you? You changed my life for the better. You were like the breath of fresh air I'd been needing for years. You helped me out of my comfort zone, held my hand, and embraced me as I am. You saw the real me when no one ever bothered to see past the surface…and along the way, I fell deeply in love with you." She was crying silent tears now. My throat closed up at the sight and all the affection I felt for this one goddess of a woman. "You're my best friend, my other half, my soulmate. I want to spend every waking moment with you and make memories that we'll cherish until we're grey and old." I kissed her knuckles, my vision blurring. "Will you make me the happiest man in the world and marry me, doll?"

She nodded frantically, wiping her tears. "Yes! Yes, I'll marry you, Hunter!"

I slid the ring on her finger and stood up to kiss her, a row of fireworks going off behind us.

"I love you," she whispered in between kisses. "I." *Kiss.* "Love." *Kiss.* "You." *Kiss.* "So." *Kiss.* "Much."

"I love you too, Gabriela," I whispered and laid my forehead to hers, gazing into the eyes of my beloved.

And just like that, our happy ever after had begun.

The End

ACKNOWLEDGEMENTS

Thank you so much for reading *My Treasured Obsession*. I hope you loved it and these characters, including our girl Luna <3 This was one of the best and smoothest writing experiences I've ever had and I'm so glad that I got the chance to share Hunter and Gabriela's story with you. This entire project took nearly eighteen months from start to end and could not have been finished without the help of my amazing team.

To Annie and Alicia, I know I'm going to sound like a broken record, but thank you again from the bottom of my heart for being alpha readers. I appreciate all the hours you spent reading (and sometimes re-reading) my chapters, giving your thoughtful feedback, going over the artworks, and just being there for me throughout the journey. One of the reasons why this story wrote itself so seamlessly was because of you and your endless love for my characters/story world. You always sent me encouraging words, checked in with me, and proved once again that one of the greatest gifts in life is friendship. Couldn't imagine doing what I do without you here. I'm so happy our paths crossed and blessed to have you both in my corner. In case I don't say it enough, I love you dearly.

To my mom, thank you for your unwavering support and love. I wouldn't be here without your blessings. I love you so much.

To my best friends J and K, your friendship means the absolute world to me. Thank you for supporting all my creative endeavors and always hyping me up. The way you constantly show up for me lights me up from within. Here's to more decades of shared laughter, inside jokes, and memories we'll always cherish.

To Emma, thank you so much for beta reading with your busy schedule, helping with the Italian in this book, and for answering all my questions. I'm so grateful for the feedback you provided. Adore you.

To Lima, thank you for reading the ending of this book on such short notice and providing your medical expertise. I couldn't have completed this project without you!

To Emily, thank you for editing *My Treasured Obsession*. Fifth project under our belts and I'm so thankful to be working with you. It's always such a pleasure. I promise to write faster for you lol!

To Manuela and Gabriela, thank you for creating such gorgeous illustrations—for the cover and the inside of this book. You always do such a fantastic job bringing my characters to life and I'm so glad to have you on my team <3 I always look forward to your emails with new artwork and I can't wait to work on more projects with you.

To Nada from Qamber Designs, it's been such a joyful experience working with you for nearly five years. You always make my books so beautiful. I love how the typography/border turned out on this cover, alongside the stunning interior formatting. Thank you for everything!

To the lovely ladies from the Instagram/TikTok community (Blake, Danni, Ellie, Ellen, Himani, Mahbuba, Niss, Norhan, Sahra, Sil, Smiqa, Sabrina, Yas, Zahra and so many more), forever grateful for your kindness and support!

And lastly, to my wonderful readership, thank you for reading my stories and showing me so much love <3 I started writing online over a decade ago and it warms my heart to know some of you have been with me since the beginning. Anything I write, I always write with you in mind. You know this. Love you to the moon and back. xo

If you enjoyed reading *My Treasured Obsession*, I would appreciate it if you left me a review on Amazon and Goodreads. It's a huge help and I can't wait to hear your thoughts!

Love always,

WHAT'S NEXT?

Book #2 in the **My Everything Forever**
series will be about Sam & Anna.

Follow me on Instagram and sign up to my newsletter
to stay in the loop about upcoming publishing news!

OTHER WORKS

If you'd like to read more from me, you can also check out the books of the other couples in my story world:

Ella & Cade: Trapped With You (Remastered)
(Sins of Montardor series – Book #1)

Darla & Zeno: Corrupted By You
(Sins of Montardor – Book #2)

Mabel & Liam: The Guy For Me (Novella)

ABOUT THE AUTHOR

Marzy Opal is a romance author who writes about soulmate energy and everlasting love. Her stories contain empowered heroines, obsessed dirty-talking heroes, and lots of swoon-worthy and steamy moments. Aside from writing, Marzy has a strong passion for lattes, reading, and watching reruns of her favourite shows!

CONNECT WITH ME

Enjoyed *My Treasured Obsession*?
Make sure you stay connected for upcoming books and series!
My social media handles are @marzyopal and you can find me on:
Goodreads | Instagram | Facebook | Marzy's Queens Readers' Facebook
Group | Pinterest | Spotify | TikTok

Lastly, don't forget to subscribe to my newsletter on my website:
www.marzyopal.com/newsletter